THE GOD IS NOT WILLING

THE GOD IS NOT WILLING

The First Tale of Witness

Steven Erikson

TOR

A TOM DOHERTY ASSOCIATES BOOK
NEW YORK

THE GOD IS NOT WILLING

Copyright © 2021 by Steven Erikson

Maps copyright © 2021 by Neil Gower

A Tor Book
Published by Tom Doherty Associates
120 Broadway
New York, NY 10271

www.tor-forge.com

Tor® is a registered trademark of Macmillan Publishing Group, LLC.

The Library of Congress Cataloging-in-Publication Data
is available upon request.

ISBN 978-0-7653-2359-0 (hardcover)
ISBN 978-1-4668-8120-4 (ebook)

Our books may be purchased in bulk for promotional, educational, or business use. Please contact your local bookseller or the Macmillan Corporate and Premium Sales Department at 1-800-221-7945, extension 5442, or by email at MacmillanSpecialMarkets@macmillan.com.

First published in Great Britain by Bantam Press, an imprint of Transworld Publishers, Penguin Random House

First U.S. Edition: November 2021

Printed in the United States of America

0 9 8 7 6 5 4 3 2 1

For dragging me online, and for the friendship, this novel is
dedicated to Lenore Kennedy

Contents

Acknowledgements

Many thanks to my advance readers, Dr A. P. Canavan, Baria Ahmed, and Mark Paxton-MacRae; and to my agent, Howard Morhaim, and my editor, Simon Taylor. Special appreciation goes to my fans frequenting the Steven Erikson Facebook page, and to all the You-Tubers now discussing all things Malazan: you delivered the shot in the arm when it was needed the most.

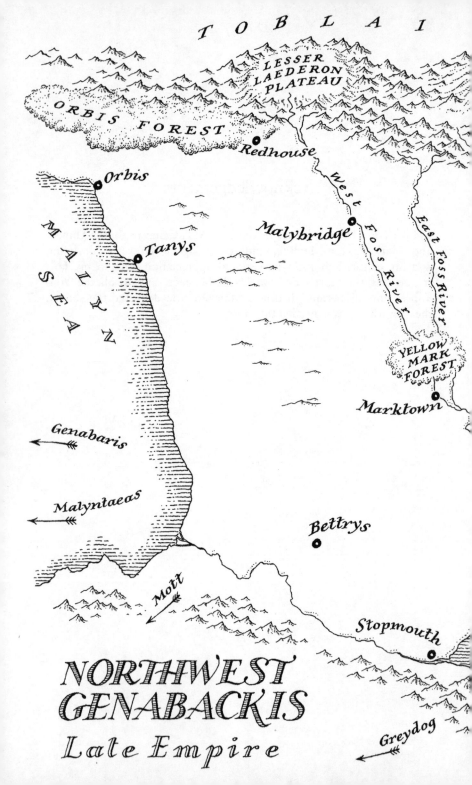

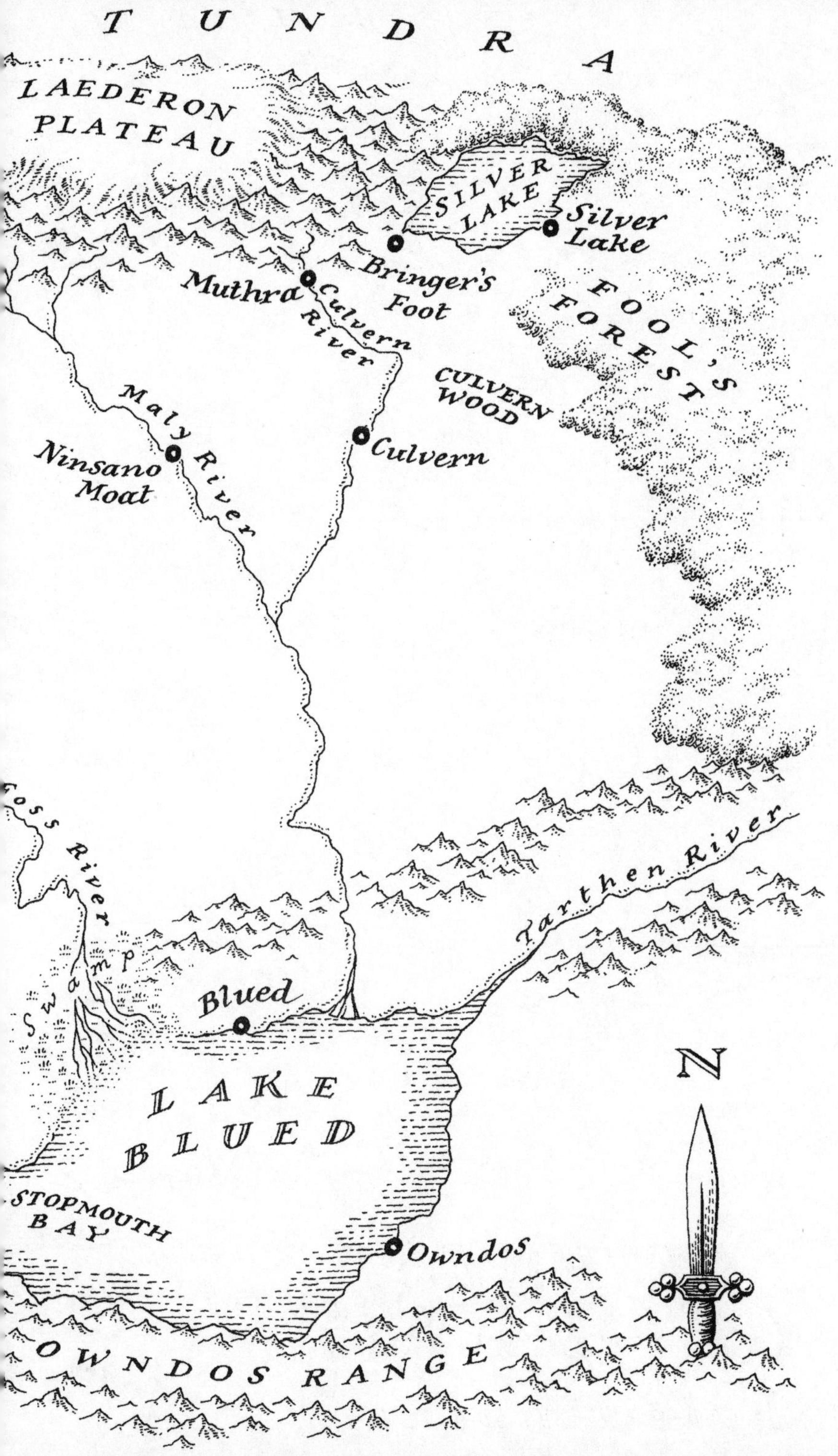

TUNDRA

LAEDERON
PLATEAU

SILVER
LAKE

Silver
Lake

Bringer's
Foot

Muthra
River

Culvern
River

FOOL'S
FOREST

CULVERN
WOOD

Maly River

Culvern

Ninsano
Moat

Goss River

Tarthen River

Swamp

Blued

LAKE
BLUED

STOPMOUTH
BAY

Owndos

N

OWNDOS RANGE

DRAMATIS PERSONAE

Rant, the half-Teblor bastard son of Karsa Orlong
Damisk, a hunter and tracker
Gower, Lord of the Black Jheck
Nilghan, a warrior of the Black Jheck
Sarlis, Rant's human mother
Three, a Shi'gal Assassin

XIVth LEGION, 2nd COMPANY

Captain Gruff, company commander

Spindle, sergeant, 3rd Squad
Morrut, corporal, 3rd Squad
Oams, 3rd Squad
Paltry Skint, 3rd Squad
Benger, 3rd Squad
Say No, 3rd Squad

Drillbent, sergeant, 4th Squad
Snack, corporal, 4th Squad
Stillwater, 4th Squad
Folibore, 4th Squad
Blanket, 4th Squad
Anyx Fro, 4th Squad

Shrake, sergeant, 2nd Squad
Undercart, corporal, 2nd Squad
Daint, 2nd Squad
Given Loud, 2nd Squad
So Bleak, 2nd Squad
Clay Plate, 2nd Squad

THE TEBLOR

Delas Fana, a daughter of Karsa Orlong
Tonith Agra, a daughter of Karsa Orlong
Karak Thord, a warrior and son of Delum Thord
Pake Gild, a warrior and daughter of Widowed Dayliss
Widowed Dayliss, widowed mate to Bairoth Gild
Valoc, a Sunyd ex-slave
Elade Tharos, a warleader
Sathal, a warrior
Bayrak, a Sunyd ex-slave
Galambar, a Rathyd liberator of Sunyd slaves
Sivith Gyla, a Rathyd warrior
Toras Vaunt, a Rathyd warrior
Salan Ardal, leader of the Sunyd
Kadarast, a Rathyd warrior
Hestalan, a Rathyd warrior
Bagidde, a Rathyd warrior
Sti Epiphanoz, a Bright Knot scout

OTHERS

Bliss Rolly, a master sergeant of the Malazan regulars
Horser, a corporal of the Malazan regulars
Trand, a Malazan regular
Flown, a Malazan regular
Amiss, a Malazan regular
Lope, a Malazan regular
Gund Yellow, a Malazan regular
Nast Forn, Lieutenant, Silver Lake Garrison
Silgar Younger, mayor of Silver Lake
Storp, a barkeep and retired veteran
Creature, a weasel
Monkrat, a mage
Blowlant, a camp follower
Varbo, a camp follower
Fist Sevitt, commander of XIVth Legion
Daisy Broke, a battalion commander, XIVth Legion
Deader, a battalion commander, XIVth Legion
Hayfire, a captain of the XIVth Legion
Wheeze, a sergeant of the XIVth Legion
Sulban, a sergeant of the XIVth Legion

Bellam Nom, a sergeant of the XIVth Legion
Pestle, a marine
Goodnight, a marine
Olit Fas, a marine

Tangle-Witch, a tribal spirit
Nistilash, a Ganrel warlock
War-Bitch, Goddess of the Jheck
Casnock, Lord of the White Jheck
Pallid, a Hound of Shadow

Andrison Balk, Commander of a mercenary company
Ara, Lieutenant of Balk's Company
Stick, sergeant in Balk's Company
Sugal, sergeant in Balk's Company
Bray, sergeant in Balk's Company
Scabbe, mage in Balk's Company
Cranal, mage in Balk's Company
Vist, mage in Balk's Company
Flap, night-blade
Bairdal, night-blade
Paunt, night-blade
Orule, night-blade
Palat, night-blade
Fray, night-blade
Irik, night-blade
Rayle, night-blade

What to make of this? The Lord of Death is dead. The Sire of War rests silent in a broken crypt. Light and Dark have fled into Shadow, and Shadow dreams of sunlight. Houses lie abandoned. Heralds cry out unheard; masons sift dust through numb hands; mistresses wait alone in the night. Queens weep and kings stumble. All the world is in flux, truths dying with every breath spent and every word uttered.

An old woman walks a corridor, lighting candles one by one, but the hollow wind steals every flame in her wake.

But now I see arrayed before me a new field of battle, greeting dawn with heavy silence. Soon, in the fraying gloom, the darkness shakes apart to reveal two armies facing one another. Banners flap like wings, the ranks plume and steam; the rising sun makes a strewn treasure of weapons and armour.

Then rises a single figure between the foes, spire of flesh and obdurate will, iron-boned yet shattered of visage. He is no one's champion, yet everyone's god. He is the warrior's red blessing, yet the lover's sweet kiss; he is witness to every corpse, and the maker of children. He is history's gilded prow, rearing fierce through the spume, yet dwells at ease in the space between barrow and menhir. He is heavy footfall and he is feather touch; cold stare and fleeting glance. For him, all is surrendered; for him, all is sacrificed. In his name nations fall; in his name, gods will kneel. If empires burn, blame him not, nor again in the moment the lover turns away. To witness is to begin to see. To see is to begin to know. To know is to recoil. Yet he stands fast, unarmed, un-armoured against this future, and I do know him: he is the Unwilling God, the Helpless God, the Slayer of All and None.

The foes do not move. The sun unfurls its golden light across the surface of the world. Will this be a day of war? Let us see . . .

'Hanascordia'
Visions of the Last Prophet
Third Karsan Apocrypha
(Darujhistan, in the Year of Feral's Challenge)

PROLOGUE

Above Laederon Plateau, Northwest Genabackis, Teblor Territory

THE ASCENT HAD TAKEN SIX DAYS. BY MIDDAY ON THE SEVENTH they reached the top of the escarpment flanking the near-vertical wall of ice that had been on their left for the past two days. The face of that wall was ravaged by past melts, but at this height winter still gripped the mountains, and the winds that spun and tumbled down from high above were white with frost, bleeding rainbows in the sharp sunlight.

The escarpment's summit was a sloping, ragged ridge, barely level enough for the four Teblor to stand. The wind howled around them, tearing at loose weapon straps and furrowing the furs they all wore. That wind periodically shoved at them, as if incensed by their audacity. These heights and this world did not belong to them. The sky was too close, the air too thin.

Widowed Dayliss of the Teblor drew her wolf-skin cloak closer about her shoulders. Before them, the slope fell away in a steep, rock-studded descent to a mass of broken ice and sand and snow that skirted the shore like a defensive wall.

From where they stood, they could see beyond that saw-toothed barrier, out to the lake itself. Buckled ice rose like islands, shattering the level snow-covered surface of the lake. Some of those islands were piled high as fortresses, as if a hundred tyrants warred to rule this vast empire of frozen water.

No one was yet ready to speak. Widowed Dayliss lifted her gaze and squinted northward, where the lake presumably came to an end. But all was white in that immense distance. Hovering like vague clouds above this whiteness were the higher peaks, the highest of the range, and the sides facing south were bared of snow. The sight of that alone was appalling. Widowed Dayliss turned to the young warleader standing upon her right.

3

It still startled her to find a Rathyd accompanying them, as if a thousand years' worth of feuding and murdering meant nothing, or at least not enough to keep this warleader from venturing among the Uryd, from seeking out warriors to accompany him to this place.

Everything was changing. She studied him for a moment longer, and then said, 'Your people could see, then.'

Elade Tharos was leaning on his two-handed bloodsword, its point jammed into the glassy ice that filled a crack in the stone at his feet. 'In the high summer camps,' he said, nodding. 'The White Faces were white no more.'

There had been few Uryd, having heard Elade's tale, who came to comprehend the significance of this news. Life's pace was slow, the measured beat of seasons. If it had been colder this past winter, why, it had been warmer the winter before that. If the thaw came in fits and starts; if strange draws of warm air swept down from the northern heights; if snow fell for day upon day, deep enough to bury a Teblor; if the forests themselves now climbed higher upon every mountain side, while trees much further down died to summer droughts and pestilence . . . why, just as one chooses a different high pasture each summer, so too would the ways of the Teblor shift and adapt and accommodate.

This news, they muttered, was not a thing to fear. Oh, perhaps the Rathyd – those few settlements left, in their hidden, remote places, cowering from the hungry slavers of the south – had taken to suckling fear from a beaten bitch-dog, and would now start at shadows in the sky . . .

Such words should have darkened Elade Tharos's visage. Instead, he had smiled, teeth bared in a silent snarl. Drawing a breath, long and slow, he had then said, 'The slaver-children are all dead. Or did you disbelieve even these rumours? Has my name no meaning here? I am Elade Tharos, Warleader of all the Sunyd and Rathyd. Warleader of the free and the once-enslaved. The heads of a thousand slaver-children now mark our victorious trail back to our homelands, each one riding a Sunyd or Rathyd spear.' He paused, contempt a feral gleam in his grey eyes. 'If I must, I will seek out a few Phalyd warriors for this journey north . . .'

And that had done it. After all, what tale would Elade Tharos bring to the hated Phalyd? *'The Uryd fled into their huts and would not hear me . . .'* Even without comprehension, there was now no choice, for pride was every warrior's master.

This Rathyd warleader might be young, but he was no fool.

'The eternal snows have been shed,' said Karak Thord. 'In itself an impossible thing.' His mien was troubled, but he was not staring at the

4

distant mountains. He was staring at the lake. 'The question, then, of where they went, has here been answered.' Karak turned to Elade. 'And this drowned valley? Has it ever been thus?'

'No, Karak of the Uryd. A river once, yes, that ran clear and cold over rounded stones and pebbles and sand. A place where gold was gathered in the shallows. To cross, no deeper than one's hip.'

'When was that?' Karak Thord asked.

'In my father's time.'

There was a snort from the other woman among them. 'Have you pried his memories, Warleader, to glean what century it was when he last visited this place?'

'No, Tonith of the Uryd, I have not, for he is dead. Understand, my family line has long held the gift of gold-gathering. We travelled the deepest reaches of the range, in ways no other Teblor had. All the gold traded among the Teblor was found by my family.' He paused for a moment, and then shrugged. 'I was to have followed, of course, and so my education began early. Then the slavers came and we were driven from the south, we who escaped. And when at last we thought ourselves safe, why, a raiding party came upon us. There, my father was slain.'

Widowed Dayliss studied the warleader again. Her mouth was suddenly dry. 'The raiders, Warleader, they were Uryd.'

'They were,' he replied with little inflection.

Karak Thord was now staring at Elade with wide eyes. 'My kin . . .'

'Just so,' said Elade. 'It was not difficult to learn of their names – after all, do not the Uryd still sing of Karsa Orlong, Delum Thord and Bairoth Gild?' He levelled his gaze on Dayliss. 'And you, Widowed, whose child was born of Bairoth's seed. Are you not now among the new believers of the Shattered God?'

'You know too much of the Uryd,' she replied, a blade's edge now hovering beneath her words.

Elade shrugged. Seeming to dismiss them all along with the subject of their conversation, the warleader fixed his attention once more on the frozen lake. 'Look well,' he said. 'Before us is not a lake, but an inlet. Beyond the Godswalk Mountains, where tundra once stretched, there is now a sea. High lands to the west keep it from the ocean. To the east, it stretches across a third of the continent.' He halted abruptly and tilted his head. 'What do I know of this continent? More than any of you, I am sure. You imagine us in a small world, these mountains and valleys, the flatlands directly south and beyond that, a sea. But it is not the world that is small, it is Teblor knowledge of it.'

'But not for you?' Tonith Agra's tone was harsh, whispering of a fear she would mask with contempt.

'The once-slaves had much to say. All they knew serves to enlighten. And, I have seen the maps.' He now turned entirely round. 'The ice-wall holds back the sea. We have climbed with it at our side these past two days. We have seen its cracks, its rot. We have seen the ancient beasts once trapped in it, knots of foul fur studding the cliff's face. More emerge with every spring, drawing in the condors and crows and even the Great Ravens. The past offering up a bounteous feast for the carrion-eaters. And yet,' he added, 'to see it is to see the future. Our future.'

Widowed Dayliss had understood the significance of the bared mountain peaks. The world's winter was dying. She had understood, as well, the purpose of this journey. To see where the meltwater had gone. To see why it had not come into the lower ranges, where drought still plagued them every summer. Now she spoke the truth. 'When this ice-dam breaks—'

But Warleader Elade Tharos was not one to yield to her the utterance. 'When this ice-dam breaks, warriors of the Uryd, the world of the Teblor ends.'

'You said a sea,' Karak Thord said. 'Against that, where can we flee?'

Now Elade Tharos smiled. 'I have not simply come among the Uryd. I have been elsewhere, and before I am done, I will have all of the Teblor clans with me.'

'With you?' Tonith asked. 'What would you have us avow? The great Rathyd Warleader, the Liberator of the Sunyd and Rathyd slaves, the Slayer of a Thousand Children of the South! Elade Tharos! Why yes! Now he will lead us into a war against a flood that not even the gods could stop!'

He cocked his head, as if seeing Tonith Agra for the first time. For certain, there had been few words between them since they'd left the Uryd settlement. 'Tonith Agra, your fear shows its pattern beneath skin too thin, and every word you speak is its brittle beat.' He held up a hand when she reached for her bloodsword. 'Hear me, Tonith Agra. Fear stalks us all, and any warrior who would deny that is a fool. But listen well. If we must feel terror's icy wind, then let us have it at our backs.'

He waited.

Widowed Dayliss made a sound – even she could not describe what it meant. Then she slowly shook her head. 'You feel yourself in the Shattered God's wake, don't you? In his shadow. The Rathyd whose father fell to Karsa's bloodsword. Or Delum's, or Bairoth's. So now, you would step out from that shadow. And the glory of what you will lead will push the Shattered God into the ditch.'

Elade Tharos shrugged. 'Here is the glory I seek, Widowed Dayliss, and if the Shattered God is to play a role in it, then it will be at the end of my bloodsword. Tonith Agra has the truth of it – we cannot wage war against a flood. The water will come. Our lands will drown. But the drowning of Teblor lands is only the flood's birth. Do you not understand yet?'

She nodded. 'Oh, I do, Warleader Elade Tharos. That flood will come down from our ranges. It will inundate all the lands of the south. Where dwell the slaver-children. It will destroy them all.'

He shook his head. 'No, it won't. *We will.*'

Abruptly, Karak Thord's weapon was out. He faced Elade Tharos and then knelt, raising his bloodsword between them, parallel to the ground and resting on his upturned palms. 'I am Karak Thord of the Uryd. Lead me, Warleader.'

Smiling, Elade touched the blade. 'It is done.'

A moment later, Tonith Agra did the same, and despite the clash so recently unveiled between them, the warleader accepted her without a qualm, without even a moment's hesitation.

Widowed Dayliss looked away, although she knew that the Rathyd had now turned to her and was waiting expectantly. She neither would nor could deny him. A savage heat burned in her veins. Her heart was pounding. But she held her tongue, long enough to peer into the distant south.

'Yes,' Elade Tharos murmured, suddenly close at her side. '*Before the water, there shall be fire.*'

'Perhaps it was my husband who killed your father.'

'It was not. With my own eyes, I watched Karsa Orlong cut him down. I alone among the Rathyd men survived the attack.'

'I see.'

'Do you?' he asked. 'Tell me, where is this Shattered God? Has Karsa Orlong returned to his homeland? Has he come to gather up his blood-kin, his new followers? Has he begun the great war against the children of the south? No. None of these things. Tell me, Widowed Dayliss, why do you cling to such false hope?'

'Bairoth Gild chose to stand at his side.'

'And died for the privilege. I assure you,' Elade said, 'I shall not be so careless with my sworn followers.'

She snorted. 'None shall fall? What manner of war do you imagine, then? When we journey south, Warleader, will we not paint our faces black, grey and white?'

His brows lifted. 'To chase our own deaths? Widowed Dayliss, I intend for us to win.'

'Against the south?' The others were listening, watching. 'You say you have seen the maps. So have I, when Karsa's first daughter returned to us. Elade Tharos, we cannot defeat the Malazan Empire.'

Elade laughed. 'That would be an over-reach of even my ambition,' he said. 'But I tell you this: the imperial hold on Genabackis is weaker than you might think, especially in the lands of the Genabarii and Nathii.'

She shook her head. 'That distinction makes no difference. To bring our people south, to find a place in which to live that is beyond the floods to come, we shall have to slay them all. Malazan, Nathii, Genabarii, Korhivi.'

'True, but it is the Malazans alone who have bound all of those people into a single foe, upon the fields of battle. Where we will meet them and crush them.'

'We are raiders, Elade Tharos, not soldiers. Besides, we are too few.'

He sighed. 'Your doubts do not discourage me, and I will welcome your voice in the council of war. Are we too few? Yes. Will we be alone? No.'

'What do you mean?'

'Widowed Dayliss, will you make the vow? Will you hold high your bloodsword to take my touch? If not, then our words must end here and now. After all,' he said with a soft smile, 'we are not yet in a council of war. I would rather, in the time of your doubts, that you gave your voice to all of those who share them yet would remain silent.'

She drew her weapon. 'I will,' she said. 'But understand me, Elade Tharos. The daughters of Karsa Orlong have journeyed from our lands to where their father, the Shattered God, will be found. They have done so many times.'

'Yet he does nothing.'

'Elade Tharos,' she replied, 'he but draws a long breath.'

'Then I shall look forward to hearing his war-cry, Widowed Dayliss.'

I think not. But she held her silence. And then settled down on one knee and held up her wooden blade. 'I am Widowed Dayliss, of the Uryd. Lead me, Warleader.'

The sun had reached its highest point in the day. From the vast frozen inlet of the mist-shrouded inland sea, groaning sounds broke the silence. The thaw was beginning. From the wall of ice, now on their right, there was the drumming rush of water, somewhere behind the green and blue columns of ice. It was the same sound they had noted with each afternoon during the climb, when the warmth was at its peak.

In the ranges of the south, the clans would be pleased at this onrush of seasonal run-off. This summer, they would say, the drought shall end. Do you see? There was nothing to worry about at all.

Soon, she knew, such petty matters would lose their relevance. When the warleader came among them. Bringing with him the promise of retribution against the hated children of the south. Bringing with him the promise of war.

When he at last touched her blade and voiced the words of acceptance, she straightened and held out a hand. 'Let us consider this our first council of war.'

Karak Thord said, 'Dayliss, this is hardly—'

'But it is,' she cut in. She met Elade's eyes. 'Warleader. There is a secret we four must now agree upon, a silence we must vow not to break.'

'What secret?' Tonith demanded.

She held her gaze on the warleader. 'Deliver to all the clans of the Teblor the promise of a war against the children of the south. Speak of retribution. Speak of vengeance for all the crimes done upon our people by the slavers and bounty hunters. Speak of the new settlements that sought to encroach upon our territories. Tell them of your past victories. Win them over, Warleader, with words of blood and glory.'

Tonith stepped between them. 'What of the flood? That revelation alone is enough!'

'Many will choose not to believe our words,' Dayliss replied. 'Especially among the most distant clans, who are perhaps content in seasons that have not changed, and so know nothing of travails or scarcity.'

None spoke for a time. But the shifting of the ice began to find its voice once more.

Elade Tharos then nodded. 'I am prepared to do as you suggest. But to win over all of the clans, I cannot stand alone.'

'That is true. And that is why we three shall be with you, Warleader. Rathyd, Sunyd, and *Uryd*. This detail alone will make them listen to us.'

Karak Thord grunted. 'Could we find us a Phalyd, why, the mountains would shake in wonder.'

Elade Tharos turned to him. 'Karak of the Uryd, I *have* a Phalyd among my followers. Thus, it shall be Rathyd, Sunyd, Uryd and Phalyd.' He faced Widowed Dayliss again. 'Wisdom. Let us then avow silence and hold fast to this secret. Until such time that we are all four agreed that it must be revealed.' He looked to the others in turn, and each one nodded. Even Tonith Agra.

Only then did they begin their descent.

While the water drummed through unseen caverns behind gleaming walls of ice, and the sun's growing heat made the rocks steam.

BOOK ONE

KNUCKLES

As the helpless and wounded and young fled, it is said a line was made behind them, across the narrow cut of the pass. Twelve Teblor adults, bearing whatever weapons they could find, each took their last link of broken chain and hammered spikes through it, deep into the rock. Now bound by ankle shackle to the length of their chains, there they would stand against the ferocity of the slavers and their enforcers, the pursuing army seeking to regain its wealth in flesh.

It cannot be verified, of course, if this in truth occurred. What can be said, however, is that the flight of the liberated Teblor succeeded, thus bringing to an end the institution of slavery in the Malyn Province of Malazan Genabackis, which in turn saw the fall of the final hold-out of this wretched trade in flesh.

Valard of Tulips did make a curious recount in her *Geographa 'ta Mott*, however, of the eponymous Teblor Pass, a mere three years later, noting the presence of a bone ridge in a certain line, there at the narrowest section of the trail, while upon the downward slope was found a deeper scatter of other bones. As if, she wrote, 'a thousand men had died fighting a single line of defenders.'

It should be noted, as well, that Valard, being a devout Mystic of Denial, would have been entirely ignorant of both the Slave Rebellion of Malyn, and the local legend of the Stand of the Spike.

Gaerlon's History, Vol. IX
The Great Library of New Morn

CHAPTER ONE

Inauspicious beginnings often deliver the deadliest of warnings.

Sayings of the Fool
Thenys Bule

Sliptoe Garrison, Culvern Crossing, east northeast of Malybridge, Genabackis

A PALE SKY MADE FOR A COLOURLESS WORLD. THE SEASON HAD yet to turn. The thickets to either side of the cobbled road leading to the fort and the town that crowded against one of its sides remained a chaotic hue of browns, dull reds and duller yellows. Buds had finally appeared, and where there had been ice in the drainage ditches and in the fields beyond, there was now water, stretching out in grey puddles and shallow lakes reflecting the blank sky.

Someone once said – Oams couldn't recall who – that the world was heaven's mirror, the tin kind, scratched and mottled and pitted as if to mock heaven's own face. No doubt, a point was being made by the observation. Strange how things said that made no sense could stay in the memory, while all the truths just fell away, abandoned in the way of things that had little relevance.

Any soldier who denied the lust for danger was a liar. Oams had been in the ranks since he was fifteen. Twenty-one years later, he'd been running from that truth for his entire adult life. While it was hardly alone back there, all the other pointless truths stayed in its shadow. The addict's pleasure was always a guilty one, to be sure, the towering stalker he always found at his side when he stood looking down on a corpse that, had things turned out badly, could have been Oams himself. Living was easier, he reflected, when you could kill your fear. Then stare at its bloodless face, waiting for your heartbeat to slow and your breaths to settle.

13

And tomorrow was another day, another fear, another face, relief flowing like the sweetest drug in the veins.

He was a soldier and he couldn't think of ever being anything else. He'd die on a battlefield, showing his killer his bloodless face, and probably he'd see, in his last moments, his enemy's own towering stalker. Because everyone knew, death was the one truth you couldn't outrun.

The north forest was at his back. His mount was weary, and it wouldn't do to stay unmoving for too long, lest its muscles tighten up, but Oams remained motionless in his saddle. A few moments longer wouldn't kill either of them. He hoped. At least enough time for his heart to slow down and his breaths to settle.

When it came to a spirit rising up from the worn cobbles in front of a person, there was no telling the mischief it might have in mind. It'd be a mistake to confuse sorcery and its warrens with the unseen worlds where the dead were far from alone. And the pantheon of gods and ascendants, caged in their temples, rising and dying like flowers as one age gave way to another, belonged to a realm different from all those inarticulate primal forces hanging on in the Wilds and other forgotten places.

The tall, spectral thing before him now was almost formless. Barely human, outlines vague and elusive, its central mass a dark stain through which jagged streaks of something flickered as if agitated, trapped. All dull as the sky, dull as the lakes and puddles.

He'd been waiting for it to say something, wondering why his horse was paying it no attention at all. And as the moment stretched, his mind wandered over past battlefields – especially the last one – wondering if there was something he'd missed. Something like his own death. After all, did the dead even know they were dead? Was there a memory back there that he'd flung away, in some spasm of horror and regret? The savage burn of a spear-point sinking into his chest? The agony of a stomach wound, an opened throat, a bleeder in the thigh?

'Is that it, then? I'm dead?'

His mount's left ear flicked, alert and awaiting his next words.

The answer the apparition gave was unexpected. It swirled towards him, its darkness filling his vision, the chaotic skein of *something* arcing and slashing on all sides, and its embrace rushed through him, a shudder, and then a shiver that rolled like a wave. He tracked it passing over, around, and within his body.

And then it was gone.

Blinking, he looked around. Nothing but the dull, colourless world, a cool morning of early spring, the faint sound of trickling water, barely a breath of wind. His gaze dropped slightly to the road, to the place directly beneath the apparition's appearance, and his eyes focused on a single cobble, mud-smeared but somehow different from all its companions.

'Shit.' He dismounted, reeled momentarily in the wake of that embrace, and then stepped forward and crouched down, wiping at the cobble's surface, stripping away the sheen of muddy water. Revealing a carved face. Round, empty eyes, grooves to frame the nose into a rough, elongated triangle, a downturned mouth.

'Fuck Genabackis,' he muttered. 'Fuck Culvern Wood, fuck all the dead people long gone, fuck all the forgotten spirits, gods, spectres and fucking everything else.' He straightened, swung back to his placidly waiting horse. Then he paused as he recalled that ecstatic shiver. 'But most of all, whoever you were, if that was a fuck, I'll fucking take it.'

Edging the north side of the fort was an abandoned graveyard, a strange mixture of beehive tombs and mounded urn-pits along with mostly sunken, tilted platforms, hinting at more than one ancient, long-forgotten practice by equally forgotten peoples. When the Malazan 3rd Army had built the fortification, way back during the conquest, the trench and embankment had cut into the cemetery where the various grave markers edged onto the level area mapped out by the engineers. Some of the upturned stones, brickwork and platforms had been used to lay the foundations for what began as a wooden wall but was now mortared limestone. The unearthed bones had been discarded and left scattered here and there among the high grasses flanking the trench and cursus; some still remained visible, the shards splintered and bleached white among the tangled stems.

Messy work back then, but necessity was a harsh master. Besides, the damned cemetery was in the middle of nowhere, leagues from the nearest town, with only a handful of villages and hamlets within a half-day's trek – not that the locals bothered, since they one and all insisted that the graveyard wasn't theirs.

The southern side of the fort was marked by the *new* graveyard, with small rectangular stone-block crypts in the Genabarii style and a single longbarrow packed with the mouldering bones of a few hundred dead Malazan soldiers, on which a small forest was now growing. This cemetery was flanked by the fort wall through which a new gate had been built, and otherwise surrounded by the town that had grown up with the imperial outpost.

The land beyond the eastern wall was maintained as a training and marshalling ground, settlement prohibited, although sheep were allowed to graze there to keep the area from becoming overgrown.

The fort had been raised a hundred paces from Culvern River. In the intervening decades, the spring floods had been steadily worsening, and now the river's bank was less than thirty paces from the fort's western wall. In this narrow strip, the 2nd Company of the XIVth Legion had made their camp.

The sergeant had walked away from the sound of the rushing water, as he did every morning, since it was a sound he hated. Heading inland and skirting the fort to his right, he strode into the overgrown snarl of the abandoned cemetery, remembering the first time he'd seen it.

They'd been bloodied by an unexpected clash with the Crimson Guard, and news from the south was making the name *Blackdog* a curse word. One of the problems was that the Bridgeburners had been split up, two companies sent off to support the 2nd Army up here in the northeast, while the rest went down towards Mott.

The sergeant settled onto a slightly tilted stone platform, staring across the embankment to the solid stone wall of the fort. He remembered when it was nothing but wood and rubble. He remembered how his back ached between working the spade and swinging the pick, breaking up grave markers while the wood teams cut down an entire nearby copse to raise the first walls.

There had been a rawness in the air back then, or perhaps that was just him. Certainly wilder out here, on the very fringes of civilized settlement. It was the early days of the Bridgeburners being thrown into one nightmare after another. So, hope was alive, but it'd been getting fragile.

Peace had settled its suffocating blanket since then, snug around traders, innkeepers, crafts-people, sheep-herders and farmers and all the rest. Stone replaced wood, empty land sprouted a town. None of that seemed, or looked, real.

He hadn't ever expected to return here. Not to a place where he'd twice pushed a spade into the earth, first to build a fort, and then to dig out a barrow, watching red-splashed friends being rolled into it. A soldier's loyalty died to a thousand cuts, until it seemed there was no hope of finding it again – not to an empire, not to a commander, not even to a faith. He'd seen companions slip away, deserting, even among the famed Bridgeburners, too far gone and too alone in their heads to meet anyone's eyes. He'd been damned close to that himself.

Years later and far to the southeast, in the rain outside Black Coral, High Fist Dujek Onearm had unofficially dissolved the Bridgeburners. The sergeant remembered that moment, standing in the deluge, listening to that torrid rush of water from the sky, from the mortally wounded Moon's Spawn hanging almost directly overhead. A sound he had come to despise.

He should've done like the others, then, the few who were left. Just walked away. But he'd never been one to settle down anywhere. Not even the tempting delights of Darujhistan could hold him. Instead, he wandered, he circled, wondering what it was about loyalty that haunted him.

Was it any surprise that he found himself in the Malazan ranks once more? And had anything changed? The squads of marines never seemed to, despite the endless succession of faces, voices, histories and all the rest. Commanders came and went, some good, some bad. Years of peaceful postings were punctuated by nasty scraps, the restless oscillation without end. It was, he could see now, always the same. The Malazan Empire's last moment, he had become convinced, would be when the last marine went down, on some useless battlefield at the back-end of nowhere.

No, nothing out there had changed. But inside, inside the one ex-Bridgeburner still serving in the empire, it was a different story.

Black Coral. After the rains, after the white salt had been scuffed from the shoulders of his leather jerkin, and his dry eyes had been pulled from what he had been, not yet finding what he would become, he had walked to a barrow. A glittering mound, sparkling like all the world's wealth, where he left his sigil of silver and ruby, his fire-licked burning bridge.

Strange, how a man he'd never met could have changed him so. A man, he had been told, who gave his life to redeem the T'lan Imass.

Itkovian. You of the single mad gesture, the appalling promise. Did you imagine what it would make you? I doubt it. I don't think you spared that a single Hood-damned moment, when with clear eyes you went and forgave the unforgivable.

He'd not known much of that at the time. But in his near-aimless wandering, he closed a circle upon his eventual return to Black Coral, to see what had been made of the place where the Bridgeburners died. And had come face to face with the birth of a god, a faith, a hopeless dream.

You still didn't blink, did you? So newly born, you gave only a wry smile at your impending death. While so many of us stepped forward, driven to defend you. Strange compulsion of loyalty, not to you, but to an idea, what you embodied.

No amount of abuse, no extreme of sensation, emotion, terror or lust; no place in all the worlds real and imagined, could disavow or discard this one, loving need.

Redemption.

Now *there* was a loyalty no mortal could shake, a need a mortal couldn't help but turn back to, eventually, when all the distractions turned brittle and hollow and a long life neared its end.

In all his years, a soldier among soldiers, then a wanderer among strangers, a veritable sea of faces had been brushed by his searching gaze, and in each and every one of them he had seen the same thing. Often disguised, hidden away, but never well enough. Often denied, with bold defiance or uneasy diffidence. Often blunted, by drink or smoke.

Longing. Look for it, in every crowd, and you will find it. Paint it any colour you choose: grief, nostalgia, melancholy, remembrance, these are but flavours, poetic reflections.

And it is the Redeemer, holding redemption in his hands, who would answer our longing. If we but ask.

As it turned out, he wasn't quite ready to do that, and even had he been, how would it look? Play out? *What comes when longing is at last appeased?* Was salvation something to be feared, the removal of the last thing to live for? Was longing for redemption no different from longing for death? Or were they fundamental opposites?

Distant motion drew his attention and he saw his night-blade, Oams, riding in from the east. So, that work was done. Still, it'd be worth hearing the report first-hand, before the call to gather came.

The sergeant stood, hands on his hips as he arched his lower back. Two days ago, not far from here, he'd been shovelling another hole. For the spill of familiar faces into the ground, *and good night, one and all.*

When Oams caught sight of his sergeant out among the old graves and tombs, he angled his mount off the track and rode to meet him. He was still thinking about that apparition, to be honest. Hard to drag his thoughts away. Nothing like that had ever happened before. It should have frightened him, but it hadn't. He should have recoiled from its embrace, but he didn't. And maybe that stone head, driven down into the ground and now part of an imperial cobbled road, had nothing to do with the spectre.

He had been thinking about the soldier's lust, that cold light in the eyes, thinking about the trouble soldiers slid into when they finally buried the sword. And it had been the man now awaiting him at the edge of the cemetery that brought on those thoughts. The man too long in the ranks, but with nowhere else to go.

Oams reined in and dismounted. Hobbling the horse, he walked to meet his sergeant. 'It was what you figured it would be, Spindle.'

'And?'

'Sorted,' Oams replied. He shrugged. 'I didn't have much to do, to be honest. He was already taking his last breaths. Only thing keeping him alive was all that rage. In fact, he might've tried thanking me for killing him, but couldn't get the words past all the blood in his mouth.'

Grimacing, Spindle glanced away. 'Now that's a comforting belief.'

'I thought so,' Oams said easily. After a moment, he shrugged again and said, 'Well, I'd best stable the horse. And then it's the tent and a whole lot of sleep—'

'Not yet,' the sergeant cut in. 'Captain's called us all to meet.'

'New fucking orders? We just got ourselves seriously slapped down. We're still licking wounds and ignoring all the empty chairs at the game table. Company's down to three fucking squads and they want to send us off again?'

Spindle shrugged.

Eyeing him, Oams remained silent for a few moments, and then he looked around. 'This place gives me the creeps. I mean, bodies on a battlefield is one thing – that all went down at once, half a day's worth of work. It's the role we play, so I'd better be comfortable with it, right? But graveyards. Generations of the dead, one on top of another on top of another and so on. For centuries. It's depressing.'

'Is it?' Spindle asked, now studying Oams with an unreadable expression.

'Smacks of . . . I don't know. Futility?'

'Why not continuity instead?'

Oams shivered. 'Aye. The being dead kind.' He hesitated, and then asked, 'Sergeant, you ever think about the gods?'

'No. Should I?'

'Well, was it them who made us? And if they did, what the fuck for? And if that's not bad enough, then they go around messing in our affairs. It's like they can't leave off and let us go our own way; like some damned chaperone who refuses to leave the fete, and there you are, breathing mutual lust with some beauty and both of you looking for some bushes to hide behind, and . . .' Seeing the incredulous look on his sergeant's face, Oams let the thought drift away. He rubbed swiftly at his face and offered up a sheepish smile. 'Iskar take me, I'm tired.'

'Go stable your horse, Oams,' said Spindle. 'You might have time for a bite or two before we gather.'

'Aye, I'll do that.'

'And well done on the . . . mission.'

Oams nodded. And then returned to his mount.

The sun was a brighter white in a white sky, not yet noon. The sound of meltwater trickling in the narrow trench running parallel to the wall hung in the background. The rooster that had been crowing since dawn suddenly let out a strangled sound, and then fell ominously silent.

Stillwater stood watching the big, heavy soldier shrug his way into his mail shirt. Once again, iron links snagged strands of his long, filthy hair, tearing them from his scalp so that, here and there on his torso, golden glints floated above the blued iron. While he never made a sound when he did this, a few of the plucks were always savage enough to redden his pitted face and make his blue eyes watery.

With the mail shirt settled and pulling down his already sloping shoulders, he collected up his belted sword. Somehow, there were long wispy strands of red-blond hair caught up in the bronze fittings of the scabbard, too. Cinching the belt tight above his hips, he paused to scratch at his flattened, crooked nose, surreptitiously wiping at a tear leaking down from his left eye, took another moment to brush at his worn leather leggings, and then faced her.

'Iskar's limp, Folibore, we're just walking to the command tent.' She pointed across the compound's central marshalling grounds. 'There. Where it's always been.'

'I have always believed that preparation is the soldier's salvation, Stillwater.' He squinted across the compound. 'Besides, the most deceitful paths are the ones that look easy. Should I get Blanket for this? He's in the latrine.'

Stillwater pulled a face. Blanket made her nervous. 'Well, how long has he been in there?'

Shrugging, Folibore said, 'No telling how long it'll take.'

'Why, what's wrong with him?'

'Nothing. I told you. He's in the latrine.' He paused. '*In* the latrine. Dropped that amulet his grandmother gave him.'

'The amulet with the inscription? The one that says *kill this boy before he grows up*? What kind of keepsake is that? Blanket's not right in the head, you know.'

Looking uncomfortable, Folibore shrugged again.

'Never mind,' said Stillwater. 'Let's go. I doubt the captain'd be happy with a Blanket covered in shit anyway.'

They set out.

'Ignore the others,' Folibore said. 'I for one appreciate your natural wit.'

'My what?'

'Your natural wit.'

She glanced across at him quizzically. Heavies were a strange lot. What was it that made the mailed fists in every squad so weird? They had one task, after all, and that was to plunge face-first into whatever maelstrom was coming at them. Get up front, weather the onslaught, and then punch back. Simple.

'You don't even need to be literate,' she said.

'Back on that again, Stillwater? Listen, reading's easy. It's what you do with all the words now in your head that's hard. Consider. Ten people could read the same damned words and yet walk away with ten different interpretations.'

'Uh huh.'

'That's why it's a rule to keep us heavies away from written orders.'

'Because they confuse you.'

'Exactly. We get trapped in all the permutations, the nuances, the inferences and assumptions. It's all so problematic. What does the captain *really* mean, after all? When he writes, say, "advance to the front". The front of what? What if I'd had a run-in with some loan-shark and now there's a contract out on me? Then it would more accurately be "*retreat* to the front", wouldn't it? That is to say, if I took that order personally.'

She glanced at him again. Too big for comfort, bony brows and massive, squarish head under that patchy long hair, a flattened face mostly swallowed up by the red beard framing the huge battered nose, small blue eyes with the most delicate lashes. 'You're saying that's what happened to First Squad? The heavies got hold of the orders and half a bell later, they're all dead?'

'I'm not saying that's what happened to the First,' he replied. 'Merely one among a long list of possibilities. And you'd probably know better than me.'

'So what do *you* think happened to the First, Folibore?'

'You're asking me? How would I know? How would anyone know?'

She scowled. 'Someone does.'

'So you keep saying. Listen, forget the First. They're gone. Dead. A real mess.'

'What kind of mess?'

'The real kind, obviously.'

They were nearing the command tent when Corporal Snack appeared from one side and intercepted them. 'Just the two I was looking for!'

Stillwater winced at the knowing look Folibore gave her. Him and his warnings about easy paths.

Snack was struggling to cinch his belt, pawing bemusedly at his prodigious belly as if surprised to find it there. 'Where's Blanket?' he demanded. 'We need the whole squad for this. Captain's waiting.'

'He's down in the latrine,' Stillwater said. 'Swimming in piss and shit looking for his amulet.'

'The one he keeps up his butt hole?'

'That's a good guess,' Stillwater said.

'The one that once shot out of his butt on a spear of flame?'

'Best fart fire ever seen, sir,' Folibore said, nodding solemnly. 'Bet you're still sorry you missed it.'

'Sorry ain't the word,' Snack said. 'Well, go get him then. Both of you, that is. So there's no argument.'

'Then all three of us are going to be late,' Folibore pointed out. 'You might want to reconsider that order, based on the exacerbation being compounded, sir. One soldier not here right now, but then three not here. That's half the Fourth Squad, sir.'

'More than half,' Stillwater chimed in. 'No one's seen Anyx Fro for days.'

Snack's heavy brows lifted. 'Anyx is still in our squad? I thought she got transferred.'

'Did she?' Stillwater asked.

Those brows now knitted. 'Didn't she?'

'Wasn't there an order come down?'

'I never saw no order.' Snack threw up his hands. 'And now Anyx Fro's been transferred!'

'No wonder she's not been around,' Folibore said.

'Hold on, Snack,' said Stillwater. 'As our corporal, how come you didn't know about any transfer or orders or anything? It's not like our sergeant never tells us anything.'

Snack stared at her in disbelief, fleshy face reddening. 'Yes it is! That's exactly how it is, you dim-witted witch! He never tells us anything!'

'Anyway, more than half, then,' Stillwater insisted. 'The heavy's got a point. Who's all here for the Fourth? Right, the corporal and the sergeant. The rest of us are taking a bath in the fucking latrine. Won't that smell bad when all the sergeant can do is shrug about his missing squad?'

'Oh, Stillwater,' said Folibore, 'you should know I'm laughing inside.'

'What?'

'Such an innocent expression on your sweet face. And oh,' he added, looking over her shoulder, 'here she is now.'

Stillwater and Snack turned to see Anyx Fro slouching her way in their general direction. The corporal stepped forward. 'Anyx! Over here, damn you!'

It wasn't quite a straight path that she took, but it was a good try. Anyx was looking pale, but then, she always looked pale. That said, her eyes were drooping a bit more than usual. Cursed with a sickly disposition, was Anyx Fro. 'Poor Anyx,' Stillwater said as the woman joined them.

'Why poor me anything?' Anyx demanded. 'Why are you all looking at me anyway?'

'Corporal Snack said you'd been transferred,' Folibore told her.

'Have I? Oh, thank the gods.'

'No!' Snack said. 'You haven't been transferred, damn you. But you've been missing for days.'

'No I haven't. I knew where I was the whole time. Look, wasn't there a call for the Measly Company to meet up?'

'We don't like that name,' Snack said.

'Who's we?' Anyx asked. 'Not the we that calls us the Measly Company, that's for sure. Which is pretty much everyone, Corporal.'

Their conversation was interrupted when Sergeant Drillbent emerged from the command tent.

Suddenly flustered, Snack said, 'All here, Sergeant, except for Blanket who's shitting amulets in the latrine. I mean—'

Stillwater, being merciful, cut in, 'He means Blanket's in the shitter for real.'

'Oh,' said Folibore, 'I do love you, Stillwater.'

'What?' she demanded. 'What did I say now?' She returned her attention to Drillbent. 'Point is, Sergeant, Blanket's no loss for this meeting. Since without his amulet he can't whistle out of his butt anyway.'

'Captain was not impressed—' began Anyx.

The sergeant's grunt stopped her, and everyone else. All eyes were now on Drillbent, who then glanced up at the mostly white sky. After a moment he squeezed shut his mild, hazel eyes and briefly pinched the bridge of his oversized nose, before swinging about and heading back into the command tent. A faint gesture told them to follow.

Stillwater gave Snack a quick shove against one shoulder. 'After him, idiot. It's all good.'

The command tent was crowded. But then, with all the soldiers of the 2nd Company of the XIVth Legion in attendance, save one, it should have been a lot more crowded. Impossible, in fact. Stillwater tried to imagine twelve squads crammed in here and she had to fight a smile as she moved to find a canvas wall to put her back against, as was her habit. It wouldn't do to smile, after all, given the paltry state of the 2nd, and all the faces she'd never see again.

For a brief moment, she wondered what was wrong with her. The general mood was bad, and it should be. Three pitiful squads left for the captain to command, at least until the new recruits arrived, and when would that be? Probably never. And then there were all of her dead friends to consider, and that was the problem. She never considered them at all, since they were dead.

Arms crossed, she watched the captain scanning the ring of marines. In a moment or two, he would stand up and begin speaking, and anybody who'd never met him, who knew of him by name only, would stare in open disbelief.

The captain's name was his given name. Had to be. Not even long-dead Braven Tooth could have made it up, not this time, not for this man. It was too idiotic to fathom. She studied him, watching the performance as the captain glanced down to check his lavender silk shirt, paused to adjust the cuffs and then examine the thin leather gloves covering his long, thin fingers. Now came the sudden, fluid rise from the stool, his left hand angling up to hover close to his ear, fingers fluttering, and his painted face, so white as to be deathly, shifted into a smile that almost parted his red lips. 'My dearest soldiers, welcome!'

Yes, ladies and gentlemen, this is Gruff, our beloved captain.

Paltry Skint stood as far away from her sergeant as she could manage. She'd put Oams, Benger and Corporal Morrut between her and the man, and she would have shoved Say No in there, too, except Say No, being left-handed, always fought on Paltry's left side, and nothing was going to budge the woman from her habit.

It was not because Paltry didn't like the sergeant, or trust him, or anything like that. Problem was, he stank. Well, not personally. It was his hairshirt that stank.

She'd heard a rumour that Spindle was the last living Bridgeburner, but she doubted he'd ever been in such infamous company. There were always rumours like that, swirling around certain soldiers who had a way about them. People needed it. The Malazan armies needed it.

Uncanny hints, curious mysteries, all the whispered tales of a lone figure seen wandering out beyond the camp, deep in the night, communing with the Horse-Spirits of Death's Company. With Iskar Jarak himself, the limping guardian of Death's Gate.

Only the last surviving Bridgeburner would keep such company, or so the argument went. Old friends, long dead, their bodies thin as mist and their horses sheathed in frost. Battered comrades still splashed in the blood of their deaths, swapping jokes with the sergeant in his hairshirt. That stank of the dead.

Well, she'd never once seen Spindle out in some field beyond the campfires, gabbing with ghosts. And his hairshirt stank of the dead because it was made from his mother's or maybe his grandmother's hair. But maybe that bit was made up, too. Who'd wear something like that? While Spindle could be strange every now and then, he wasn't insane. Then again, the hairshirt came from somewhere. And that could well be an old woman's hair, grey and black and patchy with crinkles.

But what good were explanations? Knowing or not knowing made no difference to the stink. Anyway, Bridgeburners were said to have had tattoos on their foreheads, a bridge in flames – obviously – and all Spindle had on his high forehead were pock-marks that could have come from anything. Some childhood illness was a lot more likely than the spatter from a Moranth munition. Besides, no one had seen any of those for ten years or more.

Bridgeburners. Bonehunters. Coltaine's Crows. The Malazan Empire had plenty of lost armies in its history. All dead but never forgotten. But that was the problem, wasn't it? The dead needed forgetting, but like Say No was always saying, remembering's one thing, but the reason for remembering is quite another.

She glanced at her fellow heavy, always there on her left. Say No looked over, and then shrugged.

Say No was always saying that, true. But what in all the world's black feathers did it mean?

Captain Gruff finished preening and then stood.

Daint and Given Loud of the 2nd Squad had found a bench to share, and it was a tight squeeze, since they were both big men, but neither one was inclined to budge and though seated, they were locked in a titanic battle, shoulders, hips and thighs pressed against their opposites, trying to push the other body from the bench seat.

Their breaths had grown loud, whistling from nostrils, and the bench was creaking under the strain. Neither man looked at the other. There wasn't any point. Even their features were physically matched: stolid, blunt, scarred, bearded, small eyes between flat noses, mouths seemingly incapable of smiling.

Almost within reach of Given Loud, So Bleak studied them from where he stood, slightly to the back of the rest of Shrake's squad. He'd come over from the 1st Company when its remnants were broken up. Before that, he'd been a regular in the XVIIth until the Gris Mutiny rose up and was put down at the cost of half the damned legion. While So Bleak had a way of surviving, that had stopped being a good thing. Now he was a man known to leave wreckage in his wake. Unsurprisingly, a warm welcome to this squad had yet to materialize.

But he'd done passably in the scrap against Balk. There was that, at least. Courage had never been an issue. He'd even managed to get his shield between a spear-point and Corporal Undercart's chest, which had earned a reluctant nod of thanks. Unless it wasn't a nod at all, just the man looking down to make sure his chest was intact.

It had been the two heavies who'd done most of the work anyway. Daint and Given Loud, it turned out, were somewhat competitive, especially when fighting. In fact, So Bleak was beginning to realize, the pair had taken their rivalry to pathological extremes. It was now seething hatred. The two men never exchanged a word. Never even looked at each other. Never shared a canteen. And yet, were never apart, lest one get a step up on the other.

A less unlucky man would find it amusing, So Bleak mused. For himself, the endless battles between the two heavies had acquired the qualities of morbid fascination. And at this present moment, he was waiting for the bench to explode.

'Alas,' Gruff said after his warm welcome, 'every region has its bandits.' Both hands lifted to stifle a protest that, as far as Stillwater could see, no one seemed inclined to make. 'I know, darlings, I know! How many bandits can field what amounts to a full company of well-equipped and exceptionally well-trained and most impressively disciplined troops? The Fist assured me, yet again last night, that the formidable nature of Balk's forces was not even hinted at in the scouting reports.' He paused and studied the faces surrounding him. 'Accordingly, our company paid a high price in defeating him.'

'But we didn't,' said Sergeant Shrake of the 2nd, twisting one end of her lone lock of long black hair. Her languid gaze slid across to Spindle. 'If not for capturing Balk himself, and if not for the surprising loyalty his troops showed in laying down their arms once Spindle put a knife to the man's throat, well, none of us would be here right now.'

'I assure you, Shrake,' Gruff said with a smile, 'I was getting to my praise of the Third Squad's impressive coup in capturing the bandit leader.'

Corporal Morrut spoke up from his usual position beside Spindle. 'It was your plan to start with, Captain. Spindle always says credit where it's due, sir.'

'With the intention of cutting off the snake's head, to be more precise,' Gruff noted, since for all his affectations, he was not a man to polish his own horn. 'Well, probably not the best way of putting it,' Stillwater amended. The captain went on, 'Since was it not obvious that Balk's sub-commanders were one and all able to continue prosecuting the engagement? Thus, Balk's demise would have achieved little by way of salvaging the situation. That said,' he added, left hand dangling once again, 'Spindle's *threat* of killing the man, without actually doing so, yielded a most opportune effect. In short, my dears, we were fucking lucky.'

This time, nods all around.

Stillwater was in the habit of wearing a ragged scarf, a tattered length of unbleached linen that had once covered the eyes of a corpse. It wasn't like the corpse needed it, since the crypt was unlit anyway, and even if there'd been cracks between the barrow-stones bleeding in the odd tendril of daylight, the dead didn't need eyes to see, so a cloth covering those eyes didn't do anything. Thinking logically was a talent of hers.

Her old friend Brenoch had been with her in that witch's barrow, she recalled. The problem with looting crypts and whatnot was that, without fail, some other looter had gotten there first. In some places, robbing the dead was a crime and the punishment was death and she was all for that, especially if it meant she could find just one damned barrow that hadn't been picked through first.

Brenoch had been kicking through some rubbish near the back end, where the arched ceiling sloped down. He'd caught a glint of something, he said. She left him to it, happy enough to be standing beside the open sarcophagus, seeing the crowbar scars on the limestone rim where that bastard thief who'd beaten them to it had prised loose the lid to send it crashing down on the other side. And that detail was only interesting in reminding her that they could do with a couple of prybars the next time they busted into a barrow. What made her content was the witch's shrivelled corpse and all the pretty linen that had been draped over it.

Most looters were men and men had no understanding of the finer things, and even if the linen shrouds were all speckled and crusty with flecks of dried skin and stained here and there with that mysterious liquid that leaked out of dead people, the stuff her mother had called *Hood's Honey*, they were still linen, and linen was pretty.

So, Stillwater had taken the strip from the corpse's eyes, and that's how she found the two gold coins that'd been left underneath, neatly wedged into the sockets. She'd hidden them away quickly, but Brenoch had caught something, enough to be suspicious. In the end she told him about the coins, if only to silence his badgering. Brenoch had been furious, and then jealous, and then avaricious, until finally she had to kill him when he went and stole the damned things, and never mind all his protestations to the contrary. Poor Brenoch, joining that long list of friends she'd once had.

These days, Stillwater wore the scarf to hide the rope tattoo encircling her neck. Some might mistake it for a noose tattoo, which was ridiculous since a noose tattoo was just asking for trouble. But a golden finger-thick rope, looped round her neck, no beginning, no end, signifying her vocation and devotion to killing as many people as necessary, well, that was *elegant*.

Being an assassin had its risks. She would have avoided the profession altogether if not for her night of revelation. Which old friend had that been? Ah, Filbin. Who had a few ways with sorcery. Rashan, in fact, the sweet magic of shadows. And was idly teaching her a few things, when it suddenly hit her. *Cotillion, my patron, Lord of Assassins. The Rope. But wait, he was only half of it, wasn't he? It'd been him and Shadowthrone, together, who'd carved out the empire. The dagger and the magic, bound as one. Rope and Shadow. But who needs to be two people for that? An assassin mage! Why did no one ever think of it before?*

She would be the first, and the best. She'd gone on to learn all she could from Filbin before she'd had to – well, poor Filbin.

The key was keeping the magic secret. And that made the tattoo useful when it might at first seem idiotic. Imagine, announcing to everybody your devotion to the Lord of Assassins! Who would do that? She would, especially when it served as misdirection. *It's one thing to know someone's a killer and might be out to kill you, so you focus on all the ways to block an assassin. Leaving open the shadowy path of magic. And before you know it, here I am, stepping out from your very shadow and stab-stab-stab!*

Drillbent knew what he had in Stillwater and he employed her talents accordingly. He never once asked why she'd joined the Malazan marines, when she could have chosen a life of demure opulence in some big city of the empire, taking contracts from the endlessly feuding nobility. When she could have worn silks and kept her jet-black hair long, shiny and clean, and besides, she knew how to do *sultry* or at least was pretty sure she did, only there wasn't any call for *sultry* in the marines. No, not once had he asked anything about her.

There'd been assassins in the marines before. There'd been Tosspot, and Lurvin Waifwater, and Kalam Mekhar. Sooner or later, there was night-work to be done, and that's what he had her do.

She wore the scarf for modesty, so as not to frighten her fellow soldiers. Oh, they all knew about her tattoo, but something about it gave them all the shivers. Unless it wasn't the tattoo at all that made them start and act all edgy whenever they glanced at her neck. Maybe it was the twin Hood's Honey stains on the scarf, the way they looked like eyes. When of course that was impossible. Even the dead couldn't look through gold coins, could they?

She'd always wondered where Brenoch had hidden the coins. Probably swallowed them. Careless of her not to think of that at the time. She could have cut his belly open and retrieved them.

'That wasn't much fun,' Snack said as they walked back to the squad's modest circle of tents. There was plenty of room in the barracks but none of the survivors seemed in the mood to bunk there, with nothing but empty echoes to listen to all night.

'Never is,' said Anyx Fro. 'Silver Lake. Wasn't that the place of the Teblor Uprising? Heard half the town burned that night, and since the slave trade dried up there's no money coming in. What's the point of going there?'

'The orders are complicated,' said Folibore, and glancing over, Stillwater saw his knotted brow.

'No they aren't,' she told him. 'We're to reinforce the garrison there, indefinitely.'

But Folibore shook his head. 'But that's just it. How long is indefinite? We could grow old there, wasting our years away until we die of old age and end up buried in a grisly mound. Winters are cold beside that glacial lake, you know, as if being dead isn't cold enough. No, I don't like it, and besides, I'm not sure the captain was precise enough. Word is, that garrison got chewed up by the slaves. There's only, what, seven of 'em left? So, strictly speaking, they'd be reinforcing us, not us reinforcing them.'

Their sergeant was walking a few paces ahead of them, but as usual, Drillbent made no effort to settle things.

Snack tried. 'We're riding north to Silver Lake, Folibore. That's all you need to know.'

'Then why did Gruff ask Spindle to wait behind? Doing some quiet talking, right? There are implications to that, inferences to be made, even.'

'Spindle's Spindle,' said Anyx Fro, as if that explained everything.

Folibore squinted across at her but said nothing.

Arriving at their camp, just beyond the fort's western wall, they found Blanket at the hearth, making tea. Anyx made a gagging noise and retreated to her tent. Drillbent did the same but without the gagging, plunging into his tent without a word. Snack went to find his tin cup but in passing close to Blanket, he evidently changed his mind, and set off for the Trader's Inn just up the road, one hand over his nose and mouth.

Folibore sat down on a log beside his fellow heavy. 'Blanket, you stink.'

'But it's a triumphant stink.'

'Found it, then?'

'You'd be amazed at what you can find knee-deep in shit and piss with a sieve in your hands.'

'A sieve?' Stillwater demanded, keeping her distance. 'Where'd you get a sieve from?'

'Borrowed it from Clay Plate,' Blanket replied.

'Does he know?'

'Doesn't have to. I already returned it.'

At that moment there came a bellow of outrage from the 2nd Squad's encampment. The three soldiers glanced in that direction, but only for a heartbeat or two.

'I take it you didn't clean it,' said Stillwater.

'Do I look clean?'

'There's a well in the fort.'

'They wouldn't let me near it. Those garrison guards don't like us.'

The tea was ready. Folibore produced a cup and Blanket showed his manners in pouring it full first, before filling his own cup. Gestures like that made Blanket strange. Stillwater didn't trust people with manners. Considerate, kind, helpful people – what was wrong with them? Something. You could be damned sure of that.

'We have our new orders,' Folibore said around blowing into his cup. Then he sipped noisily before adding, 'Silver Lake.'

'Now that's troubling,' said Blanket.

'I know,' Folibore replied. 'I said so, but no one was listening to me. And the captain's having a private chat with Spindle.'

'That's even worse.'

'That's what I said.'

Blanket puffed out his shit-smeared cheeks. 'Silver Lake. Where the God of the Shattered Face had his first run-in with the empire.'

'What?' Stillwater asked, startled.

'I was going to add that,' said Folibore, 'but no one was listening anyway.'

'Blanket,' Stillwater ventured a step closer, only to retreat again, 'what was that you said?'

'The God of the Shat—'

'You mean the Toblakai. But he rose out of the ashes of the Sha'ik Rebellion. Seven Cities. Raraku, not Silver fucking Lake.'

'Before Raraku, Silver Lake,' insisted Blanket. 'Not a true Toblakai, either. A Teblor. That fallen, benighted mob of mountain savages to the north of here. Remember the story of the Idiot Attack? Three Teblor charging a garrisoned town? That was Silver Lake.'

'Was it? I thought that was Bringer's Foot.'

'Bringer's Foot didn't even exist back then,' Blanket explained. 'Silver Lake was as far as the settlers got. No, the Idiot Attack happened at Silver Lake, Stillwater. And it was led by the one who would become the God of the Shattered Face.'

'Portents,' muttered Folibore between slurps. 'Permutations . . . implications . . . things stirring beneath a deceivingly placid surface.'

'And one of the three thought he was a dog.'

Bewildered, Stillwater stared at Blanket. 'What does that mean?'

Blanket shrugged. 'Hard to say.'

'But significant,' Folibore said.

Both men nodded at that and resumed drinking their tea.

Stillwater shook her head. 'I thought the Idiot Attack was, I don't know, a hundred years ago. Obviously,' she added, 'not at Bringer's Foot, since as you say, that settlement's new and all. Well, ten years old. I don't know why I thought it was at Bringer's Foot, since I also thought it happened a hundred years ago. It's not like I'm an expert on the settlements in the north, am I?'

'Clearly not,' Blanket agreed.

She scowled. 'Fine, you don't have to make a big deal about it. The point is, I never connected Toblakai to the Idiot Attack. Never connected him to anywhere on Genabackis at all. You're saying he's Teblor? Which clan? Sunyd or Rathyd?'

'Neither,' answered Folibore, holding out his cup for more tea, to which Blanket obliged. 'There's more clans further north, higher up the mountains. The Sunyd and Rathyd were the ones the slavers cleaned out, though not all of them, as it turned out. The Uprising was in fact a liberation, by kin. If I had to guess, we're heading to Silver Lake because something's stirred up the Teblor. All over again.'

'The God of the Shattered Face is what's stirred them up this time,' said Blanket.

'*What?* He's *here?*'

'No, Stillwater, he's not.' Blanket then frowned. 'At least, not that I heard. But then again, who knows where gods go, or what they do.'

Folibore said, 'The God with the Shattered Face lives in a hut outside Darujhistan.'

Stillwater stared. 'He does? Well, what the fuck for? What's he doing there?'

'No one knows,' answered Folibore, 'but he hasn't moved in years. It's said he refuses his ascension. It's said he beats all his followers whenever they show up. And you know what that does? Brings him more followers. I know, there's no making sense of people. Never was, never will be. Just like badly written orders. You can tell someone to go away and the someone leaves only to come back the next day with a friend, or three.' He shrugged.

Blanket said, 'But the cult's among the Teblor by now, I'm sure.'

'Oh,' murmured Folibore, 'that's a point.'

There was a loud scuffle of canvas from Anyx Fro's tent and her head poked out between the front flaps. 'Will you all shut up? I'm trying to sleep.'

'It's the middle of the day, Anyx!' snapped Stillwater. 'That tent must be boiling inside!'

'That's why I wanted us camped on the *east* side of the fort.'

'But that'd mean early morning light and waking up in a pool of sweat, like we told you.'

'And I told *you* all that I'm an early riser!'

'So go pitch your tent on the other side of the fort!'

'I just might!' Her head withdrew.

It was quiet for a few moments, and then Stillwater asked Blanket, 'Find a safe place for your amulet now?'

'Want to see a fire fart?'

Captain Gruff was pacing. 'Still, I'd like to see you try.' He paused to study Sergeant Spindle. Odd, wasn't it? A genuine ex-Bridgeburner. But he looked perfectly normal. Save for that foul hairshirt, that is. Gruff always had a secret delight in seeing outrageous expressions of fashion. But there were limits.

Still, here the man was, slouched in that saddle-chair, one of the Legends. Granted, not precisely one of the *famous* ones. But since there was no one else left, just being the last survivor had to earn some prestige. Of a sort. Being the last, and yet, quite possibly, also the *least*. Made for a strange outlook, Gruff assumed, which no doubt accounted for Spindle being the tersest man he'd ever met. 'You will try, won't you?'

'Loyalty's an issue, sir.'

Gruff spun deftly on one heel and resumed pacing. 'You might be surprised, my dear fellow, that I have few concerns in that regard.' He paused for a glance. 'Do you wonder why?' At the single raised eyebrow, Gruff continued, 'Yes, curiosity is a virtue indeed. I shall appease you forthwith. But first, I cannot help but admit to some concern, specifically with regard to how my company will take the announcement.'

'They'll take it,' Spindle said.

'Ah! A vote of confidence? What a relief!'

'They'll take the announcement, sir. Living with it's another thing.'

'Oh. Hmm, I see the distinction.' He brightened. 'Then again, a wise, calming word from you? Surely that would be more than enough . . . Oh dear, you don't seem convinced.'

'I can live with it,' Spindle said after a few moments.

A statement uttered with a most severe lack of inflection was not one to reassure the listener. 'Oh sweetness, this is sorely testing my faith, Sergeant.'

'I can see that, sir.'

After a moment, Gruff flung up both hands. 'Listen to us! Getting ahead of ourselves again. One bridge at a time – ah, as the saying goes. Well, rather. The first and thus far only relevant question to be answered here and now, my sergeant Spindle, is: will you do it?'

Spindle rose to his feet and then spent a moment kneading his lower back. 'Won't be easy.'

'Oh?'

He shrugged. 'Introduced myself with a knife pressing his throat, sir.'

'Bygones, surely!'

'Now you want him and his company sewn up with ours.'

'I assuredly do, and is the solution not poetic?'

'Aye, like a draught of poison for the soul, sir.'

Gruff blanched. 'Dear me, what sort of poetry do you read? Never mind. It remains an elegant solution to our depleted state.'

'They depleted that state, sir, in case you forgot.'

'Bygones!'

Spindle stared, as if once again not quite sure of his commanding officer. 'You said something about being confident.'

'Indeed. It's Balk's pedigree, Sergeant. We are of a like, he and I.'

'You are?'

'Station, my dear. Station. Certain virtues will persist.'

Spindle was quiet for a moment, and then he asked, 'His rank, sir?'

'Ah . . . oh, I know. *Lieutenant* Balk. Why, that even *sounds* fetching.'

'Aye, sir.'

'Spindle, you do understand that it must be you who does the asking. Definitely not me.'

'Not quite.'

'Because it was your knife! It was you who forced them all to surrender.'

'Makes me their favourite marine, does it?'

'Well, had you *cut open* Balk's throat . . .'

Spindle stared a bit more, until Gruff realized, with a sigh, that something more *direct* was required. He met the sergeant's eyes and said, in

33

a somewhat cooler tone, 'If it had been me with a knife to Balk's throat at *that* moment, Sergeant, I'd have sawn his head off.'

Spindle's stare widened slightly. Silence stretched, and then the sergeant grunted. 'I'll ask him, then.'

Relaxing, Gruff smiled. 'Excellent, my dear Sergeant Spindle.'

At the command tent's entrance, Spindle paused and looked back. 'Captain?'

'Yes?'

'Ever got your hands wet . . . that way?'

'Sweetness! More times than I can count.'

Spindle said nothing and then, with a parting nod, left the tent.

Idly, Gruff wondered why admissions like that seemed to startle people. One would suppose fellow soldiers to have tougher hides than that. Most curious.

Shrugging, he sat at his officer's desk and lifted up a mirror, and humming softly, began reapplying paint to his lips.

CHAPTER TWO

Something's always happening.
It's why misery gets no rest.

Karsa Orlong

THE BANDIT LEADER, BALK, WAS SLOUCHED ON THE CELL'S wooden bench, his back to the stone wall. This cell and three others were on the opposite side of the compound from the barracks that had been turned into a prison for Balk's Company. Normally, the gaol was reserved for the occasional murderer or drunk, someone from the company ranks, where some private adjustment of behaviour was required. Usually with fists, only occasionally with a knife across the throat.

Spindle sent the garrison guard out of the corridor and drew the stool the guard had been seated on up closer to the cell's bars. Balk glanced across at him briefly before returning his attention to the floor, where three dead rats – necks obviously broken – made a tidy small pile.

Something about the scene made Spindle frown. 'You're not a necromancer, are you?'

There was a faint gleam of bared teeth. 'No. I am not.'

Relaxing, Spindle sat down. 'He's dead,' he said.

'Who?'

'The self-styled Baron Rinagg of Fool's Forest. Seems he was pretty sick to begin with. Dying, I'm told. But we got what we needed out of him before he died.'

'And what did you need from him, Sergeant?'

'He had something on you, and it was enough to extort your participation.'

'Participation in what, exactly?'

Spindle shrugged. 'I take it you were a mercenary company, and what started out as a basic contract of service eventually turned into something else. Banditry.'

Balk glanced up a second time, his eyes mostly hidden in the shadows pervading the cell. 'The baron was asserting his right to rule the region. Tithes and tolls. Not banditry.'

'Aye, I get it,' Spindle replied. 'But tithes and tolls are administered by the empire. Those imperial title-holders who manage that also hand over most of the taxes to the regional collector. No one appointed Rinagg, and he handed over nothing.'

'The baron had been a soldier,' Balk said. 'He'd fought against the invasion.'

'Yes, well, he lost.'

Neither man spoke for a time. Then Spindle rose and rubbed at his face. He arched his back and winced slightly. 'You are nobleborn, or so my captain believes. A man of honour. Your followers certainly think so.'

'They should've ignored my fate,' Balk said.

'Had I killed you, I'm sure they would have.'

'And then you would have lost.'

'Probably. So, I'm wondering, what were you doing with a company of four hundred veteran mercenaries, wandering through Fool's Forest? The empire doesn't hire mercenaries. It couldn't have been to take Rinagg's coin. Not at first.'

'And why not?'

'Because the man was a nobody. Even with his taxing the caravans and loggers in the east, he couldn't afford you for long. Whatever he had on you was serious enough for you to work against a loss, probably emptying out your own holdings all the while.'

Balk looked away, seemed to study one of the walls. 'Know much about mercenary companies, Sergeant?'

'Ran up against a few, aye. Years back. Most of 'em barely held together even when the going was good. Show them a mailed fist and they'd scatter more often than not. It takes a special kind of fool to give up a life for coin. With a few exceptions, the empire would buy them out and then break them up.'

'And the better ones?'

Spindle moved to lean his back against the wall opposite the bars. He crossed his arms. 'There were two, maybe three,' he said.

'The Elin Shields? The Tulip Troop? Amberstone?'

Spindle sneered. 'Runts, all three.'

'Fool. You've never dealt with any of them, have you? Tulip masses eight whole companies—'

'The days of the ones worth anything are long gone, Balk. Aye, yours could bloody a nose, and did, but only because we were understrength. Ill-informed. We went in expecting a hundred or so losers.'

'You went in with all you had.'

'All comfy, aye. Had we known better, your soldiers would've risen in the morning to find all their officers dead, you and the baron included.'

'Nothing up front, then. Just knives at night.'

'Aye, short and sweet.'

'You really know nothing—'

'Oh, Balk,' Spindle said, resting the back of his head against the wall. 'The Crimson Guard. The Grey Swords.' He cocked his head. 'Mott Irregulars? Not sure whether I'd count them, to be honest. Less a company than a tribe, and us trespassing.'

'Liar.'

'Don't think I can count the Tiste Andii of Moon's Spawn either,' Spindle went on. 'Not as mercenaries. They took coin from no one. As for the Grey Swords, well, thankfully we met up with them not to fight each other, but to join forces. Liberating Capustan . . . that's a day I'll never forget.'

Balk had climbed to his feet and drawn closer to the bars. 'You really expect me to believe you, Sergeant? Why play this game?'

'I don't think I trust you, Balk,' Spindle said, now eyeing the man from beneath half-lowered lids. 'But Captain Gruff has an offer. Your previous employer is dead. The Second Company's understrength, but we need to garrison Silver Lake. The local Fist has approved a six-month contract. You'll earn enough to restore your holdings. For purposes of command structure, you would rank as Lieutenant.'

'A contract? Not broken up and folded into the Legion?'

Spindle pushed away from the wall and headed for the door. He wasn't in the habit of repeating himself. 'Decide, and then inform your guard.'

'It's against his nature,' Stillwater pronounced.

'What nature would that be?' So Bleak asked, leaning forward to stack the wooden chips. 'The white paint's coming off.'

'It's not paint,' Clay Plate said. 'It's lead. Keep stacking and stacking 'em and your hands will turn blue. Then rot and fall off. But you won't care, because you'll be insane by then.' He jabbed a finger at Anyx Fro. 'And I told you, Anyx, you want proper paint. Crushed limestone and birdshit and a few drops of linseed oil. Better yet, just gild the damned things.'

'Will you kindly shut your word-hole?' Anyx said calmly. 'Just let the man think.'

'Benger doesn't know how to think,' Clay Plate replied.

Stillwater groaned and rubbed at her eyes. 'This is the problem,' she said. 'Right here. Anyx, little carved chips of wood ain't a Deck of Dragons, no matter what you say. Besides, the whole point of Fiddler's Gambit is it's a card game played with a Deck of Dragons.'

'Well,' Anyx retorted, 'have *you* got a Deck, Stillwater? Have you even *seen* one?'

'Once,' she answered. 'In G'danisban. Three-Finger Herahv, just before he deserted. Last thing he said was something about finding the old Path of Hands. Poor Herahv.'

Clay Plate snorted. 'Ha ha hah!'

Stillwater scowled at him. 'What?'

'Guy with only three fingers goes looking for hands! Ha ha hah!'

Benger straightened and slapped down a disc. 'I'm countering with the Mistress.'

'That's still in Death's Company,' Clay Plate said. 'You can't win the game hiding behind the Gate.'

'I'll think about winning later,' Benger replied as he collected up his tankard and drank deep.

Stillwater made a sound she'd intended to be amused but it came out like something caught in her throat. She took a quick drink from her own tankard, wondering why things like that kept happening to her. 'It's all just surviving right now, right? Like I said, not in his nature. Push Benger against a wall and he'll look for a window to close.'

'Push me against a wall and I'd do the same,' Clay Plate said to her. He laid out a pair of chips. 'Icari to blank the past, giving me a free play. Unloved Woman to break the Mistress.'

Frowning, So Bleak slid a chip into play. 'Black feathers to flank.'

'Ganging up on me!' Benger hissed. 'Come on, Stillwater, do something!'

'Who made me your friend, Benger? But if you hand over that Korabas you're hiding in that stack . . .'

'No trading!' Clay Plate shouted.

'Who says?' Stillwater asked.

'This is the problem in a game without any rules,' Anyx Fro observed. 'Every company I've ever been in plays a different version.'

'But ours is the official version,' Clay Plate said.

'There is no official version!'

In the meantime, Benger had sent the Korabas chip skidding across the table, to vanish under Stillwater's right hand.

'There,' she said, 'that wasn't so bad, was it?'

'You've ruined my victory,' Benger grumbled. 'But this way I won't go out weakest, either.'

'True enough,' Stillwater said. 'I play Church of the Eel. The Unblinking Eye, the Lord of Omens. The Unloved Woman turns away and the Shroud descends. Tears flow into the River that runs through the Gate. It's a flood of disaster, swelling the depleted ranks of Death's Company. You all miss a turn in confusion and here comes Korabas, Slayer of Magic. The world ends. I win!'

'You gave that victory to her!' Clay Plate snarled at Benger.

'To make sure you end up in the weakest position, aye, I did! Now, give me that Twice Alive chip. I get open-of-play next time, because her Korabas ending knocks her off the pedestal.'

'I don't want to play any more,' said Clay Plate. 'Politics and betrayal and back-stabbing, why am I even surprised?'

'Just as well,' Anyx Fro said, 'give *me* all the chips. They need repainting.'

'Just remember who owns Twice Alive.'

'I will, Benger. Maybe.'

'Cheat me and I'll curse you, Anyx.'

'Fine. I need to test the Iron Maw anyway and you'll be as good a target as any.'

'Not much of a threat,' Benger said with a grin. 'An invention that doesn't even work, and looks stupid, besides.'

Anyx used her forearm to sweep all the chips into a hide sack, which she then cinched tight. 'Remember Benger's words, everybody. We can repeat them over his grave. Well, the hump of earth containing the few bits left of him, that is.'

'Poor Benger,' said Stillwater.

Clay Plate was nursing his ale. 'It's Blanket who should be cursed. Benger, I'll ally with you next game if you curse that redolent piece of animated shit.'

'I don't need allies, since I got Twice Alive.'

'Maybe,' said Anyx Fro. 'You ain't gonna make many friends with all that cursing people stuff. Besides, you're supposed to be a healer, not a curse-spewing asshole.'

'Curse-spewing asshole?'

'That would be Blanket, actually,' said Clay Plate.

Everyone but Stillwater laughed. She wondered what they'd found so funny.

The Trader's Inn was crowded, but not as crowded as it used to be. Most of the three squads were here, the heavies all at one table and arguing about something. The only sergeant in sight from where Still-water sat was her own, Drillbent, who was at a small table with only a jug of ale for company.

It wasn't that nobody liked Drillbent, Stillwater reflected morosely. It was just that nobody knew him. Well, they knew him, but they didn't know him, either. They knew him enough, after all these years, to know that they didn't know him, was what she meant to think.

And the corporals had a table of their own, with Oams taking the fourth chair but sitting well back from Morrut, Undercart and Snack. It was probably the only seat he'd found. She'd worked with Oams. He was competent, one of the last of the sappers but also a night-blade, since sappers didn't count the way they used to. They had a handful of munitions to work with, but those were touchy. Not Moranth, of course. Just imperial copies. Oams was always complaining. Every fourth one was a dud. Not consistently, of course, but that's how it averaged out. And the flamers had a way of blowing up in one's hand, which wasn't good. She didn't understand sappers.

There was a vivid memory of the last battle, out on the outlying flank edging the tree-line. Pithambra from the 7th Squad, facing down a half-dozen of the enemy with a single sharper, which he threw at their feet. But the clay was too thick, Oams later explained, so it bounced instead of exploding, and in the next breath Pithambra was dead. Someone stepped on the sharper later, took off both legs. Too little, too late.

She remembered pointing that out even as she pointed at the legless bandit who'd died upright. Those within hearing had laughed for some reason. Thinking on it again made her scowl deepen. Imagine, laughing after having had the crap beaten out of the company. And whenever someone talked about that whole scene now, they ended it by describing that bandit, whom they had named Too-Little Too-Late, and then laughing all over again.

Malazan marines seemed to like laughing at all the wrong things. She didn't get it at all. Now, stealing from a dead witch, that was funny.

Anyway, poor Pithambra.

Benger and Clay Plate left the table, followed a moment later by So Bleak, leaving just Anyx Fro for company. Stillwater eyed the woman. 'You look sick.'

'I am,' Anyx replied. 'Sick of you always saying I look sick. I just happen to have a porcelain complexion.'

'A what?'

Anyx brushed one cheek and fluttered her eyelashes. 'Creamy—'

'Colourless.'

'Delicate.'

'Deathly.'

Anyx fell silent.

'Go on,' Stillwater prompted. 'Let's hear your description of those bags under your eyes.'

'They're my mother's.'

'So why do you have them?'

Anyx frowned. 'I just told you. They're my mother's!'

'So why did she give them to you, and why did you agree to take them in the first place? What did she say? "Oh here, darling, I'm tired of carrying them." And you said, "Yes Mummy," and now here you are, looking like you live under a rock.'

'It's just an act, isn't it? I mean, it's a good one. You've got all the heavies convinced, anyway.'

'Convinced of what?'

'That you're thicker than a gangplank, Stillwater.'

'I should've joined the Claw. Then I wouldn't have to deal with all these insults. In the Claw they talk about killing and that's all they talk about, and really, what else *is* there to talk about? Especially in the Claw.'

'Oams was in the Claw,' said Anyx Fro. 'Might be he still is.'

'Oams? I don't believe you. He never talks about killing.' She glanced over at the man sitting with but not with the corporals. Something obviously poked him about her attention, since his head turned and he met her eyes, and then made a face. She made one back and returned her gaze to Anyx, who was busy tucking a wad of rustleaf into her mouth. 'Yesterday afternoon all he was talking about is the jumpy thing.'

'The jumpy what?'

'Thing. Inside his body. Jumping this way and that.'

'What kind of thing?'

'The jumpy kind, I guess.'

Anyx Fro's look flattened, and her eyes thinned. 'It's got to be an act.'

'Oams? He's got no act. I mean, he couldn't. Besides, now he's all jumpy.'

'Doesn't look jumpy. Looks half asleep, actually.'

'And he was asking me about spirits and spectres and gods and did they like to fuck mortals and what if one did?'

Anyx emptied a stream of brown spit into a spare tankard on the table, then looked down at it and moved the tankard away. 'And what did you say, Stillwater?'

'I said what anybody'd say.'

'Which is?'

'Oh, I said: "No, Oams, I'm not fucking you, so fuck off already."'

Anyx nodded. 'No argument there. So . . . which one are you?'

'Which one what?'

'Spirit, spectre or god? Goddess, I mean.'

'I didn't fuck him, so it wasn't me in the first place.'

'So you think one did?'

'Oams? Why would anything fuck Oams? No, he's just fishing.' She sat back and crossed her arms. 'And that's why he's not a Claw and never was.'

'You might have a point,' Anyx conceded. 'He's got no magery in him, after all. Most Claws do, you know.'

'They do?'

'Of course. They're mage-assassins, Stillwater. It's pretty much required to even be considered for admission into the ranks.'

Stillwater stared at Anyx Fro. She made a sound that meant . . . that meant something, but she didn't know what. Then she swore. 'It's always the way, dammit! Just like the barrows – someone always gets to them first!'

Clay Plate swung by at that moment, collected up his tankard, drained it, set it back down, and then walked away.

Stillwater looked at the tankard and then at Anyx, who met her eyes and then looked at the tankard, and then they were both looking at the tankard. After a long moment, Anyx rose from her chair, shouldering her bag of wooden chips. 'Got some painting to do.'

'More lead-paste paint?'

'Why not? Got a whole jar of the shit. Just don't stack 'em and stack 'em, that's all.'

'Maybe that's what's making you look so sickly, Anyx.'

'Not sickly. Porcelain.'

Sergeant Shrake dipped the tip of her braid into the wine and then slipped it between her full lips and sucked.

'Do you really have to do that?' So Bleak asked.

'We cast knuckles, So Bleak,' she said around the braid, which she was now chewing. 'I lost.'

'You were also short in your squad.'

'Been short before. Your reputation preceded you. It's not a good one.'

'Nothing changed,' So Bleak said, in some exasperation, and it didn't help that he was a bit drunk. 'Luck is luck. The Lady's pull. Then someone decided that it was everybody around me getting the Lord's *push*. That's not fair.'

'You're right,' she replied. 'The Law of Fair has been broken. I suggest you register a complaint with the universe. Best way, of course, is to scratch it on a piece of pottery and then throw it into a well. I'm told that works every time.'

'You should really be considering me your charm.'

'I would, if you were at all charming. Truth is, you're plain, So Bleak. And besides, you came in with that name of yours, meaning you'd already earned it.'

'I earned it because I'd lost too many friends. Because your miserable universe doesn't *have* any laws.'

Shrake dipped her braid back into her wine and made stirring motions. 'My universe isn't miserable at all. It's all flowers and meadows and butterflies under a bright sun on a warm summer's day. Want in?'

'Do I ever.'

'Never happening. You're too plain and besides, you're bad luck to have around. And now we're stuck with you and if you go and outlive us, I swear, So Bleak, I'll break the Gate Guardian's other leg to get back here and haunt you for the rest of your Lady-kissed butt-polishing life, and I'll be bringing my marines with me.'

He glared at her while she slid the braid-end back into her mouth and sucked, somewhat noisily. 'I hope you choke on that,' he said.

'Just my luck, or, rather, yours. Now go get more drunk and puke in someone else's lap, will you? I'm waiting for Spindle.'

He rose and wobbled momentarily, and then swung about with as much dignity as possible and made his way outside. He didn't like Trader's Inn anyway, especially on the night before they all shipped out. Worse yet, something wasn't right about this time. He couldn't pin it down, of course, but it was the kind of feeling he'd had before. Usually on the night preceding disaster. Then again, it wouldn't do to talk about that to anyone, especially since the last time he'd had this feeling, they'd been about to slap down a hundred or so useless bandits.

His life seemed to have found a new trajectory. He was tumbling down the stairs, one agonizing step at a time.

Once outside, he paused, letting the night's cold breath wash over him. He decided that he hated Sergeant Shrake. With her wine-stained braid and big squishy lips, her eyes so veiled and languid like pools of water, her pointy chin and wide, flaring jawline, her big-boned chest and the slight inward turn of her left foot making her walk look tentative despite her bouncy back-end. He especially hated how smart she was, all that sarcasm oozing out like snake venom. But most of all, he hated the fact that she could swing that broadsword of hers the way she could. Imagine, cutting a man halfway through at chest-level! He wouldn't have believed it if he hadn't seen it with his own eyes.

That'd been right after he'd saved Corporal Undercart's life. Or maybe it was just before. One or the other, anyway. True, she was a bit beefy on the shoulders, but still, she'd left her feet to do it, at the end of a sudden charge, and she'd come at the man from a flank – he'd not even seen her, and both his arms were up for some reason, so she got in under that. Ribs snapping like a sapper's knucklers. *Snap! Snapsnap!* And then gushing blood, and down he went choking on red gore.

He hated her all right. Hated her so much all he wanted to do was fuck her.

But plain men had no luck with women like that, making him hate her even more. So that was the truth of it all right. This miserable universe only ever showed him its bleakest face.

Then he reeled at a sudden insight. *Your universe, So Bleak? Why, it's your perfect reflection. That's all it is and all it ever will be. Now be a man and chew on that!*

A pox of black feathers on the Lady's pull. Next time, next scrap, next whatever, he was going to march straight into it, praying for the Lord's push. *End it. End it all, damn you!*

Then he dropped to his knees and puked.

'It's all about the greater good,' Blanket was saying, 'and if that meant chaining some poor fools to a damned wall, well, better that than a whole damned continent under water and thousands and thousands drowned.'

'Easy to say,' Paltry Skint retorted, 'since it wasn't you chained to the Stormwall.'

'I was speaking in terms of principles, Skint, which is what we have been addressing all this time.'

'But your principles are just your way of glossing over the nasty details, Blanket. And that's why I'm saying that what Stonewielder did was the right thing.'

'We don't really know what Stonewielder did,' Folibore pointed out.

Paltry Skint turned on him. 'That's so typical, Folibore. This may shock you, but your ignorance does not constitute a defence of your position. It simply highlights its flaws, not to mention the appalling paucity of your education.'

Folibore blinked. 'Whilst you in turn engage in personal attacks, that being the last refuge of the indefensible.'

'Wrong. My last refuge is this fist in your face.'

'Hah!' snorted Blanket. 'As if physical violence isn't the first choice of the intellectually challenged.'

She pointed her finger at him. 'Exactly! And what did Stonewielder do on the Stormwall? He stopped fighting! All that killing and dying had to stop so that's what he did!'

'"And in the icy waters rush,"' intoned Say No, '"the white waves scythe / until the stone stands alone. / On their salt-maned horses they ride / circle the single tower. / You would swallow the heart / of the Fallen God? / Ascend the stairs to confront / his beautiful broken daughter? / Then heed this granite blade / that rises no more . . ."'

The heavies sat silent, a few eyes made damp.

Folibore leaned back, sighing. A little poetry was all it took, to keep the fists from flying.

'How does the rest of that go?' Blanket asked hoarsely.

Say No shrugged. 'Can't recall, to be honest.'

'Something about "the blinded eye",' ventured Daint.

'Wrong song,' Given Loud said in a growl, glaring at Daint. 'You're thinking of the Lay of Ipshank—'

'No, I'm not,' snarled Daint. 'The Lay of Ipshank is on a four-three-four cadence and needs a tusk-drum dropped down an octave—'

'Not without the thumping heel dance on the counter-beat!'

'Only in Dal Hon! Nobody else cares a whit about a thumping heel dance, you damned fool!'

Folibore startled everyone by pounding his fist on the table. Wine and ale spilled. 'We were discussing principles in the matter of what constitutes true ethical virtue, my friends. Paltry Skint elected to focus on the fate of Stonewielder upon the Stormwall, and the Washing of Tears that thereafter cleansed Kolanse. Might I now take the opportunity to counter with The Unwitnessed—'

'Not again!' Paltry Skint shouted. 'If the damned Fall of the Bonehunters was *unwitnessed*, how can we ever know what happened in the first place? That history is all fake! No, it's worse than fake. It's *made up*!'

Blanket half-rose in his chair, teeth bared. 'And what's so wrong with "made up"?'

'"Our fates unknown,"' sang Say No suddenly, '"where ends the magic road / and the wings cannot give shelter . . ."'

And once more, as she continued, everything settled back down. But Folibore knew that it was going to be a long night. He eyed Say No, praying to all the gods that she'd memorized enough stirring poetry.

When Shrake saw Spindle entering the tavern and approaching her table, she also took note of Drillbent getting up and heading over.

Drillbent arrived first. Shrake used a foot to push a chair away from the table and he gave her a curt nod before slumping down in it.

'No one's going to like it,' he said, flicking a glance at Spindle when he pulled up another chair.

'So Bleak's getting drunk,' said Shrake.

Drillbent frowned at her. 'So?'

'Bleak.'

'No, I heard you. I meant, so what?'

'The old stories are true. We have proof. When it's going to be a shitstorm, So Bleak gets drunk first.'

'We ain't in any shitstorm.'

'Yet.'

'Well,' Drillbent said after a moment, 'too bad you couldn't distract him.'

'I told you, Drill, it's a bad idea. Look, I'm having a hard enough time keeping my hands off him. He's so . . . puppy.'

Spindle and Drillbent exchanged looks.

'Fuck off you both. It's bad form, crotch-grinding one of your squaddies. You know it.'

A waiter arrived and set down a jug of the cheap Nathii wine and then walked off.

'He forgot your cups,' Shrake observed, defensively corralling her own lest anyone get ideas. 'But you can swap the jug back and forth.'

Spindle said, 'So the braid thing didn't work?'

'Oh, he made disgusted noises, but he couldn't take his eyes off it. In other words, it went the opposite way. I suppose if I start picking my nose . . . but no, nothing's working. We're like lodestones on a tabletop, slowly crawling closer and closer. Pretty soon . . . *snap!*'

'Four-legged back-beast,' said Drillbent. 'Little Shrakes, little Bleaks.'

'Did you call him ugly?' Spindle asked her.

'I called him plain.'

'Try ugly next time.'

Drillbent breathed loudly through his nostrils. 'Calling him ugly doesn't change the fact that he's good-looking, at least as far as you're concerned, Shrake. Me, if I had to get up every morning looking at that face, I'd probably hang myself.'

'But that's because you hate everybody.'

'I don't hate everybody, Shrake. They just bore me.' Then he blinked. 'Present company excluded.'

Spindle cleared his throat. 'Lieutenant Balk will lead his column. We'll camp a bit apart on the way to Silver Lake, but I'm still expecting a few catcalls and maybe a scrap or two. We need to keep our soldiers tightly reined. The captain wants that understood. Meals will be communal.'

Shrake leaned back and started dipping her braid-end into her wine, and then yanked it away with a scowl. 'I foresee an epic food-fight with losses on both sides. I suggest we get ours in first by having Oams spike a few bread-rolls with knucklers. I know, they're used to scare horses but I'm sure one blowing up in a mouth will be surprising enough.'

Sighing, Drillbent said, 'The empire ain't what it used to be. Hiring mercenaries. And if that's not bad enough, how about ones we just locked horns with?'

'Their previous employer is dead,' Spindle pointed out.

'Look at us,' Shrake suddenly said. 'Three left.'

'Makes for short meetings,' Drillbent said, and then held up a hand. 'I know, bad taste. Sorry. We need to be more like Stillwater.'

Shrake's eyebrows lifted. 'Stillwater? That knify mage of yours?'

'But no one knows she's a mage,' said Drillbent.

'What are you talking about? Everyone knows!'

'*She* doesn't know that.'

'Which makes her an idiot,' Shrake said. 'And you think we should all be like that? Idiots?'

'She doesn't see the real world,' Drillbent explained, 'including all the people around her. She lives in her own little place, and what a place! Crowded with dead friends and living friends who will soon be dead, and meanwhile, everything else doesn't even exist!' He sat back. 'I envy her.'

Shrake dipped her braid into her wine and then sucked at it.

The two men at the table with her watched.

She scowled, yanked the braid from her mouth and said, 'Fucking men, you're all alike.'

CHAPTER THREE

Fist Sevitt commanded the North Malazan Provinces on Genabackis at the time. Not much is known about Sevitt, and likely never will be now. It is curious how history can line up before us like witnesses all in a row, and among the faces straining to speak, only one in ten, or twenty, does not stand there with mouth tightly sewn shut. The past is often mute, yet that which shouts to us in the present makes mockery of presentiment. I would indeed wager that each and every ruined monument is a testament to stupidity. Nothing of wisdom survives. Only the vainglorious travesties of pride and idiocy.

Now, where was I? Oh yes, Fist Sevitt . . .

Cahagras Pilt
Preface to the Introduction,
Preliminary Thoughts Towards Rethinking History
The Great Library of New Morn

Silver Lake, Malyn Province

THOUGH HE'D BEEN A HUNTER FOR MOST OF HIS LIFE, NOT ONCE during the night did he entertain the thought of awakening others in the town. He was getting on in years. He'd seen a lot, enough to know when it was time to set aside the bow, to find a good perch, and to sit in silent witness to something wonderful.

Animals had habits. It was easy to think that's all they were. Eating, breeding, raising young. Running from danger, standing ground when cornered. He had seen animals acting in fear, in terror, and from places of pain and anguish. He'd even watched them run off cliffs to their deaths, when a herd became a single beast, blindly fleeing what it could not even see.

He had seen other animals, the hunting kind, in their relentless pursuit of prey, and how necessity was often cruel, remorseless.

Life had its patterns, some small, some so vast it was a struggle to comprehend them. Plants, animals, people. They all fit into that pattern, whether they liked to or not, whether they admitted it, or not. Time pushed everything forward; either you flowed with it or you didn't.

In the night only now ending, the lake's surface had found a new pattern of its own, one the hunter had never seen before. Beneath the broken half-moon, wreathed in silver and fulminating, with the soft roar of clashing antlers filling the still air, caribou swam the lake. Thousands, perhaps even tens of thousands.

The lake's north shore was a tumble of boreal forest, a succession of ravines and gorges making a rumpled pattern running east–west. Those cuts had probably been there long before the lake's appearance, and whatever drainage occurred from that shore did so through cracks in the bedrock, through seeps and underground passages. The rumpled pattern worked northward, skirting the worn edge of the Godswalk Mountains, eventually levelling out into a muskeg swamp and beyond that a tundra that stretched for a hundred leagues, if not more.

The herd had habits, but they had never included migrating this far south. The hunter knew that for certain. The caribou wintered in the forest and, come the spring, they usually ventured *north*, across ancient trackways cutting through the muskeg, and out onto the rolling tundra.

The hunter had never been that far upland, but he had heard tales from the forest dwellers to the northeast, the traders in fur, amber and wild rice. And he had, on occasion, hunted caribou in the forest.

It had taken most of the night for the herd to cross. Had this event taken place twenty years ago, he might well have rushed into the settlement, gathering up as many hunters as possible, and they would have conducted a slaughter, thinking of all that meat, all those hides, all the wealth on hoof.

Bloodlust, he now decided, was the last thing to go, but go it eventually did. He was tired of killing.

So he sat, watching the spectacle beneath the moon's silver light. The thousands made into one, the one broken free of its seasonal habit. It wasn't enough to simply wonder why. There could be a dozen reasons for that and perhaps they were important, something worth taking notice of, but what took hold of his soul, what occupied his thoughts as the night slowly worked past and the beasts surged up onto the shore and then spread out, heading south across pastureland and the vast swaths where forests had once been, was something far more profound. People looked at the beasts and saw every habit as instinct, as if those beasts were slaves to their own natures.

In many ways, perhaps they were. But what this night revealed to the hunter was that any animal – every animal – was more than just a collection of instincts. Making animals no different from people. Each life, properly *alive*. Alive in the way of people. Hopes, possibly even dreams. Desires, oh, yes, for sure there were desires.

I do not wish to drown.

I do not wish for my calf to drown or be dragged down by wolves.

I do not wish for an arrow to stop my heart. Or puncture my lungs to make me cough blood, weaken, stagger, fall to my knees.

As the sky began to lighten, the last of the herd left the lake, flowed overland into the mists of the south. Cheeks wet, he watched them leave.

His fellow hunters would be furious. Many would set out after the herd, and animals would fall to their arrows. But their weakest, most vulnerable moment had passed.

Only then did he descend from the outcrop, collect up his string of hares, and head down to the road, on this, his last day of hunting. Ever.

The tavern called the Three-Legged Dog was at one end of a row, nearest the lake, occupying a corner with the Shore Road on the left and Silver Lake's main thoroughfare along its front. Beneath the balcony's overhang and above the tavern door was mounted a massive horse skull, almost twice the size of a normal horse's skull, at least by southern standards.

Inside the tavern, above the stone-framed fireplace and facing the bar, hung the smoke-stained skull of a grey bear, missing its lower jaw. Mortared in among the rounded stones of the fireplace was a Teblor's skull, with everything above the brow cracked and broken.

Whenever Rant gazed northward, across the lake, or to the hazy mountains in the northwest, he imagined a world where he was small, beneath notice by beast and warrior alike. When he was younger, little more than a child, he'd been fascinated by the three skulls of the Three-Legged Dog, but that fascination – all his fiery imaginings – had not survived the succession of growth-spurts that then afflicted him, when his few friends of similar age had stopped playing with him and had instead begun fleeing from him.

Other truths were not long in coming. Everyone in town knew of the madness afflicting his mother. They knew it by that name, when for most of Rant's life until that point, she had been his only guide into the strange world of the grown-ups, and so he had thought of it as being normal. Grown-ups, he had concluded, possessed hidden faces. They showed one during the day, out on the street or in other public places; and they showed another at night, or in the privacy of their homes.

He had even believed, for what seemed the longest time, that his mother's red teeth were normal. Until he realized otherwise, and somewhere in the midst of that confused revelation, he'd heard the words *'the whore's blood-oil smile'*. And this was added to his list of things that didn't yet mean much, but someday would.

In what he believed was his ninth year he was a head taller than the tallest grown-up in Silver Lake. And his old friends, now gathered into a protective gang, would throw stones at him from across the street. Two years later, grown-ups looked up at him from chest-height. And from his old friends, the stones they threw got bigger. Not long after that the people in town called him *'that Teblor half-breed'*, and they then flung upon him all the venom that followed the slave uprising.

Of course, he had seen the Teblor slaves, and he had come to understand that the skull in the fireplace also belonged to a Teblor. But for the longest time he had not connected them with his own life, his growth spurts, or the widening breadth of his shoulders, his raw strength.

The uprising, when it came, had been brief but brutal. Teblor savages, unbowed by shackle and chain, had come down to free their kin. They had killed anyone who sought to oppose them. It happened in a single night, and all he had seen of it from his room with its single window facing onto Shore Street, was the lurid glow of flames from the burning holding pen off to the far right, and a scatter of motionless forms on the muddy street below, with the occasional scream in the distance making his skin crawl.

Since then, hate had been added to the fear, and Rant, who had grieved over the loss of his friends, desperately searching within himself for the source of their fright, now found himself more alone than ever, more alone than he thought a person could ever be.

He could not look to his mother for much comfort. This truth had been slow to come into Rant's mind, this realization that she was unreliable, unknowable, that the fierce, fevered look in her eyes that he'd once imagined to be love, wasn't anything of the sort. It was *madness*. And that her smile was not a display of affection. It was *'the whore's blood-oil smile'*, a thing of hunger and need.

From his loft bedroom, on the bed positioned as far away as possible from the one whole side open to the main living area below, he remained motionless, curled up around his confusion, the straw ticking of his mattress damp under the burlap, smelling of things he had never smelled before.

While she skittered about every now and then below, voicing small giggles punctuated by sobs, and with the sobs came the sound of her fists beating at her own face, bruising it, puffing it up, skin splitting where it had swollen the most.

From where he was, eyes fixed on the porthole window with its dull lake-gleam and smudge of distant mountains hovering blurred and colourless through the dirty glass, he could not see that face. But he knew what it looked like.

After all, she had been giggling, sobbing and beating her own face even as she straddled him, hips thrusting, and he looked up at her, not knowing what was happening, even as strange feelings tingled everywhere between his legs, and the thing his pee came out of was now hard and long and aching. And inside her.

Eyes of madness. Blood-oil smile. Sudden flashes of horror. Fists against her face until cuts bled, nostrils bled, eyes bled. While a part of him speared her, and he thought about one of the other names they now gave Rant. *Blood-oil bastard.*

He didn't know what Blood-oil was. Their family name, perhaps. The word 'bastard' meant that he had no father. He knew that much, and besides, it was obvious, since 'father' was a word his friends used, and he never did, while 'mother' was one they all used.

Some 'fathers' had been killed in the Uprising.

Confusion rushed upon him everywhere his thoughts went. Not just his mother's madness and what she'd done which she'd never done before, at least not to him. He'd seen her with men, since that was her work. And the men paid her and that was how they lived. Rant decided that he would now have to find something to pay her as well. And it wasn't just the mystery of *Blood-oil*, which might be his father's name, but not his only name – that father he didn't have – since Drunk Menger who owned the Three-Legged Dog had tried kicking him in the alley behind the tavern, where Rant was in the habit of hiding and playing with the town's two feral dogs, and while the kick had missed, Menger's face stayed twisted with hate as he cursed Rant.

'Get yer fecking carcass away from here! Y'think yer the only bastard that fecking Shattered God left behind 'im? Karsa Orlong's half-breed bastard! No, you ain't, or wasn't, only we done for the rest of 'em – years ago! Cut 'em down as soon as they showed that fecking Teblor sign, and we shoulda done the same wi' you! Blood-oil bastard!'

And that was what troubled him the most. *Karsa Orlong.* The same name his mother chanted as she rode him, eyes of madness, smile of Blood-oil, while Rant frantically tried to think of some way to pay her for the work, because without work they couldn't eat.

And he was always hungry.

After she was done and had clambered down from the loft voicing a chorus of sobs, he rolled onto his side, drew up his knees, and waited for the sun to come up.

Now, in the burgeoning light, he stared out the tiny window. Across the murky lake, into the blurry black line of forest, up the jagged slopes of the so-far-away mountain peaks.

'Rant!'

He shifted at her rasping call. 'I don't got anything,' he said, as sudden tears welled in his eyes.

'Rant! Listen to me! Are you listening? You have to go.'

'Go where?'

'Get out. Run away. Leave town and never come back! I can't. I won't. There's no. It's the unspoken law! I didn't. Never meant.' Low muttering then, followed by: 'Listen! Go find the Teblor, them that escaped – they know about you. They protected you, but now they're all gone, understand? People'll kill you here, and soon! It wasn't me. It's the fever they pay for, understand? They get a taste, just a taste, and they come back and back and you, you . . . no. Get away. I can't. I won't.'

Fists against the face.

He winced. 'Don't. No more, please.'

The fists stopped their thudding. Her voice changed, suddenly flat. 'Go. Today. Right now. If you don't, I will kill myself.'

'I can pay! You'll see!'

She shrieked then, and the ladder creaked sharply as she was upon it, scrambling up. He curled tighter.

'I'll pay, I promise.'

'Nobody gets enough, Rant. You stay and it'll happen to you, too. And I won't. I won't. Lie there, then. Know that I love you with all my heart. And that's why I'm now going to cut my throat wide open.'

He might have cried out then, though it was not a sound like anything he'd ever made before, so he couldn't be sure, but with it came a surge of movement from his own body, as he twisted past her, still gripping his blanket, and slipped over the edge of the loft, his height more than matching the height of the ladder she'd just climbed.

Lunging for the doorway. 'Don't!' he screamed, not daring to look. 'Don't!'

Then he was running, down the main street, straight for the strand of pebbled beach fringing the shore – and there were animals there, coming up out of the water. Like tiny horses but antlered. Lots of them. They bolted away from him even as he plunged among them, smelling their wet hides, seeing their pluming breaths in the cold morning air, the heat rising from their backs.

He slid, slipped on the mud, fell among their legs.

The world was awash in tears. His mother had cut open her own throat. Because she loved him. Because he couldn't pay.

The pounding of hoofs dwindled, and he looked up. The animals were leaving. He rolled onto his side in the stony mud just up from the beach and looked out across the choppy lake.

When they found her body, the men would gather their bows and spears, and they would set out after him.

He continued staring northward, to that distant black line of forest on the far side. The place where the giant beasts lived. And the Teblor.

Rising to his feet, he found that he still held his blanket. He'd outgrown it long ago. He balled it up in his left hand and then walked onto the beach, and into the icy water.

He began swimming.

The dogs were still barking in the nearby farms, even as the last hundred or so caribou left the churned-up fields, continuing south towards what remained of forest this close to the town. Eyes on those caribou, the hunter wondered at their fate. He feared a slaughter would soon descend upon them, as word spread.

His traps had snared five hares, one of them a female swollen with unborn pups. He regretted that. And with the winter as hard as it had been, there wasn't much meat on the others. The truth was, the borders of the wild had retreated, as they always did. Settlements rose up, sank down roots, spread out in a flurry of swinging axes and brush-fires, and before too long, the role of the hunter more or less faded away.

Were he a decade or two younger he would be resentful, his anger stirred up, and already preparing to flee the civilization that had arrived. The world seemed vast, but he wondered if there would come a day when the last wild place vanished, when old hunters like him would sit in taverns, drunk on ale and weeping with nostalgia, or stumbling pointlessly down stinking alleys and streets, yet another victim of progress.

But even these thoughts simply skittered across the surface of his mind. The only progress that mattered was what a single life had to deal with, day by day. The rest was someone else's problem. He wasn't one of those who could think themselves into a white rage, reaching too far ahead like a skeletal hand erupting from a grave, or reaching back in a pathetic attempt to make things the way they used to be.

Still, when the animals went away, something terrible took their place.

The road leading into town was muddy, stones overturned, filled with ruts that cut across its width. Work-crews might have to come out to make repairs. There'd be swearing and cursing, and if the day was warm and the smell of growth was heavy in the air, few would even notice the new season's gift.

Glancing left, he scanned the lake, taking note of the water close to the shore, its milky silts spreading in clouds. Here and there, he now saw, carcasses broke the surface. Those waters were cold.

Then he halted, eyes squinting. Something still thrashed out there. He watched for a time, until he was certain that he could see a bare arm, rising and falling. He scanned for sight of an overturned boat hull, but the figure seemed to be entirely alone.

And doomed.

But not trying to help would haunt him, he was certain. Turning away always carried a price, and he was tired of paying it. He set off, picking up his pace as he crossed the bridge over Foul Creek, making his way towards the beach where the fishing skiffs were all drawn up. This early in the season, the fish and eels were still sluggish, still down deep. The eel-run into the shallows and up the feeder-streams was still a month away. Even here, the year still had its lean times, and this was one of them. Most of those boats hadn't moved since last autumn.

There was no one down on the beach. It was still too early. But he saw Capor's old skiff, pulled up on the strand alongside his new one. It was battered and leaked and hadn't been used at all last summer, but the hunter settled on that one, since Capor wouldn't yell too much at him for using a boat he'd pretty much left to rot.

Reaching it, he dropped the string of hares and flipped the boat over. Flinging the hares into the boat, he began pushing the craft towards the water. A glance showed him the swimmer still out there, although the arms were slowing down.

A few moments later the skiff was in the water and he clambered aboard. He left the mast stowed since there was no wind to speak of, and instead pulled out the oars, dropping them into their sockets in the weathered, warped gunwales.

Rowing was brisk work, the kind he wasn't used to, and it wasn't long before he worked up a sweat. Facing the shore, he saw the first townsfolk to be up and about, dark figures crossing Centre Street. Then a lone fisherman appeared, carrying a bucket down to his skiff. Not Capor. Probably Vihune, with that bow-legged gait. The figure paused upon seeing the hunter out on the lake, but then continued on. Vihune had little imagination and rarely wondered about things for long.

The hunter paused, twisting round to catch sight of the swimmer. For a few breaths he searched in vain. The arms no longer flashed upward in their flailing strokes. The hunter shipped the oars and carefully stood, feet planted wide to keep the skiff steady. Then he saw it. Still out there . . . or not. Floating, but motionless.

Probably nothing but a carcass. I came out here for nothing. And that carcass was far away, too far to be the swimmer. Still it looked big, and the colour . . .

'Shit.' He sat back down and collected up the oars and resumed rowing.

His eyes weren't as sharp as they'd once been. But that was a man clinging to a bloated caribou. He was sure of it. Shoulders aching, he pulled fiercely on the old oars.

Rant dreamed that he had grown very small. His legs had vanished first, then his arms and now most of his body. He was now nothing but shoulders, neck and head, all of that resting upon the smelly soaked fur of the strange animal that floated like a fresh log. But he could feel how the fur slid up his cheek, so he knew that he would not be long upon this strange island. Soon, even his shoulders would disappear.

It was now obvious to him that all those years of growing bigger were being reversed, shrinking him down and down. Being so tall had shown him too much of the world, too much that was frightening and confusing, full of hard words and harder rocks. So, he was going back, un-growing, and the sun was warm on one cheek and the water he floated on wasn't cold any more, and it all seemed very reasonable to imagine himself becoming so small no one would ever see him again.

But then he was being jostled about. It was too much effort to open his eyes, but he heard splashing, grunting, the squeal of wood. A bend of rope slapped lightly on his cheek. Then his head was being moved round, every motion wonderfully smooth. Something like a knot brushed one shoulder, and where it touched, pressure was building. He felt his shoulders being pulled up, and the big floppy things attached to them bumped here and there as they were lifted upward. His cheek left the fur and he moaned at the loss.

He heard a faint, far-away voice. 'Alive after all, then. Thawing's going to hurt, I think. A lot. Sorry for that.'

More movement, an eternity of it, until the back of his head crunched vaguely on gritty wood, and he could smell fish-scales, and the sun had flipped over to the other side of the sky, drying the cheek that had been warmed by fur, and everything was rocking for a time until the motion settled into rhythmic surges announced by someone's grunting.

The un-growing had stopped, and now he was growing again, in patches of sunlit fire.

'It's said some of you half-breeds got two hearts. If you was one of the unlucky ones with only a single beater, you wouldn't have lived this long anyway. Those half-breeds weaken in only a few years, when their bodies get too big for just one heart. And today, lad, you needed that extra one. Damn me, the scale had me all confused. You swam more than half of the lake. Hard to believe.'

Rant concentrated on the voice, not because he understood what the man was talking about, but because it was better than concentrating on the pain, as the fires spread and spread.

'Let the sun thaw you, nice and easy. Can you open the fingers of your left hand? That sodden blanket needs to be squeezed dry. Right now it's just a ball of ice, I bet.'

Rant could feel water now, sloshing around him. It was cool, not cold. It was getting deeper.

'Can't talk much more, I'm afraid. Need my breath. We're sinking. It's the north shore or we're done for. You won't survive another dunk and on this side it's all fresh melt. I see chunks of ice.'

Rant lifted one arm, and then the other. He managed to let go of the blanket. Then, opening his eyes, he sat up.

The man at the oars started. 'Gods below, this fast? Never mind two hearts. You must have a dozen beaters or more.'

Rant recognized the man. One of the hunters, one of the men who used to track escaped slaves and led slaving parties deep into Teblor lands, who'd once been a soldier, too. The man, in fact, who had killed that grey bear, the skull of which was in the Three-Legged Dog. 'You hunted me down,' Rant said from where he found himself slumped up against the stern-wall, his words slurred. 'They say you are the best. Now you're going to take me back and they will kill me.'

'Kill you why?'

'Mother cut her own throat because of me. Because I couldn't pay for her work.'

'You're the one they call Rant.'

Rant nodded.

The hunter pulled on the oars, but the craft barely moved. The water was halfway up now, slapping the underside of the wooden bench. 'I ain't taking us nowhere.'

Rant gestured. 'Give me the oars.'

'You?'

'So I don't think about things.'

'Things?'

'The fire. Mother.'

The hunter hesitated, and then released his hold on the oars and moved round to make his way forward. There was a wooden bailer tied to a brass loop in the gunwale. He collected it up and began bailing.

Rant pushed himself up onto the bench, twisted round and took up the oars. He dipped the blades in and pulled.

The boat lurched forward, knocking the hunter onto his knees, making him curse at the icy water. But then he resumed bailing, and when Rant made another stroke, he obviously rode the surge since there was no pause in his scooping water.

Strangely, the rowing eased Rant's pain. It made him take deeper breaths, too, and now it was his bare feet in the water that burned, but it seemed that the hunter was getting ahead of the leaking.

It was only then that he noticed the rope-rigging tied round his chest, felt the twin knots against the muscles covering his shoulder-blades, and the large brass loop at his sternum. Slave's rigging. He'd seen it before. 'These ropes,' he said.

'I always carry rope,' the hunter said. 'Brass rings, leather string. And a fire-kit, which we're going to need once we land on the north shore. Got meat, too, a bit pickled now from the salt Capor used on his catch.'

'This rigging.'

A moment's pause from behind Rant, and then: 'Aye. But those days are done.'

'You'll get a reward,' Rant said.

'Did you see your mother cut her own throat?'

'I ran first,' Rant replied. 'She said—'

'Words can chill the blood, but they can't spill it. I'd wager she never did what she said she would – oh, I know she's mad, your mother, but taking a blade to her own throat? Especially with the Blood-oil Curse? That's lust's own fever. She wanted you out of Silver Lake. Good reason to, in fact. Still, what a gods-awful way to get you running.'

'My name is cursed?' Rant asked. He wasn't prepared to believe the hunter about his mother. Not yet.

'What?'

'Blood-oil, my family name. You said it's a curse.'

The question must have offended the hunter, because he made no reply. The wooden scoop was scraping the hull now, picking up only dollops of muddy water. Rant's ankles were out of the water as well, and prickling, as if swarmed by biting ants. He continued rowing, not daring to ask any more questions.

'Slow up, Rant. Twist round. See that dip, beside the fallen log there? Angle us in.'

They were almost upon the shore. But it had only moments ago been so far away, with the old boat going nowhere. Rant was having trouble believing the truths of the world. He had been grown, only to un-grow, only to grow again. But this time he was differently grown from the first time. This time, the world wasn't too small for him, yet parts of it were.

The prow crunched up on sharp rocks just under the water and clattered into the heavy brush hanging above it. The hunter threw a loop of rope to snag those branches, and he used them to steady the craft. 'Okay, climb out, lad. Collect up that string of hares, and my bag there. Oh, and yes, blanket, too. Good idea.'

The water was only knee-deep when Rant stepped over the side of the boat, but it stung fiercely. He quickly scrambled onto the shore. The hunter followed, holding his rope in one hand and his unstrung bow and quiver in the other. He then made to tie up the boat, only to fall still.

'Why bother? It'll sink down right here anyway. See those new splits? That was you, Rant, you weigh more than this lake's biggest sturgeon, I'd wager.' He retrieved his rope, slipping one end out from the brass loop at the prow. 'Now, up and inland, lad. We'll find us a flat perch and make us a fire. We've both worked up an appetite, I'm sure.'

'You will make smoke from the fire, then?' Rant asked. 'So they can see and come get us?'

The hunter glanced up at Rant, his expression flat. 'No smoke, lad. I'm taking you to the Teblor.'

Confusion again. 'Why?'

The hunter shrugged. 'Half-breeds are trapped between worlds. But maybe the Teblor one will treat you better than ours did. It's worth a try.'

'But why?'

'Your family name, Rant, it's not Blood-oil. It's Orlong.'

This new world had too many truths he couldn't trust. 'So . . . what is Blood-oil?'

'It's complicated, that one. Maybe later.'

'I've forgotten your name, but you're the one who killed the grey bear.'

'The last grey bear this side of the Godswalk,' the hunter said, grimacing. 'People don't get it. I killed it out of pity. My name is Damisk.'

He knew that name, from the slaves. 'The Teblor hate you,' Rant said.

'With good reason. I'll take you as close as I can to whatever village or camp we stumble on. The rest is up to you, because I'll be hightailing it for the southlands.'

Rant nodded. That, at least, made sense. He lifted up the string of soaked hares. 'I'm hungry, Damisk.'

'Aye. A full stomach brightens the day.'

'You saved my life.'

Damisk shrugged. 'No such thing as saving a life, Rant. Better to say I happened by to prolong it. Now, those hares are gutted, but we need to skin 'em—'

'I know how to do that,' Rant said.

'Good. You do it, then, and I'll build us a fire.'

Rant still carried his knife, the only gift he'd ever received, from a Malazan marine when a troop passed through Silver Lake once, back when he was five or six. He pulled it out. The blade was icy cold. 'Damisk, did you see all those antlered horses in the lake?'

'Aye, I did.'

'What was that about?'

'I expect we'll find out. Or not. Either way, the Lady's Luck to 'em.'

He led Rant up the slope, into the forest proper, collecting up branches, twigs and lichen from trees as they went. The sun, it turned out, was as warm on the north shore of the lake as it was on the south shore. A big world, Rant reminded himself. But smaller, too.

CHAPTER FOUR

The XXXI Legion barely mustered two-thirds strength upon arriving in Nathilog, as the ocean crossing had been disastrous, beset by unseasonal storms. If this was not enough for the beleaguered soldiers, rumours of the Desert Plague among the ranks forced the harbour-master into quarantining the fleet in the bay, patrolled by fire-ships. This delay in disembarking was but one error in all that followed. Why make note of it as being of particular significance? Let us just say that the mood of the soldiers was not pleasant.

Brath of Worthless Ingot
History of This and That
The Great Library of New Morn

THERE WASN'T MUCH IN DAMISK'S PAST THAT HE WAS PROUD of, and there wasn't much of the world that he liked. At least, not when it came to the world of people. Too many of them were stupid. They couldn't think clearly enough to save their lives. The worst part was, they didn't know they were stupid. Every failure had an excuse, every loss was someone else's fault. Stupid people always had a reason to be angry but didn't have the capacity to understand that they were angry because they were frustrated, and they were frustrated because they didn't understand, and they didn't understand because they were stupid.

But stupid people could be excused for doing and saying the things they did. They couldn't help it, after all. It was the smart people who had no excuse. And that was another thing: even smart people could be stupid on occasion, or stupid about some things even if smart about others. More often than not, in Damisk's experience, many

61

people were smart about everyone around them, yet stupid about themselves.

Was there ever a civilization, in all the world's history, where honesty wasn't rare? The honesty that looked both ways, that is. Inward and outward.

At the end of all these thoughts, however, Damisk ever returned to a simple truth about himself. He wasn't particularly smart, but neither was he particularly stupid. When he revisited the conclusion that he didn't much like people, he always included himself.

'It's not about good and evil,' he now said to Rant, as they sat at the small fire with its bed of coals and almost smokeless heat. 'And I should have warned you earlier, a hunter spends a lot of time alone. Too much time alone, in fact. So, when that hunter finds company, why, he tends to have a lot to say. Do you mind?'

The huge half-breed shook his head, the lower half of his face still greasy from the meat. He was barefoot, but the soles of those feet looked toughened. He had taken his hide tunic off earlier, pounding out some of the water, only to then put it back on, since it would dry tight and brittle otherwise. That tunic was slave's garb, probably the only clothing available in a size that would fit the lad. Damisk had helped remove the harness and returned it to his pack, out of sight. It was still undecided, in the hunter's mind, whether Rant was stupid or smart, especially since Teblor were slow to mature, not physically, but mentally.

'Good and evil, Rant. Sages talk and write about them all the time. Temple priests. Magisters, executioners. And they talk about those two things as if someone was around to judge, some god or gods, maybe, or even the universe itself. But no one is, or if they are, they ain't talking. So those mortals, the sages, priests, magisters, they make themselves tall and stern and then claim that they're the ones entrusted to do all the judging. And they back up that claim in the usual way. Holy texts, Imperial Law, the City Watch, soldiers, the typical sword-in-the-shadows always there, hovering, hiding behind the sweet talk.'

Damisk paused. It was hard to tell if Rant was understanding any of this, or even listening. Stupid people could put on masks of concentration and attention, but they were paper-thin masks, and behind it was something small and lost in the fog.

'My point is, your mother's not evil. Neither are you. Let me tell you what the Wilds have shown me, way out beyond civilization and its web of lies.' He held up his hands, palm tilted to catch the last of the day's light. 'No good and evil, no right and wrong. The real scales upon which we are all judged are much simpler, Rant. Take a life, no matter how short or long. What's it made up of? Well: choices, deeds, promises, beliefs, mysteries, fears, a whole list of things – whatever you care to think of, in fact. That's what makes a life. Want to see it in terms of good and evil, of right and wrong? That's not the way of the Wilds, because those words are really about people judging other people and the problem with that is, you can't find truth studying the scales if your own eye's skewed. And everyone's eyes are skewed, whether they admit it or not.'

Damisk studied his upturned palms. 'A soul collects marks, Rant. Like you'd find on a factor's ledger. Some are burned into the surface. Some are placed there with a kiss. Forget good and evil, right and wrong. Think instead in terms of suffering and blessing.' He paused, studying the half-breed's heavy-boned face. 'That's the only ledger that counts. Take a life, like I said before, and now look back on it. Choices, deeds, promises. Which ones made for suffering, and which ones blessed?'

He lifted his hands higher and then let them drop. 'Every mortal soul lives a thousand lives, even more, but that don't mean a thousand ledgers for each soul. No, it's just one ledger, the same ledger. The soul brings it with it every time it lands in a body, and that body plays out its life, adding one mark at a time. Suffering. Blessing. And there's no escaping it, no cheating, no hiding it all away. What I call the Wilds is just raw nature, the universe itself, and it misses nothing and never blinks. And that's how souls pay for every choice, every decision, every promise, broken or kept.'

'Pay how?' Rant asked.

'Whatever you put in, you get back. Spend a lifetime making others hurt and suffer, your next lifetime delivers the same upon you. No escaping it. Those scales of justice, Rant, they ain't out there somewhere. Those are just flawed reflections.' He jabbed his own chest. 'They're in here. Justice doesn't exist in the Wilds, you see. I spent a lifetime looking for it out there, never found it. No, justice resides in each soul. So, when you cheat and think you got away with it, you didn't. When you cause suffering in someone, either directly or with your own indifference, the ledger inside records it. And the scales tip, and that suffering will return to you, and your soul will one day know the anguish you delivered.'

He studied Rant's face for a moment, and then shrugged. 'Your mother was raped by Karsa Orlong, caught up in the blood-oil curse, and you came of that. And she was stained by that blood-oil, driven half-mad, and that's never gone away, and yet somehow, she managed to raise you, keep you safe for as long as she could. Rant, she *suffered*, but it's not your fault. In fact, you, you're her *blessing*. And that's why she sent you away, to keep you safe.'

If a spoken word could brand itself upon a listener's face, then *'blessing'* did so now, and Damisk watched the eyes widen, the shock's sudden slap slowly sinking deep its sting, until what had at first hurt now delivered warmth, like a woman's caress. This was a boy who didn't know he'd been loved by anyone, especially not his mother. Damisk had worried that Rant hadn't followed the track of what he'd said. He needn't have. The lad was a long way from grown-up and that made him seem slow, clumsy, a simpleton. He was none of those things.

A life unloved was slow to awaken. It often never did.

'Damisk?'

'Aye?'

'My mother worked with men in the village. In her room. And they paid her. But then she worked with me, that last night. But I couldn't pay her.' He paused. 'I don't think I'm still her blessing.'

Damisk stared at the boy. He struggled to keep his voice calm. 'And after that happened, she drove you out of the house?'

Rant nodded.

'And said she'd cut her throat if you stayed.'

He nodded again.

Damisk wanted to put his hands to his face and weep. He drew a deep, shuddering breath, and then another. 'That was the blood-oil fever. What she did to you, it was the blood-oil. What she did after – driving you away – that was the real her. The mother who raised you and loved you. Two different people, Rant, in one body.'

'I never liked the blood-oil one. She scared me.'

'She did something terrible to you, Rant, that night. Something no sane mother – or father – would ever do. Most that do that to their child don't have the blood-oil as an excuse. And the marks they burn on their ledgers promise a dire retribution. I can't even pity people like that.' He struggled to keep his hands from trembling. 'The curse of the blood-oil is a madness. Your mother must have fought against that desire for years. When you stopped looking like a child, she lost the battle. And then, as the fever passed, her guilt devoured her whole.' He paused, not wanting to say what he was thinking. But Rant needed to understand. 'If she did take her own life, it was the guilt and shame and horror and fear that made her do it. Not you.' He studied Rant's face.

'She was beating her own face,' he said. 'So much I barely recognized her.'

'Maybe, as a final, desperate act, she didn't want you seeing her face when memories of that night start to torment you. Abide by that if you can. It wasn't her, not your mother at all. But someone else. Someone else who did that wrongness to you.'

'That one didn't bless me, then.'

'No, that one *cursed* you, Rant.'

'But my real mother, she loved me and blessed me.'

'The only way she knew how, yes. If you can, forgive your mother, but never forgive the blood-oil woman who raped you.'

Rant wiped at his eyes. 'I don't know how to do any of that, Damisk.'

'I don't think I do, either,' Damisk confessed.

'Damisk?'

'Aye?'

'I think you saved me to tell me this. But not for me, because I'm nobody special. I think you did it to leave a mark on your soul, a good mark. Because . . .'

'Because of all the bad ones?' Damisk brushed his hands together and grunted to his feet, his legs feeling weak under him. 'Toss those bones into the fire, will you? There'll be a wind tonight. We'll need to move deeper into the forest.'

As the lad set about his work, Damisk collected up his bow and quiver, forcing his thoughts back to the present. *Leave the rest for now. It's too much for us both. All the madness in the world – what can one man do? What can one child do?*

All my talk of justice, and then he tells me that. Karsa Orlong, you have a lot to answer for. When this bastard son of yours finds his anger, when he realizes the full extent of the betrayal – not by the woman who could not help herself – but by the man who cursed her with blood-oil, by you, Karsa . . .

Damisk rubbed at his face, drew another deep breath to take stock of his surroundings, of this moment. The passage of the caribou had chewed up everything underfoot. Every twig and branch up to a certain height had been swept away, making the forest look different. No obvious game-trails remained, and he didn't know this particular stretch.

Slow going, in other words. He stood facing the rough climb that awaited them, until Rant was done and had moved up alongside him. Then Damisk turned to the half-breed. 'My soul's next life will arise in the rotting bones of the bleakest, blackest valley, and there it'll stay.' He scratched at his beard. 'One mark of blessing? Well, it's a start.'

The ridge they found that seemed unbroken was well inland. The lake could not be seen, even though Damisk knew they were walking parallel to its shoreline as they trekked westward. But even this uplifted ribbon of bedrock was rumpled, fissured and pocked with sinkholes. In most of these places, there was only black mud left, the beds of lichen and moss churned up by countless hoofs. They would need to move past the land the caribou had crossed before they could hope to find standing water. Damisk hoped they would reach such an area before it got too dark.

Few of the jack-pines and black spruce along the ridge grew to their fullest height and girth, and from many of them their roots snaked over the bedrock like ropes or limbs as they sought out cracks and declivities, making the footing uncertain and treacherous as the gloom slowly descended. The cool air shifted into cold, but without winter's bite: a sure sign that the season of growth was upon the world.

The season for hopes, for renewed ambitions and enlivened resolve. The season for all the delusions to rise up once more, filling the fresh night air with their haunting promises. Damisk's mood soured. He'd seen too many of these seasons, felt all too often the hollowness at the core of renewal, the rot hiding within.

In the course of his single lifetime as a hunter, he had seen the game disappear in an ever-widening circle, with the settlement of Silver Lake at the centre. Too many believed the world was unchanging, eternal in its cycles. The roll-over of one season into the next, year after year, deceived them into believing this. To Damisk's mind, that most comforting lie was among the foremost traits of stupidity.

Nor was change unpredictable. It was in fact the very opposite. With eyes open and thinking fully engaged, so much of what came was not only predictable, it was inevitable.

He thought to explain this to Rant, the giant child at his side, laying out his theory of how the world worked; that its most powerful constant wouldn't be found in natural laws, in the needs of eating and sleeping and breeding. Wouldn't be found in how places rose and then fell, either. Wouldn't be found in seasons, or traditions, or all those borders animal and human scratched out on the ground.

Lad, the most powerful constant is stupidity. Nothing else comes close. Stupidity kills all the animals, empties the sky of birds, poisons the rivers, burns the forests, wages the wars, feeds the lies, invents the world over and over again in ways only idiots could think real. Stupidity, lad, will defeat every god, crush every dream, topple every empire. Because, in the end, stupid people outnumber smart people. If that wasn't true, we wouldn't suffer over and over again, through generation after generation and on for ever.

But the lad was young, too fresh to the world for such grim lessons. He had enough horrors to deal with. Besides, it did nothing to tell someone such things. Stupidity needed no allies among the wise, because there was nothing out there that could challenge it.

The shadows lengthened, darkness taking the ridge. But at last they were clear of the swath left by the herd. Ahead was a tangle of toppled black spruce and beyond it was a broad depression in the bedrock, filled with a pool of meltwater.

'This will do,' said Damisk, eyeing the vertical root-walls of the fallen trees.

Rant settled into a squat, his expression troubled. But he was not yet ready for words, so Damisk chose not to prod him. Instead, he walked close to examine the walls of roots, stones and dirt, where despite the failing light he'd seen pale glints of something amidst the tangle.

Bone didn't survive long in this area: the soil was too acidic, and the forest was filled with scavengers, both small and large. Usually, little was left, barring antlers and the rare fragment of jawbone, held together by hard teeth, and these he'd find scattered here and there on the bedrock, or nestled sun-bleached in beds of lichen and moss. Black spruce had short lives, thirty or forty years, so these root-walls were not especially large.

Strange, then, that these root-mats were studded with what looked like canine teeth, wolf or wolverine, or bear. He plucked one loose and squinted at it in the gloom. Then he drew out a second one. 'Shit,' he muttered. He replaced both fangs and turned to Rant. 'Sorry, not here. We have to leave.'

The young Teblor half-breed looked up, his brow knotting in confusion.

'I didn't think they came this far south,' Damisk said, unslinging his bow and quickly stringing it. He drew out an arrow made for larger game, the iron point long and x-shaped, and nocked it.

Rant unsheathed his knife.

Night had settled around them.

'Quiet now,' Damisk whispered, 'and follow me.'

They set off westward along the ridge for a half-dozen paces, and then Damisk led his oversized charge down onto the flanking slope facing the lake, to keep them both below any sight-line from inland. They were forced to slow down, stepping carefully among the tumbled, sharp-edged rocks and the boles of fallen trees, slipping on dead branches with the spaces between them draped in cutworm silk.

Damisk's mouth was dry. He considered guiding them down closer to the lake's rocky shore, but even there the water could only be reached by descending sheer cliff-faces of rotten rock, and that didn't change for the rest of the lake's reach into the west, until it curled southward at its far end. He cursed himself for not filling his flask at the pool of meltwater. Panic had taken him, if only momentarily.

They arrived at an overhang, slightly hollowed out, and Damisk drew Rant into its meagre cover. They crouched down. Damisk held the nocked arrow in place with the index finger of his bow-hand, gesturing the boy closer with the other hand. 'Saemdhi,' he said in a low voice. 'Hunters from the north, said to dwell on an island ringed in ice. They must be tracking the herd, but there's more to it. The fangs I found were put there probably today – we might well have passed right through them. Meaning they know about us.'

'What fangs?' Rant asked in a whisper.

'Among the roots. Sealion, bigger than a bear's canines. The Saemdhi hunt seal when they don't hunt caribou. Those fangs are claiming territory.'

Rant's face, barely visible in the darkness, seemed to be regarding him blankly.

Sighing, Damisk said, 'The lake's north forest is Korhivi hunting land, only the Korhivi don't have the numbers of the Saemdhi. And if the Saemdhi are down here, then they've already gone through the Korhivi.'

'Gone through?'

'Killed them, Rant. All of them.'

'All?'

'There've been no Korhivi fleeing into the settlements. That I know of. Given the chance, they would've, since we trade with 'em and we get along, mostly. The Saemdhi, well, that's a different story. Nobody gets along with them. I said they hunt seal and caribou, and that's true enough. But none of that's part of their rite of passage into warriors. No, for that, they have to head north, as far north as they can go, and each one does it alone. And doesn't come back unless they're carrying the head of a White Jheck.'

'What is a White Jheck?'

'Ah, Rant, the world's big but it ain't empty. If I told you that white bears and even grey bears will run from the White Jheck, will that do?'

'And these Saemdhi hunt them?'

'Aye.'

'How?' Rant pointed at Damisk's bow. 'With that?'

'Maybe. Poison-tipped? That'd be the safest option, at a distance and quick-acting besides. You can get poisons from some lichens. To be honest, I can't imagine any other way, except for snares and traps. Nobody said the White Jheck were smart, after all.' He paused, and then shrugged and said, 'Unless of course it's all made up. It's not like

I've ever actually seen a White Jheck. But I've seen a Saemdhi warrior, and that's worrying enough for me.'

'If they know about us, why haven't they killed us, too?'

'If I had to guess, you're keeping us both alive, Rant. Or more accurately, the Teblor blood in you.'

'The Saemdhi know the Teblor?'

'Some of the oil in blood-oil comes from them,' Damisk said. He shrugged again. 'Seal, whale, or something similar. Traded with the Teblor for mountain hardwoods. If we meet any, we're likely to see Teblor-style weapons among them, just scaled down.'

'I have seen a Teblor wooden sword,' said Rant.

Damisk nodded. 'The dried-out one behind the bar at Three-Legged, aye. A properly cared-for sword in the hands of a Teblor can cut through a soldier's chain-and-leather hauberk. Crumple Malazan shields, too, not to mention helmets.' He scratched at his beard. 'Doubt a Saemdhi could, though. Still, it's not like I'm armed for fighting, is it?'

'I wonder . . .' ventured Rant, and then he fell silent.

'What do you wonder?' Damisk asked. 'Out with it.'

'Well . . . if they saw us when I was wearing the slave rigging.'

Damisk could feel the blood draining from his face and limbs. He sagged lower, the arrow tilting up from the string, the notch suddenly freed. 'Ah, shit, you ain't dumb at all, lad, and here I am wishing you were.'

'But we took it off,' Rant added. 'They would've seen that, too.'

'If they know me for a slave tracker, that might not matter.'

'I'll protect you, Damisk. I'll tell them.'

Damisk re-nocked his arrow. 'I doubt they'll stop to chat, Rant, but I appreciate your words.'

'What are we going to do?'

'I'm tempted to leave you here. For now,' he added quickly. This boy had seen enough abandonment. 'I can move fast and quiet and give 'em a good chase. They might swing back to find you, but even if they do, it won't be to hurt you. Just tell them you want to join your people.'

'You just said you were coming back.'

'If I can, I will. That's a promise. Wait through the night, maybe into midday tomorrow. If I'm not back by then, I'm dead. Follow the lake-shore, west. When you get to the far end, keep the nearest mountain on your right and follow the cut. It's a bit of a climb, but it'll take you to a pass. You're looking for old stairs, Rant, cut into the rock, and bones, lots of bones. And a waterfall.'

'And then?'

'Climb and keep climbing. Sooner or later, you'll be spotted by a Teblor tribal. Phalyd or Kellyd.' He tossed over the two remaining hare carcasses, both of which had been slow-cooked earlier.

'You are expecting to die,' Rant said.

'I'll see you before noon tomorrow,' Damisk said. 'Bed down here and try to get some sleep.' He turned to make his way back up the slope.

'Damisk?'

He paused and glanced back. 'What?'

'Is my father truly a god?'

Damisk hesitated, and then said, 'He wasn't back then. Just a warrior, a raider. What he is now I don't know. Stories are just stories, until you come face to face with the truth of things. Don't live by 'em, Rant.'

Rant looked down. 'Just a raider, then.'

'Lad, he was a warrior like none I've ever seen. Like none of us in Silver Lake had ever seen. Aye, we chained him. For a time. But they say he lives still, far to the south. Free. Unbowed. And maybe that's all it takes to become a god. I wouldn't know either way.'

'I would like to—'

'It may not be worth it,' Damisk cut in, hearing the harshness in his tone, but that was needed. For this, at least. 'You were born of rape, and rape is a brutal act, and what happened to your mother, at Karsa's hands, well, that was worse, because it was from the blood-oil. Karsa brought it to his lips out of desperation and rage – the whole raid had gone into the shit-hole. His friends were dead or about to be. What he did to her wasn't about power, or domination, or any other pathetic need. It was the act of a rabid beast, unthinking, unfeeling, uncaring. And that's what he left her with. That, and you. Don't look to Karsa Orlong for anything, Rant. Stay with the Teblor. Make your life among them and leave it all at that.'

Rant might have shrugged in response; it was too dark to be sure, but it was clear, after a long moment, that the lad wasn't going to reply. No empty promises at least.

Damisk turned back to the slope and began climbing. He'd done what he could.

Maybe blood-oil was just an excuse. There were always excuses, weren't there? He shook his head. Truth was, he wasn't fooling anybody, not himself and not, it seemed, a half-grown half-breed.

Damned drakes gang-raped hapless ducks every damned spring, after all. There were whole strands of nature that were, simply put, utterly fucked up. Threads of madness, bitter and frenzied. But in the Wilds, what creatures did, they did unthinkingly, without the wits to know better. People didn't have that excuse.

Except for the blood-oil. Except for the fact that Karsa Orlong, wounded and hunted, had been kicking through doors, crashing into rooms. If he'd found a fucking cow, he would've raped it. Instead, he found Rant's mother.

He didn't know for certain, but any child produced of that fever might well have blood-oil deep in his body, like a fuel awaiting a spark. Enough townsfolk thought as much, and they eyed Rant with fear and because of it, they would have killed him eventually. For all Damisk knew, they were right.

But what blood-oil did to a Teblor wasn't the same as what it did to a lowlander. Teblor weathered the fever, broke through the frenzy, and came back to themselves. A lowlander's mind simply snapped. And Rant had half of one and half of the other. Among the Teblor, then, he might be safe. Among lowlanders, possibly not.

The moon was behind clouds and still low on the horizon. The forest was silent as Damisk slipped back onto the ridge, staying hunched over. He stilled, holding his breath, eyes tracking. Nothing. Still, the hairs lifted on the back of his neck.

Aye, they're out there.

Rant had never been in a forest. His entire life he had spent in Silver Lake. The houses, the alleys, the beach where the boats were drawn up and the gulls fought over fish-guts, the main street and the old gates still unrepaired after the Uprising. The garrison barracks and the factor's house, which had burned down twice and had been rebuilt only once in Rant's memory, leaving charred ruins where he'd hidden when the stone-throwers were on the prowl. The only wild things he'd seen were the town's feral dogs. Every other beast was already dead – brought in by hunters – when he set eyes upon it. That, and the skulls, of course.

If he'd thought of the forest, he'd imagined it crowded with terrible beasts, and savages and Teblor raiders. It had never occurred to him that it was mostly empty, mostly quiet, and so unrelievedly dark as soon as night fell.

Yet Damisk said there were hunters out there. Murderers of all the Korhivi, those strange quiet people wearing furs and hides who crept to the town's edge to trade their wares, once in the spring and once just before the winter snows. They would never come again, now. He tried to picture them all dead, lying on the needle-carpeted ground in their camps. Slain children and babies left to starve or die to wolves or bears. Places of blood and hearths heaped in ash.

There was no prowess in such killing. No reason for it. No glory. And there was another worry, one that now gnawed at him. If these

Saemdhi thought nothing of slaughtering whoever got in their way, then Silver Lake itself might be in danger. His mother, and all the children and everyone else.

There was hardly anyone left in the garrison.

He looked down and found that he was still gripping his knife. The blade's dull gleam made him think about the Malazan troops that used to visit the town. It had been almost two years since the last time. Their arrival had made some people happy, while others would curse under their breaths, because the Malazans belonged to an empire and that empire had invaded Genabackis and conquered all the Free Cities, and now no one was free any more.

If the Saemdhi attacked Silver Lake, who was there to defend it?

He could go back. Warn them.

Rant crept out from the hollow. He could see patches of glimmering from the lake, between branches and twigs. If he made his way down to the shoreline, he could follow it back to the boat. He could row it across and be the hero, and who would kill a hero?

But maybe the Saemdhi wouldn't keep going. They had no boats, after all, so how could they hope to cross the lake? What if he warned everyone in town and the Saemdhi never came? Then they would kill him for sure.

He didn't know what to do.

'*Sanc fris ane orol.*'

The voice was a woman's, coming down from directly above the overhang, and thus out of sight.

Chest pounding twin beats, Rant crouched lower, motionless, the grip of the knife suddenly slick in his hand.

'*Tre'lang ane Teblor?*'

Was she speaking to a companion at her side?

'I was telling you to avoid the lake,' said the voice. Faint scraping sounds, and then a figure dropped down to land lightly in front of Rant.

He ducked deeper into the hollow, knife out.

He could not tell her age, but her face was pale as moonlight. She wore furs but they were matted and clogged with something black. Sticks jutted from her – no, not sticks. Arrows. He counted six that he could see, two of them buried deep in her chest. Her hair hung long, loose and tangled.

'The half-breed,' she said. 'Shattered son for the Shattered God. I once thought to kidnap you. Save you from your fate. But it seems you've saved yourself.'

'How do you live?' Rant asked her.

'You think someone could survive this? Don't be foolish. I am dead. Quite dead. But . . . restless. It wasn't the best way to go. They made sure of me first, knowing I was their greatest threat. I hit the ground before the first one stepped into the camp, and being dead, I could do nothing to stop what followed.'

'Korhivi.'

'You call us that, but our ties to the Korhivi are few. You lowlanders never asked, but we called ourselves by another name.' When she shrugged, he heard fletching move like stiff brushes among the twigs at her back. 'Does not matter now, as we are gone.'

'The Saemdhi.'

'They don't know what to do about the lake. Six of them track your friend, but the rest are above the shore. Their Bone-Throwers say nothing, hiding their fear.'

'Why do they fear the lake?' Rant asked.

'It was not always a lake,' she replied, taking a step closer and then settling into a squat. Now he could make out her face. It had been pretty in life. It wasn't pretty any more, and nothing shone from eyes that sat deep and dull as stones. 'Lowlanders call it Silver Lake. We call it Tarthen'ignial. The Valley of the Tarthen Stones. Before the waters came, it was a sacred place, with tall stones standing in rows down the length of the valley, and in the centre a mound of skulls. Tartheno and Imass. It's said the Imass skulls remain alive, even now, looking out into a flooded world of silt and dead trees.'

Rant's gaze edged past her, out to the gleaming water of the lake. 'I swam half of it.'

'And they watched you, I'm sure. Waited for you, even, to drown and sink down, to sit before them as have so many others. Were they disappointed? Who knows.'

'But it's all under water now,' said Rant. 'We fish in the lake, drag nets and hook-lines.'

'You do, and nets have been lost, yes? Those standing stones are now webbed, old rope and lines tangled about them like offerings. You doubt me? I have been down there, walking among them. There are advantages to being dead.'

Rant considered that and was unconvinced.

'The Saemdhi will not harm you,' she then said. 'Your friend they will kill.'

'He saved my life. If I tell the Saemdhi—'

'Most of them don't understand Nathii, the language you speak. Forget him, you'll not see him again.'

'What do you want with me?'

'The ice of the north was created by the Jaghut. Omtose Phellack. But the Throne of Ice lost its power long ago. It's said the Lord of the Ice has returned, and that the great war with the Imass is over.' She paused to cackle, and then spat out something the colour of lake-water. 'How can I argue any of that, with Death's Gate now guarded by The Bird That Steals? But if the Throne is again occupied, the one sitting in it has done nothing. And now the magic fades. Tell your Teblor kin, the ice of the north has melted, all of it, and the floodwaters are coming. Tell them they must flee.'

'I don't understand.'

'But will you remember my words?'

He hesitated, and then nodded.

'Did you see the herd?'

'Yes.'

'Fleeing the waters. And now the Saemdhi, also fleeing the waters. More will come. Wolves, bears, the Jheck.'

'Why would the Teblor believe me?'

'You are the Son of the Shattered God.'

'Why would they believe that?'

'They will know.'

Rant settled back. 'I will do as you say, but only if you save Damisk.'

'The pup would bargain? With a dead witch, no less!'

'Save him.'

'It may already be too late. Besides, I haven't got much longer like this. Already I can feel the tug of oblivion. Soon I will leave this body and my powers in your realm will be much diminished. The dead can only haunt when they are filled with hate. I am not. The Saemdhi may have angered me, with their wanton slaughter, but because I understand their panic, I cannot hate them.'

'Save Damisk.'

The dead witch scowled, making a face that Rant knew he would see again in his nightmares. 'This is what I get for being helpful? Very well. I will try. As for you, stay here tonight, in your little cave. Then head west, into the—'

'I know. I will find the Teblor. Damisk told me.'

She studied him in silence for a long moment, and then turned away. 'Who heeds the dead?' she muttered.

If the question had been meant for him, she didn't wait around long enough for him to think of a response. Now he was alone once more, the silence of the night closing in again. Rant settled deeper into the hollow, putting his back to the ragged stone. What did it mean to travel west, skirting the lake for as far as it went? To climb into the mountains on narrow trails? To find a staircase made of bones and carved rock? He closed his eyes and tried to imagine these things, seeing himself in these strange places, many days from now.

But the only sensation he felt, welling up inside, as if eager to drown him, was loneliness.

He missed his mother. He missed Damisk. He even missed the dead witch. And, for the briefest of moments, he missed being in the settlement, dodging the stones being thrown at him.

What was it like to feel safe? He didn't know, and he wondered if he ever would.

The massive outcrop of shale-stone sat tilted on the bedrock, some lone remnant of this place having once been different from what it had become. Damisk was two-thirds up the cliff-side, lying prone on a ledge covered in guano. Almost within reach above him, on the under-side of a projecting shelf of slate, was a row of swallow nests, silent and, he suspected, still unoccupied this early in the season. He was thankful for that, as it meant no shrill alarms from birds huddled atop eggs. He held his bow horizontally, out over the lip, an arrow resting on the grip's small indent.

At the base of the cliff, five shapes slipped among the brush and fallen trees, bodies and limbs wrapped in leather and strips of fur, heads covered in scalps cut from the Korhivi. One was armed with a short recurved bow made of antler and horn, and the arrows in her quiver looked long. She'd yet to nock one to the gut string, but he knew that the point would be as long as his forearm, a barbed thing of bone polished and gleaming, the shaft immediately above it probably smeared with poison.

The other four carried javelins, stone atlatls sheathed at their hips.

Damisk slipped his fingers around the string of his bow and slowly drew it back. The woman with the bow was bigger than the men, broad-shouldered and heavy-boned. She remained a half-dozen paces behind the others, pausing every few steps to scan the area. She'd yet to lift her gaze to the cliff-side.

He waited until she paused once more, and then let fly.

The arrow sank into her between shoulder and neck, the angle taking it down the length of her torso. When she fell to the ground, the Korhivi scalp slipped away to reveal a shaved pate mottled with dried blood.

Damisk withdrew his bow and sank deeper into the shadow beneath the overhang. He heard sudden motion below, but no voices. They were converging on their fallen comrade. When they saw the arrow's entry angle, they would turn to the cliff, scanning it as their eyes worked to the very top. Seeing nothing.

This spur of shale could be slipped around, paths found to take them up onto the ridge. Two would go to the right, two to the left. They would close in on the spot directly above Damisk.

Thirty heartbeats later, Damisk edged out slightly to study the base. The woman's body had been flipped onto its back. The bow and quiver were both gone. The other four Saemdhi were nowhere to be seen. His gaze returned to the corpse. There was a blackish stain on her forehead – he couldn't make out much more than that, but he knew that the woman's own knife had been driven to the hilt between her eyes, to take into the precious iron blade her soul. And, somewhere nearby, that knife had then been driven into the trunk of a tree. Her spirit now belonged to this place, and this place now belonged to the Saemdhi.

Damisk moved out and began climbing down. There was moonlight now, both a boon and a curse. Without it he would never have managed to kill the woman with the bow, nor seen his hunters approaching the base of the cliff. But his enemy could see as well as he could, possibly better. His only advantage was that they were dwellers of the tundra, not the forest. Like any hunter, they knew how to remain motionless, drawing slow, deep breaths. But when they moved through the underbrush, they made noise.

Damisk didn't.

Reaching the base, he crouched for a few heartbeats, checking his own gear, making certain it was closely bound and unlikely to catch twigs and branches, and then approached the corpse. As he expected, his arrow had been broken, the iron point cut out of the body and pocketed.

The dead woman's broad, flat face held a peaceful expression, despite the black slit dividing her forehead. He set off for the tree-line.

He'd only begun his circuit when he found the knife in the tree. Antler grip, a bone spinal disc for a hilt, and a cheap blade of trader's iron. It snapped with little effort.

Now you wander lost, and long may the Korhivi ghosts chase you. Only fools believe that vengeance does not live on past death, and by the spirits I hope it finds you.

He moved in among the trees again, heading westward. He doubted he would catch up to the two hunters ahead, so he didn't try, angling instead back towards the lakeshore – the route he'd be least likely to take.

Forty paces along, he came across a low game-trail cutting inland, and there found the corpse of another Saemdhi. The man's neck had been broken. A dozen Saemdhi arrows had then been pushed into his chest, mouth, eyes and ears.

A Korhivi survived, then. An angry one at that.

Shaken by the sight, Damisk stepped over the body and continued on.

Good and evil belonged nowhere in the world outside a mortal's thoughts. Even blessing and suffering, which surely did exist, could turn slippery in the hand. Was a quick death a blessing? Did saving a life doom it to years of suffering?

He didn't know. Everything was slippery, if you thought about it long enough.

Damisk wanted to be hopeful for Rant's fate, not just for the journey, but among the Teblor, too. Half-breeds skidded in the blood between two worlds. Often, neither world welcomed them for long.

Rant was Karsa Orlong's son, and that could be his salvation, or his death-sentence.

But of the two, which is more merciful?

Far more quickly than he anticipated, the hunters were on his trail once more. This time, they moved without heed against making noise. Anger, then. A knife found broken, a new battle born, one of curse and counter-curse. Should they catch him, his death wouldn't be quick.

He ran fleet as a deer through the black woods.

CHAPTER FIVE

It's said that Orbis was a pretty coastal town.

Barhawk
'Idyll Beneath the Waves'
The Great Library of New Morn

'SO I'M A SERGEANT NOW?' SUGAL SNORTED EVEN AS HE SAID IT, his tilted eyes narrowing as he watched Balk pulling his mount away from the front of the Malazan column and then heading back at a slow canter. Sugal twisted in his saddle to regard the troops of their own column. 'This is stupid. We could fall on 'em now and line this damned road with Malazan heads. Sweet payback for the way they did the captain.'

'Lieutenant now, not captain,' Bray said. 'Balk's been busted down a rank.'

'Well, they can call him whatever they like. Doesn't change for us, does it? We're Balk's Company. I don't recall getting in line at any Malazan recruiting station, do you?'

'It's a contract,' said Stick as she wiped her hands on her leather leggings and then swung back up into the saddle. 'The rest ain't our business, Sugal. You think too much, about business that ain't yours to begin with. You think it matters a fuck what your opinion is. You think anyone gives a shit what you think.' She lifted her canteen and took a deep draught, then wiped her mouth before scratching at her tangled mass of dirty yellow hair, wincing as she pulled through knots.

Sugal glared at her. 'And I bet you think you finished your piss down in that ditch,' he said. 'Instead, here you are, spraying it at everyone.'

'Not everyone,' she replied, her moon-like cheeks puffing as she shifted about on the saddle. 'Just you, Sugal. Because you ain't good with thinking. In fact, the only thing you're good for is busting skulls. I keep telling you. We'll all be happier once you just stop thinking and, more to the point, stop talking.'

Bray grunted. 'You two about done? Captain's here.'

The three 'sergeants' fell silent as their commander rode up and reined in. 'No,' he said to them, 'we're not sending a hunting party after the damned caribou. Gruff says to leave them be.'

'Waste,' muttered Sugal.

'The scouts took down a couple dozen as it is,' Balk added, shrugging as he ran a hand through his brown hair, a detail Sugal noted Stick watching with half-lidded eyes. 'We haven't got the time to cure the meat, though they put half the kill in bags of salt.' He gestured at the waiting troops, drew his horse round and they all resumed their trek.

Something about Balk, Sugal mused as he looked away from both their captain and Stick. Didn't need much by way of giving orders, since everyone's eyes were on him anyway. Just a vague wave, and now the whole column was back on the move. That was a talent or something. One day, Sugal would be the same. All eyes on him, even Stick's. He'd enjoy that. Putting her in her place. Same for Bray, who never said much but always sided with Stick.

The three of them had been together for almost seven years. It was a wonder they'd not killed each other by now. But then, they'd found something in common. A certain secret pleasure in seeing the life fade from a fool's eyes. Any fool. Preferably, lots of fools.

Two years and counting with Balk, but that might not last much longer. Balk would rather take coin from living merchants than rob their corpses. Said it made for a better investment in the long run. But what did Sugal care for the long run? Balk was holding the three of them down, simple as that. Even Stick was chafing, which was why she was drinking more these days. Sugal didn't much like Stick when she was drinking. She just got nastier.

Worse, she'd got it into her head that she was in charge of the three of them. Like the leader or something. But Sugal had always outranked her, even back when they first met in the Tulips city guard. It had been his arrangements that had put them in coin, at least until the Claw came in and wiped out all the loan-sharks and sent the three of them fleeing for their lives.

No, Sugal reflected, he didn't like Malazans. None of them did. The only thing to do with Malazans was to grab them, take the slow knife to them, and laugh while they begged for their miserable, useless lives. He, Bray and Stick had done that more than once, but since hooking up with Balk they'd been having a dry spell.

'Our sworders ain't happy, Captain,' Sugal now said as their horses plodded along the field's muddy edge. 'This whole business with the Malazans.'

Balk glanced across at him, one eyebrow slightly lifted, but he said nothing.

Sugal shifted on his saddle, glanced across the field to his left, squinting at the distant line of forest, where grey shapes were moving in the shadows beneath the trees. Caribou, in their hundreds. Like deer, only rougher-looking, and they didn't hold their heads as high either. Built for winter winds, Stick said, but she didn't know shit.

She spoke up now, 'It's Sugal who ain't happy. The coin, like you told us, is damned good. No point in hard feelings either, since we already whupped them, meaning they got to treat us nice and all. Nobody's complaining but Sugal, Captain.'

Sugal scowled at her. 'You talking for me, Stick?'

'Someone with brains has to, Sugal, especially when you decide to talk for everybody else.'

'Enough, you two,' said Bray. 'It does no good to the sworders to see the sergeants bitchin' at each other. Think of all the eyes on you right now.'

Captain Balk then said, 'Now there's an idea. The three of you, fall back to your platoons. And Bray, call up Lieutenant Ara for me.'

So much for cosying up to the captain. Sugal fixed a glare on Stick, but she wasn't even paying attention. There might come a day, he reflected, when he did the slow knife on her. Unless, of course, she got to him first. No, that wasn't likely. He was better than her in every way, after all. And look at her, swaying half-drunk in her saddle.

None of them said a thing as they fell back, Bray angling his mount towards Ara to pass on Balk's invitation to the lieutenant. Sugal caught the look of black hatred Stick threw at Ara as soon as the lieutenant rode up past them. Sure, that made sense. Ara had been with Balk longer than anyone else. That detail alone made her an obstacle. No, an enemy, in fact.

One day, Sugal would be leading this company. When the Malazans netted Balk back in the forest, it had been Ara who commanded everyone to lay down their arms. She was the reason they were all in this mess. If it had been Sugal commanding, he'd have let the Malazans slit Balk's throat, and then he would have unleashed his enraged sworders and they would have cut down every last Malazan, probably saving that hairshirted sergeant for the end. For a long night of the slow knife.

But none of that had happened. Ara had a lot to pay for.

Sugal brought his horse close alongside Stick.

'Leave me alone,' she said. 'I got platoons to lead.'

'Ain't we all,' Sugal said, leaning towards her and adding in a low tone, 'When it's Ara's turn, she's all yours, Stick.'

Stick smiled. 'Generous of ya, but don't make me have to remind you of that come the time.'

'I won't.'

'Good enough,' she said. 'Now get out of my sight.'

As she rode away, Sugal glanced over at Bray. 'You heard?'

Bray shrugged from under his boar-hide hauberk. 'Enough.'

'Good, remind me when it happens, so I don't say nothing to piss her off.'

Lieutenant Ara came up alongside Balk. She draped her reins in a loose loop around the saddle horn, and then settled back. 'We need to kill them soon, Captain.'

Balk sighed. 'It's not enough knowing what they are, Ara. For justice to be seen, they need to be caught in the act.'

'Waiting for a victim? Fuck me, Captain, that's almost as cold.'

'Depends on the victim,' Balk replied. 'I seem to remember hearing you calling on a dozen or so nasty spirits to have their way with Spindle. Would you weep if our three sergeants had half a night to work on him?'

'Weep? No. I'd feel pity, and that's a problem, Captain. I don't want my hate for Spindle all clouded up with feeling sorry for him. In any case, it's not just the obvious victims we have to think about here. Those three would just as easily take the knife to you or me, and you know it.'

Balk smiled. 'Sugal wants to replace me as head of the company. But he's not smart enough to succeed. Stick wants the same, and she is. And she has Bray with her.'

'When she's not drunk.'

'Oh, I doubt her drinking would slow her up much,' Balk replied. 'Probably the opposite, in fact.'

'So let's just kill them,' Ara urged. 'This kind of situation, the one who makes the first move is usually the one who wins.'

'Oh, I will,' Balk promised. 'When it's tactically expedient.'

Ara fell silent. Their column continued flanking the Malazan company with its massive train of wagons, most of which were intended to resupply the garrison at Silver Lake. She'd heard that there were only seven soldiers left in that garrison, leaving her to wonder at the sheer bulk of equipment accompanying this venture. There was also the matter of billeting once they arrived. Balk's Company alone would probably double the town's population.

'Captain, ever been to Silver Lake?'

'Once,' Balk replied. 'I was young, accompanying my father who was delivering horses from our estate. One thing you can certainly say about the Malazans: they pay fairly for the things they want.'

Ara flinched, looked away. 'I don't think,' she said, 'this is a good idea.'

'I know you don't.' It seemed as if he would say no more, then he continued, 'Ara, my father backed the Greydog Army. It lost the battle, was scattered to the winds, and the Malazans punished the nobles who mustered and then supplied that army. We were left destitute, and if not for the horse-breeding, we would have lost our lands. That is our history. There's no escaping it.'

All hope of freedom is lost when the past is a prison you will not leave, Andrison Balk. But there was no point in her telling him that. The estate had survived. Barely. And Andrison's father had died younger than perhaps he would have otherwise, if spared the vicissitudes of Malazan justice. And Ara's own family would not have lost its land, thus severing the betrothal that would have seen her married to the man now riding at her side.

'I chose to become landless,' Balk said. 'I chose to place myself in a position where I no longer owed them anything. And you, Ara, chose to accompany me. But nothing holds you here.'

And there it was again. He kept kicking open that door, even though they both knew what it would do to him if she walked through it, if she left. She suspected a part of him wanted that wounding, one more scar added to the rest.

'Yet,' Balk continued, 'the contract was accepted, and you said nothing against it at the time.'

She had no response to that. They'd had this conversation before. It never went anywhere. She thought to change the subject. 'Sugal needs to be—'

'We have time,' Balk cut in. 'This posting gives us what we need to lick our wounds, to resupply. The Malazan Empire is stretched, exhausted, sinking into complacency. When you've proved to be unstoppable, you eventually come to believe in your own immortality. You believe that your sheer immensity guarantees your survival. But that's a delusion. No empire is too big to fail. And fail it will.' He grunted. 'And it may well begin here, on Genabackis.'

She felt a stirring of anger. *Men, such fuckwits*. 'I lost more than you did, Captain. You seem to forget that, there atop your solitary mountain.'

'Then how can you not be with me?'

Not? Where the fuck am I, then? She gathered up the reins and swung her startled mount around. 'I'm going to check on the troops.'

Stillwater liked marching on roads. Of course, not as much fun loaded down with one's kit and weapons and whatnot, but with all the supply wagons trundling along in their wake, even the leather satchel on her shoulders felt light. No need to carry food, spades, picks, rope and line, tents, tent-poles, stakes, mallets, hatchets, cooking gear, extra water, spare boots and all the rest. In fact, with the sun pleasantly warm and the mild breeze keeping the blackflies down, with only the occasional dump of horseshit to step over – and really, it was amazing how much shit a mere dozen horses could dump in a day – this was as close to contentment as one could get. True perfection, of course, would be the addition of a few throats to slit open along the way.

She didn't consider herself particularly bloodthirsty. She just liked her work. A lot. The only troubling thing in her mind at the moment was all those Imperial Claws who'd stolen her idea. Credit where it's due. Was that so hard? But to be honest, the sweet marriage of sorcery and assassination was obvious, in retrospect. And did it really matter whether she was the first? The one who'd thought it up before anyone else?

Well, yes, dammit.

'Just an outing in the woods,' said Corporal Snack, marching beside her. 'And me just a scrawny thing.'

She glanced across at him. He was puffing, sweaty, his beard glistening. 'What you got in that pack, Corporal? You're dying there.'

'Thanks for the offer but no, I'm fine.'

Stillwater frowned. 'What offer? Did I make any offer?'

He scowled at her. 'I was telling a story.'

'Yeah, the same story, the same damned story, always that story.'

'Because you never let me finish it! I keep starting and then—'

'Exactly,' she cut in. 'And it's driving me crazy.'

'So let me finish it!'

'Why? It's already boring and you just started it.'

Folibore spoke a step behind them. 'It's a fine story, Still. You really should hear it. And that way, the corporal never has to tell it ever again.'

'Oh, really? But here you are, Folibore, about to hear it again. So what you just said is a lie. It is, isn't it? Admit it.'

He sighed. 'You're right. I've heard it a few hundred times.'

'You're both miserable shits,' said Snack. 'It was when I was very young, on a day that—'

'Wish it'd been your last day, for ever, I mean,' Stillwater said. 'Poor Snack, cut down before his time. Think of what he could've become! If only he'd kept his mouth shut, stopped blabbing on with his fucking story shit, why, he never would've gotten his throat slit.'

Folibore and Blanket both snorted, sounding like horses trying to drink through their nostrils. Stillwater checked over a shoulder to make sure nothing new was smeared on her pack-flap, and then turned back to Snack. 'Get this into your head, Corporal. I don't like stories. They don't interest me. Every story is about somebody being stupid. I'm dealing with stupid every day.'

'But Stillwater,' said Blanket, 'the value of stories about people being stupid is that you learn the lesson of their stupidity without having to pay the full price.'

'Oh I pay it all right,' she retorted. 'I pay it in boredom.'

'Fine then!' snapped Snack. 'Have it your way. Tell me, Stillwater, what do you want to talk about?'

She turned her head and nodded towards the company marching parallel to them. 'Those. I don't trust them.'

'Really?' Snack asked. 'Why is that? I mean, we were only trying to kill each other a couple weeks back. Only got half our friends cut down in the process. Whole squads wiped out. And ours on Spindle's flank with all those fucking arrows flying while he jumps Balk.'

'It's not that,' Stillwater said. 'Why aren't they on the road? Why are they happy marching across muddy fields? It's fishy.'

Snack rounded on her. 'That's why you don't trust them?'

'That's what I said, isn't it? Why don't they just fall in behind the supply train? This is a perfectly good road. Malazan marines, the first legions stationed north of Betrys, they built this road. It's a fucking Bridgeburner road.'

'Maybe,' ventured Folibore, 'they're making a point.'

'You're all idiots.' This came from behind the two heavies, where Anyx Fro walked all by herself, which was the only way they let her walk since she never walked straight and any soldier trying to march alongside her ended up getting bumped into over and over again. Something was wrong with Anyx.

Blanket said, 'Thank you, Anyx, for your pithy contribution to this discussion.'

'It's a stupid discussion. If any of you bothered looking through my new eyeglass, you'd see the sneaky savages keeping an eye on us from those woods over there.'

'What sneaky savages?' Snack demanded, now squinting to the distant tree-line. 'Those aren't sneaky savages. They're caribou.'

'Never mind the stupid caribou, Corporal. Besides, half of 'em aren't caribou at all, just sneaky savages wearing caribou skins and antlers on their heads.'

'That's ingenious,' said Folibore. 'And I imagine they stick together in pairs, to give us four legs to see, too.'

'Maybe,' Anyx Fro said, lifting the massive eyeglass once more. 'But all that disguising stuff don't work with me, does it. Because I can see their fucking nose-hairs.'

'Why would you look at their nose-hairs?' Stillwater wanted to know. 'What's so important about their nose-hairs?'

'It's a subtle thing, Still,' said Blanket, 'but it's how you can distinguish one forest tribe from the next. The Western Ganrel twist theirs into braids, stiffened with snot. But the Eastern Ganrel, well, they curl them up round the outside of the nostrils.'

'You're making that up,' Stillwater accused.

'Of course he is,' said Folibore. 'It's actually the other way around.'

'Let's get back to the sneaky savages,' said Snack. 'I still don't see any. Just caribou.'

'Then get back here, Corporal, and take a look for yourself.'

Snack's face was blotchy, the way it always looked when he got irritated. He swung round and shouldered his way between Folibore and Blanket. The pack on his shoulders clanked a bit and the strange sharp bulges jabbed dangerously, forcing both heavies to step quickly away.

'What's in there, Corporal?' Blanket demanded.

'How many times do I have to tell you all: it's none of your business.' Snack joined Anyx Fro and tugged her by an arm off to the side of the road. 'Now, give me that thing.'

The rest of the squad followed suit, leaving Sergeant Drillbent marching in front of a gap where his squad used to be. Stillwater didn't think he'd notice and sure enough, he didn't.

In a few moments the first wagon on the train would arrive, closing the gap.

Snack now noticed that the others had joined him and Anyx. 'What do you fools want? We're going to lose our place in the line. You, Folibore, get back up there and keep us a place.'

'I want to know about the sneaky savages, Corporal. I think it may be important, possibly even significant, in an ominous way.'

'More than ominous,' Blanket added solemnly. 'Portentous, in fact.'

'Ominous and portentous,' Folibore nodded.

Snack turned to Stillwater, looked at her for a moment as if about to order her to do something, and then changed his mind. He took the silver and iron eyeglass from Anyx and edged round so that he could rest it on Fro's shoulder while he peered through the eyepiece.

Anyx scowled. 'Why didn't I think of that?'

'Because nobody walks with you,' Stillwater said. 'Hence, no shoulder to scry on.'

Folibore and Blanket made snorting noises again. Stillwater ignored them. Anyx just glared at her for some reason. Stillwater shrugged. 'Look, it's an easy fix. You want a pole, about that high, with a notch on top to take the weight of the eyeglass. Also, given that all of your inventions are stupidly heavy and stupidly bulky and mostly useless, that pole could come in handy for lots of them, too.'

'Or,' drawled Anyx Fro, 'I could just use someone's shoulder.'

'What do you see, Corporal?' Folibore asked.

'Sneaky savages.'

'Really?'

'Told you,' said Anyx Fro.

Stillwater now looked in earnest at that distant tree-line. 'Check their nose-hairs,' she said.

'Either that,' added Snack, 'or very devious caribou.'

'So which is it?' demanded Blanket. 'Sneaky savages or devious caribou?'

'Maybe both.'

Stillwater watched the two heavies exchange significant looks, and that was enough for her. 'I want to see,' she announced.

Anyx Fro ducked under the weight of the eyepiece, which suddenly angled it up, poking into Snack's eye. He yelped and staggered back, but Anyx managed to catch the eyeglass before he dropped it. 'Not a chance, Still. Find someone else's shoulder. Better yet, find someone else's eyeglass.'

'I don't have to,' Stillwater said, dragging her pack free of her shoulders and setting it down. She began rummaging. 'In case you all forgot, my secondary training is surveying.' She pulled out a small eyeglass made of brass and ebony. 'This here's a five-lens, which I found near Brightgo's Barrow outside Nathilog.'

'Near?' Blanket asked.

'Okay, in. An antique, but with this thing, I can *count* nose-hairs.'

Anyx Fro now held her eyeglass like a club, and even took a step towards Stillwater before Folibore gently pulled her back and disarmed her.

Stillwater extended the eyeglass. It made a smooth *snick* sound when it locked. She peered through it.

'Well?' Snack asked.

'I see a leaf. It's huge. In fact, you could hide an army behind that leaf.'

'We need Oams to go out and check this out,' decided Snack. 'Whose squad is he with again?'

'There are only three squads,' said Folibore. 'How can you not know?'

'But which three squads?' Snack demanded.

'Well, we're one, leaving, uh two.'

Anyx Fro snorted. 'Can people actually be this idiotic and still live? Oams is in Spindle's squad, Corporal. That would be the Third Squad. And we are all in the Fourteenth Legion, even though most of that legion is back in Betrys or somewhere. Our captain's name is—'

'Okay, just shut your gab-hole,' Snack said. 'Head on up there, Anyx, and tell Spindle about the savage caribou spying on us.'

'Maybe that should go through our own sergeant first, Corporal,' Anyx Fro said slowly. 'What do you think?'

'Fine. Sure, tell him along the way. Get going now. They could jump us any time.'

'If *we* jumped *them* we could have something to ride,' Blanket pointed out.

'That's stupid,' Snack said, rolling his eyes. 'You can't ride caribou. They're too short.'

'Can't ride spying savages, either,' Folibore added. 'Not like that, anyway.'

Anyx Fro still hadn't left. 'What if Spindle doesn't want to send Oams?'

Snack frowned. 'What? Well, who would he send, then?'

'Stillwater.'

Stillwater lowered her eyeglass. 'That's not my kind of work. But he won't send Oams anyway, since it's broad daylight and there's no way to sneak across a stubbly field, is there?'

Anyx Fro's sudden smile looked evil. 'Exactly. But a killer witch who can slip into shadows that aren't even there, why, *she* could.'

'No,' Stillwater said. 'He won't send anyone, because this whole thing is stupid. And what's all this talk about magic? Not me. I'm just an assassin . . . what are you all looking at?'

Snack pointed at Anyx. 'Just get on up there.'

'I will, as soon as Folibore gives me back my eyeglass.'

'There's an art to this,' Benger was saying. 'But you should know this, Oams, more than most. Every mage practises sleight-of-hand, even when Mockra's not their chosen warren. It's down to hiding what you got, right? Keeping it all under cover. Not letting anyone sniff you out, and if you don't do what you need to do to hide what you are, you're dead.'

'Benger,' said Oams, sighing, 'everybody ends up dead.'

'Right. Dead fifty years from now, or dead tomorrow. Choose.'

'And nobody chooses, either,' Oams said.

Benger was Dal Honese. Though it probably wasn't true, a handful of scholars of the magical arts believed that Mockra was born in the jungles of Dal Hon. The Old Emperor probably began as a sorceror of Mockra before stumbling onto whatever he stumbled onto. Or so most mages surmised. And he'd been Dal Honese. Maybe. Or maybe not. Oams mentally shook his head. Just thinking about Kellanved started up a cloudy haze of confusion, as if to invoke any memory having to do with him in turn triggered a latent spell that spanned the entire world. Which was ridiculous.

'I'm trying to help you out here, Oams.'

'Sorry, Benger, I've forgotten what we were talking about.'

'It's a question, isn't it? I mean, how *does* one cross open ground without anyone actually seeing it being done? You know, when there's a few hundred savages with painted faces hiding out in a forest, every one of them squinting in your direction and all.'

Oams scratched the stubble on his jaw. 'Get Stillwater.'

'I agree, in principle. But Spin said for us to check it out, didn't he?'

They were walking a dozen or so paces back from their sergeant, with the two heavies, Paltry Skint and Say No, forming a big swaying wall of backsides in between. 'Well,' said Oams, 'it's something to ponder.'

'No it isn't,' replied Benger. 'Everybody knows you're a Claw, Oams. There's a dark warren swirling around you. Don't know why I never noticed it before.'

'I'm not a Claw,' Oams insisted. 'And even if I was, I'm not any more, and even then, not all Claw are mages, so if I was, once, it wasn't the magicking kind anyway, not that I was ever a Claw in the first place. The point is, I don't know what you think you're seeing. Whatever it is, it ain't me.'

'Okay, maybe it's not you, but whatever it is, it likes you a lot.'

'Look,' said Oams, 'why don't we just saddle up a couple of horses, ride out there, and ask them what in the Crow's name they're doing?'

'I hate horses and more to the point, horses hate me.'

'Sure, they can sense things.'

'Oh, really?' Benger removed his helmet to scratch at the few wisps of crinkly white hair on his betel-brown head. 'You remember that Arthani cavalry charge outside G'danisban? Five hundred horses slamming right into our line of pikes?'

'What about it?'

Benger put his helmet back on. 'It's a question, isn't it?'

Oams rolled his eyes. One of Benger's favourite statements. Playing along was the easiest option, so he offered up the required 'What is?'

'Well, which were stupider: the horses or their riders? I'd call it about even. A quarter bell later, they were all dead or dying.'

'How is any of that relevant here, Benger? We're not going to charge the local tree-fuckers, are we?'

'It's relevant because I'm not going to put my trust in a wild-eyed beast with a turnip for a brain.'

Oams grunted. 'I'm sure they feel the same way about you.'

'Besides, that's too much to work with, under the circumstances. Anyway, thanks for the distraction. I'm sure they're convinced.'

'What? You there already?'

'I am.' Benger suddenly vanished.

Cursing, Oams moved up, pushing between Say No and Paltry Skint – no easy feat – and ignoring as best he could their unpleasant suggestions once he managed to squeeze through. Reaching Spindle and Morrut, he said, 'He arrived and then something went wrong.'

'Went wrong how?' Morrut asked.

'I don't know, only the illusion broke. Could be he saw something that distracted him, messed up his concentration. Or they've got a warlock or witch who sniffed him out and slapped him down.'

Spindle said, 'Corporal, saddle us four horses. We'll ride over.'

'Four ain't enough to rescue Benger if he needs rescuing,' Oams pointed out as Morrut hurried off.

'Three, actually,' said Spindle. 'The fourth horse is the spare, for Benger.'

'So you think he's fine, then?'

Spindle shrugged. 'It may not seem that way, but probably.'

'We could collect up a detachment from Balk's troop along the way,' Oams suggested, somewhat reluctantly.

'No point in making this any more confrontational,' his sergeant said. 'Stay here and wait for Morrut. I'll fill in the captain.'

Oams watched Spindle jog up to where Gruff rode with Sergeant Shrake, whose bad ankle always got worse as soon as the word 'march' was mentioned. He couldn't blame her, really. They'd had enough mounts back at Culvern, but this was the third straight year of drought and two failed crops had left Silver Lake low on feed, and until the weather fully turned, forage was chancy. Nobody liked watching animals starve. So, that meant slogging on foot. Shrake hated marching as much as Benger hated riding. *Ah, well, no such thing as a happy world full of happy people. Someone always pops up with something to complain about.*

But this dark warren thing that Benger mentioned. That was troubling.

'Just the mage I was looking for.'

Oams turned to see Anyx Fro arrive, carrying her eyeglass. 'I'm not a mage.'

'What's with all these mages denying being mages?'

'I'm not like Stillwater, Anyx.'

'Huh, so the mysterious airs thing is just an act? Nothing but vapid posery?'

'Posery?'

'Posing! Posery. The act of posing.'

'You mean like "posturing"? Or pomp and pretence?'

'Stop fucking distracting me, it won't work. We're being spied on from the tree-line.' She lifted up the huge eyeglass. 'Couldn't hide from this.'

'Couldn't hide from Spindle's own eyes, either,' Oams said.

'What? You're lying.'

'Obviously not. Anyway,' Oams added, 'Benger magicked up and went over for a look-see. But then his illusion that was walking and talking beside me went *pffft*. So we're going to ride over there.'

'Keeping it subtle, huh? Why bother going at all? Benger's probably dead by now. There's a warlock over there.'

'How do you know that?'

'I saw him,' and now she smiled triumphantly. 'Obviously, Spindle didn't, and now Benger's dead. I call this yet another breakdown in communication slowly whittling away the Malazan military, one stupid mage at a time.'

Paltry Skint spoke up behind them. 'There are many interconnected factors contributing to the decline of the Malazan Empire, and while the military's growing dependence on magery is a significant and disturbing trend, I would suggest that the primary source of decay is Anyx Fro and her stupid inventions.'

Anyx offered up a rude gesture, somewhat truncated by the eyeglass in her hands. 'You heavies don't fool me, Paltry.'

'Nonsense, our posery is clearly successful,' Paltry replied.

'Oh, look, irony.' Anyx returned her attention to Oams. 'I bet Spindle didn't see what Stillwater saw, though.'

'Which was?'

'Leaves. But apart from that, she thinks there was some kind of signalling going on.'

'Signalling? Between?'

'Them and Balk's.'

'Oddly disturbing,' Paltry Skint murmured, and Say No grunted agreement.

Spindle returned and a moment later Morrut arrived leading four saddled horses. 'Got more to report, Sergeant,' Oams said as he swung up onto a mount. 'Can fill you in on the way.'

'What kind of signalling?' Corporal Snack asked Stillwater.

She shrugged, folding up the eyeglass. 'Hands. Gesturing.'

'You mean, like, waving?'

'That's exactly it, Corporal. They're just waving hello. Like this,' and she made a gesture at him, 'only completely different.'

Folibore snorted. 'That isn't waving hello, Stillwater, and you know it.'

'And those savages weren't fucking waving hello, either.'

Snack turned on her. 'But you just said—'

'She was being sarcastic, Corporal,' Blanket explained.

'Well, how am I supposed to know that, Blanket? This is how it all breaks down.'

Stillwater sighed. 'Feather's itch, Snack, you're as bad as Anyx Fro.' She fell silent then when, up ahead, Sergeant Spindle, Oams and Morrut rode out from the column, trailing a lone horse.

'That's not a good sign,' Folibore said.

'Benger,' Stillwater muttered. 'They probably caught him. Killed him. Poor Benger.'

Sergeant Drillbent dropped back, his battered, pitted face dark and glowering. He pointed a gnarled finger at Stillwater. 'You, magic up and get out there.'

'I'm not a—'

'Stop fucking around,' Drillbent said. 'I'm giving you an order.'

'I need to go behind a wagon,' she said. 'Then I'll drop into the stubble, blend in based entirely on my sneaky skills, and squirm my way across the field. Because you got that sorcery thing all wrong.'

'Just get over there and back 'em up in case they need it.'

'Can I assassinate that warlock?'

'Don't know. Can you?'

That sounded like another order to Stillwater. She smiled, and then shoved her pack into Folibore's arms. 'Don't lose it.'

'Why would I lose something I plan on looking through?'

'In other words,' she said, 'respecting my privacy doesn't stand a chance against your creepy fetishes.'

'That's about right.'

'Stillwater,' growled Snack.

'I'm going!' She dropped back and edged round on the opposite side of the first ox-drawn wagon. The driver stared down at her. She scowled back up at him. 'Look away, asshole.'

The Shadow Realm had always been an ugly warren, full of strange folds, some of which could be moved through, while others seemed crammed with horrid, vengeful demons who only occasionally listened to reason. Even more alarming, cracking open a doorway into the warren was no guarantee that where you ended up was where you wanted to end up. She'd heard tales of mages stepping onto demonic battlefields, or even into the maw of a Shadow Hound.

'You're still staring.'

The driver was chewing something that left his lips stained purple. He looked like that kid she once found completely entangled in black-berry vines, bawling even as he stuffed his face. Except that this man was old, possibly even in his forties.

'I need to hide,' she told him.

'So hide,' he said in a thick drawl, and then sent out a stream of purple-black juice off to one side.

'What's that you're chewing?'

'Who said I was chewin' anything?'

'Just look away.'

'You called me an asshole, for no reason at all.'

'You're giving me a reason to call you an asshole right now.'

'You hurt my feelings.'

From around the wagon came Snack's bellow. 'Stillwater!'

Stillwater drew out a knife. 'If you don't look away, I'll kill you.'

'Well, why didn't you say so in the first place?' The man looked away, upwards, studying the clouds or something, his bushy jaw working on whatever he wasn't chewing.

She studied him a moment longer, just to make sure, and then with a faint gesture, she opened the Warren of Shadow. The only visible sign was some odd blurring of the air and the ground before her. So far, so good. Sheathing the knife, she quickly slipped through.

The sky overhead was suddenly darker, dimmer, a vague yellow hue to the solid iron-grey overcast. The road and field, columns and all the rest were gone, although if she squinted, she could make out a few ghostly outlines, and a handful of bright smudges from mages and healers, who – to her eyes at least while in her warren – always leaked. The brighter glow from the ox next to her was a bit startling, but some animals had a nose for magic, or an ear, or just hackles. When the beast lowed, the sound came through as if from a distance. As she went in front of the ox, she flicked its nearest ear. It lowed again.

She could make out the tree-line, there on the other side of Balk and his troops, but it was as if everything had been roughly sketched against the backdrop of the landscape before her, which stretched out a rippled sweep of black sand studded here and there with sharp rocks and larger, rounded boulders. Streaks of paler sand cut diagonally across a nearby hill in strange ribbons, and some kind of four-legged beast was standing on the crest, watching her. Hard to tell how big it was, since distances played tricks in this warren.

When she set off towards the tree-line, it didn't follow, so she decided to ignore its steady, burning stare.

Less than a dozen swift strides brought her past Balk and his column, and then, suddenly, the tree-line loomed before her, rising spectrally through a heap of boulders that struck her as curious – but something to think about later.

Faint thuds of horse hoofs behind her, and she turned as Spindle, Morrut and Oams rode up.

Stillwater started. Oams was dully glowing, something sickly and dangerous, and she wondered if she'd seen it before. He was a sapper who did knife-work. Was he a Claw like they said? Hard to know. Some people lit up for no reason, like they were skew-eyed or something. In any case—

Glancing at Spindle gave her a bigger shock – even though she'd been expecting it, since he did every time she had looked upon him while in her warren. *Crazy . . . something. Something. What in Jarak's name is that?* Filaments of waving energy, too wild to be a web, flowing around the sergeant as if tugged every which way by invisible currents. With a full third of them stretched down and wrapped about the barely visible form of his horse, as if holding it under him, and the animal's spirit was shivering as if terrified.

Morrut, meanwhile, had all the presence of a dead clam.

Stillwater moved to one side to let the trio pass, and was startled a third time, since something was following Oams, and it was big and heavy – she sensed a hint of fiery mane, hands with dagger-long nails or talons, and masses that hinted of the feminine – floating along, hovering close behind Oams.

'Who are you and what do you want with Oams?'

The apparition appeared to not hear her. Stillwater grunted, watching it slide past, noticing how it kept Spindle at a distance, as if uneasy about those waving filaments that looked ready to snag anything that came too close.

Was Spindle a mage? If he was, he'd never tapped it, not once in her memory. And if his hairshirt truly was haunted, that too was well hidden. No, Spindle was just Spindle. Though he might be cursed. But if he was, why hadn't Benger lifted it long ago, since along with all that Mockra he used, he was also an adept of Denul?

They'd halted their mounts. Stillwater could hear Spindle's voice as if through a wall or two. 'Stay here with the horses, Morrut. Looks like our guests have fled, but we need to find Benger.'

'Fled but not too far,' Oams said. 'And I smell blood and guts.'

Morrut spoke. 'Might be butchered caribou, Oams.'

'You think so, Corporal?'

'No. Just my feeble attempt at being optimistic.'

Spindle and Oams dismounted. Stillwater watched those filaments tug free of Spindle's horse, at last releasing the beast's quivering soul.

'Take the lead, Oams,' said Spindle.

They moved in beneath the mostly leafless canopy, Oams now cradling his crossbow. Lagging a dozen paces back, Stillwater followed. That warlock was close but well disguised, probably wrapped up in the spirit-tangle of this remnant pocket of what had once been an ancient forest that covered most of the continent's northlands. All the farmed land around here had the ghosts of trees if you had the eyes to see them, and this particular stand of aspen, elm and alder seemed restless – she suspected the thousands of caribou that had passed through it and the few hundred that still remained had brought with them their own primordial something, muddying the elemental waters.

Stillwater's immediate problem, however, had to do with clambering over the heap of boulders in the realm she now travelled. The stones were greasy, patchy with moss, black as the pits of the Widow's eyes. She scrabbled up its flank, and then hissed a curse. Stillwater had looted enough barrows to know one, and this pile of rocks was a damned barrow.

A barrow in the Shadow Realm. She paused in her climb, licked her lips. How often did that happen? *How about . . . never!* It didn't even look very old, did it? Any piled-up heap of boulders got swallowed by turf and sod in no time at all. Grass and then shrubs and then small trees. Three hundred years later and few would even know it was there. But even the moss she kept clawing through was only a few years' worth, if that.

Looted? Not likely! This is Shadow, full of demons, and revenants, and Hounds!

She resumed her scramble and quickly reached the top. Not twenty paces ahead in a small clearing stood Spindle and Oams. With that fire-haired heavy apparition circling the glade like a dog on a scent. And there, at the sergeant's feet, was what was left of Benger. Arrow-studded, scalped, eviscerated, throat-slit and eye-plucked.

Poor Benger. Oh well, nothing more for me to do, then. And those two still alive, they look fine, especially with that giant bloated hag with the talons stalking about like a whore in a barracks. And that warlock's nowhere – nothing glowing within sight. He's bolted for sure, couple of nice round eyeballs in his mouth like river pebbles, bloody scalp at his belt, a man who had himself a good day. Poor, poor, poor Benger.

Meanwhile, someone had thrown this giant barrow right into her path. Couldn't be accidental. The universe didn't work that way. *This – this is just like in the epic poems about all those Ascendants and gods and stuff. Convergence. Right here, right now. Me . . . and this barrow.*

She clambered along the spine of boulders, towards its higher end, where sure enough she found a massive, oblong lintel-stone, over-hanging an inset slab door. Dropping down in front of it, Stillwater paused. That barrier looked big and heavy, and here she was, without a pry-bar.

Momentary inconvenience. She quickly glanced round. Spindle and Oams over there, backs to her, demon hag suddenly nowhere to be seen and good riddance. Perfect. She dropped her warren, took two rapid steps forward, and then, with a quick gesture, jumped back into Shadow.

To find herself in darkness. Musty smells, dead smells, but none of the smells as old as they would've smelled if the crypt wasn't new.

I'm in! 'Hello, Mister Dead,' she murmured. 'I've come shopping.'

The passageway ahead was low, forcing her into a crouch as she edged forward; the dry earthen floor sloped, dropping away with each step she took. She knew she'd reached the edge of the tunnel when both hands which had been held out to the sides to track the passage's stony walls suddenly found empty air.

Stillwater halted. Settling into a squat, she whispered a few words and waited until a faint glow painted the crypt's curved walls.

A four-legged wooden bier filled up the centre, roughly hewn and bound with leather strips instead of iron nails, fetishes of feather and rat-tails dangling from the sides. The body lying on it belonged to someone tall, thin-boned and now desiccated inside a snugly fitted deer-hide sack, its wrapped feet closest to the tunnel entrance. A mask of lacquered wood covered the body's face, features carved into an exaggerated grimace, with long grey hair spilling out to the sides. There were no eye-holes in the mask but eyes had been painted on, wide and staring. 'Look,' she whispered. 'Lead paint.'

On one side near the head, a small iron-bound box rested on a three-legged pedestal, lid sealed shut with a ribbon of beeswax covered with stuck moths and other dead insects. On the other side was a full helm with plated cheek-guards, the black iron bowl half caved in.

'Should've ducked,' Stillwater muttered.

The legs of the bier were of foot-stool height, leaving space underneath. Stillwater dropped to her knees and then bent forward and peered into the gloom beneath the body.

A scabbarded sword lying lengthways. The hand-and-a-half kind, with a cross-hilt of twisted iron and a spherical pommel of what looked like amber. She reached under and dragged the weapon close for a better look. A bit of work with her knife got the pommel-stone loose and she quickly pocketed it. She was curious enough to pull the sword a third of the way out of the scabbard and pause to admire all the patterning on the blade. But she didn't have any use for swords, and besides, it looked too big to be attractive to anyone else in the squads. So she pushed the weapon back under the bier. Low priority, but if she had a hand free, she'd take it with her to sell it on, maybe in Silver Lake.

Settling onto her knees, she studied the wrapped corpse once more. Then slit the hide lengthways and spread it wide to look at the body underneath. The glint of gold caught her eye in the folds of the woollen cloak the figure had been buried in. A brooch. She cut it free of the cloth and added it to the pommel in her belt's pouch. There was a necklace, too, made from hundreds of tiny canines. Rat-sized? She wasn't sure. She couldn't remember the last time she'd examined a rat's canines. Blanket would know; he knew all sorts of things. She pulled it round until she found the clasp and moments later added it to her loot.

She lifted free the nearest arm. It made crackling sounds. 'Ooh, nice vambrace.' She unclasped it. The left arm ended just above the elbow. 'Ouch. Should've dodged, too.' But it looked like an old wound. This warrior's luck was the Lord's every time. She even found the sword-thrust that probably helped kill him – along with the bashed-in head and lead paint – just to the left of the breast-bone, a horizontal cut that had slipped between ribs to pierce the heart. 'Should've flinched.'

That was the thing with dead people. They were dead because they never listened to advice. If she'd been at this man's side, he'd probably still be alive. Wall-eyed and drooling because of the paint, but alive.

Anyway. No torcs, which was too bad. No rings, either, but him being a fighter, that wasn't surprising. Nothing more painful than a ring pinching in the middle of a knife-fight.

She gave the mask another look. It was interesting. Painting wasn't too bad, but no inlay. Some rich noble might buy it and not give a thought to whatever nasty spirits lurked in it. Stick it up on a wall and forget about it while his whole bloodline rotted and fell apart. He'd probably pay a lot for it, too. Idiot.

She lifted it free of the face. The withered visage beneath wasn't human. Stillwater scowled. 'Tiste. Should've guessed.' The skin covering the sharp-boned features was grey, but then, that wasn't too surprising, since the man was dead and all. And sure enough, his right temple was bashed in, skin mottled and torn and black-stained with old blood. 'See? Duck, dodge, flinch. I could charge a fortune for advice like that.'

She slipped the mask beneath her blouse, where it sat cold against her left tit.

And now, at last, it was time for that pretty little box.

Her knife-point slid easily through the beeswax. The lid tilted back with a faint squeal.

Gold coins. Stacked, each coin glued to the one above and below by more beeswax. She counted twelve stacks, twelve coins to the stack. Which made for . . . a lot. 'And here's some more advice,' she told the corpse. 'Because you're dead, you can't keep this. But because I'm alive, why, I can. And you can't take it with you into the dead-place, either. But I can take it wherever I please. You sat on it like it was an egg and all for nothing, because now you're dead.'

She drew out a slightly bigger pouch, this one made of softened leather. In good times, it held whatever sweets she could find from whatever nearby market there happened to be. Empty since before Culvern Crossing. Tragic but now convenient.

The stacks each came away with a bit of tugging and twisting and quickly filled up the bottom of the sack. She knotted the mouth and hefted the weight. Damned heavy. The coins were pretty big, bigger than a Daru Council, bigger than an Untan Old Sovereign. And thick, too. And by the weight, solid gold each and every one.

'I'm rich. Come by honestly, too. Hard work and nobody lending a helping hand. No soft inheritance, either. Do I look soft? Bloaty and saggy and perfumed and sniffy? Not me. This is proper recompense, and nobody's going to—'

The linen scarf round her neck tightened fractionally. Stillwater dived to one side, even as a dagger blade cut hard diagonally down between her shoulder-blades – failed back-stab! Not deep enough to reach skin – she twisted as her knees landed on the lower half of the corpse. Stubby wooden legs snapped, at least two of them, and the body rolled on top of her, neatly putting itself between Stillwater and the tattooed, savage form that leapt at her, blade flashing.

That dagger punched hollowed chest.

'Missed!' Twisting free, Stillwater slashed out with her own knife, felt its tip nick the attacker's chin. His head jerked back.

'Warlock! Sneaky bastard, hiding in here!'

He tried closing again and she kicked him in the face, sent him back over the half-collapsed bier.

As he scuffed about trying to regain his feet, she swung the sack of coins into the side of his head. The impact made a satisfying *crunch*. Blood spattered the stone wall and the warlock reeled back, landing on his backside.

Stillwater lunged at him, forcing him onto his back as she stabbed with her knife. The blade punched in above his left collarbone.

He countered with a sideways thrust that scored deep along the bone of her left shoulder-blade. 'Ow! Fuck, that hurts!' The sack of coins was no use this close in, so she let go of it and jammed her thumb into the warlock's right eye. The eye popped like a grape.

He tried bringing his knee up between her legs, but she blocked it with her right thigh. 'Not gonna work – I'm not a man! Hah!' He tried again and connected with her crotch. 'Ow! Ow! Still hurts! A lot!'

She rolled off, in agony, slashing blindly with her knife.

It laid something open and blood gushed onto the back of her weapon-hand. 'Got you!'

Bursts of pain lanced deep in her left thigh. 'Ow! Fuck you!'

She kicked out with her right foot and got her heel deep into the man's gut. Breath whooshed out. She kicked again, heel into his jaw. Dislocated it sideways.

Stillwater flung herself back onto him, stabbing him twice in the chest. A salty thumb plunged into her mouth and she bit down, and then began chewing. A few moments later, she realized that the warlock was motionless beneath her. She spat out his mangled thumb and sat back.

His moccasined foot slammed into the side of her head, pitched her on her side, stunned. 'Fucker, you should be dead by now,' she mumbled. She'd dropped her knife. 'Why aren't you dead?' As she groped for it, she heard the warlock get to his feet and then stagger up the passageway. 'Getting away? Unbelievable! Not a chance!'

Her fingers found her knife, but the wrong end. 'Ow, fuck!' Her other hand grasped the sack of coins. Bursts of agony from her left thigh every time she put weight on that leg. Slowing her down. 'Get back here, un-killable bastard!'

She plunged into the passageway. He was nearly at the entrance, and its massive door had been dragged to one side. *When did that happen?* She saw his silhouette blotting out the pale light beyond, and then it vanished.

She heard strange noises outside as, head spinning and neck feeling wrenched, she crabbed her limping, half-hitching way up the incline. Then plunged out through the mouth of the barrow.

A Shadow Hound stood not five paces away, its mouth crammed with the lower half of the warlock, the upper half presumably already inside. The noises she'd heard were the man's bones breaking. The beast dipped its head slightly to fix lambent eyes upon her.

Stillwater laughed and pointed. 'Look at you! Got your mouth full! Can't do—'

The Hound's head snapped up, both tattooed legs sliding almost bonelessly down the beast's throat.

'Oh, shit.'

Stillwater opened the warren, a jagged rent spitting energy, and dived through even as the Hound lunged down at her.

She felt a sudden tug on her leather poncho, and then was tumbling onto mulch-strewn ground beneath a cloudy but warm sky.

She heard the faint hiss of a sword leaving its scabbard and lifted both hands. 'I surrender!'

'Stillwater!' Oams knelt above her, setting aside his crossbow. 'You look a mess!'

'I'm stabbed, Oams,' she snarled in reply, 'and head-kicked and neck-broke and my squishy's one giant bruise and not in a good way. How do you think I should look? Look at me! Leaking blood everywhere!'

'Squishy?' Oams asked.

Spindle was now on the other side, standing, looking down, his short-sword in one hand. 'That's not all your blood,' he said.

'Fucking sneaky warlock, hiding in a damned barrow. In the Shadow Realm! Can you believe the nerve?'

'Where is he now?' Oams asked.

'Dead. And let me tell you, it wasn't easy.' She sat up, gingerly. 'Ow, my back's cut wide open, and look at that hole in my leg!'

Oams was still kneeling, now a bit behind her. 'The bottom half of your poncho is missing, Still. What happened there? Big hole down right at the—'

'Shadow Hound. Almost got me.'

Spindle was still staring down at her. 'Shadow Realm, barrow, warlock, and a Shadow Hound. Did I miss anything?'

She drew her leather sack of coins up close, eyes narrowing suspiciously. 'Nope. That's it, Sergeant.'

'Fuck sake,' Oams muttered, straightening and collecting up his crossbow.

Scowling, Stillwater said, 'What? I killed that damned warlock, didn't I? Okay, maybe too late for poor Benger, which is really annoying, since who's going to heal me? But still, he wasn't up to any good, that warlock, was probably going to kill you both.' She paused to wipe at her face, the back of her hand coming away smeared with blood and bits of dead skin from the corpse. 'And that warlock, he had a skin disease, too.'

'Oams,' said Spindle, re-sheathing his sword.

'Not sure, Sergeant. Somewhere close.' Oams then turned to the glade and raised his voice. 'Benger! Warlock's dead, you can come out now!'

Thrashing from a nearby tree-top, and then there was Benger, climbing swiftly down.

Stillwater looked over at where the other Benger had been lying in a big glittery stain of fluids, blood and gore. And watched it all fade into nothing. 'I knew it,' she said. 'Arrow-studded, scalped, eviscerated, throat-slit and eye-plucked. Who do you think you are, a Tiste?' Then she waved at Benger. 'Healer! Hurry up, I'm dying!'

Lieutenant Ara rode up alongside Balk and together they watched in silence as the small troop of Malazans emerged from the tree-line, four astride mounts and one on foot. The woman on the last horse looked to be covered in blood.

'It wasn't the trading that changed my thinking,' Balk suddenly said. 'Any tribe will happily engage in handing over a bundle of furs or whatever for an iron pot or a knife or hatchet. Useful things. More durable and efficient than whatever they replaced. That simply makes sense, but the habit's addictive, and too many less pleasant things come with it.'

Ara said nothing. Balk's need to justify the decisions he made spoke to some lingering doubts, she assumed. The Malazans had clearly clashed with the Ganrel. Unnecessary, of course. But also not surprising, all things considered. No one was here to trade, and this was imperial land. There were rules when it came to unpacified forest people. Besides, the mages among the marines would have sniffed out that something unusual was going on.

'But those villages deeper into the Wilds,' Balk resumed after a few moments, 'that's where I discovered the first Nathii refugee, a lowborn peasant who'd been facing a life of toil and poverty, trapped in a system designed to keep him down – a system that would then do it all over again to his children. He ran from all that. Was terrified I was there to drag him back into civilization. But I wasn't. Instead, I was curious, and I listened to his story. And when he told me there were others like him, deep in the Wilds, living lives without coin or class, without back-breaking toil or in squalor, well, that didn't surprise me, either.'

In the distance, Spindle had swung his mount and was now riding towards them at a slow canter.

'It landed on me all at once,' Balk said. 'Revelation.'

Ara's gaze narrowed on Spindle. She still wanted him dead. She still hated him for the way he had forced her hand. 'He'll want to know what the fuck's going on, Captain.'

'Nothing was going on.'

'Yet.'

They said nothing more as Spindle rode up and reined in alongside Balk. 'Lieutenant Balk.'

'Sergeant?'

'There was a warlock, waking up the land's spirits.'

Balk shrugged. 'They do that. Easier to track game.'

'If it was game they were after, Captain, they didn't need any magic. You can't go twenty paces in those woods without bumping into a caribou. These Ganrel are deep into our territory, but I imagine you treated with them often enough in Fool's Forest.'

'In trading season, certainly.'

Spindle nodded equably, seeming at ease in the saddle. 'Lots of reports,' he then said, 'all along the north borderlands. They're on the move. Incursions in strength. A few clashes here and there. Not trading.'

'Will that be our task out of Silver Lake, Sergeant? Chasing savages off imperial land?' There was timbre to his tone, edging towards indignation and contempt. 'Shall we set their heads on poles? Or just collect scalps?'

'Not the Malazan style, Lieutenant,' Spindle calmly replied, his attention on something ahead, squinting in the afternoon sunlight that had finally burned through the thin overcast. 'We're here to protect the settlers, maintain the imperial roads and patrol the borders.'

'You rode into those woods, Sergeant. Three mounted and leading a fourth horse. Then rode out with four riders and one on foot. One wounded.'

'A warlock working the land spirits can use them to track enemy troop movements.'

'Are we at war now, Sergeant?'

'I'm thinking someone is,' Spindle answered. Then he shrugged and gathered up his reins. 'No matter. The warlock's dead. Not really what we had in mind, but he wasn't interested in conversation.' Tapping heels to flanks, he rode away.

After a long moment, Ara hissed; 'Nistilash dead? I don't believe it.'

Balk was now studying the marines marching on the road, where the riders had arrived and were rejoining the others. 'Less than twenty of them,' he muttered, 'and yet, somewhere in that mix, there is someone who is *very* dangerous.'

'But Nistilash, Captain? The Ganrel will never recover from this.' She gestured towards the marines. 'Those bastards just cut out their fucking heart.'

'That death has weakened them, yes,' Balk said, 'but enraged them as well.'

'Spindle doesn't trust you, Captain.'

He spat to one side. 'It's mutual.'

Ara considered, and then said, 'Sugal, Stick and Bray can have Spindle for a night of knife-work. With my blessing.'

CHAPTER SIX

The present age is only unique because you live in it. When you die, you cease to care about that age. And you know this. Which is why you don't care about anything past your own life. Why should you?

It follows, quite reasonably, that every generation is righteous in cursing the one that precedes it. Namely, yours. And the vicious fighting withdrawal that is your own conservatism – this bitter, hate-filled war against change – is doomed to fail, because no age lasts for ever. One follows upon the next and this is an inescapable fact.

So step aside. Your day is done. Any regression into childish tantrums makes a mockery of wisdom. The age dies with you, as it must, and you now show its face to be that of a mewling child who can no longer hold on to what has ceased to exist.

Synthraeas
After the Last Day of Defiance
The Great Library of New Morn

RANT WANDERED LOST. FOR THREE DAYS HE HAD WALKED bedrock that was a cracked maze of folds and fissures twisting every which way, the crevasses snagged with fallen trees and often swallowed in darkness, the high ridges forming a series of overlapping, broken ribbons. He had lost sight of the lake two days ago. The sun had grown hot, turning the lichen brittle underfoot, filling the air with insects.

He finally came to a place where large boulders were scattered across a flat sweep of bedrock, and he sat down on one in the shade cast down by a jack-pine, the bole of which was strangely twisted up its entire height. He had found a handful of puff-balls among the lichen and was eating them one by one. Like crumbling cheese in his mouth, but without much flavour.

A weight of truths was settling upon him. He had not learned how to live by himself. There was more to surviving than finding food and water or curling up in a shallow cave or hollow when night arrived. These things happened or they didn't, in the way that an island or sand-bar could save an exhausted swimmer. But life's greatest struggle was between such refuges, in all the moments between here and there, with every breath drawn in what seemed an exhausting fight against unseen currents.

He didn't know what to do with these empty stretches. The voice in his head, which Rant assumed belonged to him, had begun to sound like a stranger's, a frightened child pacing the confines of what few thoughts it possessed. Round and round they went, not at all helpful or useful.

The sun was going down, shadows lengthening. He scratched at insect bites, wiped the blood from his fingertips on his thighs. The snow-melt pools were almost gone; he had to pull moss away from cracks and dips in the bedrock to find what water he could. This latest high-ground he had found had opened out, no longer a ridge flanked by crevasses, and pockets of forest rose up wind-bent for as far as he could see in any direction. Mountains showed their tops in what he imagined to be the west, but they also loomed northward. It seemed that he could walk towards either of them by following this vast plain of bedrock.

He couldn't be certain, but he thought that the boulders made patterns, as if they'd been pushed into place, but wherever they began to form a line, it would end in a jumble of shattered rocks, or boulders tumbled away. This world looked to be broken, maybe on purpose.

Damisk hadn't found him. It left an odd feeling inside. When the old hunter had come into Rant's world, he had somehow filled it, and now he was gone. Alive, and then probably dead, and now, if his ghost were to suddenly appear, Rant knew he'd weep with relief. Anything to stop being so alone.

He'd eaten all the mushrooms, but his stomach still felt hollow. There would be no more food tonight, and he saw nowhere that might give him some shelter against the chill that would come when the sun was gone. The voice in his head told him that there weren't many choices left to him, but the easiest one among them was to just give up, to lie down in a hollow in the rock, and when death finally arrived, why, he wouldn't fight it at all.

Shadows were lengthening, painting the undulating bedrock in strips that stretched out from the boulders and scratched black scars from the trees, as if throwing their branches onto the ground. Patterns of webs and bottomless pits spreading out around him.

Safer, then, to not move at all. Rant slid down from the boulder and then curled up against its base. No matter how small he made himself, the lone blanket he had could not cover him. His feet and ankles were already swollen and red with mosquito bites, so he carefully covered them, even though the rough cloth made the itching worse, and then settled down to await night.

If Damisk spoke true, then his mother was still alive. He was glad for that, and without him and his complaints about always being hungry, at last she'd now know some peace. And she could save some coin, too, maybe enough to fix the leaks in the roof. He made up a picture of her in his head, the last of the men gone for that night, so she could settle down in her bed, and there'd be no creaking sounds from the loft to mark his restless sleep. He could see her face, all the worry-lines soft-ened now that he was gone, and all the bruises faded to nothing and the scabs fallen off. So pretty.

While out on Centre Street, his old friends wandered with rocks in their hands and no one to throw them at. And Drunk Menger was out in the back alley behind the bar, leaving buckets of scraps for the dogs. Capor and Arko and Vihune were in the tavern sitting at the table closest to the fireplace, because they were old and old people were always cold. They talked about the same things they talked about every night: fishing and nets and hooks and boats that needed new paint.

This same cloudy moon now rose over the town on the other side of the lake. The same stars sparked to life in the deepening sky. Nothing was as far away as it seemed, and yet beyond reach, too. The only thing he possessed that was free was his thinking, the way it winged through the night not caring how far it went, and as the darkness closed in, the stranger in his head fell silent, yielding to the world around him.

He could hear bats, the muted chirp of huddling birds, and overhead stretched the starry road that belonged to spirits. On this night there was no wind, so the biting insects swarmed him.

His father was no god. He couldn't be. Gods could stride across mountains with only a single step, could wade the deepest lakes and pluck trees like flowers. They stood so tall that no one far below mattered to them.

Most of the people in Silver Lake were Nathii. They'd been pushed there by the Malazan invasion all those years ago. They'd gone as far as they could, and the empire then swallowed them up. But somewhere in all of that, there'd been the trade in slaves, and at first those slaves came from the north forests and they were people no different from the people in the town. But then the slavers found the Teblor, in numbers too few to fight against them. There were people who wanted to own other people, which Rant didn't understand, but the Teblor worked harder and lived longer than any forest savage. That made them valuable.

Silver Lake had grown rich. Everyone lived in nice houses and led good lives, and no one was hungry. But the Malazans didn't like slavery. Their empire outlawed it. In the Malazan Empire, no one owned anyone else. So it was a fight between money and the law, and it took a while for the law to finally win.

Damisk had explained all of this while they walked. Damisk had talked like he had too many words in his skull and he needed to get them out. He said that history was a collection of truths, sometimes hidden or mixed up, even twisted into untruths, but if you picked at them hard enough, those untruths unravelled. Only most people didn't want to pick away at anything, not if the untruths made them comfortable and happy, or rich.

History lived in memory; only each person's memory was their own and nobody remembered things the same way. So history was also an ongoing argument between truths.

'And here's the other thing, Rant. History isn't the past. The past is gone, behind us all, with no going back to it, ever. No, history is what we carry in us right now. It's the story of our memories of how things were, in our own life, in the life of everyone who's gone before. And the further back you go, the fewer the memories, so we take all the gaps and fill them up with how we imagine things had to be. You might think your imagination is good at that. But it isn't. The more limited your life experience, the weaker your imagination.

'But what about children, you ask? Don't they disprove what you just said? Yes and no. Their imagination is the strongest thing they possess inside, and that makes the world wonderful. Until it's crushed under heel. Sooner or later, a child's taught to leave it behind, abandon it, stop feeding it. So it withers.'

And Rant had nodded. Yes, he told himself, I am withered. I feel it inside. Too many stones striking his body, too many curses sent his way for being who and what he was. Being a child meant being half-blind to what was and growing up was finally seeing how things really were.

'Your father is Karsa Orlong, a Teblor warrior. Maybe now a god. That's where your life's story begins, Rant. It's a truth. History. It's a wonder they didn't kill you long ago. So why didn't they? Have you ever wondered that?'

No, he hadn't. He hadn't really known that people wanted to kill him, not until the last few days. Not liking him wasn't the same as wanting to kill him, was it?

'*Fear,*' Damisk had said then. '*The spawn of a god. What if Karsa Orlong learns of the fate of his son? What if Karsa Orlong returns to Silver Lake? Is it wise to anger a god?*'

No, that didn't seem wise.

'*But your mother knew not to trust that. She knew the danger you were in. The way hate loses its mind and does things it shouldn't ever do. Another reason for sending you away. She made sure you would live and if that isn't an act of love, why, nothing is.*'

But now he wanted to die. To fade into history, to be forgotten. The way, with a wave of a hand, a god might erase the bad things it had once done. Like making Rant.

He heard a sound and opened his eyes.

Three figures stood facing him, bathed in the moon's hazy light. Two women and a man. Their limbs were tattooed in spiral patterns that seemed to glisten as if catching the moon's silver glow. They wore necklaces of teeth, and bird-bones hung snagged in their long, unbound yellow hair. Scalps adorned their hide belts. The man carried a bow made of horn, so polished that it looked like it was made from amber. He was broad-shouldered, bandy-legged, his face hidden by a mask made from bone pieces. The woman on the left held a javelin in her right hand, the shaft resting on her shoulder. She was young, her body almost plump, her face round and pocked with black spots. The other, older woman was unarmed. All bones and weathered skin, she looked to be dying. The shelf of her brow was massive beneath hair so pale it was almost colourless, and her eyes were buried deep, each one a distant, glittering and cold star.

Rant slowly sat up. 'Saemdhi,' he said.

The crone scowled. '*Sae Imas hedi.*'

He stared at her, uncomprehending.

The younger woman voiced a string of foreign words in a tone Rant recognized as contemptuous. Despite that, he marvelled at their beauty, so song-like that he smiled at her.

The man grunted what might have been a laugh, and then added a few words, equally melodic.

The round-faced woman puffed out her cheeks but said nothing more.

'*Sae Imas hedi,*' the crone repeated, more slowly this time. 'People of the Cold Seas, Toblakai-child.'

Mindful of Damisk's words, he replied with, 'I am Rant, the son of Karsa Orlong, and I greet you.'

The three were silent, as if measuring him against his claim. Then the crone spoke again. 'I alone understand Nathii. But your father's name is known to us all. We have heard of you, the god-spawn child in Silver Lake. We did not think they would let you live.'

'I fled,' he explained, shrugging.

'You are weak.'

Rant nodded. 'I do not feel like the son of a god.'

The younger woman began speaking again, harsh and dismissive, and while she went on, the man wearing the mask stepped away and began circling the area, sliding a long, barbed arrow from his quiver as he did so. When the girl was done she drew her javelin down and pulled from her belt her throwing-stone.

'They want to kill me,' Rant said.

'No,' the old woman replied. 'But there is danger here.' She came closer and settled down opposite him. From a hide bag she began laying out dried meat and scorched strips of what looked like fat. She then offered him her waterskin. 'In the time before the world broke, this was an island in the ice. Do not drink too much, else your stomach rebel. Food now, chew slowly, yes, like that. An island, God-spawn, made of the world's own skin, raised up as a sanctuary, or a prison. Sometimes a refuge makes the strongest cage, for one then has little interest in testing the bars.' She paused, and then said, 'Here dwelt the Jheck, thinking themselves safe against the breaking of the world.'

'I don't know who the Jheck are,' said Rant, 'but I have seen no one.'

'Following the breaking of the world, the ice died and was reborn many times. In the times when there was no ice, we came upon them, knew them for Jheck, and we hunted them.'

'They are like herds?'

Her smile revealed oversized, squarish teeth, stained and worn down. 'No, God-spawn, not like herds. They are hunters like us, eaters of meat. Our warriors must test themselves against the Jheck.'

'Why?'

The question seemed to leave her confused. 'Jheck are the enemy.'

'But why?'

'It has always been so,' she said, now clearly irritated.

'Have you killed them all then?' Rant asked.

The old woman sat back, wrinkled lips compressed, the glint of her eyes colder.

The man wearing the mask returned to them and lowered into a squat, the bow resting across his knees, arrow nocked and casually pointing at Rant. '*T'eth sin veral. Nallit.*'

Rant saw now that the mask wasn't made of bone, but pieces of turtle shell.

'*Ihm fal e'rath*,' the crone answered. She jerked a nod towards Rant. '*Sae g'nath Toblakai.*'

The masked face regarded him for a moment, and Rant could see pale eyes in the slits, steady and unblinking. Then the warrior rose, turning to the younger woman who was now seated on a nearby boulder, javelin leaning against the stone. He said something that elicited no reply from her, then he shrugged and moved off once again.

The crone made a clucking sound that didn't sound friendly. 'God-spawn, you are seeking your own kind.'

'Teblor, yes.'

'Do they want you?'

'I don't know. What would that feel like? To be wanted?'

'I do not think you will make it,' she said. 'The one you travelled with – where is he?'

Rant shook his head.

'We hunt him, too. He's killed too many of us. We will find him and kill him. Does that please you? It should. He leaves a trail of blood, that one.' She retrieved the waterskin and what remained of the meat and cooked fat. Then she slowly climbed to her feet. 'You will die on this ancient island. Your father was careless, to so abandon you. To that, we need make no answer. Some streams do not travel far. Some streams die of their own accord. But you may be of some use yet.'

They left him then, without a single backward glance.

Rant settled his back against the boulder once more. Food and water, yes, but no friendship. But it seemed that his one friend, Damisk, still lived. Fleeing somewhere out there, perhaps on this very island of bedrock. If he could, he would find him. The crone could think what she liked. With Damisk at his side, Rant would survive.

From a distance came something like a shriek. Rant rose and faced the direction the Saemdhi had gone. He could see nothing, the moon's light too weak. Was there movement? Fast-moving blots of darkness?

Then into view came two figures, running towards him. One was limping, then it staggered, and a moment later a blackness seemed to rise up around it and pull it down. Another shriek, of raw terror, now closer, coming from the last one who still ran.

Her javelin was gone. Her face was twisted, blood-splashed.

He watched her drawing ever closer. Some instinct made him draw his Malazan knife.

Something swept in from her left, shoulder-height and elongated, a black smear in the darkness.

Rant shouted a warning and rushed forward.

Too late. It struck her from the side, sent her spinning through the air, limp as a doll. The creature met her again as soon as she struck the bedrock. Jaws closed round one thigh and then the woman was being whipped side to side in a terrible snapping of bones.

Rant found himself running for them. His mind was blank, but it seemed that he was moving through a horror that had flooded the night, while he cut through it strangely untouched, empty of panic or fear.

From the corner of an eye he caught a flash of motion, and he spun.

The wolf hammered into him, snarling darkness, fangs and fur. He staggered at the impact, his left thumb somehow jammed into one side of the lunging beast's mouth, pulling its head and jaws away from his throat, until with a twist those jaws brought their jagged molars down on that thumb, crushing it.

The pain shot fire up his arm. He answered it with a snarl of his own, and now the knife in his other hand started stabbing the blade deep into the beast's chest. Three, four, then five times, knuckles slamming into blood-soaked fur.

The wolf crumpled onto its side.

Even as he straightened, another beast struck him from behind, leaping up to clamp jaws on his neck.

The impact threw him onto his hands and knees, and the animal's heavy weight rode him down onto his stomach.

Writhing, Rant brought the knife up over the side of his head. The point found an eye socket, drove deep. The jaws on his neck spasmed and then went slack. Rant pushed the carcass off and regained his feet. He stumbled towards the wolf still savaging the young woman.

Two more wolves struck him, one to each side and from slightly behind, the attack perfect in its timing. Jaws fastening about his upper arms, tearing and grinding through meat as the beasts sought to drag him down.

Instead, Rant straightened, raising his arms. For a moment, both wolves dangled in the air. Somehow, Rant's left hand caught hold of a hind leg. He bent it until it snapped. The wolf on that side released his arm as it shrieked in pain. Ignoring the other wolf, Rant swung round and got his grip under the animal's snout, even as he brought his knee down heavily on its back. Then he pulled the head up and back until the neck broke with a meaty *pop*. He realized that he was weeping but had no idea why. With his left hand now free, he made a fist – leaving out his mangled thumb – and punched it hard into the second wolf's belly.

Fluids burst from the back-end and the wolf seemed to curl round his fist, jaws pulling free of his arm as the beast convulsed.

He brought the knife down through the top of its skull, hard enough to drive the weapon's point into the bedrock itself. The impact made the steel ring like a bell and its shock numbed his hand so that he lost grip.

Turning back to the wolf that had attacked the young woman, he found the beast facing him. Its flanks were wet with blood and an antler-handled knife jutted from one side of its chest. The young woman lay motionless a few paces to one side.

Rant stared into the beast's amber eyes.

Then the animal slowly settled onto the bedrock, and a moment later sank onto one side, jaws agape and tongue lolling as it panted.

Still eyeing it, Rant walked over to the young woman. She was a mass of torn and shredded flesh, but her face was unmarked, eyes closed and looking peaceful in death.

She'd not liked him much, Rant knew. He reached down and tenderly moved some blood-soaked hair from her brow.

There was a grunt and then a wet cough and Rant turned – and the wolf, he saw, was no longer a wolf, but a huge, hairy, barrel-chested man, slowly pushing himself into a sitting position, even now reaching up one flat, wide hand to pull the knife from the right side of his chest. His eyes – still amber and bestial – now fixed on Rant, and a flash of white showed amidst his bloody beard. 'You were the bait, then. Fools.'

The man spoke Nathii, but with an accent Rant had never heard before. 'Bait?'

'They meant to spread out, with you at the centre. Thinking we'd find in you easy meat. And then attacking while we fed.'

Rant shook his head. 'They were kind to me.'

'Sound carries out here,' the man said, pausing to spit out a gobbet of blood. 'You don't understand their tongue, do you? The language of the Imass. Well, we do, and once veered, our ears are keen indeed.' He jutted a nod towards the young woman. 'Her idea, in fact.'

Rant looked back down at that pretty, round face. The black pocks, he now saw, were tattoos of some sort that left raised scars.

'As if we would attack a Toblakai,' the man said. 'Can't think of a single damned creature on this whole world that's fucking harder to kill.'

'But you did,' Rant pointed out. 'You attacked me.'

'And there you are, proving my point.'

Rant straightened. He was dripping blood everywhere and he felt lightheaded. 'I think I'm going to die now,' he said.

'I doubt it.'

'Are you going to? Die?'

'Five of my six dead, four by your hand, Toblakai. Lung-stabbed, too.' His heavy brow knotted briefly, and then he said, 'No. But I'll be a while mending. That is,' he added, eyes narrowing, 'if you don't decide to finish me off now.'

'I don't like killing,' Rant said. 'And I'm tired and I want to sleep. But then you could kill me.'

'I won't. I got in too deep here. If you'd left the Imass to me, right now we would be sitting around a fire, drinking brewed tea and swapping lies.'

'Lies?'

'You're young. They'll all be lies, coming from you. As for me, well, no guarantees either way. So, Toblakai, when did you decide you don't like killing?'

Rant thought about it. 'Just now, I guess. I've never done it before.'

The man was silent for some time, and then he grunted, 'I am Gower, Lord of the Black Jheck. I travel to the Toblakai with a promise. You?'

'Rant.' He hesitated, and then added, 'Bastard son of Karsa Orlong. I am going to the Teblor – who I think are your Toblakai, since you give me the same name.'

'Delivering a promise?'

'No. Seeking one, I suppose.'

'Let's not kill each other, Rant. Sleep sounds infinitely better.'

Rant sat down a bit more heavily than he'd planned.

'I see that you're a youth, Rant,' Gower then said, with a voice that seemed far away. 'Woe betide the enemy when you're full-grown.' He might have laughed then, but the sound fell away as darkness closed in and Rant's mind slid into nothing.

*   *   *

Damisk had been a soldier once. He hadn't liked it much. Then he'd been a tracker for the slavers. That, too, had rankled. And for a time, he had been a guide for a dozen or so cultists worshipping a body under a rock. That venture had nearly killed him. It took a certain kind of person, he eventually realized, to be comfortable taking orders. Such people weren't rare, either. In fact, there were more of that kind of person than any other.

On the ledger's other side were the ones who liked *giving* orders, and most of them were dangerous idiots. Their reasons were often suspect, usually something to do with ambition and a hunger for power, as if they could only measure self-worth when they had a heel on someone's neck. In fact, Damisk couldn't think of many bosses he hadn't wanted to kill, or at least pound to a pulp.

He was flawed, no doubt. Good leaders existed, somewhere. People who saw their position as a service, a responsibility, even a burden. He might follow someone like that, or rather, he would have ten or twenty years ago. Now, he was probably too old, his skin of patience worn thin.

His style of hunting demanded that he work alone. Solitude had been his final refuge, a way of looking kindly upon the world rather than cursing it with every second breath. But solitude had its price.

The Saemdhi had driven him northward for the past two days and three nights, out beyond the undulating sweeps of exposed bedrock that still bore the scars of ice, and up against the very edge of the wetlands. He'd killed a half-dozen warriors thus far, and twice he'd thought he'd shaken off pursuit, only to find a new war-band on his trail.

Slightly off to his left rose the first peaks of the mountain range that stretched westward all the way to the ocean, but even these were days away. Before him was the same maze of wetlands he had been skirting for a day and a half: sinkholes filled with black pools, stands of knee-high trees lining ribbon-like ridges, sweeps of marsh grasses choking channels wherever water flowed. High islands of mud fringed in reeds and at the centre of each hill, a ragged tree-stump so old it was as hard as stone. Mosquitoes and biting blackflies swarmed the air amidst cavorting swallows gorging themselves in flight.

Behind him to the south, boulders and the dips and folds in the bedrock had provided him with some cover, but the last thousand or so paces had been across open ground, a flat-land of gouged stone that gently tilted downward to the edge of muskeg.

Five figures were now visible emerging onto that flat-land. His pursuers.

To venture out into the bog would see him hip-deep in icy mud before he'd gone four paces. The Saemdhi could keep their distance and fill him with arrows the way they would a moose driven into a mire.

Damisk had seven arrows left in his quiver, all lightly pointed, intended for taking down fowl. Most of his heavier arrows now jutted from bodies in his wake, the pursuit too relentless to allow him to retrieve any. He nocked an arrow as he turned to jog slowly westward, skirting the edge of the muskeg.

His pace was slow. He was exhausted, driven solely by stubborn determination, a refusal to make it easy. Besides, there was something beyond the wetlands that held his attention, a mystery that gnawed at him. The north horizon floated, shimmering, casting off blinding flashes here and there, but not nearly as many flashes as he expected, since those reflections came from ice. The entire horizon to the north should be a solid line of sun-painted flame. But it wasn't.

Even as his hunters spread out and drew closer, Damisk glanced again and again into the distant north. He could swear that the golden flashes were *moving*.

But now something directly ahead caught his attention. A low heap of tilted slabs of stone, rising from a broad depression like some shattered monument. Still two or three hundred paces away, the edifice looked to be as big as a keep, each elongated slab of stone three or more man-heights in length. They reached skyward, one leaning haphazardly against another, with no suggestion of order or intention. As if the very skin of the bedrock had erupted in violent up-thrust. It did not look natural, but neither did it seem deliberately assembled. No matter. It looked to be a good place to make his stand, especially if he had the time to clamber up among the tilted slabs, using them for cover.

The Saemdhi clearly saw the same and they now picked up their pace. Two carried bows, the remaining three javelins held at the ready. They didn't need to reach the stone-pile first. Arrows at seventy paces could be dodged, so long as Damisk saw them coming. Javelins at forty paces, the same. But at forty paces, arrows would join those javelins, and they were likely to take him down. Sweat blurring his vision as he ran on leaden legs, he tried to gauge the various distances.

He wouldn't make it in time.

Readying his arrow, Damisk waited until the moment when none of the Saemdhi seemed to be looking his way, then he swiftly let fly a high, arcing shot.

When the arrow landed less than two paces in front of the lead hunter, she and the rest suddenly scattered and Damisk heard their cries of alarm. Bird-arrows didn't have much fletching and what there was of it was thin, suited to passing through thickets and among branches. That made these arrows hard to see, especially against a blue sky. Too bad he'd missed, however; the disruption hadn't been enough to make any difference.

He prepared another, but it was likely he wouldn't try again, as the Saemdhi were now staying vigilant.

To Damisk's surprise, his pursuers began slowing up, and now they were shouting at him, waving their weapons. He didn't know their language and, clearly, they didn't know his. The one in the lead began gesturing, a knife in one hand making exaggerated slicing motions across her own neck.

Damisk shifted his attention from the Saemdhi towards the rock-pile. No more than thirty paces away. Where had the time gone? Oddly, the resemblance to a fallen keep was now sharper, although no brickwork was visible. But a new detail had revealed itself. Swaths of something like hides were draped all over the tilted stones, blackened stains of blood everywhere. And now he saw the swarms of flies surrounding the edifice. Between two massive leaning slabs was something that looked like a cave-mouth.

The hides were of human skin. Saemdhi. He could make out entire bodies, including arms, legs, palms and soles – even fingers and toes. Scalps of pale, colourless hair fringed the flanks of the cave, stirring to some unfelt breeze from the cave's mouth, and on the cracked bedrock surrounding the edifice thousands of bone shards were scattered amidst the rubble.

Damisk glanced back at the Saemdhi. Now he understood the lead woman's gesturing. She was promising him a quick, merciful death, as befitted a worthy enemy. They had all halted fifty or more paces away. Not a single weapon was trained on him.

Amidst the growing stench of rotting flesh Damisk caught the scent of wolf.

Jheck.

'Ah, fuck,' he muttered. 'I'm dead either way.' Still, deep in his chest remained a burning defiance when it came to these damned Saemdhi. Offering him a quick blade across the throat was all very well, but then one of them would wear his scalp at her hip, and that rankled. *Let the Jheck have that trophy. Let my skin ride this rock.*

He offered up a rude gesture towards the Saemdhi, and then swung round and approached the rock-pile.

The buzz of the flies was almost deafening at the mouth of the cave. Damisk could see that the path leading inward sloped down to impenetrable darkness, bedrock worn by the passage of feet, paws, whatever. That path made him pause, as he tried to comprehend how many centuries could have worn down those ruts, smoothing and then polishing all the edges. From the distance he had thought the stone slabs were fragments of the bedrock itself, broken and pushed upward, but that wasn't the case at all. The slabs weren't the native black stone shot through with veins of milky white quartzite; instead, they were dull green, creased but smooth. They looked to be solid serpentine, or even jade.

The realization made him bark a sour laugh. Here, before him, was wealth unimaginable.

From deep within the cave, a muffled grunt answered his laugh.

'Aye,' said Damisk, raising his voice. 'You have a new guest. Another fool to scalp and skin and eat the rest, but I'm bound to sit ill in your stomach, Jheck. Bitter and old, that's me, Damisk of Silver Lake.'

The voice that drifted out was a woman's. 'Not another Imass youth, then, seeking glory.'

'Staying alive is glory enough,' he replied.

'Damisk of Silver Lake, broken Teblor souls haunt your shadow. And animals uncounted. I see others, your own kind. All dead by your hand.'

Shaken, Damisk licked dry lips and said, 'No Teblor died by my hand.'

A pause, and then, 'They are unconvinced.'

'There were . . . slaves. I but did my job.'

A heavy sigh, too heavy to belong to a person. 'A stunningly sound defence. Mere chains, not murder, the hand staying clean. Unsullied, even.'

'I do not think you are Jheck,' Damisk said.

'No? Then what am I?'

'Teblor.'

'Will there be a day in your life, Damisk of Silver Lake, when the true paucity of your imagination confronts you? Will it be today?'

He scowled. 'Insulted by the mouth of a cave, then.'

'More apt than you might think,' she observed in a wry tone. 'For us both, all that has passed before the stony regard of this Hold of the Azath is likely inconceivable. I would think even a god might recoil at this memory's vista.'

'An Azath House? They are found in cities, made of brick and cut stone. This pile of rubble is no Azath House.'

'Shall we argue? Why not. It's been too long. No, Damisk of Silver Lake, not a House. A Hold, such as arose in the time before the first village. This one belongs to the Jheck and this is entirely appropriate, since the Jheck still haven't learned how to make a house. Or a village, for that matter.'

That wry tone had become mocking.

Damisk glanced back to see if the Saemdhi remained. All five now crouched in a half-circle. They seemed to be sharing a meal. Should he somehow manage to evade the expected death here, they would be waiting. For how long, he wondered?

'I need to sit,' Damisk said.

'Your courage impresses me. Just within, you will find some boulders, roughly shaped but sufficient to your desire.'

'Should I enter your abode,' Damisk said, 'will I ever be permitted to leave again?'

'That depends on how long you choose to stay,' she answered.

'And if I say: "not long"?'

'Then, unless you manage to deliver such profound insult to me . . . well, even that. Let it not be said that I have become thin-skinned in my old age. Yes, you will be able to depart my sweet company whenever you like. And fling yourself upon the mercy of those Saemdhi hunters who now skirt my borders.'

'And if I test their patience?'

'As opposed to mine? As I said, there are risks to staying here too long.'

'Your rumbling belly?'

'I now begin to weary of this veiled bargaining. Sit on the fucking rock or don't, Damisk. Enter or remain where you are. Or indeed, climb to the highest peak of this Hold and perch yourself there.'

Damisk cocked his head. 'The highest peak? Why would I do that?'

There was a long pause, and then, 'Why, to escape the worst of the flies.'

'One last question,' Damisk said. 'Forgive me, but once I find this boulder to sit on, will I see you?'

'I haven't decided that, yet.'

'Will you at least tell me your name?'

'It is Jheck – and now you know. Difficult to pronounce in your language, alas. But I have a few titles, gathered up here and there. The one I prefer the most is, I think, War-Bitch.'

And then she laughed, a sound that chilled Damisk to his marrow. But she'd called him courageous, forcing him to now prove it. Returning the arrow to its quiver, he quickly unstrung the bow and then edged his way down the slick slope of bedrock, and into the gloom.

The boulders were arranged in a rough semicircle, each one crudely hacked, to make seats that faced into the cave. Ten or so paces deeper in, almost swallowed in darkness, was a broad pedestal flanked by elongated slabs of stone that tilted inward as they rose, likely meeting high above the pedestal. The arrangement had all the makings of a throne, but not one suited to anything two-legged, as the pedestal had no back and the steady flow of cold air was clearly coming from somewhere behind it.

Lying at the foot of the pedestal was a white-furred wolf, its emerald-green eyes watching him curiously as he moved to settle down on the nearest stone seat. *War-Bitch. Ah, now I see.* 'How do words come from those jaws?'

'No need,' came the reply, clear and sharp, as if it was the cave itself that spoke. 'My words assault the barriers of your mind, vanquish all resistance, and so flower in your skull at my will.'

He grunted. 'I'd wondered at your facility with the Nathii tongue.'

'Your facility to wonder finds a low ceiling, Damisk of Silver Lake,' she replied. 'What of this ancient temple? This long-forgotten beast-throne? What of those countless generations that once worshipped here, once venerated this sacred abode? What of the ice that once laid siege to this temple, its grinding pressure piled so high it swallowed mountains, yet could not defeat a jumble of tilted stones? Will you not even wonder at my presence here, lingering for years, my solitude broken only by idiotic Imass youths feeding a hatred so old they are oblivious of the crime that birthed it? And whose crime was it to begin with? Not the Jheck's, I assure you, and I should know, because I was there when it happened.'

Damisk said, 'I merely commented on our mutual understanding, War-Bitch. But your grasp of it turns out not to be as sound as you might think. To wonder about something is not the same as a *sense* of wonder.'

'Pedantry is no virtue,' she retorted. 'Rather, the product of a small mind, a confined misery of obsessive precision. My answer to you wondering was mere free play, a poetic digression. But no, the man wants to sit on a rock and speak Nathii, in discourse of such wit as to leave me breathless.'

He fell silent, too weary for this by far.

'Feelings are hurt, oh my.'

Fur and rotting meat made pungent the chill air of the cave. He could now hear the hollow wind that flowed outward from some deep recess behind the throne, like a thousand voices in mourning. Of course people had died by his hand. He'd been a soldier, after all. He'd worked for slavers. And now, he was being hunted by Saemdhi, War-Bitch's Imass – and what if they *were* Imass? Not the undead kind, thankfully. People could get lost in the world. It was big enough for that, he supposed. Lost, until found, and with the finding, why, trouble started.

Were the Jheck driving the Saemdhi southward? He thought again of that north horizon. 'Ah,' he then said, 'advising against staying here too long. Suggesting the highest points of this temple, not because of the flies at all.'

'I set out a hint or two,' she said in a murmur.

'The thawed permafrost. The new wetlands. There will be flooding.'

'More than that, Damisk of Silver Lake. It nears the time for me to leave this place.'

'To go where?'

'The Jheck may not know how to build a house or live in a village, but they are not stupid.'

'They're not fish, either,' he said. 'Will you guide them to safety, then?'

Her laugh was a bark, erupting from the wolf lying before him on the pedestal, and then the beast lithely rose and lifted her head.

Damisk flinched back. She was as big as a horse.

'Safety?' she asked. 'Heed my title, you foolish man.'

'War? Against the Malazan Empire? Now who is the fool here?'

The wolf stretched. 'Remain here this night, Damisk of Silver Lake. Rest yourself.'

'And the Saemdhi outside?'

'Not my concern. Who knows, upon seeing me emerge, they might conclude that you are dead. Assume that they will cease to plague you. Avoid returning southward, and do not even think of making your way back to Silver Lake. There are ten thousand Saemdhi between here and there.'

'*Ten thousand?*'

She grunted. 'Imass breed like flies, spilling out now that the walls of ice have gone. So, neither south nor east. Not north, obviously.'

'I was already heading west.'

'What awaits you in the west, Damisk, will kill you.'

'Then you offer me no true options.'

'I have no obligation to offer you anything,' War-Bitch answered, moving up past him.

'What lies behind the throne?' Damisk suddenly asked.

She paused, her massive head turning, eyes fixing on his own. 'You would walk the ways of the Holds? Probably unwise.'

'Do you know them? Have you been there?'

'Not recently.'

'Why not?'

'The last time, I barely escaped with my life.'

She moved up to the cave-mouth, momentarily blocking most of the red-tinted light reaching in from the setting sun beyond, and then was gone. The spill of light that then flowed back into the cave's entrance was the hue of blood. Damisk thought of his victims, the dead trailing him wherever he went.

After a moment he rose, setting off to explore what he could of this cave, hopefully finding a niche or hollow out of the wind's cold path. For a man crowded by ghosts, he felt very alone.

*   *   *

The air seemed to be spinning. Rant was not at its centre, yet he could watch and feel it flowing over him on its way inward to the place where stood the tree with the twisted trunk. This was why that trunk was so twisted. Because it had grown inside an endless spiralling of energy.

The flow was the softest caress over the unmarked skin of his arms and one shoulder. He saw that he was naked and lying on his side, bearing no wounds, which made no sense because there had been wolves. Or a man who thought he was six wolves and perhaps he had been, not just the leader of a pack – his words had been confusing. They had fought, and then spoken once they decided not to fight any more.

The wind settled what felt like a soft hand on his brow, making the skin tingle. A woman's voice then said, 'Close your eyes and walk with me.'

She held his hand and they were crossing the flattened bedrock in which every hollow was now filled with fine sand. He kept his eyes shut, though this made him stumble every now and then. He couldn't recall having stood up, or whether he had taken her hand, or if she had taken his.

Now she spoke. 'It is a dangerous thing to fall unconscious in the mouth of an ancient gate. The vortex possesses a current that drags at a mortal soul, but not the flesh. Yours has pulled free and was soon to make passage into another place – it could not sink into the tree, for that is already occupied. Indeed, should you dig into its roots, you will find a cache of stone spear-points and stone knives, each one having once belonged to a Bonecaster. In this manner, every soul remains bound together, generation upon generation. Here, the Imass of old made a stretch of rock sacred, marking it with boulders.'

'Who are you?' Rant asked. Her hand was so soft, so warm.

'I am unsure. I may have forgotten. It has been so long.'

'You are a soul without a body?'

'I am. Very good.'

'Trapped in this . . . gate?'

'Yes, I think so now that you mention it. I have been.'

'For how long?'

'Yes. You remind me that time passes beyond the gate. But here, between all the worlds, it does not.'

He thought about that. Still they walked, and the flow of energy whispered over him, sometimes warm, sometimes cold. He kept his eyes tightly shut, believing somehow that to open them would shatter all of this, even send away the woman who now guided him. 'Then where are these Imass Bonecasters?'

'The Jheck came and broke things. The Bonecasters are now trapped in the twisted tree, a tree that has ceased to age and so will never die.' She paused, and then said, 'I knew them, I think. These Bonecaster souls. They would sing. Most beautiful, their voices.'

'If the Jheck broke things, why does the gate remain?'

'The gate existed long before the Imass arrived here. They found it and made it their own. The energy does not care. It flows indifferent to all claims.'

'Is this gate . . . a warren?'

'No, but it may be that this is what warren gates are made of. Warrens and Holds, all dependent upon some ancient, long-forgotten sanctification of these whirlpools between realms.'

'Then why do you not travel through the gate?' Rant asked.

'I told you, all is present, all is now in this place.' She halted him. 'Now, slowly kneel. Yes. I will take hold of your other hand, and guide it slowly, with great care lest you injure yourself.'

He felt her take up his right hand, her own fingers sliding over it and then easing his hand forward and down.

A moment later his fingertips brushed something, and she moved his hand over it so that he could feel more of the object. A shock of familiarity made him gasp. 'It is my knife, my Malazan knife.'

'Careful of the edge,' she cautioned. 'Grasp it lightly by the handle. Feel how solid it stands, buried in the rock? This was a thing that you did, will do. Indeed, if you listen to the energy currents, you can hear its eternal reverberation.' She sighed. 'Imagine, driving a knife into solid rock. Strength of the wielder to match the strength of the iron itself.'

'What has my knife to do with . . .' Rant's question fell away. 'I trapped you here? With my knife? But how is . . .'

'Then, now, one day. You cannot feel it, nor can you see it, but the iron has become twisted, deep inside the blade. I doubt this weapon will ever break. Like the tree, it now holds within it this timeless place, this eternal energy.'

'And you are in it? Your soul?'

'I think so.'

Rant fully took hold of the knife. 'Then I will break it and free you.'

'You cannot. But, should you draw it free, then when you leave here with it, I will come with you. Is this a better fate? Do I so thirst for blood that I will delight in every wound you deliver? Every life you take with this weapon?'

'I don't want to deliver wounds or take lives,' Rant said. 'You might grow very thirsty.'

'Or I may not. My memories are mostly gone. Who I was, what I was like. My hopes, fears, loves, all gone.'

'Then,' ventured Rant, 'you have room for new ones.'

'Yet a knife holds my soul. I will taste the world by its edge. I will know cold and heat and the play of light. I will bathe in blood.'

'Perhaps I could find someone, a sorceror, who can free you.'

'You would trust me in the hand of a stranger?'

Rant scowled. He was only trying to help, but her every response forced him to think. He didn't know what to do, what to say. He could leave the knife, driven deep into the bedrock, for someone else to happen upon it. But it belonged to him. A Malazan soldier had given it to him. He remembered that day, that moment, and the entire memory shone like the sun's own fire.

'What are you doing?'

He had been dodging stones. 'Playing with my friends.'

'Call this playing, do you?'

He'd nodded. His upper lip had been split and it hurt to talk. There were small bruises on his chest and back.

'See this?' A huge knife he then pulled free of its sheath. 'See how the water mark plays on the blade, like ripples in a pond? Aren Steel. This is a fighting knife, a weapon. Do you understand? No whittling with it, no cutting up vegetables or butchering a carcass. No throwing it into trees.' Back into the sheath it went. 'Take it, it's yours now.'

Heavy in his hand, the wooden sheath battered and worn with only a few flecks of gold and red paint filling the carved patterns that ran like serpents up its length. The pommel smooth but dented and scarred, the cross-hilt short and stubby. 'Why?'

'For when you get tired of playing.'

A Malazan soldier. A marine. A weathered face full of wrinkles and white scars, eyes like almonds and black as pitch. Now walking away, leaving Rant with the knife.

One of Rant's friends had then rushed up to the marine, begging for a knife of his own, or even a sword. The back of a gauntleted hand sent the boy reeling, his face a welter of blood, and the marine turned to face Rant's stunned friends. 'That knife stays with him. If I find it in one of your hands when I come back this way, I'll skin the lot of you, then gut the ones who spawned you. Hood's breath, I'll torch this entire cesspool of a village.'

Rant's friends made no efforts to steal his knife. But after that day, the stones got bigger. And it would be years before Rant decided he was tired of playing. In fact, he had only decided it in this instant.

I am tired of playing.

The words burned in his mind as he straightened. He began trembling.

'This I recognize,' the woman at his side said.

'What – what is it I'm feeling?'

'Anger.'

Anger. He thought back to his fight with the wolves. All had been calm, almost lifeless within him. But what he was feeling now was the opposite. It devoured him, and then yearned to lash out.

When he sank to his knees, her hand was pulled from his clasp as he made fists. 'I . . . don't . . . like this.'

'You have never felt this way before?'

'No! I don't like it!'

'Anger is the demon within us all. When it triumphs, there is ruin. When it is unleashed, there is madness in the world.'

Rant was now weeping. 'They weren't my friends!' he shouted. 'They were *never* my friends! They – they *hurt* me!'

When she touched his cheek, that raging fire winked out. Cold silence filled his skull. The trembling was gone, the anguish nothing but ashes. Stunned, he blinked away his tears, and found himself staring out into a formless void. He quickly turned his head. Even with his eyes now open, he saw nothing of the woman. The feel of her soft, cool fingertips was all there was of her.

'I have taken it,' she said. 'Deep into the blade. Chained the demon. Now, all you have left is forgiveness.'

He recoiled at the thought, and then, as a new thought entered his mind, he said in a hard, bitter tone, 'I will defend myself.'

'Always,' she replied. 'Always.'

Something in her tone made him want to weep all over again. Instead, he crouched down, grasped hold of the knife's leather-bound grip, and pulled it free of the stone.

'Good,' she said. 'Now, close your eyes again. In your mind, give me form as I stand before you. I will add to it what's needed. Yes, like that, and yes again.'

'You are beautiful.'

'Yes, I cheated.'

'Like my mother.'

'No, not like her. I am not here to mother you. Nor will I mould you into my lover. You are too young. Consider me a sister. Can you do that?'

He thought about it. There were boys he knew who had sisters. Older, younger, even a twin. 'Older,' he decided. 'What is your name?'

'I cannot recall. Choose a new one.'

'Three.'

'Three?'

He nodded firmly.

'I am Three. Do you have me now in your mind's eye? Good. It seems I have added something of my own, something I once possessed, perhaps. But I see no value in it. So, beloved, raise up the knife, and cut off my wings.'

He could see them, leathery like a bat's wings, rising up behind her in folded shrouds of black. Yet it seemed that they belonged. Rant focused once more on her heart-shaped face. And there, riding the high, flaring cheeks, a hint of scales. Vertical pupils nested in lavender regarded him – he had never before seen eyes like those. 'I don't want to,' he said.

'I have a suspicion,' she said then. 'That what I once was no longer dwells in the world. Its time has passed. My kind have slipped into the shadows, and the shadows have died in the darkness where all lost memories go. If I hold on to what I once was, I may awaken more of myself.'

'Wouldn't that be a good thing?'

'It might be a bad thing.'

'I'm not cutting them off, Three.'

'Very well. Trapped as I am within a knife's blade, they have no function beyond the unease they stir within me, which I shall learn to live with.'

He started. 'Oh. My name is Rant.'

She smiled. 'Tartheno Thelomen Toblakai. These are the names I recall that describe your people. It is your kind's habit to hoard souls. It seems you have begun.'

Rant looked around. 'Take me back, please. I left someone there who's hurt.' He didn't want to think about hoarding souls. Not ever.

She reached out her hand and he grasped it. 'Close your eyes,' she then said. 'And we shall walk the spiral back out.'

Sometime later her hand dissolved in his and he halted, opening his eyes to find himself standing near the twisted tree. It was mid-morning and the air was surprisingly warm. Nearby a fox and her three pups were feeding on the young Imass woman's body.

He saw that Gower was sitting with his back to a boulder, watching the small animals. Two ravens had landed and were hopping cautiously towards the foxes and their grisly prize.

Rant looked for his new friend, but there was nothing, not even in his mind. But he held the knife – was her soul truly within it? Or had he dreamed the whole thing?

'Nice trick.'

Rant frowned at Gower. 'What?'

One blood-crusted hand waved feebly. 'Vanishing for two days, then coming back all healed.'

'There is a vortex.'

'Oh I know. Dangerous in there. Most don't return. Well, some-times pieces of them do. Vortices. We Jheck usually avoid them out of caution, that being our natures. Indeed, our ritual of avoidance begins with running away in screaming terror.'

Rant approached the huge, hairy man. He could see that he had suffered. Although the wounds on his body had closed, still they leaked, the blood glistening. His lips were cracked and scabbed. 'I have no water,' Rant told him, 'but maybe I can go find some.'

'I've healed enough. If I don't get off my ass soon I never will. Besides, watching the beasties get fat is making me even hungrier, and don't believe what you might've heard about the Jheck, we're not in the habit of eating Imass flesh. If we can help it.' He started working himself upright, grunting and swearing.

'Are there other Jheck nearby?' Rant asked.

'I hope not. In fact, if I don't meet kin any time in the next year, I'll consider myself blessed by every spirit of sky, rock and sea. Being a Lord means being ready to face any challenger and right now a Saemdhi toddler with a gourd rattle could beat me senseless.'

Rant sheathed his knife. 'Do you need me to help you walk?'

'The capacity of a child to insult his elders seems unending. Shall I suffer this ignominy? What if someone sees us? No, what you suggest is impossible. I shall walk on my own or die.'

He managed three steps before falling over unconscious.

Rant threw Gower over one shoulder. Facing the direction he believed was west, he began walking.

BOOK TWO

STARWHEEL

Make my ending a whisper. Let yours be a shout.

Fisher kel Tath

CHAPTER SEVEN

All was in tumult. New flavours now flowed through the Warrens, and it seemed that something of the underlying structure – the very bones of magic – had begun to show through in patches, as if the skin had been stripped away.

From the far land of Letheras came the tale of an ancient Ascendant who had, in the course of but a few days and nights, raised into being an entire new assemblage of Warrens and Aspects, all born from his fevered brow.

While many are inclined to discount such rumours, that disinclination itself serves no answer to the changes now apparent. And so I must conclude that, in absence of alternative, the Letheras tale is most likely true.

Who this Ascendant was invites closer examination, and on that subject, let's hope someone undertakes to pursue it, because I can't be bothered.

Musings of Lazy Bark
The Great Library of New Morn

THE IMPERIAL ROAD LEADING FROM CULVERN UP TO SILVER Lake more or less paralleled Culvern River before angling towards Silver Lake, swinging northeast, cutting across an ancient floodplain that had once been forest but was now farmland. The raised, cobbled track crossed strip-fields of black mud demarcated by low stone walls, the only trees remaining in sight being those that sheltered farmhouses and abandoned stone-cutter huts.

It wasn't a landscape that inspired, Spindle decided, being little more than a smudged mix of muddy browns and greys, a place where the holdings were small and the peasant farmers pulled their own ploughs and seeded the rows by hand, and no matter how many local stones went into the making of the road and all the boundary walls, more turned up every spring in the surrounding fields. Collected and heaped in piles here and there, they made the area look like a plain of tombs.

The day was drawing to a close as the column came within sight of Silver Lake, a few slate-tiled roofs visible through wreaths of wood-smoke above the earthen embankment that defended the town on the three landward sides. A few more recent buildings now flanked the north side of the road outside the berm, partly obscuring Spindle's view of the New Gate and the bridge span directly before it. None of these buildings looked completed, and the stacks of planed wood next to them were grey and rotting. The end of the slave trade had emptied this town's coffers.

As they drew closer, a rank stench rode the onshore breeze, coming from the drover's field and the slaughterhouse to their left. Even in the gathering gloom, Spindle could see row upon row of caribou hides stretched out on racks in the field, over which ravens wheeled.

'Venison stew tonight,' Oams said, riding at Spindle's side. 'And tomorrow night, and—'

'Ride ahead, Oams,' Spindle cut in. 'See if we have an official retinue awaiting us.'

'—and all of next week, too. Aye, Sergeant. And if there isn't?'

'Then get me a table at the Black Eel, just the other side of the gate.'

'Been here before, Sergeant?'

'No.'

After a moment, Oams kicked his horse into a canter, somewhat startling Captain Gruff up ahead when he rode past. Gruff then reined in and waited for Spindle to come alongside.

'My dear Sergeant.'

'Sir?'

'It's my thought that Lieutenant Balk's Company should camp south of the town, just outside the earthworks. What do you think?'

'The common pasture? Aye, that'll do.'

'I see a watchtower atop the berm.'

Spindle nodded.

'Are we understood?'

Spindle nodded again.

Up ahead, on the stone bridge just before New Gate, Oams had met three locals. Dismounted, he stood beside his horse, facing the approaching column. As Spindle and Gruff rode up, Spindle studied his soldier's expression, but could read nothing from it. His gaze then tracked to the locals, one of whom stepped forward.

'You are a welcome sight, Captain. I am Lieutenant Nast Forn, commanding the imperial garrison here. My non-military role is as Imperial Administrator for the region.' He hesitated, and then continued, 'Since the last Administrator was killed during the Uprising. Presumably her replacement is with you?'

Gruff dismounted and a moment later so did Spindle. The column had halted on the road behind them.

The captain answered, 'Alas, Lieutenant, no. It seems you will have to continue to be burdened with your additional responsibility, onerous as it no doubt is.'

Nast Forn looked to be in his early thirties. The strips of bronze on his leather breastplate were polished to a coppery sheen. A vambrace was strapped to his sword-arm and the short-sword in the scabbard at his left hip showed a silver pommel capped with a sizeable ruby. His name sounded Untan, leading Spindle to wonder at the ill fates that had brought this likely highborn officer to this remote posting. At Gruff's news, his expression grew bewildered. 'Surely there's been some mistake, sir. My last missive was addressed to Fist Sevitt herself. The list of reparations and material loss has the entire region in a state of disarray—'

The other man among the trio now stepped forward, talking over the lieutenant. 'My pardon, sirs, I believe I may be able to speak to that more directly.'

'How delightful,' said Gruff with a smile. 'And you are?'

'Silgar Younger, Silver Lake's mayor and the regional factor, and in said capacity I lead the community's petition for imperial reparation following the Uprising. Our patience, I must admit, is wearing thin.' He gestured. 'As you can see from the half-built residences you just passed, our efforts to rebuild and, indeed, to grow our community have stalled. The failure of the imperial garrison to defend us and protect our town is directly responsible for our present plight, and it is unseemly that the empire is delaying our just recompense.'

Gruff's smile had not wavered. 'What an extraordinary and most elaborate argument, good sir. But as you might now recognize, if belatedly, such topics are best suited to private discussion at a later date, since I do in fact carry with me documents providing the empire's response to your request, in detail. At present, however, we have more pressing needs.' And he beamed at the mayor. 'Billets for the marines, if you please, in the town. Our mercenary company will encamp outside the south berm, for now. Further, you will note our extensive supply train. We shall need it guided by the best route to the garrison grounds.' His attention shifted to the lieutenant. 'Lieutenant Nast Forn, I would hear of the disposition of your troops. Perhaps you and I can walk together?' He handed the reins of his horse to Spindle. 'Sergeant Spindle, can you liaise with the mayor as regards the billeting?'

Spindle glanced at the third local and said, 'I'm sure our billets are ready and waiting.'

The woman, decked out in somewhat worn marine gear, met his eyes and grinned. 'Clean and spiffy, in fact.'

Pausing with brows lifted, Gruff turned to her.

She snapped a salute. 'Master Sergeant Bliss Rolly, sir.'

'Good gods! Indeed? But what in Jarak's Limp are you doing *here*?'

'Hiding, sir. Not well, it turns out.'

Gruff now swung back to Nast Forn. 'Were you aware of the hero in your midst, Lieutenant?'

'Not only aware, Captain, but most appreciative, since without her here, not one soldier in the garrison would've survived. Nor, I think, most of the town.'

'Ah, of course. Not surprising, hearing this. And I would hear more! Come!' Hooking his arm in the lieutenant's he set out for town.

Silgar Younger was staring with his mouth open. Then he recovered, turning to Spindle. 'Yes, about those billets! Three of the finest residences in the town have been appropriated – no, *stolen*.'

'Were they occupied?' Spindle asked.

'Well, not officially—'

'Excuse me, but what does that mean? Were there people living in those houses or not?'

'Slain in the Uprising,' Silgar replied, 'and with no one left to inherit the holdings, ownership fell to the community itself, said disposition to be determined—'

'By you?' Oams asked innocently from where he stood off to one side.

'As mayor—'

'Right. By you, then.' Oams came forward and took hold of the reins of Spindle's and Gruff's horses. 'I see a tavern right here, Sergeant, with a nice long hitching post. Shall I?'

Spindle nodded.

'As I was saying,' began Silgar Younger.

'Put it in writing,' Spindle said, striding over to take Bliss Rolly into a tight embrace. '*Damn woman*,' he whispered into her thick black hair, '*you shoulda run further.*'

Stillwater slumped heavily in the chair and reached for the tankard of ale in front of her. 'Now this is the life,' she said. 'All except this cut on my finger, and you know what Benger said? He said, "You cut it on your own knife, so live with it." Can you believe that?'

Folibore clunked his tankard against hers. 'You're always cutting yourself on your knives, Still. They're too sharp.'

'Of course they're too sharp, you idiot. I'm an assassin. Anyway, that's beside the point. Benger's the problem.'

'He healed you up.'

'Except for the finger!'

Anyx Fro was sitting opposite them, with Blanket slumped beside her, already asleep. 'I still think you're lying about that scrap. Shadow Hound ate the warlock? Ridiculous.'

'You saw the bite on my poncho,' Stillwater retorted. 'What did that? A mole? It was a Shadow Hound and it nearly got me. You should've seen that old warlock get gobbled up. Snap, pop, gulp! So fast!' She drank down a mouthful, brows lifting at how good the ale tasted, and then sighed. 'Poor warlock.'

'And you robbing a barrow,' Anyx said in disgust. 'Some dead man's coins jangling your bag. Only you, Stillwater.'

'I tracked the warlock into that barrow, I'm telling you. It was just a bit of convenience, me finding that loot. A genuine convergence.'

Folibore choked on his ale and spent a few moments coughing.

'Can you believe it,' Anyx said in a different tone. 'Bliss Rolly. Here, in this fucking ass-hole of a town.'

Stillwater shrugged. 'Gotta be somewhere, so why not here? And of course Spindle's all tight with her. Because, why? Because he's Spindle, that's why.'

'Bridgeburner,' said Folibore now that he'd recovered.

'Oh,' moaned Anyx Fro, 'spare me. There ain't no Bridgeburners left anywhere. All dead. Withered corpses floating around in Moon's Spawn. Dead. Sure, Spindle's a veteran, I ain't disputing that. He's seen things, done things. He's one of those sergeants who never get promoted – the army's full of them.'

'Good thing, too,' said Folibore. 'The backbone, the iron spine.'

'Yeah, all that. But a Bridgeburner? Forget it.'

'We got to do something about Benger,' said Stillwater, studying the long red line of the cut on her finger. 'Healer's supposed to heal. When he don't, what use is he?'

'Not just Denul,' Folibore pointed out. 'Mockra.'

'I'm just saying. Assassin with a cut finger's no good to anybody.'

'Assassin looting barrows isn't either,' Anyx said.

'A convergence of powers,' Stillwater pronounced. 'Me, that warlock, that Shadow Hound, and don't forget, the dead Tiste Edur, too. With his necklace of rat teeth.' And she lifted it from under her shirt to show it off. 'Probably ensorcelled.'

'Cursed, more like it,' Anyx said. 'It wasn't a Shadow Hound trying to bite your ass off, it was a giant undead mole, looking for his teeth.'

Stillwater glared at her. 'It's not my fault nothing interesting ever happens to you, Fro.' She then looked over to where the sergeants were sitting. They were in conversation with the Black Eel's proprietor, Storp, who was old and grizzled and had *veteran* written all over him, especially on his face and neck where he was badly pocked by Moranth acids, probably from a Burner. 'And then Spindle tells us this is where us soldiers drink, even though that Three-Legged Dog place is way closer to our new house. Only he says he's never been here before. How does that make any sense?'

The door opened and in came Bliss Rolly leading three of the garrison soldiers who claimed a table that had been reserved – if the knife jammed into its centre meant anything – while the sergeant went over to the sergeants' table because that's what sergeants do.

Stillwater nudged Folibore, brows lifting as she eyed the soldiers who'd come in with Bliss Rolly. 'The ones who survived the Uprising, and what a sorry-looking lot. No heavies. Those two look like sisters, and that other one looks like a three-day-old beached fish.'

'That's a little harsh, Still,' said Folibore. 'His gills are still flapping.'

'Right, so throw him back.'

'Listen to you two,' said Anyx Fro, not turning around for a look. 'They're Malazan soldiers. Regulars. And obviously they can stick a sword, else they wouldn't be alive, would they?'

'Depends,' Stillwater said. 'They could've been the fastest runners.'

'Right,' Anyx snapped, 'and Bliss Rolly would've let them do that, sure. And now I bet they're eyeing you all and saying the same shit. "Oh, look at that frowning cow with the cut finger, what good's she for? And that heavy who obviously takes longer getting dressed than a damned princess on a first date." The point is, we're the newcomers here, so it's on us to buy 'em the first round, so cough up some of those Tiste coins, Stillwater.'

'Don't be an idiot. That loot's not for spending. Folibore, you got some spare coins. Use 'em.'

'Me? I'm broke.'

'Well, Blanket, then.'

They looked to Blanket. He still had one hand wrapped round the tankard, which had about a third of the ale still in it. Blanket never got through a whole tankard. Ale knocked him out. He could handle wine, though, except that he got maudlin when drunk. Asleep, Stillwater decided, was better. 'Go on, Fro, see what's in his pouch.'

'You want me to reach into his pouch? Are you insane?'

'There's coins in there,' Stillwater said.

'How do you know? How do you know *what* he has in that pouch?'

'Well, what else would be in there?'

'I don't plan on finding out,' Anyx Fro announced, leaning back and crossing her arms.

Stillwater sighed. 'Go on, Folibore, rob your buddy here. You can pay him back later.'

'With what?'

'That bit's not my problem.'

Grunting, Folibore got up and edged round the table. He collected up the leather pouch dangling from Blanket's belt, opened it up, reached inside, and came out with three silver jakatas.

Stillwater looked pointedly at Anyx Fro. 'Now who's the insane one?'

'They're sticky,' Folibore said.

Anyx Fro bared her teeth in triumph. 'Told you.'

'I mean, *really* sticky.'

'I think I'm going to puke,' said Anyx.

'What're you doing?' Stillwater demanded of Folibore as he bent to the pouch again.

'Putting them back.'

'So who's going to pay for the drinks?'

'Too late anyway,' said Folibore. 'Just saw So Bleak buy 'em the round.'

'Second Squad beat us to it, again! Damn you, Anyx, this is all your fault.'

'I don't want any new friends anyway,' Anyx announced. 'More names to try and remember and really, what's the point? Besides, you're the one who's flush but too cheap to pay for anything.'

'But now we won't be friends with Bliss Rolly, because if we're not friends with her soldiers then she won't be friends with us.'

Anyx Fro's stare was a bit disconcerting. 'How old are you again? Never mind.' She leaned forward. 'Here's the thing about heroes, Stillwater dear. Last ones standing, right? Well, that's the detail worth noting right there. All those bodies around that hero? *They're all dead.* Trust me, you don't want to hang around Bliss Rolly.'

Folibore cleared his throat. 'But Anyx, it was you insisting we buy 'em the first round.'

'As a courtesy, aye.'

'You don't want to be friends with Bliss Rolly?' Stillwater asked, now bewildered.

Fists tight and whitening at the knuckles, Anyx Fro said through clenched teeth: 'No, Stillwater, I don't.'

Stillwater settled back. 'Then it's all worked out, hasn't it? So Bleak's doomed and we didn't spend a thing! Hah hah! And that leaves us all night trying to decide what to do about Benger the traitor!'

So Bleak frowned. The soldier opposite him was named Trand, and he smelled. His clothes were filthy. His studded black leather vest looked like it had bird shit on it. His long hair hung in greasy ropes. 'What's wrong with my name?' So Bleak now asked, his frown shifting into a scowl as he studied Trand's wary expression. 'I earned it.'

'Maybe that's the point,' ventured the older sister, Flown, one finger tracing the wide scar on her right cheek, up and down, up and down. 'Earning a name like that. Whole legions wiped out in your company. Are you in the Limping God's pay or something?'

'This is what I get for buying you all a round?'

'Oh,' smiled Amiss, the younger sister, 'we appreciate that. Honest. Storp's ale is the best, but it ain't cheap. Speaking of which, we got back-pay owing, lots of it. That supply train got a quartermaster with it? It'd be good if someone told us, you know. Our tab here could buy a damned keep on a hill with a moat full of fish and apple trees in the yard. Storp's been easy on us but even so, the man's gotta live. Did you know he was a regular in the Third Legion? The *actual* Third Legion. Right, that one. Fought alongside the Bridgeburners, did Storp, in the sapper auxiliary, in fact, and I bet you didn't know that the sappers had their own auxiliary, but they did, on account of needing crews on all that engineering stuff. Mining under walls and things like that. He nearly died in a tunnel at Nathilog during the Conquest. And you got Spindle. That's amazing. Bliss Rolly's always talking about him, his way with animals and such, and then—'

'I'm sorry,' So Bleak cut in, somewhat desperately, 'what was that about Spindle?'

Amiss glared at him, her lips pressing into a thin, affronted line.

'Now you've done it,' muttered Flown. 'Interrupting's bad manners and Amiss won't abide that. You better hope you're never back-to-back in a scrap, cos she won't have yours, So Bleak. In fact, she'll leave you to the wolves and smile when they rip out your throat.'

A chill crawled up So Bleak's spine, as the young woman's glare was now murderous. 'I'm sorry,' he said again, this time with more feeling. 'It was just something you said caught my attention, about Spindle and, uh, animals. Didn't mean to interrupt but I couldn't let that one pass by, in case you changed the subject.'

'So there was only one thing interesting enough to make you sit up,' Flown said, shaking her head. 'In all that Amiss was telling you? Just ignored all the rest, did you?'

'Including,' Trand added, leaning forward, 'that bit about our back-pay.'

'I'm a fucking marine,' So Bleak snapped. 'I haven't got a fucking clue about your back-pay.'

'Now he's all sweary,' Flown said. 'The man responsible for slaughtering his own armies, on account of the Lord's push being his best friend, is now sitting here all red-faced and angry because he insulted my little sister. I'm not sure I like where this is going.'

'Right.' So Bleak took a deep, settling breath. 'How about we start over?'

'Another round on you?' Flown's smile was wintry. 'That's nice, but no. You can't buy our good feelings, you know. All things considered, it might be better if you just rejoined your friends over there, where you can explain how you mortally offended us.'

So Bleak slowly stood. 'Your friend Trand needs a bath, but when it comes to foul smells I guess none of you notices, which is a bit telling.'

Flown showed raised brows to her sister. 'I think he just insulted us.' She looked up at So Bleak. 'Not sure you want to be challenging us, since can you really say your squad's with you no matter what? I mean, a name like yours and all. Besides,' she added, her gaze flicking away, 'Corporal Horser, Gund Yellow and sister Lope have all just arrived. Horser might like a bit of a fight, you being marines and all.' She smiled again and resumed tracing the scar on her cheek.

'Now I get it,' So Bleak said. 'Though I doubt Storp would be pleased with the mess this is going to make of his bar. Anyway, I'm calling your bluff, Flown, because with Spin and our other sergeants sitting with Bliss Rolly, none of this will get past posturing. But if you all think you got something to prove, do your best.'

After a moment, she looked away. 'Was just having a bit of fun, So Bleak.'

'That's what that was? If—' All at once two large presences flanked So Bleak, and a heavy arm settled over his shoulder. Startled, he found his face a bare hand's width from Daint's mashed, flattened visage. On the other side, he saw, was Given Loud. 'Gods below,' So Bleak breathed.

'Having a nice chat with the regulars, then?' Daint asked, showing the few front teeth he had left with a broad smile.

'Looking very nice, that chat,' added Given Loud, grooming his beard with his sausage-fingers.

So Bleak tried to recall the last time he'd heard these two heavies say anything, anything at all. He couldn't. In fact, these were two voices he realized he'd never heard before now. 'I think we're fine, Daint,' he managed.

'Oh, we're fine all right,' Daint said.

'We're finer than fine,' Given Loud said, adding his heavy arm to Daint's, the weight of the two making So Bleak groan. And sure enough, both men began pressing against him.

Flown was studying all of this with growing bewilderment.

'I think,' So Bleak said in a grating tone, 'we can go back to our table now?'

'You sure?'

'You sure?'

Gods, they even sound the same. 'Absolutely sure.'

'Not even introducing us?'

'Not even introducing us?'

'Given Loud, Daint, Flown, Trand and Amiss. There, done.'

Like three dancers entwined, the two heavies wheeled So Bleak around – his feet barely scraping the floor – and led him back to the squad's table.

'*What're you two doing?*' So Bleak whispered.

'You may be bad luck, So Bleak,' said Daint, 'but you're *our* bad luck.'

'Hands off is what he means,' Given Loud said. 'Fuckin' regulars.'

'Uh, why, now I'm feeling all warm inside,' So Bleak said. 'But I think that's because you're both crushing me.'

Reaching the table, the two heavies pulled away, leaving So Bleak to collapse on watery legs into his chair.

'I knew it was a mistake sending you,' Clay Plate said. 'But our idiot corporal thought it'd be—'

'Watch your mouth, Plates,' Undercart warned in a growl. 'Call me an idiot one more time and you're up on report.'

'Fine, I'll put it this way. Our genius corporal just went and made an idiotic decision, but hey, it happens to the best of us.'

'I'm having trouble with the distinction,' Undercart said.

'Thought I made it clear enough, sir.'

'It would've been, except for it all drowning in sarcasm. Kind of clouding up the sincerity.' His fist flew out to box Clay Plate on the left ear. 'There, that's better.'

'Ow.'

'Sir.'

'Ow, sir.'

'So Bleak, let's hear your report.'

Reaching for a tankard, So Bleak shrugged. 'Assholes.'

'Now here's a man who knows how to make a report. Succinct, definitive. Well done, soldier. Now, how about we have us another round? Your turn, Plates.'

'No it— *ow!*'

Corporal Horser leaned with both hands on the table between the sisters. 'Now, what the fuck was all that about? That looked a heart-beat away from a scrap.'

Flown twisted to look up, all innocence. 'Just a marine being rude, sir.'

'You hankering to get the crap beaten out of us all, soldier?'

'Wouldn't have come to that,' Amiss said.

'Not when those two heavies showed up,' Trand added. 'That said, that poor fool stuck between them looked to be having his bones start snapping if that went on any longer. Weird.'

'Is that bird shit on your vest?'

'Fuckin' gulls, sir. They're targeting me like they're Loqui Wyval.'

'Well maybe if you didn't look like a fuckin' bird nest, Trand.'

Flinching, Trand looked away.

Sighing, Horser straightened. 'Stop being idiots and that's an order. They're here now and be thankful for it, what with the local forest tribes acting so snarly of late. Besides, I have good news. We're getting paid.'

The three soldiers sat up at that.

'And for you three, all of it's going straight into Storp's cashbox.'

They slumped again.

'She just might kill you, you know,' said Oams.

Benger's bushy brows lifted. 'Stillwater? It's just a wee little cut. Besides, she doesn't scare me.'

Oams leaned back in his chair and eyed Benger. 'What a ridiculous thing to say.'

'All right, maybe a bit, then. Okay, she's terrifying, especially when she gets that look in her eyes. Know the one? Cold, dead, blank, un-wavering, like looking into the eyes of a fucking crocodile.'

'So heal her up, then.'

Benger tilted forward, hands wrapping around the tankard in front of him. 'Every damned time! Half the wounds on her are self-inflicted! I once saw her drop her knife on her own foot, went right through the leather, then through to jam in the sole. You know how dangerous punc-ture wounds are? Imagine, a clumsy assassin – why is she even still alive?'

They were sharing the table with Say No, Paltry Skint and Corporal Morrut, all three of whom were in an argument about the billet the squad had been given. Say No and Paltry were having a spat so each one wanted her own room. But there weren't enough to go round. Morrut had just announced he wasn't going to cook for the squad any more, since his culinary efforts went unappreciated, and since Spindle was getting the master bedroom, it only made sense that the corporal should get the second biggest bedroom, the one on the same floor. But there was only one bedroom on the ground level, besides the kitchen and a sitting room that was now full of smelly gear, and if the rest of the squad had to cram into that one room, too bad.

Oams didn't care. He wasn't expecting to spend much time in that ex-slaver's house anyway.

Benger was doing that stifled laughing thing that he did, shoulders jumping, mouth split wide, eyes watering with mirth, and all of it utterly soundless.

'What's so funny?' Oams asked.

'There's a second bedroom on the ground level,' he said, low so the others wouldn't hear. 'They just can't find the door!' And he began laughing again.

'You don't think they're going to wonder where you keep disappearing to?'

'Big mystery, but that's Benger for you, right? Anyway, I suggest you lay out your bedroll between Say No and Paltry. They're going to make up and you know it. Probably tonight. Who knows, you could find yourself in the middle of something amazing.'

'And now Benger shows his creepy side. Uh-oh,' he added as a figure loomed up behind Benger.

An insanely sharp knife-blade settled down just above the man's left ear. 'I'm going to cut this one off,' Stillwater announced.

Everyone at the table fell silent. Benger had stopped laughing, his eyes wide and wild.

'Why that one?' Morrut asked. 'The other one's just as ugly.'

'Oh I'll get to the other one, if Benger decides he still won't heal my cut finger.'

Paltry Skint was shaking her head, expression sad. 'Bad idea, Still. Never good threatening a healer.'

'It's not a threat. I'm just telling him what I'm about to do. Hold still, Benger. I'll make it clean and quick.'

'Okay! Stop! Don't move it! I'll heal your damned finger!'

She edged round and held it out. 'Look at it. All red and swollen. And is that pus? Am I seeing pus, Benger?'

Benger grasped the hand. He closed his eyes and muttered something under his breath. The cut thinned, paled, and then vanished. 'There! Happy now?'

Stillwater withdrew her knife. 'Not really. I was all excited about cutting off your ear.'

She walked back to her table. Sighing, Morrut resumed informing the two heavies about the sleeping arrangements, cooking tasks, and laundry.

Oams tilted closer to Benger. 'I did warn you.'

'She's a madwoman!' Benger hissed, wiping at the sweat on his brow. 'She was going to cut my ear off! I'm the last serious healer left – did she think I wouldn't make her pay for that?'

'You should've just healed that finger along with all the rest,' Oams said.

Benger leaned close and whispered, '*But I did!*'

Oams frowned. 'But you – she – oh, fuck.'

'*I do it every time!*' And Benger started laughing, shoulders jumping, face deepening its hue, mouth wide, eyes starting to stream tears.

'Fucking illusionists.' Oams stood. 'My watch beckons. One day, Benger, someone's going to kill you – not the enemy, but one of us.'

'You can try!'

CHAPTER EIGHT

It takes a small mind to believe that the world is as simple as
it seems.

Mad Rivet on his Day of Execution

THE BLACK EEL HAD BEEN LOUD, A LITTLE TOO WARM WITH ALL
the bodies, and definitely overripe. Outside, standing on the
cobbled street that curved its way into the heart of the town,
Oams paused to breathe in the cool night air. Directly opposite the
tavern and on the other side of the street, there was a narrow ditch and
then the slope of the south embankment, the earthworks thick with
dead winter grasses only now starting to show new growth.

Drawing his half-cloak tighter round his shoulders, he set off,
jumping the ditch and then quickly ascending the berm's steep slope.
Classic Malazan construction, Oams noted. On the outside of the
embankment the slope would be just as steep, the ditch much wider.
As defence-works, the berms surrounding the settlement were never
intended to be held, since the local garrison couldn't house enough
troops for that. But the steep bank on the inward-facing side would
send the enemy tumbling, and the narrow ditch was perfect for
breaking ankles and legs. Of course, all that would come after being
overrun. Before that even happened, the defenders could line the
ridge, firing arrows into the approaching forces. Then retreat behind
the berm if the enemy started firing back. Lob more arrows over the
embankment, with the crossbow-equipped close-contact soldiers
crouched and waiting for the silhouetted line of the first attackers
appearing atop the berm.

*Kill and wound enough of them with arrows and quarrels, and the
rest will get second thoughts about closing. Street-to-street fighting is*

a nightmare, and us Malazans are damned good at it. Forest savages? Not so much.

He scrambled to the top of the embankment, but stayed low once there, moving quickly towards the wooden watchtower rising in a somewhat ramshackle, leaning mass of wood off to his left.

In the field beyond the berm's outer ditch, Balk's Company looked settled down, only a few campfires still glowing, and even fewer lanterns within the tents all laid out in ordered rows.

Balk's discipline was good, especially for a man who'd never served in any real military. His followers were tough and well-equipped, including decent armour. That cost money. Most mercenary companies eventually dissolved because maintaining fighting readiness was expensive. The ones that survived understood first and foremost that it was a business and needed to be run like one.

The best ones, of course, knew how to win engagements, ideally without a fight. Winning made reputations and reputations were everything.

Reaching the gaping doorway at the foot of the stairs, Oams paused. *Damned thing's almost derelict.* He could smell burnt wood and some of the framework had seen fire. Enough to weaken the structure? Hard to tell. He edged through the doorway and then began ascending the switchback staircase.

Creaks, the rustle of mice or rats scurrying away. Dust and old smoke heavy in the damp air. The smell of sawdust and rot coming from the walls.

There were five landings, but only the top one had windows. A rusty iron tripod commanded the centre, an old and battered signalling system of mirrors, hinges and gears set atop it, its oily workings fuzzy with windblown seeds and dust. Swallow nests crowded the lintels of each open window, with guano heaped high on the ledges. A few nests were inside the room as well, up in the corners beneath the roof's rafters, so the floor was a mess, crunching underfoot as Oams positioned himself so that he could look out on Balk's camp.

He settled into a squat, wrists resting on his knees. East of Balk's camp, about fifty paces distant, the forest began in a row of young aspen, elm, alder and birch. The line of trees was uneven, as bites had been taken out of it, and here and there stacked cordwood waited to dry.

Whatever the mercenaries were up to with the local forest tribes wasn't something they were keen to reveal. The thought of a powerful warlock tracking them up from Culvern was troubling. That said, Stillwater killing the fool might well have started a blood-feud, possibly even a full-blown war.

Restless borders had a way of staying restless. Even with the slave trade long gone, something about this place felt like a wildfire waiting to happen. Spindle and even Gruff knew something was going on. Oams could sense their unease.

His breath caught as a pressure swept in from behind him, engulfing him in an unseen embrace. He felt something like bands – or the fingers of hands – close around his wrists from behind. Not tight enough to hurt, but solid and firm.

'All right,' he muttered under his breath, 'now what?'

A woman's voice spoke in his head. '*Sleep.*'

Stick tapped her knife-blade against the tent-pole and a moment later came the low invitation to enter. Sugal behind her, she ducked and slipped within.

Balk was seated on a three-legged leather camp-stool. His armour was off, his long hair no longer bound but hanging loose. The lantern's wick was cranked down, giving off barely a glimmer of light.

'They're bound to have someone watching,' Balk said. 'That old watchtower.'

'You think they know?' Stick asked.

'No. Just being naturally suspicious. Who do you recommend for some knife-work?'

'When?' Sugal asked.

'Tonight. Right away. They've just met up with the garrison here. Not marines, but regular soldiers. Haven't yet taken their measure. A dead marine in the watchtower could be anyone's work. It'll certainly make cooperation unlikely.'

'Setting the marines against the locals,' Stick said, nodding. 'I like it.'

'So, who?'

'Why not me?' she asked.

Balk shook his head. 'None within my command. Not you, Stick, or Sugal, or even Bray. Give me someone who can get to that watchtower unseen, with enough skill to make sure it doesn't go sour.'

Stick glanced at Sugal, who shrugged. She said, 'Flap, I'm thinking. He's half Korhivi.'

Balk frowned. 'One of my better scouts. He does knife-work?'

'More than that,' Sugal said. 'He's got a bit of forest-magic about him. Besides, he likes the dark, eyes like a cat's.'

'All right. Send him out.'

Flap lay motionless in the high grasses, almost at the foot of the watch-tower. He was smiling, though that wasn't a problem, since his teeth gave off no gleam, being stained deep brown by betel juice.

Beyond this land's pain, there was anger. Rage, even. Flap could taste it in the chill night air. There had been centuries of dying here, dying and suffering. Plenty for him to feed on. Swirling currents of hate, trapped energies spinning in vicious eddies. The land was in ferment, bubbling with heat.

It had taken a long time for him to reach this point beneath the tower, moving in slow increments, just another patch of shadow on the ground; and with plenty of clouds obscuring the moon, he was almost certain that he'd been unobserved. The captain had ordered the main cookfire relit, sent out a squad to tend it. Anyone with eyes on the camp would lose their night vision. Captain was a smart man.

He was about to kill another Malazan. Another knot to tie into his hair. Seven was a good number, a magical number. The spirits would delight in his fortune. The six knots already in his hair had made him nervous. Six wasn't a good number. There were six islands on death's white river, six challenges a soul must master on its journey to the Place of Antlers and Horns. Tangle-Witch had six teats that she used to feed her demon children. Flap didn't like six.

He could hear faint murmuring above him, coming from the swallows in their nests. They weren't happy, because they had company. Flap could almost hear the fool's breathing. He began snaking forward, working his way past the front facing of the tower that looked out onto Balk's camp. Around the corner, into high greasy grasses, then the second corner, coming opposite the gaping doorway, where he slowly rose into a crouch.

The wooden floor and stairs would be a problem, covered in dried guano likely to crunch underfoot. And the stairs themselves would creak and groan to his weight. He would have to move very slowly indeed.

Flap drew out his narrow-bladed long-knife.

Each footfall settled slowly, without much weight on it until it was firmly set. It took forty heartbeats just to reach the stairs. He bent close to the first wooden slat, tracking with his fingers until he found the square-headed nails. Where they were still deeply set into the old wood should take his weight without creaking.

One foot per step, balanced like a heron in the reeds. Not a single tick or creak and he was at the first landing. Now he could see the scuff-marks of boots left by the soldier above him.

The land was silent in its suffering. It had no voice except what the wind gave it when sweeping through tall trees: scraping branches and the rocking of tree trunks, but this was a seething hiss devoid of feeling. The leaves chattered nonsense, never understanding how short their season of life would be. What rotted and crumbled made little sound barring the occasional wet sob. And where the spirits lingered, in bog-holes and caves, in spring-pools and streams, all anger was borne by their unblinking eyes. The only voice the land possessed belonged to its dwellers.

This night, Flap would speak with his knife. The honed iron edge whispering across a throat, the bubbling gasp of shock that followed.

Last landing, his head slowly rising above the last step, to see a figure slumped in sleep near the south-facing window.

Lazy, useless Malazans. This marine was to be feared? A fool who couldn't even stay awake?

Flap straightened from his crouch, made quick work of the final three steps on the stairs, and now edged across the floor towards the sleeping soldier.

Stabbing pain into the sides of his neck. Agonizing pressure on the sides of his head. He was lifted upward on spattering streams of blood, torn savagely to one side, and in the last few moments of consciousness, Flap saw his headless body more than an arm's reach away, crumpling to the floor. He continued staring as the scene tilted to one side, and then the floor rose up to meet his forehead, whereupon he rolled and rocked before darkness arrived with a final thought.

Six was a bad number.

A solid kick in his side startled Oams awake. Cursing, hand drawing his knife, he scrambled upright.

Anyx Fro stood opposite him, blinking. 'Thought you were dead. But you were asleep. Asleep! I can't believe it! What if they sent another one when the first one didn't come back? Didn't that even occur to you? You witless, pathetic—'

'Be quiet!' Oams hissed. It was late, at the edge of dawn when the darkness seemed to get still darker, and yet Oams could smell the reek of blood and spilled bowels. He saw that Anyx gripped her short-sword, the iron's gleam seeming to hover like smoke. On the floor close to the tripod was a humped form.

'And what did you do to this poor bastard, anyway? Look at the neck – his head looks *torn* off.'

As his eyes adjusted, Oams could see the head she'd indicated, the skin of the throat and neck ragged, tendons dangling. He angled his gaze to study the face. 'That Korhivi scout of theirs.'

'Flap,' Anyx said. 'The one Stillwater said to look out for. What's wrong with you?'

He hesitated. Panic had blossomed in his chest and gut. His heart thumped hard against his ribs. 'Ensorcelled, I think. Something knocked me out.' He stepped forward and nudged the head with the toe of his boot, making it rock slightly. 'This bastard.'

'Threw magic at you, did he? Was that before or after you tore off his head?'

'Before, obviously. But I must have resisted it at first, enough to close on him and—'

'Tear off his head. With your hands and scrawny arms. Got it.'

'Sure. I was offended, wasn't I?'

'That he made it all the way to the top of the stairs without you hearing a thing? Give it up, Oams. You fell asleep. On watch. In the old days, that's execution, and Spindle's old guard all the way. Well, it was nice knowing you.'

Sheathing his knife, Oams settled into a squat and covered his face with his hands. 'Wasn't like that,' he said.

'Can't quite hear you through your fingers, Oams.'

He dropped his hands and glared up at her. 'Something's attached itself to me. Big, nasty. It rose up out of the ground in front of me, just outside Culvern. Been haunting me ever since. Showed up tonight, knocked me out somehow.'

'Have I got this right?' Anyx asked. 'You got a spirit for company. Puts you to sleep, then kills anyone sneaking up on you?'

'Looks that way.'

'Didn't kill me.'

'Well, no. Didn't have to, I guess. You weren't planning on cutting my throat.'

'If I'd known you were sleeping and not dead, I damn well would've. Just to teach you a lesson.'

'Then there'd be two heads rolling around on the floor.'

'You sure about that?'

'Of course not,' Oams snapped. 'I'm not sure about anything.'

'What's this spirit look like? Horns, three eyes, two mouths full of fangs, one of them in the forehead? Bat wings? Snake for a tail?'

'What? No. You ever see something like that?'

It was getting light, light enough to make out her round face, and at his question her expression changed. 'No. Don't be an idiot. I mean, not while I'm awake. Or sober.'

'She's more or less human, but big, like Paltry Skint, only bigger. Oh, and long talons.'

'Paltry Skint has talons?'

Sighing, Oams straightened. 'Your watch. I got to find Spindle and make a report.'

'Your report, aye. Why not rehearse it first, you know, just to be safe. Pretend I'm Spindle.'

'That won't work. He's prettier.'

'Just pretend.'

Oams looked away, stared at the surprise frozen on Flap's dead face. That embrace had been . . . exquisite. And her voice – he'd like to hear it again. But still, the whole thing was bad news. 'Fine,' he said. 'Balk's Korhivi scout tried to kill me but my spirit guardian Giant Clawed Woman ripped the man's head off. Oh, and Giant Clawed Woman knocked me out first, so you might have to take me off night-watch duties for a while.'

'Knocked you out? Where's the bump on your head? Show me.'

'No bump. Just sleep.'

'Sleeping on watch?'

'It was sudden. She embraced me and whispered "Sleep", and that was it. I was out. Instantly.'

'A new detail! Giant Clawed Woman talks!'

'I guess so.'

'So tell her to go away.'

'We don't actually *talk*. It was only the one word. That's all she's ever said.'

'How many times has this happened before, soldier?'

'Never! But I can't guarantee it won't happen again.'

'That's a problem,' Anyx Fro said. 'I'm going to have to kill you.'

'He won't say that.'

'Maybe not, since Giant Clawed Woman might appear and rip his head off. Lucky you, Oams. Wish I had a guardian Giant Clawed Woman protecting me. But not if she looks like Paltry Skint, though. Anyway, ask Spindle what he wants done with little Flap here. I'd rather not spend the morning with him for company, you know? I'm offering you that by way of distracting Spindle from the fact that you fell asleep at your post. You can thank me later. If he doesn't kill you. But he probably will, so better thank me now.'

'Thanks,' Oams muttered, heading down the stairs.

'That didn't sound very sincere!' Anyx Fro shouted down after him.

'Get out of my tent,' Stick said. 'It's barely dawn. Go away, Sugal.' She fell back and pulled the furs over her face.

'You got a problem,' Sugal said from where he stood just inside the tent's entrance.

'You're about to have one.'

'Flap never made it back.'

After a moment, Stick sat up. 'That's not good.'

'He fucked up, obviously,' Sugal said. 'Balk wants you. I wasn't going to suggest Flap. I was thinking Bairdal. But you said Flap, and now you got to answer to the captain.'

She started getting dressed. 'You didn't say nothing, Sugal. If you figured Bairdal would've been a better choice, and then you didn't say nothing to me and Balk, then it was you who fucked up, not me.'

Sugal scowled. 'I'd opened my mouth and everything, but then you cut me off.'

'Never happened.'

'I say it did.'

'You still could've objected.'

'But it's you Balk wants to see, not me.'

Throwing him a dark look, Stick pushed past him. It was a chilly morning and she hadn't had enough sleep, but anxiety had her mind racing. She set off for the captain's command tent.

The problem, she knew, wasn't about who went out. Flap or Bairdal or anyone else, for that matter. The problem was that the assassin was now either dead or in Malazan custody. If the latter, it might not be too bad, since Flap wouldn't talk and the Malazans didn't bother with torture. If you answered, you lived. If you didn't, you died.

It didn't seem likely that the Malazans would just hand him back. No, best assume that Flap was now dead. Either in the night and in that tower, or this morning in the company of Spindle and Gruff.

And that made it easier. A problem, yes, but not an insurmountable one. Flap had a history of hating Malazans, after all. He'd gone rogue before. *Besides, why did you have a soldier in that tower, watching over us? I thought we were in your employ? Allies, even? For all we know, Flap saw movement in that tower and went to check on it. Whole thing could've been a misunderstanding, and now one of my men is dead.*

No, she decided with a small smile, this wasn't a problem at all.

The building that housed the Imperial Administrator was one of the few cut-stone constructions in Silver Lake, rising two and a half storeys with a slate-tiled roof, suitably imposing and conveniently close to the town's cemetery. Captain Gruff sat in the office on the second floor, looking out on that graveyard which spread out just beyond a squat wooden house with a flat roof, on which sat a fat old man eating a pigeon, raw. Feathers drifted on the morning wind.

Mayor Silgar Younger was still speaking, but the captain had stopped listening. He hadn't slept well for some reason despite the rather comfortable quarters he'd commandeered. The report on the now-dead warlock was troubling, and a few moments earlier, Sergeant Spindle had been called away by one of his soldiers. Gruff could see them standing on the corner outside that wooden house. Oams was talking. Spindle was listening. That was troubling, too.

Lieutenant Nast Forn was seated behind his desk, drinking from a clay cup full of cider which was probably only mildly alcoholic. He too looked bored, although an undercurrent of anxiety revealed itself in the way he fiddled with the imperial seal.

Silgar Younger raised his voice. 'Must I repeat myself, Captain?'

'Hmm?'

'The list of reparations, sir. It has been years! Material losses itemized, and all the lost income that followed said losses. Did you not mention that you have arrived with the official documents from the Fist in Tanys?'

'Indeed, sir,' Gruff said. 'I have in my possession the official reply and am authorized to enact it at my convenience.'

Silgar blinked. 'Your convenience?'

'Just so, but I admit to some hesitation.' He glanced out the window. 'It's such a fine morning, after all. As if summer is but moments from arriving. I daresay it might even be veritably *hot* come the afternoon. Assuming the sky stays clear. Tell me, are clouds in the offing? Seasons are variable and so forth and surely you know well the local habits of weather and whatnot.' He smiled.

'Good sir,' said Silgar, 'forgive me for sensing that you are not taking this seriously enough.'

'Oh pish, of course I am, Mayor Silgar. But please, allow me to indulge in a moment of sympathy for good Lieutenant Nast Forn here. After all, he has experienced the brunt of your displeasure for quite some now, hasn't he?'

'In his role as imperial administrator—'

'Just so, a burden the young man certainly did not ask for.' Gruff slapped his hands on his thighs and rose. 'But very well. Dear Mayor, given the nature of the Uprising and its focus on the heinous practice of slavery, the Fist has authorized me to announce the following.' He then stepped forward, both hands grasping Silgar's brocaded lapels, and in a single motion, Gruff lifted the portly man from the chair he had been sitting on, dragged him close and said, 'Fuck you and your reparations.' He then flung the man against the nearest wall.

The back of Silgar's head crunched against the plaster, making a pink dent, the pink flowing in streaks as he slid to the floor.

Gruff examined his nails. 'Damn, is that a tear? No, just a scuff. Thank the gods.' He turned to Nast Forn, who sat staring with his mouth open. 'Lieutenant, I believe the mayor's servants are in the waiting room below. I fear he requires assistance leaving the premises. Are you satisfied that this meeting has concluded? I am. I further assume you have back-pay to distribute, meaning you have a busy day ahead. I will see you at the barracks at the fifth bell? Excellent.'

Gruff collected his soft leather gloves and strode from the room.

Oams was sweating in the bright sun, blinking rapidly as he studied Sergeant Spindle's face. Not a hint of emotion all through his lengthy, increasingly desperate report. Not even a question asked, seeking clarification on this point or that. And now Captain Gruff emerged from the stone-walled house and walked over.

'Dear Sergeant Spindle, your evident perturbation disturbs me.'

Oams squinted at the captain. *What perturbation?*

Spindle turned. 'Well timed, sir. Oams had the middle watch at the South Tower. Was visited by a night-knife, sent by Balk. That assassin is now dead.'

'Excellent outcome!'

'His head was torn off,' Spindle added.

Eyebrows lifting, Gruff regarded Oams with renewed interest.

'Not by Oams's hands, sir. If you recall, Benger took note of a rather intimidating spirit that seems to be following Oams around. Well, it stepped in last night. While Oams slept.'

'Slept?'

'At the spirit's behest, sir,' Spindle said.

'Oh dear.' Gruff continued studying Oams. 'Is this a common event, soldier?'

'First time, sir.'

Spindle cleared his throat. 'Captain, there's the matter of the body.'

'Send it to Balk. Without comment.'

'Understood, sir.'

'Now I need to retire for a time, to buff a nail. Carry on.'

Oams watched the captain head off. Then he turned to his sergeant. 'Balk won't be happy. Flap's head all torn off like that. He'll have questions.'

Spindle grunted and then said, 'Don't we all.'

'I guess I'm off night watches now?'

'What? No. You'll just be paired up from now on.'

'With who?'

'Benger.'

Oams sighed. 'I didn't know he'd sniffed out my . . . companion.'

'Your spirit friend isn't subtle,' Spindle said.

'Can he get rid of it?' Even as he asked, Oams wasn't sure he wanted anyone to get rid of it.

Spindle shrugged. 'I didn't ask him to try. The spirit's presence is a mystery, but one we shouldn't ignore. It's awake for a reason, and it picked you for a reason. Let's see where that takes us.'

'I guess I can't complain,' Oams said. 'It saved my life. But then, if it hadn't knocked me out, I would've heard Flap coming up the stairs. Could've taken him alive.'

Spindle frowned. 'Why would we want him alive? Off you go, Oams. Get some sleep. Real sleep, I mean.'

'Aye, sir.'

He set off for the squad's house. *I'm not tired. In fact, I haven't felt this well-rested in years. Giant Clawed Woman, next time, let's try for a longer conversation, so you can tell me what the fuck you want.* Something stirred in his gut, strangely delicious even as it was disquieting.

He decided to head down to the lakefront.

You ripped his head off. Did Flap really deserve that? Also, I need to give you a better name. Giant Clawed Woman? Nah. Lacks subtlety. Typical that Anyx Fro clearly liked it, though. How about . . . Rose?

CHAPTER NINE

Refugia made for an interesting experiment, in the manner that the Jaghut predilection for experimenting on lesser beings is interesting. Isolate a population within towering walls of ice, yet keep its island refuge rich in resources, the weather passable, and see what happens.

The sentient mind has an infinite capacity for assembling rules of behaviour into an intricate nightmare of carefully crafted madness. Ignorance is like a seed and where it is planted in the guise of a virtue, it becomes a weed that chokes the mind until all reason is lost.

Berate if you will this obsessive curiosity of my kind, our calculating indifference to tragedy and suffering, but know this: in our cool regard, we but mimic the gods.

Think on that the next time you kneel before the altar, and so fall under the shadow of your god's inhuman gaze. Their minds are not your mind. Their desires are not your desires. Their pleasures are not your pleasures. Kneel then in the cup of your god's hand. But be warned. He or she might simply squeeze. Call it the predilection towards curiosity.

Many a night in my long life, I have been startled awake by an immortal's softly whispered *oops!* Another life gone, reduced to a red stain on finger and thumb. *Oh well.*

Gothos
Gothos' Folly

D AMISK LAY IN SHADOW AT THE CAVE'S EDGE. THERE WERE now twelve Saemdhi encamped a short way off, with more approaching in the distance. They must have witnessed

War-Bitch leaving, he was certain, but that had been two days past. It didn't seem likely that they believed he still lived. Something else was going on.

He was hungry. There was nothing in the cave he was inclined to eat. Near one wall, water leaked from a fissure, forming a pool in a depression in the bedrock, which then drained into a deeper crack against the wall. This alone kept him alive. The cold wind sighing out from the cave's throat had seeped into his bones, and even here at the lip of the entrance's slope, he shivered incessantly.

Three of the Saemdhi had moved out from the camp, none visibly armed. Bonecasters, he suspected. He watched as they separated from one another, eventually taking positions thirty or so paces apart, in a curving line facing the Azath Hold. Though Damisk could not ascertain from where he lay, he suspected that there were other camps and more Bonecasters, and that the Hold was now encircled.

A ritual was in the offing. If War-Bitch still resided within the cave, Damisk suspected, none of this would be happening. These Saemdhi would have fled the area. In the way of most northland dwellers, their ability to communicate across vast distances was uncanny. Perhaps some talent among the Bonecasters – yet he had heard tales that suggested that even hunters possessed this ability to converge from opposing horizons, as if the language of the land and the sky was infinite in its details, if only one possessed the senses to heed it.

This ritual was opportunistic, and Damisk was pretty sure it was an attack on the Azath Hold.

Audacious. Insane.

The three Bonecasters had lit fires at their feet, feeding them with small knotted bundles of grass, lichen and dried moss.

A gust of frigid air rolled over Damisk from the depths of the cave, cold enough to make him gasp. *And the Hold answers. Limper's fucked knee, I'm in the wrong place.*

These Bonecasters might bring down the edifice on top of him. But where could he go? If he attempted to flee, the hunters in the camps would see him, and this time there would be no outrunning their arrows.

The Bonecasters were singing, their voices reedy and faint. They had drawn out stone blades and were cutting their forearms and thighs, threads of blood lifting into the air like torn strands of web, stretching higher and higher. In the distance came the dry crackle of thunder.

The wind coming from the cave rose into a howl, sending icy tendrils beneath Damisk, fierce enough to bodily lift him. Cursing, he rolled to one side and kept rolling until he came up against a tumble of sharp-edged rocks, where he twisted round to find handholds.

Thunder rattled the air on all sides now, drawing ever closer. The tilted slabs groaned and rocked. The howl was deafening.

Can they kill it? What happens if they do? Aren't the Azath some kind of prison? What the fuck might get loose?

As if in answer to his fears, a savage spray of gravel and fragments of ice spat out from the cave's mouth, the few that struck Damisk leaving spots of blood. He pushed himself flatter against the uneven boulders.

Something made a snuffling sound, followed by a low-throated cough.

Lightning struck the top of the highest slab, the impact loud as a cusser. Shattered rocks rained down. The towering slab lurched slightly.

Then something huge filled the cave-mouth. Damisk stared up at it.

The grieving grey bear he had killed years ago had stood as tall as two men. This one was twice that, big as a carriage. Icy dirt cascaded down from its colourless, half-rotted fur. The low-slung head moved past Damisk, a head too wide to fit through a normal doorway, the eyes nothing but hollow pits, dust streaming from its dry, gaping mouth and gusting out from its nostrils with every ragged, rattling exhalation.

The ground shook with its footfalls as it clambered out from the cave-mouth, up the slope.

Damisk heard a distant shriek cut through the thunder and whirling wind.

The bear roared, then launched itself forward like an avalanche.

Damisk scrambled to his feet, in time to see the bear reach the first hapless Bonecaster. Whatever was then thrown skyward from the beast's jaws no longer resembled anything human. The Saemdhi in the camp were in full flight, but they might as well have been crawling. The giant bear's speed was breathtaking, terrifying, and it attacked with an intent so deliberate and so plain that it was clear that it intended to leave not one Saemdhi alive.

Damisk stumbled back into the cave. The thought of trying his luck evading the beast out on that featureless tundra made his knees weak. Inside, the wind had fallen off. Even the cold was fading, and water was trickling like sweat down the stone walls and flowing in thick threads from the ceiling. Still half-numbed with horror, Damisk edged round the altar and continued on, deeper into the cave than he had ever gone before. The passageway made a crooked, narrow-walled descent – in no way wide enough to permit the passage of that giant bear. So where had it come from?

He continued onward, deeper, the air growing colder, his hands now held out as the darkness was absolute. His steps slowed at a thought. *I could hide right here.*

Until the beast comes back, taking up residence on the other side of the altar – and no chance of getting past it then, is there?

And if I'd left the boy to drown in the lake? I'd be in the Three-Legged Dog right now, drinking myself into a quick, miserable death. Guilt will do that . . . to those of us with any decency left.

No, Damisk, no regrets. You gave him a chance. It'll have to do.

He kept walking, one foot at a time sliding forward, his hands outstretched. Nothing to see, nothing to hear, not even the sound of trickling water.

What if being dead is just like this? The soul lost and blind to all, drifting through oblivion? What if what we're given in our lives is all there is? No hand of judgement, no weighing of deeds. A lifetime of decisions yielding no final answer. No ledger and from that, no justice.

The thought horrified him. He'd seen too much cruelty and too many betrayals. *Some bastard had damn well better be waiting on the other side. Iskar Jarak, fix your cold, lifeless eyes upon each soul that arrives. Ignore the wheedling, the self-pity, the cries that we didn't know any better. We did know better. We've always known better.*

Abruptly his hands met something that burned his palms, sending him back a step with a gasp and then a curse. *Ice. A vertical wall of ice.* He edged forward, running the fast-numbing tips of his fingers along the slick surface, until his right hand dipped into empty air. The ice here had been shattered.

Damisk moved into the gap. It stank of bear. *It was frozen here? Held in place by ice?* He turned, expecting to detect a faint glow from the distant cave-mouth. Instead, there was only blackness. Too many twists and turns in the passageway? Possibly. He set out, retracing his steps.

After a dozen paces, his arms outstretched and expecting at any moment the touch of cold stone, Damisk halted again.

I'm lost. The way out is not the way in. I'm in the Beast Hold, the oldest warren of all. Now what?

A sideways breath of air sighed over him, faintly warm. He slowly turned in that direction. The scent of wet earth, and now, the tang of salt.

The sound in his ears could be the susurration of blood in his body, or something else. Damisk walked forward, into that sighing breath. The floor began sloping upward, and then, ahead, a faint glow, slowly outlining the cavern he traversed. He continued on, climbing the slope.

The cavern narrowed into a choke-point where the ceiling hung low, forcing him to duck. As he did so, however, he paused. Dim though the light was on this side of the passage, he could see odd black stains surrounding the choke-point. He peered closer. The imprints of hands, short-fingered, wide-palmed. The paint could be red or black – there was no way to tell. But every palm had been pressed against the edge of the opening, as if the hands had been holding back the edges or seeking to widen the passageway.

Beyond, the diffused light showed him a steep ascent, narrow and winding, a floor made of soft white sand littered with twigs and dry leaves. The walls on either side had been carved into an array of beasts, with every natural fold and crease serving to give them shape. He saw many he recognized, but far more that he did not.

Damisk picked up his pace as he ascended the passage. That hissing sound was louder now, not the swish of his blood in his skull, but coming from up ahead.

Harsh sunlight flooded in at the next bend in the passage, revealing a levelled floor of white sand and, near the cave's mouth, a small ring of stones surrounding a black stain. The sky he could see was bright blue, the air sweeping in surprisingly warm.

He clambered to the cave's mouth and came out upon a narrow ledge. Four or five man-heights below was a narrow strand of beach. He was perched halfway up a cliff-face. The sea before him was cerulean, its white-foamed waves rolling up onto the strand below. In the distance, almost opposite him, there was the hint of land on the horizon.

'Fuck.'

*   *   *

It was hard to tell if the mountains were getting any closer. The undulating stretches of lichen-covered bedrock continued, it seemed, to the very foot of that distant range. At least now there were dips in which still water could be found, black and warmed by the sun.

It was midday. Rant set down the still unconscious Jheck – careful to not let the man's head crack against the stone – and paused to study Gower's sun-burnt face. Rant had been carrying him for three days now, and not once had Gower awakened. His breathing was deep but slow, his wounds red but no longer leaking.

Rant straightened to stretch out his cramped shoulders and aching back. Was it just weariness that made it seem that Gower was getting heavier, heavier than he should be? Sighing, he made his way to the nearest pond.

The pool was swarming with mosquito larvae, so he used a handful of moss to filter the water he poured into a sun-bleached skull-cup he had found a couple of days back, bringing the cup to Gower's lips and letting some water trickle through. This always made Gower cough, and Rant could never be sure if any water was getting down. Even hacking coughs did not stir the Jheck from his sleep.

Damisk had once described himself as a man who lived mostly alone, and when he was in company, all his words just came out in an endless stream, as if to relieve the pressure of too many solitary thoughts. That made sense to Rant now. For a time he had tried talking to the spirit in his knife, but that spirit's ability to answer seemed to have ended when it slipped fully into the iron blade. Then he tried talking to Gower, but that hadn't worked either.

And now he was full of words, full of thoughts that had nowhere to go. He imagined that this was what it meant to be lonely. An entire inner world with no way out, no audience or witnesses. If there was beauty in there, none could see it. If there was torment, no one could hear the cries for help.

He sat on the ground beside the motionless form of Gower, his eyes on the empty skull-cup. It looked human. He'd noticed a few bone fragments scattered around it when he'd first come across it, pieces of jaw and face-bones, all bedded in lichen. But no sign of the rest of the body. The edges of the skull had been gnawed by mice.

Perhaps one day his own skull would be lying out here in its nest of moss. With Gower's a few paces distant. Bodies dragged off by scavengers. And like any scatter of bones, nothing but mystery remained. So much of the world was and would be for ever unknown.

Silver Lake had seemed so big when Rant had lived there. There were alleys and streets that he knew, yet others he'd never explored. Buildings he had never been inside. *Most of them, in truth.* Yet now, even the thought of Silver Lake felt too small, shrinking in his mind with every day and night that passed. He did not think he would ever see his birthplace again.

And if I did? Years from now, returning, walking through Culvern Gate?

And the first stone thrown at me?

Into his mind flashed the memory of killing wolves, snapping bones, driving a knife-blade through a skull. Shock rippled through him. He would answer the first thrown stone with broken bones and shattered heads. Thinking on the truth of that made him feel cold and lifeless inside, and that in itself was frightening. Confused, shaken, he stood and walked back to the black pool.

Another piece of emerald green moss into the skull-cup. Then he dipped his hands into the water and filled the cup. Carefully lifting the moss up he studied the water. Only a few squirming larvae. Rant picked up the cup to drink and then froze.

A man was approaching.

On the stranger's left shoulder rested a heavy haunch, butchered from some massive animal. Flies swarmed it, making the red slash of exposed muscle almost invisible beneath seething, glistening black. In the man's right hand was a strange weapon, made from a long jawbone, its outer edge glittering with inset chips of obsidian; he held it at its narrow end, both his hand and the grip hidden by hide straps. At his back was a spear with a long point made from some reddish, waxy stone.

'Wake him up,' the man said in a harsh growl as he drew closer. He spoke Nathii. 'I challenge him.'

'You cannot,' Rant said. 'He is injured.'

Bright white teeth flashed amidst the black beard. 'That makes it easier.' He dropped the haunch, triggering a burst of buzzing flies, and drew a stone knife from a sheath at his belt. 'I'll just cut his throat. The great Lord Gower, tyrant of the Black Jheck, spilling his blood out like piss on the ground.'

Rant moved between the stranger and Gower. 'He is under my protection. Go away.'

'This is Jheck business,' the stranger said, eyes narrowing. 'Nothing to do with Teblor. He feared my challenge and so left the den. I followed. I will be Lord of the Black Jheck.' His gaze strayed to study Gower. 'He lost his pack. A formidable enemy, to have so weakened him. I found Imass dead, but not enough to explain this.'

'It was me,' Rant said. 'I killed the others in his . . . pack. I almost killed him as well. I'm sorry for what I did, and have now vowed to protect him, until he recovers.'

The stranger snorted and glanced away. 'Teblor and their vows.'

'Don't make me kill you,' Rant said, drawing out his Malazan knife.

The Jheck scowled. 'That puny thing?' He turned back to the haunch and crouched beside it to begin hacking off a large section. 'We trade. This food to fill your belly. I'll build us a fire. We'll eat, and then talk, late into the night. Deeds of valour and prowess – will yours match mine? I doubt it, pup that you are. In the end you will have to admit defeat and have no choice but to curl up in that little blanket of yours and go to sleep. Come the morning, you will greet the new Lord of the Black Jheck.'

'It will not be like that,' Rant said. 'I am his protector.'

'Was he awake to hear you, he would likely die of shame. Lord Gower, in need of a half-grown Teblor protector? A boy with a knife?' The stranger set the slab of meat to one side and began gathering small stones to build his hearth. 'But this lie of yours intrigues me. Veered into six, Gower is master of the hunt, the ambush, the kill. If you had been his intended prey, you would not be alive, and if somehow you managed to survive the battle, to indeed kill five of the six, why, you'd be a mass of wounds. So I conclude that you lie.' He paused to grin over at Rant. 'It was this way. Gower fought a hundred Imass, maybe more. A running battle, a path I did not cross until the end. He killed the last of them and then fell senseless, too wounded to carry on. You then found him, or, rather, you found a large wolf, bleeding out. You were starving – that much I can see. So, being the coward that you are, you thought to carry the beast until it died, and to then eat what you could of it.'

'No,' said Rant.

The Jheck's grin remained, his eyes like chips of stone. 'He must have climbed back into consciousness, if only for a moment or two, else he could not have sembled back into his two-legged form. Suddenly, you found yourself carrying not a dead wolf, but a man, still dying, but not dead yet. Would you eat a man? The question haunts you. This is why you still carry him, waiting for him to die. The question will be easier to answer then.'

'Then why do I not let you cut his throat?' Rant asked.

The man nodded. 'A good question. But I have worked out the answer. You would deceive me with all this talk of honour, of vows and duty, so that I do not kill you once I've killed Gower. You seek to convince me that you are a worthy companion, one I might welcome at my side when we return to the den. As a new Lord, my hold on power will be shaky for a time. You will vow to stand at my side as the Lord's guard, because it will be a continuation of the vow you have already made.'

'It will?'

'A vow to protect the Lord of the Black Jheck. And I will be Lord of the Black Jheck.'

Rant shook his head, watching as the warrior drew out his fire-kit and began striking sparks into a small heap of crumbled lichen in the hearth, leaning close to begin blowing once the first tendrils of smoke appeared. Flames licked awake. Rant said, 'My vow is to protect Gower, not the Lord of the Black Jheck.'

'Upon the new shore,' the stranger said, now rummaging in the heavy hide sack that had been strapped to his back, 'there is driftwood. Heavy as stone, that wood, and yet it burns. Slowly, with great heat, enough to melt red metal and even black metal. As for bhederin meat, ah, this shall be a feast to remember.' He drew out a few sticks of grey wood. 'See how generous I am? Jheck rarely bother cooking meat. But I know of the Teblor and their delicate ways. I do this for you.'

'I will not let you kill Gower.'

The stranger shrugged. 'Let us put that aside for now. I see your hunger. I choose to be generous with my kill. We shall eat.' From his pack he drew out a barbed bone skewer, impaling the slab of meat. Feeding the wood into the fire, the man then began adding more stones to the hearth, building up high points on which to rest the skewer. 'My name I now give you – another honour you likely do not deserve. I am Nilghan, the only Black Jheck to have scaled the great ice, to have indeed journeyed into the southlands beyond. Ten years I spent among humans. I have seen the high walls of Blued, the world's greatest den, where the human packs breed like lemmings. I learned this language we speak, and I know you for a half-human bastard – not by how you look, mind you, but by how you smell.' The meat sizzled when he set it over the flames.

'I am Rant, from Silver Lake. My father is Karsa Orlong.'

Nilghan grunted. 'You are bold in your lies, pup. I admire that. I was a scout for the Blued den, out on the eastern marches, when I heard of the attack on Silver Lake. Three Teblor warriors, only one surviving. That one captured, beaten, made into a piteous slave. He was then sent by ship – a large dugout – to the den of Seven Cities. His name was Karsa Orlong. But he is long dead or worse, a grovelling slave in a puny village across the western water, drinking horse piss and fucking sheep – which are strange little animals with lizard eyes.'

'He lives, in Darujhistan.'

'That den name is known to me, but no den in the world is as big as Blued. Four, maybe five times as big as Silver Lake, if you can believe that.' Nilghan flipped the meat.

The smell was overpowering. Rant could barely keep his eyes off the steak.

'Why wander these lands, Rant of Silver Lake? The Imass have followed the herds. We Jheck follow both. The wall of ice is gone. There will be slaughter in the south. As Lord of the Black Jheck, I will avoid all vows. Instead, we shall track all those who would fight; we shall pick off the weak ones, feed on their corpses and grow fat and rich with blood's sweet wealth.'

'I journey to the Teblor in the mountains.'

Nilghan snorted again. 'Better hurry.'

'I was travelling with a friend. A hunter named Damisk.'

The Jheck warrior's gaze snapped up, fixing on Rant. 'Damisk. Who journeyed among the Imass when they first camped on the shore, who thought to trade with them and barely escaped, leaving a score of bodies behind him. Damisk? Let it not be said that Nilghan is churlish in his praise. He is a hard man to kill.'

Rant tilted his head. 'That was praise?'

'Among the Jheck, no praise is higher than to say someone is hard to kill. Now, make use of that fancy knife of yours and cut off some of this meat. Eat until your belly aches.'

'My knife is not for cutting meat,' Rant said.

'You have a talent for hinting at things, Rant,' Nilghan said, using his own stone knife to saw through the steak. 'It may be that I'll have to kill you sooner or later. Then I will have your fancy knife for myself.' He offered Rant the meat.

He took it. Charred on the outside, raw on the inside. The juices covered his chin and his hands. 'What is bhederin?' he asked after swallowing the first mouthful.

'Before the ice fell, we knew but one kind of bhederin. But I have seen the bhederin the Rhivi of the south herd and hunt. Those are small, their horns are short. Killing one would be effortless.' He gestured his knife at the haunch lying behind him. 'This is the proper kind. Twice the size of the southern ones, with long horns out to the sides, like this.' He spread out his arms. 'Packs must work together to take one down.'

'But you are alone.'

'This one was freshly dead when I found it. The wounds made me think of a grey bear, but too large for that. Also, no signs of feeding, or even marking the kill. I admit to being plenty nervous as I cut off a share. A grey bear with paws big enough to crush all the ribs on one side? Impossible.' He shrugged. 'I cannot in truth say what killed it.'

'It is delicious.'

'Of course it is. I learned to cook among the humans of the south.'

CHAPTER TEN

In the habit of changing one's mind
are born a multitude of worlds
a spinning away of possibilities
and imaginings where women walk
between shadows and men kneel
round clay bowls filled with ashes.
Where will you wander in this turnabout
among the sowed fates even as the truth
is unveiled and each track that seemed
so without consequence is now revealed
as flesh of earth and blood of time?
In the heart hides every history
of what might have been and each step
you now take carries with it deeds
you believed abandoned to idle whim.
Thus is set upon you the burden
of your universe in which dwell
infinite universes.

The Spirit of Lull Apocrypha
The Book of Crows
The Monks of G'danisban

DAMISK HAD CLIMBED DOWN FROM THE CAVE'S LEDGE AND now wandered the strand of beach. There was plenty of driftwood, possibly more than there should be. He scanned the weathered, sun-bleached detritus that had been thrown up along the tideline, seeking signs of working: adze or axe marks. Nothing. The only curious detail was that most of the wood had come from uprooted trees, the kind one often saw after a flood.

The day was hot, and beyond a small sculpted crescent the water of the bay seemed to drop off into sudden depths. When a storm came the waves would hammer this inlet, sending spray possibly as high as the cave itself. This beach was no certain refuge.

Damisk removed his moccasins and walked out into the shallows. The water was warm, soothing his battered feet. He waded out to the very edge of the drop-off and then turned to face the cliff. Above the cave's mouth was an overhang, and three man-heights above that what looked like the summit, the edge thick with sedges. The climb above the cave's overhang would be difficult, as the strata were sharply canted, further proof that waves had carved out both the cliff and the inlet.

His only way home, he suspected, would be found in the cave, or rather, in the ancient warren hiding in the cave's depths. But that was hardly a sure thing. Besides, he was hungry, and the thought of plunging back into that chilly darkness with an aching belly and diminishing reserves was not appealing. He needed to hunt.

He returned to the shore and sat on a log, waiting for his feet and shins to dry before pulling on the moccasins. A short time later, with his bow unstrung and strapped to his back, his few remaining arrows secure in the quiver, he began the ascent.

It was not easy; he was weaker than he thought, and secure hand- and footholds above the cave's overhang were difficult to find, though he did manage to rest at one point with his knees jammed against a narrow ledge, twisting above the hips to press himself against the hot, dry stone. The bird nests he found in the cliff-side were long past the season's end, torn and shredded by winds and disuse. No eggs or chicks, alas. In fact, he realized, he'd seen few if any birds at all. Finally, he reached the thick tufts of sedge bundles rooted in crumbled stone and sand. A few moments of unease when he gathered handfuls and tested them with his weight. But the roots held, and he managed to drag himself over the bundles, rolling onto relatively flat ground.

Lying on his back, he caught a glimpse of something to his right. Shifting his gaze in that direction, he found himself staring at four floating mountains of black rock perhaps half a league inland, looming so close to the ground that, had he been directly beneath one, a decent bow-shot might well reach its tooth-rotted base. Moon-spawns. He'd thought there was only one, and hadn't it been destroyed years ago?

Birds wheeled round them, but never straying far. He squinted at them. *Great Ravens? I hate Great Ravens.* He remembered the Malazan invasions; he remembered the Tiste Andii, who had fought against the imperial tide. Uncanny, alien, empty-eyed, and how the great black carrion birds followed them like a promise. And then the battlefields, with those ravens filling the skies, descending in deafening raucousness to feed.

I don't like this world.

Having caught his breath, Damisk climbed to his feet. He quickly readied his bow and set an arrow to the string. The plain rolling away from the coast was undulating, thick with grasses. Beyond the four moon-spawns – each one like a ragged black fang against the blue sky – the land rumpled its way into hills, and there a forest began.

He saw no sign of game on the grasslands, and that was strange. To reach the forest, he would have to pass directly beneath the moon-spawns. Sighing, Damisk set out.

His pace was slow; he had little energy for anything else, but he continued scanning the landscape, his gaze returning again and again to the four giant suspended mountains. No doubt the Great Ravens had seen him, since nothing else moved on this plain. But his approach did nothing to alter their lazy wheeling about the edifices.

Eventually, he passed into the shadows cast down by the moon-spawns, and here the air was suddenly colder, unnaturally so. He had removed a layer of quilting and hide whilst walking in the sun's light. Now he quickly donned them once more, his breath pluming. The sooner these looming monstrosities were behind him, the better.

Damisk recalled a fur-trapper who had set off into the north tundra, seeking white hares. He had departed in the early spring, before the hares' fur changed into the summer hues of dun and tan. But then the season had reversed itself, a late blizzard arriving and temperatures turning bitterly cold for weeks on end. When the man returned, he was barely recognizable. He had left hale, young, a hunter in his prime. The creature who staggered back into town walked bent-backed, his flesh reduced to nothing more than ligament, tendon and gristle. Starving and lost in the wastelands, his body had devoured itself.

Damisk suspected he was edging into that stage. He knew he had lost weight, his clothing hanging looser. He had already added two holes to his belts since leaving Silver Lake's shore.

The average man could carry two, perhaps three weeks' worth of food on his back. On longer journeys, he would have to hunt or fish, and neither enterprise was guaranteed to succeed. At the wrong time of year that man might find no beasts at all, or the fish had moved out of the shallows, seeking deeper, colder waters. The migrating birds might well have gone too.

He had not set out well-supplied. He had eaten only when he managed to kill something. To enter into the Wilds required planning. From the very beginning on the north shore of Silver Lake, his every step had been ill-considered. When people died in the Wilds, it was always at the end of a succession of mistakes. *And look at me, the veteran hunter, here at the end of too many mistakes to count.*

He staggered clear of the preternaturally cold shadows, back into late afternoon summer heat. Before him, the first trees emerged from the drainage channels between the hills, spreading out well before the summits. Damisk moved towards the nearest channel, skirting its edge. He could see now that the forest was a northern one, thick with entangling undergrowth made up of dogwood, elm and alder, with taller aspen trees rising here and there, their knotted dusty boles stark beneath pale green leaves. This was no canopy forest. Moving through it would be a nightmare.

He spotted a tangled sprawl of blackberry along one edge of the channel, the small fruits ripe and hanging in thick clusters. Whispering a prayer of thanks – to no god in particular – he headed over. The berries were sweet, many so ripe they melted between his fingertips even as he tried plucking them loose. Not a single bird had partaken of this feast, and that absence – none but Great Ravens in the sky, and the forest and thickets silent – sent a faint shiver through him.

He really did not like this world.

He ate berries for a time, knowing he would pay for his greed with plenty of straining the next time he shat. Better than dying of malnutrition. Some energy returned to him almost immediately. Wiping his stained hands across his thighs, he once more took stock.

Deer were in the habit of bedding down in these overgrown channels during the day. Damisk selected a decent-sized gorge and carefully made his way towards it. He descended into the thicket, slowly working his way through. His only hope was in spooking a deer into motion, and often they would not move until one very nearly stepped on them.

It was close to dusk when he finally clambered out from the thicket, having traversed its length without finding any evidence of deer – no beds of flattened grasses, no scat, no trails even. Covered in spider-webs, scratched by thorns, he emerged near the summit of the hills, where the aspen trees now dominated, along with poplar and the rare birch. Moving between the boles was an easier task, though not by much.

Damisk found an old hollow and sat down within it, resting his bow across his knees. He was sore, frustrated and worried. A world devoid of animals? Was such a thing even possible? There were hardly any insects.

He glanced back the way he had come. The moon-spawns showed to him their shadowed flanks, black as tears into night. Apart from the

Great Ravens – now drawing in to roost as dusk approached – none showed any sign of life.

Movement on the plain. Damisk sat up, slipped into a crouch, and then slowly stood.

What are those . . . things?

There were hundreds, loping on two hind legs, many seemingly burdened with packs or . . . *beasts. Slaughtered, butchered beasts.* 'You fuckers. You've killed and eaten *everything.*'

He liked to think most hunters wise. He liked to think they understood the necessity of being sparing, of ensuring the game would be there the next season, and the one after that. But that naivety had been stripped away from him long ago. A hunter took what was offered, each and every time. If they could kill more than one beast, why, that's just what they did.

And I was no different. Couldn't think past my fucking nose. Couldn't? No, Damisk, do not lie to yourself. Wouldn't. Because to think like that – to think at all – stays the hand. Assuming you're not batshit insane, that is. Assuming you're not some bitter cauldron of bloodlust, drunk on cruelty, thinking that standing with your foot on an animal's blood-spattered neck makes you something.

He spat onto the ground as he watched the mass hunting party draw closer to the moon-spawns.

I know these. Never seen one. Never imagined they were even real. There are no Tiste Andii in those floating fortresses. Damn, I wish there were.

Fucking K'Chain Che'Malle. Fucking lizards. Why in the Limping Man's name can't the Elder Races just . . . go . . . away?

Once the hunters were in the gloom beneath the moon-spawns, there was all kinds of activity, a flurry of motion, with things like platforms descending empty from the rock fortresses, rising up again loaded with dead animals.

Damisk spat a second time.

Those moon-spawns will move soon, find new land to bleed dry, leaving nothing behind.

A sudden buffeting of air made him duck and then look up.

Not Great Ravens at all. The creature hovering above him was a reptile, skin-taut wings hammering at the air, its fanged head tilted down with its eyes fixed on him.

And now Damisk saw a small group of K'Chain Che'Malle emerge from the deep shadows beneath the nearest moon-spawn, loping towards the first of the hills. Armed with swords and long spears and headed straight for him.

Should've thought of that. After all, they take everything.

Sudden rage whispered through Damisk. He had an arrow to his bow before he knew what he was doing, and then that arrow shot upward. Up among the leaves, a dart vanishing—

A fucking waste! What was I thinking—

Heavy crashing from above, snapping branches. Damisk flung himself to one side as the flying reptile plummeted to the ground, landing with a bone-breaking *thump* amidst broken branches and fluttering leaves.

He stared at it, uncomprehending, saw the fletching of his bird-arrow snug tight in the creature's left eye socket.

The icy rage inside returned, and this time, there was a surge of pleasure.

A chill crackled up his spine. *This land has spirits. Gods. It must have. And one's using me now.*

Below, the K'Chain Che'Malle hunters were closing.

With a half-snarl, Damisk set off deeper into the forest. Before long he was deep into the thickets. He could hear more of the winged lizards overhead, voicing cries that sounded frustrated. It was impossible to move without making noise, but Damisk struggled to keep it to a minimum, ducking and shifting sideways to slip between branches. Somewhere behind him he heard heavy thrashing sounds – the K'Chain Che'Malle hunters were in the forest now.

God or no god, this won't end well.

He was already beginning to tire once more. *Maybe I'm done. All this struggling, the sheer stupidity of a man's stubborn will. It's all catching up. My last decent act was saving that half-breed. And see the stream of blood still flowing from that. If I—*

Heavy thumps ahead, a flash of leathery wings slapping heavy on the ground. He could make out a clearing, into which two of the winged lizards had fallen. From high above, others shrieked in rage or fury, and now he could make out their shapes in the gathering gloom overhead as he reached the clearing's edge – and it was clear that none dared land.

An enormous figure crouched in the centre of the clearing. At first, Damisk thought it was a statue, something hacked from grey stone, its rough, rude angles worn smooth beneath rain and wind. Three sets of arms sprouted from its elongated torso, the highest pair gripping a stone bow and even now notching another arrow into a bowstring that glistened like diamond. The other hands held an array of stone weapons. Scattered around the pedestal it crouched on were the severed heads of something vaguely human, lying like grey boulders on the grass.

The creature's face was blockish and angular, its eyes deep-set above prominent cheekbones, its jawline as gracile as any human's. Long hair the colour of its skin hung in a ragged mane. Nothing of its face suggested the demonic, yet the body beneath was monstrous.

Damisk watched the bow flex as the creature's torso arched, and an arrow hissed upward.

A high-pitched scream rang in the darkness, followed a few moments later by a heavy body crashing down through trees.

Behind Damisk, the hunters on the ground were rushing closer in an explosion of branches and leaves, the ground reverberating with their footfalls. 'Not again,' he muttered, hesitating between impossible choices. Cursing under his breath, he scrambled into the clearing, another arrow ready on his bowstring. The feel of the ground under his feet was strange, as if beneath the thin layer of humus and grasses there was solid stone.

The creature saw him and brought the bow round, another arrow shimmering into existence on the string.

Damisk gestured frantically behind him. 'Don't waste that fucking thing on me!' Breath held, he spun to face the forest, readying his own bow.

The first K'Chain Che'Malle appeared, huge bladed weapons bound to its forearms. Its entire body was held parallel to the ground above two massive hind-limbs and a splayed tail, and it charged forward with jaws spreading wide.

A stone arrow sank deep into its chest. The K'Chain Che'Malle swerved drunkenly, claws tearing up the turf as it struggled for balance. Then it pitched forward onto the ground.

At the same moment, stone and iron clashed behind Damisk, and he spun round to see that two other K'Chain Che'Malle had attacked the creature on the pedestal, one from each side. In terms of size, they were well matched.

He saw a stone mace lash a path that would intersect a hunter's head, before an iron blade rose to block it. Sparks burst, and then the sword was in pieces, shards spinning. The mace slammed into the hunter's skull just behind an eye socket, crushing bone. The eye spurted in a bloody stream, the impact savage enough to nearly tear the head from the neck.

On the other side, blades danced in feint, thrust and counter-thrust, gleaming and glittering in the darkness like moonlight on a mountain stream.

Only now did Damisk notice the shackles wrapped round the grey creature's ankles, the chains embedded in the pedestal.

'Hardly seems fair,' he whispered, drawing and sending an arrow towards the K'Chain Che'Malle.

The arrow either bounced or skidded off hide, but it seemed to momentarily distract the hunter. Blood sprayed and it reeled back, one arm nearly severed at the shoulder, and an instant later a rapier point sank into its throat, followed by a short, wide blade thrusting from below, gutting the beast. It fell, curling up around its spilled intestines.

Silence, beyond the drip of blood on leaves.

Damisk settled to his knees, fighting to slow his frantic breathing, his pounding heart. If there were more of the reptilian hunters close by, they remained in the forest, beyond the grey creature's reach. The three that had entered the glade were all dead, and nearby lay the humps of at least two of their winged kin.

He lifted his gaze to find the chained creature studying him, every weapon ready, an arrow pointed directly at him. Damisk flinched. 'It wasn't me you used, then? Out at the forest's edge?'

Nothing, and then, slowly, the bow's bend relaxed, the arrow dipping.

Damisk nodded. 'Aye, it was you, and that was me.'

Was it moonlight that turned everything in this glade grey and life-less? Was Damisk looking upon a living creature, or some arcanely animated statue? He sighed. 'I'm not from this world. I came through the Hold of the Beast. I was hungry. I thought to hunt, but the K'Chain Che'Malle have left nothing. Now, I simply want to find my way back to that damned cave.'

It stared at him.

Great, a mute god.

'There are four moon-spawns over the plain.' He hesitated, and then said, 'Maybe you can destroy all who come into this glade, or fly above it, but let's be honest, that's not worth much. They're killing everything out there.'

The god lifted one foot, rattling the chain.

'I saw,' Damisk said, nodding. 'If I had to guess, I'd say your worshippers did that. To keep your wrath – and your reach – tightly circumscribed.' He shrugged. 'It's what we mortals do, given the chance. It always astonishes me how naive gods are – at least in legends and myths and, uh, here. Anyway, if I had to guess a second time, I'd say that all your worshippers are dead. Dust and mouldering bones. Crumbling ruins, mournful ghosts. Those heads surrounding you. In other words, chaining you was a fatal mistake. For them.' He sat, leaned back, stretched out his legs. 'I doubt you're sympathetic.'

The chain rattled again.

Damisk squinted at the god. 'You think I can break those chains for you? And if I did?'

The god lifted its face to the sky.

'You'll go after the K'Chain Che'Malle. After the moon-spawns. Are you that tough? Fine, shall I try?' Wearily, he climbed to his feet, walked over to the pedestal. The god watched him, the mace and a few bladed weapons still dripping blood.

Damisk clambered onto the pedestal. A single thrust or slash and he was dead, but he'd ceased to care. He reached down and lifted the chain. Stone links, heavy in his hand. He saw no seams, not even at the shackle fittings. He gave it an experimental tug.

The links snapped like fragile glass.

'Ah! Needed a mortal, did you?' He quickly broke the other chain and then stepped back fast, nearly falling from the pedestal as the god straightened to tower over him.

Looking up, he met its flat stone eyes.

It blinked, and then darkness swept in to engulf Damisk, and he knew no more.

He awoke to bright sunlight on his face and the soft sound of birds flitting through the thicket. Groaning, Damisk sat up.

The giant grey creature was gone. On the stone pedestal, placed between the broken chains, was a hide-bound object, its smeared surface crawling with flies.

Damisk slowly stood, joints aching. He paused for a moment to settle a wave of vertigo, and then approached the pedestal. He unwrapped the hide to find slabs of marbled meat, roughly hacked and mostly bled out. Damisk's stomach clenched at the sight.

He drew out his dagger and cut away a small slice. The flesh was tough – too fresh – yet delicious. He cut himself another slice. Too much at once and he knew he'd lose it all; even now, faint spasms troubled his gut. He risked a third piece, and this time chewed for a long time, until all flavour was gone, before swallowing it down.

He sat on the pedestal. The sun was warm, the air of the clearing filled with insects. A glance southward revealed nothing but empty sky. *Wise enough to have fled, then. Who'd want to face an angry god?*

After a time, he decided that what he'd eaten would stay down. Wrapping up the meat once more and slinging the package onto a shoulder, he collected his bow and quiver and set out. Back to the cave and, hopefully, back home again.

Before seeing the boy drowning in the lake, he had thought his time to be more or less done, all his deeds behind him, his adventures nothing more than tales he'd tell any fool careless enough to listen. A life spun into lies – what history wasn't? All the times he'd slipped Hood's shadow and claimed prowess over luck, skill over the wayward tug of fate.

Sitting in the smoky tavern, too deep into his cups as yet another pointless night crawled past, a man spilling everything but confessions. There, then, on his last patch of ground, deeming it worthy of defending until his last breath. Wasn't this how every survivor ended their time in the mortal realm? The slow crumble taking it all away, until only delusions remained? He thought he'd earned it, the way a drowning man earned his beach, there to lie gasping amidst the roar of surf and the screaming gulls. At life's end, he was done with expectations, done with ambitions, done with hope. Sitting on the tavern's porch in the shade, watching the great dramas of Silver Lake's few hundred denizens. Watching them walking in the sun or in the rain or in the snow, blurry figures trailing their stories.

Man and woman both, there was an age that, when reached, made the world beyond seem to fall away, drained of colour, devoid of significance. To live as a thing no longer desired but tolerated, at best humoured. To reach that age was to know the light in the eyes dimming – the first spark to wink out, and from that moment on, the shadows just crept ever closer.

Damisk sighed. Instead of all that, here he was, dragging his battered hide and bones across unknown worlds.

Well, better this than being a chained god, helpless to prevent the rape of his world. I did that much at least—

Damisk clambered free of the last thicket, staggered out onto the plain once more. And halted, blinking, struggling to comprehend what he was seeing.

The four moon-spawns had not fled. Their shattered remains covered the plains. The carcasses of dead K'Chain Che'Malle rose in elongated mounds, like beach-ridges, the wrack of storm-debris driven high onto shore, in masses of snapped limbs and gaping wounds. And virtually everywhere else, where broken chunks of black rock did not lie like rubble, he saw the carcasses of the winged lizards, arrow-studded, twisted in death.

A handful of crows waddled drunkenly in the spattered gore not twenty paces from where Damisk stood.

Gods below, get me out of here.

*   *   *

Grainy-eyed, Rant watched Nilghan stir awake. Grunting, sighing, a short hack of a cough and then the Jheck warrior slowly sat up, scratching vigorously at his black beard. A moment later he glared across at Rant.

'Full belly. You were supposed to sleep.'

Rant shook his head.

'Instead, I was the one to fall asleep. You could have cut my throat. It's what I would have done. And now, how will you survive the day? I see your exhaustion. When you stumble, I will pounce. Not to kill you, unless I have to, but to kill him.' And he nodded towards Gower's motionless form. 'Look at him. As good as dead already.'

Rant stood.

Nilghan edged back. 'Teblor are too tall,' he muttered, reaching for his strange bone and obsidian weapon. 'My right hand is wedded to this, bound in the promise of death.' He worked at the straps, tightening them with his left hand. 'It seems we must now fight. I will kill you swiftly. Very little pain.'

'I'm not fighting you,' said Rant.

'You are right to be afraid.'

'I'm not afraid. I am sad.'

Nilghan paused to study Rant, his red-rimmed eyes narrowing. 'There are white bears that live on the ice, kin to the great cave bears. Kresimlha Arot is the white she-bear of the sky. Her tongue flashes at night, in all the colours of flesh, blood and life. And all creatures that dwell upon the earth have suckled at her teats. Is it sustenance that she offers? No, it is not. It is sadness.' Shrugging, he climbed to his feet. 'Sadness is what all living things share. You think you are alone in what you feel. I tell you that you are no different from the rest. To live is to be sad, and to be sad is to know . . . well, your every breath rides the stream of flesh, blood and life.' He widened his stance and faced Rant directly. 'Now then—'

Rant leapt forward, his fist slamming into Nilghan's face. Nose shattered, eyes rolling up, the warrior toppled onto his back.

Frothy bubbles from the red ruin of the nose revealed that he still drew breath. Satisfied, Rant crouched beside the unconscious warrior. He untied the weapon and used the straps to bind Nilghan's wrists. He dragged Nilghan over to where Gower was lying and left him there. He then tied the remains of the bhederin haunch to his rope belt, as well as the jawbone weapon. The spear he looped over his back before turning to the two Jheck warriors.

It was awkward getting each man onto a shoulder, but at last he managed it, bringing his arms up to hold both in place. Breathing heavily, he began walking.

*　　*　　*

Damisk squatted facing the cave. The surf thundered behind and below him. Salty mist settled on his face and hands. It seemed that the freeing of the god had unleashed a fury of storms. Climbing down the slick cliff-face had left him still trembling, half in exhaustion and half in fear. And now before him waited an unknown fate.

The Beast Hold clearly opened to many worlds. It was possible that he would never find his way home; that he might wander strange realms for the rest of his days. But even that seemed to be a better alternative than staying where he was. Delivering mercy to a god was no guarantee of benign regard in return. Indeed, the thought of a god's attention in any capacity made him uneasy.

Sighing, Damisk straightened, and then began his descent into the cave. The warmth quickly drained away and after a few twists and turns the reflected light vanished as well, leaving him to slowly grope his way forward.

I am so sick of caves.

His outstretched hands contacted a wall of ice. Damisk paused, closing his eyes.

You again. Good. Now, just let me trace you here, until . . .

A gap. He hesitated, tempted to whisper a prayer, but to which god? *Ah, fuck them all.*

Damisk stepped forward. The cold battered him, stole the breath from his lungs. Eyes stinging, he pushed on. The stone floor was slick beneath his moccasins but level so far.

Something brushed his left cheek, just beneath the eye. Damisk flinched. Motionless, he waited. When nothing further touched him, he turned slightly and reached out. His fingers settled upon something smooth and somewhat yielding. Tracking it, he grunted in sudden fear. A face.

Damisk stepped back, one hand drawing his knife.

After a long moment in which the only sounds he heard were his own breaths and the thumping of his heart, he edged forward once more. Settled the fingertips of his left hand upon the face.

Frozen. Lifeless. He touched open eyes, lashes that crumbled under his touch.

Gods, what a fate.

Damisk moved on. Three, four strides. With his fifth, the ice-laden floor sloped downward. Unbalanced, he fell, and then began sliding. Breath held, hands outstretched but finding no purchase, he slid, picking up speed.

His hip struck something hard that pitched him around. Desperate, Damisk stabbed his knife-point into the icy floor. He slowed as the iron point carved a deep furrow. Then the blade snapped, and he plunged onward.

Sudden daylight and then stony ground slammed into him. He heard his bow splinter, one jagged end ripping through his hide jerkin and then the padding underneath. The other end whipped round to strike his face. Cursing in pain, he rolled over the hard stones and finally came to a halt.

Slowly, he gathered himself, and then, wincing, he sat up.

Behind him rose the towering fangs of rock. He seemed to have fallen out from the Hold through solid stone. Disbelieving, he looked around.

Carrion-eaters had found the mangled corpses of the Saemdhi. Bits of them lay scattered over the ground on all sides.

Distant movement caught his eye. Damisk climbed to his feet. Squinting, he studied the strange apparition staggering towards him.

It was slow going, but at long last the figure reached Damisk and halted.

'I've been searching my memory,' Damisk said, 'and nowhere can I recall advising you to collect Jheck warriors, Rant.'

Red-rimmed eyes blinked wearily at him. 'Damisk.' The word was a croak. 'You look awful.'

CHAPTER ELEVEN

On this day and all the others
I track the furrow of your latest plough
The sod upended, the roots helpless
It is no admission of weakness
To say the land of my soul is thin
Now that the herds of old are dust
You set a level gaze on the task ahead
I am upended, flailing in the absence
Of mercy – what dreams you must cherish
Demanding the splitting of earth
The bleeding out of the wild
Have you seen as I have a world exhausted
By the flat gazes of the unfeeling
Heavy is the plough's iron fang
Mindless its unyielding passage
We cannot speak you and I
The shared language barely disguises
Our mutual incomprehension
I am unashamed by the blood on my hands
While you ever remain a step back
Where the silence greets you as a friend of old
And the cleaving fang carries the burden
Of all that you have murdered
Lift that pale hand and open your palm
So innocent an altar for your day's bread
And think of me no longer
I am riding with the herds in the silence
Of dust.

Death of the Plains
Erit (the Rhivi)

THERE WERE SIX WAGONS IN THE TRAIN OF RHIVI TRADERS that came up from the Inland Road, skirting Balk's encampment before drawing up outside New Gate. Stillwater eyed them from her post. The oxen in their yokes were a sorry lot, old and swaybacked, their ochre hides patchy, worn to pink skin where the yokes rubbed against the shoulders. Their eyes were duller than the sky.

'Me or you?' Anyx asked from the other side of the track. 'As you can see, I'm all comfortable here, and that should count for something.'

Stillwater glanced over. Anyx was leaning against the gateway's upright on her side of the road, a battered marble column dug up from who knew where. The upright next to Stillwater was a tree trunk. Oak or something like that. Its flanks were studded with iron nails, a few of them still bearing tattered, sun-bleached strips of cloth. There was no leaning against something like that. 'Not fair, Anyx.'

'What's not fair?' Anyx retorted. 'You got the stool.'

'Sitting's more comfortable than leaning,' Stillwater replied. 'Which means my repose trumps yours, so you can talk to them, see what they're trading and stuff like that.'

'Repose, is it? You even know what that means?'

Stillwater snorted, stretching out her legs. 'Means I keep sitting. Go on, woman, I had the last bunch.'

'That last bunch was two old women with a cart of wrinkled apples. Barely counts.'

'Counts enough. Hurry up, they're almost here.'

Sighing, Anyx pushed off from the column and walked over. 'At least give me one of them apples, Stilly.'

'No. They were a gift.'

'A bribe.'

'A gift, because I smiled so sweetly at them.'

'The eyes on your scarf scared them so bad their bladders leaked,' Anyx said, now stepping forward and raising one hand to halt the lead wagon. 'Hold up there!'

The old, flat-faced Rhivi who had been walking alongside the oxen flicked his switch in front of the nearest beast's nose, halting it. His plains accent was like music as he spoke in Genabarii. 'Trading here four years now, soldier. We usually draw up in Buyer's Field. No problems.' His thin eyes flicked towards Stillwater. 'No tithes either. What we sell they want.'

'Oh yeah?' Anyx ambled closer. 'Like what?'

'Medicines, spices. Feathers, perfumes, jewellery. Raw copper, amber, some hides, loom-weights, spindles.'

'Is that all?'

'Baskets, sandals, bone needles, yellow-thorn, fire-sage, rat-tails, duck eggs, ferrets, weasels, snake-skins, bowstrings, arrow-shafts.'

'And what about the other three wagons?'

Stillwater sighed and stood, brushing at her leggings. 'Stop being such a bitch, Anyx.'

Anyx scowled back at her. 'You could fit all that in a kit bag, Stilly.' She faced the trader again. 'Well?'

The old man scratched at his hairless jaw. 'That would be a dangerous kit bag,' he said in a murmur.

'What do you mean?'

'The ferrets and weasels are live, soldier. Good for ratting in barns and crawl-spaces.'

'That's a relief,' said Stillwater, moving up alongside Anyx. 'Beats live snake-skins.' She pointed to the wagon at the rear of the train. 'But that's no trader, that one.'

The Rhivi shrugged. 'Shrine of the Monk. We do not ask of its chosen path, for it is free to travel where it wills beneath the sky.'

'Monk?' Stillwater asked. 'What kind of monk?'

The Rhivi said nothing.

'All right,' announced Anyx, 'you can draw up in Buyer's Field, but first, let's see those weasels.'

'Anyx,' Stillwater warned.

'Shut your trap, Stilly. I saw how your eyes all lit up at the rat-tails.'

'Only because of this necklace of teeth I got. Rats' teeth and rats' tails, get it?'

'Oh I get it,' Anyx replied. 'You're insane.'

'Stay on post, and let the trader wagons on through,' Stillwater told her. 'I'm going to interview the monk.'

'What for?'

'Because I think he's lying.'

'Who? The monk? You haven't even met him yet!'

'Not him,' Stillwater replied. She pointed at the Rhivi trader. 'Him. I asked him what kind of monk and he didn't answer. That counts as a lie.'

'Saying nothing counts as a lie?' Anyx snorted. 'Like I said. Insane.'

Ignoring Anyx, Stillwater spared one final glare at the Rhivi and then began making her way towards the last wagon. It reminded her of a Trygalle carriage, all black lacquered wood and ornate carving. The lone ox pulling it was huge and in better shape than the others.

Behind her, the Rhivi trader spoke. 'The witch watches with unkind eyes.'

Stillwater swung round. 'What's that?'

'A warning.' The Rhivi shrugged again.

'Didn't sound like one,' Stillwater observed. 'It sounded like some weird mancy, or worse, some stupid Rhivi saying that's supposed to sound profound and meaningful but really it's just stupid.'

The Rhivi's gaze was fixed on her scarf. 'Well, it's true that we Rhivi make up stupid sayings to whisper into the ears of credulous foreigners, but that wasn't one of them. A spirit rides you, or perhaps it's just her curse. You'd be better off burning that cloth.'

'But then everyone'd see the rope tattoo.'

The Rhivi blanched slightly and stepped back.

Pleased, Stillwater continued on to the last wagon. An old legless woman was positioned on the high bench, traces wrapped round one gnarled hand. She was smoking a pipe, the smoke of which was the same colour as her skin and hair. And eyes. 'Gods, woman, why hasn't no one buried you yet? Is the monk inside, watching all this through a peep-hole? I bet he is. You, in there! Unlock the latch, I'm coming in!'

A small panel slid open beneath the high bench, down where the old woman's legs would have been, and a darkly tattooed face appeared. 'At your peril, soldier. I have curses. I have mighty warrens at my beck and call. A dozen Gates hover here inside this carriage. Besides, the witch's eyes aren't welcome.'

'What a stupid place for a window, Monk,' said Stillwater. 'You've got a legless old woman for a hat.'

'Keeps me warm. Now leave us!'

'That's disgusting. You don't know where she's been. And is that a Malaz Island accent I'm hearing?'

'Stilly!' Anyx Fro rushed up and thrust a small, black, snarling thing at her. 'Look what I bought!'

The hissing weasel bared its white needle-teeth. Stillwater stepped back in alarm. 'Why didn't you get a ferret? At least you can cuddle those. That thing'll chew your nose off first chance it gets.'

'Maybe yours,' Anyx said, stroking the creature's small head. 'We've already bonded.'

'Well, you do share the same mad look in your eyes. Fine, I'm happy for you. Now take it away before it sprays on all of us.'

'And look at this,' Anyx went on, 'see how it just slides in here?'

Stillwater grunted. 'I see that your cleavage now has a black hairy head, and teeth.'

'So warm!'

'You really are losing it, Anyx Fro.'

'I'm bored!'

The first three wagons had rattled on through the gate, into the town proper. The old woman on the monk's carriage was glaring down at Stillwater.

'Fine,' Stillwater said to Anyx. 'Go on, take the stool and don't blame me if the thing pisses down your tummy. Stuck in there, I know I would.'

'What are you going to do?'

Stillwater rapped one fist against the side of the carriage. 'I'm escorting this monk to Headquarters, because I don't think the captain's going to be happy about a Malaz Island sorceror-monk farting warrens and curses here in town.'

The face disappeared from the small window and the panel slid shut with a snap.

'Captain might kill him,' mused Anyx.

'I'm hoping,' Stillwater replied. She looked up at the old woman on the high bench. 'Come on, then, hag, you just follow me in, and no funny stuff.'

Captain Gruff was tapping his front teeth with a long, blue-painted fingernail. 'North Fool's Forest, but not yet South Fool's Forest?'

Oams glanced at Spindle and then back at the captain. 'Not yet, sir.'

'And you're certain of the tundra tribes?'

'Sir, the woods are crawling with all types. I only guessed that some of them were from up north. Wearing seal skins and the like. Big ones, those people. Wide, ugly.' He shrugged. 'A few of the closer forest bands and whatnot looked to be in thrall to the big ones. But also Bright Knot.'

Gruff's teeth-tapping stopped. 'Bright Knot? The all-women warrior clan? Are you sure?'

'Well, can't be *all* women,' Oams said. 'Related to the old Mott Irregulars, unless I got that wrong.' He shot Spindle another look but the sergeant said nothing, didn't even nod or shake his head. 'Thing is, sir, I once saw some Bright Knot armour, down east of Mott Wood. It was a bit of a mess, pulled out of swamp-muck and an arm and a shoulder still in it. The sapper who found it thought it was an alligator hide. And it was, only fashioned into armour. Saw the same among the women warriors I spied in the woods here. Cutlasses of some sort at their belts, and lots of throwing knives. Fits the description I heard from . . . somewhere.'

After a moment, Gruff stood and stepped out from behind his desk. He stared out the mottled window-pane to the street below. 'A fell gathering indeed. Sergeant Spindle?'

'No movement from Balk's camp, sir. But they have to know what's in the forest.'

'No increase in pickets?'

'None that we could see.'

'Thus . . . not afraid. Hmm, this, my dears, could endanger my sleep, and you know how I cherish my sleep. After all, a well-rested captain is less inclined to invite a bloodbath simply because he's in a foul mood. And did I mention the unsightly dark pouches beneath my eyes? No, darlings, this won't do. At all.' He swung round. 'Sergeant, can we hold?'

'As is? Not a chance, sir. A fighting retreat? Maybe.'

'And then,' Gruff said, sighing, 'there's the townsfolk to consider. And let us be truthful, I'm no Coltaine, and you're not Wickans.'

Spindle grunted.

Oams couldn't be sure that was an amused sound. It could as easily have been his sergeant choking on something.

'Oams,' Gruff now said, 'you weren't seen in your scouting venture?'

'Seen? Oh yes, sir. No doubt at all. They have shamans. Mages. Spirit-Dancers. Fat Whelps of Tangle-Witch.'

'Fat – what?'

'Followers of Tangle-Witch, sir. That's what they call themselves.'

'Ah, and here I thought you were being uncharacteristically unkind. So, Oams, since you claim you were seen, is it too indelicate of me to ask: why weren't you killed?'

'One, I think they wanted me to know they'd seen me, sir.'

'Is there a "Two"?'

Oams nodded. 'My, uh, shady friend.'

'She who rips off heads?'

Wincing, Oams hesitated, and then nodded. 'Aye, sir. Those tribals cleared us a path, sir. Out of fear or respect.'

'Fear or respect, is there a difference? Never mind. Sergeant Spindle, one of our gate guards is waiting for you outside, in the company of a ghastly carriage and an even ghastlier old woman perched on the bench, and when I say "perched", I am, as always, being precise.'

Spindle rose.

'As for you, dear Oams,' said Gruff, 'let's do some scouting here in town.'

'Sir?'

'Head-count. How many would need to be carried, or on a wagon or cart. Number of young children. That sort of thing. Oh, and don't simply query the mayor for the information. He would have us compensate for a town consisting of ten thousand people, even if seven thousand of them will be found in the cemetery. No, gather a few soldiers and make discreet enquiries.'

'Yes, sir.'

'And well done, Oams. Do blow your shady friend a kiss from me, will you?'

*   *   *

Stillwater smiled at Spindle and then scowled at Oams who stepped out a few paces behind the sergeant.

'Stillwater,' said Spindle, halting in front of her.

Since Oams made a face at her and so she had to make one back, it was a moment before she returned her attention to Spindle. 'Sergeant. There's a monk in this carriage. I think he's a spy, tagging his wagon on the tail of a bunch of Rhivi traders. A clever ploy, but not clever enough.'

'I see.' Spindle squinted at the carriage. 'A monk, you said? Not two . . . necromancers?'

'Well, who knows who else is in there with him, Sergeant? Could be ten necromancers for all we know.'

'Why not wake up your warren and find out?'

'If I was a magic-user that's what I'd do all right.'

They stared at each other.

After a long moment, Spindle stepped past her and knocked on the carriage door. There followed muted sounds of locks and latches clunking and rasping, and then the side door opened a crack.

Stillwater drew her dagger. 'I could go in first, Sergeant, removing all threats. Shouldn't take long. But I get first claim on anything pretty inside. Or worth lots of coin.'

'I think not, Stillwater. That will be all.'

'You're dismissing me? Then going in alone?'

'I believe Oams could do with some assistance. Catch up with him and he'll explain.'

'But I was on gate duty.'

'And you're not there now, are you?'

'This was temporary, Sergeant. Should I really leave Anyx Fro all on her own back there? Her and her weasel?'

'Her what?'

'Her new pet weasel. We'll probably have to kill it. Don't you think I'd better get back there? I mean, after I'm confident you didn't get your throat slit inside the carriage?'

'And why would a monk slit my throat, Stillwater?'

She shrugged. 'Who can figure out the mind of a monk?'

Sighing, Spindle said, 'Very well. Since you seem to have a clear aversion to helping Oams, return to your post, Stillwater. As for me and my throat, on my head be it.'

Stillwater frowned at the faint smile on Spindle's face, but only for a moment. Sergeants were idiots. 'Yes, Sergeant, thank you, Sergeant. You're right, let's leave Oams all out on his own. It's all he deserves.' Smiling back at Spindle, she walked off.

Spindle turned, opened the carriage door, and clambered inside.

'Figured I'd find you here,' Oams said, sitting down opposite Benger. The Three-Legged Dog was Benger's favourite kind of tavern: the haunt of locals. Oams glanced around, making out figures in the gloom, hunched over small tables. *All six of them.* 'That is, if you're really here.'

'Of course I am,' Benger retorted with a scowl. 'Where else would I – oh, fine. You're right. I'm actually lying in my hidden room, playing with myself.'

'If you are, I'll have to head over there and start kicking through walls.'

'Are you sure you really want to do that? Think what you'd see if you found me. All right, that was just a joke.'

'Interesting that you admit to calling it a joke.'

'What?'

'You playing with yourself.'

Benger's scowl deepened. He sighed. 'Yes, I'm really here. Honest. You need to stop being so suspicious, Oams.'

'That's probably the stupidest thing I've ever heard you say.'

'So you found me. What do you want?'

Oams said nothing while the barkeep shuffled up and set down a tankard, pausing to lick spilled beer froth from his grubby hand before shuffling back to the bar.

'Take it as a good sign,' Benger observed, 'that he's actually drinking his own swill.'

'Should I?' Oams took a sip, grimaced, frowned, and then shrugged. 'Could be worse, but it ain't Malazan Dark.'

Benger snorted. 'You idiot. You never had Malazan Dark in your life and you know how I know that? If you'd had, you'd be dead.'

'Really. And why is that?'

Benger leaned forward. 'Malazan Dark is a joke, you see. An inside joke.'

'Inside what?'

'Deadhouse, is my bet. It's the drink of the Shadow Moon. A metaphor, right? Old soldiers who've just been through the worst shit they've

183

ever known, they'll say "but it ain't Malazan Dark". Get it?' Benger leaned back with a smirk. 'But here's the problem, Oams. Because I had to explain it, why, it loses all its power. So, if anyone asks me who messed up that old saying, why, I'll tell them. You.'

'Why is it that conversations with you turn out to be so frustrating?'

'Well, that's the problem, isn't it?'

Oams closed his eyes for a moment, and then sighed. 'Okay, what problem?'

Benger swallowed down a mouthful of ale. 'See that skull above the fireplace? See the skulls set in the stones around it? See that three-legged dog-hide hanging between the kitchen and the main room? Those, dear boy, are history. Right here. Teblor horses and hounds. Teblor skulls, in fact.'

'Karsa Orlong.'

'The God with the Shattered Face, aye. I get shivers just sitting here.'

'But here you're sitting.'

'Well, sure. I mean, I like shivers.'

Oams rubbed at his face. 'Fucking mages are so weird.' He settled back, thinking. *The problem, as Benger would say, with being haunted by a giant red-haired woman spirit, only really gets irritating when she has nothing to say. I can handle the rest, even her nightly embraces. Okay, especially her nightly embraces. Now that's a shiver to love. Icy, prickling, something sinking in. Spooning.* Two nights past she'd actually moved one of his arms out of the way, to better wrap round him. But nary a word, not even a whisper, or a warm breath against the ear. It was maddening.

Benger's strange huffing laugh made him look up. 'What now?'

'Whatever you're thinking's made her blush.'

'What? She's here? You can see her?'

'Soaking in your lust is my bet. Such a lively glow. You two want to borrow my secret room?'

'No point.' Oams drank some ale.

'There's more than one kind of sex, Oams.'

'What do you mean?'

'I mean, for some things out there, just touching your beating heart makes 'em squeal. Or feeling the heat from your body. Or sipping from the bowl of your life-force, for that matter.'

'You make her sound like a parasite.'

'Maybe that's exactly what she is. But no, you want to attach squishy sentiments to this whole thing. There are bats that nip the ankles of cows and then lick up the blood. Eels that ride the stream of your piss and live in your cock. Spike-worms that crawl into your ear and eat your ear-drum, make a cocoon out of wax, and then come out as a big yellow and black beetle that lives in your sinuses.'

'Spike-worms? I've never heard of spike-worms.'

'Falari Islands. Explains why most Falari are insane. My point is, she's getting *something* out of canoodling you. And what are you getting for all that attention? Scant little, is my bet.'

It was hard to argue against any of that. 'Gruff wants a head-count of the locals. Who can walk, who can't.'

Benger's eyes narrowed. 'Walk? Or run?'

'Well, we can start with walking, then worry about running later.'

His pitch dropping, Benger said, 'You know what this signifies, don't you? And it's your fault, the whole thing.'

'How's it my fault?'

'Because you scouted the woods.'

'And if I hadn't, Benger, we'd not know how bad it's gotten.'

'Exactly. Peace of mind.'

'Fatal delusion, you mean!'

Benger shrugged. 'Semantics.'

The tavern door creaked open and Oams shot a quick glance over a shoulder, and then turned back to Benger. 'Who else to help us?'

Benger's tone was strangely flat. 'The heavies. Paltry Skint, Say No, Daint, maybe Folibore. I'll send squirrels to mess their hair.'

'You'll what?'

Benger blinked. 'Sorry? I said I'll round them up.'

'That's not what you said.' After a moment, Oams turned around a second time. The woman he had just seen come into the tavern was now sitting alone at a table a half-dozen paces away. There was something odd about her. He faced Benger again. 'You're looking spooked.'

Benger's gaze flickered. 'Hairs rising on the back of your neck?'

'Now that you mention it.'

'Blood-oil.'

Oams started. He leaned forward. 'That's her? I've heard about her,' he whispered. 'Sells a hint of it.'

Benger's brows lifted. 'You want a taste?'

'No, I don't. The addiction spreads.'

'I'm sure she's kept busy, aye.'

'Poor woman,' Oams muttered. 'It'd be nice if something could be done for her.'

'There's ways,' Benger said, 'assuming she even wants it.'

'Why wouldn't she? There are? Ways?'

'High Denul, the highest.'

'You?'

'Maybe.' He shrugged. 'I'd be willing to give it a try. But it might cause trouble. Locally, I mean.'

'Ah, I see. Well, maybe bring it up with the captain. I mean, we're soldiers. If we ain't here to do some good, what's the point?'

Benger smiled. 'Oams, you're a rare one indeed. No wonder they kicked you out of the Claw.'

'I was never in the Claw. I don't know why people keep believing that nonsense. Now, you going to ask her if she wants help?'

'No. I'll wait for the captain's say-so.'

'He will.'

'I know.'

'Drink up,' said Oams, 'and let's get to work.'

Folibore accosted the man on the boardwalk that ran along the east side of the main street. 'You. You're number fifty-seven. Remember that number.'

The man stared.

'This won't work,' Blanket announced behind Folibore.

Folibore turned and scowled. 'You shouldn't have come along. Oams and Benger were very precise in who they volunteered for this. Me, not you. Daint, not Given Loud. See the pattern, Blanket?'

The man tried edging away but Folibore grasped his arm and yanked him back. 'Number fifty-seven.'

'Look,' said Blanket. 'I'll throw him to the ground and pin him. You carve the number into his forehead. Easier that way.'

'I broke my knife. Last night.'

'Doing what?'

'Never mind,' Folibore replied. 'The point is, I only have my sword.'

'I don't care how big you carve the number, Folibore.'

'I'm fifty-seven!' the man shouted.

'See, Blanket?' Folibore released the man. 'Let's go find another one.'

The man hurried off, skidding wildly across the muddy street, and then darted towards an alley. Folibore and Blanket watched until he was out of sight.

'He ain't forgetting nothing,' Blanket asserted. 'But how come I'm always playing the bloodthirsty one? Why don't we switch it up?'

'There are many points to your statement, Blanket. Let me address each one in turn.'

They set off down the street, eyes scanning for the next hapless citizen of Silver Lake. 'First off, you weren't volunteered. That alone puts you in a subservient position, here on my indulgence as it were. Two, it was my scheme, not yours, so I get to choose who says what.

Three, it's obvious that I'm nicer than you. Anyone can see that . . .' He paused and pointed at a woman rushing into the street to avoid meeting them. 'You!'

'Nineteen!' she shrieked.

'Hmm,' said Folibore, 'thought she looked familiar.'

'No she didn't. We've never seen her before. Something's awry here, Folibore.'

'And five, I'm the one who has to keep the count in his head. While you're here as potential back-up, you are in fact mostly redundant.'

'I have proof that I'm not redundant, Folibore. You missed number "four" in your points.'

'I didn't miss it, Blanket. Four is the basic fact that you actually *are* bloodthirsty. I figured we could take that as a given.'

'Me? The sword thing was your idea!'

'I really did break my knife last night.'

'Doing what?'

'Never mind,' Folibore replied. 'The point is, I only have my sword.'

Blanket frowned. 'You already said that. Those exact words. You just repeated yourself.'

'You started it.'

'I started it hoping, indeed, *expecting*, a different outcome.'

'And if bloodthirsty isn't egregious enough, you're also stupid. Really, Blanket, sometimes I despair.'

They rounded a corner and ran into Daint and Given Loud, grappling, hands about each other's throat.

'Hey!' barked Folibore.

The two heavies paused and looked over.

'You weren't volunteered, Given Loud. You shouldn't be here.'

'I got fourteen all on my own!' Given Loud snapped.

'And I got sixteen!' Daint retorted. 'Only what do I find? Some one-legged woman who's both fourteen and eight!'

Blanket frowned. 'One-legged? Really short hair, skew-eyed?' He looked at Folibore. 'But she's twenty-three.'

'My friends,' Folibore said, 'I believe we have stumbled upon a flaw in Blanket's scheme.'

'*My* scheme?'

'He has a point,' Daint said. 'I mean, how are these people going to remember all their numbers?'

The interior of the carriage was plush, the benches stacked with pillows, small lanterns hanging from hooks casting a yellow glow that played along the gilded edges of the woodwork. Other hooks near the back held a heavy brocaded curtain, drawn across the sleeping area. Thin brown pelts from some small creature had been stitched together to make a blanket, which was wrapped around the shoulders of the monk sitting opposite Spindle.

'Stillwater thinks you're a spy.'

'Those days are behind me.'

They were speaking Malazan. The monk lifted into view an ornate carafe and poured out two gold cups full of dark, thick liquid.

'What's that?' Spindle asked. 'Molasses?'

'Kelyk – oh, don't give me that face. This version's pretty much neutered. Not even harvested from leaking bodies any more. There was a god at the heart of that foul brew, remember. No longer.' He offered Spindle a cup. 'A touch bitter still, but pleasant in its own way.'

'I'll pass, thanks.'

'I should have thought of that. Bad memories.'

'What I remember is giving you a Hood-damned shake, Monkrat. I probably should have killed you outright. That's the punishment for desertion, after all.'

'You weren't a soldier of the empire at the time, I seem to recall. Lucky me.'

Spindle leaned back on his bench. 'Braven Tooth gave you that name, but it was just a name. Only now you're playing the role for real, it seems.'

'The Monk of Rats. And my cult is growing. Just think, Spindle, your old friend here is on his way to becoming a god.'

'I figured this was just a scam. You seem to be doing well by it. What happened after you left Black Coral?'

Monkrat sighed, sipped at the kelyk, and then sighed again. 'Dark days, darker nights. I faced my soul and found it wanting. Everything you said to me – you were right, and right to do it. And, in a way, you shoved me onto this path I'm now on.'

'You were being an asshole and I called you on it. That's it.'

'It's hard to believe,' Monkrat mused, eyes on the black liquid in the cup he cradled in his hands, 'some assholes will tell you they're assholes, with a gleam of . . . something . . . there in their eyes. Pride? Defiance? The silent scream of a desperate fool?'

'Usually all three.'

Monkrat nodded. 'It's pathetic, really, that pointless avowal. The pride is hollow, the defiance the thinnest shell. While the scream deafens.'

'You always had a way with words,' Spindle observed, 'when you bothered to use them.'

Monkrat shifted the cup to one hand and waggled the fingers of the other. 'See the stains? Not kelyk. Ink. I am writing my own Holy Book.'

'Had no recollection of you being the worshipping type.'

'Oh but I was, Spindle. I worshipped the worst in people. Gave me all the excuses I needed for being who I was, for everything I did. I bowed to the truth of misery and suffering, looking out only for myself.'

'Then it all changed.'

Monkrat half-smiled, not at Spindle, nor at anything in the carriage's chamber. Perhaps a memory, tinged with regret. It looked far away and long ago. 'The priestess of the Redeemer. Remember her? Poisoned with kelyk, dancing the dance of death and destruction.'

Spindle nodded.

'Imagine turning a thing of beauty into something like that.'

'I doubt she'd appreciate being called a thing, any more than you would, Monkrat.'

'I didn't mean her face or body. I didn't mean *her*, Spindle. I meant the dance, the ecstasy of worship. Falling into your god's lap – I saw that and it humbled me.'

Spindle's gaze narrowed. 'Exactly what manner of god are you hoping to become?'

'Does it matter? Braven Tooth named me Monkrat and you know why? I befriended a rat in the barracks, that's all. It'd been knocked in the head, wouldn't have survived if I didn't feed it and keep the ratters away. Anyway, it couldn't balance quite right on its hind legs. So it would dip all the time, as if bowing to me, while I fed it.'

'And how did Braven Tooth see all that? That man never left his office.'

'He didn't. And even stranger, he named me before any of it happened.'

'So, if he hadn't given you that name, you would never have befriended that addled rat? Is that what you're saying?'

'No. More like Braven Tooth could see into our souls. Knew who we were before we did.'

Spindle thought about it, and then shrugged. 'It's possible.'

'Then it was the flavour of my magic, taking me even deeper into all of that. I charmed rats, made use of them. I could ride each one, see through its eyes, hear what it heard.'

'Good for spying. Yet you joined the Bridgeburners.'

'I didn't join the Bridgeburners and neither did you. It grew up around us and you know it. And I found use for my talents anyway. Rats are the sapper's best friend, damn near kin, in fact.'

Spindle grunted.

'I went west,' Monkrat said. 'After Black Coral. Like everyone else, I was flush with the Redeemer's blessing. Made me wish I hadn't deserted when I did, made me wish I'd seen the god when he was just a man.'

'Itkovian. If you'd stayed, you probably would have died in the tunnels under Pale, long before we ever crossed Itkovian's path.'

Sudden fire lit Monkrat's dark eyes. 'Wrong. That's just it. You wonder what haunted me? What broke me? Think, Spindle! What do rats do before it all comes down?'

'They flee.'

'They would have come pouring out from those tunnels the moment Tayschrenn stepped out onto the battlefield! Don't you understand? I could've saved the Bridgeburners. I could've saved them all!'

Spindle sat back, slowly closed his eyes. Remembering . . . and then shutting those memories down. He opened his eyes again and looked on Monkrat. 'No point in thinking that, Monkrat. Besides, if not the tunnels under Pale, then some other catastrophe. The Empress wanted us gone. Or Tayschrenn did, as if the distinction matters. We were already dead and we knew it, and *that's* why you deserted. Our first rat to flee.'

Monkrat lowered his head and was silent.

'I don't think deciding to ascend works,' Spindle said quietly. 'You can't will yourself into becoming a god.'

Monkrat looked up, a speculative cast to his expression. 'You mean you don't – you haven't— Gods, Spindle, when did you last use your warren?'

'Years and years. No good ever came of it. Why?'

'So you don't know . . . you don't know *anything*!'

'What are you talking about?'

'The pantheon got blown apart – sure, you know that much, aye. But then new warrens arrived. Crazy ones, batshit *insane* ones. Gods fell, and new ones are rising. There are Dragon Decks out there with Houses you've never seen before – scores of them!' He paused to toss down the kelyk and then reached for the second cup. 'Never mind the Runts,' he added, wiping his mouth.

'The what?'

Monkrat's eyes flickered. He rose from the bench and slid open a small panel in the carriage wall behind him and then swung back round cradling a small box made from lacquered wood. Sitting down again, he shook the box.

Spindle heard clattering within. 'Coins?'

'Yes. No. Runts. Not currency—' he rasped a laugh. 'Not in any sane way, I mean. Those new warrens – oh, some Deck Mancers have tried working them in, but it's an awkward fit. No, these warrens use the Runts for divination.' He set the box down on his lap and carefully unlatched it. 'I've done my readings and nothing's changed. I'm not doing one now.' He glanced up with almost fevered eyes. 'They're a bit wild, those readings. Worse, time drags while doing it.'

'It drags how, exactly— No.' Spindle shook his head. 'Never mind. I'm not that interested, to be honest.'

Monkrat drew out a few of the coins. Spindle saw flashes of silver, gold, iron and copper. 'The metal's important, aspected, in fact. So, some Runts have one kind of metal on one face and another on the opposite face.' He grimaced. 'That's why they don't work well as currency.'

'I see a gold one there, both sides.'

Monkrat plucked it from the others and tossed it over.

Catching it one-handed, Spindle drew it close. 'This is solid gold.' The face he looked at showed a spoked wheel, not as lines but as tiny bumps. 'White gold.'

'Aye. Starwheel. And the other side?'

Spindle flipped it and his brows lifted. 'A red tinge to the gold. Showing a sword. Single-edged.'

'Fury,' said Monkrat. 'Icari's own blade.'

'Icari? Icarium? Ah, *Runts*.'

'Some say he created these new warrens – they're not all new, of course, but even the familiar ones are twisted. Light and Dark, Life and Death, they don't go where they're supposed to.'

Spindle tossed the coin back. 'I'm surprised those ones aren't melted down. The weight of that's easily ten Daru Councils.'

'Closer to twelve, but it's a known curse to melt these things down, or split the facings, or hammer them flat, cut them in half, spit on them, or gamble with them. As for damning the dead, why, imagine placing face-up Oblivion, or Misfortune, in the corpse's mouth. Vicious. Still, there are hawkers selling curse-Runts for precisely that. It's an abuse. I wouldn't do it, and I wouldn't buy one from them either.'

Spindle shrugged. 'Things change. The world changes. But what changes here may not be the same as what changes somewhere else. I don't think—'

Monkrat cut him off. 'Do you think I've just been wandering the Rhivi Plains for ten fucking years? Spindle, I went to Seven Cities. I only returned a couple of years back. The Crow Cult – that's *Coltaine* they're worshipping! It's swept the entire continent! And there are others. Icari with and without the Runts, Twice Alive, Iskar Jarak—'

'I know who Iskar Jarak is, Monkrat.'

'And his Knights of Death? They're fucking *Bridgeburners*.'

'So you missed your chance.'

'I didn't, Spindle. That's just my point. Didn't you feel it flow over us? Us Bridgeburners still living? Have you even a clue what I'm talking about?'

'You deserted.'

'It didn't matter.'

Now it was Spindle's turn to look away, and memories he had pushed to the back of his mind returned and there was no stopping them. Moon's Spawn, broken and dying, weeping an ocean of tears onto the battered plain. The dead Bridgeburners interred within, an unexpected blessing, and something cool, soothing as a balm, flowing into him, easing the grief, the terrible loss.

And he'd seen, in the eyes of the others – Picker, Antsy, Blend, all of the ones left alive – how it flowed through them as well.

And down came the black rain. And later, we each offered the Redeemer what we had, our frail tokens, to build his barrow. We walked among the living, us handful of survivors, like ghosts.

Only to then blow away, scattered to the winds.

He faced Monkrat again. 'You felt it?'

'Hungover and fevered in an alley in Mott. Something cool kissed my brow. Something seeped down into me. I felt it, aye, and thought it some god's bitter mockery.' He cocked his head. 'And you? Did you know it for what it was?'

'No. I doubt any of us did. We were . . . numb. Broken. Ruined, in fact.'

'And now?'

'Sometimes I feel . . . watched over.' Abruptly he shook his head. 'Just a feeling.'

'Not just a feeling, Spindle. Come now, think, man! The Limping Soldier at Death's Gate, that's *Whiskeyjack*. And they're with him. Our friends who died. They're all with him. They were *blessed* in Moon's Spawn.'

'Who blessed them in Moon's Spawn?' Spindle demanded. 'Not the Redeemer. Not Caladan Brood.'

'Twice Alive,' Monkrat replied. 'Ganoes Fucking Paran, Master of the Deck.'

'What makes you so sure?'

Monkrat shrugged. 'The flavour. No,' he amended. 'I don't know for sure. Just a feeling, Spindle. Who else was there? Who else had the power to bless? It was Paran.'

'You weren't even there.'

'No matter. I talked to enough people who were.'

Spindle was unconvinced, although he could not be certain why. 'Could have been Korlat, who gave her heart to Whiskeyjack. Could have been Anomander Rake himself.'

But Monkrat shook his head. 'That would taste of Kurald Galain. This blessing was clean. Fired by grief and regret. Why don't you believe me?'

'Captain Paran became the Master of the Deck, aye. And now he's ascended. Now he's Twice Alive, Lord of Divination, Guardian of the Deck. A god like that isn't about blessing. He's about sanctification. Of invested cards and Houses and all of that.'

Monkrat's gaze had narrowed. 'So you're not as uninterested as you make out to be, are you?'

'I just think the Bridgeburners began their own path to Ascendancy long before then. In Seven Cities. And that's why the Empress needed to destroy us. She witnessed Kellanved's trouble with the Logros T'lan Imass. She didn't want a repeat of that.'

Monkrat smiled, leaning back. 'Then she was a fool, Spindle. Killing us just pushed us all the faster into Ascendancy. The T'lan Imass? Interesting comparison. Just think. A thousand years from now some fool necromancer will call upon the Knights of Death, and some damned army of undead will show up. Iron swords instead of flint, but otherwise? Probably damned near identical to the T'lan Imass. Some ideas are so deadly you just can't keep 'em down.'

The notion left Spindle shaken. *Is that where we're headed, us few Bridgeburners still among the living? Whiskeyjack, did you really want your own army of undead? Are you actually* happy *about all this?* He scowled at Monkrat. 'What are you doing here?'

'There are rats in the forest.'

'We know—'

'No, I really do mean rats. Tundra rats. Big bastards, thick fur, pick a body clean in a dozen heartbeats. I was on the Rhivi Plains, you see, and my power is – well, I can sense rats. I know, weird, but that's how I am now. Anyway. Those Tundra rats – the Saemdhi call them *vel'ay*, by the way – they're on the run, down from the north. They've come as far as the Rhivi Plains already. On the run, Spindle.'

'From what?'

Monkrat shrugged. 'Something bad. So, here I am, then. First to flee the first time around, and now, the first to tell you, *flee, Spindle. In Iskar Jarak's name, get the fuck out of here!*'

CHAPTER TWELVE

If you draw near
My dark fire
Be warned of
Unpleasant heat
I linger for but a moment
On the staircase
Until my breath resumes
And with each
I am lifted
To the next step

I have little tolerance
For deflection
These games
Of intellectual dishonesty
You wrap round
The grisly confessions
Chorused in your
Legion of fears
And blades of cold hate
When into my wake you go

Fool's Debate
Simaron

MALAZAN MARINES – THOSE NOT ON PATROL OR GATE OR tower duty – crowded the Three-Legged Dog tavern. Accordingly, the locals had fled, all of them shouting out various numbers as they did so.

Folibore cleared his throat and then said, 'I would like to call this meeting to order—'

'Will you shut your trap, Folibore!' Oams snapped. 'Listen, all of you. This wasn't a hard mission. So how in the Weeping Child's name did you manage to utterly mangle it beyond all recognition?'

Folibore pursed his lips and said, 'Which one of us would you like to start?'

Oams put his hands to his face. 'Gods below,' he muttered.

'I would suggest seniority,' offered Blanket. 'Only, the four of us heavies all joined up at the same time. As for Benger, well, who knows? Now Oams, Oams has been at this a long time, I'm sure. Longer than any of us, given his Claw origins.'

'*I was never a Claw!*'

Everyone nodded, and Blanket continued, 'So I think it comes down to Benger or Oams, but since it was Oams who asked for an explanation, well, that eliminates him. Unless he wants to explain the debacle to himself, in which case I think the rest of us should head off to the Black Eel and leave him to sort out the mess.'

'It's got to be Benger, then,' said Folibore. 'By process of elimination.'

'And seniority,' Daint chimed in.

'And seniority, Daint, yes.'

Oams thumped his palms down on the table, making everyone start. 'It was supposed to be on the sly. Quiet, no fanfare. A basic head-count and a handful of salient details like who's housebound or crippled or blind, and the number of children under marching age.'

'"Salient",' said Given Loud, brows lifting. 'Now that's a complication.'

'It is,' Folibore agreed. 'Open to an array of interpretations.'

Oams's palms slammed the tabletop again. 'Only there's the mayor chasing me down in a blind panic,' he ground on, 'because the story's out they're all being evacuated. Probably at sword-point. Off to the mines—'

'What mines?' Daint asked. 'I didn't know there were mines.'

'*There aren't any mines!*'

The door opened and in strode Stillwater, Anyx Fro and So Bleak. More chairs were dragged across the filthy floor. Armour clanked as the three newcomers settled down.

Anyx smiled at Oams, and then stuffed her mouth full of rustleaf, her face getting paler the longer she chewed.

Oams stared in distracted fascination, until So Bleak cleared his throat and spoke.

'There are two thousand two hundred and eighteen residents of Silver Lake.'

'But I only got to twenty-nine,' said Folibore.

'Sure,' Daint cut in, 'but your Twenty-Nine was my Seventeen, Given's Twelve, and—'

'Be quiet, please!' Oams begged. He faced So Bleak. 'And how did you get that count?'

'I asked the undertaker. He keeps a list, and it gets better.'

'Better how?'

'Precise numbers, Oams. There are two hundred and nineteen children under the age of eight. Another three hundred and fifty-seven between ages eight and sixteen—'

'This town's gone fuck-crazy!' Stillwater exclaimed.

Oams pounded the table a third time and then pointed at So Bleak. 'How does the undertaker know all of that?'

'It's obvious,' offered Paltry Skint. 'Fiscal projections to establish the expected timeline of supply and demand. Coffins.'

A long moment of silence, and then So Bleak said, 'No, not that. The undertaker's also the local healer.'

Anyx grunted and spat a brown stream onto the floor and then said, 'So he's a bit of a pessimist, is he?'

'Let's get back to the fuck-crazy,' insisted Stillwater. 'I'm right, aren't I? That's a whole lot of little people!'

So Bleak raised a hand. 'It is. But after the first raid, there were lots of dead locals. And then after the Uprising, even more dead locals. The past mayor started paying women to have babies and the present mayor continued the practice.'

Anyx snorted. 'There's better ways of getting women pregnant.'

Stillwater tried slapping Anyx but missed. 'He didn't personally stick coins up their baskets, did he?' Then she paused and looked round. 'Did he? Check those babies, So Bleak, see if they all look like the mayor.'

'He paid them to get pregnant,' explained So Bleak. 'He didn't *get* them all pregnant.'

'How much did he pay them, So Bleak?' Anyx demanded, and then looked around. 'Hey, if it's a lot—'

'You're not a local, idiot!' Stillwater said. 'The mayor won't pay you to get pregnant, understand? Besides, if he did, the rest of us – who know you – would all chip in to pay you even more *not* to get pregnant. Why? Because one idiot leaf-chewing cow looking like you is enough, that's why!' Then she faced Oams. 'So I heard we're executing all the locals anyway, is that right? I'm all for it – where do I start?'

'We're not executing anyone!' Oams shouted.

Stillwater blinked. 'Oh, well, how about just one? I volunteer Anyx Fro, *before* the mayor gets her pregnant.'

Anyx snorted. 'I'm not a local, and besides, you're all about to make me rich. Unless the mayor's good-looking.'

Folibore leaned forward and said, 'She has a point, Stillwater. About not being local, I mean. Not the getting rich thing, however. After all, her getting pregnant means she gets booted from the marines and while that's sad, it's not that sad. Besides, the mayor's ugly. In any case, I recommend we kill the undertaker last.'

'That makes sense,' said Stillwater, nodding. 'Not all of it. Some of it. You're getting better, Folibore.'

'No,' said Oams, close to weeping. 'None of it makes sense.'

'I'm not getting pregnant, then,' said Anyx Fro. 'Besides, I wouldn't want an *ugly* mayor's baby no matter how much he paid me.'

'Well that's just great,' moaned Blanket. 'Now we've got a heart-broken mayor to deal with on top of everything else.'

Stillwater nodded. 'Poor mayor.'

Oams stood up. 'So Bleak, come with me to report back to the captain, will you?'

So Bleak shook his head. 'No need. I already did.'

'So I'm off the hook?'

'You are, Oams. And you're welcome.'

'Bless you, So Bleak, and never mind what your squad-mates all say about you.'

'Wait – what do they all say?'

Oams stepped round the table and briefly settled a commiserating hand on So Bleak's shoulder as he walked off. A moment later he was out the door.

No one spoke for a time, and then Daint sighed. 'That was fun.' He straightened and looked around. 'Where's the bartender gone?'

'He ran out,' said Blanket, 'around the time Stillwater passed on the news about us executing all the locals.'

'So . . . free drinks!'

'No, Stillwater, we can't do that.'

She glared at Folibore. 'Why not?'

'Because they'll take it out of our pay, that's why. As soon as the confusion is all cleared up and people can start breathing easy again, the owner will be back, and if he finds his casks all empty, he'll report it and deliver a tab to the captain and then we'll all be in trouble.'

Stillwater frowned at him. 'You mean we're not killing all the locals? This is no fun. We *never* have any fun any more!'

Amiss sat with her sisters at a table in the Black Eel. They were all eyeing the lone marine at a nearby table, who was sitting far enough away not to hear them talk about him, and other things related to the marines. Even so, his presence was unnerving.

Lope, the youngest of the sisters, was pouring cheap wine into her hookah. Her eyes were glazed but that was pretty normal for her, and it didn't help that they were a dull green, like dusty leaves. After two bowls of rustleaf, her voice was raspy as she said, 'We can't trust them. It's not like how it used to be.'

Amiss rolled her eyes. 'You're barely seventeen years old, Lope. How would you know anything about how it used to be?'

'When Bliss Rolly drinks too much, it's me she talks to.'

'That's because you look innocent,' said Flown. 'You're not, of course. In fact, you're the worst of us.'

'That's beside the point,' Lope said. 'It used to be that the legions or even the armies had just a handful of mages. High mages. Scary as shit. Oh, there were always a few others in among the squads, but they were low-grades. Little bits of this and that. Now that's all changed. No more High Mages – the Emperor knows he can't trust them. So he took the marines and packed them full of low-grades and some a little bit nastier, too. Magic fucking everywhere.'

'It's down to the Moranth munitions drying up,' said Amiss. 'Sure, we're now making our own but those aren't as reliable. So, if the marines still want to be a gnarly fist that punches through the enemy, they need to compensate for the loss of the Moranth munitions. Mages instead of sappers, got it?'

'Who's doing the explaining here?' Lope demanded behind a fresh cloud of sickly-sweet smoke. She squinted over at the lone marine. 'And he's a mage.'

Flown grunted. 'Shows no sign of that.'

'Of course not,' Lope replied. 'That's the point. If I had to guess, I'd say more than half of the marines now here are mages of some kind.'

'If you had to guess?'

Lope scowled at Amiss. 'Fine, that was Bliss Rolly's guess. You got problems with that, take it up with her.'

Three newcomers entered the tavern. Amiss carefully collected up her tankard and drank. Lope made more clouds. Flown hunched her shoulders and leaned forward onto the table, reaching for the pitcher. In a low tone, she said, 'That's unexpected.'

'Balk's Company,' muttered Lope. 'Had to happen sooner or later. Even mercenaries got to drink every now and then.'

'Ha ha,' Amiss said in a flat tone. 'Storp said they'd been buying casks from him and carrying them back to their camp. No, those three, they're fishing.'

'Heard a rumour,' said Lope, pausing to pull on her mouthpiece.

'Our drunk sergeant again?'

Lope shrugged. 'Maybe. They got a scout of theirs killed by a marine on watch. All a terrible accident, apologies all around. Thing is, it was brutal work. Eye-popping brutal.'

Now that was interesting. Amiss studied her sister. 'Go on. Eye-popping how?'

'Like the body showed up in one bag, the head in another.'

There was silence at the table for a long moment.

Lope grinned. 'That's right. Be careful about walking up behind a marine and tapping a shoulder. Reflex motion: sword out and straight across your neck and your head rolls and that's that. "Oops," says the marine.' She held up two fingers. 'Two bags.'

'Which marine?' Flown asked.

'Does it matter?'

They fell silent as the mercenaries, each carrying a tankard of ale, now walked over to the table next to the three sisters.

Two men and a woman. The woman looked half-drunk already, and something about all three made the hairs crawl on the back of Amiss's neck.

'Regulars,' said the woman, 'right? Pleased to meet you – you look like sisters. I had a sister once. She drowned in a pond. Five years old. Broke Mother's heart.'

'Terrible,' said Amiss. 'Sorry for you and your mother.'

'I was only a year older,' the woman went on. 'Tried reaching out to her when she fell off the bank we were on. Missed. I knew how to swim, but it was a long drop. I was too scared to jump. By the time I climbed down, it was too late.'

'Bet that broke your heart, too,' Lope said tonelessly.

The woman shrugged. 'Might have. Little girls, they get over things fast, don't they? I'm Sergeant Stick. This is Sugal and Bray. We lead companies in Balk's legion.'

'Legion?'

'About right, numbers-wise,' the man named Sugal said.

Lope grunted. 'And that's all it takes to make a legion, does it? Numbers.'

Sugal's answering smile was without humour. 'Before the empire here coughed up a contract, we'd hammered those fucking marines – if you'll pardon my language, and being regulars, I'm sure you will. Strange, isn't it, how you're cutting up someone one day, then marching beside them the next.'

'Coin is coin,' said the woman, Stick, draining her tankard. 'It's all down to being professional.'

'Heard one of those marines said hello to one of your scouts the other night,' said Lope in a drawl.

Nothing much changed in the expressions of the three sergeants and that detail alone sent a chill through Amiss.

Stick twisted round towards Storp who was behind the bar. 'Another ale, keep!' She swung back. 'Those marines aren't your friends,' she said. 'But we might be. That's why I'd like to buy you three a round of drinks. Then we can get all friendly.'

'How did it feel?' Lope asked.

'How did what feel?'

'Pushing your sister over that bank. Into the pond. Watching her drown. How did all that feel?'

Amiss was fast drawing her knife, but the bigger man, Bray, was faster. The table skidded hard towards them, driven by a kick, and two long-knives flickered in the dull, low light as Bray advanced a step.

The table had jostled all three sisters, but their blades were out, the only problem being the wall at their backs.

Fuck. Those long-knives weren't bar-room weapons. *He's going to gut the three of us like fucking fish on a dock.*

Stick was standing back, a smile playing on her lips. Sugal had a short-axe in one hand, ready to slide in behind Bray.

Then someone calmly strode between them.

The marine. 'That's enough,' he said.

Bray raised his long-knives, his teeth bared and his eyes glittering.

'No, you don't want to try,' the marine said.

'You think you can draw that stupid short-sword before I cut you open?' Bray asked, his smile broadening.

'Not a chance,' the marine replied. 'But if you look back to the bar, you'll see Storp has his crossbow out and he's aiming at the back of your head. I suppose you can try ducking, but I doubt that'll work. Besides which, by then, I'll be busy killing your two companions, and no, I don't need a short-sword to do that.'

Bray didn't seem like he was going to back off. Instead, he looked a moment away from charging the marine.

Then Stick said, 'Relax, Bray. I was the one insulted by that smoky kitten over there, not you, and I'm already over it. Sheathe the blades, friend, and pull us that table back so we can sit and—'

'No,' cut in the marine. 'You can get the fuck out. Captain Gruff's orders. No mercenaries in the town. Storp sends you ale and wine and you get fed right in your camp.'

Stick smiled. 'All right. Can I get your name, Marine? You know, for the next time we meet. I'm Stick.'

The marine smiled. 'See? That wasn't hard. I'm Clay Plate, Second Squad. Next time we meet, be sure and say hello.'

'Oh I will,' said Stick. She waved to her companions. 'Let's go.'

'Pay up what you owe first,' Clay Plate added. 'Keep Storp happy.'

'Aye,' said Stick, 'we'll do that.'

Heart still pounding hard in her chest, Amiss slid her knife back into its scabbard, and then sat. After a moment her sisters followed suit.

Clay Plate returned the other table to its proper place. He paused to watch the mercenaries leave, and then dragged a chair up and sat down, facing Amiss. He smiled.

'Two of you were pretty obnoxious to one of my squad-mates that first night.'

'Apologies,' said Amiss. 'We've been here too long.'

Clay Plate nodded. 'That happens. I just want to clear things up here, if you don't mind?'

Flown opened both hands in an inviting gesture.

'You're regulars in the Malazan Army. Yes, it's not the most exciting posting you could've gotten. But that don't matter, and that especially don't matter to us marines. While we're here, we've got you all nice and warm' – he gestured, one finger poking beneath his vest – 'right here. Cosy as can be.' He then jerked a thumb to the door behind him. 'Those three. Paint stripes on 'em. They're not right.'

'I noticed,' said Amiss, her mouth dry.

Clay Plate then pointed at Lope. 'Just because you've sniffed out what's true about that drowned sister, don't mean you have to say it out loud. But you know that, yet you did it anyway. Almost got you and your sisters killed. That's stupid. Stick'll come for you sooner or later. Because you saw through her charm, saw what she thinks she can keep hidden from everybody.' He rose. 'We'll keep a close eye on proceedings, but be careful.'

'I can take care of myself,' said Lope.

'Oh, lass, she won't go *straight* for you. She'll kill your sisters first, to make sure you suffer. And your friends, too.'

Lope went pale, and she half rose. 'Fine, I'll cut her to pieces first—'

After both Amiss and Flown had dragged Lope back down, Clay Plate smiled again. 'Patience, soldier. It's not time to heat things up. Not yet.'

They watched him return to his lone table where, after a moment, Storp joined him.

Lope relit her hookah with shaky hands.

Turning on her, Amiss said, 'They would've killed us and you know it.'

After a moment, Lope gusted out smoke and nodded. 'Sorry, sisters, I pushed too hard. That woman, though.'

Flown sighed. 'You know, I hate to say this, but being tucked inside that marine's vest, up in his no doubt smelly armpit, well, it feels pretty good right about now.'

Amiss nodded. 'Amen to that.'

Spindle stepped into the office. Captain Gruff had his vambraces out on the table, working in a red-ochre stain, polishing until the leather gleamed. His long fingers looked to have been dipped in blood. 'Dearest Spindle, glad to see you alive. Please sit. There is wine. It's not good wine, but it's wine.'

Spindle slowly sat but shook his head at the offer of wine.

Gruff glanced up. 'Well?'

'About as expected, sir.'

'And?'

'He wants us to run, sir.'

Sighing, Gruff leaned back. He frowned briefly at his crimson fingers. 'Heartfelt advice, I'm sure. Alas, not a soldier's lot. He came for you in person, yes?'

'I suppose so,' Spindle replied, shrugging slightly.

'Bit of a risk for a deserter. After all, you're obliged to kill him on sight.'

Spindle glanced away. 'Sometimes, sir, mercy does more to punish than killing.'

'But the lesson is surely lost on others.'

'Only you and me, sir, know who Monkrat once was. Now, he's the Monk of Rats. A self-proclaimed Ascendant, closing in on godhood. If I had a concern, it's what his past is doing to his present. Hard to know precisely what kind of god he'll turn out to be.'

'Hmm, perhaps you should have killed him after all, as an act of mercy to the rest of us.'

'He came with good intentions, sir. I have to honour that.'

Gruff sighed, and then lathered out another lump of red staining grease. 'Since you put it with such delicacy, I have no choice but to respect the compact between the two of you. Hence, I'll not cut his throat.' He fluttered shiny fingers. 'He can leave in peace.'

Spindle nodded. 'Thank you, sir.'

'Assuming, of course,' Gruff went on, 'you can satisfy me in explaining what really drew him here, beyond that simple warning – and speaking of that, does he count us blind fools? No matter. The rest, dear Sergeant, the rest.'

This is a man you can't dance around. Not that way, at least. 'The Ascendancy of the Bridgeburners, sir.'

'Iskar Jarak's Dead Legion? What of it?'

'Not just the dead ones, it seems. I would think that's what's propelled Monkrat to what – and who – he is right now.' Spindle hesitated, and then added, 'There's not many of us left this side of Death's Gate, but it seems that none of us were left out of . . . whatever happened after Black Coral.'

Gruff was nodding, his eyes closed, his hands still on the vambrace he held. 'Your confession, and its implication, does not surprise me, beloved. Anything else?'

'He tossed me a Runt.'

Sudden attention, Gruff's eyes glittering. 'I have been led to believe you knew nothing of such things.'

'I didn't. I don't. He explained it, and I still don't.' *Led to believe? In what way? By whom?*

'Yet you inform me of this detail. Why?'

Spindle shrugged. 'Instinct, sir. Something told me it needed saying.'

'It did. It does.' Gruff smiled, but it was a cold smile. 'Which Runt, if I may ask? You need not answer, since such things are private, and privacy demands respect.'

'Starwheel.'

'You are certain? When you first beheld the coin in your hand, it was the Starwheel face? Not the face of Fury?'

'Aye, sir. A wagon-wheel made of dots.'

'Not dots, my friend. Boulders. The Starwheel lies upon the ground, forever facing the sky.'

'Ah,' said Spindle. 'I've seen a few of those. Somewhere.'

'Ever walked within one?'

Spindle scowled. 'I'm not an idiot, sir.'

'Of course not. Forgive me. These new warrens are fraught, often fundamentally misunderstood. I am tempted, I do admit, to visit your monkish friend.'

'For a casting? He'll ask for gold. Lots of it.'

'They always do.' Gruff set down the vambrace. 'These are perfect. Now it's time for the breastplate. I foresee a long evening of rubbing and caressing.' The look he shot Spindle now was sly. 'Best leave now, yes?'

Lieutenant Ara led the three company commanders into Balk's command tent. At a gesture they halted a few paces in, Stick wavering slightly amidst the fumes of alcohol.

Balk, seated on a camp stool, regarded the three in silence for a long moment, and then said, 'Lieutenant Ara has delivered the report of your fishing venture, passing on to me all that you said to her. Not difficult, since you said very little. Sugal, you seem the least inebriated, so I will ask you to elaborate, in detail, the events as they occurred at the Black Eel.'

'Yes, sir,' Sugal replied. 'We'd thought to sow some discord, maybe get the regulars on our side of things. Or at least stir things up a bit.'

'The regulars?'

Sugal nodded.

'All seven of them. Well, yes indeed,' Balk said, his tone dripping, 'that would shake things up all right.'

Sugal shifted uneasily. 'We knew it could go the other way, and figured that wasn't bad, either. Three dead regulars. In answer for the man we lost, you see.'

'I'm confused,' Balk said, glancing over at Lieutenant Ara. 'Do you recall, Ara, me voicing the opinion or the desire for some kind of retribution for the death of our night-knife?'

'No, sir.'

'Mhmm, yes. In fact, I seem to recall saying something about patience in this matter.'

'You were explicit in that, sir,' said Ara.

Stick suddenly snorted. 'Fucking marines are down to a handful, sir, because we cut 'em to pieces. They aren't nothing to be afraid of—'

'You stupid, drunk idiot,' Balk said, his tone hard as iron. He rose. 'Shall we return to that day? Our clash with that undermanned company of Malazan marines?'

'We cut down two-thirds of them!' Stick said in a belligerent rasp.

Balk stepped in front of her. 'So we did. Hardly surprising, since there were a thousand of us. And afterwards, after they'd forced Ara into laying down arms, did you take note of our losses? No, I didn't think so. You three, commanding companies in my legion, don't give a fuck about your own losses. Very well, allow me to inform you of the total body-count incurred during our engagement with *fifty* marines.'

'We had 'em, sir,' hissed Stick, glaring at Ara.

'Three hundred and nineteen dead,' Balk said. 'Seventy-three wounded and of those, only ten able to fight again. Ever. You three, so fucking busy chasing down their flankers in the bushes, weren't even there to see those marines take out entire squads, one after another. And defending only, mind you, as they held us in place while three of their squads went around us – somehow – and took down my guards and put a knife to my throat.' He stepped right up to Stick, one finger pressing against her chest, forcing her back a step. '*Defending* action. Not counter-attacking, which they should have done – perhaps even would have – except for the orders they had to take me alive.'

Balk moved back to his stool, visibly trembling with rage. 'So,' he said in a calmer tone, 'you found three regulars in the tavern. Why aren't they dead?'

Sugal cleared his throat. 'There was a marine who got in the way. We could've taken him, sir, but we were mindful of your orders not to bother with the marines.'

'And that damned keeper behind the bar,' Stick added. 'Crossbow trained on us.'

'Storp, you mean,' Balk said, turning to face them again. Three nods answered him. 'Malazan Second or Third Army veteran.'

'Old as fuck,' Stick said. 'Next time, Sugal will just camp out in his face—'

'There will not be a second time,' said Balk. 'You three, like everyone else in this camp, are *restricted* to this camp. Disobey and you won't just be stripped of your rank. You will be executed. Am I understood?'

Ara saw Stick's mouth twist into a sneer, but the fear was bright in the eyes of all three commanders. The acknowledgements came reluctantly, first from Sugal, then Bray, and finally, Stick.

'Get out of my tent,' said Balk.

They were gone in a moment.

'That was close,' said Ara after the tent flaps had settled. 'The leashes are fraying on those three.'

Balk grunted, sitting back down on the stool. 'Not much longer, or so I have been assured.'

'I hope you're right,' said Ara.

'I wonder,' Balk muttered.

'You wonder what?'

'Well, which lone marine it was who made them back down. Even with Storp and his crossbow.'

'I would think,' Ara ventured, 'one of the ones we know about. Stillwater, maybe. Or Oams. Or Benger.'

'If there comes a day when we cut those leashes, Ara, we point them straight at those three. Understood?'

She nodded. 'And let's hope they all kill each other.'

'That would be perfect,' said Balk. 'In the meantime,' he met her gaze, 'be careful, Ara. They already hated you. And now, having brought them to me after this debacle, they hate you all the more.'

'I know.'

'You advised we kill them weeks past,' Balk observed. 'I rejected that, and still do. But the longer I wait, the more in danger you get. I don't like this, Ara. I want you to understand that. For now, I need them.'

'And me, Balk? Do you need me?'

'Yes, I need you. More than I need them. Tonight, I almost decided to gut all three and have done with it. The only thing that stayed my hand is the notion of using them against the three nastiest marines we know of – if they fail, I won't belabour the loss. If we're lucky, they'll at least wound the enemy.'

'The simple distraction might be enough,' said Ara.

'Soon,' Balk muttered.

'Do you wish to be alone?' Ara asked.

'Not tonight, no.'

She reached up to remove her cloak.

Spindle found Oams and Benger at a table near the back wall of the Three-Legged Dog. The two men fell quiet as he sat down facing them.

'Well done on the head-count,' Spindle said to Oams.

'But I—'

'So Bleak told me you sent him to the undertaker. That was clever.' He paused and then shrugged. 'Getting the heavies involved in anything logistical was my mistake. Though I'm sure they had fun screwing it all up.'

Benger snorted. 'You shoulda heard 'em, Sergeant. It was a fuckin' opera.'

'But I didn't—'

Spindle cut in again, 'It's time for you to ride, Oams.'

Oams blinked. 'Aye, sir.' Then he frowned. 'You said "ride". So, not the forest again.'

Benger punched Oams on the shoulder. 'Get the cobwebs outa your head, idiot.' He squinted at Spindle. 'On the quiet, right? I'll need to think on that.'

'Think fast,' Spindle said. 'I want him out tonight.'

'Man and horse together won't be easy,' Benger mused. 'All the way out and past Balk's camp. That's not seeing and not hearing, maybe even not smelling. And if they got extended pickets we're talking near two thousand paces. Minimum.'

'I don't smell that bad,' Oams said, scowling.

'And if your horse farts? Sergeant, I can glamour things, but I'm thinking a diversion. Something to get everybody hunkering down.'

Oams groaned. 'Not this again, Benger.'

After a moment, Spindle nodded. 'Very well. Get Undercart in on this. Oams, gather your gear and meet us at the stables.'

Oams was glaring at Benger. 'How many ponchos am I going to need this time?'

Benger's teeth flashed in a grin, his shoulders hunching in his huffing laugh. 'We're going to have to wake up Undercart. You know what he's like when he wakes up.'

'You're doing this on purpose,' Oams accused in a harsh whisper. 'I can see it in your eyes, Benger. You could glamour this all on your own and you know it.'

'Better safe than sorry,' Benger replied, suddenly serious.

When Spindle rose, the others did the same.

Oams and Benger left coins on the bar counter, since the proprietor had yet to return.

Corporal Undercart sat at the table in the main room of the commandeered building, one long end of his moustache in his mouth. Apart from the rhythmic bunching of his jaw muscles and the strange chewing sounds, he was both silent and motionless.

Benger sat opposite, fingers tapping the tabletop.

The corporal stirred. 'My skull's about to explode.'

'What are you calling up?'

'Haven't started yet. The warren's fighting me.'

'Why?'

Undercart shrugged. 'Happens sometimes, especially Blueiron. I have a theory.'

'Oh wonderful, let's hear it while Oams waits outside.'

'I'm detecting contradictory sentiments in that invitation, Benger. Would you care to clarify?'

'No, and don't even think of punching me in the side of the head. I ain't in your squad.'

Undercart leaned forward, still chewing on his moustache. He tapped his temple. 'Lightning in here, Benger. It's how our bodies work.'

'Oh really?'

'Aye, or so I theorize. I've seen experiments, made with lodestones and copper wire. I've seen the dismembered legs of frogs made to twitch.'

'What kind of fucked-up brain thought up *that* experiment? Never mind. Just kick your way in and let's get on with this.'

'My point is,' Undercart went on, 'you can overload – in your head – if you're not careful, and the Blueiron opens up too fast, too strong. You waking me up means I'm tired and tired means I can't keep my walls up – the walls that protect my sanity—'

'Those failed years ago. Hurry the fuck up, will you? We need the darkness. Oams needs it. I need it!'

'Fine! But I want healing right afterwards.'

Benger rolled his eyes.

'Promise me, Benger!'

'All right! I'll heal your poor hollow achy head.'

From outside came the dull rumble of thunder.

Benger grunted and then said, 'That's a league or more away. Pull it in, Undercart. Right on top of us.'

The corporal shook his head. 'And Oams rides out under it? Do you hate him or something?'

Benger grinned. 'He'll get soaked through and won't be able to get outa the saddle for half the night at least. He'll chafe something awful and won't get any decent healing for who knows how long. It's perfect!'

'And you have the nerve to call *me* insane?' Undercart shook his head a second time.

When the storm broke above the town, Oams bellowed a curse as lightning flared and then cracked like the snapping of a giant god's bones. Thunder descended somewhere inside an almost solid sheet of rain. Fighting his panicked mount as the street instantly turned to mud, Oams pulled the beast round and drove his heels into its flanks. The horse slewed under him for a brief, terrifying moment, and then found its footing.

Not Undercart's fault, oh no. Benger's gonna pay for this. He glared up at the cacophony erupting over him and knew that half of the ferocity was all illusion, because Benger was an asshole. The rain pelting his face stung like darts. Ducking his head made a roar in his ears as the rain pounded on his helm.

'You little shit!'

He could barely make out the gate he rode through, and the high cobbled road was a dull gleam off to his left as he rode south. The fires from Balk's camp weren't even visible, likely drowned in the deluge.

A moment later a heavy embrace closed on him from behind and above, and the roaring sounds died away even as ecstatic shivers rushed through him.

Oh fuck. Dear lady, you are a blessing.

Even as the thoughts sang through his mind, a deep undercurrent of unease rolled into its wake. That embrace was *tight*.

The lightning ceased, even though the thunder continued, as if the mountains across the lake to the north were shaking beneath drumming fists. *That* was all Undercart.

Gods below, we're a scary bunch.

BOOK THREE

ROOTS OF STONE

Today, we become spokes of the wheel.

Elade Tharos,
Warleader of the Teblor

CHAPTER THIRTEEN

One of the accursed Blood-Posts was found outside the burning Sunyd village. Like the wooden weapons the savages employ, this was infused with Blood-oil, leaving it strangely glossy and virtually indestructible. On it were carved the names of children sacrificed to their demonic gods. If this was not horrifying enough, the women of the village will sing a song interweaving the names of each and every child given to the Faces in the Rock. They sing with joy, tears of happiness in their eyes.

If there is consolation to be had in this, it is the fact that none of those children grew to adulthood. None became warriors. Which of course saved them from slavery and death. Even so, would that their blood was on our hands. At least then, their deaths would be clean.

I Hate All Gods
Goru of Plaited Tail

DELAS FANA OF THE URYD SAT RESTING IN THE HIGH GRASSES of the escarpment's summit, one hand on the hot back of Sculp, the solid muscles of the dog's shoulders rising and falling as the beast panted in the heat. The climb had been arduous and the shift from night-time travel to that of daylight made her eyes grainy, her limbs heavy. Off to her left the other two Teblor hounds, Muck and Cromb, were hunched over the desiccated carcass of a mountain goat that had died in the past winter. Bones crunched in jaws and the musty reek of withered gristle drifted along the ridge. On the escarpment's steep, grassy slope below her, butterflies danced among the alpine flowers.

Almost home. The air was crisp and clean despite the unseasonal warmth, smelling of raw stone and water. There had been people in Darujhistan whose faces had displayed scepticism, even disbelief, when she spoke of the scents of various stones, or the myriad flavours of water that rode the air. Standing water smelled sickly. Spring-fed water was metallic. Rain possessed a smell she could only describe as *sky*.

Azure Lake, she recalled, was foul on the edges of the city, but its scent was strangely cold and icy further out. The smell of temple stone was different from that of tenement buildings. From the cobbles underfoot came the sick greasy tang of humanity and animals, but on the bridges spanning the small, dying rivers that wound through the lower city, the limestone smelled of sea-bottom. She had never walked a sea's murky floor, obviously, but there were veins of similar stone high in the mountains, mostly made up of crushed shells. When water splashed a newly exposed vein, a redolent mist arose, and this was what she had smelled on the bridges of Darujhistan. She could make no sense of that.

Sculp lifted his massive head suddenly, and Delas Fana felt the muscles stiffen under her palm. She scanned the valley below, but its deepest regions were still swallowed in shadow. Movement? Possibly.

'Are we pursued?' she asked in a low murmur. She had made this journey more than once now. More often than not with her sister accompanying her. They had been careful but confident as they trekked the lands of the south. The children who dwelt there posed little danger, and only once had a group – bandits, she supposed – accosted them, seeking the highly prized weapons of the Teblor which, she later discovered, sold as art objects in cities like Darujhistan. Expensive art objects.

She and her sister had left no survivors, and of the horses they had subsequently captured, only one was young enough to eat. Searching the broken bodies of the bandits had yielded few of the small coins the southlanders used, and so the only reward she and her sister received for their trouble was a full belly.

Travelling alone, however, had proved more adventurous. She'd had to kill more than a few acquisitive southlanders, especially in the more remote areas, and so she had taken to travelling by night, avoiding towns and villages, cities and forts. But now, at last, she had reached territory claimed by none. Once home to the Sunyd, these highlands had reverted to wildness, with only a few scattered ruins to attest to those now gone from the world.

The last she had heard, the Sunyd survivors, ex-slaves and the few who had remained free, were now among the Rathyd.

Sighing, Delas Fana collected up her spear and rose to her feet. Off to her left, the westernmost arms of Silver Lake gleamed with reflected sunlight, but the town itself was not visible, lying close as it was to the vast lake's southeastern end. Standing, she no longer needed Sculp's sharp senses to warn her of company. A small band of figures were now visible on the escarpment's slope, slowly climbing out of shadow.

It had taken her all morning to ascend the slope, so the strangers were little more than spots far below. She would have to wait to make out details. But one was taller than the others.

A Teblor? Possibly.

Muck and Cromb joined her, their breaths acrid with carrion stench. The three Teblor hounds had been awaiting her in the valley below. They had travelled far from the nearest Uryd village to find her. How they could do such things was a mystery. All of Gnaw's offspring possessed such uncanny talents. No other tribal dog did. Another legacy of her father's ascendancy, she assumed.

The thought of her father made her scowl. Old, obstinate, communicating in grunts, he infuriated her. He was a god. Did not the Teblor need a new god, now that the Faces in the Rock were no more? What to do, when the god was not willing?

Breath hissing in frustration, Delas Fana shook her head. It would do well if these below were bandits. She was in the mood to kill something. The same mood that always followed thoughts of her father, she knew. To simply conjure in her mind's eye Karsa Orlong's tattooed face, the impenetrable walls of his eyes, the hint of the smile that never came to his thin lips, made her want to draw her bloodsword and send heads flying on fountains of blood.

The handful of acquaintances in Darujhistan whom she might consider to be friends, lowlanders all, would bark their harsh laughter at her anger, and all the desires flooding into her mind with its arrival. They would nod and say, *Aye, a true Teblor you are. Slaughter and mayhem are your answers to everything!*

Such accusations irritated her. If left alone, were not the Teblor peaceful? Beyond the inter-tribal wars, raids, feuds and the like, they only desired to be left alone, isolated from the outside world. Southlanders died too easily for it to be sporting, at least when it came to individual combat. They only caused trouble for the Teblor because there were so many of them. That, and the inherent weakness of being *Sunyd*.

Of course, isolation came with a price. She glanced down at Sculp. 'On the One Day, all those years ago,' she said, 'there were hounds to match you on the streets of Darujhistan, my friend.'

The beast looked up, sand-hued eyes fixing on her.

'Never mind the children of the south. Where they dwell, other things will be found. Things worthy of challenge. Hounds of Light and Hounds of Shadow. But also Eleint. And even among the children, ascendant warriors most formidable. And yes, gods. Many gods. Would you like to taste a god's throat between your jaws, Sculp?'

The eyes gleamed brighter for a moment – or perhaps she but imagined it, and since desire was a powerful seducer of the imagination, she felt no guilt at the pleasure the notion delivered. 'Soon, I will take you and your brothers with me into the southlands. To Darujhistan itself. We will set out each night into the streets of the city, to hunt. Sorcerors, demons, Hounds and dragons, what times we shall have, my friends, there in the City of Blue Fire.'

And her father? Would he object? Would he at last rise from sitting on his slack ass and actually *do* something?

Delas Fana snorted. Probably not.

The figures below were closer now. And one was indeed a Teblor. The other three looked to be children of the south, and the two hairy ones were arguing, their guttural voices rising up to where she stood.

All three Teblor hounds suddenly growled, hackles rising.

Delas Fana sniffed at the air. 'Jheck.' She settled a hand on Sculp's broad brow. 'Not an enemy, friend, despite their wolf-stink.' She paused, and then added, 'But there are many fools among the Jheck. Perhaps one of the two below is such a fool and he will challenge you. Do not attack first. But remain wary. I am told some Sunyd Teblor scout for the southlanders. Do the Jheck do the same? Let us wait and find out.' She glanced down. 'Muck, Cromb, hide on the flanks, stay unseen.'

The two hounds ducked low and slunk away, Muck to the left, Cromb to the right, both vanishing in the high grasses.

'At last, they have seen us, Sculp. The Teblor, he has lifted his head. Ah, he is young. Not even armed. What a strange band this is.'

It would still be some time before they came within range of conversation. At least the two Jheck had stopped their bickering, if only for the moment.

Spear leaning on her left shoulder and Sculp now sitting at her right side, Delas Fana waited.

'Whatever she is,' Damisk said, 'it's not Sunyd.'

Gower grunted. 'That matters to you, Tracker? You think your name is not known among the other tribes of the Teblor?'

In a rare moment, Nilghan nodded agreement. 'The weak and frail Lord of the Black Jheck is right. You'd best leave us now. Flee like a hare.'

They were ascending the steep slope towards the escarpment's high ridge. Although the grasses were thick underfoot, this being a south-facing slope, here and there loose scree beneath those grasses made the climb treacherous.

'I will see the lad accepted first,' Damisk said. 'I promised that much, at least, and I will hold to it.'

'Thank you, Damisk,' said Rant. 'If she isn't nice, I will protect you.'

Gower swore under his breath. 'I foresee many complications being bound to you, Rant. It seems that, if the need arises, I too will block her path to you, Damisk. Not because I like you. It is Rant who holds my life in his hands.' He swung a sneer on Nilghan. 'Do you even understand such things, you thick-skulled *bara'id*?'

'I understand that he alone is the reason you still breathe, you limping grey-snouted excuse for a Lord. Him and Damisk, to be honest. So I will be pleased when the Tracker runs away. Rant, next time you will have no chance to knock me on the head with a jawbone – for that is surely what you must have done. But I will seek to only wound you, even if you deserve death for having ambushed me with that whalebone. Because,' he added in a gentle tone, 'you are but a pup still, and one must be forgiving of the mistakes that pups make.'

'I but punched you,' Rant explained, yet again.

'A lying pup makes forgiving more difficult.'

Damisk shook his head, saving his breath. It was a wonder the pair had not killed each other, and he suspected that it was only Gower's lingering weakness that prevented the Jheck Lord from slaying his rival. Nilghan was working hard to convince himself that Rant had somehow deceived him, flourishing some unseen weapon and catching the warrior unawares, but the effort sounded thin, not least because Nilghan's nose was still broken, flattened by knuckles and driven to one side of his broad face. Most of the red swelling was gone, but his nose was in the habit of bleeding when the wheezing grew too fierce. As it was doing now.

'The banded spear she carries looks Uryd,' Damisk said to Rant. 'That is fortuitous. Your own clan.'

'Not mine,' Rant said. 'My father's.'

Gower spoke. 'What makes either of you think the Uryd will look kindly on any spawn of Karsa Orlong's? He has abandoned them. He grows fat in a southlander city. They will build a temple around him, bathing him in whale-oil and fondling his testicles.'

Unable to help himself, Damisk snorted in laughter. 'Is that what worshippers do to their god, Lord Gower?'

'Southlanders,' Gower replied.

Nilghan was finished wiping his nose. 'What does the Lord know of the southlands? I alone – and perhaps Tracker here – have journeyed into those lands. I have seen the great dens where chickens live in stacked cages and people buy clay masks no one dares to wear. I have seen the temple priests eating flies and building black-feathered wings they tie to their arms – but can they fly? No, of course not. Still, on one day each year one of them leaps to his death from a high tower. Then the broken corpse is dragged to a square where it's nailed to a cross made of wood and left there for the crows to pick clean. But what I never saw was any fondling of testicles!'

'The Uryd will have no choice but to know you as kin,' Damisk said to Rant as the two Jheck fell to more bickering. 'Once I see the acknowledgement of that, I will indeed leave you.'

Rant nodded. 'I don't want you hurt, Damisk. You are my first and best friend. If Gower is bound to me because I saved his life, then I am bound to you in the same way. But I will miss you.'

'You fared well when I was nowhere close enough to help you, Rant. I think you might well have managed the entire journey on your own. You underestimate yourself.' He edged slightly closer as they climbed and added in a low tone, 'And do trust in Gower. He will honour his vow.'

'Nilghan still wants to kill me,' Rant whispered.

'Too bad your punch didn't break his neck as well as his nose. But again, Gower won't let it happen.'

'But Nilghan wants to kill Gower even more than he wants to kill me.'

'And Gower still refuses his challenge. The Jheck are strange folk, Rant. I cannot tell you what is allowed and what isn't when it comes to such challenges to leadership. But something prevents Nilghan, and it has nothing to do with us or Gower's weakness.'

Behind them, Nilghan raised his voice. 'What are you two whispering about now? Will you kill me in my sleep? Poison the water in my flask? I should warn you both, I have prepared a curse to utter with my last dying breath. You will pay for murdering me a thousand-fold!'

'In the meantime,' Gower said, 'we pay for Rant *not* killing you a hundred-thousand-fold.'

'O Lord of the Black Jheck, your wit is as tiny as a rabbit plop. I have no understanding why you were made Lord of our people. Imagine, a Lord who has never left his tribal land, never seen the wonders and dangers of the outside world!'

'I have left it now,' Gower replied.

'You lack not only wit but wisdom. It was but chance that saw the walls of ice die during your reign. Before then, I was content to let you rule us. After all, nothing ever changed. The Saemdhi hunted us, we hunted them. The seasons came and the seasons left. Is it any wonder I fled to the outside world?'

'And I wish you'd stayed there.'

'I could not, and do you know why? I saw, with my own eyes, how small our world truly was – us Jheck. Few even knew of us not five days south! As if we did not even exist, making you Lord of nothing, trotting in aimless circles scattering rabbit plops in your wake! The Jheck needed to hear the truth.'

'They heard it,' Gower said. 'How could they not? You never shut up.'

'Yet you did nothing!'

'Did I not?'

'No! Instead, you fled your own people! This is why I set out to track you, to kill you, to return to our people as the new Lord of the Black Jheck.'

'Where you would be challenged ten times a day, Nilghan, because people are tired of listening to you. An avalanche of words buries all wisdom, something you still haven't learned. With all your babbling, we see how the southlands infected you.'

'I have seen, you fool! Chickens in cages! Wolf furs stacked to the ceiling! The hunger of the southlanders will never cease – not even when the last living thing is gone from the world, no, not even then. When that day comes, why, they will kill and eat *each other*.'

'Silence, Nilghan.'

Something in the Lord's tone made Damisk finally turn around, as did Rant.

Gower had halted and he now held up a hand. 'Listen to me, Nilghan.'

'Why should I?'

'You misapprehend so much. You want words from me? Very well. I now give them.'

Sneering, Nilghan crossed his brawny arms.

'I left, yes, because I heeded the truth of what you witnessed in the lands of the south. Indeed, there were more truths in your words than even you understood. I set out to find War-Bitch.'

Damisk saw Nilghan's eyes widen.

Gower went on. 'I was close on her scent – I knew it no matter how many generations have passed in our prison of ice. No matter how long since we last beheld her presence. I sought her and failed.'

'Why am I not surprised?'

Gower shrugged. 'The lands were crawling with Saemdhi Imass. It seemed they all wanted to kill me.'

'Of course they did,' said Nilghan, nodding. 'Everybody wants to kill you. You're like that.'

'And then I erred in judgement.'

'Of course.'

'Crossing jaws with a Teblor youth.' Gower paused and glanced over at Rant. 'After I fell into the Healing Sleep, Rant carried me. He carried me past War-Bitch's den. But it doesn't matter, because she wasn't there.'

'No,' said Damisk. 'She left.'

Gower started, and then scowled. 'You met her, and survived? This I doubt, Tracker.'

Damisk shrugged. 'As you like. I'll say no more of it in any case.'

After a moment, Gower returned his dark gaze to Nilghan. He drew a deep breath, and resumed, 'It doesn't matter. I have her scent again. We are tracking her even now.'

'To what end?' Nilghan demanded.

'Our prison of ice is no more. We are unleashed. So howl our warriors, night and day, or are you deaf even to that?'

'They are right to howl!'

'Perhaps. But take a moment, Nilghan. Consider our prison of ice. View it another way. Not as a prison, but as a *refuge*.'

Nilghan's brow clenched, the blood starting from his nostrils once more, glittering thick and red in his moustache and beard. He opened his mouth to speak, and then closed it again.

Gower nodded. 'This, warrior, at last.'

'They will find us.'

'If we did nothing. If we stayed where we were – but you and I both know that such a choice is impossible, anyway. I comprehended, Nilghan, the many truths of this.'

'If you saw true, Lord, why did you not gather all the Jheck clans? Why did you not take up the Black Blade? You should be leading us into the southlands even now! To kill them before they kill us!'

'War-Bitch will lead us.'

'She is a myth,' snarled Nilghan. 'There is no scent of her. And now even Damisk joins your lies!'

'We will need her,' said Gower. 'But even she won't be enough, will she, Nilghan? You, who have journeyed into the southlands, know this, yes?'

'Of course,' Nilghan snapped. 'I dream not of victory, you fool, just a legacy of slaughter such that the Jheck will never be forgotten, not for a thousand years!'

Gower was grinning, and that grin chilled Damisk. 'And now, Nilghan,' the lord asked, 'where do we find ourselves? You and me?'

'Too far west!'

'Too far? Or *almost there*?'

'Where?'

'War-Bitch clearly understood. She seeks what I set out to find. Allies.'

In the silence that followed that statement, as the climb resumed, Damisk edged a step closer to Rant. 'My friend,' he muttered, 'if I could, I'd leave right now. I have finally made sense of everything I've seen. My people need to be warned.'

Frowning, Rant lifted his gaze to look upslope. Finally, he could make out the Teblor woman's features. The giant dog at her side must be a Teblor hound – he recalled the huge skin he'd seen at the tavern in Silver Lake. Neither woman nor beast had moved in all this time and even now they stood motionless, watching. Waiting. Suddenly, Rant felt a whisper of fear.

'Damisk, will another ten paces matter to your desire?' He watched as uncertainty warred in Damisk's lined face.

After a moment, Damisk nodded. 'Very well. Ten more strides up this slope, so that words may be exchanged.'

'If she readies her spear,' Rant said, 'begin running back down. I will place myself between her and you for as long as I can.'

'Ah, friend, if she raises her spear, do nothing. She'll do it to distract you, as her war-dog comes for me – and *that* beast you will not stop. No, consider me dead then, Rant.'

'I will protect you, and so will Gower. He said so!'

Sighing, Damisk said, 'Ten more strides uphill, friend. Shall we?'

Delas Fana waited another few moments, to let them draw nearer, and then she held out her hand. 'That is close enough for now,' she said in the Nathii tongue. 'Which among you leads? Who will speak for you? These are Sunyd lands. Teblor lands.'

'I am Nilghan—'

'And so he is,' cut in the other Jheck. 'But he speaks only for himself. I speak for the Black Jheck, however, for I am Gower, possessor of the Black Blade and Lord of my packs. Name yourself, Uryd.'

Delas Fana sighed. 'You have travelled far, Lord Gower. It seems the vast barriers of ice have failed in keeping you and your kind where they belong. The Saemdhi traders who visit us speak often of you, and none of it pleases the ear.'

'Saemdhi!' snarled the one named Nilghan, his outburst accompanied by a spray of blood from his nostrils. Cursing, he spat, and then spat again. 'An iron hammer swung in the night, catching me in my sleep! Beware the treachery in our ranks, Uryd. Even Lord Gower stands wide-legged on thinnest ice. He speaks of War-Bitch.'

'I know nothing of any war-bitch,' Delas said, shrugging. Her gaze shifted to the youth who carried naught but a knife at his belt. 'You, Teblor. Half-blood. Are you a Sunyd slave? A traitorous scout?'

'I am Rant,' the youth replied. 'From Silver Lake. I was born there, but I was never a slave. And I know little of scouting.'

She had more questions for him. Even at this distance, she could see fear in his eyes. Perhaps he did not possess the freedom to speak openly? Her attention finally shifted to the southlander. 'I cannot decide about you. You are too old to be such a fool, so you must be weary of life and will welcome its end. Because you will not leave here alive.'

Rant moved to place himself between her and the southlander. 'He is not to be harmed. He saved my life and guided me here. He has brought me to my people.'

'Your desires are not relevant,' Delas Fana said. 'Nor are mine, to be honest. He was dead the moment he stepped onto the slope.'

Rant glanced back. 'Run now, Damisk. I will—'

'Damisk!' cried Delas, and the hound beside her suddenly rose to its feet. 'Now *that* is a name I know.' She tilted her head up and shouted, 'It is Damisk!'

As her words echoed, other Teblor hounds appeared, rising from the thick grasses beside and behind the strange group, eight in all, and a moment later five Teblor warriors came into view, four of them on foot and quickly edging downslope to take flanking positions. The fifth was mounted, walking her horse up alongside Delas Fana, with two more hounds appearing on her left.

'We have guests, sister,' Delas said.

'They tracked you?' the rider asked.

'Possibly.'

'Foolish decision.'

Below, the Black Jheck lord spoke. 'This is poor greeting for an emissary. If you would make this a fight, then I will welcome the exercise.' He drew from under his leather jerkin an obsidian knife and grasped the blade with his other hand. 'I will break this the moment you attack, even as I veer, and when I do, all the Jheck will know we are at war with the Teblor.'

Delas Fana said, 'If an emissary you truly are, Lord Gower, then no harm will come to you. I am Delas Fana of the Uryd, and she astride my horse is my sister, Tonith Agra.' She hesitated, and then added, 'I have come from the southlands, from beyond Lake Azure, and so I know nothing of events here of late. But I will tell you this: the Teblor will not turn their backs on any war, so if you will it, then by all means do so, and all the Jheck will regret your decision. But if you are indeed an emissary, then put away the blade.'

Gower hesitated.

The other Jheck warrior grunted a laugh. 'Now the dilemma strikes him! My lord would have the Teblor as allies. But he is bound by a vow to defend the tracker, Damisk. Why? Because the half-blood wills it. Which matters the more to you, O Lord Gower of the Black Jheck? The Teblor as allies, or enemies in a war no one wants?'

Rant turned slightly and looked at the warrior. 'Nilghan, if you will not help protect Damisk, then please move away from us, and if you seek to attack Gower unawares, I will have to kill you.'

Brows lifting, Delas Fana glanced up at her sister. 'He's a bold one, isn't he?'

'Deluded,' Tonith replied in a rasp.

Delas Fana faced the surrounded party again. 'Does your warrior speak true, Lord Gower? You are oath-bound?'

Gower looked miserable. 'I am.'

'And how do the Jheck weigh such things, as against the desire for an alliance between our peoples?'

'I've not yet decided.'

There was motion, and Delas Fana's gaze shifted in time to see the tracker Damisk slowly raising both hands into the air. 'I can solve this,' he said. 'Rant, it's not your fault how this has turned out. I absolve you both of blame and of responsibility. The Teblor have good reason to hate me, to desire my death.' He paused, and then said, 'And I have good reason to surrender to them.'

Rant wheeled round. 'No! You cannot!'

'I can and I do, Rant. Lord Gower, sheathe your blade. Be the emissary as you originally intended.'

Tonith Agra spoke then. 'Tracker Damisk, your death will be a slow one, a painful one. Alas for you, I do not possess the mercy to slay you quickly. You must be handed to our Warleader, who now calls both Sunyd and Rathyd his kin. Is that not fitting?'

Damisk nodded. 'It is fitting.'

The Teblor half-blood closed in and embraced a startled Damisk. Holding him tight, he spun round to face Delas and Tonith. 'No! He is not to be harmed!'

Delas caught the hidden smile in her sister's words: 'You would challenge the Warleader, then? Your . . . knife, against his bloodsword?'

'I will!'

'So be it,' Tonith said with a shrug. She shifted her attention to her sister. 'Delas, when the kin of Gnaw set out from the camp, I knew the reason, and so I followed.'

'That is a long journey to take, sister,' Delas Fana replied.

Tonith smiled. 'Not as long as you think.'

Rant felt chilled and no amount of exertion as they crossed the escarpment could allay it. Fear gripped him inside, fear for his friend, Damisk. His icy hand felt for the knife's grip again and again as he walked.

The Teblor hounds were bigger than any dog he had ever seen. Even Gower's wolves were no match for these beasts. They encircled the group and when any one of them edged closer to Gower or Nilghan, hackles lifted and canines were bared, and it would take a sharp command from the mounted woman before the beast pulled away, stretching the distance once more.

Four of the six Teblor warriors were women, none as tall as Rant. The two men matched him in height. One was thin, almost emaciated, with a haunted look clouding his features. He bore the old scars of shackles on his wrists. The other wasn't much older than Rant himself, although leaner, offering Rant a sneer every time he glanced the man's way.

This was not how he'd thought his first meeting with kin would turn out. In his mind, he had envisioned something less fraught, something gentler. Perhaps not embraces and hearty welcomes, although that would have been nice. At the very least, they would have accepted him. Instead, every gaze he met was either contemptuous or openly hostile. Faces and expressions, in other words, he knew well from Silver Lake.

This sense – that nothing about him had changed – threatened to overwhelm him with despair. There seemed to be no point in Damisk risking his life to deliver him to the Teblor, and no point in Rant attempting to find a home among his kin. It was not too surprising, he supposed. After all, not everyone in Silver Lake got along with each other, despite their all being human. He had been foolish to think he could join a family. Families, after all, were for other people.

And now he would have to kill a warleader to save Damisk's life. They would hate him when he did that.

No matter. He and Damisk would leave. They would give up the whole idea of Rant living anywhere in the company of others. They would find a valley somewhere, a place no one visited, and build a home there, and as the years passed and Damisk grew old, Rant would take care of him, in the way that a son took care of an ageing father.

His hand had settled on the dagger's grip for some time now, and he found that it was warm – almost hot – unlike his other hand. He decided that the spirit within the blade was close, and so in his mind he spoke to her.

You will taste blood soon. I have to kill a man to save a man. This is how things now are, it seems. This is a world where people fight each other. Not like in Silver Lake, where most people got along even if they didn't like each other. Oh, there was fighting there once, too. When the slaves got free. But I did not see much of that. Mostly, I lived in peace. Except for the stones.

The forest frightened me. So did the tundra. I think I've been frightened ever since I tried to swim the lake. Not the kind of fear that makes a dog cower, not like that at all. This is the deeper kind.

Out here, I don't think people care for each other. Out here, it's all about who's stronger, or smarter. Who commands and who obeys. This is what Damisk has been trying to tell me all along, with his old man's wisdom, the kind of wisdom a father offers to his child, the kind my true father never did.

So I found Damisk. And I found Gower. But now these Teblor want to kill Damisk, and Gower must speak for his people. And Nilghan . . . I don't understand Nilghan. I think he is too full of words. But I like him anyway, even though I do not trust him.

So what is it that I fear? I think I understand it now, because it's been with me all along.

Being alone is what I fear.

The knife grip was hot in his hand, nearly burning his palm. He wondered what that meant. Perhaps, he thought, she was telling him that as long as she was with him, he wasn't truly alone. Of course she would tell him that. What value a weapon without the hand wielding it?

But she could not walk beside him now, nor ever. She could not give him the companionship he desired. It was strange to think that this woman's soul, bound to the blade of a knife, was more at home in this world than he was.

One thing I do not understand, he told his knife: *if I am but a half-blood Teblor, why am I bigger than all of them?*

Damisk walked beside Rant, his thoughts in turmoil. Not quite what he'd planned from the start. No chance to slip away like a ghost, leaving the lad to his own kind. To make matters worse, he was now a prisoner. There would be no warning to bring to his people, no one to tell them that the tribes of the north were coming south, that there would be war.

But even this realization fell away from his thoughts, crowded out by his growing fear for Rant's fate. In so many ways, this hulking figure at his side was still a child. The Teblor Warleader would kill him. Even had Rant been a skilled fighter – which he was not – no knife could defeat a sword. That was a simple, irrefutable fact. *Perhaps, if thrown . . .* but the weapon Rant now gripped at his side was not the kind one could throw with any accuracy. Its balance was off – Damisk need only glance at it to see that. And the lad had slipped it beneath a leather strap that served as a belt, but on the right side, so that he now held the grip as if the weapon were an icepick.

Worse still, Rant was clearly terrified. He would freeze when he faced the Warleader. Conjuring the scene in his mind's eye, Damisk felt his heart breaking yet again. Deep pain, grief and self-recrimination.

And if I broke away right now – rushed between the dogs?

A simple command and the beasts would take him down, pin him to the ground. But not kill him.

He carried a skinning knife. None among the party had been disarmed. It was the typical arrogance of the Teblor. *So, can I take my own life? That would stop this madness in its tracks. That would save Rant.*

With the thoughts whispering through his mind, the decision was made. It would shock the lad, to be sure. It would wound his soul. A betrayal of sorts. *Aye, Damisk proves at the end to have no faith in his friend. Damisk chooses to abandon him, leaving him to his fate among kin who hold him in contempt. The half-blood is doomed to be an eternal outcast, accepted nowhere.*

But it's better than dying for no reason, because they will kill me after they kill him. A life thrown away.

Still, it wasn't much of a life, was it?

Ah, Damisk, now the coward in you speaks. You don't want to kill yourself. You know that nothing about it will be clean. You know how many wounds your death will deliver.

But it's still the best option. Rant, of course, will never understand that.

He drew a long, slow breath, his right hand stealing across his belly. There probably wouldn't be time to bring the blade up to his throat. But up under his ribcage would suffice. A quick thrust and then a twist, falling forward to drive the blade as deep as possible. *Let them rail. I'll save a breath for Rant. Tell him to live on, no matter what. Tell him I'm sorry. Tell him none of this is his fault.*

His hand edged further until it touched the hilt—

A heavy force struck him from behind, sent him sprawling onto the ground. Wind knocked from his lungs, he nevertheless twisted round and pulled free his knife.

Savage jaws closed on his wrist. Bones snapped.

Damisk screamed.

Until a boot slammed into the side of his head.

Horrified, Rant straight-armed the young warrior who had kicked Damisk – sent him flying backward – and then grasped the hound by the thick hide of its neck with one hand and brought the other down to grasp the snout as the beast continued to savage Damisk's wrist.

A sudden wrench split the dog's jaws so far back, most of its face was torn free of the skull underneath, the crushed wrist spilling loose. He then lifted the beast into the air, twisted, and drove it down onto the ground. Blood, splintered bones, a body mangled almost beyond recognition. Still holding the twitching form one-handed, Rant tossed it away and pulled free his own knife, whirling to meet another Teblor hound.

The knife twisted of its own accord, reversing his grip, and then, as if two hands closed onto his wrist, he was yanked forward into an awkward lunge.

The knife buried itself in the second hound's chest.

At the thudding impact, the beast seemed to explode, ribs punching outward through muscle and hide, stomach and lungs bursting in a welter of fluid and blood.

Rant stared in horror, but the knife was far from done. He heard and felt the heavy buffeting of wings – shadowy forms snapping out on either side, as if riding his shoulders – and he felt himself lifted into the air as his knife-arm twisted him round, dropping him into a crouch now facing the first warrior – who had regained his feet and was closing in, spear readied in both hands as he thrust the point forward—

The knife-blade snapped up in a flickering parry that shattered the spear shaft.

In a blur Rant found himself drawn up close to the warrior, their eyes meeting. The knife had already done its work, blood pouring down over Rant's right hand. The look in the warrior's eyes was one of blank astonishment. Until the clouds of death closed in and the head fell back, following the body as it collapsed, pulling free of the blade.

Sobbing, Rant staggered back a step, and then another, finding himself standing over Damisk's motionless form.

A sudden flurry as beasts moved in close – but not the Teblor hounds. Wolves, a dozen in all, snapping and growling as they encircled Rant and Damisk, all angling to face the outer ring of Teblor hounds and warriors.

'Hold!'

The command came from Tonith Agra as she fought her panicked mount. The Teblor hounds that had been closing in, a breath away from attacking the wolves, suddenly pulled back.

The other male Teblor warrior had drawn close to his companion's body and was pulling it clear. 'Dead, Tonith! Galambar is dead, gutted like an elk!'

'Hold, everyone!' Tonith shouted. Her eyes, wide with horror, were fixed on Rant. 'Will you now kill us all, demon?'

'Damisk lives! I promised!'

Tonith's sister now spoke in a quavering voice. 'Half-blood, your friend was about to cut his own throat. We knew it was a possibility. You are bound in loyalty – *all* of you, it now seems, even the one named Nilghan. See how they protect you? But Damisk, he sought the coward's escape. Fearing the pain promised him—'

'I said I would fight your Warleader—'

Delas Fana frowned. Her tone hardened. 'Sorcery was not part of the bargain. Nor the demon-blood you hide within you. Such allies are not permitted in a duel.'

'I have no demon-blood,' Rant said, now trembling. 'I am but the bastard son of Karsa Orlong and a southlander woman. If there is a demon within me, its name is Blood-oil.'

In the silence that followed, something seemed to drain away. Delas Fana watched, with narrowed gaze, as the dogs among the pack that were kin to Gnaw all turned away, suddenly indifferent to the threat the half-blood and his D'ivers allies posed. Her sister then dismounted and strode to where Valoc crouched beside the body of Galambar, a Sunyd weeping over a fallen Rathyd. The other two women – both Rathyd – remained poised to attack, spears at the ready, hate-filled eyes fixed on Rant.

Tonith Agra had said little of the vast changes that had evidently come to the Teblor since Delas was last among her people. They had barely spoken while in the company of strangers, and Delas had felt the questions stacking up in her mind. Uryd, Rathyd and Sunyd all travelling together. The hounds of two tribes not at each other's throats. And now her sister calling Elade Tharos a warleader.

Tonith Agra had clearly intended for the revelations to come all at once, in the camp that waited ahead – likely where the escarpment was cut into by still higher mountain passes. Her sister liked to play such games, a hoarder of secrets and habitually inclined to torment Delas Fana with pointless evasions and a smug expression of superiority.

Occasionally, a price was paid. Delas Fana had been close enough to perhaps flank Galambar, to intercept with an oblique thrust slicing into Rant's wrist as the knife moved to gut the warrior. She might well have saved the Rathyd's life, disarming the half-blood in the process.

But Delas held no loyalty to any Rathyd. Even now, she felt only a vague bemusement as she watched Tonith and Valoc begin preparing the body for burial.

Glancing over, Tonith said, 'Keep an eye on them, sister. Our hounds are acting strange.'

'Proof to his words,' Delas Fana said. 'They know the father's scent.'

Tonith grimaced, shot a momentary glare towards the half-blood, who still guarded Damisk's prone body. 'Later,' she snapped. 'We have kin to bury.'

'Kin?'

Valoc swung to face Delas. 'Galambar cut my chains! By his hand I was made free!'

'I do not question your grief, Sunyd. Why should I? Besides, you were always the weakest among us. If the southlanders had not made you slaves, perhaps the Uryd would have. Is this now the case, sister? Have the Uryd forced to kneel both the Rathyd and the Sunyd?'

Tonith's gaze was flat. 'Warleader—'

'Elade Tharos,' Delas cut in, lip curling. 'You invite a Rathyd to lead you, Tonith Agra? Perhaps you accepted what he set before your hut and are now his wife, now a woman among the Rathyd?'

'Warleader Elade Tharos leads all of us now, sister. All the tribes of the Teblor. Even the Lanyd and Phalyd. I remain Uryd. Elade Tharos is not my husband. He is my Warleader.'

'Our father is the only Warleader the Teblor require.'

'Then why is he not at your side, Delas?'

'This is not the time to speak of such things.'

'No, you're right. It isn't.'

Delas Fana glanced over at the half-blood. The Jheck had sembled back into their two-legged forms. Both looked utterly miserable. She sighed and said to her sister, 'Bury him, then. I will guard.'

'As you guarded Galambar?' asked one of the Rathyd women, sneering.

The other said, 'She is not one to rely upon, Sivith Gyla.'

'No,' said Delas Fana with a smile, 'I am not.'

Tonith and Valoc pushed Galambar's intestines back into the cavity they had tumbled out of and then arranged the body into a foetal position facing east. They brought the hands together in front of the face that still bore its surprised expression. The two dead hounds –

both Rathyd – were dragged close, arranged so that one curled above Galambar's head and the other at his feet. Then Valoc set out to find stones to build the cairn, refusing Tonith's assistance.

After a time, one of the Rathyd women set down her spear and went to join him. They began by arranging boulders in a ring around the bodies, while Tonith continued working on Galambar's corpse, stripping the clothing of ornaments, collecting all the jewellery, as well as the knife and its scabbard and belt. The shattered remnants of the spear were placed near the hands, the long iron head pointing north.

Tonith Agra then walked to her horse and, after removing the saddle, began grooming the beast.

More boulders were added to strengthen the base of the ring, and then smaller rocks began to fill the interior. The nearest supply of stone was a hundred paces away, where mountain rubble had been pushed by ice into a ridge that stretched across the escarpment. The other Rathyd woman soon joined her companion in assisting Valoc. Despite this, they would not be finished before dusk.

Damisk was still unconscious. Rant now sat close to the man, one hand resting lightly on the chest – minutely rising and falling with breath. Rant's red-rimmed gaze fixed on the shadows stretching across the escarpment. Gower had bound the torn remnants of Damisk's wrist, draped a fur cloak over the man and made a pillow of his bedroll. He'd then moved a short distance away and lowered himself into a squat, watching the Teblor building the cairn.

Nilghan paced for a time, muttering under his breath, until finally settling down close to Gower.

'You have failed,' he said to Gower. 'Failed the Black Jheck. You chose the half-blood over your people. Your rule is at an end. I am now Lord of the Black Jheck.'

Gower grunted in amusement, but it was a sour grunt. 'If I failed, then so did you.'

Nilghan's shoulders slumped. 'I was ensorcelled. It is the only possibility. On black wings a fierce rage stole into my body. It filled my liver, my hearts, all my lungs. It was foreign. I was caught unawares. It shall not happen again.'

'Foreign? No argument there, truly a stranger to your soul—'

'What are you talking about?' Nilghan growled.

'That foreign thing, Nilghan. Not sorcery, but *loyalty*, a notion you still do not recognize.'

'Am I to be loyal to a demon half-blood who tried to break my neck?'

'It seems you are.'

Nilghan snarled, and then fell silent.

Gower glanced over at Rant. 'He may never awaken,' he said. 'Prepare for that.'

Rant shook his head. 'He but sleeps now, Lord.'

'A sleep that may well be eternal.'

'I will protect him.'

Gower bared his teeth. 'That we have seen, young friend. Your knife is possessed.'

'I know.'

Brows lifting, Gower shot Nilghan a look. Their eyes met. Nilghan scowled.

'Has it always been so, Rant?' Gower asked.

'No, Lord. It was given to me when I was a child, in Silver Lake. It is Malazan.'

'It is Aren steel,' said Nilghan. 'I have seen such blades in the great dens of the southlanders. Very rare, very expensive. When Rant is dead I will claim it.'

Ignoring Nilghan, Gower scratched at his beard, contemplating the young half-blood. 'You used it to kill one of me.'

Rant nodded. 'Through the skull, yes. But the blade bit deep into the rock beneath.'

Nilghan snorted. 'Even an Aren blade could not—'

'It did,' said Gower. 'I witnessed it myself. The sound it made still echoes in my skull.'

'It was not possessed then,' said Rant. 'She came after.'

'She?'

'My friend, the one who now dwells in the knife.'

'Winged, was she?'

'In her first form, yes.'

'That first form, Rant . . . two legs or four?'

Rant frowned. 'She stood upright, Lord Gower. Taller than me, but very thin. Her eyes were serpent eyes. Her wings were as those of a bat. I sensed . . .' His brow clouded.

'What did you sense, Rant?'

'She . . . lived a solitary life. There was blood on her hands.' His frown deepened. 'I almost hear . . . echoes of truth.' He looked across to Gower. 'The blood of matrons.'

'Matrons?' Nilghan asked. 'She killed mothers? What point to that, when they're already mothers? I have seen how the southlanders breed! You need to kill the women *before* they become mothers, or there's no point to it!'

Irritated by Nilghan's expostulations, Gower waved a dismissive hand. 'Be silent, will you? Rant does not speak of an Eleint, despite those wings. He speaks of an *assassin*.'

'Pah! Those tales are mere inventions, brother.'

Rant's head lifted suddenly. '"Brother"?'

Nilghan's scowl deepened. 'Aye, was that not obvious?'

Sighing, Gower said, 'Would the child that I was had strangled you in your cot.'

Nilghan snorted. 'Even then you feared me.'

'You? No. I feared Mother.'

His brother shivered. 'Mother. Yes, to be feared indeed.'

Gower faced Rant again. 'An assassin, winged, with serpent eyes. Slayer of matrons. That which possesses your knife is a K'Chain Che'Malle, a Shi'gal Assassin.'

'She had no memory of being . . . such things,' said Rant. 'Nor do I recognize the names you use. She dwelt in another place, one that lies over what we can see. But my knife pinned her to the ground – the rock. Trapped her in this world – my knife was the only place she could go.'

Nilghan said, 'They won't let you use it. Her. That knife. They will give you a spear or a sword instead, and the Warleader will kill you. And then he will kill Damisk, if he is not already dead. Then I will challenge my brother and slay him and become Lord of the Black Jheck. And an alliance shall be made with the Teblor.' He barked a sudden laugh and slapped his thigh. 'And then there will be glorious slaughter!'

Rant's gaze was bleak, and yet empty at the same time. 'If you hold this as a promise, Nilghan, then I will have to kill you before I kill the Warleader, and against you, I will use my knife.'

Eyes widened in Nilghan's bestial face. 'Not fair!'

'And you killing a weakened brother is?'

Gower snorted. 'It's all words, Rant, as it has always been. In our den, not a morning came when I did not hear Nilghan challenge my right to rule. But he fears what he claims to desire and in that, he's wiser than he thinks.'

Nilghan rose suddenly – the motion sending the remaining hounds to their feet. Low growls surrounded them. Glaring, Nilghan planted his hands on his hips. 'Shall it be this way, then? The Jheck warrior seeks to piss in the grass and these dogs quiver in terror? Hah! Watch me challenge them!' He strode off.

The Teblor hounds backed off and watched him pass. After a few moments, the beasts settled down into the high grasses once more.

Darkness had come, but the clunking and scraping of stone against stone continued as the Teblor built the cairn. Gower could just make out the two sisters standing near the horse that one rode and the other claimed. They were speaking in muted tones. If veered into his pack, Gower would be able to hear the words they exchanged. But not as he was now.

He had expected to die when protecting Rant and Damisk. His strength was frail, his defiance short-lived. Now he squatted, exhausted, heartbroken. If Damisk lived, the man would lose his right arm below the elbow. They would have to cut off the ruined limb before rot set in. The kick to Damisk's temple had been fierce – when Gower had lifted the man's head to set it upon the bedroll, he felt and listened for the crunch of broken vertebrae, but there was nothing to indicate a snapped neck, as far as he could tell. He well knew that the act of raising the man's head could have done yet more damage – and Gower had secretly hoped it would, if only to save Damisk the agony of what was coming.

The warmth of the day was fast ebbing in this high mountain air. Overhead, the stars were flaring to life like the campfires of a vast army.

A Shi'gal Assassin. Old legends, ancient titles and names – does nothing ever just go away? It remains a strange thing, the thought that this Teblor half-blood child could slay an Eleint. With a knife. After all, it is said that Shi'gal Assassins have done just that: slayed dragons.

But the Teblor warleader will bring a swift end to the lad's life, a quick slice of the blood-rope that binds soul to flesh. And, as it may well pass, a Teblor warleader will take as his prize the deadliest of weapons.

'Rant.'

'Yes, Lord?'

'This soul within the blade – does it know loyalty? Does it care who its master is?'

'I don't know. We spoke. She seemed nice.'

Gower winced. He hesitated, and then said, 'In the event you fall, the one who slays you will claim it.'

'If I fall, who takes the knife no longer matters to me.'

'If you could choose?'

'Damisk. But my death will mean his. So, you, Gower.' Rant shifted to fix his gaze on Gower. His tone was suddenly older, almost leaden. 'You desire it, Lord? Shall I give it into your hands? Is that what you want to ask me?'

'Not for me,' Gower said. 'War-Bitch.'

Rant's pale face angled away. 'I do not know this War-Bitch.'

'Of the blood of Togg and Fanderay, the great sky-wolves of my people, Rant. The mother, perhaps, of all the Jheck. The First D'ivers,

231

or among the first brood. Where things are born is quickly lost to time. The details are smoothed away in service to the tale being told, and retold. Few among my own kind even believe in her any more. Yet her scent rides the wind. It sings to my blood.'

'Why does she need a knife?'

'To keep it out of Teblor hands,' Gower said.

'But they will be your allies, Gower.'

'This camp of theirs, Rant, the one we shall find tomorrow. There are commingled scents.'

Rant glanced over again. 'What do you mean?'

Sighing, Gower looked down at the ground, seeing only blackness. He continued staring in silence, until within the darkness he saw the first glimmers of flame. He nodded, unsurprised. 'Saemdhi. The Teblor already have allies, it seems.'

Rant was silent for a dozen breaths. Then he spoke. 'Yet War-Bitch is there?'

'No. But she's close. I think, Rant, she but awaits my arrival. Me, and the Black Blade.'

'And she will need the knife – against the Saemdhi?'

'Bonecasters. I fear this, yes.'

'If the Teblor Warleader is a true leader, Gower, he will insist that the Jheck and the Saemdhi become friends. Allies all.'

Gower grunted. 'If he is capable of that, Rant, he is capable of anything.'

Nilghan returned. 'They're done with the damned rock-pile. Bedding down, if you can believe it. There will be no fires, no meal. These Teblor, brother, are barbarians.'

CHAPTER FOURTEEN

I've seen this art before
The narrowing gauge the twisted
Extrusion
The pattern selected from which
The silent bitter thrash
Is drawn
Has minute labels the frayed
List so petty and piteous
The prick of hurts
The scour of spite
It narrows and narrows the gauge
As if to kneel in the shit
Is not enough
Tear off the ratty rags all that remain
Of your wailing flagellation
Topple forward and take a
Mouthful
To spew in the face of the glorious
Passion
I've seen this art before
Betraying itself

I've Seen This Art Before
Ormulolgen

THE TWO RATHYD WARRIORS FLANKED VALOC AS THEY FACED the cairn and sang with their throats the *Nine Tents of the Dead*, the language not even Teblor, but Tartheno-Toblakai, the words stretched so deep into the past all threads were lost.

Delas Fana had learned more of such histories, the host of fragmentary lies and truths assembled here and there in ancient tomes invariably penned by a human hand or, in one instance at least, the hand of a Jaghut. Those long-lost Toblakai ancestors of the Teblor had been pre-literate, as far as anyone could tell. Their histories were woven by memory and voice, in poems and songs and the droning rhythms of throat-singing – and it was said that even this last was not originally Toblakai but appropriated from the Imass.

Her education had been intense during her time in Darujhistan, a thirst her sister did not share. She knew now that her kind were found in many places in the world, bearing many names. Tartheno. Fenn. Toblakai. Thelomen. Thel Akai. Arakyan. But few of these isolated tribes knew of their distant kin. They had been scattered, perhaps even torn apart, lodging like battered survivors in remote places.

Now, it seemed, the only things they shared with unknown tribes belonged to the eternal stony faces of birth and death. Cries of pain and cries of grief echoed down the generations, true language and words floundering into mere sounds.

The temples and libraries of Darujhistan had been her only worthwhile investment during her years spent prodding her father. That and the friendship she'd forged with Samar Dev, who either was or wasn't Karsa Orlong's lover.

As the voices reverberated in the night air, Delas Fana watched her sister hobble the horse and then walk a short distance away to lay out her bedroll. After a time, Delas strode over to join her, even as Sculp, Muck and Cromb appeared, settling down to offer the heat of their bodies against the chill.

Tonith Agra lifted a hand. 'Listen! Galambar's soul enters the first tent, only to find another within—'

Delas Fana cut in. 'Mistranslation, sister. There are no Nine Tents of Death. There are nine *skins* of death. Each must rot in turn until the soul is finally freed of all worldly substance. The Tartheno were in the habit of skinning their enemies and then tanning that skin, thus chaining the soul to the mortal realm. Their warriors would take to wearing strips of such skin, thereby binding those they have slain into their wake. This is why the war-cry of a hundred Tartheno was said to come from a thousand throats.'

Tonith Agra's eyes glittered, cold as the stars overhead. 'And this is your gift, Delas? Dismantling our traditions in the name of what?'

'Well, how about in the name of truth?'

'What purpose has this truth of yours?'

Delas Fana settled down onto the ground, cross-legged. She drew her fur cloak tighter about her shoulders. 'The Teblor imagined themselves alone. And perhaps we have believed this for many, many generations. That is no surprise. We were surrounded by children and their strange ways were not ours. When the Faces in the Rock came to us with their deceptions, we set aside our oldest beliefs. That was a mistake.'

Tonith Agra snorted softly. 'Your truth seeks to do the same. It seeks to tear from us all those traditions and beliefs that survived the false usurpers—'

'Not at all, sister. My truth, as you call it, isn't mine at all. It is ours. The Teblor were never alone. We weren't even unique. Is it not important to understand that the things that define us are the things we share with kin we have never even met?'

'That makes no sense.'

Delas Fana looked away, fixing her gaze on the Rathyd and Sunyd now pacing a circle around the cairn. A dull cadence of mumbled words accompanied their steps. 'If a Thelomen warrior came to us, we would deem him an enemy. If a Fenn met a Tartheno, they would fight. Just as Uryd fight Phalyd or Rathyd—'

'No longer,' Tonith said. 'You have been away too long. Our world has changed. We are united at last.'

'This astonishes me, sister. Our father is not known as Teblor. He is called Toblakai.'

'I know this,' snapped Tonith Agra.

'In the eyes of children we are all the same. Yet we demand something different, clinging to our tribal names as if the distinctions mattered. They don't. Is this the message of your new Warleader?'

'You would change the world in a day? He does what he can.'

Delas Fana was silent. After a time she sighed and shrugged, the gesture likely unseen by her sister. 'I have no loyalty to any but my own tribe, yet I seek one for all the Tartheno and Thelomen and Toblakai. For the Fenn of Quon Tal. For the Arakyan of Genostel. I am not blind to the contradiction.'

'It seems you are.'

'No, the difficulty is complicated, sister. One of my hearts holds to one truth and the other to another. Even kinship is no guarantee of loyalty. We were born among the Uryd, taking their name, because we were the prizes of war. Is it any wonder we are so divided within?'

'I am divided no longer,' insisted Tonith Agra.

'Indeed,' Delas Fana murmured. 'And so you would give the life of your half-brother into the hands of a Rathyd warleader.'

Delas Fana heard the breath caught, and then the low hiss of anger, proof that her seemingly disconnected thoughts, and the list of confessions that followed, had drawn her sister unawares to the precipice now facing them both. And now, even as Tonith Agra silently battled herself, Delas Fana pressed on. 'There is so much of our father's face in his, I chastise myself for not seeing the truth at once. And the mass of his body, the set of his shoulders – his mother seems to have given him nothing—'

'Not so,' Tonith Agra said in a bitter tone. 'His eyes belong to her. They are not Karsa's. There is nothing of Karsa at all in those eyes. Too soft, too weak, too . . .'

'Vulnerable?'

Tonith's savage hand gesture was a chopping blur. 'A pup's weakness. It does not belong in one of his age.'

'He was, we must presume, raised by his mother. A southlander swallowed in the madness of blood-oil. Think on that, sister, if you dare face the horror.'

'You would twist my hearts to his side?'

'Since he gave us his name,' said Delas Fana, 'I have not ceased to think of his birth, his raising, his poor mother.'

'Southlanders are weak. She must have been raping him every night, before even his cock knew how to stand. In her frustration, she would beat upon him until it did. Is he father to brothers and sisters? Do the southlanders even care?'

'Ah,' said Delas Fana in a quiet voice, 'your thoughts have not ceased either.'

There was a sudden shuddering sound from Tonith Agra, and then, in tones chained tight, she rasped, 'I would howl to the Wheel of Night, Delas, if I could. But I gave him to Elade Tharos. What choice did I have? He would keep the tracker alive when that tracker deserves death a thousand times over. What are we to do?'

Delas Fana rubbed at her face. The cold air was making it numb. 'He has his father in one more thing, Tonith Agra. Look at those who are with him. To earn such loyalty is, as we well know, a deadly gift.'

'Your point?'

'Does Elade Tharos possess the same?'

'He does, in his own way. There is a secret, sister, you will soon learn. A truth, if you will, that will change your world in a single day.'

'Not relevant,' Delas Fana replied. 'We are no different from those Jheck. Before us awaits a fateful choice. How will you live with your half-brother's blood on your hands?'

'*Not mine! Elade Tharos's!*'

Ignoring that fatuous defence, Delas Fana continued, 'And what of this loyalty you claim for your new Warleader? Will it survive his murdering a near-helpless pup who shares your blood?'

'Sister – that winged apparition, what was it?'

'I do not know,' Delas Fana confessed. 'As I said, this bastard son of a god has his father's talent for allies. Tell me, do all the Uryd now follow your Warleader?'

'They do. Even Widowed Dayliss.'

'That . . . impresses.'

Tonith Agra hissed out another breath. 'Elade Tharos will not stand long in Karsa Orlong's shadow.'

'Oh? Well, he might well proclaim the sun upon his face, and do so for ever, since our father continues to do nothing. But should that change—'

'You don't understand, sister. It does not matter that our father does nothing. It does not matter that he remains in Darujhistan. Before too long, Elade Tharos will come to him. We all will.'

Delas Fana stared in shock. 'That is madness!'

'The madness of the world, sister, is indifferent to our sensibilities. Did I not speak of a secret? We shall invade the southlands. We shall set the lands ablaze. And we shall not cease our march until we are at the walls of Darujhistan.' Tonith Agra spat onto the ground. 'Our father has failed his people. Elade Tharos has already usurped him.'

'Elade Tharos is not a god.'

'Nor is Karsa Orlong! How can he be, when he does nothing? When he refuses the title and all the responsibilities it demands of him?'

'He vowed to return to the Teblor—'

'He broke that vow.'

Delas Fana fell silent. Her sister was right, giving voice to her own internal battle, the siege of doubts surrounding her fading, failing convictions. After a time, she said, 'Perhaps news of this will stir our father into action.'

'Do not flee us again, sister. He will learn of it by other means.'

'I will not,' Delas Fana said. 'I cannot, because the bastard son is here, and he knows not that we are his sisters.'

'What if he did?'

'You are bringing him to Elade Tharos, to a duel, to his own death. If he knows you as his half-sister . . . well, I suspect all he has ever known in his short life is betrayal, so consider his lack of surprise a mercy to your conscience.'

'Mine alone? I think not.'

'I'm afraid it is,' said Delas Fana. 'For I will challenge Elade Tharos first. In defence of Rant's life. Did I say defence? I meant apology.'

'You cannot apologize for something you knew nothing about—'

'I know now, Tonith Agra. A belated apology is better than none at all. Better than betrayal.'

'If you were not my sister, Delas Fana, I would kill you for that insult to my honour.'

'Insult? I speak only the truth, Tonith Agra. You have chosen. You have given our half-brother to Elade Tharos. When you did so, you did not know him as kin. But you do now, and yet your promise – uttered in a cloud of ignorance – still demands your obeisance. That, sister, is a choice.'

'Elade Tharos will kill you.'

'And then kill your half-brother. Two of your kin will fall to Elade Tharos. How will you answer that?'

'This is impossible!'

Delas Fana collected up her bedroll. 'Sculp, to me,' she commanded. The beast rose. She turned to her sister. 'Deal with it.'

Hound at her side, she went off to find a suitable bed of grass.

Rant woke up on his side, curled up against the chill, but there was solid warmth at his back. Blinking sleep from his eyes, he slowly sat up to find a hound pressed against him, the animal twitching as it dreamed. He looked across to Damisk, a motionless form beneath furs. It took a few moments before Rant detected the slow rise and fall of the man's breathing.

'What is it with you?' Gower demanded from where he squatted a few paces away.

Rant considered the question. 'There is nothing with me, Lord.'

'You killed two dogs and yet this one gives you its warmth? No, Rant, there is indeed something about you. Your father is a god. That must count for something.'

'Perhaps it but sought *my* warmth.'

'Are you warm?'

'No.' Rant rubbed at his eyes, and then slowly climbed to his feet. The Teblor warriors were readying to depart. He saw the one named Delas Fana now approaching, her gaze fixed on him. Rant closed a hand on his knife's grip. Seeing the gesture, the woman shook her head.

'You are safe from me, son of Karsa Orlong.'

Rant let his hand fall away. 'Yes, I am for the Warleader.'

'Perhaps.' She halted a few paces away, glanced over at Gower. 'And how will you answer this pending travesty, Lord Gower of the Black Jheck?'

'I have been considering the problem. Damisk freed Rant from the binding of life to life. But Rant refuses to be free. He is stubborn, almost as stubborn as a Jheck.'

'You will surrender your role as emissary? Perhaps the other will take it.'

Gower's grimace was sour. 'Nilghan would if he could. Alas, it seems life to life binds us all. Nilghan, for my sins, is my brother. He may rail, but the brood of mothers know no greater loyalty.' He paused, and then added, 'Besides, there are Saemdhi ahead – in the camp we now journey to. Mortal enemies of the Jheck. This obscures everything.'

'I see.' Delas Fana studied the Jheck lord for a moment, and then swung her attention back to Rant. 'They will stand in your stead, bastard son.'

'I don't want them to.'

'I am told Elade Tharos is a mighty warrior, but there is more to this than that. He is the lone survivor of a Rathyd camp that your father attacked and destroyed. His hatred of you will be a white fire consuming his soul.'

'That does not make my killing him any easier,' said Rant. 'I wish to kill no one.'

'Without that ensorcelled knife, you will not kill anyone, Rant.'

Gower barked a laugh. 'Your Warleader is in for a surprise. Oh – do not look at me like that. I fought the lad before anything ever came to that knife. He damn near killed me.'

'Can he wield a sword? A spear?'

'If the Warleader is open to hand-to-hand combat, Teblor, I'd wager on Rant.'

Tonith Agra now joined her sister to listen in on the conversation. She looked exhausted, as if sleep had eluded her the entire night.

Delas Fana turned to her with brows lifted. 'Will he eschew weapons, sister?'

'Of course not,' Tonith Agra said, her tone fierce with some unknown emotion. 'He will kiss the edge of his sword and leave blood on his lips.'

'Then not a duel at all,' Gower said in a growl. 'Simple murder.'

'He may not get the chance,' said Delas Fana.

'Fully recovered,' said Gower, 'I might indeed kill him. As for Nilghan, well, he may prove a tougher challenge, especially if I hurt the Warleader first. Which I intend to do.'

And now the other Teblor were gathering, the surviving dogs among them, except for the beast that had slept beside Rant. That animal now sat beside the half-blood.

'The Warleader will be sorely tested indeed,' said Delas Fana, colour high in her cheeks. 'As it seems even Nape will stand for you.'

Rant looked down at the creature. 'That is this one's name? It is a good name.'

'The third born to Gnaw. Your father's beloved hound.' Delas waved at the dogs drawn closest to her. 'Sibling to Sculp, Muck and Cromb. They know you, Rant. They will, I think, even fight for you.' She smiled. 'You shall come before Warleader Elade Tharos as a small army, your own tribe, even.'

Startled, Rant looked around, gaze moving from Gower to Nilghan, and then to each Teblor dog that Delas Fana had named. 'But,' he said, bewildered, 'I have no tribe.'

Delas Fana had been studying her sister while Rant spoke, but now she shrugged and stepped forward, drawing her bloodsword as she did so.

Gower and Nilghan both growled.

Shifting the wooden blade so that it rested athwart her palms, Delas Fana met Rant's eyes, and then kissed her blade and slowly knelt before him. 'I am Delas Fana, daughter to Karsa Orlong. Born of rape. Rant, you are my half-brother. We are kin. If Warleader Elade Tharos refuses to face you unarmed, then I will challenge him first.' She still held his gaze, kneeling before him. 'Today and from this day forward, you have family.'

Tonith Agra hissed a vicious curse even as she drew her own wooden blade, kissed its gleaming edge, and then knelt. 'I am Tonith Agra, daughter to Karsa Orlong. Born of rape. If my sister falls to Elade Tharos, I will challenge him next. Know also this. There is a third sister, to you a third half-sister. She awaits us in the camp ahead. We are your siblings in truth – Rant – do you have others? By your mother?'

Mute, Rant shook his head. His soul, he realized, was weeping, but he didn't know why.

'The blood-oil didn't take her to you?'

'Once,' grated a voice off to one side. Damisk, leaning up on the one elbow that still worked, his eyes red smears in hollow, dark sockets. 'Only once. Then she drove him away.'

Delas Fana hissed. 'A woman of great courage, then. Of great strength of will.'

Rant stared at her. *My mother was brave? Strong?*

Damisk spoke, trying to raise his voice, 'Accept them, Rant. Accept your half-sisters as kin. As family.'

But Rant hesitated, and then shook his head. 'I cannot. If it means they die defending us, Damisk. I cannot.'

'As stubborn as a Jheck!' Gower roared, startling everyone. He straightened, glaring at Rant. 'You damned pup, do as you're told!

Do you think I want to die today? Does Nilghan? With three Teblor warriors standing between us and that fucking Warleader, our triumph is assured!'

'No,' said Rant again. 'It must not be. None will stand for me. None will die for me! Not even the dogs.'

'Then Damisk dies and he dies badly,' said Gower.

Rant shook his head. 'I will defeat the Warleader. But I won't kill him if I can help it. This is the only way.'

Abruptly, Tonith Agra began laughing. She stood, sheathing her blade, still laughing. 'Oh, he is assuredly Karsa Orlong's son!'

'But one ignorant of our ways,' Delas Fana said, still kneeling before Rant. 'Listen to me, half-brother. If you refuse our blades, you refuse us. What you decide now cannot be undone. Are we kin or not?'

'No one fights for me.'

Damisk was now on his feet, weaving unsteadily, his mangled arm dripping blood. 'It's not you they're fighting for, Rant. It's me. Will you stand in the way of my best chance at living?'

Rant frowned. 'I will let no one kill you, Damisk.'

'Your pride pretty much guarantees it, Rant.'

'You believe I will fail against this Warleader?'

'You're not thinking this through,' Damisk said wearily. 'Even if I am spared, they will not let me leave. They cannot.'

'We will both leave,' insisted Rant. 'We can do so now.' He looked at Delas Fana. 'They will not stop us.'

'They will,' said Gower. 'No word can be brought to the south-landers, as Damisk will surely attempt. If he can, which I now begin to doubt. The tracker is already half-dead.'

Nilghan spoke. 'I am of a mind to kill him myself! Oh, pup, do not look so wretched. If I do it will be an act of mercy.'

'I'll not resist,' said Damisk, head bowing. 'Be swift, Nilghan.'

The two Rathyd warriors moved to place themselves between Damisk and the Jheck warrior, their own hounds among them.

Nilghan snarled. 'Heed this, Rant. The Teblor will not relinquish the tracker, not now, not ever, no matter what you do.'

'Oh,' sighed Tonith Agra, 'do stand up, sister. This bastard rejects us.'

'No!' Rant shouted, facing them again. 'I don't! But I don't know what any of this means! What are half-sisters? Are there other women out there like my mother? Other women cursed with the blood-oil of our father? And . . . what is rape?'

'Ahh,' Gower said in something like a ragged sob, 'shit.'

*

The shock of Rant's bewildered confession was like a solid blow against Delas Fana's chest. She struggled to speak. *We are such fools – we thought him a near-man, but he is still a child. He understands nothing of this.* 'Rant, please touch the blade of my sword.'

'Will you fight the Warleader before me?'

She shook her head. 'There will be no challenge, no fight between you and Elade Tharos.'

'None,' added Tonith Agra, her face strangely twisted, tears filling her eyes. 'Elade Tharos has honour. This I swear.'

The confusion on Rant's face deepened. 'I don't understand,' he said again in a small voice. 'Damisk—'

'You cannot fight for him,' said Delas Fana. 'No Teblor will allow it. Rant, I beg you, touch the blade!'

He reached out and did so. Tonith Agra stepped forward, drawing her own weapon again and holding it between them. 'We are half-siblings, Rant. Same father, different mothers. It is the Teblor way to claim a night with the wives and daughters of age of any warrior they slay. They lie with them, and sometimes a child comes of that. Because the wife and daughters must agree to this or forfeit their lives, this is called *rape*—'

'By the southlanders,' cut in Delas Fana, rising at last from her kneeling position. 'Among the Teblor, this is a warrior's *right*, be that warrior male or female. Obviously, only a male lying with a female can produce a child. This is accepted among our people.'

Rant touched Tonith Agra's blade.

'Barbarians,' Nilghan growled.

Rant turned to Damisk and then walked towards him. 'Damisk, what is going to happen? Why can't I fight for you? I promised—'

Weakly, Damisk sat back down. He waved his uninjured hand. 'Rant, remember that Malazan marine who gave you the knife? The tale you told me of the other children trying to take it from you, and how that soldier sent one flying with the back of his hand?'

'Yes, but—'

'What if that marine had drawn a sword and cut the boy down?'

'He wouldn't—'

'Why not?'

'Because—' Rant frowned. 'Because a soldier wouldn't do that.'

'No honourable adult would, and for the Teblor, honour is everything. Rant, among your people, you are not yet a man. The Warleader cannot fight you, for the same reason the marine could not – would not – cut down that child.'

Rant turned back to meet Delas Fana's eyes. 'Is this true? I'm to be treated as a child?'

'Because you *are* a child.'

'I am almost fifteen years old!'

Tonith Agra spoke. 'For you there has been no Night of Blood, Rant. Until then, in the eyes of all Teblor, you remain a child. But more than that,' and she turned to the two Rathyd warriors still standing between Nilghan and Damisk, 'it is the purpose of every adult Teblor to protect you, no matter what tribe claims you. Do I not speak the truth, Sivith Gyla? Toras Vaunt? Valoc?'

The Sunyd man and both Rathyd women nodded.

Tonith faced Rant again. 'There is no more solemn vow a grown Teblor holds to, none to challenge the protection of a child.'

'Yet,' said Damisk in a rasp, 'you call us *children*.'

'Because you are small,' Tonith Agra snapped. 'Because a child cares for no one but itself. Because each one of you lives as if right and wrong is someone else's problem. Because you are without restraint, consumed by greed – you would stuff the entire world into your mouth given the chance. You are what a Teblor child would be *if it never grew up*.'

Rant said, 'I am none of the things you say a child is, Tonith Agra.'

Nodding, she smiled at him, but it was a fragile smile. 'No, Rant, you most assuredly are not.' She hesitated, and then said, 'It seems you have been quickly raised into the virtues and responsibilities of adulthood. Likely not by your mother, strong as she may have been. No, I now think . . .' she looked to Gower, and Nilghan, and then to Damisk, 'your friends here have guided you well.'

'Then if I do not behave like a child—'

'The law,' Delas Fana cut in, 'remains. Until your Night of Blood, you are a child.'

'Damisk,' said Rant, 'what are we going to do?'

'You do nothing,' the tracker replied. 'This is between me and the Teblor.'

'They will kill you!'

'I've lived a long life. It wasn't all good and I won't say otherwise. In a way,' he added with a wry smile, 'this is fitting. Some people tell themselves that their past is behind them, as if being responsible has a time limit and if you live long enough, you've outrun it.' He shook his head. 'It all catches up, sooner or later.'

Delas Fana spoke to one of the Rathyd warriors. 'Sivith Gyla?'

The taller of the two women glanced over.

'Bind Damisk's wound, else he bleeds out before we can reach the camp.'

Rant turned to her, expression darkening. 'I am not Teblor, not part of your tribe! That law is your law, not mine.'

'But you are among us now,' Delas Fana replied. 'All that follows will be among the Teblor. Our laws. Our ways.'

Tears streaked Rant's cheeks, and his hands were fists, the knotted knuckles white. He faced Damisk. 'I have killed you,' he said.

'No,' said the tracker. 'Understand this, Rant. It was me who tracked runaway slaves. Me who led the raiding parties. It was my idea to kill all the game in the Sunyd lands, weakening the people, driving them into starvation. And for these crimes, the fate awaiting me is just.'

Now horror replaced the grief in Rant's eyes. 'But . . . why did you do that, Damisk?'

He shrugged. 'The child would devour the world, if he could. We choose to do things for the simplest of reasons. Coin. And from coin we buy food, clothing, a place to live. Each of us strives to meet these needs, Rant. Whatever we do to get that coin, well, we justify it, because everyone has a right to live, don't they?'

Rant wiped at his cheeks. Delas Fana could see how deflated he had become. Broken, as if Damisk's words had stolen the honour of their friendship. But she understood Damisk. She understood what he was doing. It just wasn't easy to listen to.

Tonith Agra caught her sister's attention, gesturing. Sighing, Delas Fana joined her and they strode a dozen paces away from the others. They faced the escarpment's steep descent, the tracks through the high grasses left behind by those who climbed it the day before still visible.

'What is this story about slaying all the game in the Sunyd lands?' Tonith Agra demanded. 'Such a thing is impossible.'

'He probably lies,' Delas Fana replied. 'He builds up his crimes to sever Rant's loyalty.'

'The other things he said are true.'

'I know. But perhaps they are not enough. After all, a tracker is hired to do such things.'

Tonith Agra grunted. 'We never doubted the courage of Damisk Tracker.'

'Perhaps,' ventured Delas Fana, 'your Warleader can be convinced to give Damisk a courageous death.'

'He will be given the chance to be brave,' Tonith Agra replied.

Delas frowned. 'Why would Elade Tharos do that?'

'To remind us all, sister, that the southlanders have brave warriors among them. That they are not to be underestimated.'

Delas Fana snorted. 'Too late for that. You have already underestimated them, if you believe we shall march all the way to Darujhistan.'

'You have not seen the army that has gathered. Teblor tribes we'd thought to be mere legends, lost in time, are now among us. Vathyn.

Menark. Tryz Roke. All from the Rippled Lands. Saemdhi in their thousands, with Bright Knot among them. And soon, perhaps, the Jheck.'

Baffled, Delas Fana shook her head. 'How did Elade Tharos achieve such a thing? The Rippled Lands are far from any Malazan or Genabarii threat. The Saemdhi and the Jheck are from the ice-lands. Again, no southern enemy assails them. This makes no sense, Tonith.'

'It will, soon,' promised her sister. 'Now, we must walk west, to the very end of the escarpment.'

Delas Fana made a sour sound. 'Walk I shall, since you've stolen my horse.'

'Borrowed, sister. The beast needed a rider after so long without one. But if you like, you can ride her now.'

'No, it is fine,' said Delas Fana. She swung round to regard the strange party. 'Our poor brother,' she murmured.

'He has older sisters now,' Tonith Agra said in a hard tone. 'Protectors. Imagine Sathal's face when she learns of this – when she first looks upon her new kin. We will take care of him, Delas Fana. We shall be his wall of swords.'

Delas Fana smiled and then slowly nodded. 'Sisters three.'

CHAPTER FIFTEEN

Warfare is a restless art. It may suit the tellers of tales to fix it in place. It may suit the creators of tapestries, frescoes and paintings to set upon battle-scenes of the distant past the modern phalanx, the panoply of common weapons: hauberks of chain and visored helms, the sky raining arrows and great siege engines battering the walls. The truth is: ways of killing define progress, not just in our civilization, but in all civilizations. These things evolve and as they evolve, they become more lethal.

In the late years of the reign of Emperor Mallick Rel, the Malazan legion shared only the trappings of its earlier predecessors. It was, in fact, utterly transformed from preceding periods of Early and Middle Conquest, and if it is said (by numerous contemporaries of that time) that the standard legion of regulars had declined in training, discipline and combat effectiveness, none would challenge the corresponding rise of the Marine Legion . . .

> Introduction to 'The Last Day of The North'
> Resling's *History of Now*
> The Great Library of New Morn

'EVERYBODY WAS ALWAYS LOOKING AT MY CLEAVAGE SO NOW IT looks back,' said Anyx Fro, sitting in a chair with muddy boots propped up on the edge of Folibore's bed which was fine since Folibore was off on patrol.

Stillwater tugged at her linen scarf. It was feeling tight these days, like a noose slowly constricting, no matter how loose she wrapped it around her throat. 'That's all very fine, Anyx, but your cleavage's eyes are little buttons of insanity.'

Scowling, Anyx patted the weasel on the head, which made sense, since its head was the only thing visible above her woollen shirt, tucked snugly between her breasts. She was about to say something but the door to their room thumped and then burst open, revealing Corporal Snack's muddy backside as he dragged in a huge sack across the threshold.

'Wrong room again!' Anyx and Stillwater shouted in unison.

Hunched over and still backing his way in, Snack twisted to look. 'That's fine,' he said. 'I'll just be leaving this here, for safe keeping.'

Stillwater sat up on the bed. The sack clanked and clunked. It was filled with knobby things. 'That's not your usual sack of useless shit, is it?'

'I'm adding to my collection,' Snack said, grunting as he dragged the sack up to the foot of Folibore's bed. 'Besides, this isn't your room either, neither of you. This is Folibore's and Blanket's room.'

'Our room smells,' said Stillwater. 'That weasel is crapping and pissing and spraying everywhere.'

'I'm still training it,' objected Anyx Fro. 'That's what the tray of sand is for.'

Stillwater glanced over, met the weasel's beady stare. 'Training it to do what, shit and piss and spray everywhere? You've done a bang-up job, then. Here I was worried it was untrainable, being a mangy rope of fur with a head stuck on one end. And when are you going to give it a name?'

'I have. Its name is . . .' Anyx Fro frowned. 'Creature.'

Snack was doubling and then tripling the knots on the sack. 'Nobody go prying,' he ordered. 'This is private business.'

'Relax,' said Stillwater. 'We already checked out your original sack. This looks like more of the same. You've got a problem, you know that? We're all agreed. You need help.'

Straightening, Snack glared at her, his face flushing. 'Where's your decency? Your respect for the possessions of someone else? A superior officer at that! You're all worse than scum, damn you.'

'Not me,' said Anyx Fro. 'It's obviously a fetish which makes help impossible. Everyone else got all worked up about it. I didn't.'

Snack fixed his glare on her, but whatever he was going to say never came out. Instead, his face went redder still, his eyes bulging slightly.

Anyx Fro shot Stillwater a knowing look. 'See? Where did his gaze go first?'

'That – that looks unhygienic,' Snack managed.

Stillwater nodded. 'I know. It's a wonder it isn't dead. Poor Creature.'

More boots on the landing and a moment later Folibore entered, followed by Blanket. They paused, expressions clouding with confusion.

'Wrong room,' said Stillwater in a sudden flash of inspiration. 'You guys are across the way. Don't know what you do in there but the place stinks. Just passing by the door is an ordeal.'

'Oh,' said Folibore. 'Sorry. Anyway, Still, you and Anyx are due for the street patrol.' He paused and nodded to Snack. 'Corporal.' Then he looked over at Anyx Fro and nodded again. 'Creature.' Turning around, he said to Blanket, 'Come on, then, it's the wrong room.'

'But why are my things in here?'

Folibore halted at the threshold. 'Don't tell her I said anything, but I think Anyx Fro has a thing for you, but she knows it's hopeless, so she just steals your stuff instead.'

Blanket scratched his beard, and then shrugged.

They went out, closing the door behind them.

Snack looked at Stillwater. 'That was mean,' he said.

'In a bell's time they'll realize they've been duped,' Stillwater explained, rising from the bed. 'And come storming in here all hot and offended. But we'll be out on patrol. Anyx, let's get going, shall we?'

'But it's raining outside.'

'That's what ponchos are for.'

'Creature doesn't like them. Creature can't see.'

'That's fine, because Creature is not going out on patrol. We are. Creature is a weasel, in a constant state of rage because it's just smart enough to know how stupid it is. I suggest you leave it in Folibore's and Blanket's room.'

Anyx brightened. 'Good idea.'

They stepped out into the corridor. Anyx reached between her breasts and pulled out what looked to be a near-comatose weasel. 'Don't!' she snapped when Stillwater reached out to poke its face. 'Creature hates you. Creature will bite your finger right off.' She knocked on the door opposite.

After a moment Folibore opened it, but he was wearing a cloth tied tight around the lower half of his face. 'Yes?'

Anyx ducked slightly and let Creature jump out of her hands. It dashed for the shadows under the bed Blanket was sitting on. 'Just for now,' said Anyx Fro, smiling around a mouthful of rustleaf. 'You know, like last time.'

'Oh,' said Folibore. 'Right. Well,' he added in relief, 'that explains the tray and all the sandy shit.'

'And get Blanket to toss me my poncho, there on the peg beside the bed.'

'Ah,' said Folibore with a sage nod, 'it seems the obsession goes both ways. You two should do something about this, you know.'

'We would,' said Anyx Fro, 'if we didn't hate each other.'

Corporal Snack stepped out into the corridor. 'Get going, you two. Benger's waiting for you outside.'

'Benger?' Stillwater asked. 'What's he want with us?'

'How should I know?' Snack retorted, bushy black eyebrows beetling. 'It's Benger.'

Stillwater tugged at Anyx whose head had disappeared beneath the poncho as she struggled into it. 'Let's go.'

'But I can't see!' came the muffled complaint.

'Come along,' said Stillwater, dragging her companion down the corridor. 'I'll let you know when you hit the stairs.'

'Ah,' said Benger, 'women!'

'Bit of a stretch,' said Stillwater, glancing sidelong at Anyx Fro.

Benger straightened from the wall he had been leaning against, out of the rain if not the wind. He drew up his poncho hood. 'It's important that you have tits and stuff,' he said, 'for what's coming.' He stepped off the wooden walkway, splashing into the ankle-deep mud of the street, and then turned and stared up at Stillwater and Anyx Fro, who had not moved. 'The thing to do now is follow me.'

'Because we have tits and stuff?' Anyx Fro demanded. 'I don't think so, Benger.'

'Are you sure you want us to follow you?' Stillwater asked. 'I mean, if I had my knife out and slipped or something. Poor Benger, that's all I'm saying.'

He stared up at them for a moment longer, and then gestured with both hands. 'Oh, it's nothing like that. This is officially sanctioned by the captain himself. But you see, I couldn't use Blanket and Folibore. I need women.'

'Tits and stuff?' Anyx said.

'Exactly, now you have it, so come along you two, we're on an errand of mercy.' Neither woman moved. Benger scowled. 'Fuck sake, now what?'

'Well,' said Stillwater, 'you're good at talking, and we all know that, right? So it's not too shocking that you caressed the captain's downy ear-lobe about the need for a woman—'

'Or two,' Anyx Fro added.

'Or two, well, almost two, I mean. And no doubt at all that we're talking supreme acts of mercy here.'

'On our part,' said Anyx Fro. 'Maybe even getting mentioned in dispatches, possibly a commendation or two.'

Stillwater nodded. 'Thing is, Benger, I'd rather get beheaded by a five-year-old with a dull axe than fuck you.'

'A *blind* five-year-old,' said Anyx Fro, crossing her arms – the gesture of defiance mostly unseen as it was beneath her poncho.

Benger said nothing for a moment, and then giggled. 'You two crack me up. Sleep with either of you? Let's find that blind five-year-old and he can start on me first.' He waved again. 'Stop pissing around. This is marine business we're about here, not indulging the twisted sexual fantasies of a witch-haunted night-creeper and a can't-walk-straight soldier who stinks of weasel spunk. Now, march!'

He set off again, and this time both soldiers followed, if the uneven heavy splashes of boots in mud was any indication, and a glance back assured him it was. He shook his head. Women pretended otherwise, but they obsessed about sex just as much as any man. Or maybe it was just these two – no, Sergeant Shrake was even worse, sucking on that mouthful of silky hair and whatnot. *And the way she walks. I mean, seriously?*

They crossed the street up near the corner that faced onto the main street, and then crossed that as well.

Behind Benger, Stillwater hissed and said, 'You're taking us to the Three-Legged Dog? I told you, Benger, we're not—'

'Wait!' interjected Anyx Fro. 'If he buys us drinks first?'

'We're not going to the fucking bar!' Benger snapped.

They continued on, heading towards the lakefront. Arriving at the last house before the boat-yards, Benger halted and swung to face the soldiers. 'All right, we're here.'

'We're not anywhere!' objected Anyx Fro, looking around.

'She's . . . wrong,' said Stillwater. 'Oh. Hold on, Benger – have you lost your mind? We're talking *blood-oil* with this one!'

Anyx Fro spun to stare at the narrow, ramshackle house. 'This is *her*? You been taking sips, Benger? That's not good. We can't help you. Except maybe, lethal poison.'

'High Denul,' said Benger, scowling at both women. 'Listen. This is the problem as I see it. It's the problem of what the fuck are we doing here? We're Malazan marines and here is where we've been posted, so what's our job? Clanking around looking tough? Drinking all their ale and wine? Taking over houses and getting in everybody's face? Sure, all that. But there's more, too, isn't there? We help where we can.'

'And you think you can?' Stillwater asked.

'Maybe. I mean to try.'

'So what do you need us for?' Anyx Fro asked. 'I don't do that kind of magery and neither does Still. We're the wrong – oh, tits and stuff.'

'But not local, so you two got no reason to be nasty, right? Well, have you?'

Anyx Fro shrugged. 'It's a bad way for her, aye.'

'Stillwater?'

She studied Benger with narrowed eyes. 'You're really going to try, Benger?'

'Aye, I am.'

'Pull this off and maybe, just *maybe*, I'll fuck you.'

Benger blinked, rapidly, and kept blinking. 'Huh? But, I mean, ahh, I see. Because I'm not the shit you think I am.'

'I'm not forgetting you never heal me when I accidentally cut myself,' Stillwater replied. 'What I'm saying is, you do this, Benger, and you're a good man in my eyes. For a while.'

Anyx Fro, who had been staring at Stillwater with incredulity, was now frowning. 'So that was the offer of what, a metaphorical fuck?'

'Exactly,' said Stillwater.

Benger rubbed vigorously at his face and then said, 'The other point is she shouldn't be afraid of you, because she doesn't know you. Yet.'

Someone else was walking up the street towards them. A local man, face hidden by a dripping woollen cowl. Startled when he almost collided with Stillwater, he swore out loud and sidestepped in an effort to pass her. Stillwater got in his face again. 'Not tonight,' she said. 'Go home to your wife before I gut you for being a shit.'

The local man retreated, quickly, and then paused and turned round. A small sack appeared from under his cloak. 'Food,' he said, 'for Sarlis.'

At Benger's nod, Anyx Fro went over and collected it.

'All right,' said Benger, facing the door, 'Let's do this.'

Sarlis had few memories left of her childhood, and even fewer of her teenage years. All that she was had been torn away in a single day. Now, images like ragged tatters of cloth floated through her mind, stained red by blood-oil. On her small, knobby knees on the lake's stony beach, moving stones aside to expose the finer sands beneath, which were mostly made of what looked like glass beads, in a dazzling array of colours. Crying out at their glinting magic.

There were times, when the fever was upon her, that she saw those handfuls of glittering sand, and the sunlight igniting all the hues brought pain to her eyes. Terrible pain, yet she could not stop staring, the pain crawling like fire beneath her skin, spreading out to engulf her face, then neck, then chest, shoulders and arms and hands.

Sunlight and colour like venom in her veins.

Another day, this one of ice on the lake, a vast stretch of blinding white, the surface sculpted by the winds that came down from the north. A man and a woman – her parents? Possibly. The air was cold but fresh, and whatever she was wearing made her immune to its bite. Plumes of breath riding laughter, excited shouts, the crust of snow breaking when she fell.

In the heated cauldron her body had become, crimson steam would rise to flood her being. That cauldron was home to a red serpent. She would watch it uncurl and lift into view, the snake's head breaking through the lake's ice, and the water welling up around it wasn't water, but blood.

There was no value in holding on to the memories of the girl she had been. Each one succumbed to who she was now. Yet they lived on, untethered to anything. She came to believe there was a purpose to this. Every scene of innocence existed in her mind as pieces awaiting corruption, and it was her fate to witness that poisoning again and again.

The serpent was stirring. She sat in the attic, in the room that had been her son's, looking out the mottled window. Days of rain were preferable. The water devoured the distance, made all things grey and blue. Few people moved about on the muddy street. Smoke from chimneys sank downward rather than lifted skyward. The outside world was in the habit of disappearing when heavier sheets of rain came ashore.

The first man would come at dusk. He would bring food and a few coins. They all brought food, because it was no easy thing leaving the house, hated as she was by most of the town's denizens, especially the women.

The fragmentary nature of her memories belonged only to her life before the blood-oil. Everything that followed was burned into her with vicious clarity. The blood-oil clung to her nerves, heightened every sense, and it seemed there was no limit to what could be seared onto her soul. Every cry of anguish and ecstasy that broke her lips still echoed in her mind; every convulsion still trembled through her flesh. Echoes and ripples unending. She thought this to be her fate, past into future, an unbroken succession that would only end when age claimed her – when no man or woman would want her any more. And then? Why, only madness.

But now that had changed. There was one memory that cut through all the others, one memory that seemed immune to the red stain. Its edge was cold and sharp, and to linger over it, almost lovingly, was to feel something new, unexpected, delicious.

She could defeat the blood-oil. She could spit into the face of the serpent. This was the message behind the memory. *Freedom.*

Sarlis found herself smiling, an expression that was coming to her more and more as each day and night passed since—

A shudder ran through her. What preceded that perfect memory were other ones, terrible ones. Depravity's depths knew no bottom; it just went down and down, and down. But she could escape that as well. All this was possible now.

Still smiling, Sarlis reached out and lightly traced with one finger a line across her throat.

Where the knife's iron blade had rested.

The knock at the door below didn't sound right. Sarlis knew most knocks from her customers. She descended from the loft, poured tea into a clay cup and then sat at her kitchen table, its surface scarred and gouged by years of manic fingernails. The knife awaited her, freshly honed and resting within reach.

The knock came a second time, and that in itself was unusual. Those who came to her normally entered after the first rap of knuckles. Sarlis hesitated, wondering if she should rise and walk to it. Instead, she said, 'Enter.'

The snake within stirred and stirred. She could feel its flicking tongue, and everywhere it touched grew hot, eager.

The door opened and three hooded figures entered. Soldiers. She had wondered when the first would come to her door. But three? The one in the lead shook off rain and then pulled back his hood.

Something made Sarlis flinch.

Behind the man, the withdrawn hoods revealed two women. The taller of the two nodded and said, 'Most women do that when they see Benger for the first time.'

'I still do,' said the other woman, her face broad and pale, strangely sensuous. 'I've just learned to hide it. You know. Cough. Sour belch. Like that.'

'Don't listen to them,' said the man. 'They're just here as examples of women who don't fear or hate you. To put you at ease.'

The serpent inside was twisting now, anguished or irritated. 'You want them to watch?' she asked.

'They can do what they like,' the man said, looking momentarily confused. 'I'm the one you're going to talk to.'

'Talk?'

The taller woman snorted, clomping over to the pot of stewed herbs. 'Is this tea? Smells like tea. Can I have some? The thing about Benger, you see, is that he's a nitwit about some things.'

'Most things,' corrected the other woman. 'Pour me one too, Still, unless you've decided to take rudeness to the next level.' She began removing her poncho. 'It's hot in here. Is it hot in here?'

'I'm Benger,' the man said to Sarlis. His poncho differed from that of the others in that it had clasps on the front, and he'd begun tugging them loose. 'We're marines, Fourteenth Legion. That's Stillwater pouring the tea and the one who's reacting to your blood-oil, that's Anyx Fro.' There was sweat on his pocked brow. 'And she ain't alone in that, gods below.' He slapped his cheeks and shook himself like a dog shedding water, then clapped his hands and dragged the only other chair opposite Sarlis. Sitting, he blew out a heavy breath. 'Concentration won't be easy.'

'What do you want?' Sarlis demanded of all three, her eyes flicking from one to the next, finally returning to Benger.

Stillwater was standing with two clay cups in her hands, frowning down at Benger. 'That's a big chair you're sitting in, Benger. Low seat, though. You could prop a bear in that thing.'

'My son's,' said Sarlis.

There was a moment of silence, the two women exchanging glances that meant little to Sarlis, and then Benger cleared his throat. 'There's the problem. One of them, anyway. Is he here?'

Swirling pain, horror and guilt flushed through Sarlis. She looked away. 'He's gone. I sent him away.'

'Still in town?'

She shook her head.

'How old would he be by now?'

She didn't like Benger's eyes. They were too sharp but not in the way of blood-oil's hunger that she saw in others who came to her. She looked up to see Stillwater studying her. One eyebrow slowly lifted, and then the woman winked. Sarlis looked away again. 'I have work to do—'

'Not tonight,' said Stillwater, not harshly.

'Oh,' said Anyx Fro, bending to rummage under the poncho she'd left on the floor. She lifted into view a sack. 'Food. We won't make you go hungry. But tonight your business is with us.'

Sarlis nodded, rose and began lifting her shirt.

'No!' barked Benger. 'Stop! Sorry for shouting. She didn't mean it that way. Listen, I've got some questions I'd like to ask, if that's all right. To start. Where it goes from there is . . . well, we'll decide that then. Your son, how old is he?'

'I don't know,' Sarlis said after a moment. She sat back down, her gaze skittering across the knife on the table. There was a way out. She knew that now, drew strength from it. It didn't matter if these soldiers wasted her time. 'I was pregnant for so long.'

'A year?' Benger asked.

She shrugged. 'Maybe two.'

A foreign curse hissed from Stillwater.

'And the child,' Benger pressed, 'took his time growing, didn't he?'

'Years and years. He mixed up his friends whenever one group grew past him and another group showed up – he thought they were the same, the same friends. They weren't. They weren't his friends, either.'

'You thought his mind was weak, or broken,' said Benger, nodding. 'Stunted, even. But that's the Toblakai part of him. It's slow. Years and years of slow. And then there's his father – you know him by name?'

'Karsa Orlong. It is said he lives in Darujhistan, a city far to the south. A city beside a lake. It is said he is now a god.'

Benger tapped fingers on the table, and then his attention shifted to it. Sarlis watched him looking at the deep gouges, the crisscrossing scars. Glancing at her hands he probably saw the blood crusted around her nails. Something flickered across his face. 'Blood-oil,' he said, meeting her eyes, and this time she did not look away. 'Anyone ever sat you down and explained it to you?'

'Explained? Explained what?' Hysterical laughter bubbled suddenly in Sarlis, but she fought it back down. 'What is there to explain? A fever. A disease. A madness. Yes, a madness.'

Benger's eyes hardened. 'All these years, and no one's had the mercy to tell you anything?'

'There is nothing to tell.' Something like anger made her add, 'I am inside looking out. You are not.'

'She has a point,' said Stillwater, passing one cup to Anyx Fro and then tugging at the scarf around her neck, as if it chafed.

'I know that!' Benger snapped at his soldier. He paused, drew a deep breath, and spoke in a quieter tone. 'Your name, I'm told, is Sarlis. Yes? Good. Very well, Sarlis. Blood-oil is a restless tide. It doesn't just spread, doesn't go in just one direction, ever outward as it were. This has been studied. It flows back and forth. Even now – and this is important – it's flowing between you and Karsa Orlong. Between you and your son and between your son and his father.' He waved a hand. 'Doesn't matter how many leagues apart you three are. Flowing, back and forth, back and forth.'

Sarlis stared at the man, and then shook her head. 'My son is not . . . not . . . not like me. No fever. No . . . needs. And his father? I do not think of his father. Ever.'

'Toblakai—'

'Teblor,' cut in Anyx Fro. 'The tribes here are named Teblor, Benger.'

'Fine. *Teblor* do not succumb to the curse of blood-oil. Not the way humans do. It's not permanent, for one thing. It's quickly expended.'

Expended, yes. In me.

'But its essence remains, a lingering component in Teblor blood. There are elements of otataral in blood-oil, making Teblor resistant to magic, but that immunity is not consistent. Some Teblor are more immune to sorcery than others. Karsa Orlong is . . . very immune. But the problem I'm getting to, Sarlis, has to do with that ebb and flow, the tide itself. You see, what comes back to you from Karsa Orlong – in that unseen stream – is now coming from a *god.*'

'Widow's empty nights,' muttered Stillwater, 'that doesn't sound good. You giving up on this, Benger? What can even High Denul do against that?'

'My son is not like me,' insisted Sarlis. She'd barely understood most of what Benger was saying.

'He won't be,' Benger said, 'I don't think. His father's blood is strong. But I'm also thinking . . . it needs to be stronger.'

'Stronger?'

Another flicker in Benger's eyes, but he nodded. 'Just to make sure he's safe.'

'How can he be made stronger?' Sarlis wanted to know.

'And that's the problem all right,' he said, hands flattening on the table as he leaned back. 'And I think I have a solution, the kind that solves two problems all in one.'

'Tell me,' Sarlis said, body now taut, 'how can Rant be made stronger?'

'That tidal flow, Sarlis, the one coming to you from Karsa Orlong. I think I can divert it. Into your son. I think I can bend it away from you entirely. And once I do that, I think I can end your curse of blood-oil.'

It was suddenly hard to hear anything. Sarlis stared, saw Benger's lips moving, but no sound reached her. Something was filling her head, hot as the sand beneath a hearth. She could vaguely hear the drum in her chest, the beating thing held fast in the fist of blood-oil, thundering louder and louder – but all at a distance.

Benger waved a hand in front of her face. She ignored it – no, untrue. She had nothing left within her that could react to it, or to anything else.

Inside looking out.

Stillwater appeared, plucking Benger from the chair, taking her seat to face Sarlis, pushing a cup of tea into Sarlis's hands, lifting both hands to her lips, making her drink. She said something but the words arrived in a meaningless murmur. After a moment, Stillwater removed the cup and set it down on the table. She stood and came around to position herself behind Sarlis, leaning over to whisper in one ear.

At first only the breath reached Sarlis, warm and damp. Then there was something like a snarl, and for a brief instant Sarlis saw a vision – a memory – not her own. A thin cloth upon lifeless eyes, that were suddenly no longer lifeless, the point of view shifting until *she* was the one looking up through the gauze.

'*This bitch is worse than useless! One day I'll strangle her, rope or not, I swear it! Listen, you sad tortured thing. Take Benger's offer. Leave him to turn the tide away from you. But understand one thing: once it's severed, once you're on dry land, the stream between you and your son will be gone, too. No choice.*'

At that, a wail rose from deep within Sarlis, moments from finding voice.

'*Stop that screaming! Listen! You want Rant safe? You want him free of the curse? You've got to cut yourself away from him, for ever. For his sake. You've got to take that on – it's the price you must pay. Will you do this? Answ—*'

'—Denul, Sarlis. This is what we do. Benger's better at explaining this than me. In fact, you wouldn't think any of this can come from me at all. If you knew anything about me, that is. But listen. It's what it means to be a Malazan marine. We save people. That's why Benger is here.'

That last voice belonged to Stillwater, the words hot against Sarlis's ear. She drew a sobbing breath, and then nodded.

A calloused soldier's hand gripped her shoulder briefly, and then Stillwater reappeared, collecting up the cup again and offering it to Sarlis.

She took it, met Benger's eyes. 'The curse?'

Sighing, Benger held up both hands. 'I'm not sure. But once I isolate you, once I get the flow from Karsa Orlong stopped, then I can take a closer look at the blood-oil in you. I can't promise, but I have hopes of healing you, yes. That's the problem and that's the plan. What say you?'

Only tears answered him.

Spindle had walked down to the lake and now stood on the beach to the west of the docks and jetties. The rain was marching in sheets across the water, the far shore not even visible. The air was warm now that spring was giving way to summer. Drops fell from the brim of his poncho's oiled hood. Undercart's sorcery was slow to dissipate, or perhaps this was just the season's normal course.

Rain on the still water of a lake made a peaceful sound and it had a way of quelling the turmoil in Spindle's head. He had been haunted by memories of Black Coral, the pilgrims' camp and the children he and

Monkrat had saved. There had been harsh words between them, but in the end, Monkrat had remembered the soldier's vow.

The fear in the man's eyes, there in the carriage outside the company's headquarters, when he hissed his last warning, still burned in Spindle's mind.

He heard boots crunching on the pebbled beach and turned to see Bliss Rolly tramping towards him. When she arrived she halted at his side and faced the lake as he had been doing.

'I figured this to be out of the way,' she said after a moment. 'Peace and quiet was what I wanted. The slaving pissed me off. Against imperial law, but the captain of the garrison was being paid on the sly.'

'Where is that captain now?' Spindle asked.

'Mostly in the lake. One of the escaped slaves tracked him down, I suppose, put a knife up the underside of his chin. We found the body in a burned-down shack, gathered what charred bones we could and fed them to the lake.'

'Not a barrow?'

Bliss Rolly wore no poncho. Water soaked her hair and trickled down her face. 'I had him charged for corruption, officially. Dead or not, he was stripped of rank.' She paused. 'Didn't deserve to lie with our fallen soldiers.'

'"Malazan justice doesn't stop at the grave's edge,"' said Spindle, nodding.

'That sounds like a quote.'

'Rel's Fifth Edict. It's what allowed you to posthumously charge your captain.'

Bliss grunted. 'No wonder it went so smoothly. I just figured, since he wasn't there to defend himself . . .'

'The Emperor's new code of laws is pretty damned extensive,' said Spindle. 'Mallick Rel may be a bastard but he doesn't lack zeal, or intelligence. I have no problem serving him.'

Bliss Rolly sighed. 'Eight years of peace, barring a few bar-fights here and there. You have a point, friend.'

Spindle managed a slight smile. 'Bar-fights? Bliss, what you found yourself in on the Jhag Odhan was *not* a bar-fight.'

'I guess not,' she admitted, and then added, 'What it was, was stupid.'

'Never poke a Jaghut,' said Spindle. 'Especially now that the T'lan Imass are gone.'

Bliss Rolly blew air out in a spray of water. 'Spindle, the Saemdhi north of here are Imass. Flesh-and-blood Imass. Very few flint weapons, though. Bone and antler. Ugly, nasty things.'

'The Saemdhi or their weapons?'

'Both.'

'I doubt these flesh-and-blood Imass are bound to any war with the Jaghut,' said Spindle.

'Agreed. I was wondering, when do you expect Oams back?'

'Not sure. Soon, I hope.'

She nodded. 'It'd better be.'

They were silent for a time, and then Bliss Rolly spoke again. 'That captain of yours, Gruff. He's . . .' She shook her head.

'Aye,' agreed Spindle. 'That.'

'This whole thing with Marine Legions now,' she resumed, 'did it come from the Emperor or one of his cronies?'

'The Emperor.'

She edged round to face him. Seeing her face, the flushed round cheeks, the deep brown eyes, Spindle felt a flutter in his chest. 'Are the rumours true?' she asked.

He shrugged. 'Probably.' He wasn't prepared to add to that at the moment, as he was too busy chastising himself. He was too old to be thinking – feeling – this stuff. Holding her gaze, as she searched his eyes, wasn't easy.

'No worries about Gruff then?'

'None at all.'

She jerked a single nod, faced the lake again. 'Good.'

'Did he see you coming?'

'No. Sometimes I wish he had.'

'You made it mercifully quick, Bliss Rolly. It ill behooves you to regret that.'

'I know. I definitely enjoyed torching the shed, though.'

Spindle fixed his attention on the lake and its sheets of grey rain. 'There's Malazan justice, and then there's *Malazan* justice.' He glanced over at a faint sound from her.

A sudden grin had stretched Bliss Rolly's plump lips, a cold chuckle already fading away. 'As one battered and bruised Jaghut on the Odhan now knows.'

'Any time you want back into the fold, Bliss . . .'

Now her smile was turned on him – the flutter becoming something else in his chest – and she shrugged. 'We're shoulder to shoulder right now, Spin. That suits me fine.'

He was startled when she hooked her arm in his and pulled him into motion. 'Let's head back for a hot drink in my room. I'm sure the coals have warmed it up by now.'

'Well,' he managed, 'these old bones will welcome that.'

'Aye, we can share complaints . . . after.'

The sound of rain on still water followed them all the way to the docks.

Stillwater and Anyx Fro stepped outside and stood beneath the eaves to stay out of the rain. Benger was setting up his ritual and the woman at the kitchen table was still crying. There was no one visible on the street.

Benger had loaned Stillwater his pipe and pouch of rustleaf, since what Anyx Fro used didn't burn well, which was a good thing since she stuffed it into her mouth. If it had to be lit that would probably hurt. Then again, Anyx Fro's mouth on fire wasn't too bad an image, or, rather, it shouldn't be. Something about what was going on inside left Stillwater feeling kind-hearted, even towards Anyx Fro. So she put away the image to be used at some later, more appropriate time, and kept herself busy filling up the pipe-bowl. When she was done she held it out towards Anyx Fro, who grunted in irritation and then tapped the side of the bowl with one finger. Smoke rose and wafted into the air.

'Filthy habit,' Anyx Fro said, punctuating her pronouncement with a brown stream into the puddle opposite her.

'Said the Lady of the Brown Teeth,' Stillwater replied while puffing vigorously on the pipe.

'Camouflage for night-work,' Anyx explained. 'That white flash of yours gives you away every time.'

'I only smile when I'm finished,' Stillwater replied. 'It's the thing to do when you're standing over a corpse watching the blood pour out like kelyk.'

'What did you whisper to her anyway?'

'What?'

'In there. You whispered to her. When she was about to lose it. And it calmed her down. I didn't know you had that in you, Still. In fact, what I figured you had in you was mostly blood-curdling nightmare stuff.'

'Nightmares? I don't have nightmares.'

Anyx Fro grimaced and then said, 'That's not what I meant.'

'I feel sick.'

'That's because you don't use rustleaf. I'm surprised you're not coughing your lungs out and puking.'

Stillwater puffed some more on Benger's pipe. 'Special occasions only. I don't cough because I learned how a long time ago. I was six when my sister taught me.'

'Six? Nobody told her you were a bit too young? Wait, *what* sister?'

Stillwater frowned. 'Well, she was five at the time. I never told you about my sister? Or my brothers? Or the estate and all the stupid dresses our servants stuffed me and my sister into so we could stand around getting bored at banquets? At least until we got drunk and passed out under the settee in the hallway.' Her frown shifted to a scowl since Anyx Fro was staring at her, mouth open to reveal a dark brown mass of rustleaf on the verge of tumbling out. 'What's the matter with you?'

'Uh, nothing.' The mouth closed and Anyx Fro looked back out onto the street. 'What happened to her?'

'Who?'

'Your sister! In fact, what happened to all of them? Brothers, parents? That estate? Those fucking banquets? *The dresses!?*'

'What are you so mad about?'

'What the fuck are you doing *here*?'

Stillwater looked around. 'Silver Lake? We're on—'

'Gods below! What made you join the marines?'

'To get away from them, of course. To get away from all of it. It's all poison, Anyx Fro, take it from me. Being rich fucks people up, in their heads. Their hearts, too. They pamper the outside to hide the rot inside. Well, not me.'

'Oh, right,' snapped Anyx Fro, 'better off being an assassin! What better way to coddle your own soul!'

'Exactly,' said Stillwater. She puffed some more, and then said, 'What did you ask me again?'

'Whispers!'

'I told her about soldiers, of course. About our purpose. Like Benger said, we're not here just to kill and maim and destroy. You've got to balance the fun with other stuff, in your head, I mean.'

'Go on,' invited Anyx Fro, one cheek bulging so much it had a white spot, the other cheek sweet and rosy, her gaze strangely piercing as she studied Stillwater.

'It's obvious, isn't it? We're not in charge, right? Benger's explained it often enough. Weren't you *ever* listening?'

'I was, but that was coming from Benger, not you.'

'Even our officers aren't in charge,' Stillwater resumed. 'No, we're here as servants of every citizen of the empire. Any soldier who forgets that isn't worthy of the title. And that's why I became a marine.'

Anyx Fro blinked. 'What?'

'Being a soldier is the opposite of being rich, and if you'd grown up where I did you'd know that. And that's another thing. My father and all the other rich people, they have no problem seeing soldiers as their servants. Problem is, they expect those soldiers to be serving only *them*. Not anyone else. Not the poor, that's for sure. And why do they expect that? Why, because they're rich! Real trouble starts when the soldiers buy in to that and end up serving only them. That's fucked up. And that brings me to the marines, where not giving a fuck about how rich someone happens to be is pretty much our credo.'

Anyx Fro snorted. 'More like we don't give a fuck, period.'

'But we do! And that's why Benger's doing what he's doing. Basically, I was whispering that we actually care.'

'You amaze me, Still.'

'You made my pipe go out, damn you.'

'Give it here, then. I got better rustleaf than Benger's horse-piss-soaked barn-hay.'

'Great, thanks, and then we'd better go back inside. He said he wants us close by in case bad stuff happens. But first, I may have to puke.'

High Denul was a curious magic, more than a little mysterious. It was either one warren that could infect every other warren, or it wasn't a warren at all, but something closer to the raw stuff of Chaos. It worked by interfering with everything else. Some illnesses depended on a fierce and deadly kind of order, after all. Cancer and other tumours, for example. Others involved too much chaos, as in wounds and bone-breaks and internal bleeding. Sometimes, High Denul repaired things, restoring order. On occasion, something entirely missing, such as a limb or an eye, could be regrown, and that drew on High Denul's chaotic power to make something out of nothing. At still other times, High Denul could be used to break natural laws, defying entropy itself.

Practitioners tended to find themselves more adept at one of these expressions than any other, and this imbalance could be seen as a kind of specialization. Benger suspected that his own chosen Warren of Mockra was closely related to High Denul, although the connection might not seem obvious. If it existed, it was at a fundamental level, once again spun tightly around elemental chaos. Illusions also conjured something out of nothing, after all.

Accordingly, his own approach to High Denul remained at that foundational level, sliding back and forth between it and Mockra and Mockra's little sister, Meanas. The mind had a role to play in healing, of that he was certain. It also, perhaps, had a role to play in reality itself.

Was it an illusionary trick to fashion the mental image of a vast, blood-red river within the mind of Sarlis? To make it seem utterly real, gravid with sound and light, the currents thick, the reeds of the banks tugged by an inexorable flow? Was it mere sophistry to bodily shove the woman into that river, the waters relentlessly pulling her out from the bank, out to where the river's own heart-line ran in a single-minded stream? Far from either shore, lost and carried onward?

And now the forces of his will: massive stones splashing into the surging waters. What would it take to divert such a vast river? A mountain crushed to rubble. The convulsions of sand and gravel, solid clays to seal each and every layer of broken rock. Building ever higher. Silty foam and straining, confused currents, a war begun between stone and water, between the laws of flow and the explicit defiance of unyielding barriers.

Such forces in contention were easy to visualize, easy to comprehend. Still, he wondered why such a scene came so easily into his imagination, bold as a shout of warning.

No matter, there was power here, threaded through and through with High Denul. This, he could work with.

Sarlis was drowning. No, she had already drowned. She watched her limp body twisting and tumbling in the deep currents, scraping along the bottom, limbs thrashing in blooms of silt – each cloud whirling away like plucked wings, vanishing into the gloom.

She was bloated with blood-oil, and though her flesh was dead, still the curse burned like fire. Her eyes were blank walls, unseeing yet seeing. She could look upon them even as she looked out through them. And now there were versions of her, it seemed. The torrent of the river was suddenly filled with them, body after body. Those that struck the strange walls of stone now appearing were then broken, shattered or shredded by the impact. Torn apart. The entire current seemed to be breaking up as it hammered against the stone, blunted, twisting into savage eddies – something was happening.

She wondered where the soldier-mage had gone. She wondered where her home was, the cramped kitchen, the sagging, stained mattress of her bed. How could the world vanish so utterly?

The deep currents continued to savage her many bodies. Limbs tumbled past. Viscera uncoiled from huge wounds like serpents escaping into the silty flow. She saw the flash of bone, thin streams of blood and swaths of dark hair.

And then, suddenly, only one body remained to her. It had rolled through blinding mud up against the stone wall. She moved in and out of it, looked down upon it, looked up through its eyes. The currents sought to sculpt a hollow for her, a grave into which she could sink, yet, even as the pit beneath her deepened and widened, she felt herself rising, tugged upward along the ragged boulders.

The darkness began to fade, the boiling silts surrounding her lightening as she was pushed towards the river's surface.

Hands reached down, grasped hold of her.

And then she was being dragged from the water, roughly pulled across wet stone that tore at her skin. Blinking water from her eyes, she stared up at a red sun blazing with heat.

On one side was something warm, pressed against her shoulder, and she turned her head to see Benger. He was sitting beside her, soaked through, gasping and spitting river water.

'What – where are we?' Sarlis asked.

He ran hands over his face to wipe away the water. 'It's all down to finding something you can use, something that makes sense to both of us.'

She studied him. He looked exhausted. 'Why are you doing this?'

'You didn't deserve it.'

'I can still feel the blood-oil.'

He jerked a thumb skyward. 'Aye, there it is. That sun, with its ring of copper and all this heat. You might think blood-oil flows all through your body – and I suppose in one way it does. But there's a core, ringed in magic-deadening otataral. What reaches into your body are its flames. Tendrils of heat, igniting your nerves, filling you with desire and desperate need.'

Sarlis sat up. She was now dressed as she had been in her kitchen. The clothing was dry. *All Benger's doing. None of this is real. And yet . . . it is.* The sun's raging heat beat down on her like a weighted fist.

They were on a raised road or bridge of stone, perhaps three carts in width. On one side was the river, a rushing torrent of brown froth that ran towards one bank, where it pushed inland, clawing at hillsides and crumbling cliffs as it forged a new channel. The other side of the river's old pathway, far below, was nothing but mud and red-tinted puddles and ponds, all visibly drying in the heat, stretching away into the hazy distance.

She stared up at that sun. 'How do we reach that?'

'You don't. I will.'

'But . . . how?'

'I'm still trying to work that out.'

'It's impossible. You tried, sir. No one else has. I'm grateful.'

He flashed her a grin. 'I'm a Malazan marine. Fuck impossible.' Grunting, he climbed to his feet. 'Two Runts to build this so far,' he said. 'Stone and Water.'

She saw in one of his hands a silver coin.

'Now Air, to make a bridge.' He flicked it upward.

The silver gleam flashed and flashed and then vanished.

'This would be costly if I wasn't making it all up.' He drew out from somewhere another coin and held it up close to his face as he squinted at it. 'That sun up there begs the question: what's it doing there? Well, it's all about unravelled time, you see. That fiery thing in the sky exists in the moment of Karsa's assault on you, in the very instant that the blood-oil entered your body. If you went to it, Sarlis, you'd re-experience the entire rape. In a way, you do re-experience it, but as the rapist, not the one being raped. Those men and women who visit you every night – they're your victims, even if they don't see it that way. But it's not you doing the raping: it's the blood-oil.'

'I don't . . . it's the fever.'

'Aye, as good a way of describing it as any. Unravelled time.' He showed her the coin. 'Starwheel. I need it to keep building, you see.'

'No.'

Benger shrugged. This time, when he flipped the coin into the air, it shot upward, fast enough to crack the sky with a thunderous eruption that echoed like a drum-roll. 'Now it gets difficult. The Runts are limited. They have plenty of raw energy, aye, but that only goes so far.' He set his hands on his hips and fell silent.

She studied the sun again. It was vast, ferocious, virulent. She thought of this lone man, this *Malazan marine*, somehow reaching it, striding into the flames. She saw him burned to ash.

Benger's voice startled her, as if he had spoken into one ear. 'I think,' he said, 'I need a dragon.'

' . . . a dragon.'

'What did he say?' Anyx Fro asked.

Stillwater frowned. 'You heard him.'

'Okay, maybe I did. And I'll ask again: *what did he say?*'

The kitchen was unbearably hot, which didn't make much sense since the ancient iron bowl Sarlis used for cooking held little more than a few glowing embers in a bed of ash. Stillwater had removed her poncho and was now loosening the ties of her hauberk. 'Stop blubbering and try thinking for a change. This is Mockra shit. Not a *real* dragon.'

'I get that!' Anyx Fro retorted as she started checking her weapons and armour. 'But that's insane, Still. Benger may be good at faking shit, but to conjure the illusion of an *entire* dragon? He'd have to be a High Mage to do that!'

'There are no High Mages any more in the Malazan Empire.'

'I know!' Anyx Fro drew on her helmet and affixed the strap under her round chin. 'That's my point!'

Stillwater paused to eye her companion. 'It's mine, too,' she said.

After a moment, Anyx Fro's eyes widened. Then she drew her short-sword. 'Where do you want me?'

'Just get ready,' Stillwater said. 'We don't know yet which way to jump. Not until Benger decides on one.'

'On one what?'

'Dragon, of course!'

'Well – wait. How many dragons does Benger know about?'

Stillwater dropped her hauberk to the floor. 'How should I know?' She moved to bend down in front of Sarlis, but the woman's eyes remained closed, her breathing only a little fast. Straightening, Stillwater checked all her knives. 'Just follow me in and be sure to take my flank.'

'I know, I know, stop hectoring me. Wait – he won't be picking a . . . you know . . . a *dead* one, will he? Cos I've heard of bad things happening when you conjure up something that's dead.'

'Of course n—' Stillwater scowled, turning a glare on the somnolent Benger who sat there with an utterly stupid expression on his ugly face, eyes jumping behind closed lids. 'I fucking hope not.'

He'd seen a tapestry once, in Nathilog, or maybe Genabaris. A scene of pitched battle, since weavers seemed to be obsessed with such things. Probably somewhere around Mott, during the Malazan Conquest. There was a forest in the foreground, seen from a high vantage point, and two armies spilling out from it locked in combat. Out on the plain beyond, phalanxes clashed against a long defensive line six ranks deep that seemed to encircle a modest high-ground. Atop that hill were banners thrashing in the wind.

The reason why the banners whipped every which way was the two dragons flying above the battle, one crimson and one black, the former highlighted with gold thread, the latter with silver. Beyond all of this, like a giant black turd floating in the sky, was Moon's Spawn.

Benger didn't know much about dragons. He'd never seen one and didn't know anyone who had – except perhaps for Spindle, if he really *had* been a Bridgeburner. It was said that a crimson dragon – the very one pictured in the tapestry – dwelt in Black Coral, but he'd never been that far east. Probably a stone carving atop a tower, painted gaudy red and gold, something to signify that there'd *once* been a crimson dragon, and that it had nested or something near Black Coral. Tales always grew in the telling.

He thought about that tapestry now, trying to decide which dragon to conjure. Either one would do, he was sure. The problem was, the only dragon he thought he knew in that tapestry was the black one. Of course, it wasn't that he didn't know *anything* about the crimson one. It might have been the one sighted at Black Coral. But what if that one was a different one? And in the end, did it even matter? The crimson one looked scary.

The black one . . . well, there were enough stories about that dragon. Terrifying stories to be sure, but what else would one expect when it came to stories about dragons? That was the problem right there. *All* stories about dragons were terrifying.

It wasn't that he didn't believe in dragons. That would be idiotic. Of course there were dragons! Reputable people had seen them! Fought them, even – unsuccessfully for the most part. They existed, same as dhenrabi and bhederin and dogs and Jaghut and undead K'Chain Che'Malle.

Benger frowned. *Well, with my own eyes I've seen . . . dogs. Gods below! That's it? Dogs? What if it's all made up!? That fucking tapestry nothing but a tangled web of lies! Moon's Spawn itself! That probably never existed! It was just a big black cloud that looked like a face or something!*

Dhenrabi? Bhederin? Undead K'Chain Che'Malle? All lies!

Groaning, Benger sagged and then fell onto his knees. He looked up suddenly and glared at everything surrounding him and Sarlis. 'I'm in trouble,' he said.

'What is wrong?'

He clawed at his face and moaned. 'Mockra's Curse. It can come on you suddenly. Illusion magic – illusions! They're a problem, a big problem. You create lies and lies and lies and what does that do to your head? What happens when you realize that maybe it's *all* lies! Everything! Reality? *What's that?* It's nothing! Made up!' He stared at her. 'Don't you see? We're all in an illusion! A grand lie, bullshit on the cosmic scale, all of us the product of some deranged mage trapped in a closet!'

She studied him, expressionless.

Benger leaned towards her and whispered, '*Do you even exist?*'

'I wish I didn't,' she replied.

Benger made fists and raised them skyward. 'All a lie!'

The hand that cracked the side of his head had very hard knuckles. Cursing as he fell onto his side, he clutched the throbbing spot on his temple, and found himself staring up at Stillwater. A moment later, Anyx Fro was there as well. The two women looked down on him.

'Not again,' Anyx Fro said.

'Poor Benger,' Stillwater sighed. 'Mockra's Curse.'

'Existential crisis,' Anyx Fro said, nodding. 'When you're running across a field of horseshit you're bound to step in it sooner or later.'

Stillwater turned to her. 'What does that even mean?' Then she reached down and dragged Benger to his feet. 'Snap out of it. We're here. You said something about a dragon. I just want to point out that you might consider conjuring something not-a-dragon. For instance, a giant ladder. Assuming it's that red thing in the sky you need to get to, and knowing you, it is. It is, isn't it? Don't you think you could have made your illusion *easier*? I mean, what's wrong with a set of stairs?'

He gaped at her for a moment, and then scowled, pushing her hand away. 'You don't understand anything! These things build themselves!' He pointed skyward. 'That's inside a shell of otataral! Of course I had to put it far away!'

Anyx Fro spoke. 'Just get on with it, Benger. We're here in case it all goes wrong. But bear in mind that if something goes wrong and that wrong has a dragon face and dragon teeth and dragon claws, we're all going to get ripped to pieces. It's a small detail, something to do with being hopelessly outclassed, right?'

Benger pointed again. 'I need to conjure a dragon!'

'So start conjuring!' Stillwater snapped. 'Just don't—'

The world darkened, cold air pouring down from above. Sarlis screamed. Or Anyx Fro. Someone screamed. Staring upward, Benger was silent. He could see nothing but black looming directly above them, so deep and solid that the blazing red orb could not penetrate it. And it was huge.

'What the fuck is that?' Stillwater demanded. 'That's the worst rendering of a dragon I've ever seen!'

'I can see wings!' Anyx Fro shouted.

'No you can't,' replied Stillwater. 'There's a name for that.'

'I said I can see wings!'

'Honestly—'

'She's right,' cut in Benger. 'It's in there. The dragon.'

'So clean it up! It's your illusion, after all!'

'I can't.' Benger rubbed at his face, wishing his beard was long enough to tug, or thick enough to comb through in a satisfying manner. But it was neither, so he rubbed. 'This is unexpected. That black . . . cloud.'

'It's not a cloud,' said Anyx Fro. 'It's pure power. It's Elemental—'

'Dark,' finished Stillwater. 'It's Elemental Dark! Benger, you idiot! What dragon – no, not *that* dragon! Benger, you've conjured up an illusion of *Anomander Dragnipurake*! Have you lost your mind?'

Benger stared at her with wild eyes. 'It was in a tapestry,' he whispered.

'But that dragon is dead!' Anyx Fro shouted. 'Anomander is dead! Conjuring illusions of dead things – you just don't *do* that any more! Not since Hood bailed on that whole Lord of Death thing and Iskar Jarak stepped in – he just guards the gate! No throne, no rule – no *rules*! Benger! The spirits *hate* it when you conjure up their bodies!' She threw up her hands and swung to Stillwater. 'We're all dead. It was nice knowing you – no, not really. Let's call it tolerable—'

'You're babbling again,' Stillwater said, still squinting up at the black cloud. 'I still don't see any wings.'

Benger moaned – he was doing a lot of that at the moment – and then said, 'He's coming. Maybe he won't be mad. I mean, it's in a good cause, isn't it? If I just explain things—'

Now Stillwater could see the wings, and a whole lot more. A massive snout, head emerging on its long neck, the eyes a luminous blue shot through with silver.

'Blue eyes,' she whispered to herself, 'are an abomination.'

A soft male voice filled her head. *'It is difficult enough being remembered, resurrected in the minds of all who once knew me, all who once saw me. I dwell in Darkness without form. No other existence is possible for me. If you will hold me here, Illusionist, be brief. They are coming.'*

Stillwater turned to Anyx Fro. 'Did you hear that?'

The woman, face pale as a moon, nodded.

Grunting, Stillwater turned to Benger. 'And you? Please say yes, and don't even bother asking who's coming because I don't want to know. Say your piece and let's get this done.'

He gaped at her. 'What was I thinking? I was thinking about the *crimson* dragon. I swear it!'

'Benger!'

Abruptly, Benger fell to the stony ground, where he lay in a motionless heap.

Anyx Fro stepped close to him, looking down, and then spat a brown stream into the river roaring close by. 'Did he faint, Stillwater? Did our High Mage just faint?'

Shaking herself, Stillwater crouched opposite Sarlis – who was sitting with her knees pointing in strange directions, like a gawky adolescent. 'What did Benger want the dragon to do? Did he say anything?'

'C-can't you wake him?'

Stillwater looked to Anyx Fro. 'You keep nudging him with your boot, he's going to roll into the flood and drown.'

'That's the general idea,' she replied.

'Stop it. Try waking him instead.'

'Oh? How, pray tell?'

'Surest way is a knife-point under a thumbnail.'

'I could just cut the thumb off – my knife's too big to get the point under a nail.'

'I know that, Anyx Fro. That's why I suggested it. Start digging!' Stillwater turned back to Sarlis, trying not to think about how patient or impatient the giant thing above them was. 'Think back, please!'

'Something about otat – ota—'

'Otataral. Right. There's otataral in blood-oil. Deadens magic.' She frowned. 'Not so effective, however, against *Elder* magic.' Stillwater straightened and looked up at the dragon. 'This woman is cursed with blood-oil fever. We're trying to rid her body of it. We're trying to cure her. Oh, and I was wondering, who's coming?'

'The ones I killed hunt me eternally. Without form I cannot be found. They are coming.'

'The ones you killed? Well, can't be *that* many of them, right? Oh, hold on. You mean the ones you killed with that horrible sword?'

'Among others.'

'Stillwater . . .'

'What *is* it, Anyx Fro?' Stillwater hissed. 'Can't you see I'm talking to a dragon?'

'There.'

She saw that her companion, still kneeling above Benger, was pointing to the drained river channel. Something was seething along it from the hazy horizon towards them, black, roiling, iron weapons flashing red in the glare of the sun. Wide as the river-bed. An army. Lots of armies, or one big one. Or lots of big ones – *Jarak's Prick, it doesn't matter!*

Stillwater licked her lips and then faced the dragon again. 'If we can't wake Benger up, are you stuck here?'

'I am. My hunters are spirits and shades, but they are many.'

'Anyx—'

'I've made a bloody mess and nothing!'

'The other thumb then! And then his fingers!' She addressed the dragon again. 'Lord of Dark – is that what you were called? Never mind, it's what I'm calling you because I really don't want to use your name. Listen, can you, you know, destroy that big red thing in the sky?'

'Your reason?'

'To save a life.'

The dragon hovered above them, wings slowly fanning, the dark cloud swirling around them. The eyes seemed to be fixed on Stillwater alone, piercing through to her very soul. She felt a rush of something that left her knees weak. *Sadness? Weariness?*

'No other is required.'

Wings thundered and the black cloud with the dragon within it began rising. Stillwater stared, watching it climb ever higher.

'Stillwater!'

'What now?'

'He's so far gone he's as good as dead! I've gone through all his fingernails!'

'So reach in between his legs, right in there, Anyx, and start working his you-know-what.'

'What? Gods below! This is madness.'

Stillwater had to look. 'Huh,' she grunted. 'Didn't think you'd do it.'

'It's not working!'

'No, why should it? You have no shame, Anyx Fro, you know that?'

Sarlis stared in wonder at these strange women. Benger was a healer. He'd told her his desire, described his wish to see her healed. His eyes had been kind, but it had taken her some time to recognize what she was seeing in them. It had been so long since she'd last seen that look in anyone's eyes.

Disgust. Contempt. Hunger. Desire. These were the faces turned upon her and no other expression ever warred with them. Though she had understood most of what Benger told her, his face and those eyes had baffled her, even frightened her.

Even so, Benger made sense. She knew why he was here, why he'd done what he'd done, even if he'd now failed at the last moment. But the women sharing this uncanny scene made no sense to Sarlis at all.

Fear and frustration battled on Anyx Fro's round face, and she was now jumping up and down on Benger's body and Sarlis could hear bones breaking.

'Wake up! Wake up, damn you!'

Meanwhile, Stillwater was dividing her attention between that black cloud that had now risen to swallow the blazing red sun, and the thousands of horrifying creatures surging towards them from the river's old channel. Yet her breathing had not changed, slow and calm, and nothing tightened her features. It was as if she had no feelings at all, not even ones born of self-preservation.

'Give it up, Anyx Fro. What was unconscious is now dead. Benger's dead. Poor Benger.'

'Poor us!' Anyx Fro shrieked. She gave Benger's corpse one last kick and then rushed to Stillwater's side to stare at the seething army. 'We can't stop them! And why are they still coming? He's way up there in the sky!' She started pointing upward and shouted, 'Look, you idiots! Up there! You don't want to tear us to pieces – you want to tear *him* to pieces!'

'Well they can't reach him, obviously,' Stillwater observed. 'Accordingly, they are going to take out their frustration on us.'

'That's not fair!'

Stillwater tugged at her stained linen scarf. 'I swear, this thing's trying to strangle me.'

Anyx Fro's eyes bulged as she stared at her companion, but her tone was suddenly calm. 'So take the fucking thing off. You're going to need the attention of the Rope for what's coming, anyway. I'll take the right – assuming they can climb this wall and yes, I'm sure they can. You take the left. We stand here and chew them up some, and if we're lucky, that dragon will finish devouring the sun in time for the curse to end, and then one of us grabs her and we bolt out of this insane Mockran nightmare.'

Stillwater licked her lips, cocking a hip as she considered, and then she nodded. 'All right. I mean, I wanted the right but if you really want the right, fine, you can have it. It means I'm on the fucking left which I hate but that's all right, I suppose. Since it's so important to you.'

'*Now* is the time to go all passive aggressive?'

'The dragon's going to be annoyed when it sees that Benger is dead,' Stillwater said in a musing tone, even as she began working loose the scarf's knot. 'Stuck here with all those past victims hounding it. If it was me, I'd probably turn us into melting goo before we ever get a chance to bolt. Or worse, the damn Lord of Dark chases after us.'

'Not our fault! Benger's!'

Stillwater nodded. 'Good point. You can explain it to him. With gooey lips and a diffident expression on your melting face.'

The army was suddenly frighteningly close, the lead line of creatures breaking into a charge towards the base of the stone wall. Sarlis stared at them. Hundreds of different forms, only a few humans in this first wave. Demons? She didn't know what demons looked like. Some were big, shambling, monstrous. Others ran on three legs with heads like those of horses, a massive single eye socket in their foreheads. Still others swarmed across the mud as if scuttling like crabs. A bestial roar lifted from them, rising up to sweep over the wall.

Sarlis wondered at her lack of emotion. The world felt disconnected from her, thinning as if in a fading dream. She looked skyward and saw the black cloud convulsing, contracting. The red sun was nowhere and even its reflected light was fast dying.

And the fire in her body winked out.

The first spectres reached the wall, began flowing up it.

Looking down, Stillwater finally got her scarf free of her neck. 'Anyx! See that big one with giant swords for hands? That one's yours.'

'No it isn't! That's on your side! Why me?'

'I don't like it,' Stillwater replied.

'Fuck you!'

But an instant later that spectre vanished inside an explosion of flames. 'See, Anyx? That wasn't so hard.'

'Fuck you all over again! Wait – is that a *Jaghut*? That's a fucking Jaghut!'

'Your side for sure,' Stillwater replied. As she moved to tuck the scarf safely around her knife-belt, a sudden updraught plucked it free of her hand. 'Shit!' She reached, fingers clutching, and found herself completely overbalanced. 'Crap, I'm falling.'

Swan-diving into a mass of spirits and spectres wasn't ideal, she reflected as she plunged downward, both hands plucking knives free. Even so, it was spectacularly unexpected in so far as the army went, when she landed atop a seething tide of dead-smelling bodies. Her knives lashed out everywhere as she twisted and slipped and slid through the heaving press.

She heard distant thunder – was that Anyx Fro? Seemed pretty loud for her, though. The thunder crashed again, much closer this time, and the mass of bodies she was entangled with shuddered like a single beast.

'Ow! Fuck!' A blade had scored across her right side, flaring pain down her ribs one by one. Stillwater twisted and double-stabbed a brawny upper arm and then angled the blade-edges in opposite directions and ripped the limb wide open on either side of the long-bone. 'Now the next time you wave at a friend half your arm will fall off! Ha ha!'

Suddenly, she bumped over a huge knee that buckled under her, and then slid down to the churned mud of the river-bed.

'Aagh! Smells!'

The thunder this time erupted right on top of her, the sound deafening, the concussion making everything in her skull ring like a thousand bells, even as an enormous fist of air pressed her deep into the mud, pinning her fast.

She couldn't breathe. The world was black. Her mouth was packed with mud and the mud was packed with – she frowned – *scales? Oh, fish-scales! Of course!*

She thrashed to climb back out of the mud, kicked until she kicked air, pushed and stabbed and slashed until both hands and arms were free, spat out mud and fish-scales as her face reached air, and then planted her elbows and tried sitting up. Failed the first time, her elbows sinking deep. It was as if something had a tight grasp of her buttocks and not in a pleasant way, especially with the sucking sounds added in. The second time the mud gave up with a regretful gasp, and she managed to roll onto her side, onto her hands and knees, and then to her feet, where she stood reeling in a vast, vacated ring lined in shattered bodies.

'Look at this! I'm amazing—'

A strange, ethereal figure moved up beside her. Stillwater leapt away, spinning round to bring both knives up between her and the newcomer.

It made no move to attack her.

Stillwater saw her scarf. It was wrapped about the figure's head, the old twin stains that looked like eyes perfectly positioned to be above whatever eyes the creature had. Wild rotting hair sprang out in all directions; the face that she could see was withered and sunken, the body all knobby bones beneath tattered funereal clothes. 'Give me back my scarf!'

The head turned with a creaking sound, the painted-cloth eyes regarding her. 'You hopeless tomb-robbing back-stabbing cow, are you truly that stupid? I'm the witch around your neck!'

Stillwater reached up to touch her own throat – the gesture was instinctive, as she was looking at the scarf – and so she scowled. 'Well, why aren't you still there?'

The army was spilling up against the shattered bodies, moments from surmounting them to close back in and swallow them both.

'Shattered Holds,' the dead witch sighed, 'you amaze me.' She pointed at the wall behind them. 'Go on, I'll handle this.'

'I want my scarf!'

'So come and get it when I'm done! Errastas' Hold isn't going anywhere soon, is it?'

Stillwater blinked. 'Just how old *are* you?'

'Now she insults me!' The witch pointed again at the wall behind them. 'Go!'

The mass of spirits and spectres finally poured over their shattered kin and rolled like a wave towards them.

Snarling, the witch spread her arms. Thunder hammered into the churning mob. Bodies broke and spun and flew into the air, leaving behind a huge gap of smouldering mud and a few lower limbs still standing here and there.

Stillwater stared. 'Okay, I'm going now,' she said.

The monsters had reached the top of the wall on all sides, with only Anyx Fro standing between them and Sarlis. The soldier was swearing non-stop. She had her short-sword out and was chopping into the skull of something she called a Jaghut. It was on fire but that wasn't stopping it as it sought to rise over the wall's edge. But the soldier's attention was being constantly pulled away by other creatures gaining the wall, each one demanding a quick gesture that made them burst into flames. Figures staggered about in fierce fire, bones snapping and shedding black flakes that drifted and danced in the roiling air.

None of this seemed even possible to Sarlis. How could one woman— and why was Sarlis so unafraid? So emptied of . . . *everything.* She floated inside, untethered and unconcerned. She watched Anyx Fro incinerate one monster after another, in between smashing the Jaghut's hairless skull into something resembling a broken pot.

'Fuckyoufuckyoufuckyoufuckingdie!'

At last, the Jaghut lost its grip on the wall and fell back. Anyx Fro spun to ignite a dozen creatures rushing in on one side, and then turned the other way and paused, her soot-stained face growing smooth and childlike as the deep frown disappeared. 'What did she do down there? There's no one on her side any more!' She staggered closer.

Sarlis pointed down to the river-bed. Thousands of shattered forms lay in heaps. The entire front of the endless army on that side had piled up in windrows of destruction. 'A blindfolded woman is destroying everyone down there.'

Anyx Fro spat another brown stream – she'd been spitting brown streams between curses since the whole battle began. 'Where's Still-water? I don't see her.'

Sarlis shrugged. 'Ever since she fell, I've not seen her whenever I looked. I don't know.'

'She fucking bailed through her warren! I can't believe it! Left me here!'

'But who is that blindfolded woman?'

Anyx Fro chewed a bit and eyed the distant figure as it marched relentlessly into the army on a slow but savage drum-roll of thunder and tiny flying bodies, and then shrugged. 'Stillwater's ugly as a boar's backside, but she isn't that ugly.' Another wave was cresting the wall on the other side. Anyx Fro sighed and adjusted her grip on her sword. With her other hand she gestured. Figures lit up in flames that danced from head to head. 'Look, I'm getting tired, dammit.'

Sarlis glanced skyward and gasped. 'They're gone!'

'What?' Anyx Fro did the same. 'He did it! But how did he – gods below!' Anyx sheathed her sword and grasped Sarlis's arm. 'It's done. Time to go.'

'But your friend Stillwater—'

'She's no friend of mine! She's probably already back in your fucking kitchen, pilfering the bread-box!'

'No I'm not!'

They turned to see Stillwater climbing onto the wall. She was cut and bleeding from dozens of shallow wounds, her thin leather shirt slashed almost to ribbons. She was also covered in mud.

'Thanks for leaving me doing everything!' Anyx Fro yelled.

'Just go,' Stillwater said, settling onto one knee to catch her breath.

'What about you?'

She straightened and pointed at the distant blindfolded figure. 'She's wearing my scarf and I want it back!'

Sarlis saw Anyx Fro staring, stone-faced, at Stillwater. 'Right,' she said. 'Have fun.'

Stillwater watched them vanish. More ghastly creatures were on the wall now, converging on her. She glared. 'You stupid brainless idiots – do you see Anomander Dragnipurake? Do you? He's gone!'

As one they paused, and then wailing anguish rose up from a dozen, then hundreds, then thousands of throats.

'That's right! Back to having no body, no form at all! Really, what's the fucking point of chasing him?'

That seemed to be the wrong thing to say, as their attention returned to her, and as one they surged forward, weapons waving.

'Oh, typical. Even the undead can't stomach the truth.' She spun about and leapt over the wall, opening her warren even as she fell, into the Wilds of Emurlahn.

'I'm coming for my scarf!'

Blinking, Sarlis found herself sitting in her chair at the kitchen table. She flinched when Anyx Fro stepped into view, removing her sword-belt and flinging it to the floor.

Benger was sitting opposite, puffing on his pipe.

Now Anyx Fro had a knife out and was advancing on Benger. 'You devious piece of shit—'

A hand shot up to forestall her. 'Did you think I had it in me to nego-tiate with Anomander Dragnipurake? I nearly shit myself! Think on it, Anyx! Who has never *ever* been afraid? Of anything? Who just gets on with it no matter what? Who's got that innocent-looking face that could sway the bitterest god?'

Anyx Fro glared for a moment longer, and then hissed a curse and sheathed her knife. She wiped at the soot around her eyes. 'Fear? Yeah, she doesn't know what it *means*.'

'Exactly,' said Benger. 'By the way, where is she?'

'Probably dead. Torn to pieces because she's . . . she's . . .' Anyx Fro shook her head. 'I don't know what she is. Was.'

Benger made his weird huffing laugh. 'She's Stillwater and that's all you need to say, right?'

Nodding, Anyx Fro abruptly sat on the floor. 'And it's done? It looked done. Is it done?'

Benger set down his pipe. Meeting Sarlis's eyes he leaned forward and took one of her hands in both of his. 'Is the water clear?' he asked.

She frowned at the strange question. Then, in a warm rush of realization, she saw that it wasn't strange at all. 'It's clear, sir. It's very clear.' *Gods below, I'm not – I was and now I'm not, and all that I've done—* She burst into tears, a cry rising up from deep inside, so harsh it ravaged the back of her throat.

Benger sat, gently patting her hand, while Anyx Fro went to build up the cookfire to make tea.

'No witch can outrun me,' Stillwater muttered. She was standing in the street, plucking dried chunks of mud from what was left of her clothes. She'd have to go back to Sarlis's house to get her gear because sure as Hood's dead Anyx and Benger wouldn't have thought to collect it up.

It was very late, almost on the edge of dawn. The town of Silver Lake was as silent as an unbroken-into tomb would probably be, not that she had any plans on finding out any time soon.

She reached up to make sure the scarf was back, snug round her neck. It was.

Sighing, Stillwater walked to the house of Sarlis.

Question was, what was Sarlis going to do now? It was gone. Gone from her and not ever coming back. Townsfolk wouldn't get it or wouldn't like it. *Damn, she'll have to join us, become a camp follower.* But not in that way, of course. The company needed cooks and menders and grooms and whatever those people who do laundry were called.

Of course, she might never want to see us again. Bad memories. Benger's ugly face. Anyx Fro's even uglier one. And she might hate Stillwater for diving off the wall like a coward or something. Like she didn't care whether Sarlis lived or died.

It was all the scarf's fault.

She reached the door, was surprised to see a thin crease of dull gold light beneath it. Shrugging, she knocked.

A few moments later it opened. Sure enough, Sarlis cried out and—

And suddenly Stillwater was wrapped up in a fierce embrace, and kisses were making wet patches all over her cheeks, and the thin arms kept tightening and tightening around her.

Stillwater didn't move and let Sarlis do whatever. The fact was, she couldn't understand people at all.

CHAPTER SIXTEEN

Death has but one gate leading in
Yet infinite ones leading out
Life has but one gate leading in
Yet infinite ones leading out
Your life has but one path
It leads in and it leads out
Each step you take has infinite choices
And each step taken reduces to one
This morning seven birds crossed the sky
Moving as if bound into one
Yet I thought of tail-feathers and wings
Each in turn making minute adjustments
No two the same, no two ever the same

In the Age of Simplicity
Elder Fisher kel Tath

RANT SLEPT DEEPLY, SENSELESSLY, UNTIL THE MOMENT THAT something seemed to strike him from behind, fierce as a bolt of lightning against the base of his skull, but the impact did not awaken him. Instead, he found himself lying in swaddled furs upon the ground, at the very edge of the vast encampment of Teblor and their allies, and all of this – the low campfires, the figures moving or standing in the night – matched in every detail the world he knew before sleep had taken him. This dream – if a dream it truly was – altered but one thing: he struggled to move, his limbs leaden as he sought to crawl across the ground, away from the thing that had struck him.

Even crying out elicited but a guttural moan. The words he attempted came out drunken, slurred.

It was impossible to know how much time passed as he struggled, dragging himself forward one hand at a time. His body was not the one he knew, but one he remembered from long ago. He was small, a child of but few years. And he was crawling to his mother, though he could not see her. There was fear but it felt muted, distanced.

An eternity or an instant later he awoke, finding himself lying motionless within the furs, having crawled nowhere, having not moved at all. The darkness around him seemed crazed, filled with chaotic streaks of almost-light. Chills rippled through him as he revisited the dream, tasting once more its peculiar sensations.

Rant rolled onto his back, watching the strange fulmination of night surrounding him. He thought back to the dusk of the day just gone, when they had arrived at the place where camped the Great Army of Elade Tharos. When so many warriors of the Teblor closed in around them. The raw emotions of grief and anger and confusion, the edge of violence drawing close again and again. The mass of Saemdhi voicing murderous cries as they encircled Gower and Nilghan, weapons waving. Forest people scurrying like curs underfoot on all sides. The mighty roar that answered the news of Tracker Damisk's fateful capture.

Rant had felt small, insignificant. He had felt as if he was drowning in the lake all over again. But no hands were reaching down to grasp him and pull him to safety. All the warriors, all the people and hounds and dogs, all the tents and yurts, the smells and sounds – he'd been overwhelmed.

When the Warleader Elade Tharos stood before Rant and spoke, Rant had understood nothing. The language was Teblor, and among all his kin, only Delas Fana and Tonith Agra spoke to him in words he could understand, and in that meeting neither was permitted to speak, not even to translate, because it was the Warleader's responsibility to greet all newcomers.

Elade Tharos's tone had been challenging, defiant, mocking. Much of what he said drew laughter from the crowd gathered around them, dismay from Tonith Agra, and dark fury from Delas Fana. Rant had understood that he was being belittled – that had happened to him before, many times, in Silver Lake. He didn't need to comprehend the actual words to understand: the tones were enough. He also realized that Elade Tharos was performing. More than once he heard the name 'Karsa Orlong', delivered in contemptuous tones and gestures of dismissal.

The Warleader's greeting of Delas Fana had been perfunctory, ending with Elade Tharos making a demand of some sort, to which Delas Fana sneered and turned away. No rage answered the insult. Instead, the Warleader had but smiled and then shrugged. Thereafter he ignored Delas Fana.

The third sister that Delas Fana and Tonith Agra had spoken of, Sathal, looked nothing like her siblings, being very pale and red-haired, and almost as tall as Rant. Their reunion was one of brief embraces and then muted but heated conversation. When Sathal had at last turned to face Rant, he found himself looking into the bluest eyes he had ever seen. Blue as the ice of Silver Lake. She'd made to approach Rant but was stayed by Tonith Agra's hand on her arm.

The gesture filled Rant with regret. He would have liked company at that moment. Even Gower and Nilghan had been kept at bay. There were warriors everywhere, spear-points like liquid as the dying sun cast the iron in hues of red and gold. Threats were shouted at the Jheck, mostly from the Saemdhi who followed their snarls and curses with peculiar dances, miming the slaying of beasts or some-such. But every time Gower and Nilghan attempted to move closer to Rant, they were pushed back, and Rant could see the temper of the Lord of the Black Jheck growing ragged.

It might have gone badly then, but at that moment, Damisk had been dragged into view.

Lying in his furs, beneath a paling sky, Rant felt tears filling his eyes. He would have fought for his friend. He would have killed Elade Tharos and taken pleasure in doing so for all the contemptuous things he was saying. This was no greeting of kin, after all. This was no different from Silver Lake, no different from all that Rant had known growing up among humans. He was tired of it, tired of being singled out for ridicule.

Should he blame his father? That seemed too easy. He'd wondered, as he looked upon Elade Tharos, how Karsa Orlong would have answered the Warleader. Would he have pushed his way to where they held Damisk, drawn a knife or a sword and stood over him, challenging all who sought to harm the old man?

With Damisk twenty or more paces away, a dozen Teblor warriors between them, Rant had turned from Elade Tharos in the middle of delivering yet another half-dozen insults. Drawing his knife, he had walked towards his friend.

The first two Teblor warriors who stepped into his path then backed away, as hounds suddenly surrounded Rant, heads slung low and teeth bared. The massive beasts made no sound at all as they edged forward.

Bewildered, Rant followed. He counted ten Teblor hounds encircling him, protecting him, including the three he already knew were kin of

Karsa Orlong's beloved dog. Behind Rant, Elade Tharos shouted something, and then repeated the phrase.

The warriors holding Damisk quickly retreated, dragging their prisoner with them, and yet more Teblor moved in to block Rant.

A moment later Delas Fana was at his side. 'No further, Rant, I beg you.'

Rant pointed at a mob of young Teblor. 'They have stones in their hands. They were about to throw them at Damisk.' He raised his knife. 'I don't like stones.'

Delas Fana turned to Tonith Agra. 'A clean death for Damisk, sister – you said he would grant that. Tell him, before this turns bloody.'

'I will,' Tonith replied, moving off to speak to Elade Tharos. The Warleader looked furious. He had more to say, more to perform, but now he was being ignored.

'I don't like the Warleader,' Rant said to Delas Fana. 'Does he not know the southlander tongue?'

'Of course he does,' Delas Fana snapped. 'Only a few of the more distant tribes do not. He did this to ensure you would have nothing to say. He mocks your ignorance and refuses your claim to kin.'

Rant shrugged. 'I refuse his, too. I would not want him as my brother, or uncle. I would not want him as my Warleader.'

'The name of Karsa Orlong hangs over him,' she said in a low tone. 'Sathal has told me – Elade Tharos has been waging war against the faith of the Shattered God – against your father and his ascension. He would wrest away such worship and demand it for himself.'

'Let me fight him, Delas Fana. Tell them that I am an adult. That I have passed my Night or whatever it's called. Let me kill him.'

'With your knife you might well succeed, Rant, but the Rathyd warriors who were with us have already announced that your knife is demon-possessed. They have also announced that you are still a child.'

Rant could no longer see Damisk – he had been carried deeper into the camp. 'I have no kin here among the Teblor,' he said.

'You do, Rant. You have your sisters.'

'Sathal's eyes are cold.'

'Their hue is misleading.'

'Where is she?'

'Gone to find Widowed Dayliss – another potential ally. Those who worship the Shattered God now look to you, Rant. None of them were pleased by the Warleader's words. Now, I beg you, sheathe your knife. If not, your Jheck friends will fight and they will die to Saemdhi spears. These hounds here will all die as well. Your sisters, too.'

Rant put the knife away. 'I don't know what to do.'

'Do as your father does.'

'Which is?'

'Bides his time.'

Tonith Agra returned. 'It is done,' she said. 'He likes it not, but Damisk's death will be clean.' She hesitated. 'As clean as he can make it.'

'How did you convince him?' Delas Fana asked.

'As we agreed, sister. Southland courage is a lesson well considered.'

A moment later Elade Tharos was standing opposite Rant once again, but this time almost within reach. 'You need to learn the Teblor language, pup.'

Rant met the Warleader's eyes. 'You are invading the south?'

'I am. And this—'

'Then I need not learn your language,' said Rant.

Elade Tharos turned to Tonith Agra. 'He is your kin now. See that he behaves. As for you, Delas Fana, all warriors here have sworn to me. We are but days from marching, and all who march with me must have so sworn. You have until then to decide. Present to me your sword or challenge me.'

'I am already sworn,' Delas Fana replied.

Elade Tharos scowled. 'You risk banishment, Delas Fana.'

'And you risk ridicule, Elade Tharos, if you cannot stomach a single unbound warrior in your army.'

The Warleader said nothing to that, and a moment later walked away.

Tonith Agra hissed under her breath, and then turned to her sister. 'You knelt before Father? He accepted your blade?'

Delas Fana shrugged. 'I don't like being given ultimatums, sister. This Elade Tharos does not impress me. I have seen little of him, but what I have seen is petty.'

'You have much still to learn,' Tonith Agra replied.

'This army here seems vast, but we both know what awaits us in the south.'

'This is but *one* of the Warleader's armies, Delas. You must understand. This is not an invasion. It is a *migration*.'

Delas Fana faced her sister. 'But why?'

Tonith Agra took her arm. 'I will explain. But not here. Come, let us go find Sathal and Widowed Dayliss.'

Delas Fana hesitated. To Rant, she said, 'Find a place to sleep close by. If you can, join the Jheck. But stay near, so that we can find you.'

They left him then, alone with the hounds. The mass of warriors was breaking up as darkness crept into the camp. Rant saw Gower and Nilghan. He went to them.

'My mouth was wet,' said Nilghan. 'I could feel seven hearts beating in my chest. I was prepared to die and was filled with the glory of seeing you wield your knife, pup. Death and blood on the ground. That strutting Warleader sitting down with his head cradled in his lap. His expression of surprise would have carried me sweetly into the realms of the dead.' His face twisted in disappointment. 'Then you sheathed it.'

'I was told to be patient,' Rant said, kicking a few stones aside to make a place to sit down. 'I do not like being patient. They will hurt Damisk and I will do nothing. Patience, it seems, can be cruel.'

Gower was studying the ten hounds now settling down around them. 'These beasts are unlike the other Teblor dogs,' he said. 'They are indifferent to the scent of wolf. Formidable allies, Rant. Karsa Orlong gifted you with life, but it seems he's not yet done with gifts.'

'Now even the Saemdhi avoid us,' muttered Nilghan, frowning down at the ground as he circled a patch. 'Where hides War-Bitch, brother?' After the third circle he sat and made himself comfortable. 'All of the Saemdhi are here in this camp. They shit and piss everywhere. Too long in this place and disease will come. Did you see all the caribou carcasses? Not short of food, but do they offer us any? This Warleader chooses to not even greet the Lord of the Black Jheck. In all manner we are insulted and left to starve.'

'Soon,' growled Gower, 'you will have spoken as many words as there are Saemdhi in this camp. Be silent. I must think.'

'Then I shall not speak to you but to Rant, as he alone appreciates my wisdom. Do sit, pup. Nothing more will occur this night. Your sisters are doing what all sisters do, whispering and gossiping in their pack. Decisions will be made, and all the rules men once thought inviolate have now changed, though they know it not. Nightly, women reshape the world. It has always been this way.' He paused to scratch under his furs. 'In the great dens of the southlands, on a certain day – I forget which – women gather in the streets to celebrate a goddess called The Unloved Woman. She is the matron of widows or plain women or something. I don't know. It's a woman thing. In a central square there is a ritual, hundreds, even thousands, of women standing in a vast circle. The High Priestess steps into the cleared space, wearing plain Malazan armour and wielding a sword with two edges. Her enemy approaches, fully armoured, her head covered in a helm with a face made of iron scales or maybe coins. She too holds a sword, in her right hand. The crowd sings something horrible to my ears, so loud it hurts my head, and they get louder as the enemy approaches the High Priestess.' He paused, squinting at Rant in the gloom. 'Are you awake, pup?'

'I am,' Rant replied.

'More's the pity,' Gower said under his breath.

'But it is the left hand that rises between them,' Nilghan said. 'And even as it does so, the High Priestess strikes! Her sword cuts down her enemy! The crowd roars and suddenly everyone is weeping and they're dragging off the body leaving a streak of blood—'

'She truly killed her enemy?'

'No. All faked. I was so disappointed. What manner of faith is this charade without real blood? But the crime does not end there. For that night, all those women will lie with each other, not with men. Husbands are ignored. Lovers are denied. Even bold warriors of the frozen north, superior in all ways imaginable, are left abandoned, their needs unmet. The southlands, pup, are strange.'

'But what—'

Nilghan raised a grimy finger. 'I'm not yet finished.'

'Spirits of moss and bone,' moaned Gower.

'You have sisters now, and so I am warning you. Sisters are not like mothers, not like grandmothers and not like daughters. It may even be that they are their own D'ivers, an uncanny pack of demons who but choose to mimic your form. They will decide things for you. They will decide things *about* you, too. They will chart the map of your future, not because they expect you to follow it, but to ensure their own disappointment when you don't.'

'Do you have any sisters, Nilghan?'

'No, and each night I thank The Unwanted Woman of the southlands.'

'I thought she was The Unloved Woman.'

He waved a hairy hand. 'Unwanted, Unloved, Unfriendly, whatever.'

'I think,' said Rant, 'I will sleep now.'

The sun's light was painting the eastern sky. Rant sat up. Ten hounds lifted their heads to regard him. They had slept in a circle around him, Gower and Nilghan. The two Jheck snored in tandem beneath heaped furs.

The dream bothered him. The fierce blow to the back of his head had not been painful, simply shocking. Nothing like a fist or anything solid at all. Had he somehow imagined it? And how could it awaken him yet not awaken him, flinging him instead into a dream?

He had crawled, seeking his mother. Yet he had never reached her. A weakling child who could barely lift his limbs – he had no memory of ever being such a child. Strength had always surrounded him. Stones had bounced off his back and he had laughed at their impact, even as a part of him, deep inside, wanted to curl up and hide.

But what good did his strength do him here?

Others were awakening. Fresh smoke was rising from fire-pits and hearths. Somewhere a dog barked. Rant saw Delas Fana approaching. He rose, drawing his furs around him. The air was cold, but the clear sky promised heat.

'Brother,' she greeted him, 'you slept well?'

'No,' he replied. 'What will they do to Damisk?'

She glanced away momentarily. 'It's already done.'

'He's dead?'

'No, but he soon will be.' She hesitated, and then said, 'It is not pleasant. Best you stay away, as there's nothing to be done. Leave Damisk to his fate.'

'I will see him,' said Rant. 'I will speak to him.'

'Rant—'

'He is my friend and I will have . . . last words with him. Or is Elade Tharos frightened of even that much?'

'To the contrary,' Delas Fana said with a sneer twisting her lips, 'he would delight in your witnessing, and might well attend the moment, to see for himself the pain you will feel.'

'I don't understand. Why would someone else's pain please him?'

'Your father killed his father and brothers. Your father destroyed his home and took its women to his bed. These wounds are old but still they bleed.' She shrugged. 'I know little of Elade Tharos, but it is my thinking that he is the sort of man who will suck the blood and pus from those wounds until his last day of breath. He will tell you it is his strength. But his eyes are dead and only come alive when others are wounded in kind. For Elade Tharos, pain is what binds us. He dwells in a cold place, Rant, and would see it cover the world.'

'I want to leave here.'

'He won't let you,' Delas Fana said. 'Nor me, come to that. Could we slip away? Possibly. But I am told this camp breaks today. Thunder has been heard in the north.'

'Thunder?'

Once more she looked away. 'An omen. It is as my sister has said, the secret behind this . . . migration. The Teblor will follow Elade Tharos because they must. So too the Saemdhi, the Bright Knot and all the other peoples of the north.'

'There will be war?'

She nodded.

'What of Silver Lake, where my mother lives?'

'You can hope,' she said, 'there is time to flee. There will be no conquering and holding of land, Rant. Once the Warleader's armies begin moving, they will not stop.'

'So Elade Tharos would kill my mother, too.' Rant rested his hand on his knife. 'Why should I care about the laws of the Teblor? If my knife is demon-possessed, it is still *my* knife.'

'Would you battle this entire army?'

'They are so eager for a fight, why not?'

'Then your sisters will die with you. The Jheck as well. These hounds. All will die with you.'

He faced her. 'You have chained me, Delas Fana. You and the others – you have all chained me.'

'Family,' she answered in a flat tone. 'Now you begin to understand.' After a moment she plucked at his arm. 'Very well, come then.'

'Where to?'

'Damisk.'

It hadn't been entirely the truth, nor a lie. The Sunyd had been weakened by a concerted effort to reduce the game in their territory. Wholesale slaughter was the first stone in the avalanche. Everything that followed was inevitable.

In his youth, Damisk had questioned little. He'd thought that taking the world as it was marked him as a wise man. Not one for ideals or dreams or even faith. Nothing humans did could inspire the young tracker with the creases around his eyes – eyes weathered by vast distances and landscapes so overwhelming they belittled the witness. The northlands made a man small, but this in turn made a man's decisions monumental. What path to take? When to turn back? The arrow that sped from his bow ended a life again and again. Animals lying on the ground, losing the light in their eyes as their cries faded, the stuttering rise and fall of each breath slowing until stillness arrived and silence settled all around.

The trees and rocks cared not. The sky never turned away. Clouds did not suddenly weep tears of grief. But a thread of life had been cut, and Damisk would draw out his knife and his rope, scanning nearby branches. He would hitch the carcass up, head down, and open the throat so all the blood drained out. He would run hands along the hide, gauging its worth. He would think of a full belly and scan the sky for the first sight of condors and vultures and ravens. Hunting had its place in the Wilds, because the Wilds needed their wolves and daggercats, their bears and wolverines, owls and hawks, the snakes in the leaf litter, the kingfishers above the streams.

Did it need people?

He had believed, back then, that he had a place in the Wilds. That people belonged here, no different from wolves and bears. And as long as the Wilds stayed wild, this belief was beyond challenge. But the Wilds were only wild because people had not yet arrived in sufficient numbers, not yet swung the axe and lit the fires and cut nature's thread.

Every beast could be slain, the hunting animals among them left to starve. The mountains would not crumble. The sky would not lose its colour. And if the rivers grew fat and murky and lifeless, still they flowed.

Damisk was among the first arrows to speed unerringly into the Wilds. What followed was none of his concern. People arrived because people always arrived. There was nothing here to question, nothing at all.

Such were his years of contentment, with no hint of the restlessness that would take his soul as his body aged. When the time came to see more paths and trails behind him than those waiting ahead, a clear-eyed man could not help but turn to look into his wake. If denial was a habit, he might look and still feel nothing.

The sky and mountains mocked denial. The empty eyes of slain beasts held their lifeless stare, until turning away became endless flight. Denial was a fool's game. It belonged to the dim-witted. He had looked into too many lifeless eyes, had wondered too often at where life's light had gone.

Dimness of thought and lack of introspection made many humans less than human, surrendering their precious gifts to a headlong plunge forward, always forward. He'd had his own benighted years, when he would proclaim that he lived only for the present. He had willed himself stupid, because it was an easy thing to do.

The pain in his wrists had faded to a dull throb. He shivered every now and then from blood-loss and, perhaps, fever. With his body lying on the flat rock, the back of his head against stone, he stared skyward as the day's heat built in the sun's glare. He could hear the camp breaking, as he had listened to the Saemdhi depart en masse just before dawn, the same deep murmur of movement, footfalls on bedrock, the cries of babes and the shouts of children. But now a new sound had come, very distant, somewhere far to the north. Thunder. Cracks in the air, as if lightning was striking, followed by drumming that made the bedrock beneath him shiver.

Yet, with all these sounds surrounding him, he was thinking of the silence. When the clatter of antlers among branches and brush had ceased, when the beast was revealed, lying on its side, panting and blood coming from its nostrils. The silence that followed the light and the light that fled in an instant, leaving dull, empty eyes.

He remembered, the last few times, standing over the carcass, ready to do the work of dressing and skinning and quartering, and being frozen in place by that silence as it filled his head like roaring blood. And he would realize that he was the deliverer of silence, he was its weapon come to the Wilds, and in his wake nothing moved.

The Sunyd had been few in number, relative to the area they claimed as their own. Because they were sedentary, they hunted only the herds that migrated through, from heights to valleys, from forests to high plains. Mostly, however, they had kept goats, horses and a strange, long-furred breed of cattle, as well as pigs. Hunting was not a necessity but a pastime.

Damisk had joined in the drives to slaughter the herds, not in Sunyd lands, but in the lands south, so that no herds returned to the high forests with summer's end. If the Sunyd were weak, there were other reasons.

Of course, he knew, they hadn't been weak at all. There just hadn't been enough of them once the southlanders arrived.

We are the bringers of silence. For a time. Until the axe and flame, the roads and wagons.

The stupid knew better than to look into their wake. The wise could not help it and so suffered greatly. This was humanity's great divide, and many a time, Damisk had envied the stupid and all the obstinate incomprehension he saw in their eyes and faces. *In the end, it takes wisdom to scream.*

Iron spikes had been driven into the bedrock, through wrists and ankles. He was naked, his skin burning even as chills racked his frame. The Teblor had then left him alone. Left to the Wilds.

The mountains did not crumble. The sky did not turn away. No clouds appeared to weep for him. His only company, for the moment, was biting flies. His chest rose and fell, rose and fell. Blood crusted his nostrils and one side of his head throbbed. His mouth was dry, lips split. His broken wrist, tightly bound in leather to make sure he could not tear it free of the spike, was now numb, the hand lifeless.

He'd seen a god in chains. He'd freed it to unleash unimaginable slaughter. *In that world, at least, the Wilds fought back. Would that he join us here and now. Because here and now, surely the first soul he would rip from its body would be mine.*

Instead, the Teblor will be my justice. Nailed to the bedrock in a place where people don't belong. I . . . I have no complaints.

A shadow fell over him. 'Damisk.'

Blinking, he sought to focus, and then managed a rasping sigh. 'Ah, Rant, you shouldn't be here.'

The half-blood was weeping.

'Be at ease, lad. I was already dying.'

Water filled Damisk's mouth as Rant poured from a bladder. He coughed, then managed a swallow. When it continued pouring he turned his face aside. The bladder moved away and out of sight again. A moment of hilarity struck Damisk and he smiled. 'Aye, that's a thought. Drown me and cheat them all.'

'Damisk. I have failed you. I asked for a few more steps, remember? I should have freed you when you wanted it.'

'My choice,' Damisk said. 'Not the best of them, aye. But it was the path I took.'

'Delas Fana says the Saemdhi have gone to attack Silver Lake.'

Damisk frowned, and then asked, 'Only them?'

'Other tribes, too, I think.'

'No Teblor?'

'Sunyd, for revenge. Ex-slaves.'

'And the rest?'

Rant shook his head, reaching up to wipe at his eyes and cheeks.

'There's a legion, lad. Malazan marines. Somewhere south of Culvern the last I heard.'

'You couldn't warn them, Damisk—'

'Ah, my conceit. I'd wager they've caught wind of trouble with or without me. What I'm telling you, Rant, is there's still a chance. This could go bad for the Teblor and their allies. Not likely, but possible. Hold to that. Hold to that.'

'This isn't the only army, Damisk. There are others, east of here. Every Teblor tribe.'

'Bloody days ahead, then. Stay out of the fighting, Rant. It's not your war.'

'I won't fight, Damisk. Unless it's to protect Gower and Nilghan, and . . . my sisters.'

Damisk nodded but said nothing. He'd run out of words.

'Will you live long? Don't live long.'

He shook his head. *Not long.*

'You were my first friend,' Rant said, weeping again. 'And because of me you're going to die. You should have let me drown in the lake. My mother should have cut my throat, not her own.'

Damisk shook his head. *She didn't cut anyone's throat.*

'I know. I believe you. And now she's going to die along with everyone else in Silver Lake. This world is too big for me, Damisk. I wish I could go home. I wish I could die with my mother.'

Now Delas Fana came into view, just past Rant's shoulder. Her hands were on him, seeking to pull him away. 'It's done, Rant. I doubt he's even hearing you any more. Not long now. Possibly even before we leave this place.'

Rant turned on her. 'You call this a clean death?'

'It is the Teblor way. A criminal alone with his guilt. If there is torment, he will deliver it upon himself. This, Rant, is clean. He will be gone soon.'

Aye, Damisk thought, *it is clean.*

He let his eyes close, struggled to slow his breathing. He understood Delas Fana. If death wasn't as close as she said it was, he would pretend otherwise.

Rant's sobbing tore at him. He struggled against one last look – but then, who would want to see a child's face at this time? After a long, deep breath, he let his face go slack.

The cries moved away. Sunlight once more burned against his face, lit the world orange behind his eyelids.

Distant horns sounded. And the deep murmur of footfalls rose up like a tide.

I didn't cry out when they drove in the spikes. I didn't rail, didn't curse. I didn't give them anything.

I don't think they expected otherwise. Still, I wonder if they understand. I'm a southlander. I'm from lands that have known more wars than the Warleader can conceive. We may be rubbish at peace – who isn't? – but war . . . ah, war we know.

The Warleader was the arrow speeding into the south.

But the south wasn't wild. It knew all about the silence that comes after the last drop of blood. And the last breath.

Something stirred him, nudged at his attention. A sound, perhaps. He couldn't feel his body. Damisk opened his eyes. It was late afternoon. The army was long gone. Not a single footfall reached his ears.

The thirst was unbearable. His skin was afire, wrapping dead flesh.

A snuffling sound – yes, that was it – coming from one side. He turned his head, struggled to focus.

A grey bear, standing on its four limbs for the moment, head slung low and slowly shifting from one side to the other. A sow, less than ten paces away, wet udders at her belly.

A smile came to Damisk's lips, audibly cracking them. He tasted blood.

Oh, this place was full of smells the bear knew to avoid, the mass of hunters who would kill her at a moment's notice. But they were gone, leaving but one, and from that one came the smell of blood.

'I took your mate,' Damisk whispered, though he knew it wasn't true. 'I took him down. I stole him from you – do you remember? He'd wandered too far. On the wrong side of the mountains. I killed him.'

Still the huge beast hesitated. There was garbage in the abandoned camp, things to eat had been left behind. The bear didn't need him.

'I killed him!' Damisk cried, his voice hoarse. 'Now I'm here for you! Where's your courage, damn you?'

The bear huffed and then ambled closer, a few strides, only to pause again, half rising up to look around with nose testing the air. A moment later a cub appeared well behind her, and then a second one. Both hung back. This winter's brood, already the size of a normal black bear.

Damisk shifted his head again and again, trying to snare her gaze. Eye contact, he knew, would do it. *All we need here, lady. Meet my eyes!* But her head swung away again and again, her wet nostrils flaring. 'Look at me!'

Their eyes locked.

When she moved on him, it was in a blur.

Damisk had not screamed once when the spikes were driven through his limbs. Not once.

He screamed now. For a long, long time.

CHAPTER SEVENTEEN

The cult of Coltaine, the Black-Winged God, first arose in Seven Cities. Within half a dozen years it had become the dominant religion on that continent. It quickly entered a period of schism, numerous subsects arising, many of them secret, decidedly gnostic.

Temples of the Black Feather appeared in every major settlement. The site of the Fall became a place of pilgrimage. Iconic symbols proliferated, some with obscure meaning. The black feather was of course common and unambiguous, as was the X-shaped form, often wrought in silver or gold. The gilded red-gold butterfly pendants and brooches were less clear; so too the temple practice of housing Wickan cattle-dogs.

Curiously, the believers did not come from the warrior or soldier class. The majority of them were among the poorest in the imperial population. The indebted, the benighted, the lame and the sick.

For a time – a grisly period indeed – certain subsects engaged in kidnapping soldiers to be sacrificed amid a ring of the destitute, in the poorest quarters of the city. As expected, the reprisals were bloody and officially sanctioned.

If anything, this had an effect opposite to that intended. True, the kidnappings ceased. But the faith became a wildfire, sweeping across not just Seven Cities, but all the territories of the empire.

Malazan armies despised the cult.

Igniting the Fires
The Birth of New Religions in the Late Malazan Empire
Faels Ebal of Aren Outside the Fall

S ARLIS WAS LED INTO A ROOM CROWDED WITH THE PARAPHER-
NALIA of war. She was guided to a table by a scrawny youth with
a runny nose. A broad-shouldered old woman sat there, iron tools
and balls of leather-string arrayed before her. She had hair on her chin
and along the line of her jaw, her flat face suggesting Rhivi blood. Dark
eyes in deep sockets regarded Sarlis, devoid of expression.

'I'm Blowlant,' she said in a rough, scratchy voice. 'You're new, so
you sits and listens and watches.'

A heap of leather armour filled one side of the table. Blowlant reached
a gnarled, stubby hand into it and pulled free a long-sleeved shirt. It
was in ribbons, bloodstains and cuts and slashes everywhere.

Sarlis recognized it. 'That's Stillwater's.'

'It's always Stillwater's,' Blowlant replied, deadpan. She bunched it
up and threw it onto the floor. 'Her favourites, she says. Always wants
it sewns back togethers. No points. Never any points. So we gets her a
new one, see, and we scars it up and sews in stitches and makes scuffs
and bunches it up and beats it with rocks. Then we gives it to her and
she's happy again. Varbo! Gets us a new ones for Stillwaters!'

Another worker on the other side of the room looked up from
rummaging through a large crate. 'This ain't Stillwater's crate, Blow.
This is Second Squad's crate.'

'So finds Stillwaters's crates!'

Varbo straightened, scratching at his flaky scalp. 'We're in town so
we weren't expecting to need it, so it got packed down in the cellar.'

'That's a stupids one on you, Varbo. Don'ts matters where we is.
Stillwaters always finds a reasons to bleeds. What idiots don'ts knows
that? Go finds us a shirts!'

Scowling, Varbo tramped from the room.

Blowlant sighed. 'He was a soldiers onces, thens he tooks a hits to the
heads. Alls he can do nows is counts things. We keeps him for count-
ings.' She pulled out another shirt. 'Sees how bads this one smells?
Blanket's. Brokens buckles. Easy fixes.'

Sarlis settled back to watch. It didn't matter that this would be dull
work. It didn't matter that Blowlant was ugly and smelled like horses.
Here, in the company's troop of followers, she was safe.

Four days ago she had been thinking about drawing a knife across
her throat. Now there were vast, empty spaces inside her, waiting to be
filled with new things. It made her feel younger than her years.

'What's thats in your eyes, girls?'

'Tears. I'm sorry.'

Blowlant stared for a moment, and then set the shirt down with a
sigh. 'It's justs a buckles, girl, and buckles breaks. Blankets breaks his

buckles because he's fatters than he thinks's. But maybe he isn'ts. Maybe it's becauses of Folibores, who sneaks when Blankets's sleepings and breaks the buckles so's Blankets thinks he's gettings fatters. Why elses would Folibores feel bads for us and buy us lots of buckles and jugs of wines? See? It's alls downs to knowings. These soldiers ain'ts pickys. But Captains Gruffs – oh, that's's a wholes different story! Leave mendings of Gruffs's to me. Luckilys Gruffs does mosts himselfs. He's likes that.' And she held a finger to the side of her hairy head and made small circling motions. 'Who can figures, eh? Bests seams-makers in the wholes Legions would rathers disembowels peoples. Wasteds talents. Wasteds! Now, gets that box o' buckles there and I'll shows you hows.'

Spindle opened the door to the captain's office in time for two of the mayor's assistants to drag an unconscious mayor from the room.

'The mayor's just leaving,' said Gruff from behind his desk. 'Do come in, Sergeant,' he invited as he frowned down on the roundish blood splash on the desk's battered top. 'Wood, it seems, is harder than bone. What a curious thing! Sit, old friend, please.'

Spindle righted the chair and sat in it. 'Captain, there's movement on the north shore of the lake. Balk's Company is stirring a bit. The western forest is crawling and the folk don't seem interested in trading.'

Gruff had found a discarded cloth from the wastebasket beside his desk and was wiping at the blood. 'There is a brand of obstinacy, Sergeant, that leaves me baffled. Other brands I understand very well. Benger, for example, and his determination to heal a local woman sorely beset by unwanted afflictions. Even blessed Stillwater and her stubborn imposition of some form of mayhem wheresoever she happens to be. Quirks of nature, if you see my meaning, the former laudable, the latter deplorable. But to stand in the face of sweet reason, suffused of visage with veins throbbing on temple and neck, why, what manner of creature wilfully succumbs to this?'

'Stupid ones, sir.'

Gruff pointed a long, perfectly manicured finger at Spindle. 'You have it, my dear! Succinct! Well done, thank you. Purchase the last of what pass for horses in this town and have the teamsters go over, once again, the condition of wheels, axles and yokes.' He flung the stained cloth back into the wastebasket and sat down. 'Top up the bags of grain and all the rest. Expand the circuit route of the patrols, especially the northwest sector from lakeshore into tree-line, and of course the west line and eyes on the south. New strings on all crossbows, fresh fins on the quarrels. Distribute the munitions—' He paused and lifted both hands. 'Dear me, listen to my prattling! To a veteran at that!'

Spindle shrugged. 'I'd forgotten about a last check on the wagons. Thank you for reminding me.' He hesitated, and then said, 'Evacuating the townsfolk at short notice still poses a problem, sir. Especially with the mayor's present . . . state of mind.'

'Unconscious? Not at all. Couldn't be more ideal.'

'Until he wakes up.'

'Groggy for days, I'm sure. Oh. Do we *have* days?'

'A week if we're lucky, sir. Bliss Rolly says not, however. Three days, maybe four.'

Captain Gruff stroked his smooth chin. 'I was considering sending the regulars as the civilians' escort. No more than a half-day to evacuate and load up. Familiar faces for the locals will assist matters, I'm sure.'

'Aye, sir. Glad to hear it. Bliss will get them out.'

'Leaving to us marines the problematic issue of holding out for the time being, if only to permit the refugees the luxury of covering some ground. We're a bit understrength.'

Spindle studied his captain for a long moment, and then nodded. 'Aye, sir, a bit understrength.'

'Paltry, Daint and Blanket for the runs and draws. Put Undercart in charge. Do that tonight.'

'Aye, sir.'

'Clay Plate, Given Loud and Folibore for the sore spot, with Benger covering. Again, tonight.'

'I'll have Morrut oversee Benger.'

'Good point – did I really put Benger in charge? Dear me. I fear I have become distracted.'

'Something wrong, sir?'

'Nothing a little make-up won't fix. Thank you for your report, Sergeant Spindle.'

Spindle rose, and then left the room.

For this patrol, So Bleak had Stillwater for company. Something about her always made him uneasy, and it wasn't just those uncanny eyes on her scarf, or even the rope tattoo hidden beneath it. On this day she was wearing an old hauberk that didn't fit very well and also had the unfortunate detail of rows of studs riveted into it, most of which were missing on the front barring two at nipple-height. This alone might have been disconcerting enough, but only one of those remaining studs was positioned where a nipple likely hid underneath. The other one was off to the side. The effect, when standing in front of Stillwater, reminded him of looking at a person with a wandering eye.

Which didn't make sense, leaving So Bleak befuddled and frustrated. He wasn't even looking at the damned studs and being a grown man who liked women and therefore had learned the subtle art of admiring breasts surreptitiously, often only via peripheral vision, everything about it made him feel unbalanced and strangely sordid.

Her acuity didn't help. 'You're just a man, So Bleak. Stop panicking. I mean, I've checked out your crotch-bulge often enough. I once even saw you naked.'

'What? When?'

Finishing the ascent of the slope, they began walking along the earthen bank on the east side of town, beyond which was a cleared killing ground of perhaps seventy paces, and then a rough line of young trees and tree-stumps leading into thicker, older stuff beyond.

'You were alone, in your tent. You had a bucket and a rag, wiping down blood and whatnot. Right after we nabbed Balk.'

'But – how in Icari's name could you see that?'

She shrugged. 'I was taking a short-cut in my warren.'

'A short-cut? We were bivouacked!'

'Okay, I felt like looking at naked men, all right? We'd just been mauled. Saw you crawl into your tent with that bucket and rag.'

'Look,' So Bleak said, 'just prise those damned studs off.'

'Not a chance. They're protecting my nipples.'

'Oh, sorry – hang on, no they aren't!'

'One is.'

He clawed at his face. 'I get it. I get you on that. I get me, too. Everybody's fucking everybody right now, because trouble's on the way. But I've given my heart to another—'

Stillwater stopped, grasped So Bleak's right arm and yanked him to a halt. 'You can't do that, soldier. Marines don't do that. It's against . . . everything. Shrake's a sergeant and I'm telling you, So Bleak, we're all disgusted how she lusts after you.'

'She what? Really?'

'Sucking on her cock-braid like that. Gives me the crawlies.'

'Cock-braid?'

'Aye, isn't that obvious? She's chewing on you plain and simple, and if that's not disgusting enough, we all have to watch!'

'I don't want to fuck you.'

'Good, then it's mutual. There's a shed at berm's end, just up ahead. Full of really old dried fish hanging on racks, but the piles of nets make for a soft bed. But I should warn you. Too much antics and thrashing and we'll end up all tied up like what happened to Undercart and that merchant's wife. Scandal! The whole town's talking.'

So Bleak stared at Stillwater, trying to make sense of her. Then he gave up. Nobody could make sense of Stillwater. The woman inside that head lived in a strange, strange world, and the proof of that was right there in her face and her eyes. Not to mention the words spilling out of her mouth. 'Let's just finish this,' he said. 'No shed, no humping. Two marines on patrol, right?'

'Sure,' Stillwater said, shrugging. 'And we'll just ignore that hairy scout in the trees who's pacing us.'

'Well, yes, it's what we've been doing, isn't it?'

'Exactly. I told Drillbent to talk to her—'

'Who?'

'Shrake. Sergeant to sergeant. But if that doesn't work, I'll just cut off her braids. Because, I tell you, we've all had enough.'

'You don't want to get Shrake mad at you, Stillwater. I've seen—'

'We all have. Doesn't bother me.'

'Who's that up ahead?' So Bleak asked. Someone had just climbed atop the bank at the lake end, struggling with something bulky and awkward.

Stillwater sighed. 'Anyx Fro. Come on, we need to see this.'

They picked up the pace. 'See what?' So Bleak asked.

'Anyx Fro invents stupid things. It's because she's basically stupid, bless her, meaning everything she invents is equally stupid. Poor Anyx.'

'Does she know you think she's stupid, Stillwater?'

'No, she's too stupid to know that, I think. Don't get me wrong, So Bleak, she's like a sister to me, the kind you try to leave behind when you go off with your friends, but then you turn around and there she is! Frustrating! So you invent a new game and it's called "tying your sister to a tree" and it all starts out great, everyone having a good time, but then when we run off she's left tied to a tree and suddenly it's no fun any more. Not for her, anyway.'

'You just make this shit up, don't you?'

Stillwater glanced over. 'Don't let Shrake fuck you, is all I'm saying.'

'I thought we were talking about—'

'And stop staring at my studs, unless you've changed your mind about the shed.'

'I don't want to fuck you!'

That was loud enough for Anyx Fro to hear, as they'd drawn much closer. She turned from the tripod she'd set up. 'Smart man, So Bleak. And here I thought you were stupid. People who fuck Stillwater end up poor, as in "poor so-and-so", which is Stillwater's way of saying "oh, dead, of course, because I killed them".' She then crouched down to pick up a heavy flaring tube of polished iron about the length of a clawfoot crossbow. It had an iron peg of some sort halfway along, which she angled into a socket on top of the tripod. She checked that it swivelled easily and then nodded. 'You two should stay back. Except maybe you, Stillwater. If you want, you can stand there, in front of the tube's big hole.'

'So this is your Iron Maw,' Stillwater said, hands on her hips.

'What's it do?' So Bleak asked.

'Anyx says it'll change everything. You know. Like, when I invented the mage-assassin.'

'You didn't invent the mage-assassin,' said Anyx Fro.

'Only to have it stolen by everybody.'

'Then they must have stolen it before you were even born.'

'It's still stealing, Anyx.'

So Bleak cleared his throat. 'Actually, I was asking Anyx Fro.'

'It's packed with a small bag of stuff, and at this end there's a mostly denatured munition mix – so it doesn't explode when air contacts it. I invented it myself, of course, because when genius strikes, sure enough you discover that you have to invent stuff to make the new invention work. That complicates things, slows progress. But now I'm ready to test it.'

'So not really one invention, but two,' said So Bleak, nodding.

'Well, more like six in all. But most of that was mechanics. The principle is basically simple—'

'Are you two going to stand around talking all afternoon or can we see it work, or, rather, not work?'

'I was meaning to do this in private,' said Anyx Fro. 'Isn't your patrol over? Why not go into that shed over there? I promise I won't aim the Maw at it. Not on purpose, that is.'

'He doesn't want to fuck,' said Stillwater. 'The world's about to end and he doesn't want to fuck. I think there's something wrong with So Bleak. I've always thought that, to be honest.'

Her arms crossed and her lips compressed, Anyx Fro looked at them both for a long moment. She worked the wad in her mouth into the other cheek, and then shrugged. 'Fine. Like I said, stand back.'

She swung the Iron Maw so that its flared open end faced the forest. 'Regulars will need a natural flame-source,' she said, 'because I mean this for regular infantry, not marines. Me, I just need to tap a finger.' And then she did.

The eruption was deafening, a huge ball of smoke gouting out from the Iron Maw, even as it flew backwards, taking the tripod with it. Fortunately, no one was standing behind it. The sky above the forest was suddenly full of shrieking birds.

Shaking his head to get the ringing out of his ears, So Bleak looked over in time to see Anyx Fro turn to him with a broad smile on her flash-burned face. 'Success!' she shouted, the cry coming as if from very far away. Then she ran over to check on the Iron Maw.

So Bleak stared after her, still not quite comprehending what had happened. A finger jabbed into his shoulder, jabbed a second time, and then again. Irritated, he faced Stillwater.

But she wasn't looking at him. Instead, her gaze was fixed on something in the tree-line opposite. So Bleak looked over there. He saw licks of flame on the ground and among the branches and twigs that surrounded a strange horizontal hole cutting deep into the forest. And something odd was in that path.

'Is that a pair of legs?' So Bleak asked. 'Just standing there? Where – where's the rest of him?'

'Our spying scout,' said Stillwater. 'Saw more than he wanted to. Poor scout.' She then turned to Anyx Fro. 'You just killed a Wilder, Anyx, a scout who was watching us. No, let me put it this way, you may have just started the war.'

Anyx Fro choked as she half-swallowed her wad of rustleaf, and spent a few moments bent over and coughing stuff out. Then she straightened and stared at Stillwater.

'And now,' continued Stillwater as she walked over to the toppled Iron Maw, 'the most pertinent question of all: how long does it take to reload?'

'About half a day.'

'Wait till the captain finds out about this,' said Stillwater. 'Poor Anyx Fro, who started a war with twenty thousand wild savages.'

Anyx Fro licked her lips with a brown tongue-tip. 'Are you saying I should have aimed at the shed?'

Bray paused and glanced back. Frowning, Sugal shrugged. They had been called to a council in Balk's command tent. The main avenue in the camp was a snarled mix of mud and flattened grasses. A plague of flies had been hounding the mercenaries for half a week and a cloud spun round Bray's head as he fixed his gaze northward.

'Did you hear that?' Bray asked.

Sugal looked towards the town. At the far end, near the forest side, a ball of black smoke was slowly dissipating in the air. 'Moranth munitions?'

'They don't have Moranth munitions any more.'

'Malazan munitions, then.'

Bray nodded. He seemed to chew the idea for a moment, and then he said, 'They blow up by accident all the time. Maybe one of the marines blew himself up. Maybe a whole squad.'

'That'd be nice,' Sugal said, impatient to resume their march as a buzzing cloud now circled him as well.

After a moment, Bray set off again.

Sugal was getting tired of Bray, though not as tired as he was getting of Stick. Despite being drunk most of the time, she had managed to push herself into Balk's Company, wedged somewhere between the captain and Lieutenant Ara. Which was saying something. No doubt about it: things had gone all twisted there. It was hard to imagine that Balk preferred Stick to Ara. The commander and his lieutenant went way back, after all. They might even be married for all Sugal knew.

He wouldn't mind a night alone with Ara, come to think of it. A night that began with some games involving naked bodies and sweat. Knives later, because a victim's screams sounded sweeter than any lover's, especially when both came from the same person. The way the look in the eyes switched from languid pleasure into horror. That alone could send waves of ecstasy rippling through him.

He'd wanted something like that with Stick for a long time. The problem was, she'd be too drunk to care much either way. Worse, she might be thinking the same thoughts he would be thinking, so it was a question of whose knife would be the first to taste blood, and Sugal hated the sight of his own blood. Hated feeling pain too, for that matter.

They reached the command tent and Bray didn't pause going in. Seeing that it was Pallat ostensibly standing guard at the entrance, Sugal slowed up.

'Soon, soldier, soon.'

Pallat's answering smile showed mostly green teeth. He was the kind of man who seemed to rot from the inside out. Dangerous with a spear, though. 'Looking forward to a line of heads on that bank, Sergeant, that I am.'

Pallat had lost friends to this company of marines. He was stoking fires. 'Just stay close to me,' Sugal said. 'When it's time, I guarantee you some fun.'

A sharp nod answered him.

Sugal stepped inside.

Ara, Stick and Bray were already seated, while Balk stood near the back wall, next to a narrow table on which rested his scabbarded sword and belt. The captain had one hand on the polished wood of the scabbard. He ran a finger along its length and then turned to his officers.

'We were under the impression that this company didn't have any munitions. Wasn't it Fray and Bairdal who were supposed to identify the supplies the marines brought with them?'

Sugal glanced at Bray. The man hadn't wasted any time with his news. That said, the explosion had been loud enough. Sugal realized that he had come in halfway through a discussion. They hadn't waited for him.

'No reason for worry,' Stick said, her words slurred. 'Word is, that stuff kills more marines than it does the enemy. Besides, none of us will break a sweat this time around. Once the forest comes alive.' And she smiled at the thought, her dark eyes glittering.

'We stay in place,' Balk said. 'We hold the south, making a bristling wall, denying retreat.'

'Should've told us from the first,' Sugal said, hastily adding 'sir.'

Balk sighed. 'Was it not obvious? We were already marching. The Baron's contract was a stopgap, a way of topping up the company's reserves.' He fixed Sugal with an expression undeniably condescending. 'Clearly, Sugal, a contract had already been agreed – it was only the timeline that was variable. The *imperial* contract – well, that was too delicious to refuse.'

Stick and Bray both laughed, as if they'd known all along how things were, and Sugal knew that for a lie.

'So whose contract is this, sir?'

'I doubt you'd believe me,' Balk replied. 'Back to the munitions. None were used when we clashed in the forest. This suggests to me that they are in short supply, and as Stick points out, they're notoriously unreliable. It would be useful to find out what just happened and if there were any casualties, but we've played too long at being uncurious. No matter, those munitions likely won't be directed our way.'

'Not when they think we're on their side,' Stick added.

'More to the point,' Balk said, 'our initial inaction is likely to confuse them.' He suddenly shook his head. 'I don't know why I'm overthinking this. There's what, eighteen of them? A handful of regulars who won't make any difference. The primary unknown is the mage-component. We've confirmed four.' He turned to Ara.

She nodded. 'Benger, Stillwater, Clay Plate and Oams, though we're not certain about Oams and besides, he's not been seen on patrol in some time. We knew,' Ara continued, 'he was venturing into the forest. For all we know, the tribes got tired of his snooping around and did him in.'

'Aren't we in contact with the tribes?' Sugal asked.

The lieutenant shrugged. 'Language barriers.'

'We have maintained some distance,' Balk said. 'They know not to attack us and that is my primary concern. Details of what goes on in the forest aren't required.' He paused, and then said, 'Their most powerful shaman getting killed has no doubt weakened them, but to be honest, that's not our problem.'

Sugal leaned forward. 'Captain, we're not going to leave the marines to the tribes, are we? I mean, not entirely? Don't we want at least some of them alive?'

A flash of distaste in Balk's face, quickly mastered as the captain's gaze settled on Sugal once again. 'I'm sure opportunities will arise, Sergeant. After all, where else will the marines retreat to? It's our camp or nowhere.'

'And the townsfolk?' Bray asked.

Balk shrugged. 'I doubt any will make it out.'

'So,' Sugal asked, 'what then? Once all this gets settled, I mean.'

'Culvern,' said Balk. 'If we're along for the ride – and no guarantee that we will be – but we would hit the garrison there, and backed by ten thousand tribals we should roll over it without much trouble. Thereafter, we would probably join a much larger army and the cities of the south are open to us. While marching in that army, we begin recruiting in earnest.'

'We will need to,' said Ara, 'once the entire Malazan Empire starts pushing back.'

Balk frowned at her but said nothing.

Ah, now I understand. Balk's lover was not convinced. Stick, meanwhile, had drool dripping from her eye-teeth. The way south was her river of blood. Sugal had a sudden fear that Stick would succeed in pushing Ara aside, maybe out of the company itself. Then she would slide her way under Balk's furs. That would be trouble, because she well knew Sugal's own ambitions.

She'll have me killed. At first chance. And she'll use Bray to do it.

The silence that had followed Ara's comment was stretching out, growing uncomfortable for everyone in the tent. Balk broke it. 'Not long now. See to your troops. Camp goes dry beginning tomorrow morning. I want everyone staying sharp.'

Sugal glanced at Stick, but her smirk had not wavered.

She had one foot on the damned pedestal, and she knew it.

Like Balk said. Not long now.

The sun was finally gone from the sky and the night would be warm, almost sultry. Folibore and the rest of the heavies were ensconced – for the moment – at the Black Eel, where Storp had lifted the huge trap-doors to the cellars to cool things down in the main room.

'Quality of life is certainly a consideration,' said Folibore. 'We dwell in a prison and frilly curtains on the barred windows won't change that fact.'

'A prison where people sleep safe at night, mostly,' observed Daint, spilling ale when Given Loud nudged his elbow the moment he brought the tankard up for a sip. Daint glowered at Given Loud. 'It's the cellmates who are the problem.'

'Everyone goes squirrelly in a cage,' said Paltry Skint. 'Just look at Daint and Given Loud. Barking mad.'

Blanket snorted. 'Squirrels don't bark.'

Paltry frowned at him. 'Don't they? I'm sure I heard one bark, once.'

'No,' asserted Blanket with a slow shake of his head. 'It's classic mis-association which is a common affliction in small brains. Squirrels. Bark. Squirrels in trees, bark on trees, thus: squirrels on bark in trees—'

'Barking,' cut in Paltry Skint, nodding to herself.

Blanket leaned back to look at her down his massive nose. 'I am not responsible for the confusion in your head.'

'Well, I think you are!' snapped Paltry Skint.

'The Wilders have it pretty good,' said Folibore, seeking to return the discussion to where it had begun. Had he begun it? He wasn't sure. No matter. 'No coin, no taxes. They don't even claim to own the land they live on. And then there's their teeth.'

'Their what?' Say No asked.

'Teeth. Next time we slaughter a few hundred, check out their teeth. No rot, and that's down to the food they eat.'

'Best way to destroy a tribe of Wilders is to introduce sweet stuff,' said Blanket. 'They get addicted to it. Bad stuff then happens.'

'Because sweet things taste good!' said Paltry Skint in a belligerent tone, as she was in a mood this evening. 'Isn't it cruel to deprive them of it? If their tribe then collapses it was because of some inherent weakness, not rotting teeth.'

Daint said, 'Cannibalism is good for the teeth.'

Sighing, Folibore said, 'They aren't cannibals, Daint.'

'If they were, they'd still have good teeth. Better teeth, even.'

'But they couldn't eat Anyx Fro,' objected Blanket.

'Why not?'

'Because she's sweet.'

'Blanket has a good point,' said Folibore, 'inasmuch as we all know he's sweet on her and he's not a cannibal, if his sandy shit is any indication.'

Say No choked momentarily on her ale. 'Sandy shit?'

'The big one he left in the tray in the room,' explained Folibore. 'I mean, once he learned to use the tray of sand, that is. I don't want to talk about what it was like before that.'

'I nearly crushed that weasel's head,' said Blanket.

'With your turd?' Paltry asked. 'How fucking big was it?'

'No, not with my turd,' Blanket explained, slowly. 'Between my knees.'

Everyone stared at Blanket, even Folibore.

'I don't want to ask,' said Say No.

'I was asleep in bed, right? And Creature likes to sleep with me, under the furs and—'

'Its own furs?'

'Well, Paltry, yes, it does have its own fur, but not the furs I meant. I meant my sleeping furs, which sadly include a few weasel strips here and there, further to which fortunately Creature does not seem to have noticed said kinship—'

'So Creature could well be using weasel furs to sleep under, in addition to its own.'

'Okay,' acquiesced Blanket. 'Valid point. Where was I?'

'Creature's head between your knees, nearly getting crushed.'

'Thank you, Daint.'

'I'm Given Loud.'

'Yes, but I happened to glance at Daint and he was mouthing your words. He does that, you know. It's uncanny.'

'Between the knees!'

'I suppose Creature wanted to get warm and why, when something warm and furry gets between my legs—'

'*Stop!*' shouted just about everyone.

A moment later, Say No snorted a laugh. 'Creature was hunting mice. Got confused.'

'The point I was trying to make,' Folibore resumed, 'is that the Wilder life is probably, on balance, easier and more relaxed than the life of a standard civilized denizen of the empire – or of any other civilized realm, for that matter.'

'Difficult to qualify,' muttered Blanket. 'Highly subjective, in fact.'

'Teeth,' said Folibore.

'I have no cause to complain,' Given Loud said, showing everyone his white, even smile.

'Marine rules of hygiene,' Daint pointed out, and even this statement, made to Given Loud, was silently mouthed by Given Loud. The two glared at each other.

'In any case,' Folibore said, somewhat exasperated, 'in the matter of our imminent invasion, I am left wondering at their motivation—'

'Sweets!'

'Cannibalism!'

'Weasels!'

'—and,' Folibore pressed on, 'I am inclined to conclude that the Wilders are invading not because they want something, but because they have to. Consider, after all, the caribou herd fleeing into the southlands, and those giant tundra rats. Something,' he said ominously, 'is happening up north.'

'Portentous conclusion,' murmured Blanket, brow knitting as he frowned.

'Possibly prescient,' added Paltry Skint. She drew out a cloth, reached up under her shirt, and began mopping beneath her breasts.

'Do you really have to do that in public?' Daint asked. 'It's disgusting.'

'What's disgusting is sweating under your tits,' retorted Paltry Skint. 'And since I've never seen you clean up your crotch, I can only conclude that it's a nightmare down there.'

'Nature,' intoned Daint, 'always finds a balance. Why disrupt such a delicate situation?'

'I've seen horses run away when you look at them sidelong, Daint.'

'Would those be the ones following you around everywhere?'

The door to the inn opened and Folibore turned to the newcomer. 'Ah, it's time to do some work. Sergeant Drillbent, isn't this a lovely evening?'

Drillbent scowled. 'Are you drunk?'

'No, of course not.'

'Not drunk? Just insane, then.' Drillbent nodded. 'The night's seething with biting flies, and you've got crawling through grasses to do. No cursing. This needs to be on the sly. Benger will help with that, I'm told. Now,' he paused to scan the heavies, 'you all got your assignments. Get off your asses.'

Everyone arose. 'Will you be joining us?' Folibore asked his sergeant.

'No. Go away. I'm meeting Spindle and Shrake here. Tonight's leaders are Snack, Undercart and Morrut. Gods below, Paltry, what are you doing?'

'Hygiene. You should try it sometime.'

'Let's go, everyone,' said Folibore, 'and leave the sergeant in peace.'

They set out. At the door, Given Loud leaned close to Paltry Skint – but not so close that the other heavies didn't hear when he asked, 'Hey, can I have that cloth you just used?'

Drillbent slumped in the chair as Storp ambled over with two tankards. Offering one to the sergeant, he sat down in a vacated chair and eyed Drillbent as he drank down a mouthful from his own tankard.

'What now, Storp?'

'In my day, heavies were idiots.'

'They're still idiots.'

'Not so sure,' Storp said. 'They've worked out that this is no normal invasion.'

Drillbent snorted. 'Took them long enough. Ten thousand caribou running south and a month later a heavy goes "Hey, that was strange" and another one nods and says "You think it means something?" and eventually it's "ominous, portentous, significant" and whatever other word they can come up with to mean the same damned thing.' He fixed Storp with a stare. 'Like I said. Idiots.'

'You're running out of time to evacuate the townsfolk.'

'They're being stubborn. Listen, Storp, maybe you could weigh in and help convince them it's either flee or die.'

Now it was Storp's turn for a level stare. He continued eyeing Drillbent as he drank down another mouthful. 'When you're soldiering,' Storp finally said, 'you don't get it. When you stop soldiering, why, then you do. It's all about anchoring down. It's about committing to a place, a whole life.'

'Speaking of which,' Drillbent said, 'you've got a decent wagon. You need to load up your kegs and casks.'

'Well now, just my point,' said Storp. 'You're not getting it.'

'Oh I get it,' Drillbent said in a growl. 'And that's why we're running out of time, because one nudge ain't enough. Even a push doesn't work. Leaving the usual last resort: sword-point.' He leaned forward. 'You really want us using that on you, Storp? We will if we have to. The outcome's the same no matter what, so why all the stamping and screaming?'

'Get old enough,' Storp said, 'you just stop running, stop going anywhere. You name a place and there you stay.'

'They're not all old.'

'They are – in their heads. You think all that wandering around you do is natural? Typical, even? Armies draw a certain breed of person, Drillbent. That can blind you to the fact that you're all in a minority.'

'You'd rather stay and die instead of go and live?'

'And you might think that's an easy choice to make.'

The inn door opened and in trooped Shrake and Spindle, followed by Clay Plate.

With a grunt, Storp rose from his chair, collecting his tankard before heading back to the bar.

As everyone sat, Drillbent frowned at Clay Plate. 'What are you doing here? I thought you were assigned to . . . something.'

'Clay Plate has a report to deliver,' said Shrake, pausing to arch her back and stretch and sweep her hair back with both hands.

'Now that's an idea,' said Drillbent. 'Let me just stand up and give my achy pelvis a good forward thrust, shall I?'

'It was just a fucking stretch!' Shrake said. 'Storp, what's taking so long?'

'He has to sew on a third hand,' Drillbent explained. 'Takes time.'

Storp arrived employing the brilliant invention of a tray to hold the three tankards of ale. Clay Plate collected his before it reached the tabletop and drank deep. When he set it down it was empty. He nodded up at Storp.

'Belay that,' ordered Spindle. 'Out with your report first, Clay Plate.'

The soldier scowled as Storp walked away. 'That's just it. It's not a report. It's just feelings.'

'We'll be sure to hug you when you're done,' said Drillbent.

'Glad you're not my sergeant,' Clay Plate said to him.

'Makes two of us.'

Clay Plate picked up his empty tankard and looked forlornly into it. Then he sighed and set it down. 'I keep to myself. Being a marine is a job like any other. That's how I see it. I'm not one to take notice of things, unless they matter. Benger did something when he cured that local. Shifted things away from here. Shifted . . . attention.'

'What kind of attention?' Spindle asked.

Clay Plate shrugged. 'Doesn't matter what kind, Sergeant. Attention is just attention and it's pretty much always bad. Then again, no attention is even worse.'

Drillbent planted both elbows on the table and knuckled his eyes. 'Gods below, is it any wonder Clay Plate's still a mystery to everyone?'

'Blood-oil's a strange thing,' the soldier said. 'One woman here, infected with its fever, for years and years. It deadened things, magically. Because something in blood-oil resists magic. You all with me so far? The point is, thanks to Benger, now it's gone.'

'And what was all that about shifting attention?' Spindle asked.

'That blood-oil was delivered by a god. That kind of attention. That's what's shifted away from here. Leaving a big hole. Only, big holes don't stay empty for long. Other things move in. Will magery be easier? Aye, it will. Will this place get crowded with possibly nasty things? Count on it.'

Spindle said, 'You're saying we should worry about the forest warlocks and witches.'

Clay Plate nodded. 'This time, when they call on spirits of the land, nothing's stopping the biggest, meanest ones of all from answering.'

'Thank you, marine,' said Spindle. 'You can go.'

The man stood, exchanged a curious look with his sergeant, and then left the inn.

'It was pillow talk, wasn't it?' Drillbent said to Shrake. 'In your own squad at that.'

'I was deflecting, damn you!'

'Because it's So Bleak you want to jump? That doesn't even make sense, because he's also in your squad!'

'Maybe I want to jump them all!'

'But especially So Bleak.'

'Yes, damn you!' She drew one end of a braid around and stuffed it into her mouth, began chewing.

'Drillbent,' Spindle said, 'hold Stillwater back.'

'She won't like that.'

'Tell her we may need her to hunt down warlocks and witches, not to mention the spirits they pull in.'

'Okay, she'll like that.'

Shrake made an amused sound and then said around her braid, 'She should take Anyx Fro with her. I saw those two legs, gone above the knees.'

Ignoring her comment, Spindle continued, 'The captain wants the regulars escorting the townsfolk out by midday tomorrow. They're bound to need help.'

Drillbent shook his head. 'The locals will probably riot.'

'More like hide in cellars and whatnot. All three squads need to help Bliss Rolly on this.' Spindle hesitated, and then added, 'Balk's Company will either react or not. Either way tells us something.'

'We're telling Balk something in return,' Drillbent observed.

'Aye. Can't be helped.'

Shrake pulled the braid end from her mouth. 'I don't get it. If we knew we couldn't trust him why hire him in the first place?'

'To get him out of the forest,' Spindle answered. 'In one place and in sight.'

'So long as Oams gets back in time,' Drillbent said.

'I still say this is a shitty way to fight a war,' Shrake muttered. 'The war we're not fighting, I mean.'

'Can't fight an enemy not willing to show up,' Spindle said. 'But that won't last. They're here, and they'll move on us soon enough.'

'You did a great job as usual,' Stillwater said, holding up her leather hauberk. 'Even got the bloodstains out. Amazing.'

Blowlant simply nodded and then headed into the back.

Seated at the worktable, Sarlis watched as Stillwater, unmindful of Varbo's ogling from the other side of the room, got out from under the old hauberk she'd been wearing and pulled on the repaired one. Once done, she collected up the old hauberk. 'Now, Varbo, come here. Got something to show you. You do studs, right? See how there's only two left up here, up front? I want you to switch them around.'

'I could add more studs—'

'No. Same two, just switched around.'

'But why—'

'So Bleak is too complacent,' Stillwater explained, shoving the old hauberk into Varbo's arms. She then turned to Sarlis. 'So here you are. You'll be going out with the locals tomorrow – we're evacuating our followers. Take the covered wagon that Blowlant uses. That way your old neighbours won't even see you.'

'Thank you,' Sarlis replied. She hesitated, and then said, 'It will be strange leaving here. I was born in this town. I have never seen any other place.'

'They're different but the same, really,' Stillwater said with a shrug. 'People make a mess wherever they are. Same mess, same smells, same shit. That only changes when you stumble into people who aren't people. Trell and Jaghut and whatnot. Tiste Andii. Jhag. Fenn.'

'How are those ones not people?' Sarlis asked.

'Well, they are. Not human is what I meant.' She frowned. 'Fake people, maybe.' She shrugged again. 'The point is, those ones don't think like us and that makes being in their company a bit off-putting. But don't worry – none of those around here, mostly. It's not like we're going to Black Coral, and the dragons left Darujhistan years ago. Wait till you meet a Moranth! Not that you will. Anyway, the southlands are the same as here. We'll rejoin you at Culvern.'

Sarlis had heard of Culvern. It was a large city four or five days south of Silver Lake. 'Why aren't you going with us?' she asked.

'We have to throw back an army,' Stillwater replied, frowning now as something had caught her attention about one sleeve of her hauberk. 'Is this a new sleeve?'

'No,' said Sarlis, 'I'm sure I saw Blowlant repairing that one.'

'Got rid of the bite marks from that Hound of Shadow, or maybe it was the warlock who did the biting. Still, I can't find a single stitched hole.'

'She's very good,' said Sarlis.

After a moment, Stillwater nodded. 'Aye, the best seamstress in the legion, barring Captain Gruff.'

The faint frown remained on Stillwater's face as she wandered towards the door.

Sarlis stared after her. She'd had another question, but it seemed there would be no chance of asking it. Now Stillwater was gone, the door slamming behind her.

Sarlis turned to Varbo, who was already busy with the studs on the old hauberk. 'Varbo, there's only a handful of them.'

Varbo glanced up. 'What's that?'

'How can three squads throw back an army, Varbo?'

He paused and studied her. 'Well, that's probably just a nice way of saying it, Sarlis.'

'Saying what?'

'That they're all going to die. But they'll hold 'em back long enough for us to get away.' He scratched the stubble on his jaw, and then shrugged. 'Marines.'

CHAPTER EIGHTEEN

There are conflicting positions when it comes to the Bright Knot tribe. Most encounters with them have been belligerent, so details are difficult and undoubtedly tainted by emotion (the primary emotion being fear).

It's a common condition among some men to fear women. Magic, after all, is a gift without conditions. Questions of efficacy are a fool's game when one's life is at stake. Prowess is only revealed when it's too late. This fear, of course, is also common between men, making the distinction doubly false and decidedly misleading.

The Bright Knot are peculiar in that their warrior caste consists exclusively of women. This is possibly due to the tribe's practice of polyandry, wherein most domestic and legal matters are handled by the guardians of the hearth, said guardians being the males of the tribe.

This gender-based distinction is rare in the world. By their very own origin myth, the Bright Knot are not even from this realm. Regardless, the tribe seems to be stable. There is, however, one oddity that may be relevant. The Bright Knot have disavowed all forms of sorcery. They have healers who make use of forest resources, but this role is not gender specific.

Proof, perhaps, of their other-worldly origins?

Beyond the Border
Tribes and Peoples Outside the Empire
Saengal of Genabaris

FOR MOST OF HIS LIFE, VALOC HAD BEEN WEAK. HE HAD BEEN eleven years old when the slavers captured him. His last sight of the camp where he had been born was his father's head on a pole standing upright on the midden at the settlement's edge. His mother died six months later. She was found lying face-down in the latrine trench that ran through the centre of the Waiting House in Silver Lake, the night before she was to be put on the auction block.

Valoc's recollection of his first eleven years was scant. The memories arrived at night like dreams of another world, an impossible world. In most of them, there was no low roof over his head, no smoke-blackened rafters with their snarls of blood-matted hair from when the grown Sunyd struck their heads against them. No stench of excrement, no nights filled with half a hundred Sunyd chained in the dark, coughing and moaning in their sleep.

The impossible world was bright, its sky beyond reach. The air was clean, the water clear. It would be untrue to hold that Valoc had known none of that in his years as a slave. He had been sold to a local farmer. He had walked muddy fields beneath an open sky. He had looked across the vast lake north of the farm, dreaming of its sweet water filling his lungs as his shackles and chains dragged him away from the light.

What made the dream world an impossible one was its freedom.

When they buried Galambar beneath stones and boulders on the high plain, Valoc had lost the man to whom he owed both his life and his freedom. Galambar had been among the Rathyd of Elade Tharos who had freed the last of the Sunyd slaves. Galambar had broken Valoc's very own chains before the Rathyd warrior drew his sword and cut down the farm's other slaves. He had pressed an iron knife into Valoc's hand and invited him to join in the slaughter. But Valoc had held back and could only watch as his fellow slaves – southlanders all – died to Galambar's blade. Galambar's lust for blood saw all children through a red haze.

The Rathyd, Valoc eventually understood, had come for the Sunyd, and none other. If the southlanders wished to enslave each other, so be it. The farmer and his family were already dead. Southlander slaves would starve in their chains and shackles or burn up when the farm was fired. Death, said Galambar, was a mercy.

Valoc had yet to take a life. When Karsa Orlong's bastard son killed Galambar, Valoc wanted vengeance, but in his mind he saw a scene where Rant was bound in chains, weaponless and pinned to the ground. A scene that saw Valoc's own shadow slide over the bastard's upturned face. And then—

And then. A scene he could barely envisage, a scene his imagination struggled to conjure in his mind's eye, no matter how satisfying it might be. *And then my hand appears. And then I swing a blade. And then ... Rant is dead. Galambar is avenged.*

Instead, all dreams of revenge had been taken away from Valoc. Galambar's death was now meaningless, product of a child's tantrum. The ways of the Teblor were still strange to Valoc. The very notion of thereafter vowing to protect the child, Rant, left Valoc physically sick.

Now, all that was far behind him. Rant had been kept close to the Warleader, under the protection of half-sisters and Black Jheck. Their army had struck south, while Valoc joined his Sunyd kin in marching with the Saemdhi eastward, along the north edge of the lake. One last time would the Sunyd find themselves in the town where they had been made slaves. With spear and blade and torch, they would scour Silver Lake until nothing remained but ashes and charred bones.

Leading the Sunyd was Salan Ardal, a woman not much older than Valoc. She had come from a camp unknown to Valoc, liberated from a valley settlement somewhere far to the west. He found her somewhat frightening. He had heard the rumour that she used blood-oil before every battle, and it was not wise to fight anywhere near her. Perhaps that explained the ferocity and hunger he saw in her eyes.

They had journeyed past the lake's eastern end and were now camped in the deep forest, the latest arrivals to a vast army of local tribes that included the White Jheck and Eastern Bright Knot. Fights broke out every night between the Saemdhi and the White Jheck, between the Bright Knot and virtually everyone else.

Salan Ardal had settled the six hundred Sunyd a short distance away from the main camp. She had just called in all the Teblor warriors and Valoc stood among them, a spear in his right hand and a copper-rimmed shield slung on his left arm. They were crowded among trees and tree-stumps. Overhead, new leaves on branches that trembled, the sunlight coming through seething on the ground, flowing across faces and bodies.

'We march tonight,' Salan was saying, 'halting at the forest edge, within sight of the town. When the sky pales, we attack. The Sunyd will strike at the corner guard station on the embankment. Saemdhi will be on our left flank. I am told there are few defenders. Once in the town, all Sunyd are free to exact vengeance. The Saemdhi and other tribes will not halt but continue south to a garrison town called Culvern. It must be understood,' she continued, scanning the crowd, 'much as we may want to, slow torture of the townsfolk is not possible. Kill quickly. Fire the buildings. All livestock are to be butchered at once, the meat salted and brought to the supply train. We Sunyd will provide the rear-guard for that train.'

Torture had not even occurred to Valoc. He had expected to be witness to the slaughter. He didn't think he would participate. But warriors in the crowd were muttering, some cursing out loud.

'There will be no shortage of southlanders to kill,' Salan said. 'This is not a raid. We are done with raids. It shall be as Warleader Elade Tharos has told us. The southlands shall know the Teblor's blades all the way to Darujhistan. Now, rest this day. See to your weapons.'

Valoc fell back as the crowd slowly dispersed. He made his way to where he had left his kit, tucked beneath the bole of a fallen tree. Once there, he paused to look around. Few warriors were nearby. Setting aside his spear and shield he sat on the trunk. He listened to distant conversations, the occasional snapping branch as the Sunyd set to making rough bedding or spaces in which to lie down.

He was thinking about freedom. Slaves possessed a place deep inside, hidden away. Where thoughts ran free, because thoughts could not be chained. Most of the time, of course, the thoughts weren't thoughts at all. They were screams. Still, this was where a slave retreated to, no matter what travails the body suffered.

The day the chains had been cut away, the shackles prised open, the walls surrounding that place had fallen. Thoughts ran free, filling his head. Emotions had assailed his mind, leaving him stunned, uncomprehending.

He remembered standing in the ruins of the farm, the bodies of his owners flung about and splashed in blood. He stood, a free man, watching Galambar killing slaves still chained, still shackled. Freedom, he realized then, was not the same as courage. It held no intrinsic honour or integrity. Freedom was Galambar's blade swinging down, smashing through arms raised in hopeless self-defence, silencing the screams. Freedom was the clear, unburdened look in Galambar's eyes when he finally turned away from the shattered corpse of the last victim.

Valoc drew from his pack Galambar's old bloodwood sword, a gift from the Rathyd warrior only a few days after his liberation. It had not seen use in years, being the warrior's first weapon upon reaching adulthood. Its polish was worn away in places, blackened in others. It was Valoc's first possession as a free man.

Valoc had not been part of the defiant stand against the slavers who sought to reclaim their property. He had been told of the glorious slaughter of the southlanders by Sunyd and Rathyd warriors at a pass into the mountains. So for Valoc, the spilling of blood – this cold freedom – was still to come. Lifting the weapon to rest the blade across his knees, he studied the translucent, amber-tinted cutting edge.

I am free to kill with this sword. Free to take another's life. I am free to remember every cruel act delivered to me by a southlander. I am free to make strangers pay for each one.

The truth was, none of that was likely. None of that fired his spirit. He was, he knew, a poor excuse for a Teblor. And he doubted that would change. Some truths cut to the bone. Vengeance was just another set of shackles. Galambar had worn his proudly, as only a free man could.

I am free to kill no one. Free to spare another's life. Free to remember every cruel act and do nothing. I am free to let this sword die of thirst.

In the dawn to come, he would find himself among a multitude of ex-slaves, yet he would feel utterly alone. At Salan Ardal's command, he would join in the rush, as if shackled to the warriors beside him. The chain would drag him forward, amidst war-cries and bloodlust.

He wanted to weep. In his mind, the face of Rant appeared, as if seen through a sheet of water. Then the details began to blur, and he saw instead the face of Karsa Orlong, as witnessed by his youthful eyes all those years ago, there in the Waiting House. He even remembered the night Karsa had escaped, only to be recaptured. The slaves talked of it for weeks, if not months, afterwards. The risks, they said, of chaining a wild beast. *An Uryd and that should not surprise. Of course he will die before too long. He will make death his freedom, and not once kneel before a master. And this is the Sunyd curse, to become too civilized.*

Because, in civilization, almost everyone is a slave. And slaves will own slaves who will own slaves, and so it goes.

But Karsa Orlong didn't die. Nor did he kneel, bowing to his fate. He was a slave who had become a god.

What will you say to me, Karsa Orlong, when I ask you about freedom?

Given the chance, Valoc would ask that question. He suspected he already knew the answer he would hear. *Only gods know the meaning of freedom, Valoc. All before me is in chains. I am not the god of slaves. I will not be the god of slaves. By my power I can see the invisible chains around all of you, your claims of freedom notwithstanding. And so, Valoc, I ask you in turn: what will it take to be worthy of my regard?*

When you at last come before me free of all chains, then will I meet your eye. This, Valoc of the Sunyd, is why I am unwilling.

Valoc started, almost losing his balance on the trunk. He had dozed off, the sword lying heavy across his thighs. That voice, drifting through his head . . . *ah, strange dream, strange words, strange . . . longing.*

He felt weak. He felt confused. He felt lost, here among his kin. He was, indeed, a poor Teblor.

At Salan Ardal's command, I will join in the rush, as if shackled to the warriors beside me. The chain will drag me forward, amidst warcries and bloodlust.

Is this freedom? I swear, I've seen it before, by another name.

Lieutenant Ara rode at Balk's side into town as the day's light began to fade. It was quiet now, the last of the inhabitants having been driven away, led south in their overburdened wagons, with seven regulars as escort.

She knew Balk had been tempted, and of course Stick was all for it a short while earlier, in the command tent. A troop sent after them, slaughter on the south road. But Balk had simply shaken his head.

It had fallen to Ara to explain to Stick, Sugal and Bray. 'There's time. They'll never make Culvern. Besides, we're not here to kill citizens. We're here to help eliminate the Malazan military presence.'

'The regulars—'

'Are irrelevant, Stick.'

'I want Bliss Rolly's head,' Stick said.

'Why?' Ara asked.

Sudden confusion in Stick's bleary eyes. 'Because,' she said. 'She's famous. That's why.'

'Plan on splashing that sweet fame all over your face?' Ara asked.

'Enough,' said Balk, rising to collect his gauntlets. 'It's time to speak with Captain Gruff. Lieutenant, you're with me.'

Ignoring Stick's glare, Ara rose to her feet. It was hot inside the command tent and she longed for the cooler air outside.

Sugal spoke. 'Is that wise, Captain? They might just kill you.'

Balk paused, brows lifting. 'I assure you, Sergeant, the charade of our alliance remains. No, the captain will not kill me. He may, however, seek to bargain.' He shrugged. 'I've yet to meet him formally. It's always been Spindle. Now, however, it's time to gauge the commander of the enemy.'

Now, riding side by side, Balk and Ara guided their mounts onto the road and trotted towards the gate.

'So,' said Ara, 'you've taken her to your bed. I suppose that's one way of keeping a closer eye on her.'

Balk glanced over. 'Have I?'

'Have you not? She's in there all night—'

'Drunk and senseless in a chair,' said Balk. 'What interest could you imagine me to have in a woman like that?'

Ara looked away, and then sighed. 'Very well.'

'Sugal waits for Stick to make the first move. While she's at my side, Sugal will do nothing.'

'You risk everything.'

'Not you, I had hoped.'

Ara felt her lips thin, mouth tightening. 'You could have forewarned me.'

'Had I believed you would doubt me, I would have, Ara.'

He had a way of turning things, did Balk. From indignation to shame, all in the span of a handful of words. Now, she was left castigating herself for harbouring such unworthy thoughts.

They drew up at the gate, expecting a marine to appear, but no one did. The post was unoccupied, the street ahead empty. 'Curious,' Balk said. 'It seems unlikely that they are unaware of . . . everything.'

'Three soldiers to a patrol on each berm side,' said Ara. 'With everyone evacuated, no reason to guard a gate, and perhaps not enough personnel to manage it. We could ride straight in with the entire company.'

Balk grunted. 'We could. That makes me suspicious.'

They rode onto the main street and headed towards the lake. Turning onto the street that led to the headquarters, they finally came upon a pair of marines. The two men seemed to be arguing, standing in the middle of the street. Both fell silent upon seeing Balk and Ara.

One smiled. 'Welcome, Lieutenant Balk. Captain's awaiting you in his office. Up the stairs. Go straight on in.'

'Thank you,' said Balk with a nod as they rode past. They reined in opposite the headquarters building and dismounted. Balk glanced back at the two marines, frowning.

But it seemed that the argument had resumed, this time in harsh whispers as the two men headed towards the intersection.

Ara snorted. 'This is getting stranger.'

'Clearly,' said Balk in a dry tone, 'they have unseen eyes on us. Still, I think this is a bluff – if the captain's awaiting our pleasure, it was a hasty preparation.'

They entered the building. A narrow corridor led to steep stairs. A room off to the left looked abandoned, empty crates piled up everywhere. Balk studied it, steps slowing, as he passed, but said nothing. Reaching the stairs they began their ascent.

Only one door was ajar along the upper floor's corridor, and from its room came soft humming, a tune Ara did not recognize, but the voice was sweet and melodious.

Balk looked at her, brows lifting. Ara shrugged. If the captain had some whore on his lap, she'd hardly be surprised. Still, it would be unexpected decadence from a Malazan officer of marines.

They reached the door and Balk hesitated briefly before stepping through. Ara followed.

The captain was alone, sitting behind his desk. The voice was his, and both hands were making elegant gestures in the air. He drew out the last note, straining slightly, and then stopped, hands frozen in place for a moment, before slowly settling. 'Lieutenant Balk and – ah, the rank confuses – oh well. *Lieutenant* Ara, as it hardly seems fitting to settle upon you a lesser rank. Corporal? No, that won't do at all. And in consideration of that, perhaps we should revert to *Captain* Balk. But in keeping with my being in command, let's call me . . . *Emperor.*' Then he waved a hand. 'Not "sire", however. Dear me, "sir" will do. Thirsty?'

A decanter stood on the desk before Gruff, along with three goblets. The man poured. 'I'm told this is decent wine, but then, said judgement came from someone named Clay Plate, so make of that what you will.'

Balk slowly removed his gauntlets, and then sat. Ara looked for a chair, but there was only the one Balk now occupied. She settled with one hip cocked, her arms crossed, a step behind her commander's chair and on his right.

'We have detected extensive activity in the forest,' said Balk. 'A large presence of Wilders is suspected. I trust you're aware of the situation, sir?'

'Awareness is an ambiguous term, don't you think? A forest crawling with savages? Why, yes. An imminent attack upon this settlement? It would be foolish to think otherwise. Other factors in play, behind, as it were, an elegant screen? You know the kind: ornate wooden frame, stretched silk, intricate embroidery in dazzling patterns. How I long for such finery in this office!' He paused, beaming, and then took a sip of the wine. And made a face. 'Dear me. Well, let us blunt our finer sensibilities with blind optimism – surely each successive mouthful will soften, if not numb, the palate.'

Balk cleared his throat. 'Your implication confuses me, sir. What elegant screen?'

'Ah! The ambiguity of awareness unrevealed, of course. Who knows what, precisely? Theories abound. Shadows move to and fro behind the silk veil.' His eyes narrowed, brow drawing down. 'All very mysterious.'

Balk shifted in the chair. 'I am somewhat astonished that the mayor proved so amenable to being evacuated.'

'Amenable? Decidedly so, Captain. What could be more amenable of disposition than a coma?'

'A coma?'

Something flat slid across Gruff's gaze. 'I wearied of his complaints. Surely, Captain, you have experienced the same from time to time. People who refuse to understand their place. Exceeding their station, as it were. Bear in mind, I was not predisposed to respect the man, after all, given his wealth and status derived solely from the slave trade.' He reached up a long-fingered, well-manicured hand to smooth down his left eyebrow. 'Deplorable profession.'

'My point,' said Balk, 'is that it seems odd to find us guarding an empty town. Undermanned as we are, what value in holding our ground?'

'Again, a mire of ambiguity surrounds the notion of "value", at least in these circumstances. Had we elected to escort the refugees the tactical situation would be difficult. The Malazan Empire has experience with that. Most unpleasant. No, better by far to raise up a bulwark well behind that train of citizens, don't you think?'

'With three squads?'

Gruff smiled. 'And your eleven hundred as well, surely.'

'This hardly seems an equitable risk, sir.'

Shrugging, Gruff drank another mouthful, grimaced, and then said, 'The coin purchases the sword, yes?'

'The sword but not suicide, sir.'

Gruff's brows lifted. 'I certainly have no intention of dying any time soon! Nor would I risk my marines in a pointless last stand, I assure you. And I am relieved to hear that you feel the same about yourself and your company. Suicide? Dreadful notion.'

'It seems you are inviting just that, sir.'

'Does it?'

'As commander of my soldiers, I require a better understanding of the tactical situation here.'

'I'm sure your task will reveal itself soon enough, Captain,' Gruff said with a smile. 'You've not touched your wine. I'd be offended if I didn't applaud your healthy reluctance. Clay Plate has earned a reprimand at the very least. I can't abide poor taste.'

Balk was clearly trying hard to rein in his temper, and Ara could see the tense set of his shoulders. 'Do you wish us to occupy the town's defences, sir? By fully lining the embankments we would present a far more formidable force in opposing the . . . the savages.'

'No, stay where you are. There will be an effort at encirclement, I'm sure.'

'Then we are to hold your line of retreat?'

'Splendid! That's settled, then. Is there anything else?'

'There is the matter of signal flags, sir.'

'Unreliable,' Gruff said, shaking his head. 'We marines prefer to be more direct in announcing our intentions.'

Balk leaned forward and when he spoke it was in a whisper. 'There're eighteen of you.'

'And each one well versed in squad-level tactics, Captain.' Gruff leaned back in his chair, frowning as it creaked. 'I thought I asked Corporal Morrut to oil this thing. He likely forgot.'

'There're thousands in that forest.'

'Probably.'

A few moments passed, the silence stretching. Ara could see Gruff's eyes locked on Balk's but from where she stood, she could not see her commander's expression, although she guessed that his face revealed a war between disbelief and deepening suspicion.

'Anything else, Captain Balk?'

Abruptly, Balk stood. 'No, sir. Thank you, sir.'

'Return to your camp, Captain, and ready your soldiers. We predict that the savages will attack at dawn.'

Nodding, Balk turned and gestured to Ara to precede him to the door.

They were silent until they left the building, and then Balk swore under his breath. 'This makes no sense at all.'

'I would not like to gamble with that man,' said Ara. 'There was a look in his eyes, just briefly, that sent ice down my spine.'

They mounted and swung their horses onto the street, began trotting. Empty, silent buildings mocked them on both sides.

In a low tone, Balk spoke. 'If it comes to this – if we're *invited* – then we know what to do. We ignore the gate – it's too obvious. We roll up the south embankment, overrun the few marines positioned on it – if there are any at all – and into the town. Cut down all opposition on our way to the headquarters building.'

'And then?'

'Then I beat that pampered asshole senseless and leave him to Stick, Sugal and Bray. My patience with this game is at an end.'

'He guessed correctly at when they'll attack, Balk.'

'No genius there, Ara. Either way this goes, it will pay to at least clear the path somewhat. I want a meeting with our mages as soon as we get back to camp.'

Ara frowned. They had three mages in the company. Of the three, only one was worthy of the title to Ara's mind. 'Scabbe has warned us again and again that strange magicks are at play in this town and on the outskirts, day and night.'

'Mockra for the most part,' said Balk dismissively. 'Probably the one named Benger. I have three night-knives ready to hunt him down.'

'Best send at least one of the warlocks with them. Not Scabbe. He's too precious. Cranal or Vist. Vist is the sneakier of the two.'

After a moment, Balk nodded. 'Vist it is. With Benger dead everything we see will be real enough.'

'When do we send the night-knives?'

'Tonight. Fuck these marines.'

They rode through the gate and Balk led them into a canter down the road.

It was dusk. Stillwater emerged from the water-closet hitching up her belt, and then paused in the corridor. 'There's something in the bottom of that hole,' she said. 'I saw its beady eyes.'

'Not Creature,' Anyx Fro said, checking between her breasts just to make sure.

'Blanket?' wondered Benger.

Stillwater exchanged a look with Anyx Fro, and then both shook their heads. 'That's too creepy even for Blanket,' said Stillwater. 'It was a beast, bigger than a ground squirrel. Maybe a beaver?'

'Strange place to build a dam,' Benger mused. 'More likely a wood-chuck.' Then he frowned at Stillwater. 'When did you see it?'

'Just now.'

'Before or after you . . . you know?'

'Before.'

'So you did it anyway?'

'Obviously, it doesn't mind,' Stillwater answered, rolling her eyes. She drew her dagger and checked the edge, and then sheathed the weapon again. 'Oams is going to complain. Unless he's already dead, his corpse rotting in a ditch. The Wilders are scouting the open land south of here – they have to be. Poor Oams.'

'They can scout all they want,' Benger said. 'Oams is Oams.'

'Benger's right,' opined Anyx Fro. 'Oams is Oams. Master Claw. Emperor's own night-blade.'

'What if he isn't?' asked Stillwater.

'Then he's dead.'

'Killed by his own lying, what a way to go.' Stillwater turned to eye Benger. 'What are you hanging around for? I've got work to do.'

'Just a moment of camaraderie.' Benger shrugged. 'I feel a renewed sense of kinship with you – even you, Anyx Fro. On account of our last job together. We made a great team, didn't we?'

'You bailed on us!' Anyx Fro retorted.

Benger flinched. 'It may have seemed that way.'

'Because it *was* that way!'

'Like I said, I'm sure it seemed that way. Point I was making is, that was teamwork at its best. Leaving me all warm and fuzzy inside. I'm almost inclined to kiss you both right now. Imagine that!'

'I will not,' said Anyx Fro with a disgusted expression.

Sighing, Stillwater checked her gear and straps and then straightened. 'I'm ready. It'd be better if I was a mage, of course. But then again, I like challenges.'

'You *are* a mage,' said Anyx Fro.

'It's a measure of my skill as a sneak that you think so, Anyx Fro. Benger's the one hiding behind magic and whatnot. Now, both of you, go away.'

Anyx Fro's gaze was level. 'So you can what, Still? Find a corner-crack in this corridor and creep along it and we standing way over there won't see nothing? All without a wisp of sorcery? You must truly think we're all idiots.'

'Well, I do, but that's not the point. With you here, I can't concentrate on being sneaky.'

Benger patted Anyx Fro on the shoulder, earning a nasty hiss from the black head between her breasts. 'Uh, let's go and leave her to her sneakiness.'

'Just one thing,' Anyx Fro said, eyes narrowing on Benger. 'You really here? I mean, I'm supposed to be guarding your back tonight. So I need to be sure I'm guarding your real back.'

Benger blinked. 'Why should that distinction matter?'

'Because I'm not going to get myself killed defending you when you aren't you, dammit!'

'Creature just told you,' Benger said. 'Wouldn't hiss and show those tiny sharp teeth at an illusion, would he?'

'Unless you magicked that too!'

Benger's eyes slowly widened. 'Mockra's Curse,' he whispered.

'Both of you, get out of here!' snapped Stillwater.

Vist held a coin in one hand. It was tin, displaying a human knuckle-bone on one side and a skull in profile on the other. The Runt was called Knuckles, but it was the skull that Vist favoured in his sorcery. Lieutenant Ara had just sent him to the three night-knives sitting opposite him, the small hearth in between flickering desultory flames amidst glowing embers and white ash. He eyed the three night-knives while one hand played with the coin.

Paunt was tying up her black hair into a single braid. There was Rhivi blood somewhere in her ancestry, but she was bedecked in jewellery that came from Black Coral. Most of it was protection magic, Vist suspected. Useful for her line of work. Her narrow face was weathered, furrowed around her broad mouth. A deep scar divided her chin.

On her left squatted Orule. He claimed to be from the city of Mott, but he betrayed the habits of a Wilder from the forest. That said, most cities in this region held a ghetto of savages who'd succumbed to civilization. A decrepit lot for the most part, doomed to poverty and disease. Orule had been lucky to get out of that. He'd shaved his pate and rubbed charcoal and ash into his scalp. There were twigs in his beard. A short hatchet was tucked into his belt, along with throwing knives in a diagonal strap across his thin chest. Betel juice stained his lips blue.

The third night-knife was Rayle. Vist liked her. She was the only professional among the three, in his opinion. Her brown hair was cut short, nicely framing her roundish face. Her blue eyes stayed cool but missed nothing. The two knives in their under-arm sheaths weren't fancy, just well-worn. Vist didn't know where she was from and she wasn't one to talk about it, or anything else for that matter. One of Balk's last hirings, he recalled, just before the clash with the marines.

It was useful studying the ones he was charged to protect. Details were important. Habits, ways of moving, inclinations, all of this needed to sink into Vist, into his mind. The sorcery he would employ this night demanded that attention to detail, lest misfortune land upon one or all of them.

When they were all done with their final preparations, and silence fell among them, Vist cleared his throat, spat once into the fire for luck, and then said, 'We're going for the mage named Benger. Face like a toad, bald on top. Probably Mockra, which is bad, since what you see may not be real. That's where I come in.' He held up the Runt. 'Misfortune will attend his every effort. Nothing but a succession of mis-casts and fouled magery. Now, for the—'

'You won't want t'be anywhere near me,' said Orule.

Vist frowned at the interruption. Savages had no manners. 'Why not?'

Orule drew out a small box. 'Won't open it here, on account of you and all.' He paused, and then in a low tone said, 'Inside is a small bag of otataral dust. Less than a handful, but enough. Cost me . . . well, I won't tell you what it cost me. I'd rather not use it tonight, but if I have to, I will. Especially since our target's a mage of Mockra.'

Vist felt sweat trickle down the centre of his back. 'This changes things. You brought it, Orule, you use it.' He nodded to the other two. 'They'll flank. I'll take up the rear. But you're on point, Orule, and when you get close, you throw that fucking handful right at him.'

Sour of expression, Orule sighed and then nodded.

Vist wasn't happy. Otataral was indiscriminate. 'But you hold off until the very last moment, understand me?'

'We weren't planning on you at all,' said Orule with a scowl. 'You fucked up how we were going to do this. But Balk wants you wi'us, so fine, you're wi'us.'

Paunt spoke. 'We were discussing maybe rubbing some into each of us.'

Vist shook his head. 'Don't do that. The effects could be permanent, making all those magicked gewgaws you're wearing worthless.'

'Not likely,' said Paunt. 'They're Tiste Andii.' She hesitated and then added, 'I'm a devotee of the Black-Winged Lord.'

Orule grunted. 'That cult's dead.'

'Not in Black Coral it's not.'

'Don't matter,' Vist said. 'I wouldn't risk it anyway, Paunt.' He glanced over at Rayle. 'You? Any glamoured jewels or whatnot?'

Her gaze fixed on his. 'Is your plan out then?'

'No, it's not. This idea of rubbing the dust in distracted me. Never mind. Don't do it. The area effect diminishes, might not even affect a mage at three paces away. Sure, magic thrown at you will die with a gasp, but I'd hardly call that good enough. Not against Malazan marines.' He held up the Runt again. 'I won't beat 'em in a contest of powers. Not my style even if I was good enough. I'm not. Instead, I taste the skull and twist and foul up the magic being thrown around. I become the enemy's misfortune, understand?'

'And otataral dust?' Rayle asked.

'Flattens me dead. So yes, I'm nervous. But Orule's got it, and it's a better option than anything I had in mind. To be honest, I wasn't expecting any of you to survive this night, but now you got a good chance.'

No one had anything to add. Vist stood. 'Three bells from now. Be ready. We meet here and we're lucky: no moon tonight.'

Stillwater sat on the embankment close to the watchtower. It was a warm night, clear with stars overhead. She had drawn deeper shadows about her but spread them out along the verge to blend with the vague one cast down by the tower. But just to make sure, she flickered in and out of Emurlahn, enough to start confusing her body, since Emurlahn was cold and damp. In fact, it was always cold and damp in Emurlahn.

People on the Falar Islands lived in weather like that all year round. They were so used to being chilled and damp the rooms of their houses were exactly the same conditions as outside, with plenty of mould on the walls to prove it. She didn't understand the Falari. As if perennial discomfort was a virtue or something. No, it wasn't a virtue. It was just bad building practices and stupidity.

She preferred Itko Kan. Always sultry. In fact, sultry was her favourite word, so no wonder Itko Kan was her favourite place. Made sense. Malaz City, on the other hand, got hot and stinking. Sure, it had one cold season but even that was a short one. She didn't much like Malaz City.

Aren Outside the Fall, however, that was—

Movement from the edge of the mercenary camp. Stillwater's gaze narrowed. A lone figure, moving low to the ground. Then two more, out to the sides. Then a last one, the hardest one to see, since something made it seem like a trick of the eye when looked at straight. Her focus continually shied away from it, filling her with doubts. There or not there? Was this Mockra?

No. It was deflection magic. 'Cute,' she whispered, leaning forward and wrapping her arms about her knees to watch some more.

—was just plain *hot*. Hot and dry, with sand whispering down the alleys and streets. Her memories of that city were spices and flies and goats on rooftops. Oh, and fanatic worshippers of the Crow God. Hawkers selling feathers everywhere. Hawkers? Feathers? That was funny. She'd made a joke, or was that a pun? Was there a difference? Well, people laughed at jokes, good ones, anyway. Puns? People groaned and moaned, mostly. Sometimes they actually hit the one who made the pun. She'd even seen a knife drawn—

The lead person, a man by his bow-legged gait, was drawing close to the base of the embankment about thirty paces to Stillwater's right, where he held up for a moment or two, visibly scanning the area. The others halted, maintaining their distance.

Then the man in front was scrambling up the side of the embankment, keeping low as he reached the crest and slipping onto the top in a lying-down position. Nicely done, Stillwater decided.

A quick slither and he was across, sliding from sight down the other side.

Stillwater continued watching as the others followed, including the last one, and this time he was more visible. A mage for certain, plucking Mockra's edges – probably didn't know it was Mockra at all. She saw a Runt at work over there, an aspected coin. Which one?

Could be Root, could be Knuckles. But the land wasn't helping, so probably Knuckles. Ah! Now she knew what he was up to! 'Misfortune,' she whispered. 'He's playing the Skull. Oh, poor Benger!'

Well, they were all across the bank now, all out of sight. Making their way into the town. Lots of shadowy alleys, empty streets, ominous silences. Feeling pretty good about themselves, too, and why not? No alarms, no patrols anywhere.

Of course, Benger wasn't easy to find. Even under normal circumstances. Besides, it wasn't exactly a tiny town, or a hamlet, or a roadside cluster of buildings. Benger could be anywhere. In a room, even. No, Benger wouldn't be easy to find at all.

Unless he wanted to be found.

Skull magic! That was clever. Didn't take much effort. Benger would never suspect it, not for a moment. He'd cast and it'd go foul. He'd swear and cast again. Swearing and casting and swearing and casting and then – oh, is that a knife sticking out of my chest? Benger dies.

Poor, poor Benger.

She rose, stretched. Then opened Emurlahn and slipped into the warren. The ghostly, half-there-half-not camp of the mercenaries sprawled before her. Glimmers of magic here and there, nothing fancy, nothing truly active. Stillwater shifted her focus and saw that Emurlahn here was a sloping plain closely matching the other world. Good.

She set out for the heart of the camp.

Orule was gesturing from where he crouched at the building's corner. Vist moved up, squeezing past Rayle and Paunt in the narrow alley. He edged down just behind Orule's right shoulder.

'What?'

'Thought I saw something.'

'Where?'

'In that open doorway opposite. Is that a bakery? In the bakery. A shadow slipped across the opening.'

Vist considered. His instincts had been right. This was too easy. They'd been invited in. More sweat ran icy fingers along his skin, this time under his arms. 'We're being baited. I'd wager eyes on us right now.'

Orule hissed a soft curse. 'Listen. Can you smell magic?'

'Sometimes. Lazy stuff. Passive stuff. Glamoured areas. But a mage wanting to hide ain't easy to see. I think we need a change of plan.' He moved back, dragging Orule with him. They hunkered down in the darkest part of the alley, with Paunt and Rayle opposite. 'I think we're being tracked,' Vist whispered. 'But there can't be that many of them capable of that. So I propose we split up.'

A soft snort from Orule. 'There's a demon in the house. Let's split up.'

Vist stared blankly, then shrugged. 'The point is, one of us needs to get to the target. Besides, that frees you, Orule. You and your otataral dust. Keeps you far away from me and that suits me perfectly. The way each of us thinks it, we're the distraction. We do things to get noticed.'

'If they have four watchers, we're doomed,' said Paunt.

Vist shook his head. 'We guessed maybe two night-knives, tops. Meaning two of us are in the clear. Even if it's only one of us, the advantage is ours. One of us will get to Benger.'

Paunt turned to Rayle. 'Our last night left alive, you and me.'

'So be obvious,' Rayle said. 'Then get spooked and retreat, just don't retreat too soon. Give Vist and Orule the time they need. Going in the opposite direction of what they expect means *they're* chasing *us*, reversing the chances of an ambush.'

Vist was impressed. She was a cool one, all right. 'Sound thinking.'

'If you say so,' muttered Paunt.

'So we head to the alley mouth behind us,' Vist said. 'Then two go right, two go left. After a bit, one goes in and the other goes on. Keep it distant, so one person can't see the both of you. Rayle, you're with me. Paunt with Orule – if the dust flies, maybe your Andii wards will hold. Now, let's go.'

There were big dog tracks right through the mercenary camp, not that anyone in the camp knew it, because those dogs had been travelling through Shadow. Stillwater paused, crouched before one set. Damned Hounds were everywhere these days, it seemed. Always sniffing around, always on the hunt, always eager to rip a poor woman's head off.

She suspected that, if someone, you know, took the time to get to *know* them. To, well, *play* a bit with them. Toss a stick or two. Why, then they'd be fine. Maybe even friendly. Instead, it was flying guts and spraying blood and crunching sounds. Could be those poor Hounds were just lonely.

She considered looking around for a stick, just in case, but the only things on hand were tent pegs. Solid enough in the real world as she threaded between rows of tents, but all wispy like smoke at the moment. Once she slipped back into the real world, she'd grab one.

It was an especially bad pun, she recalled. Who was it who pulled a knife? A heavy in the 1st Squad. Brook? Was it Brook? It was, surging out of the chair and sending it flying behind him, lunging across the table spilling tankards everywhere, giant knife flashing. And there was Cruspy, that stupid, smug, self-satisfied expression – the one that always came to people who made puns – suddenly transforming into abject terror.

'That's right, Cruspy,' Stillwater whispered as she danced lightly over yet more dog tracks. 'One pun too far.'

Screams, shouts, mayhem, a damnable brawl in that tavern. Cruspy scrambling and diving out of the way and rolling under tables and twisting around chair legs. Bleating and shrieking. Brook coming on like an avalanche, furniture flying, wooden legs snapping, splinters and spilled ale and rolling pitchers everywhere. That knife stabbing down and down, and always Cruspy managing to get out of the way at the last instant.

Until he didn't.

'Poor Cruspy,' she whispered. Too bad she couldn't remember the pun itself. Must have been a seriously bad one. The worst. The kind that peeled the skin off the brain, assuming brains had skin. Some kind of skin, surely. A pun so bad that Brook, all splashed in blood, promptly fell to the floor, completely dead, the red knife skittering out from a lifeless hand.

What a night! No wonder most people didn't want to talk about it. Or what happened to the rest of 1st Squad only a few nights later. Stillwater pretended not to know the truth. Pretended she wasn't even there. It was easier that way. Like Benger said, the mystery of what happened to the 1st Squad was useful, a healthy direction for wandering minds, and the minds of marines wandered plenty.

Now *that* tent looked interesting. She made her way towards it.

On all sides, soldiers were awake, going over their kits, getting ready for a scrap. Few sleeping on this night. Most of the hearth-fires had been left to die down, to give the impression that all was as it usually was.

Stillwater worked her way around to the back of the tent.

The problem with most jokes was that she didn't get them. Oh, she understood the words well enough, could even follow the story if there was one. But when people laughed, she didn't. She'd watch them laughing, wondering what was funny, and she'd go over in her mind every word of the joke, looking for the funny bit. But they were just words.

Stillwater drew her dagger and straightened. In the real world, she'd have to slit the tent wall. In Emurlahn it wasn't even there. Well, it was, but like cobwebs, only thinner. Couldn't block the glimmering glow on the body beyond it, though.

People laughed for no reason, as far as she was concerned. They laughed because someone else was laughing. Someone had started the laughing, so they joined in. Wasn't always easy to work out who'd laughed first. One day, she would do just that, and if necessary, why, she'd drag that person away and use some classic interrogation tactics to get the secret out of him. *'Why'd you laugh, huh? Just tell me and your nightmare can end.'*

She stepped through, and then out of Emurlahn.

The figure standing before her had been facing the wall to the right, a frown etching his pocked features.

Stillwater quietly said, 'Cranal, isn't it?'

Even as he spun to face her, she had her knife plunging up under his ribcage. When his mouth snapped open she pushed a gloved palm against it to mute any sound. But it wasn't necessary, as he was dead before he hit the ground, sliding off her blade with a queer sucking sound.

She cleaned her knife on his nightshirt. And then slipped back into Emurlahn.

She was doing what the Claw did back in the day. Maybe still did, for all she knew. Take out the ones that matter. The problem ones. The ones that always laughed first at any joke. No, wait, she'd stumbled across tracks of thinking. That happened occasionally and led to no small amounts of confusion. Temporary and, luckily, harmless.

Oams would definitely curse at having missed all this. Well, if he wasn't already dead. And who knew? He'd been gone a long time now. Maybe that giant red-haired demon-woman had murdered him in his sleep. Things like that were possible. Maybe even common, not that anyone would know, would they? Walk into the bedroom and oops, Bortho's dead!

Hang on. Who's Bortho? Did she know a Bortho once? She must have. Some fool who died mysteriously in his sleep. Ah, now she remembered!

Bortho lived in the apartment at the end of the corridor, the corner one overlooking the tiny walled-in glade, the one she'd always wanted because that would be a lovely view, far preferable to her own window which looked down on a narrow alley filled with rubbish. But no, he had that place and wasn't planning on moving so stop asking, woman.

Then Bortho strangled himself to death one night using a cord from the bedroom curtain. What a strange thing to do! But Stillwater never liked those curtains anyway and her first day in her new corner apartment, down they went. The view was lovely.

Poor Bortho.

Paunt had gone in before Orule, who was probably skirting the west side of the town, thinking about closing in from behind. But for that to work, Paunt needed to get closer. She'd been told where the squads had made their quarters, a two-storey house with a walled-in back garden, once owned by a slaver family. On this night, without even patrols on the empty streets, the marines would have drawn together. And Benger would be in their midst. Not an easy task, then, killing the man.

She paused at the mouth of an alley, and then quickly scurried across the street and into another alley. Was she being tracked? She didn't think so. One of her Tiste Andii wards, a brooch, was sensitive to things like that. Or so said the witch who'd sold it to her down on Market Street in Black Coral. Paunt reached up and touched the ornate silver brooch. Felt cool, but cool in a normal way. If there were only two watchers or trackers out there, they'd chosen other targets, and on this side of town, that meant Orule.

But he had his bag of otataral. He wouldn't be easy to take down magically. As for a knife scrap, why, she'd wager on Orule. He had a mean streak and skill besides. It was his underhanded way of fighting that made him so dangerous.

To be honest, she didn't much like him. But that didn't mean she couldn't respect him when it came to night work.

She worked her way silently along the length of the alley. She was getting close. Slowing as she approached the next alley mouth, which would open onto the street where the marines were ensconced, she drew her pair of Rhivi horse-gutters. Double-edged and the blade spreading like a broad leaf in the top third, the weapons were used in traditional feuding between clans. The high-grass ambush of warriors on horseback. Open the animal's belly from underneath, then pounce on the rider when the animal toppled.

Against an armoured opponent, they worked well enough, especially down low, a hamstring cut, or even the tendon above the heel. Send them pitching to the ground, finish them off. The challenge lay in using one of the weapons to parry or block a sword-thrust, since they weren't really designed for that, the bar knuckle-guard being short and stubby.

But she was skilled enough. A single exchange was all a proper fighter needed. The shorter the fight the better. If it turned out to be a few exchanges, that meant her odds of success were fast diminishing, and so she'd bolt before she got truly ensnared in a losing contest. She was fast on her feet and could outrun most people.

Pressed against a building wall at the corner of the alley mouth, she carefully leaned forward for a look up the street.

When she did, her eyes widened.

That had to be Benger, though he wasn't facing her, his gaze fixed on something down the street. Another marine stood near her target, about five paces distant, but on the opposite side. A woman wearing a pot-helm, scale hauberk, in her left hand a buckler and in her right a battered short-sword. Something bulged her cheek, as if she'd jammed a small apple into her mouth.

That marine then spoke in a low tone, but not so low that Paunt couldn't hear her. 'You really expecting that killer-mage to just come ambling up to us?'

'No,' Benger replied. 'He's bound to try something fancy. Do you want room to manoeuvre or not, Anyx?'

'Well, sure. Enough to be able to jump over your dead body.'

Paunt decided in an instant. That armoured woman wouldn't be able to outrun her. And Benger was nearest. She darted into the street. At the last moment, a spasm of doubt struck her. *He's Mockra, dammit!* But then it was too late for doubts, because she'd arrived. She double-stabbed, one neck-high, the other at the level of the liver.

Metal clanged twice. As Paunt's heels dug into the mud of the street in a desperate effort to halt, even jump backward, she felt fire slide through her torso, just beneath the sternum, all the way through to bite into her spine, which was when all feeling vanished. A moment later she was lying on the ground.

She heard the marine named Anyx speak, and the woman's round, bulging face was looking down on her. 'What was she thinking?'

'Thinking wasn't the problem,' said Benger, coming up alongside her. 'Seeing was.'

'What did you work up, Benger?'

'Well, she saw you as me and me as you, and us both facing the other way.'

'You mean she thought she was attacking you, with back-stabbing in mind?'

'Afraid so.'

They continued staring down at Paunt, but the only part of herself that Paunt could control was her eyes, as if they floated disembodied in a muddy pool at the feet of the two marines.

'She alive?' Benger eventually asked.

'Severed spine. If she wasn't alive you'd have to explain to me her darting eyes, and since I'm already feeling slightly nauseated, I just might puke all over you.'

'Well?' Benger demanded. 'Aren't you going to kill her?'

'I suppose it's the thing to do, isn't it.'

No! thought Paunt. *It's a lovely night – the stars—*

But Anyx stepped closer and moved her sword tip down. There was no indication that she did anything else, but when she drew it back, fresh blood smeared it.

The stars dimmed, then went out.

Orule waited until the marine straightened from her killing stab into Paunt's heart, then two knives flew out from his hands.

Both caught the woman named Anyx, one into her right shoulder, the other deep into her right thigh. Yelping, she spun and then toppled, her sword flying from her hand.

As Benger was turning, Orule already had the bag of dust, untied, in his right hand. He threw it, adding a spin to the bag with a twist of his wrist. Dust sprayed, engulfed the illusionist, who reeled back, coughing and swearing.

Drawing another knife and then his hatchet, Orule rushed forward.

Somehow, Benger had his sword out of its scabbard. Instead of backing up, he came straight at Orule.

Momentarily startled, Orule checked his attack and began to assume a defensive position with both weapons ready to parry.

Hatchets were awful at parrying, so as Benger closed in, Orule used it in counter-attack, chopping down towards Benger's wrist as the marine thrust with his sword. At the same instant, Orule brought up his knife to turn aside that thrust.

Hatchet blade chopped nothing but air. Knife hesitated.

Benger's short-sword impaled Orule's left arm, between elbow and shoulder and on the outside of the bone. He felt it savagely twist and then cut outward, severing muscle and tendons. Hatchet thudded to the ground, even as Orule spun to draw up close against Benger, his knife jabbing for the gut. The knife skittered off mail.

The short-sword came back around, stabbing into the side of Orule's neck, then punching out the other side in a gush of blood.

That blood poured down Orule's throat, burst back upward in a spray of red froth. He staggered back, turning to pull himself off the sword's blade. Thick heat filled his lungs, defied every attempt to draw breath. He fell to one knee, looked up in time to see a flash of slick iron, driving right for his forehead.

A biting punch, snapping his head back, and the night was darker than it had ever been.

Benger knelt beside Anyx Fro. 'Sorry, darling, sloppy of me, damned sloppy.'

'At least Creature didn't get hit. Just shut up and heal me, asshole.'

'Can't. Took a lungful of otataral dust. I may never recover.'

'Get me to Clay Plate, then.'

Benger straightened. 'Don't really want to move you. That leg one's a bad bleeder.' He glared up the street. 'Thought we had eyes on us.' *There!* He raised his voice. 'So Bleak! Go back and get Clay Plate!' Then Benger knelt back down and patted Anyx Fro's forehead. 'Help's coming, darling.'

Anyx Fro groaned, shifted the wad in her mouth, and said, 'That guy threw hard.'

'I can see that.'

'What happened then?'

'I killed him.'

Anyx Fro sighed. 'I keep forgetting,' she said.

'What?'

'All that magic shit, Mockra this, Mockra that. But you with a plain old sword. An unholy nightmare is what you are.'

Benger shrugged. 'Pays to have more than one skill, I guess.'

Boots on the ground, running. Benger quickly straightened. 'No closer, Clay, there's otataral here – dust, now mud. I'm also covered in it. I need a bath and quick.'

'First time for everything,' Anyx Fro muttered.

So Bleak came up and began dragging Anyx Fro by her left arm, out of the ruddy puddles. Creature's head popped up to see what was going on, and then popped back down again.

'Careful!' Benger snapped. 'Clay – the one in the thigh.'

'I see it,' Clay Plate replied. 'Stop there, So Bleak. Let me work on her.'

More boots, and Benger turned to see Folibore and Blanket coming up, both frowning.

'Problems?' Benger asked them.

'No and that's just it,' said Folibore.

Blanket nodded solemnly. 'Which makes it a problem itself.'

'Interesting point,' Folibore mused, scratching at his beard. 'Not a problem turning out to be a problem after all, but not the problem Benger might be thinking, only the opposite of that problem. The ambiguities of discourse, Blanket, surround the heart of all human misery and suffering.'

'I'm definitely suffering,' snapped Benger, 'listening to you two. What the fuck's going on? Plain language please.'

'Found a body,' Folibore said with a heavy sigh. 'We think it must be a mage.'

'Dead as dead can be,' added Blanket.

Folibore nodded. 'Pretty much so. Throat opened wide, all bled out—'

'Somewhere else,' said Blanket.

'True enough,' Folibore agreed. 'Bled white and all clammy. And then there was the coin. That was odd, wasn't it, Blanket?'

'It was,' Blanket said. 'Odd in that peculiar-discordant-that-defies-expectation sort of way.'

'What coin?' Benger demanded even as Folibore opened his mouth to add yet more rubbish to what Blanket had just spewed.

'The one resting on his forehead,' answered Folibore. 'But not really a coin.'

Blanket frowned and said, 'No, that's true, Folibore. Not a coin, not really.'

'A Runt.'

'Skull side up. Misfortune. Hah! Get it?' Blanket slapped Folibore on the back. Then he smiled at Benger and shrugged. 'Just lying there.'

'As if it was placed,' Folibore chimed in.

'Carefully.'

'Deliberately.'

Blanket nodded. 'And intentionally, too.' He glanced over at Clay Plate. 'Is Anyx Fro dead?' Now the look he turned on Benger made the man quail slightly. 'You got our squad-mate killed, Benger?'

'No, I didn't. A double ambush. Our snare caught the first one but not the second one. Clay Plate?'

'What?'

'She gonna live?'

'I don't know. Let's ask her. Anyx Fro? You gonna live?'

'Get that garlic breath the fuck out of my face, Clay.'

Clay Plate looked over at Benger and the two heavies. 'I'd say it's way too likely, aye.'

'Patch her up good,' said Benger, relieved. 'We got us maybe a scrap come dawn. As for me, I'm going to a bath.'

'You think the hunt for you is done, then?' So Bleak asked, busy cleaning mud from between his fingers.

'I do. The mage was their knuckle in the hole. Seems someone dressed him up nicely.'

'Stillwater?' So Bleak asked.

'No,' Anyx, Folibore and Blanket all said at once. Then Folibore added, 'Not her style, So Bleak.'

'So where is she and why wasn't she helping guard you, Benger?'

Benger shrugged. 'Just somewhere else, I guess. Now, let's all get off this muddy street, all right?'

A large tent near the headquarters tent was glowing and not, Stillwater decided, in a normal way. She frowned, studying it from a few paces distant, almost within arm's reach of a soldier standing guard at its drawn flap. Tents, of course, didn't normally glow at all, unless there was a lantern inside. Then it glowed, but in that yellow I'm-only-a-lantern glow, not like this, which was pulsing, fitful, vaguely blue.

Stillwater's frown deepened. What was she looking at? Magical ward of some kind? Not like any she'd ever seen. She edged forward. Some places were messy in ways that soaked through other warrens. Ancient holy sites, the ones where blood sacrifices had taken place. Places stained with pain and suffering, where the very ground had been scorched by the unhuman regard of a spirit or god.

Scabbe had found a good place to plant his tent. Chaos was close here, no matter which warren one used, sizzling just under the surface.

Killing him, she decided, would be tricky. This Scabbe was clearly paranoid. Imagining all sorts of lurkers and hunters and assassins trying to get to him. So he'd found a patch of ground black with ancient blood, every warren rotted through and through. How could someone even sleep in all that?

She shifted her focus back to Emurlahn to see how it expressed itself and grunted in annoyance. The scrubby black plain here gave way to a paved circle of grimy granite slabs, and in the centre, a low stone-lined well. The blue pulsing came up from its mouth. The challenge, she realized, was to keep from tumbling down into that well, which meant she needed at least half her vision holding on to Emurlahn, even as she sought to navigate the interior of the tent in this world.

That was the problem with paranoids. Hunting and killing them was never easy. Better if he'd just been relaxed, the way most mages were. Relaxed and confident and unsuspecting and not at all wary. She was sure mages like that existed and were pretty much everywhere. All lined up for her to kill them.

But no. Instead she was cursed to find the difficult ones.

Shrugging, she drew a dagger, and then edged through the tent wall.

Inside, it was even worse. The tent had no floor, just dead grasses and compacted mud. And part of a circle of low boulders almost buried in the earth. A cot straddled that line of stones, but no one occupied it at the moment. Scabbe was seated cross-legged near the back, facing a huge bowl-shaped brazier from which aromatic fumes wafted into the smoky air. His eyes were closed.

He was travelling. Somewhere out there, maybe in the forest and in the company of warlocks and witches. Nice way to communicate on the sly, coordinating things and such. Scabbe was this company's link to the Wilders.

The brazier stood where in Emurlahn the well was – they almost matched each other in size. Scabbe's back was touching the tent wall in this world, but in the Shadow Warren there was nothing but a few granite pavestones.

Shifting her focus to Emurlahn, Stillwater crept forward. She would position herself behind Scabbe, and then a quick knife-thrust to finish him, severing his soul from his body. He wouldn't like that at all. Suddenly, staying in the company of warlocks and witches would be suicidal, or worse. They'd snatch him out of the air. Bind him to a pebble or a knife-blade or some other useful object. No, he'd hate that and who could blame him? Poor Scabbe.

She heard the howl of a Hound, still some distance away. Nefarious dogs! Didn't they have anything better to do than hunt down inter-lopers? As if all of the Shadow realm was their backyard! And it seemed they knew her scent, too, always closing in and cutting short her time in the warren. It was getting worse and worse. Persecution!

Back out of the tent, now, but when she turned to face it, she could see the bulge Scabbe's back made in the canvas wall.

The granite flagging under her feet was greasy, treacherous. It seemed to tilt towards the well's shin-high stone wall, too, not level at all. Bending her knees slightly, Stillwater worked her way closer. Like ice under her! She needed to get out of this warren before she slid straight into that damned well!

Stillwater shifted out of Emurlahn and found herself staring at the tent wall, the night air cool and stars blazing overhead. Anyone glancing her way would see her immediately. No time to waste!

She stabbed into the bulge, heard a startled grunt.

The canvas burst into flames, blinding Stillwater even as she sought to fling herself back into Emurlahn. A hand grasped her wrist and yanked savagely. She was pulled forward, sliding on granite. In clouds of smoke and ash she found herself grappling with Scabbe. Dammit, she'd dragged him into Emurlahn.

'Trespasser!' she shouted, a second knife out now and thrusting – but he twisted his torso and the blade snagged in his coarse woollen shirt, the edge parting skin but skidding over his ribs.

Then their sliding feet struck the edge of the stone well's low encircling wall.

'Oh no!' Stillwater plunged them both back into the real world. They landed on the brazier in a crunch of glowing embers and sparks spinning up all around. Bad smells of burning cloth and then searing pain here and there and everywhere – 'Ow! Ow! Ow! Ow!'

Back into Emurlahn then, dammit! The hard stones of the low wall pounding into her left shoulder, another banging on her knee. She felt her middle sagging directly over the well mouth and Scabbe's weight wasn't helping.

'Not down there, you idiot!'

She sliced her knife's edge along his right forearm. Snarling, Scabbe released his grip on her wrist, freeing her other knife. She stabbed again, blade sinking into the mage's side. He pulled closer, one arm wrapped around her midriff, one leg up and folded over both of hers. He was dying but he was trying to drag her down into the well.

'Don't do that, you fool!' She stabbed some more, trying to prise him off her, trying to keep him from dragging her down. His leg wrapped tighter, so she stabbed that, too. 'Get off me! You're dying, Scabbe. No reason to stay mad at me, is there?'

He got a clutching mass of fingers in her hair and she didn't like that at all.

'No you don't!' she hissed, reaching up and slicing every finger she could find. Then she drove her elbow into his gasping, sweaty face. His nose cracked nicely. Twisting, she used her other knife to thrust deep into his leg – the one wrapped over hers, not the other one which was hanging down and all slick with blood that was pouring from her first stab into his back.

A Hound howled. Closer!

In the real world, ghostly figures now in the tent, swords out. Embers smouldering everywhere, smoke and ashes. Shouts and panicked cries.

No, those panicked cries were hers. This fool was so determined to take her with him! She couldn't believe how determined he was. As if it was personal or something. 'Some people!' she yelled. 'What in Icari's name is the matter with you?'

She stabbed some more, pretty much wherever she could. He trembled, then voiced a ragged sigh hot against her cheek, and slipped off.

Somehow, the sudden loss of all that weight made her lose her frail balance on the edge of the well. 'Oh crap!' She started falling.

A large hand snagged her collar, halted her plunge, and then dragged her from the well, onto the paving stones, where she lay gasping, staring up into a withered, lifeless face surrounded in filthy strands of grey hair. An apparition thoroughly horrifying.

'I've seen you before,' Stillwater said. 'Wandering around as if looking for something. From a distance, though, which was how I liked it. And I know your name, too. So . . .'

'So what?'

'Ever find it?'

The gaunt figure, dressed in rags and dangling strips of chain armour, released her and slowly straightened. In a rasping voice, it said, 'Not yet.'

'What are you looking for?'

'An answer.'

Stillwater rolled her eyes. 'To what?'

'The reason for our meaningless existence.'

Stillwater sat up, sheathing her knives. 'Good luck with that. I'm Stillwater.'

'You are anything but still.'

'And I didn't know you were in the habit of saving people's lives, Edgewalker.'

'I'm not,' said Edgewalker, head creaking as he turned to study something in the distance. 'But it would not do to fall into that well.'

'Why not?' Stillwater asked as she climbed to her feet and brushed at her clothing. 'I mean, not that I'm arguing with you or anything.'

'There are things down there.'

'Things?'

Edgewalker faced her again. There was not much in the way of expression on his features, which wasn't too surprising since he had been dead for probably a thousand years, maybe longer. But a low light gleamed from the depths of his eye sockets. 'Things,' he intoned, 'most terrifying.'

She stared at him.

'And now,' Edgewalker resumed, 'Pallid seeks to rend you limb from limb.' And he pointed with one long, gnarled finger.

Sure enough, there was a Hound, charging towards her.

'Shit.' She stepped clear of Edgewalker, drew out a tent peg and tossed it to one side.

'What are you doing?' Edgewalker asked.

'Not working, dammit!' Stillwater opened her way back into the real world, which wasn't going to be much fun when she got there but it wasn't like she had any choice, and moments before the giant corpse-hued dog reached her with jaws opened wide, she leapt through.

Into a tent full of soldiers.

Luckily, they all got distracted when the huge head of a Hound of Shadow pushed through the portal she'd made. That head twisted and the jaws closed about the torso of a soldier standing too close to do anything but shriek. Bones snapped, blood sprayed, and the Hound was bulling through.

'Holy shit!' Stillwater dropped, rolled, suddenly among all kinds of moving legs, and her knives were out and she cut through tendons wherever she could as she kept rolling until she came up against the tent wall, where she started wriggling under it.

Meanwhile, Pallid was having fun in the tent and everyone was screaming.

Stillwater slid back into Emurlahn. 'You're not here!' she shouted, back on her feet and running now, full tilt, across the scrubby plain.

Something tore through the air behind her.

'Next time,' she gasped, 'I'll bring a bigger stick.'

A glance behind showed Pallid halting, catching sight of her, and then lunging forward.

She threw herself back into the real world.

And found herself at the forest's edge, and there were three figures right in front of her. 'Warlocks and witches!' And then she was among them, stabbing and cutting.

Sharp-nailed fingers snagged the scarf round her neck, pulled her back as wiry legs wrapped about her hips and the witch's weight dragged her down. Stillwater back-swung with one knife, up over her head, and felt and heard the pommel crunch into a forehead. The fingers spasmed and lost their choking grip on her scarf. 'You cross-eyed cloth-hag! Almost killed me!' She rolled off the body beneath her.

An earlier slash had brought down one of the warlocks, and he was still thrashing about on the ground. The third one, also a warlock, was running as fast as he could back into the forest.

Stillwater pounced on the thrashing man and quickly stilled him with a knife in the throat. She glanced across at the witch, but that pommel had made a deep hole in her forehead and her eyes stared sightlessly.

Into and out of Emurlahn, running as fast as she could, howls in her wake cut off and then resuming then cut off, and on she ran. Figures fulminating in the tree-line to her right, but none venturing out. One arrow hissed past. Then she reached the embankment, scrambling up the slope. A final leap and roll into Emurlahn and then back out.

Into the ditch, buildings rising up on the other side.

And that was that!

Still a bell or so before dawn, Stillwater walked into the Black Eel. Behind the bar, Storp glanced over at her, his eyes red from lack of sleep. He nodded to her and poured out a tankard of ale.

Looking around, Stillwater saw only one other customer, seated near the back. Collecting her tankard, she eyed Storp. 'You really should've left with the others, you know.'

Grunting, Storp studied her. 'Too close to a campfire, then?'

'I saw a cloud shaped like a cow's head, once.'

'Lots of blood for a sing-along,' said Storp.

They eyed each other for a long moment, and then Stillwater made her way over to the other denizen in the bar. She sat down opposite and sighed. 'That's the problem with mercenary companies,' she said, 'they'll hire damn near anyone.' Then she tilted her head. 'You weren't at the battle, were you?'

'No. Newly hired, they left me guarding the supply camp. First I knew, Oams was riding in to tell us Balk had surrendered.'

'Did he see you?'

'If he did he didn't let on,' Rayle replied. After a moment, she shrugged. 'Probably. But Oams is Oams and gave nothing away.'

'Being a Claw he wouldn't, would he?'

'Exactly.'

'How was your night?' Stillwater asked after a most satisfying mouthful of ale.

'Just Vist. You?'

'Cranal and Scabbe.'

Rayle's brows lifted. 'Scabbe was pretty smart. Any trouble?'

Stillwater shook her head around another deep draught. She swallowed loudly and wiped her lips. 'Pretty straightforward all in all.' Then she paused, looked down at her leather hauberk. 'Look at all these burn marks!'

'Hard to notice beneath all the blood, to be honest,' observed Rayle. 'Bit gloomy in here, though. Any of that red yours?'

Stillwater brightened. 'No! At least I don't think so. How about that?'

'Did I hear a howl earlier? A very loud, very big howl?'

'Bet it was a frustrated one.'

'One of these times, Still, one of them is going to get you.'

Stillwater sighed. 'I still think they're just lonely, but I've got plans for that. Next time Edgewalker drags me out of a well, I'll ask him.'

Rayle studied her for a long, slightly unnerving time. Eventually she rose, collected her tankard, and held out her hand for Stillwater's tankard. Then she headed over to Storp for another round.

Stillwater looked around. She grunted. 'Quiet night.'

For the first time in Ara's memory, she saw that Balk was truly rattled. They stood in the remnants of Scabbe's tent. The low boulders on all sides were slick with blood. The cot was shattered, and sodden clothing flung all around. Soldiers had dragged out the last of the mangled bodies and now it was only Ara and Balk. Scabbe was nowhere to be found and Ara was fairly certain they'd not see him again.

Vanished. Just like the four killers they'd sent into the town.

The blood had drained from Balk's features. He stood staring down at the knocked-over brazier and its strew of lifeless embers. A soldier had moments earlier reported on finding Cranal's knife-stabbed corpse. In a single night, the company's mages and elite night-knives were all gone.

Had they taken Benger or anyone else down with them? There was no way of knowing, not yet at any rate. Ara suspected that the answer, when it finally came, would disappoint them.

'Gods below,' Balk muttered. Then he looked up at her, his eyes wide. 'Who in the Crow's name are we dealing with here?'

'Just mortal men and women,' Ara said. 'Highly capable, but mortal all the same. We'll see the proof of that soon enough, Balk.'

He said nothing, his eyes searching her gaze as if eager to find something he could hold on to, but she could only offer him a blithe confidence seeking to match her consoling words.

But they knew each other too well. He saw the fear growing in her eyes. Not surprising, since it was a perfect reflection of what she saw in his.

In a bell's time, the sun would break the horizon, lighting the tips of the forest to the east.

Not tomorrow any longer. Today. This is the day we have been waiting for all these weeks.

And now? Now I wish it was a year away. Ten years. Dammit, how about a hundred?

Balk passed a hand across his face, and then turned to the tent entrance. 'Time to armour up just in case,' he said in a tone that belonged in a graveyard, and then was past her, out into the growing light of day.

＊　　　＊　　　＊

Valoc was shaken from a half-sleep fraught with confused scenes that made no sense. Blinking, he found himself staring up into Bayrak's face, the warrior grinning down at him.

'Time for slaughter,' Bayrak said. 'Salan Ardal musters us. See, the sun is almost up, Valoc.'

Nodding as Bayrak moved on to find the next sleeping Sunyd, Valoc rose. He stood unmoving for a few moments, listening to the first bird-song in the trees surrounding them. His bladder was full. He was hungry and thirsty. The weapons arrayed around him looked unfamiliar and threatening.

He drew a deep breath, and then another, but they helped little. Here he was, a slave all over again.

It seemed only death could end this. With that thought, he moved off to relieve himself. Perhaps when he returned to his weapons, they would speak as if a thousand spirits were bound to each one. Promising him glory, even as the birds sang.

They would sing all day, he suspected, celebrating an innocence only they possessed.

How he envied those birds, so free to wing away.

CHAPTER NINETEEN

I knew this would come
On a bright morning exulting
In its eternal present
Nothing of night left to hold
Even the drops of dew blaze
With the sun's blinding fire
On such a morning life begins
Bursting its shout to heaven
Yet still I stand apart
Feet buried in the dark earth
Caught frozen in my upward climb
The past twisting my limbs
Etching the bark of my skin
In the knots of my eyes
Linger the whorls and worlds
In their immemorial canopies
Where remembrance illusions
Play at being alive
I will feed from the roots
Of the lost mornings behind me
Each like this one something other
It is this sensibility of estrangement
That lifts my mind like a crown
From the mortal broken brow
As if to float both free and lost
And all the unknowing
Looms like a loved one's face
I cannot recognize

The Delusion of Standing Alone
Fisher kel Tath

'**E**LADE THAROS IS DISPLEASED WITH YOU.'

'Good,' Delas Fana replied. 'It is one thing to measure a man when all goes his way. See such a man thwarted, and his true nature is revealed.'

Tonith Agra hissed under her breath and looked away.

Delas Fana straightened and looked for Rant and the two Jheck. For the moment she'd once again lost them amidst the crowds. The tents were coming down, the smoke of thousands of fires drifting like clouds descending from the mountains, obscuring the deeper reaches of the army's encampment. Animals had been slaughtered the day before and the stink of offal and blood was heavy in the morning air.

The southlands opened out before them, the last of the slopes and the deep valleys just beyond a dark mass of conifers. Somewhere past the edge of this forest was the settlement with the unfortunate name of Muthra. There was a small garrison of Malazan regulars there. By this day's end they would be swept aside, the town set aflame, with the heads of the settlers and soldiers riding spears as the Warleader led his army deeper into the south.

They would divide shortly thereafter, one arm – a third of their numbers – curling eastward to destroy Bringer's Foot and then follow the Culvern River to the larger town bearing that river's name, where they would link up with the Sunyd and Saemdhi.

Elade Tharos would lead the rest of his army to Ninsano Moat, a larger walled town wrapped around the only bridge across the Maly River. Delas Fana wondered how the Warleader would manage a siege. He was in a hurry, after all. But they needed the bridge to move onto the western side of the Maly River, which they intended to follow all the way down to the city of Blued.

Dividing the army had divided the sisters. The reason, once more, was Rant. Despite being forbidden from accompanying the Sunyd and Saemdhi, he was determined to find his mother. Reason flailed helpless against his intention – so like his father that Delas would have been amused if not for the difficulties he had forced upon his sisters.

Tonith Agra considered herself one of the Warleader's staff, not that Elade Tharos formally possessed any such thing. He held on to the tribal ways, which effectively meant disorganized chaos, clan warleaders all present and vying for his attention. But she had been one of the few to accompany him into the north, to witness the source of the coming flood. In her mind, this set her, Widowed Dayliss and Karak Thord above all others.

But Delas Fana had vowed to remain at Rant's side. She now said to her sister, 'I think Elade Tharos would be pleased to have us leave his company. He will have you and the rest of the Uryd to keep him warm at night.'

Tonith sighed. 'This matter has nothing to do with the Warleader. We have united, sister, after so many years apart. Sathal sees you as a near stranger, and Widowed Dayliss delights in your return. Now, because of the child in our midst, once again you would have us go our separate ways.'

Delas Fana shrugged. As if summoned, Sathal and Widowed Dayliss were approaching, along with the latter's daughter, Pake Gild. 'I will not kneel before him. I will not offer him my sword.'

'You have not explained why,' Tonith Agra said.

'I'm surprised that I need to, sister.' She met the eyes of Widowed Dayliss as she and her companions arrived. 'The Shattered God has bound each of us. The threads of our lives are twisted together. The ways of the Teblor cannot be denied. Your thoughts on this, Widowed Dayliss?'

The woman adjusted her cloak of wolf-fur. 'You alone among us, Delas Fana, have knelt before your father, or so you have said.' One shoulder lifted and she half-smiled. 'I well understand your frustration. Sathal managed but half a day in his company. You and Tonith Agra – well, you were there when the Lord of Death walked the streets of Darujhistan. To Karsa Orlong, you two are bound in ways the rest of us cannot match.' She held up a hand to forestall Delas who was about to speak. 'I do not disavow his godhood. I have no interest in elevating Elade Tharos into such otherworldly heights. As my Warleader, however, I am bound to follow him. The reasons cannot be refuted. We are driven by necessity – what value fighting the tide?'

'None,' Delas Fana replied, unperturbed by Widowed Dayliss's words. 'Nor do I object to the Warleader refashioning desperation into retribution. The southlanders have never been kind to us. An answer to that is long overdue. No,' she concluded, 'his steps have been unerring – no other truth could have so unified all the tribes of the north, Teblor and otherwise. This I do not object to. Rather, his display on the day of our arrival – his using of Rant to denigrate his father and our god – that offended me.'

'Had I been there,' said Dayliss after a long moment in which no one spoke, 'I would have shared your offence. It seems that Rant posed a greater threat in the eyes of Elade Tharos than I would have expected.'

'He does not travel alone,' said Tonith Agra. 'A warrior was slain. There is the matter of his Malazan knife and the demon residing within it. He came, therefore, not as a child – though he is indeed a child – but as a potential enemy, and a dangerous one at that.' She hesitated and then added, 'I too was not pleased, though I well comprehended the motivation.'

Delas Fana shook her head. 'If Rant is now the enemy of Elade Tharos, it was entirely the Warleader's doing. So be it. Since I stand by my half-brother, how could I kneel to Elade Tharos? And now, having forced my hand, he's *displeased* with me? Say what you will of our father, when at last we met him, he was not one to act in ignorance of the consequences.'

Shouts from various clan leaders. Marching order was drawing into shape. A thousand Teblor horses were being moved towards the vanguard. It was hot here, high on the slope of the last mountains. It would be hotter still in the lowlands awaiting them.

Widowed Dayliss was frowning. 'Delas Fana, I am less troubled by this than you. Recall, I knew Karsa Orlong in his youth. He was often heedless of consequences. When his pride was stung, he wounded friendships and stretched the loyalty of those who followed him. In the end of this, indeed, he left the bodies of his two closest friends lying dead in his wake.' She shrugged. 'Elade Tharos is still young, not yet versed in wisdom's scars. It takes suffering to understand. Soon, I fear, our Warleader will learn this for himself.' She then took another step forward and settled a hand on Tonith Agra's shoulder. 'Leave Delas Fana to accompany Rant, to protect him, to keep him safe.'

'She is prone to wander,' Sathal said, her tone flat as she studied Delas Fana. 'My chief memory of Delas Fana is her restlessness.'

'I do not deny it,' said Delas Fana, letting Sathal see in her eyes the fondness she held for her. 'Civilization has stained me with its eternal dissatisfaction, as I think it has done to Karsa Orlong. But this time, I am not driven away, not pulled by my frustrations and impatience. This time, my future is held fast by a vow. Rant shall not travel alone.'

'And so,' Dayliss said in a musing tone, 'your young brother gathers yet more to him. Two formidable Jheck are not enough. Nor the dogs of Gnaw's brood. Now, the most feared warrior of the Uryd, next to Karak Thord, will walk at his side.'

Pake Gild, who had been standing back in silence, now stepped forward and said, 'I shall accompany you, Delas Fana.'

Her mother turned in startlement and made to speak, but then her lips pressed into a tight line, and she nodded.

Delas Fana studied Pake Gild. She was a year older. Dayliss had been pregnant with her before Karsa, Bairoth and Delum set out for Silver Lake. Of course Delas knew her, but for some reason not well. Always quiet, always watchful. It was said she could ride any horse, broken or unbroken. 'I welcome you into our company, Pake Gild,' she said. 'Perhaps you will become a friend to Rant.' *One not bound by blood,* was what she meant.

Pake Gild frowned, as if the thought had not occurred to her, and then said, 'In truth I saw another value to my presence, Delas Fana. I now own the horses bred by Karsa's father.'

Nilghan was scowling, but then, he greeted every morning with a scowl. Why should this day be any different? The hounds surrounding Rant had grown used to the two Jheck warriors. Every now and then one of the beasts would walk up to Nilghan or Gower, sniff for a time, and then wander off again. The raised hackles were gone. The other Teblor dogs – and there were thousands of them – were all kept at bay by the brood of Gnaw. Rant had asked Delas Fana about the fate of that venerated sire but Gnaw had vanished years ago. It was assumed that the beast had limped off to die alone in the forest.

Since Damisk's death, Rant had not slept well. He woke often with his eyes filled with tears, a deep ache in his chest where the unseen wound of guilt still leaked its burning blood. Occasionally, he had woken deep in the night to find that he had drawn his knife, the blade exuding air so cold it drifted like smoke around the weapon, making the hand that held it numb. He would sit up then, and see a lone figure standing just beyond the ring of dogs, wrapped in the skin of a cave bear. Watching him, and now that he had awakened, the figure turned and walked away.

Elade Tharos was not yet done with him, it seemed. Strangely, this truth pleased Rant, because he was not yet done with Elade Tharos either. Delas Fana spoke of patience, a virtue unfamiliar to him. But he had learned to grip it tight, even if it raged between fire and ice, telling himself that the pain of restraint would be worth it in the end.

Was it fair to blame Elade Tharos for Damisk's death? Rant knew the answer to that question. The blame was with Rant, and no one else. But it had been the Warleader's command that nailed the slaver's limbs to the bedrock. As if such a thing was free of suffering, as if it had been an act of respect. There was no understanding that, as far as Rant was concerned.

'Bound,' Gower had said, 'as the slaver bound others. The answer to his crime was the taking away of his freedom. Consider, pup, what it means to be shackled by wrist and ankle. These four limbs of yours belong to you, do they not? They are your instruments of freedom, at times your weapons of will. Until the iron closes and all that is taken away. What does this do to the spirit?'

And Nilghan, seated nearby, had snorted and said, '*I would tear my own limbs off if chained they were. I am Nilghan of the Black Jheck, and Nilghan of the Black Jheck is the pack's howl of freedom itself.*'

Gower had winced, but then he nodded. '*At night, Rant, we Jheck dream of running. And running.*'

'*When as children we slept side by side,*' Nilghan had added in a growl, '*my infernal brother kicked me in his sleep. Kicked me awake again and again. I'd watch him twitch. I'd see his lips curl in a silent snarl. And I longed to close my own jaws about his neck until my mouth filled hot and salty. Hah!*'

They had broken their fast in silence, seated around a fire left to die. Nilghan's scowl only deepened when he watched the Teblor and the Ganrel and other Wilder tribes readying to depart, jostling into the column that was moments from beginning the long descent into the valley and plain below.

The hounds had gorged on cattle and goat meat the night before and their bellies were still swollen and, apparently, itchy. Rant watched them scratching, gnawing skin with their teeth.

'War-Bitch,' said Nilghan, startling both Rant and Gower, the latter looking up to give his brother a fierce glower. 'She is like a Soletaken in the midst of D'ivers,' Nilghan went on. 'A beast standing alone among packs. A creature seen on the ridge where the clan's border ends. Solitary. Doomed.'

'I sensed her close for days,' Gower said. 'Then, one morning . . . gone.'

'So you say, Oh Lord of No One. Our packs wander lost, scattered and witless. We must return to them.'

'I have whispered in my mind a summons to all of the Black Jheck, brother. Whispered, and then roared. There is a stirring in our homeland. I can feel it. We shall be joined. We shall be answered.'

'Then your gift of screaming in silence has deafened me, for I who slept not two paces from you heard naught.'

'You idiot. Do you need a summons, Nilghan? You are already here, to my everlasting regret.'

'What of War-Bitch, who has now fled us if what you say is true? If this War-Bitch was not simply imagined, conjured by wishful thinking.'

'Damisk met her, witnessed her leaving her den.'

'He said many things. Were they all true? They were not.'

Rant frowned. 'Damisk never lied.'

'And the tale of visiting another world? Freeing a chained god? Sky keeps and K'Chain Che'Malle and a slaughter to leave bards speechless? Men who live alone become the centre of the universe. Well, *their* universe, anyway. This is what drives most of them mad. Was Damisk mad? I will, out of courtesy, remain silent on that.'

Gower said, 'Your mood is especially sour this morning, brother. You would bait the pup? I've yet to remind you, Nilghan, of your place. Perhaps that is overdue.'

Teeth bared, Nilghan asked, 'Are you recovered yet, brother? I am of a mind to wrest from you the lordship, as it rightly belongs to me anyway.'

Gower slowly straightened. 'Very well. I am indeed fully recovered. Shall we do this as we are, or as packs?'

Nilghan's eyes blazed, and then the blaze guttered out. He looked away, eyes suddenly narrowing. 'Teblor women,' he muttered. 'See the intentions in their eyes? Horrid mystery makes all discourse a curse.'

Rant turned to follow Nilghan's gaze and saw Delas Fana approaching, along with another woman he knew not. He stood to meet them.

'This day,' said Delas Fana, 'we shall ride.'

Nilghan grunted. 'Impossible. No horse can abide a Jheck on its back. The nape is where the lead wolf sinks fast its jaws, after all, whilst the others close in to take fetlock and belly. Grasp and rend, drag the beast down, and then feed.' He licked his lips, as if recalling some past meal that pleased him, and then shook his shaggy head as if perplexed. 'Horses hate me.'

'I'm not surprised,' Delas Fana replied in a dry tone. She returned her attention to Rant. 'It is decided. I shall accompany you into the east, and so too Pake Gild, the daughter of Widowed Dayliss and Bairoth Gild.'

Rant studied Pake Gild. The eyes that met his were unaccountably calm, unnerving him. 'I have never ridden a horse,' he said. 'Perhaps, like Gower and Nilghan, I can walk.'

Pake Gild simply smiled.

'It is important that you learn,' said Delas Fana.

'Why?'

She hesitated, and then said, 'There may come a time when we may have to travel . . . quickly.'

'What of Gower and Nilghan?' Rant asked. 'They are my friends, and I am done with abandoning friends.'

'We shall veer,' announced Gower. 'Perhaps we cannot run as fast as a Teblor horse, but we can run for longer than any beast alive.'

Rant had never seen the Jheck actually veer into their packs. He looked on his two friends with renewed curiosity. 'Does it hurt?'

'Does what hurt, Rant?'

'Veering. Does your body break apart? Do you fall into six pieces? There will be six of you, will there not? How is it done?'

Nilghan snorted and then said, 'We surrender to the beasts within us.'

'And then?'

He shrugged. 'Then we veer.'

Gower said, 'At each moment, even as you see us now, six hearts beat within us. Perhaps only one can be seen or felt with a hand against the chest. But the others we feel, nonetheless. Only by will alone do we remain bound into one form. To veer is, as Nilghan said, to surrender.'

'Then you will have six minds?' Rant asked, marvelling at the thought. 'How can you live with six voices in your head? Who commands? Are there arguments?'

It seemed that both Delas Fana and Pake Gild were amused by his questions and Rant felt a flash of irritation at them both. The Teblor were an arrogant people, he decided, and then mused on what the world might bring that could drive that arrogance to its knees.

Gower smiled as well, but it was a warmer smile. 'My single mind, Rant, dominates the pack. But I can travel from beast to beast to beast, as needed. When,' and his smile grew ironic, 'someone drives a knife through one wolf's skull, it's best to find another, and quickly.'

'Then you've felt what it means to die?'

Gower's eyes narrowed. 'Your mind is sharp indeed. Yes, to answer you. We Jheck are well acquainted with death.'

'I'm sorry I did that, then.'

Gower shrugged. 'You killed to stay alive. Under those circumstances, Rant, no apology is ever needed.'

Something had swept the smiles from Delas Fana and Pake Gild, and both were now eyeing Rant with some other expression that Rant couldn't read. Then Pake spoke to Gower.

'The child has fought your pack, Lord Gower?'

Gower grunted. 'My first lesson in underestimating the "child", Pake Gild. There have been others, none aimed at me, thankfully. But then, the Rathyd warrior Galambar cannot offer you an opinion, since he's dead.' It seemed he was done, but then he added, 'This, of course, before any demon ever set eyes on that knife.'

'When you veer,' Rant persisted, 'what will we see?'

'You'll smell it first,' answered Nilghan, shaking himself as might a bear rising from a river. 'Then things blur and bleed, a dark smudge, a thing that roils like smoke. In the midst of this, six pairs of eyes will appear. If you are an enemy, this is the last thing you see.'

Pake Gild said, 'I shall bring us the horses. Delas Fana, will you take yours back from Tonith Agra?'

'No,' Delas Fana replied. 'Please find for me a new mount, preferably a mare.'

'Good, as mine is a mare as well,' Pake said, nodding. 'For the child, then, a gelding.' She set off.

Rant returned his attention to Gower. 'Will you veer now?'

'We shall—'

'A moment,' snapped Nilghan. 'Delas Fana, what will these hounds do?'

'I don't know, Nilghan. But this seems the time to find out, rather than on a field of battle.'

'Good point,' Nilghan said, his expression sour, a flicker of unease in his eyes as he studied the Teblor dogs surrounding them. 'Brother. Let me veer first. The injustice of your title matters less than risking the Lord of the Black Jheck being savaged and torn to pieces by a thousand ugly hounds. When you fall, it shall be to me and me alone.'

Gower snarled. 'What worth the lord who does not lead before all whom he serves? No, Nilghan, though I appreciate your grudging concern.' And with that, he began to veer.

The spicy scent stung the back of Rant's nose on the first drawn breath, his eyes filling with tears as an impenetrable gloom seemed to devour Gower. Then it frayed, like rags of black smoke, and, as Nilghan had promised, when the smoke spread out, six pairs of amber eyes blazed from it.

A moment later six heavy, hump-shouldered black wolves stood before Rant.

The hounds of Gnaw's brood were suddenly motionless, fixed in a circle facing inward and focused, Rant could see, on the six hulking wolves.

Those wolves were no match in size to the hounds, since the latter were as tall as the shaggy ponies that sometimes came into Silver Lake pulling trader wagons. But against one, even two Teblor hounds, Rant suspected a Jheck pack would prevail.

Delas Fana said, 'The Lord of the Black Jheck is formidable indeed. I would not want to face this pack. Rant, best move among the beasts, to ease the brood's worry.'

Rant stepped forward. He thought to find the dominant wolf, perhaps seeing something of Gower himself in its eyes, but no hint revealed itself.

Nilghan clearly understood what Rant had been seeking, for he grunted a laugh. 'Tactical advantage, no? Who leads? None know, until it is too late. Well, it seems my brother will not be torn apart after all – though only because of your pets, Rant – look, if you dare, to the tribal hounds beyond the ring.'

Rant did so, and a chill rippled along his spine. The Teblor dogs were swirling in their hundreds, hackles high and gazes fixed upon the pack that was Gower. Warriors bellowed commands, pulling the beasts back into the column that was now on the march. Many were reluctant to pull away.

Delas Fana joined Rant, her mien clouded. 'The Warleader had best take note of this, lest the first charge of his army descend into chaos. He would be wise to keep the Jheck upon one flank and the Teblor hounds upon the opposite. Assuming any Jheck choose to join him.'

Nilghan then veered, and once more Rant moved to stand among them, and this finally seemed to settle the brood, though no dog drew close to a wolf.

Pake Gild was returning, leading three saddled Teblor horses. Rant did not think any southlander could manage such beasts. They were each bridled with a single rein, the saddles bulky and broader than they were long. The two mares were both black while the gelding bore white fetlocks and there was grey in its black coat.

'It is said,' Delas Fana spoke from his side, 'that the Teblor horse is not a natural beast. Once, long ago, a half-blood Jaghut came among the tribes. The horses of the Jaghut are eaters of flesh, and their favourite prey was the common horse. Jaghut sorcery is powerful, driven solely by the intention of the wielder. The half-blood, as gift to the Teblor, fused together two beasts, predator and prey, into one. Thus was born the Teblor horse. I have seen venerated bones in houses among the clans. It seems they were not as large then as they are now.'

'This is true,' said Pake Gild. 'We bred them selectively. It requires subtlety and a sharp eye. Too large and their weight and muscle can snap their own bones. Too much of the Jaghut strain – which often appears in stallions – makes the animal too vicious even for a warhorse. Karsa Orlong's father was a fine breeder of horses.' She stepped forward leading the gelding and offered Rant the rein. 'It is named Chantak. Nervous for the moment, with the nearness of the wolves – but not fearful, do you see? No, Chantak eyes the Jheck packs as rivals.'

'It eats meat, then?'

'It eats like a bear eats. Meat, plants, berries, termites and ants.' She paused, then said, 'Shits like a bear, too. Black and acidic. See the elongated jaw? Teblor horses can bite through a southlander's thigh. In battle, they can take a southlander by the hip and throw him ten paces or more. A solid kick can kill even a Teblor.'

'Then it will be me who will be frightened,' said Rant.

'No, you must command. Chantak is patient. There will be time to learn.'

'So we hope,' said Delas Fana who stood by the mount Pake had brought her. She vaulted onto her mare and settled into the saddle, the rein loose in one hand.

'She is named Einal,' Pake said to Delas Fana. 'Three foals from her. A good, caring mother. Now, Rant, set your foot in that stirrup – no, the other foot. Grasp the saddle horn and pull yourself onto Chantak's back. See how easy that was? Now relax and keep the rein loose. Chantak will follow as Delas Fana will lead the way. I will ride behind you and tell you things you need to learn. Does this bother you?'

'No,' Rant replied. 'But I have never been taught anything before. I don't know what to do.'

'Just what I tell you. Had you been born among the Teblor, you would learn by observation. This is the better way of learning. My guidance will have little effect until you take upon yourself what I tell you, so for now you need only listen and remember. When you have questions, ask them and heed well my answers.'

'You are not much older than me, Pake Gild, yet you speak to me as you would a child.'

'Only because you have much to learn. I do not mean to offend.'

Rant swung his attention to Delas Fana. 'What is this special night you spoke of? The night when I become a man. When can I do that?'

'That will come soon, Rant,' said Delas Fana after an exchange of glances with Pake Gild. 'But for now, let us join the train. It seems we shall be last, behind even the elders and the lame. At least this way, the Jheck will not be bothered by any dogs.'

She did nothing that Rant could see, but her mount began walking. A moment later, Chantak stepped in behind her.

'Jaghut horses run in packs,' said Pake Gild, now only a voice as she rode last. 'Common horses in herds. Both communicate with one another in ways you cannot see. With common horses, that which drives them is fear. Among Jaghut horses, it is the hunt. Teblor horses merge the two, making them warhorses, because a warhorse must understand fear as much as the hunt. You might think a warhorse should be fearless, but such a beast will see both itself and its rider quickly killed. Fear serves, instilling caution and self-protection, and this self-protection extends to its rider.

'Does a warrior learn nothing but the attack? No, a warrior learns how to defend as well. When you ride into battle, horse and rider will both attack *and* defend. At times you will alternate, the warrior defending to protect the horse, the horse attacking to defeat the enemy. One day, you will become a single mind in battle, communicating to each other by twitch of muscle, shift of weight and balance, and where the horse's eyes fix, yours will fix in the opposite direction. Where you lash out, the horse gathers tight. Where the horse lashes out, you gather tight. By all accounts, Karsa Orlong was the finest rider among his generation – but then,' she added with a soft laugh, 'that was his father's opinion.'

Delas Fana twisted slightly in her saddle. 'Karsa Orlong now rides a pure Jaghut horse, Pake Gild.'

'He once rode his father's pride stallion, Havok.'

'Ah,' said Delas Fana, 'he chose the same name for his new horse.'

Rant said, 'There is the skull of a Teblor horse in Silver Lake. Perhaps that belonged to the first Havok.'

His comment silenced the two women.

They began the descent into the lowland valley. Rant saw Gower's pack move off, as if on a scent. Nilghan's, however, did not follow, though Rant sensed a sudden tension in the shaggy wolves that remained loping alongside the riders. Gnaw's brood continued on, seemingly indifferent to whatever the wolves did or didn't do. Nearest Rant was Sculp, trotting so close on Rant's right flank as to nearly brush his moccasin in its stirrup.

There had been children in Silver Lake who had owned dogs, but those dogs tended to flee from Rant. He had almost befriended two of the wild dogs that lived behind the Three-Legged Dog, but they too had been wary, even when he offered them food.

He had concluded that animals didn't like him. He remembered a boy getting mad at him for making his dog run away with its tail between its legs, especially since it was a big dog and the boy had always strutted whenever it walked with him. Now the animal had skidded around a building and vanished from sight.

'*Blood-oil curse is your stink, Rant. Evil and rotten. I'm getting enough dogs to chase you down instead. Ten, maybe more! Tear you to pieces! They won't eat you, though, because you're poison.*'

And off he'd run with his friends, his own pack, though it had seemed his status wasn't what it had been when he'd had his big dog beside him. He never did get himself any more dogs though, and the threat that had chewed away at Rant's insides for days, and then weeks, slowly faded. The only other time Rant remembered seeing that boy again there had been hair on his chin and one side of his forehead had been flattened by a horse-kick, which left him always smiling and drool dangling from his open mouth. And Rant's new children friends laughed at him and called him Dog-Boy because of all the drool. And threw stones at him.

One time, he recalled all too vividly, he had tried to get his friends to stop pelting the poor man, and they did. That day the stones started flying at Rant instead.

I am poison. Blood-oil cursed. Dogs run from me.

He didn't think he could trust these Teblor dogs. He wasn't even certain he could or would ever trust Chantak.

But he trusted the wolves of the Jheck, even if, for the moment, only Nilghan's pack was in sight.

'You're tensing up, Rant. Relax again. Get whatever you were thinking out of your head. Go back to something more pleasant.'

Pake Gild was pretty, but to her he was a child.

'Try harder,' she said.

Her long, thick hair was white, flowing like smoke from burning leaves. And yet her skin was onyx black, which made the emerald of her eyes all the more startling. She had fashioned a nest of sorts in the declivity of a massive split boulder, slouched on a ledge with her legs splayed forward in brazen display of her nakedness.

Sembling, Gower stood regarding her, wondering what the point of such an alluring pose was. He bowed and said, 'War-Bitch.'

'They think me long gone?'

'Yes. Even my brother believes so. Where are my clans?'

'Close, but I will tell you, Lord Gower, this is not our war. Will you resist its lure? The slaughter, the taste of blood on your tongue?'

He cocked his head. 'When you stalked my dreams, nothing was clear. I could comprehend little of your desires.'

She frowned, and then shrugged. 'I am out of practice. While you, Lord Gower, dwell in an eternal fog. What is it about this Toblakai half-blood that so haunts you?'

Gower glanced away. 'His innocence. Like a taloned hand squeezing my heart.'

'Ah,' she sighed, 'innocence will do that. And yet he is embraced by a Shi'gal Assassin, and in his blood there burns the fire of a god. Thus, while he is innocent, those with him are decidedly not.'

'Am I to fear him, War-Bitch?'

Her eyes widened. 'No, you fool. You are to *follow* him.' When she smiled, he saw that her canines belonged to a wolf. 'What a thing, isn't it? To follow *innocence*. You and I, with all our bitter scars, our cruel experience. A Shi'gal, of all things! Assassin with the blood of dragons on her hands, never mind a host of murdered K'Chain Che'Malle matrons. And in the child's *own* hands, well, let us be honest: violence is no stranger.'

'What is he? Why follow him?'

'You're asking me? You and your brother would die for him. You were ready to do so more than once. And now too his half-sisters. But tell me, Gower, will your Black Jheck agree to this? How strong is your hold on the clans? You have been gone a while.'

'They are mine,' Gower said in a growl.

'Good,' she replied. 'The White Jheck are far away. Does Lord Casnock dream of me? I know not, but I do intend to find out. If lost to me, then perhaps, one day, they will rediscover the pleasures of my embrace.'

But Gower cared little for the White Jheck. He had other things on his mind. 'Damisk is dead.'

'I know. I scoured his mind, saw the entirety of his life. It is well that he died, and in turn,' she smiled again, 'he died well.'

'Rant's first wound – I see the innocence ebbing from his eyes, and I would rail at the heavens against such loss.'

'If you seek to blind him to the world, you will fail. To live is to lose the faith you were born with to a thousand cuts, each year bleeding into the next. The eyes of the innocent see a world very differently from what you and I see. To know this is to revisit one's own loss, eye to eye with sad reflection, and to feel once more that dreadful ache in your chest.'

Gower grimaced. 'If you are in poor practice visiting a mortal's dreams, War-Bitch, you've lost nothing in understanding what it means to suffer too many truths. If we are to follow Rant, do you know anything of the fate awaiting us?'

'I know one thing, Lord Gower,' she replied. 'When it is time to move, we must move *fast*. Be sure to make Rant understand that.'

'And who will decide when that moment arrives?'

She stood, stretched luxuriously.

Gower fought back the desire he knew she was deliberately caressing awake. Goddesses could be so maddening.

'You will know it, Gower. Now, I need more reminding.'

'Of what?'

'The rewards of company,' she said, regarding him with veiled eyes.

He uttered a low growl and then moved straight for her.

It took the rest of the day to reach the base of the valley, and most of the evening for the various clans and tribes to spread out into the forests and find room to make camp. By the time the tail end of the column edged onto the valley's level basin, woodsmoke filled the forest as if it had caught fire.

Delas Fana led her small party along a terrace that marked some long-extinct river level – or so Pake had suggested – well above the valley floor. Here, conifers had given way to broad-leafed birch and aspen and the ground underfoot was mostly gravel beneath the leaf litter. The camp offered a vantage overlooking the rest of the army sprawled below, somewhere beneath the canopy of pine and spruce. Smoke wreathed the entire valley by the time Delas had built a small cookfire and prepared a meal.

Gower had returned only a short time earlier, his cheeks and neck unaccountably scratched, as if he had pushed his face and head into a thicket of thorns. Rant had not seen him semble back into human form, something Nilghan had yet to do, but Nilghan's pack had clearly taken note of its brother's state and was suddenly wary, as if hesitant to draw close.

Rant's backside and thighs ached. He smelled of horse sweat. He did not think he would ever be a skilled rider, displaying the ease he had seen from Delas Fana. Indeed, he would never be a proper Teblor. But that part he didn't mind too much. It was too strange, he decided, to think of belonging anywhere, or with anyone. Perhaps it wasn't so bad, how things had been back in Silver Lake. Wandering alone, observing the lives of others, feeling like a ghost when all was well, then all too visible when someone in anger noticed him.

Fleet of foot, he could escape most of the rocks flung his way. Even those that struck didn't hurt too much. Minor cuts. Bruises and soreness. If not for what had happened with his mother, he could have stayed there for ever. It wouldn't be happiness but then, happiness wasn't kind anyway, the way it could vanish in an instant. He might not miss it at all.

When he thought about it, he recalled seeing few happy people. Not there, and not here. In children, yes, but then they got older and their faces grew serious, their eyes cold and challenging. Something, therefore, must happen when a certain age is reached. Some secret thing, a night, just as with the Teblor. When happiness was cut away, and in its place some new truth about the world was stitched onto the soul.

'There must be words this night.'

Blinking, Rant looked up, momentarily confused. Gower was squatting opposite, the grease of the meat that had been roasted on his thick lips. Nearby was Nilghan, finally sembled and gnawing red strands from a bone, hands and face glistening. Delas Fana was using her saddle as a seat and was holding a battered tin cup filled with tea that steamed. Pake Gild was off with the horses, grooming and feeding them. Lastly, their camp was surrounded by Gnaw's brood.

Rant frowned at Gower. 'What do you mean?'

But Gower's attention was fixed on Delas Fana. 'The Black Jheck clans are to the east of here, on the shores of the great lake. Close, I believe, to the southlander settlement of Bringer's Foot. At least for the moment.'

'How do you know this?' she asked.

Nilghan grunted. 'Pillow talk is my guess.'

'I just know,' said Gower, ignoring his brother. 'When does the army divide?'

'Tomorrow,' Delas Fana replied. 'Some Teblor clans will likely grow impatient. They will travel in advance of the column and, if the enemy are few in the settlements, they will not hesitate to attack. Warriors eager to spill the first blood of this war.'

Gower's expression clouded. 'That has already occurred. Silver Lake has been attacked.'

'Again, your knowledge surprises me, Lord Gower.'

'War-Bitch,' snapped Nilghan. 'She has returned, if she ever left.' He glared at his brother. 'What purpose all this deceit?'

'My silence would have remained, if not for her appetites,' said Gower. 'She has history with the Toblakai – the Teblor, rather. As with the Saemdhi. If a god would survive, it must first learn caution. I did as she asked.'

'What news then of the battle at Silver Lake?' Delas Fana demanded.

Gower shrugged. 'A battle. The town has been burned to the ground.'

The words were simple, and they sank into Rant without raising a ripple. He found that he was hugging his knees.

'I would know more,' pressed Delas Fana. 'You said a battle, not a slaughter.'

'I did, but in that I could be wrong.'

'Who won?'

'No one won,' said Gower. 'No one will. Not in this war. I would keep my Black Jheck from it. We must journey into the south, and quickly. Best if we avoided contact, with friend or foe.'

Nilghan was suddenly on his feet. 'The goddess is ill-named!'

'The goddess has walked more battlefields than you've shat splinters of bone, brother. She has stood on a field, her white fur soaked red, wagering the cost of victory, choking on its bitter lie. She has damned those dancing on the dead and mourned the despair in the eyes of every survivor. She knows war, brother. Knows it well and indeed, too well.'

'What would she have us do? Cower in the shadows all the way to Mott?'

Gower's shaggy brows lifted. 'Mott? If that is where we are guided, then my answer to you is "Yes, Nilghan, we shall cower if we must, to the very walls of Mott." What is coming is not about victory. It's about surviving. If I can lead my clans and leave not one corpse behind, then I will have won.'

'I challenge you for the lordship!'

'Do you, Nilghan? And will you be so bold when War-Bitch slinks into your dreams, into your mind itself, and whispers of an eternity of horror?' He made to rise. 'If this is what you desire, so be it—'

But Rant found his hand on Gower's thick shoulder, pushing the man back down. 'I want the same as you, Lord Gower,' he said. 'No more dead friends, no more dead family. Nilghan, are the Black Jheck your family? Your kin? Which ones, then, will you sacrifice to this war of Elade Tharos's making?'

Nilghan's jaw dropped open. 'Not a child's words,' he whispered in a hoarse voice.

'Damisk is dead, so too my mother. I could have saved them both.'

'Ah, the child returns.'

That angered Rant, but the boiling fury quickly devoured itself, leaving behind that cold hardness that slowed down the entire world, that stilled his nerves and slowed his breathing. His other hand found the grip of his knife.

'Stop this!' said Delas Fana.

'Not your business,' said Nilghan, eyes fixed on Gower. 'The lordship—'

'Is where it belongs,' finished Delas Fana. 'You've stopped thinking, Nilghan. All of this – these valleys, all of the southlands – is about to be destroyed in a flood. We Teblor are fleeing an impending disaster that will drown our world. Do you possibly imagine that your goddess of war does not know this as true? She commands Lord Gower to save the Black Jheck and that is what he will try to do. Be at his side, Nilghan, and his chances of success increase dramatically. Fight him, and all the Black Jheck will die. Think, then, on the regard of your goddess when after death you go to meet her.'

'I am a warrior!'

Rant sighed. 'Sit down, Nilghan. Challenge your brother outside the walls of Mott, wherever that is. Please, all of you, stop arguing. I will still journey to Silver Lake, where I will bury my mother, if she is not now nothing but ashes. But this is my journey. If a flood is coming, I am taking you in the wrong direction. I no longer fear travelling alone, and I would be happy on my own, knowing that you were all safe, far away to the south.' He saw that Pake Gild was standing in the gloom beyond the fire's glow. He did not know how long she had been there, or what she had heard. 'Besides,' he added, 'I am never alone.'

'Kind sentiments,' said Gower, 'but the Black Jheck shall journey with you, Rant. I have spoken.'

'Why,' Rant asked, 'if your goddess wants you to survive?'

'Because, in the eyes of War-Bitch, you are our best chance of that.'

Dumbfounded, Rant struggled to find something to say.

'That makes no sense,' hissed Nilghan, even as he settled back down, slumping as if drained.

'Odd,' muttered Delas Fana, feeding more sticks into the fire.

'What?' Nilghan demanded.

'My instincts have told me the same thing. I begin to believe that we are not here to protect Rant, but that he is here to protect us.'

Pake Gild spoke from the darkness. 'Rant, come with me. I have listened to your words and seen what your eyes have revealed.'

Rant frowned at Delas Fana, who said, 'Formal words, Rant. You have earned your night. It is the women who decide, the women who choose, because it is the women who know.'

Pake Gild's right hand reached out. 'I have listened to your words and seen what your eyes have revealed. If you prefer a man, I will find you one.'

'A man?' Rant asked. 'For what?'

Gower grunted. 'It's simple, pup. If you would kiss someone, would you rather that someone be a man or a woman?'

Kiss? After a moment, he shrugged. 'I don't know. I don't know what you are all talking about. I've never kissed anyone, nor been kissed. I don't know why people do it.'

Gower stood suddenly. He moved away from the fire and circled round to close on Pake Gild, where he whispered something to her, his tone so low that Rant could hear nothing of what he spoke.

Rant saw shock come to Pake's features, and then pain filled her eyes. 'Then,' she said, 'it remains to be seen, but with difficulties. Rant, do stand please and take my hand. No matter what, come the dawn, you will be a man.'

Nilghan made a strange groaning sound, and then said, 'If only War-Bitch had a sister. But do as she tells you, pup. Like I told you, women know everything.'

She led him far away from anyone else, higher up on another ancient beach ridge. Not even the dogs followed. Alone in Pake Gild's company, Rant was having trouble finding anything to say. His hearts pounded hard for some unknown reason and his mouth was dry. It was as if a scent came from her, unaccountably exotic, that left him befuddled and shy.

Suddenly, he found something to talk about, but it was a new cause for worry. 'It is said that the Teblor rituals are bloody and cruel. Newborn children are sacrificed to gods of stone. Dogs slaughtered and horses skinned. There is chanting and other strange things, and spirits rise up from the earth. Will I be made to bleed?'

'When you first looked upon me,' she said as she guided him to a small clearing, 'I thought I saw desire in your eyes. Was I wrong?'

'I thought you pretty,' he said through his embarrassment, glad that it was dark so she could not see his burning face.

'You've since changed your mind?'

But he heard the amusement in her tone. 'You tease me.'

'Teasing is our greatest weapon. The skin of men is so thin, we forever test to see how easily it bleeds.'

'That is unkind.'

She found a fallen tree and dragged the trunk over. 'Sit here with me.'

He saw now that she'd brought her bedding to this place, the rolled furs lying close by. 'You have planned this from before . . . before you heard my words.'

'It was earlier this afternoon, as I advised you on horses, and as my gaze rested long upon your back, that I saw what my purpose might be here, with you. Well, one of them, as it cannot be said that I exist simply to serve a man's needs. Rather, I am free to draw close to a man, or pull far away, as I choose. I am free, also, to make myself useful in any manner that pleases me. No, Rant, there will be no blood.'

He looked around, his gaze avoiding the furs for some reason. 'What happens now? I think you were wrong. I'm not ready for anything. You all called me a child, beneath the laws of the Teblor, beneath being taken seriously by anyone. I didn't like that. But maybe I didn't like it because it was true. I am a child, and now I feel as if I'm about to lose something I was too ignorant to value when I had it.' He glanced at her. 'What is it I'm about to lose, Pake Gild?'

She sighed. 'I was warned,' she said, mostly under her breath. 'Under other circumstances, Rant, my answer would be "innocence". You would lose your innocence. But Damisk told Gower and now Gower has told me.' She fell silent then.

Frowning, Rant thought about what that thing might be. Nothing came to mind.

'It's to do with your mother,' Pake finally said, in a near whisper.

'I thought she'd killed herself because of me,' said Rant. 'But Damisk said she didn't. Is that it?'

'It was *why* she threatened to kill herself,' said Pake.

'Because I couldn't pay, like everyone else did. When she . . .' Now it was his turn to be silent. *When she did to me what she did with all those others.*

'It has nothing to do with payment, Rant. That was the curse of blood-oil, the fever of it that so takes the life of a southlander, forcing her into doing what she did. No other work was available to her, but until that night, that's all it ever was. Work. By working, she could feed the both of you, keep the house in which you lived. By working, she could care for you. But then the fever overwhelmed her, and she did something to you that should never be done.'

Rant felt like weeping, but he didn't know why, only that Pake Gild was talking her way to something and whatever that thing was, it hurt Rant inside, as if he bore a wound he didn't know was there and she was about to dig fingers into it. 'My body, parts of it, changed,' he said. 'I couldn't control any of it. She was clawing at her own face, beating herself with her fists. I didn't know what was happening. I didn't know what I should do, to make it better.'

'There was nothing you could do.'

'I was confused.'

'You were terrified,' she said.

He considered. He'd always been told about how slow his thoughts were, how clumsy and stupid he was, compared to all the southlander boys. But he could not recall ever feeling terror, at least as he understood the word, but then, perhaps he didn't understand the word at all. 'Terrified means being scared. I don't think I've ever been scared.'

'They're not exactly the same, Rant. Terror dwells deeper in the unknown than does being scared or frightened. It is confusion dragged into a silent scream, as your entire world is torn out from under you. That night, Rant, she tore away that world. That night, everything changed.'

He nodded. He could see that now. 'I ran to the lake.'

'One life ended, another begun. How did Damisk find you?'

'I was trying to swim to the north shore. It was cold. I think I was drowning. My body stopped working. My strength disappeared. Damisk came in a boat. He pulled me into it. Later, we made a fire.'

'You were his redemption,' she said. 'Well, a try at redemption, anyway. Had he saved a thousand Rants . . . well, not even then.'

'Damisk was a good man.'

'To you he was. Never mind that. It's just how people are. Warm in one direction, cold as ice in another.'

'I feel ice when I look upon Elade Tharos,' said Rant.

'Just so,' she muttered.

'But I don't like how it feels.'

She turned to study him in the moonlight. Somewhere far to the north, thunder rumbled, but the sky in that direction was dark, with no flashes of lightning. She spoke. 'On this night, we must pull apart two things. It won't be easy, but I'll do my best. On one side is the betrayal – the thing your mother did to you – and on the other is the way your body responded. You felt that it was out of control. I will teach you how to control it, and how to find pleasure in those sensations. More importantly, I will teach you how to give pleasure even as you're taking it. How we give our bodies over to trust is the greatest gift of adulthood.'

'I don't want to talk about my mother,' said Rant. 'She's probably dead.'

'If so, then understand this,' Pake replied. 'Relief rode her last breath. And had she known what the curse would make her do, she would have killed herself before it ever happened.'

There was an intensity in her eyes that made Rant's skin prickle. 'You want to do to me what my mother did, that night.'

'That was my intention, yes. But now, Rant, I have a confession. I am afraid. Not that you might hurt me. In fact, the gentleness in you shatters my heart again and again. That does not come from your father, by the way.' She drew a ragged breath. 'No, what frightens me is that I might fail, that in awakening your body with my touch, you are plunged back into the nightmare of how you experienced it the first time.'

'Are you blood-oil cursed, Pake Gild?'

'No, we Teblor recover quickly from blood-oil. Have I imbibed it? Once, yes. It is no wonder your father lost all control. Even to kiss a freshly oiled blade is to quicken the hearts and send fire . . . downward. This is part of what frightens me, to be honest. Desire is its own fever, after all, and I may well succumb to it, and in bearing seem little different from what you saw in your mother.'

'You will scratch and beat your own face? Don't do that, Pake Gild. I have decided. I will remain a child. For ever.'

She was grimacing. 'And Gower stumbles in, his face bearing the map of a woman's nails. No, Rant, I'll not deliver violence upon myself. But what I am feeling may well quicken me, and that may *look* violent, so intense the pleasure.'

He no longer wanted to be here, sitting beside this woman. He wanted to be back with his friends and his half-sister in the camp below.

'Will you trust me this night, Rant?'

'I want to go back.'

'I can see that a night such as this one will be fraught, whether it occurs now or in ten years. But the woman in your future, Rant, will know nothing of what happened to you in Silver Lake. I think of her, whoever she might be, and this makes me more determined that we do this. For her sake and for yours when you are with her.'

He couldn't think who such a woman would be, if not a woman just like the one he was sitting beside right now. Then it struck him that she might not be like that at all. He now knew four, almost five, Teblor women. And they were all different. He understood none of them.

But here was Pake Gild, trying to explain herself, telling him things, and those things in turn told him other things. His eyes widened as he studied her. 'You trust me,' he said.

A startled laugh answered him. 'Shattered Face, Rant! You are impossible *not* to trust! In that, perhaps, you are most like your father. A man of few words is a deep well, and with such a man, why, a woman will not hesitate to toss in all she has. Ironically,' she added with a snort, 'she often comes to resent that stolid silence after a few decades of their living together. *"When,"* she demands, *"will you ever give anything back?"*' She waved dismissively. 'No matter, I digress. Yes, I do trust you.'

'Then I will tell you that I am afraid, too. I want to run away from all of this. I wish I was back in the lake, with all feeling going away and so sleepy as everything starts going dark.'

'You were on death's edge, back then. Very well.' She took hold of his hand. 'Let me drag you into life's bright glory.'

'Now I am . . . terrified.'

She shook her head and smiled at him, drawing him to his feet. 'Don't be. Tonight, we start putting your broken world back together again.'

The settlement known as Muthra was empty. Everyone living there had fled, and not long past. Widowed Dayliss sat astride her horse at the edge of the ragged tree-line above the town. On her left was Tonith Agra and on her right, Sathal.

Elade Tharos had accompanied a scouting party that was even now making its way into Muthra's refuse-scattered main street. Far to the south, behind isolated copses, there was a low cloud of dust that seemed to stretch for a league or more, like a wall raised against them.

'Advance warning was expected,' Tonith Agra said.

Dayliss shrugged. 'So he says now. The smoke they would have seen above the forest could well have been from a wildfire, but they knew otherwise. This sudden evacuation was planned ahead of time and planned well.'

'An army awaits us,' said Sathal. 'That line of dust. Elade Tharos will have his battle.'

Their forces had divided the day before, with Delas Fana and Pake Gild accompanying the Rathyd and some of the forest tribes as they marched eastward, intending to strike Bringer's Foot before the day's end. And indeed there was smoke to the east as the settlement burned. Dayliss suspected they too had found it abandoned.

The Culvern River was fast and violent beneath a cloud of spray and mist where it ran up against Muthra's stone wall. Just beyond, as it reached more level ground, the waterway spread out enough to make something like an elongated lake, with two small treeless islands near the centre. A signal fire had been lit on the larger of the two islands, probably at dawn, and was now mostly burned down.

'The Malazans have known we were coming for some time,' said Dayliss. 'This does not bode well.'

'Malazan or not,' snapped Tonith Agra, 'they are southlanders, and all southlanders are children to us Teblor.'

Grimacing, Dayliss said, 'I have never liked the use of that word for the southlanders.'

'Nonetheless. Almost eight thousand mounted Teblor shall strike their line. They cannot withstand that.'

'Recall,' Sathal added, 'it is the Warleader's intent to simply drive through their defences and to then continue south. There is no time to waste. Something broke in the north – we all heard it at dawn. The flood is coming, even now, sister.'

Tonith Agra shrugged. 'And it must cross mountains, fill valleys, many of which lead to nowhere but high cliff-sides and sheer walls of stone. It may take days before it reaches these plains, and for all we know, its wrath will be spent by the time it does.'

'There is time, then,' Sathal said, nodding, 'for this battle. Once through, no force will be standing between us and the city of Blued.'

Dayliss was silent. In her mind she recalled when she and her daughter parted at midday yesterday. Pake Gild had been standing close to Rant as they readied to mount horses and ride into the wake of the Rathyd clan, and as Dayliss rode towards them, she sensed that something had changed. A moment longer and she understood.

It should not have surprised her. Rant was no child physically, after all. All he had lacked was the Teblor rite of passage. Her daughter, then, had taken him into her hands.

Even so, the look in Rant's eyes remained wary, though his nearness to Pake bespoke past intimacy. It had been, Dayliss suspected, a troubled night.

'Daughter,' said Dayliss as she reined in.

Delas Fana, the sembled Jheck packs and Gnaw's brood were gathered just beyond and Delas had drawn her horse around and was now walking it towards them.

'Mother.'

Was that a mocking challenge in her daughter's eyes, as if she expected a rebuke? 'It is good,' said Dayliss, 'that the man at your side has kept his knife sheathed. And that Elade Tharos is nowhere near us. You timed it well.'

After a moment, Pake nodded. 'There will be no challenge,' she said.

Delas Fana arrived. 'Widowed Dayliss, where are my sisters?'

'They elected to accompany the Warleader, Delas Fana, to make certain he remains distant. There was a fear that he might choose to speak one last time with the son of Karsa Orlong. I now think that they anticipated the possibility that the child would not remain a child.'

'We did,' said Delas Fana. 'Please convey to them my own cautious sentiments, that the three of you ride into battle together, that you guard one another well, and that your eyes and thoughts remain clear at all times in what's to come.'

Dayliss bowed her head towards Delas Fana. 'I shall. Thank you. What is clear is that our old world has ended. Of the future, nothing is clear. But can that not always be said, with each and every path awaiting us?'

'Some paths shout their danger, Widowed Dayliss. But the blood roars in our skulls and we hear nothing. The red mists rise, and we are blinded. The drums of our hearts promise glory and our livers burn hot with desire, clouding our minds to all else.'

'Our Warleader has spoken,' said Dayliss, her tone now cold, 'and we each have replied: *"Lead us,"* with our blades to his hand. This is his path and for us there can be no other.'

'So too avowed Bairoth Gild,' Delas Fana replied. 'And now his bones rot in the midden of Silver Lake.'

Widowed Dayliss felt her hands tighten, one upon the saddle horn, the other gripping the rein. 'It has been and always will be the Teblor way, Delas Fana. Do you speak the truth to wound me? If so, then perhaps one day soon we can revisit this moment, with our blades out.'

'Not to wound, Widowed Dayliss, but to warn.'

'If my husband and Delum Thord had not accompanied Karsa Orlong, he would never have prevailed in the Rathyd camp, and so, you would not have been born.'

'No one denies the paths behind us,' Delas Fana replied. 'And wisdom's only value in revisiting such history lies in the lesson we failed to learn the first time around. If unheeded, then wisdom's gift is lost.

Should I ever choose to revisit a path, it will not be you who I will face with my sword, but Elade Tharos.'

Sighing, Dayliss returned her attention to her daughter. But then, after a moment, she shifted her gaze to Rant and addressed him. 'You are now a warrior of the Teblor. You must be prepared to give your life to defend your kin. All Teblor are now your kin. Guard my daughter with your life, Rant Orlong.'

'I am not a Teblor,' said Rant. 'I am the son of my mother, whose blood was cursed. The name "Orlong" is not mine.'

'All warriors of the Teblor bear two names,' Dayliss said.

'Then name me Rant Bloodcurse.'

A deep chill whispered through her bones at such a horrid naming. It seemed to echo into a dark future like distant thunder that rolled on, and on. Her chest felt tight, her mouth suddenly dry. 'You reject us, then?'

'I will give my life defending everyone with me,' said Rant Blood-curse. 'But that loyalty has nothing to do with the Teblor blood in my veins. They are my friends and nothing else is needed.'

'No,' Widowed Dayliss decided, 'you are not Teblor.' Her attention turned to her daughter. 'Think well on that, beloved Pake. The warrior at your side refuses the allegiance of the Teblor. He stands virtually alone. Wolves and hounds are his tribe and a demon will command the knife at his hip.'

Pake Gild said, 'I once named Elade Tharos as Warleader. Now, I break the blade. No longer does he lead me. It is done.'

'What of that which lies between us?' Dayliss asked.

'Unchanged.'

'For now?'

'Always, Mother.'

That would have to do. Shaken to her core by the exchange, Dayliss drew up the rein and brought her mount around. She rode off at a canter and did not look back.

Now, only a day later, Widowed Dayliss studied the distant line of dust. 'One thing I do not understand,' she said. 'We know the Malazan forces are small. Only two legions to hold all of Northern Genabackis, divided into mere companies and scattered everywhere. We know, too, that the local Nathii and Genabarii conscripts are worthless and ill-equipped. So I wonder, who now opposes us?'

'Perhaps,' mused Sathal, 'they imagine us to be a small force. We Teblor never possessed their numbers, after all.'

'Either way,' resumed Dayliss, 'it seems that they have chosen to meet us. Therefore, they believe they can stop us there.' And she pointed.

'No more than a league south of Muthra.' She looked to Tonith Agra. 'Can they be so arrogant? So deluded?'

'They can,' replied Tonith Agra. 'It comes from wars against others of their kind – children fighting children – in which the Malazans usually prevail. But we shall be the fire before the flood. They are already dead and do not yet know it.'

Banners were being raised at this side of the town. 'The Warleader summons his army,' said Sathal.

They gathered reins and began their descent.

After Elade Tharos led his army through the town of Muthra, spilling out onto the farmland beyond, with Culvern River on their left flank, he rode out to face his assembled lines. Five tribes of the Teblor held the centre. Ganrel and Bright Knot were positioned closest to the high banks of the river. Upon the opposite side were a mass of Wilder tribes along with a late-arriving Eastern Saemdhi force of more than two thousand warriors wielding weapons made of bone, flint, wood and antler.

Elade Tharos had drawn his sword. It was just past noon and the sky overhead was cloudless, the sun blazing and the dusty air hot and dry. His oiled wooden weapon caught the sun's glare in lurid flashes. A headless bearskin rode his shoulders and down his back, the taloned back-paws dangling down past his hips with the forepaws crossed over his chest, pinned by an iron brooch just below his sternum. His long black hair was braided tight against his skull, awaiting the bone and turtle-shell helmet presently slung by a strap over his saddle horn. His forearms glistened as if oiled and the leather flaps protecting his elbows and knees were stained dark with sweat.

This Warleader, Dayliss allowed, looked the part. His youth was that of tempered steel, honed but not yet dulled. His jaw was free of hair and every feature was chiselled like a face in the rock. The hands, one gripping the sword and the other the rein, were large and strong. His eyes, when he trotted his horse opposite Dayliss, were clear and hard.

'They will oppose us!' he shouted. 'A decision they will soon regret! We are the wave before the wave, and when at last the waters swallow this land, their shores shall be awash in dead southlanders!'

In answer, the Teblor freed their weapons, but voiced no shout, as such displays were not the Teblor way. On the flanks, many of the tribals had little or no experience with the Teblor language, but upon seeing eight thousand wooden swords drawn, they screamed their war-cries, shamans among them bursting out of the front lines to dance in wild cavorts, blood spraying from ritual wounds upon forearms and shoulders.

'But listen well to what I now say!' roared Elade Tharos. 'Slay only those who stand in your way! We must not be halted, not slowed! We must drive a spear through their lines and then, as water breaching a dam, we pour through! Hold tight on the reins of bloodlust! Leave them to the drowning waters!'

It occurred to Widowed Dayliss that their Warleader had another option before him. They could simply ride around this entrenched Malazan position. But then, only the Teblor and the Bright Knot were mounted. The remaining tribes were all on foot, and with the elders, the lame, the pregnant women and the younger children to protect, along with what remained of their supplies, there would be no outrunning the enemy.

Though they were still too distant to make out details of the Malazan army, Dayliss was certain that some of their companies were mounted.

No, the enemy must be shattered, but as the Warleader said, it must be done quickly.

She rose on her stirrups and twisted round to look north.

The sky was strange above the mountains, grey and bruised clouds forming a solid canopy swallowing the peaks. A short while earlier the sky had filled with birds of all kinds, in places blotting out vast patches of sky. Hundreds of thousands, perhaps in the millions. She wondered what portent the Malazans read in such an event. Stranger things followed, as deer were seen bounding down out of the foothills, a few sprinting among marching tribals, eliciting surprised shouts and the occasional fruitless chase. Smaller game was everywhere, until some of the still unplanted fields seemed to swarm with its frantic retreat.

Was there time yet for this? Dayliss wasn't sure, but her hearts were beating faster, and not in anticipation of battle. As she settled back in her saddle, she glimpsed off to the west a herd of elk, among them a scattering of moose, running down a track between ploughed fields.

'We shall not wait for dawn! We must attack on this day, and by its end, the field of battle will be leagues in our wake! So ready your weapons!'

The army began to move. Elade Tharos brought his horse around, gesturing his clan-chiefs near. Dayliss nudged her mount and joined with Tonith Agra and Karak Thord as they rode to their Warleader, one and all heading south, for the moment at a walk.

Upon arriving, she saw a Wilder scout jogging towards them from the south. She had a battered Malazan crossbow on her back and was wearing bits of marine armour. A Bright Knot: others of her tribe rode to her on their shaggy ponies, lances upright and adorned with feathers and tattooed strips of human skin. The scout vaulted onto a horse that had been brought for her and moments later she and her kin drew up alongside Elade Tharos.

The Warleader addressed the scout in the Nathii tongue. 'Tell me, Sti Epiphanoz, all that you saw of the enemy disposition.'

'Warleader, this is what I have seen. There is one understrength legion of regulars divided into wings behind a ditch and a raised bank. Holding the centre is half a legion of marines formed into a wedge. This wedge stands before the earthworks. Directly behind it are three cohorts of Nathii Irregulars and local militia.' Sti Epiphanoz's expression twisted, making the silhouetted grass-blade tattoos on her face writhe across her features. 'But it is the wrong legion.'

Elade Tharos glanced at Tonith Agra and spoke in Teblor. 'Does this mean something to you, Tonith Agra?'

'I have only had passing contact with the Malazan military,' Tonith Agra replied with a shrug. 'Your scout clearly knows more than me.'

'But she is not Teblor,' said Elade Tharos. 'Worse, she once served as scout for the enemy. Perhaps she is telling us only what we wish to hear.'

Widowed Dayliss spoke. 'If indeed she once served, Warleader, then her eyes see true. Seek all its meaning from her, and then decide on its value.'

Elade Tharos faced Sti Epiphanoz. 'Explain all that is significant.'

'The legions rotate, Warleader. All over the empire. This keeps them from getting too settled, from marrying, having children, sinking roots. By the banners I could see, the half-legion of marines are the right ones. They have been here two years now. They are the Fourteenth Legion, Second and Fourth Battalions. I was in their Auxiliary, but I see none of the Auxiliary – they must be somewhere else.' She made a strange warding gesture across her face, and then continued. 'The other banners tell me the legion of regulars are the Thirty-first. I do not know where they have come from, but they were not here two years ago, and none are Nathii or Genabarii. These details are perhaps significant, perhaps not. Set them behind you for now, Warleader, and heed instead a detail I have already noted.'

'And what detail is that, scout?'

Disappointment flitted across her face. 'The wedge formation of the marines, Warleader, and the fact that they are on *this* side of the entrenchments.'

'Then they seek to stand in place? They are avowed to never retreat?'

The Bright Knot scout turned her head to say something to her kin in their own language. A few swore. Others spat. She then faced Elade Tharos again and said, 'No such vows bind them, Warleader. They are not interested in standing against our charge. They intend to *attack*.'

369

'Then they are fools,' Elade Tharos said, laughing.

'No fools among Malazan marines,' Sti Epiphanoz insisted, visage darkening. 'I did not serve long among them, but I have heard rumours—'

'Which mean nothing, scout,' cut in Elade Tharos.

Her lips pressed tight for a moment, and then Sti Epiphanoz spoke again. 'They have scouted us just as we have scouted them, Warleader.'

'What? Did you see such scouts?'

'I did. In fact, we passed one another within shouting range. I cursed them. They cursed me. I brandished my lance. They showed me their bared asses.' She paused, and then shrugged. 'I deem they won the exchange, for the asses were hairy and ugly.'

'That will be all, Sti Epiphanoz. Rejoin your flank.'

'Aye,' she replied, and then swore under her breath and said, 'Yes.'

Widowed Dayliss watched the troop ride off towards the flank nearest the river.

'We Teblor shall charge these marines,' said Elade Tharos. 'Our flanks shall engage and overrun the regulars. Is it not clear,' he suddenly added, 'that the Bright Knot fear the marines? I knew not what the scout said to her kin, but I heard displeasure and fear in their answers.'

Dayliss shifted her gaze slightly and met Tonith Agra's eyes. The truth passed in silence between them. *No, Warleader, their displeasure was with you, that you did not even note the odd placement of the marines, and from that was born, indeed, fear. But not of the marines, alas.*

'Are there provisions,' Tonith Agra asked, somewhat abruptly, 'for the swift alteration of our plan of attack, Warleader?'

'Provisions?'

'In case we must shift focus. Banners? Flags? Horns or drums?'

'The enemy shall be forced into undesired changes, Tonith Agra, not the Teblor.'

'As you say,' Tonith Agra replied in a flat tone. She edged her mount away, glanced across at Dayliss one more time, and then rode to join Sathal, who was near the head of the Uryd clans.

Widowed Dayliss sighed. *I will find you and I will guard you both. Perhaps, if needed, we can guide as well all of the Uryd.* She reminded herself to speak privately with Karak Thord as soon as she could. Of course, it could well be that her worries were unfounded. But this impending battle was not in Teblor style at all. This was not a raid, which so critically depended upon surprise. Nor was this a hunt for fleeing raiders, relying upon relentless pursuit and tenacity. Lastly, this was not the simple crossing of blades, warrior against warrior.

No, this was the Malazan style of battle. And, *gods below*, they did it well.

Suddenly, out of the dust ahead, the enemy lines appeared, foremost among them the central wedge of marines. Dayliss had no idea what the distinction was between marine and regular. She assumed the former were shock-troops, heavies of some sort, or simply the best-trained in the Malazan forces.

That wedge was already in motion, spreading its wings, flattening out somewhat but not entirely. Already advancing.

Then a detail caught her attention, even as she began dropping back to rejoin the Uryd. *Their shields remain on their backs. Their weapons are not even drawn.*

A new wave of fleeing birds swept directly overhead, adding their raucous cries. Crows and ravens, darkening the day as they swept towards the Malazans.

Screams and war-cries bruised the sky above the Warleader's forces. Weapons pounded shields. Witches and warlocks shrieked and loosed blood to the spirits. The ground trembled underfoot.

The enemy said nothing, did nothing – except, of course, for that flattened wedge drawing closer, step by heavy step. And as of yet, not one shield drawn round, not one sword pulled from its scabbard.

All at once, this day was not warm at all.

The Teblor charge towards the marines gathered pace. The confusion in the mind of Widowed Dayliss deepened. It seemed the Malazan marines were thickening their flanks, the centre now only a few ranks deep.

She rode with Sathal on her right, Tonith Agra on her left. Karak Thord had pulled ahead in his eagerness to close with the enemy. Far to the left, Elade Tharos was at the forefront, riding out in the company of his chosen warriors to form a spear-point aimed directly at that thinning centre.

She looked again at the marines. No shields were readied. No weapons were drawn, and it seemed that the attention of the entire force was now fixed on the two flanking attacks of Wilders, both mounted and on foot, and both already lagging behind the Teblor.

Widowed Dayliss drew her bloodsword. The two armies, Teblor and marines, were now half a thousand paces apart. The sound of horse hoofs was a thunder that reverberated through her entire body. Her breaths came faster, her hearts pounding hard.

Thunderous detonations suddenly rocked among the front riders off to her left. She caught a glimpse of billowing clouds of dirt and stones and pieces of horse and warrior, as the Warleader's spear-point vanished amidst a series of eruptions.

What—

Directly ahead, Karak Thord and his horse seemed to rise on a column of dirt and smoke. The explosion tore them both to pieces. Her own beast stumbled, its chest suddenly spilling blood from dozens of wounds. Another eruption, closer, and all at once Widowed Dayliss was cartwheeling through the air. Dust, savage heat, the bite of wounds all along one side of her body. She landed hard, rolled and then came to a jarring halt as she struck the legless torso of a horse. She saw her own mount, more than ten paces off, thrashing on the ground, two of its legs missing below the fetlock.

Numbed, looking about in a daze, she saw Sathal lying a few paces away. Her right leg and right arm were both gone, the last of her body's blood even now draining into the mud. Her blue eyes glittered in an empty stare.

The eruptions continued, filling the world. Deafened and still dazed, Dayliss sought to climb to her feet, but her left leg wasn't working. Looking down, she struggled to identify that leg. The entire thigh was nothing but shredded meat. Shards of bone jutted out like spikes. She sat back down in shock.

Dust obscured almost everything. It seemed that the charge had been shattered. She saw horses running in random directions, many of them no longer bearing a rider, many of them sheathed in blood. She saw warriors lying on the ground, some moving, many not. Others staggered past missing limbs or covered in wounds.

Somewhere in the distance, beyond the nearby explosions which were growing more infrequent, she heard a rhythmic roar, punctuated by more distant detonations that somehow sounded different: drawn out, like a two-person saw cutting through a tree trunk. Above this, waves of high-pitched whining, and beyond all of this, faint screams.

Sorcery?

There was no feeling in her ravaged leg. She was still sitting, somehow holding herself up with one arm positioned behind her. The worst of the dust clouds had rolled past. She could see the far right flank of Wilders. It was a line of flames, blood and death, as, step by inexorable step, that entire side of the marines marched towards the Wilders, magic pouring in erratic but almost solid waves from the front ranks.

They knew we Teblor would shrug that off, warrior and horse both. They knew it and cared not. But then . . . what struck us if not sorcery?

She could see craters in the ground on all sides, smoke rising from each one.

Munitions. Planted in the soil, sown like deadly seeds. What manner of war is this? She only now noticed that she no longer gripped her sword and could not see it anywhere. Had she still held it, she would be staring at the blade in this moment, overwhelmed by its obsolescence.

What manner . . . Even as the question clawed through her mind, engulfed in a combination of horror and indignation, Dayliss swore under her breath and shook her head. It didn't matter, did it? Elade Tharos had led them all into a deadly trap. That Bright Knot scout had been worried, alarmed, suspicious, but the Warleader had dismissed it all. Here, on this field and in this moment, she was witness to the death of the Teblor.

The roaring sound grew louder still, and the earth began to tremble beneath her. She looked for Tonith Agra but could not find any sign of her or her horse. Horns were sounding from the Malazan side. They seemed frantic.

Still, there could not have been enough of these buried munitions to kill us all. The front of the charge would have detonated most of them. Killing how many? A thousand? Two thousand? Leaving most of our warriors – she twisted to look back the way they had come.

And stared, momentarily uncomprehending.

The northern sky was half gone. Murky white columns were lifting up and out from the distant valleys. The higher passes had vanished, lost in a writhing storm of . . . *water.* She saw lesser peaks inundated in the mad rush down to lower land. She had known, but still she could not believe the sheer volume of water coming for them.

Gods below. We are all dead. Teblor, Wilder, Malazan, Nathii – all of us, dead.

Now she could see the frenzied wave devouring the settlement of Muthra, striking buildings with such force that they exploded, splinters flying upward only to then be swallowed up by the advancing, towering wall of water. Rushing forward across the plain.

'Dayliss!'

The scream drew her round. She saw Tonith Agra, thirty paces away. She was sheathed in dust and darker stains of bloody mud. It seemed that one side of her face was gone, stripped down to the bone. How she had managed to speak at all baffled Dayliss.

After that single scream, Tonith Agra stood unmoving on the very edge of the crater out of which she had apparently climbed, but still facing Dayliss.

She is in shock. She doesn't understand.

Is it not better that way?

Another warrior appeared, running, stumbling, falling to the ground. Moments later scores more appeared, many mounted, galloping southward. The first warrior made to rise only to be crushed beneath the hoofs of a horse.

Voices were shouting. Not Teblor – Dayliss turned again.

There were Malazan marines everywhere, running into the mass of Teblor. She saw them waving weaponless hands, heard their bellowed shouts. Two rushed towards a mob of Teblor that had suddenly appeared, all on foot. Children, elders, warriors.

The warriors closed on the marines and cut them both down.

Then a dozen Bright Knot rode into view, shouting at the Teblor warriors. Dayliss saw Sti Epiphanoz among them.

'They will raise sorcery!' she was screaming. 'Stop killing them! Move! Move behind them – for the centre – head for the centre!'

Dayliss shifted her attention back to Tonith Agra. A marine was running up to her. 'Can you walk? Quickly – head straight south! We're raising a wall of magic! Can you try and—'

The air cracked. Marine and Tonith Agra vanished inside a bursting cloud of dirt and stones and flames. The concussion flattened Dayliss, her face burning from a spray of gravel. Stunned, she tried blinking to clear her vision, but one eye wasn't working at all. Reaching up, she felt there nothing but a bloody socket.

Somehow, she found herself balanced on one knee, upright once more. Where Tonith Agra and the marine had been was a huge crater still gushing smoke and steam.

The marines had run onto this killing ground. They had known the risk. It made no sense.

Someone arrived, a hand closing and gripping her left shoulder. She half-turned, saw a marine, red-bearded, his face flushed and slick with sweat. 'Can you understand me?'

Dayliss nodded.

'Then call to as many of your kin as you can – get them gathered up behind me. There's no time for any more running – we're scattered all the way down Jarak's Road as it is.' He waved at a number of stumbling figures. 'These ones! Call 'em here and be quick about it!'

Dayliss followed the direction of his gesture. 'Uryd!' she shouted. 'To me, quickly! Put that sword away, Ketarst! This marine is a mage! He's going to try and—'

She stopped, turned to the marine. 'You cannot – we resist your sorcery, soldier. Too near us and it might not work at all!'

'We know that,' he growled, pausing to spit and then swear in some foreign language. 'Stay at least five paces back, that's all. It's try or give up and die.'

'What care you about us?' Dayliss wanted to know, *needed* to know.

He blinked at her, and then moved past. 'Five paces and gather yourselves up close to each other.'

'I don't—'

'I'm the bow, woman. And inside my bow-wave is your only hope of salvation. Not that I'm guaranteeing shit, mind you.'

She watched him take five paces to stand, his back to her, widening his stance and both hands lifting.

A dozen Teblor now closed in around Dayliss. None spoke.

The marine shouted, '*Here it comes!*'

An instant later, the entire world dissolved into chaos. She saw the flash of magic from the marine, saw the water strike it hard enough to push the man back half a pace. Steam poured around the marine, swallowing him, and to either side, amidst steaming spray, dark, swirling walls of rushing water ripped past, so close Dayliss could have reached out to touch them. Behind her came a single scream, as a warrior at the edge of the now huddled group was gathered away, arm and shoulder sheared off before the onrushing current snatched up the rest of him – and gone.

Overhead, light vanished as the torrent inundated the marine's wavering, hissing wedge of magic. The air was suddenly frigid, their breaths pluming.

Dayliss saw enormous boulders rolling by to either side, driven ever onward by the current. She saw a horrifying stream of bodies sweep past, but only briefly, and then more stones, gravel, uprooted trees, animal carcasses and chunks of ice.

The world lost all colour, the greyness dimming as the depths increased.

She looked again to the lone marine.

It seemed impossible. She could not imagine what it took to defy this flood. She could see how he was leaning far forward, both hands outthrust, his head bowed.

The rushing walls of water seemed to shudder.

There were two children crouched down behind her, their eyes wide.

'Fuck!'

At his curse, Dayliss snapped her attention back to the marine. His armour was falling away, shrivelled and blackened. The coarse woollen tunic beneath seemed to seethe, turning grey and then white. When it fell away, it was nothing but ash, leaving him naked.

A moment later she saw his pale skin darken to somewhere between red and purple. Then blood was streaming from ruptures all over his body. He began saying something, difficult to hear amidst the endless roar of water.

A small hand rested on her left wrist. Unable to tear her attention away from the nameless marine, Dayliss gathered up the child, and then reached back for the other one. Held them both close. 'Be at peace, my sweet ones,' she whispered. 'Almost over now.'

Then, with unnatural clarity, she heard him.

'*I'm sorry. I'm sorry. I'm—*'

She caught a glimpse of his body shredding before her eyes. And then the dark hammer descended on them all.

A score of Bright Knot and a few hundred Teblor crouched on ground growing ever muddier as salty rain poured down. Sti Epiphanoz shivered uncontrollably but was not yet ready to join her comrades who all huddled together for warmth. It was not right. Not right to duck one's head, finding comfort in the presence of kin and allies. Not right to think still of tribes and peoples.

They were alive because of a ring of Malazan marines, whose sorcery had carved out a ragged dome of salvation, now beneath fathoms of water. That ring of humanity had begun at least three ranks deep.

Now it was down to two ranks and the marines were shouting at one another, arguing over something, none of which Sti could make out from where she crouched.

Sti Epiphanoz made gestures with her hands, fingers waving, fluttering, weaving her tale of witnessing that no one would ever see. She signed for the world of gods and spirits, signed with savage intention, signed to shriek defiance at the universe.

The water seemed to be circling them now, although she was sure that was an illusion. No reason for it to go round and round, chewing away at the magic, at the men and women who were casting it, reaching in again and again to snatch up one who faltered.

I will watch and I will sing with my hands this song. The enemy met us with fire. They struck us down in row upon row. Against them we were helpless. Not one managed to close, not one to loose an arrow or throw a javelin.

I sing of that magic, that devouring maw of death. And now, I sing of the enemy who met us a second time.

To die for us. I sing my questions, not one of which will ever be answered. I sing this in wonder. Could they have prevailed, had they stayed together? Could they have saved their own comrades, there in the trenches behind them? No, that line was too long, too far away. There was no time for that, no time at all for that. Instead, they chose us.

No swords, no shields, and suddenly, no magic stealing our lives. Now, hands reaching out. Commands to get behind them.

Could they have prevailed, had they drawn tight with all their magic combined?

Could they have marched, step by muddy step, in that long retreat to dry land?

Could they have done some other thing instead of this false hope? Could they have shown mercy by continuing the slaughter?

Could they have dragged us in small groups, here, there, into a warren, a spirit realm? But not all warrens can host one of flesh and blood. Realms of fire, realms of dead air, realms of demons, realms too small, too weak, realms of all-devouring chaos. Some who could chose not to, to stand instead beside their comrades.

I sing to them dying one by one. The rain now a torrent of ice from above. I sing of the dome shrinking, the circling, circling water drawing ever closer.

I sing of the Malazan marines, who could not explain it either.

This song to the water, the water to the sky, the sky to the ground in weeping tears.

Heed this, gods. Take note of this. My song will not die.

Abruptly, a full third of the remaining marines backed away from the ring. Water gushed in, ripped at the circle, but those remaining drove it back. The marines now inside the ring rushed towards the mass of refugees in the centre.

The roar of the water was too loud for shouted commands. Sti saw the marines signalling with their hands, as if weaving songs of their own. Then she saw them splitting apart, moving into the press of refugees, corralling small groups and pulling them away from the others. Marine after marine did the same, each taking a dozen or so Teblor and Wilder.

A hand plucked at her, then she was being pushed back into a crowd, the marine doing the pushing a woman with hair so short Sti Epiphanoz could see her scalp. The tears streaming down her cheeks were red, below bloodshot eyes.

Behind her, the remaining marines began to crumple, their sorcery failing, until a mere dozen remained.

I sing the impossible—

The world darkened suddenly. Sti Epiphanoz heard screams. Curses. Someone collided with her and she fell to the ground, but her hands continued flashing, gesturing.

I sing to the gods. Against the mortal heart, you are nothing. You are—

All light vanished.

CHAPTER TWENTY

'Do you give a shit?'

First question asked of
a potential marine recruit

Dawn, two days earlier, Silver Lake . . .

CAPTAIN GRUFF STOOD FIVE PACES DISTANT FROM THE NEAREST
soldier, his leather hauberk freshly stained red, as were the thin
leather gloves on his hands. He seemed to be whistling under
his breath, though no sound could be heard. His eyes were fixed on the
tree-line. Spindle pulled his gaze away from the captain and turned to
review his squad.

The four soldiers were lined up on the berm, two paces between
them, although Say No was perhaps a bit closer on Paltry Skint's flank.
After a moment, Say No glanced over and caught Spindle's eyes. With
a sheepish shrug, she resumed the proper distance. Benger stood closest
to Spindle and Corporal Morrut was at the far end.

The dawn air was cool, the sky clear overhead. The tree-line opposite
was now a mass of figures, tribals and Teblor, jostling, weapons out,
edging ever closer to the clearing's broad swath of mud and tangled
grasses. Off to the right, all the way past the town's berm and therefore opposite Balk's camp, more warriors crowded the straggly line of
saplings and brush that marked the forest's fringe.

At Spindle's side, Benger spoke. 'We're the weak line here, Sergeant.
I couldn't illusion a flaming fart if I tried right now.' He dropped his
voice and added, 'Then there's the captain . . .'

Spindle squinted, watching the shadows shorten all along the tree-
line. When the sun's light finally reached the open field, he suspected,
the enemy would charge.

'I get Morrut anchoring the flank,' Benger continued. 'His warren is vicious and he's the furthest away from the captain. And our two heavies got plenty of shit to throw, but still . . .'

'Nerves, Benger?' Spindle smiled at him.

'Aye, worse than ever. I'm standing here with nothing but a short-sword and a shield. Feeling naked, in other words.'

'You get used to it,' Spindle replied. 'I've mostly given up on magic. If Jheck show up, however, I guess I may have to use it. I don't see any mounted among the enemy, after all, so no horses to spook.'

Benger grunted. 'You used to be an artist, didn't you?'

Spindle shot him a quick look. 'Where did you hear that?'

'Can't recall. Something about you painting Dragon decks. Something about a map table, too, maybe. And you doing readings.'

Spindle shrugged. 'Another life.'

'What was it like?' Benger persisted. 'Being a Bridgeburner?'

Spindle considered not answering. Then he shrugged. 'Each day, no different from any other day, Benger. Squads and soldiers and officers, and orders, always orders. Faces slowly fading in my memory. Friends, fools, truths and lies, and more grief than a soul can stand.'

Benger was silent for a few breaths, and then said, 'Sorry, Sergeant. Bad time to stir that up.'

'Can't imagine a good time,' Spindle replied. 'Okay, here it comes.'

Agitated motion in that distant line, the Teblor pushing to the fore-front.

'Sunyd ex-slaves,' said Captain Gruff. 'Can you see their wrists? The shackle scars? Dear me, this is a sad day, my friends. Let us hope—'

With a roar, the mass of Teblor surged into the clearing.

At almost the same moment, the detonations began.

The reverberations from the blasts rocked back everyone standing on the berm. Black, brown and red columns of dirt erupting into the air, bodies shredded, limbs torn away and spinning. The front lines simply vanished.

Spindle knew that his squad was the weakest of the three, under-manned and low on effective magery. For this reason, they stood behind the deepest field of mines.

'That should—'

But Spindle didn't hear the captain's next words. No one could, as the Sunyd kept coming.

The detonations resumed, louder, closer. Blood rained down along with body parts, some striking the embankment's slope. And still the ex-slaves came on, struggling to close up gaps, slowing as they clambered over broken bodies, sliding into smoky craters, running into billowing clouds, only to step on yet another mine.

379

The blasts seemed to be ceaseless, drawing ever closer to the embankment, and the six marines standing atop it. The sound was deafening, the entire field disappearing in smoke and raining mud.

Disbelieving, Spindle watched the hapless Teblor keep coming, now down to a few score. Close enough to see their faces, smoke-blackened, eyes wide in frozen expressions that Spindle could not – and would never be able to – read. Faces vanishing inside new eruptions, and now the blood rained down on the marines, along with pieces of meat and bone.

The last eruption echoed forlornly, slowly replaced by terrible cries of agony, and upon the killing field, none stood. In the forest beyond, figures still moved about, but it seemed they were now in flight, staying among the trees as they headed southward.

Wiping at his face, Spindle turned to his squad.

Benger stood hugging himself, his face streaked with tears. Paltry Skint was on her knees, helmet off, head hanging. Say No crouched next to her, one hand running again and again down her comrade's short, auburn hair. Beyond them, Corporal Morrut stood motionless as a statue, spattered in red mud. He seemed to be talking to no one.

A hand closed on Spindle's shoulder, drawing him around to see Gruff, his face flushed as he spoke. Through the ceaseless ringing in his ears, the captain's voice came to him as if from across a crowded room. ' . . . your squad in order, dammit! The two heavies need to go out there, but carefully—'

Spindle shook his head. 'Can't do that, sir.'

'There are wounded—'

'I know, sir, but the ground that's unexploded out there, sir, has moved. Shifted about. We won't know where to find any untouched mines. It's too risky.'

'They – they kept coming!'

Spindle understood the horror in Gruff's eyes. He understood, as well, the desperate need to do something. Anything. The faint cries continued in the field; here and there came some small motion from a body, a hand and forearm lifting from the mud, black and red-streaked. 'Captain. Listen to me. *We can't go out there.*'

For an instant, it seemed that Gruff would strike him. Then, eyes widening, he backed off, his expression flattening. 'Of course, Sergeant, you're right. Forgive me.'

'No need for that, sir. I saw you shouting, waving, trying to get them to stop their advance, but you had no hope of success. Few could even see you through the smoke and dirt.'

More detonations sounded, this time from further south, perhaps a half-dozen or so. Then they stopped. A moment later, an entirely different sound reached them.

Ah, shit. 'Captain—'

'I'm on my way. Stay here with your squad, Spindle – until you get them back on their feet at least. Then join me on the south berm if you can.'

'Aye, sir.'

Captain Gruff descended the embankment, vanished among the buildings of the town.

Spindle swung round, and with one hand grasped Benger by a sleeve. 'Come on, we have two heavies to drag to their feet. Corporal Morrut! Look lively and get over here!'

'That was strange,' said Stillwater. A dozen wolves had rushed out from the forest, followed by a few hundred Wilders. It seemed that their destination had been Balk's camp. Most of the wolves had avoided the mines, but not so the Wilders. After the first explosions settled, revealing craters and scattered bodies, the survivors staggered back in retreat. The remaining wolves entered the camp of the mercenaries.

'Jheck,' said Blanket. 'It does indeed seem that our company of mercenaries no longer works for us. This, while anticipated, still constitutes a complication.'

'Meaning, we're fucked even more than before,' offered Anyx Fro as she continued to make adjustments to her Iron Maw, which was now pointed towards the mercenary camp.

'Only modestly so,' Folibore said, 'and this may well work to our advantage, since we concentrated the mines between us and Balk's Company. After all, I counted seven going off in that field, meaning there are only five remaining this side of that tree-line. Given what was surely witnessed along the east berm, the enemy no doubt assumes a similar concentration awaiting them, well, everywhere. Hence that quick retreat.'

Stillwater turned to the heavy. 'So what you're saying is you all banked on the real trouble coming from Balk, not the forest.'

'Timing is everything,' said Sergeant Drillbent. 'Stillwater, any sneaky magic coming up on us from Balk's camp?'

She blinked at him. 'Why ask me?'

'Just answer me, for fuck sake!'

'They're cleaned out over there, Sergeant,' Stillwater replied, hoping that wasn't too obtuse even while remaining appropriately noncommittal.

'But things are volatile hereabouts,' Anyx Fro added. 'Wood spirits all stirred up about something.'

'Probably us,' Blanket suggested.

'Eyes on the forest!' Drillbent commanded.

'Damn,' muttered Folibore.

The Wilders were gathering once more, but this time opposite the southeast corner of the embankment.

'Can't someone tell them to come the other way?'

Stillwater wasn't sure who had asked that question. Probably Blanket. Or Snack, but the corporal was seriously distracted for some reason, constantly glancing northward and mumbling under his breath, so not likely him.

'Raise your warrens,' Drillbent commanded.

'That's just typical,' snapped Anyx Fro. 'And where's the Second Squad? Oh, right, picnicking on the west embankment, where nobody's facing them! Shrake always gets them the easy jobs!'

'They're hesitating,' Stillwater observed. 'Hey, Sergeant, I could, uh, sneak down there and cut up a few. Might get them to reconsider.'

'Not yet,' Drillbent said, squinting at the Wilders slowly edging out from the tree-line. 'No, let's make our suggestion a bit more direct. Anyx, Blanket, hammer them. Just once, mind you.'

'Can I use my Iron Maw?'

'No! Magic! Bloody their noses!'

Sorcery erupted from Blanket, and an instant later from Anyx Fro. Two crackling, horizontal columns of raging energy crossed the field, fast as quarrels, to slam into the nearest mass of Wilders.

Amidst distant screams and fires burning along that part of the tree-line, the world seemed to pause for a long, drawn-out breath. Then, with a roar, the Wilders charged.

'Oh,' said Folibore, 'that didn't work.'

The two Jheck had sembled before Commander Balk, both bearing wounds. Standing off to one side, having just given orders for all troops to form up facing the town's embankment, Lieutenant Ara considered drawing a few steps closer to hear the exchange. There had been a standing order, issued by Balk only a few days ago, to make no hostile actions towards any wolves sighted near or approaching their camp. A strange order that only now made sense.

She was, she admitted, astonished. But it was the only conclusion she could draw, given the circumstances.

We were hired by Jheck. But . . . how long ago?

Balk had begun moving his company in this direction over a year ago, taking small contracts along the way, the last one before the Malazans being that deranged baron in the forest. There was nothing preventing a company from holding more than one contract, after all, so long as one did not interfere with the other. Still, Balk had kept this one close to his chest, confiding in no one at all.

She felt slighted. She'd known about the continuous contacts with Wilders from the forest and had naturally assumed that those tribes had been the ones to tender the contract.

But this new complication left her in confusion, which only deepened when Balk cursed once, loudly, and then turned to find Ara, calling her over with a curt gesture.

She approached. 'We're ready to move on the town,' she said. 'Vengeance long overdue, wouldn't you say, Captain?'

'You can now set that aside, Ara, because we won't be attacking the Malazans.'

'What?'

'I finally have specific instructions. Find me three riders, I need to send a message to Captain Gruff, immediately.'

Ara blinked. 'Sir, I would imagine Gruff to be somewhat busy at the moment.'

'That's why I want three riders trying to track him down. As for our forces, tell them to stand down and begin striking the camp. We may not have long.'

'Balk—'

'Just do it! Find me three riders and be on about it, damn it!'

She stepped back, both hurt and alarmed. 'Yes, sir,' she snapped.

There would be no fast exit from the east embankment, as Wilders were returning to the forest edge, many Saemdhi among them. Spindle repositioned his undermanned squad, placing Corporal Morrut in the centre this time. He could see Bonecasters among the Saemdhi.

There were probably only a few mines left in the ground. This time it would be sorcery that decided things.

'Benger, head over to Sergeant Shrake. We may need some help, especially if these Wilders prove as stubborn as the Teblor.'

'Her whole squad?' Benger asked.

Spindle thought about it for a moment, then shook his head. 'Three at the most. The rest may be needed for the south berm.'

They could hear sorcery, but only two mines had detonated in the field between Balk's Company and the berm. 'More Wilders from the forest are harassing Drillbent's squad, I should think,' Spindle continued. 'So far. But if Balk makes his move, things could get very hairy.'

'Sergeant!'

At Paltry Skint's cry, Spindle turned to study the distant Wilders. The Bonecasters were now out in the clearing, dancing about as they began a ritual of some sort. Behind them crowded a thick mass of Saemdhi, armed with flint, antler and bone weapons.

There didn't seem to be much choice, Spindle decided with an internal sigh. 'Corporal, if you would.'

'The shamans?'

'Aye.'

'How many of them?'

'I don't like the look of that ritual. So . . . all of them.'

Morrut raised his hands to about waist-height. Slowly, the fingers half-curled, those hands began twisting inward, from supination to pronation.

The dozen or so dancing, cavorting Bonecasters began staggering, as if drunk. Then one cried out, his bared chest suddenly swelling horribly, skin splitting in red spurts. His torso exploded, the mangled organs flung outward. A moment later and the others were dying in the same fashion, bodies bursting, and every organ tumbling into view was dark, twisted, desiccated.

As the last body toppled, all movement ceased.

Morrut's hands were now fully pronated, the fingers fully curled into fists, the knuckles white as bone. Then they relaxed and he let them fall.

'Gods below,' Paltry Skint muttered, 'I will never get used to that.'

The Saemdhi should have retreated then. They had no reason for persisting in this attack. Instead, they poured into the clearing with wild, bestial shrieks.

Spindle needed to give no command. His three mages unleashed their warrens.

And the slaughter began.

Less than two thousand paces south of Silver Lake, Oams swung his mount around and cantered back to the head of the column, where rode Fist Sevitt along with the two battalion commanders.

He reined in. 'Fist Sevitt, the mercenaries have not engaged as far as I can see. This attack is coming from the forest, and I think only one squad's opposing them.'

'Strength of the enemy?' the Fist asked.

'Thousands,' Oams replied, his horse shifting nervously under him, sensing his growing desperation.

'Very well,' Sevitt said, her expression revealing nothing. 'We shall double-time our foot soldiers.' She then turned to one of the battalion commanders. 'Which squads have you selected, Daisy Broke?'

The man blinked, as if startled by the question. 'The Eighth, Eleventh and Twenty-third, Fist.'

'A captain attached?'

'No. These three will each travel a distinct warren, then act independently once arriving.'

'I understand that this is their habit,' Sevitt said, 'but I would prefer one of the sergeants to be in overall command once they arrive, to facilitate communication. Now, the sergeants for those three squads would be Wheeze, Sulban and Bellam Nom, correct?'

Oams could see Daisy Broke's astonishment, and in reply he simply nodded.

'Make it the Daru, Bellam,' Sevitt decided. 'Now, send them in immediately. I hear a growing weariness in that sorcery.'

No fucking kidding! But Oams bit back on that ill-advised response. He watched Commander Daisy Broke ride at haste back to his battalion, then cleared his throat and said, 'Fist, I request permission to rejoin my squad—'

'I understand how difficult this is for you, Oams,' Sevitt cut in. 'But no, you stay with me. If I am to parley with these mercenaries, I will need your eyes and ears and above all, your mind, since you know this Andrison Balk and we do not.'

'I barely know him at all, Fist.'

One brow lifted beneath the rim of the Fist's helmet. 'Well enough to recognize him at a distance?'

'Well, yes—'

'That may be necessary, Oams, if the man is engaged in something we'd rather not see continued, and I find myself needing to send in a Claw. Do you understand me?'

Oams nodded. 'Aye, Fist.'

She kicked her horse into motion. 'Then be at my side, soldier, we're wasting time.'

Horns sounded behind them, announcing the rise to double-time.

The cobbles of the imperial road were loud as the riders edged into a canter at the head of the legion column, but it was nothing compared to the ferocious sorcery flashing between the forest and the town's south berm. Oams took a moment to stand in his stirrups and glance behind him as the horns sounded a second time, calling for quick-time.

If the two battalions of the Marine Legion were about to head straight into a battle with Balk's Company, it would have to be in a narrow wedge formation, matching the width of the column presently still on the road. It was awkward, but Oams knew their attack would be devastating. Balk's Company wouldn't stand a chance against almost two thousand marines.

He hoped it wouldn't come to that and thought to advise the Fist riding beside him that those mercenaries wouldn't lay down weapons a second time, even if a Claw held Balk with a knife to the throat. Meaning the marines would have to attack no matter what, and if that happened, there'd be no time for the mercenaries to break. It would be all over in less than fifty heartbeats.

The squads now jogging behind him knew well the story of the 2nd Company's first clash with Balk. It was quite possible the marines wouldn't be interested in taking prisoners.

If it came to that, a lot of people were about to die.

Fist Sevitt startled him with her next words. 'If I do send in a Claw, Oams, it will be for the swift kill, you understand. Captain Balk, his lieutenant and all the sergeants.'

'Aye, Fist.'

'With their command structure eliminated, how will the mercenaries react? In your opinion.'

In my opinion. Fuck. 'Badly, Fist. For the first few breaths at least.'

'Ah. Unfortunate, then.'

She made a strange sound and he glanced over to see her face pinched as she added, 'I do hope I have made it understood to the marines behind us that the constraining orders set upon the Second Company came from me, and that the mercenaries were merely fortunate in that they avoided slaughter the first time. And that fortune may have now made them somewhat overconfident, for which they are not to blame.'

Oams set his gaze away from her and back to the way ahead. He could see smoke and dust lying like a wreath over the town. 'I'm sure you have, Fist,' he said. 'But it might not make much difference. I doubt anyone will be standing after the first punch of magic.'

Sevitt then turned to the remaining battalion commander, riding on her left. 'Sound judgement, Deader?'

'Probably,' she replied. 'It's not rational and we all know that, Fist. But there will be a little extra in that punch, no matter what we command. In that, Oams is right.'

'That is indeed unfortunate, then. Well, let us hope it does not come to that.'

This casual conversation was driving Oams mad. He yearned to stab his heels into his mount's flanks, to ride to his squad-mates. It sounded seriously messy over there, and he belonged with them.

Sudden renewed eruptions of sorcery stutter-flashed ahead.

'Excellent,' said Sevitt, 'the relief squads have arrived.'

*

Drillbent was spent, down on his knees, no magic left in him. Accordingly, Stillwater moved up to put herself between the sergeant and about half a thousand screaming savages. There wasn't much point, of course, but she'd make things ugly for whoever managed to climb the slope. A glance to her right showed Snack and Anyx Fro, the former defending against pulses of nasty spirit magic – with her warren bristling, Stillwater could see those spinning, fulminating attacks, like giant aerial fists composed of scores of small wood spirits all tangled together. Wilder magic was scary.

Anyx Fro, meanwhile, was readying her Iron Maw, since her Thyr was exhausted. Before the two of them, a few hundred Wilders had almost reached the base of the slope, forcing Anyx to angle her iron tube-thing downwards.

On Stillwater's left, Folibore and Blanket had been conducting an alternating series of messy, deadly magic, driving the Wilders all the way back to the forest's edge, where they gathered once more, moments from repeating their wild charge.

It'd be different this time, since the two heavies were spent and were now readying their mundane weapons.

Oh well. Poor 4th Squad! She'd miss them, possibly dearly.

Until she didn't.

Something made a loud, cracking sound. Stillwater turned to see if the Iron Maw had ripped itself apart – but no, instead, it had fallen over and Anyx Fro was swearing and jumping up and down – and there were more marines with them, at least two squads. That sound had been the ripping open of a warren.

4th Company. She saw Sergeant Wheeze, and there was Pestle, from Sulban's squad.

The sorcery that came from the newcomers cleared the field before them, leaving little more than smouldering ash and burnt bones. Then Stillwater saw panicked motion along the tree-line, bodies falling everywhere among the saplings, hands reaching skyward from mounds of writhing, dying Wilders.

Stillwater sheathed her knives, turned to kick her sergeant in the arm. 'Wake up, Drillbent. We're saved and it's all going fucking wrong.'

He scowled up at her. 'What?'

'Never mind.' Stillwater strode to the nearest newcomer. 'You, Goodnight, you fat cow! Cut that out!'

The scrawny waif of a woman turned in surprise. 'We're sorting this, Stinkwater, get out of my face!'

'No! Stop killing them! It's done!' Stillwater moved past Goodnight and got in front of Sergeant Wheeze. 'Call 'em off, wind-bag!'

'B-but, we're saving you, sweetie!'

'Not any more – you Serc mages got no subtlety. *Stop stealing all their air!*'

Wheeze blinked at her, his warren sputtering out around him.

Drillbent had recovered and now joined them. 'No captain again? You fucking pirates—'

'No, Drillbent! Daisy put Bellam Nom in charge—'

'Great – where is he?'

'Took his squad to help at the northeast berm.'

'What a great captain!' Stillwater shouted, throwing up her hands.

The sorcery had died among the marines, as it was clear that no one would be coming from that tree-line, where the dead were piled high in haphazard mounds and even seemingly stacked in places, in walls of twisted limbs and blue, swollen faces.

It was not a pretty sight.

Anyx Fro now stood close to Stillwater, following her gaze. 'Sometimes,' she said in a low voice, 'I think it'd be better if the enemy won. Just once. Enough to see us all wiped from the face of the world. Because, you know, Stillwater? War isn't just one thing, over and over again. It's a thing that never stops changing, and every change is just fucking worse than what went before.'

'And,' Stillwater said, 'we're the worst yet, aren't we?'

Anyx Fro nodded. 'Gods, I'm tired.'

'Did you fire your Iron Maw?'

'No. Wick was wet or something, and it guttered out.'

'Just as well,' Stillwater said.

Anyx Fro sighed. 'Aye, just as well.'

A single messenger from Balk's Company had managed to reach the town. The other two had died to mines. That lone rider had galloped up and down empty streets until entirely by chance he came upon Captain Gruff, leading Sergeant Shrake and two of her squad members, Clay Plate and So Bleak.

They had been moving quickly towards Sergeant Drillbent's position. Even as the rider suddenly appeared at an intersection before Gruff and his marines, the sounds of sorcery redoubled from the southeast berm, and the captain held up a hand to halt them.

So Bleak was only a few paces behind Gruff as Balk's messenger reined in and said, 'Commander Balk requests a parley!'

'Dear me, a parley?'

The rider seemed momentarily discomfited. 'A meeting, rather. It's, uh, urgent.'

'I'm sure it is. Has he then sighted the two battalions of marines approaching on the Culvern Road?'

The man's jaw sagged, and he shook his head. 'I know nothing of that, sir.'

Gruff turned. 'Sergeant Shrake, I believe Drillbent's position has been reinforced. Do you concur?'

'Aye, Captain. Those concussions are Serc, I'm sure of it. I'd say Fourth Company.'

Nodding, Gruff addressed the messenger again. 'Ride back into your camp and bring Balk to us. We will meet at the gate. Oh, and be sure to advise that he avoid the field between his camp and the south berm. The road, however, is safe.'

The rider gathered his reins and set off.

Captain Gruff slowly removed his leather gloves and carefully tucked them into his belt, and then faced Sergeant Shrake. 'I hear assistance to the northeast as well, and not just Undercart, Daint and Given Loud. That said, with the rest of the Legion now close, our need to hold our positions is at an end. Accordingly, send one of your soldiers to collect up Sergeant Spindle and crew.'

'So Bleak,' Shrake snapped. 'Clay Plate's slower than a tortoise in any case. Off you go, soldier.'

Nodding, So Bleak swung round and began jogging up the street. Well, this was typical. She just didn't want him around, did she? All the bad luck swirling around him – he'd seen how nervous he made her, and how eager she'd been to send him away.

Maybe he'd just give up soldiering entirely. He could retire in some city, join the one political affiliation he hated the most, and then smile as it all burned down around him.

The thought lifted his mood, when nothing else about this day could.

Balk and Ara trotted up the road and halted at the gate. Ara was startled to see the innkeeper, Storp, sprawled on a bench outside his tavern on the other side, a loaded crossbow resting across his thighs. Captain Gruff had been speaking to the old man, without eliciting any response. Then, with a shrug, the captain set out for the gate.

Balk and Ara reined in and dismounted just outside it, Balk handing her the reins to his horse.

The cobbles beneath them were vibrating from the impact of the Malazan marines now visible to the south, approaching at a steady jog. Their appearance had been a shock. It was now no wonder to Ara that the three squads in the town had been acting unconcerned all this time. They'd known what was coming.

If we'd attacked, we'd now have two thousand marines climbing up our collective asses.

Captain Gruff strode through the gate. 'Can I help you, Captain Balk? I assume you are back to preferring your old rank, yes? Thus, we meet as equals, or as near to equal as breeding and intelligence allows.'

'I am forced to cancel our services,' Balk said. 'A pre-existing contract has been invoked, requiring our immediate departure.'

'Indeed? Well, this is a surprise,' Gruff said, smiling and seemingly not at all surprised. 'Can I enquire as to the identity of your employer?'

Balk hesitated, then shook his head. 'Not relevant at this time, Captain. Our camp has been broken and we are ready to march into the forest.'

'Into the forest? You do understand, Captain, that this pre-existing contract of yours, should it require you see us as the enemy, will mean Fist Sevitt cannot let you depart. Indeed, she will likely attack you immediately.'

'The contract does not see the Malazan Empire as an enemy, Captain Gruff. There is no conflict here and if all goes well, you'll not see us again.'

'That seems unlikely, but very well. I trust you understand that your most recent payment period is now forfeit.'

Balk nodded.

A lone rider was coming up the road from the south. Glancing back, Ara saw that it was a marine, a familiar one. *Oams, is it? No wonder you'd not been seen in a while. We'd thought you dead in the forest. We were such idiots.*

Oams slowed his approach, his gaze fixed on his captain, who lifted a hand and made a gesture. Oams seemed to relax. He wheeled round and began riding back to the column's vanguard.

Fist Sevitt. *Gods below.*

'Are we done?' Balk asked. 'I am eager to lead my company out of this mess.'

'I'm sure you are. Off you go, then. Oh, and should you come across any remaining Wilders in that forest – your employers or otherwise – advise them to retreat. We have no wish to continue slaughtering them.'

'I'll do what I can,' Balk said, turning back to accept the reins from Ara. They quickly mounted and set off back towards the camp.

The sweat was fast cooling under Ara's leather hauberk, her racing heart finally beginning to slow. She glanced across at Balk. 'That was close,' she said.

It seemed that he would not even reply, but at last he gave a terse nod.

*

So Bleak climbed onto the embankment and made his way towards the group of marines hunkered down at the far end. He saw the 23rd Squad from 4th Company, the tall figure of Sergeant Bellam Nom immediately recognizable.

The heavies, Daint, Given Loud, Paltry Skint and Say No, were all crouching at the very edge of the berm, looking down at something. Spindle stood behind them, talking with Benger.

The tree-line off to the right was strewn with dead Wilders, and nothing moved in the forest beyond.

Bellam Nom's squad stayed back a few paces, silent as they watched their comrades.

Something odd was happening. So Bleak jogged towards them. He nodded at Bellam in passing and then reached Spindle and Benger.

'Time to withdraw,' he announced.

Benger glanced over. 'Not quite yet,' he said.

'Captain wants us all out—'

'*Not yet,*' Benger repeated, nodding down the slope.

A lone Teblor had been crawling towards the berm and was now at its very base. Her legs were gone below the knees and So Bleak could see the wavering twin trails of blood the woman had left in her wake. She had crossed almost half the width of the field.

'Back off,' Spindle told the heavies. 'I'll go down.'

Paltry Skint straightened. 'Beware any sudden moves, Sergeant. We saw the madness among them in that insane charge.'

'She's unarmed,' Spindle said, and he began making his way down.

The heavies readied crossbows just in case, and Bellam Nom finally called his squad into his wake and approached.

They watched as the hairshirted sergeant reached the base of the slope and then crouched close to the Teblor woman. He had a waterskin, but it seemed she wasn't interested in drinking. In fact, she looked to be dying.

So Bleak turned to Bellam Nom's squad. 'Who's the healer?'

After a nod from his sergeant, one marine stepped forward. 'Olit Fas,' he said. 'Just give the word.'

'Not my call,' So Bleak said, gesturing down to Spindle. 'But I'd say it's too late. She's about as bled out as one can get.'

'Not all the way, obviously,' Olit Fas observed.

The Teblor woman was speaking and Spindle bent low to listen. Everyone on the berm tensed.

But then her head sagged back, and after a moment, Spindle rose. He began his climb back up the slope. Glancing up, he saw Olit Fas and shook his head.

Hands reached down to help Spindle up.

'What did she have to say?' Benger asked.

Spindle stepped clear of everyone and walked back to look over the town of Silver Lake. He seemed to study it for a time, and then he turned round. 'Bellam, good to see you and thanks again for your timely arrival. If you don't mind, you can now leave. We'll catch you up.'

Bellam Nom nodded and set off along the bank, his marines falling in behind him.

Spindle waited until they were out of earshot, and then he faced those who remained. 'It's for us to decide,' he said. 'That seemed right to me, anyway.'

'What did she say, Sergeant?' Paltry Skint asked.

'Just an ex-slave,' Spindle said, turning back to look at the town. 'With a request.'

'Let's hear it,' Benger said in a low, careful tone.

'She asked that we burn the town down to the ground,' Spindle said. 'It was all they wanted, really. Just that.' He faced them. 'I'm asking for a vote on this. Hands up if you're good with . . .'

His words fell away, as he didn't need the rest.

Every hand was raised high.

CHAPTER TWENTY-ONE

A branch overhung a stone wall. Its fruit was regularly sour and unpleasant. Despite this, the offended landowner insisted that the fruit that fell from this branch belonged to him, while the owner whose property held the rest of the tree, who used its fruit to make a rather delectable wine, retorted that, if the man would claim the fruit from that particular branch, he must pay for it. As it was a matter of principle, the detail that the landowner of the offending branch typically left the fruit on the ground, where it rotted, can be deemed irrelevant.

The feud escalated. Property was damaged, reputations impugned, elaborate and bloody curses conducted, calling upon indiscriminate spirits, and eventually, lives were lost. When the case finally came before the regional magistrate, the list of charges and countercharges required an entire day to enumerate.

At issue was the initial circumstance which invoked two competing Malazan laws, one related to property and the other to the value of goods. Thus, the base arguments set forth by the relevant Acquisitors related to trespass versus wilful destruction of property (namely, the fruit left to rot).

The magistrate was new to the region. As such, he was not a member of the community and had no familial or business ties in the area. This was initially deemed advantageous in terms of a just decision strictly adhering to the laws in question.

It was quite unexpected, therefore, that he ordered the tree and both estates burned to the ground, the ground salted, and the families of both parties banished from the region.

In justifying the decision, he was quoted as follows: 'The world is full of petty small-minded bastards and in this case it was simply unfortunate that they happened to live next to each other. Now they don't.'

*Jurisprudence, Litigation and Criminal Law in the
Time of the Mallick Reformation*
(memoirs of Magistrate Ilgish the Torcher)

IF NOT FOR THE UNCEASING PAIN, HE WOULD LAUGH. IF NOT FOR the stench of torn and now rotting bodies surrounding him, the greasy feel of the grasses pressed against one side of his face, he would look into the empty sky overhead, to see the de-fleshed skulls of every god tumbling down from the heavens.

How many beliefs could one man hold in his head? Valoc knew not. But in the moment when they all left him, deluged in waves of agony and shame, he discovered that all the space they had consumed inside him, for so long, was not so vast after all.

Hollow is the head of a fool. And everyone who listens only to the echoes bouncing in his skull, believing them true, is doubly a fool. Yet these echoes are all we ever hear. Beliefs feeding into beliefs, mindless as serpents devouring their own tail.

He had believed in courage. Not his own, for he knew he had very little. But surely a righteous cause possessed a courage of its own, as fuel fed into a fire built into raging heat, pure and white and unassailable. He had believed in a future world in which he might find a place, a world that beckoned him to freedom once more.

Strip away the beliefs and a mind will prove very small indeed. Reduce the world and see how the body is the last cage, the final enslavement, with death and dreams the only escape. Dreams, of course, were illusions, their wings false, their worlds ephemeral. Death, on the other hand, offered the proper finality, the only true liberation.

How he longed for it now.

He had been in the press, three strides behind Bayrak, when something snapped underfoot, tearing the high grasses, and iron teeth sank into his shin and calf. Stumbling, bewildered, he had looked down at something that made no sense. A wolf-trap, spring-loaded, the kind his old master laid out when news arrived that a pack had been seen hunting sheep and cattle. His shin bones were broken, the flesh of his calf mangled. A chain bound the trap to the ground, held in place by a spike driven deep into the earth.

When the pain burst through the shock, he fell to the ground, and was passed on all sides by the Sunyd in their charge.

Shackled, a mere three strides out from the forest's edge. Thoughts of laughter were long in coming but come they did.

Before then, however, was an eternity in which destruction fell upon the world.

*   *   *

A silence had come to the journey once the main force of Rathyd and Wilders had passed through the abandoned town of Bringer's Foot and made their way onto the south plains, leaving the small party behind. Now Rant rode with Delas Fana and Pake Gild, in the company of hounds and wolves, and the way before them was not chewed up by the passage of thousands. The lake glimmered on their left and vacant farmland stretched out on their right.

There had been many birds filling the sky earlier in the day, all winging south. Rant only now recalled the ghost-witch's warning of a coming flood. He had not been ready to understand her warning back then, and now he feared that they might be too late, that he was in fact leading his friends and kin to their deaths.

Gower had spoken of the threat. War-Bitch's urging gnawed at Rant's mind. But he would see his old home, or what remained of it. Smoke still hung over the land to the east, and they were now drawing visibly closer to it. His stubbornness, he was told, belonged to his father. But to Rant it felt like his, and his alone. He was not thinking of his father at all, only his mother, the one person who had stood by him for years and years.

He was beginning to understand what sacrifice meant, when it came to lives lived and choices made. She could have taken her own life at any time, and yet she had endured the torment of the blood-oil curse. She had raised him, kept him fed. She had provided a home he could retreat to when the other children were at their cruellest.

If a single room could be a temple, then she had made it for him. Salvation, a place for his tears, where bruises could fade, and cuts could heal. And she had done it while enduring a life of torment.

Their last day together he would not think about. Yet heat came to his body when he thought of Pake Gild, who was still riding her horse a few paces behind him. The gentleness of her touch was only a memory, but that memory could still make him shiver. Still, this gift of manhood was a strange thing. It brought to his life a new vulnerability, one that could steal his strength, could make him weep – as he did in Pake's arms that night.

His mother's version of it had been a travesty, and only now did Rant understand the true meaning of the curse. To take away pleasure and

395

warmth from such acts seemed a crime beyond measure. To make it a thing of power and hunger and blind, selfish need, left Rant horrified. That night, he had wept for his mother. For the first time. Because, it turned out, understanding was no gift at all.

Pake Gild had not understood, he suspected, and he had been unable to give words to his weeping. She had asked again and again if she had somehow hurt him, for her desire had been strong near the end. And she had whispered to him that such powerful emotions as he was feeling were common, because to face one's own weakness could crush a frail soul.

But her embrace had not trapped him. The softness of her flesh was a comfort he had never known. He felt no weakness at all. Even vulnerability left him oddly content and, if he thought about it, fearless.

And so, he did not weep for himself at all. Instead, he grieved for the life of his mother, for what the blood-oil did to her.

Later, much later, he did think of his father. He thought about him hard, his inner eyes intent upon the black pool with all his emotions swirling somewhere beneath its placid surface. Seeking a ripple, a rising of rage.

But blood-oil was what it was. It swept away the minds of both Teblor and southlander. His father had experienced the same fire as did his mother. The only difference was in how long it lasted. It would not have mattered to Karsa if the woman he took was human or Teblor. He might well not have even noticed.

Rant could now understand how that heat tore away the future as it raised around the body and soul a wall of flames. The curse, in its moment, consumed everything. By these tracks, Rant could choose to absolve his father of all blame.

He chose not to. Had Karsa not been subsequently chained; had he not been shipped off as a slave to some distant land, would he have atoned for his crime? That, Rant decided, was the question he would ask Karsa Orlong on the day they finally faced one another. And by his father's reply, Rant would decide whether to forgive him, or kill him.

In this moment, and in every moment since Pake Gild had taken him by the hand, Rant believed it would be the latter, and his palm had brushed the grip of his knife again and again as he rode. After all, his father was in Darujhistan. Not in some far-off land with an ocean between him and his crimes. He could have, at any time since his return, journeyed into the wake of his own bloody trail. Seeking amends, even redemption.

But he had not. Karsa Orlong, it seemed, was indifferent to his own past.

There was an arrogance to this, and Rant had waited for his anger to emerge, rising in indignation and fury. But still the surface of the pool remained unperturbed, too black to reflect even a hint of light.

The spirit in his knife, he recalled, had touched him in a moment of rage and shame, and had taken from him at least the rage, if not the shame, which burned still, somewhere in the unlit depths. Was this a permanent thing? Was this why when he fought he felt nothing but calm inside, cool and detached, taking away all risk of recklessness?

Would she ever give him back his anger? Did he want it?

The townsfolk had not treated his mother well. Revisiting that truth, as he did now, yielded nothing, not even a tremble.

There were, he decided, many things wrong with him.

He saw Gower's pack suddenly loping well ahead of the party. The high banks surrounding the town of Silver Lake were now visible. They seemed stained, dotted in refuse of some sort, blackened along the top. No roofs were visible rising above those banks, which wasn't right.

Delas Fana guided her horse onto the lakeside track that led directly to the town's waterfront, and for the first time, Rant found himself riding a horse on a proper road. The endless jostling smoothed out, easing the aches in his lower back. He sighed.

'Yes,' said Pake Gild behind him, 'some things the southlanders do well.'

There were crows along the embankment, and what Rant had thought to be refuse was now revealed as bodies. Many bodies. The blackening atop the berm appeared to be evidence of fire, possibly when the town itself had been torched. But then he saw, among the bodies scattered on the facing slope, evidence that the flames had taken them as well, hot and long enough to curl the remnants of their limbs. The carrion birds were finding little to consume.

The boathouses, boats and other buildings down along the waterfront had all been burned down, the water beyond coated in a thick layer of ash that gently rose and fell with the lake's sleepy pulse.

Gower's pack had moved past all of that, vanishing among scorched trees beyond the far corner of the embankment on the east side of the town. Delas Fana led them opposite the town itself, traversing carefully what used to be Front Street, which was now cluttered with the black remains of toppled walls and raining embers. Rant rose in his saddle as he came within sight of his mother's home.

Nothing had survived the flames. The entire building was now nothing more than stumps at the corners, where the larger logs that had provided its frame still stood, if only knee-high.

Pake Gild had moved her horse up alongside Rant, on his left. She spoke. 'There was no one in this settlement, Rant. The same as Bringer's Foot. The inhabitants have been evacuated.'

Rant nodded. 'She is alive, then. She must be.'

'Would she have joined the others? Would she have been welcome?'

'I don't know. I don't think so.'

'They didn't flee in haste – can you see? No remnants of clothing or other household things on the streets. This was organized, a well-ordered withdrawal.'

'Soldiers,' said Rant. 'Malazan soldiers. They would have kept her safe. Malazan soldiers are kind and helpful. The garrison soldiers always stopped the rocks being thrown at me, when they saw it happening.'

At a shout of some sort from Delas Fana, they continued on.

There had been a fortified watchtower made of wood on the northeast corner, high atop the embankment. It was now shattered and partially burned. But what had so startled Delas Fana was what she saw beyond, between the tree-line and the earthworks.

Silent, Pake Gild and Rant drew up alongside Delas Fana who had halted her mount. The hounds and Nilghan's pack also seemed reluctant to venture any further.

The field was torn up, a mass of craters. Bodies and parts of bodies carpeted the entire area. Random streaks of scorched ground slashed out from just past the embankment's slope, and where these were the bodies were thick, so fiercely burned that they had melted into one another, forming glittering, gleaming heaps of metal, burst flesh and upthrust bones.

Rant struggled to make sense of what he was seeing. Had those been people once? It didn't seem possible. Nothing in his memory came close to the scene before him and so it couldn't fit in anywhere in his mind. When he examined his feelings, he found only relief that his mother had not been here to see any of this, that she was alive, somewhere, hopefully far away by now.

Movement at the far end of his vision caught Rant's attention. 'I see Gower,' he said. 'He has sembled and is waving to us.'

It had to have been a sound, or a shadow flitting across his closed eyelids, but Valoc suddenly knew that he was no longer alone among the dead. He opened his eyes to find a pair of wolves staring at him from only a few paces away.

The laugh that erupted, oh so briefly, from the Sunyd made the sound of a ragged croak.

Wolves, and here he lay, snared by a wolf-trap. He had known that such traps were brutal. It was said that wolves would gnaw off their own legs to escape them. A lost forelimb was probably survivable. A lost back-limb was not. Some traps were scented, to draw the questing nose of a wolf, and these of course closed their iron jaws about the animal's snout, head or neck. No animal survived that.

What was this inclination, then, that so guided a southlander's mind to chains, imprisonment, and iron-fanged suffering and death? The sheer inventiveness in devising ways to kill bespoke obsession, like a stain of poison upon the soul. He tried to imagine the mind that saw pleasure in such inventions. It must be a twisted thing indeed.

More wolves. A pack. But clearly Valoc was in his last moments of life. The scene was blurring, edges bleeding away, all the colours running like paint.

Now the wolves were gone and in their place stood a man, heavily bearded, his visage battered and ugly. He wore furs and weapons at his belt and harness.

A Jheck. Ah . . . not fever, then, not the swift rush of death.

He had heard that there had been Jheck among the forces attacking this place, but he had seen none, not before the battle, not during, and not afterwards.

Now the sound of horse hoofs, drawing closer, but he faced the wrong way to see who had arrived. Then a figure edged into his vision and he found himself staring up at a Teblor woman. She was pouring into one palm water from a skin, which she then brought to his face, wiping the soot from around his eyes. Then the water was against his cracked lips.

'Valoc,' she said.

A single swallow of sweet water. His eyes narrowed on her face. 'Delas Fana. I did not recognize you. Why didn't I recognize you?'

'You are in shock,' she said.

'I cannot move. Do you see? A wolf-trap. Much worse, Delas Fana, than any shackle I've worn. Much worse. The spike is driven too deep. I'm held fast.'

Her damp hand was on his brow, her fingers stroking around his eyes. 'Valoc. You are not snared any longer. The trap has worked through, as it will. You are lying some distance from it, and the lower part of your leg. You must have crawled before losing consciousness.'

He struggled to lift himself on one elbow, to look down the length of his body. She helped him by taking some of his weight. She spoke true. His right leg was gone below the knee. 'But,' he whispered, 'I could feel the chains. I *know* that feel. I *know* it! I feel them still . . . the shackles . . .'

'What happened here, Valoc?'

He sank back, the back of his head crunching fire-blackened earth. 'Not shackles, a trap,' he muttered, fighting back waves of confusion. 'What happened, Delas Fana? I died. That's what happened.'

'You are not dead.'

She gave him more water and the fire in his throat ebbed. 'I died with my tribe,' he said. 'The Sunyd are no more. We were slaves once, then we were not, then we were. We died here chained together by the need to avenge ourselves. This is what we did with our freedom.' He groped with one hand. 'Can you see my sword? Is it near? I never used it, not once.'

'It is burnt, Valoc.'

He saw Rant, standing behind Delas Fana, and another Uryd warrior he did not recognize. His gaze fixed on the half-blood. 'Slayer of Galambar,' he whispered.

'You are not dead,' said Rant. 'The trap saved you. There are other Sunyd survivors. There must be. We will look for them.'

Valoc shook his head, closed his eyes against the harsh sunlight now full upon his face. 'You did not see what I saw. You will find no one.'

Delas Fana knelt down, lifting his head and settling it between her knees. With a damp cloth she carefully cleaned more of his face. He didn't know why she bothered. There was a tug down near his knees and he looked to see the other Uryd woman binding the stump. He closed his eyes again.

'Valoc, was a Malazan army here?'

'Army?' Valoc smiled. 'Delas Fana, I saw the enemy, there on the bank, watching as we charged. There were six of them.'

Gower joined Nilghan who was out in the field, walking among the dead. His eyes scanned the churned-up ground, the craters. 'What manner of holes are these, brother?'

Muttering under his breath, Nilghan scowled, and then said, 'There is no glory here. No prowess. Nothing to sing of in the years ahead. Brother,' he waved a hand, 'this field was mined.'

'What does that word mean?'

'Malazan munitions, buried shallowly, studded with short iron nails driven into the clay, but not so far as to reach the powders inside. No, that takes a foot stepping down to do. And then—' Both his hands shot up, held wide, and then slowly fell back to his sides. 'See how so many of these bodies are missing parts? This is what happens.'

'My first thought,' murmured Gower as he studied the carnage once more, 'was sorcery.'

'Oh, there was that, too,' said Nilghan in a growl. He gestured at a blackened streak. 'There. A mage upon the top of the bank cast that.'

Gower glanced back to where Delas Fana and Pake Gild were working on Valoc. He saw Rant standing off to one side, surrounded by his dogs. The young warrior was looking southward.

'They never even reached the foot of the slope,' observed Nilghan.

'Look to the south,' said Gower, now following Rant's gaze. 'The whole forest's line. I see many more bodies.'

'The Saemdhi, I would wager,' said Nilghan. 'They should have simply gone around this town.'

'They could not have guessed at these buried munitions of yours,' said Gower. 'They expected the clash of weapons, a swift victory over whatever garrison held here.'

'No garrison did this,' said Nilghan, pausing to spit. 'This was Malazan marines.'

'Then they knew we were coming.'

'They knew,' agreed Nilghan.

'Nilghan, what awaits us in the south?'

His brother's eyes were bleak. 'Death, brother.'

'Unless,' said Gower, 'we are swift, unwilling to engage, perhaps even moving at night. This is what War-Bitch desires of us.'

'Where are our people, Gower? I expected to meet them before now. Then I expected to meet them here.'

'War-Bitch leads them,' Gower replied. He paused. 'I too expected to have rejoined them by now.'

'When last did she speak to you?'

He shook his head. 'My dreams and visions since I last saw her are many, each one darkness and silence, brother.'

'Is she dead, then? Was she here? Shall we find the burnt corpses of the Black Jheck somewhere here? If so,' Nilghan faced Gower, teeth bared, 'then the two of you have betrayed us.'

'They are not dead,' said Gower, though his tone revealed too clearly his lack of conviction. He continued studying the dead in this field. He knew almost nothing of the Malazans. Just another name, he'd thought, no different from the Nathii or Genabarii, or indeed the Korhivi.

He had been wrong. These Malazans were nothing like the Korhivi or Saemdhi. 'Nilghan,' he said, 'you have never before mentioned . . . marines. You spoke of Malazans, yes, and often. Who – *what* are these marines?'

Nilghan shrugged. 'I saw one once. She was delivering a message to a garrison commander. She looked like nothing special, not even frightening. I would have taken her to my bed had I the chance. A woman, then, but her uniform was not the same as a Malazan regular.'

'A type of soldier, then.'

'Yes. Sent to places with trouble. Then the trouble stops. Then they're sent to the next place with trouble. And it stops.'

Gower scanned the field. Then he nodded. 'It stopped here, too.'

Pake Gild found the shafts of two spears not too badly burned and began assembling a travois. At some point, Valoc lost consciousness, making it easier to bind him to the frame. She affixed the harness to her own horse but only led it by the rein for now, as, joined by Gower and Nilghan, they set out to skirt the tree-line on the east side of the town.

They quickly came upon the bodies of Saemdhi and other Wilders. The entire approach to the embankment revealed the same craters and dismembered corpses. Here and there a lone figure among the attackers had made a stand. These spots were marked by converging streaks of scorched or gouged earth, and the figures themselves were mostly burned away, often not much more than a small heap of grey bone splinters atop a black stain, a few fragments of skull.

'Bonecasters,' remarked Nilghan. 'Ganrel warlocks and witches. I see no rock-piles on the top of the bank. Seems they took no one down in the exchange of sorcery.' At some muttered question or comment from Gower that Rant did not catch, Nilghan shrugged and said, 'They bury them where they fall, mostly. Unless there's a bunch. Then they build a barrow to hold them all.' After a moment he spat and added, 'It's said at least one dead Malazan marine guards every border of the empire.'

Moving slowly to accommodate Pake navigating her horse and its travois over the many grisly obstacles before them, it was some time before they reached the south edge of the town. Here, at last, the scene changed.

The approach to the south embankment was unmarred barring two craters and dozens of much smaller holes that reminded Rant of gopher colonies. There were almost no bodies here at all, perhaps a half-dozen scattered Saemdhi or Wilder. Beyond it in a pasture there was evidence of a large encampment, revealed by worn tracks forming a grid, as well as four latrine trenches and a pair of middens, both downwind, on the east side and near the tree-line. Along that edge of the forest, however, dead tribals were heaped in their hundreds, so many that they seemed to form high banked rows as if mocking the town's embankments. There had been no fire to cook them and so the crows were gathered, feeding on bloated bodies.

The stench of rotting flesh was overwhelming, and flies exploded in sudden swarms as fat crows waddled and hopped about.

Delas Fana halted them halfway across the old camp. Frowning, she twisted round to study the town behind them. 'I can make little sense of this. This camp has a military look. Presumably the Malazan marines—'

'No,' said Nilghan. 'I've seen the camps marines make. They dig a trench and raise a bank, even if for but one night. They burn and bury their refuse.' His eyes narrowed as he studied the camp. 'Even regulars make a better camp, and look, this was not for only a few nights, either. This one has been here some time.'

'So who were they?' Delas Fana asked.

In answer, Nilghan shook his head.

Gower had scouted a few paces ahead. Now he returned. 'Whoever they were, they marched into the forest. Had to hack a notch in that wall of dead to do it.'

'Do they pursue the Wilders?' Pake Gild wondered.

'Only if they're fools,' Nilghan said in a low growl. 'Good way to get sniped to death. A dozen traps and ambushes for every thousand paces through that thicket.'

'I will veer,' said Gower. 'See if they formed a skirmish line on the other side of the corpse wall.'

'If it was in column,' said Nilghan, 'they didn't go into the forest to fight. The narrower the column, brother, the faster they went. If so, I gauge that to be a retreat.'

As Gower turned to face the forest, preparing to veer into his pack, he seemed to freeze in place. A moment later, Rant saw why.

Two figures had emerged from the notch cut through the heaped corpses. One was a southlander. The other was Jheck.

A lungful of otataral dust had left Benger without his magic, making these scouting missions all the more perilous. At Captain Gruff's order, Spindle and Oams had backtracked, intending to track Balk's Company. They had made use of a farmstead within sight of the old camp and had just stabled their mounts when Oams caught sight of figures close to the tree-line. Now the two marines were lying flat on the west side of the farmhouse's peaked roof, eyes over the spine.

'There were rumours of Jheck,' whispered Spindle, eyes on the distant group just beyond Balk's old encampment. 'Now at last we see them.'

'And Teblor and their terrifying war-dogs,' Oams added. 'We need to stay upwind of them, Sergeant, and keep our voices as low as possible.' He was silent for a moment and then said, 'A few thousand veered

Jheck could have changed the outcome here. Why didn't they join the attack?'

'I don't know,' Spindle replied.

Oams fell silent. It had been strange seeing his squad-mates after so long, but the reunion had been short. Not enough time for any exchange of tales. In truth, they hadn't looked good, any of them. Alive, yes, and that alone was more than Oams had expected. But sombre and mostly silent, smoke-stained and grim as they exited the burning settlement.

Spindle spoke. 'They've finished talking with the ones from the forest.'

Both watched as the entire group now made their way towards the tree-line, passing through the notch in the heaped bodies. Moments later they were out of sight.

'That travois will slow them,' said Oams. 'Sergeant, I wanted to apologize. We were a bit late. If Balk's Company had done what the captain expected it to do, you'd all be dead right now.'

Spindle grunted in reply. He then rolled onto his back and slid a short distance down the roof's slope. He stared up at the sky, pulling out from a pouch some dried meat that he began chewing on. Oams remained with his eyes fixed on the forest.

By the time he'd reached Culvern the vast barges were tied up at the river's floating docks, and two full battalions of marines had disembarked. Fist Sevitt herself was in the town, which had already been evacuated in anticipation of trouble. Oams's task had been simple enough: deliver his report and then guide the battalions north to Silver Lake.

The primary concern at the time was Balk's Company. Captain Gruff and his three squads provided the lure, keeping Balk close with vengeance so easily within reach. Spindle's knife to his throat surely still stung the man's pride. It paid to know where the potential enemy was, and sometimes, the closer the better. Still, it'd been a risky decision.

Oams knew how nervous the three squads had been during their stay in Silver Lake. He hadn't slept too well himself in his time there. Restless Wilders could be handled. A well-trained mercenary company sitting in their laps, with enough bodies to chop seventeen marines into sausage meat, was a wholly different level of threat.

At some point, however, the balance of worry had shifted to the forest, to the vast numbers of savages mustering there. Something had driven them south; something had them piling up along the entire northern border. But what had that to do with Balk and all the messages winging into the forest and back?

Oams wished someone other than Spindle was at his side right now. The sergeant was a man of too few words. Explanations had to be prised loose, and even then, one or two words didn't explain much at all. Oams didn't want to be known as someone who never shut their mouth, but this was maddening.

He studied what was left of the town, the blackened embankment, the spill of bodies that had somehow come in from the west side. He could almost hear lingering echoes from the sorcery, the munitions, the roar of flames. *I should have been there, with my squad. Now I feel as if something's been cut away, left blank.*

So they'd mined the killing fields. The long campaign of false rumours about sketchy Malazan munitions had done its job. *The era of the sapper is over. Too risky for full-scale battle. Too many duds or premature detonations.* As for all the wagons that had accompanied three measly squads to Silver Lake, why, only a madman would have risked loading them up with dozens of crates containing volatile munitions.

Maybe the hand-thrown stuff was a thing of the past, at least for the moment. But static emplacement of mines, well, that wasn't even an innovation. Fiddler's Drum had started it all years ago.

Misinformation. Let them dismiss us as nothing like the marines of imperial legend. Well, that's true enough, I suppose. We're a new breed of marine, all right. All things considered, way more lethal.

The field between Balk's camp and the embankment had been mined as a precaution. Only two had been triggered in the confused chaos on the day of battle. Oams had rejoined his squad in time to take part in digging up the undetonated ones. There hadn't been much conversation then, either. In any case, no point leaving those munitions in the ground. Why seed the future with random death?

Sighing, he slid down beside Spindle. 'So Balk's just up and left, just wheeled and marched into the forest. No wonder the captain sent us back.'

Spindle tore off another piece of dried meat, chewed for a time, and then said, 'Fist Sevitt wanted to make sure. Then there's the question of who hired them.'

'Balk thought it proper that he took our contract on top of that one?'

'So long as they didn't interfere with each other, he figured "Why not?"' Spindle chewed some more meat.

'Bullshit,' Oams pronounced. 'They sent assassins into the town, didn't they? That's how Benger caught that otataral dust, or so he said.'

'Well,' allowed Spindle, 'a bit of opportunism. Possibly thinking to do the Wilders a favour. As it turned out, it justified our pre-emptive killing of their best mages. Beyond dangling Benger as bait.'

'Stillwater?'

'And Rayle.'

'Nasty combination,' said Oams. He paused, and then mused, mostly to himself, 'Who the fuck hired them, then?'

Spindle lifted up his waterskin and drank down a few mouthfuls. 'Salty meat,' he muttered. 'That's what we're going to find out. I think I've worked it out, unlikely as the answer might be.'

'Teblor?'

'No. If them, Balk would have joined in the attack. The only Teblor here were Sunyd ex-slaves.'

'Poor bastards.'

'Aye,' Spindle agreed. After a long moment, he sighed and said, 'I wish they'd parleyed first. A lot of lives could have been saved.'

'I was wondering,' ventured Oams, 'about why you fired the buildings.'

Spindle glanced away but said nothing.

'Plant this failure at Balk's feet,' said Oams. 'He obviously had the forest contacts.'

'I think his company was hired by the Jheck.'

'What? A bunch of foul-smelling bloodthirsty wolves went and hired a mercenary company? What in Iskar's name for? And how did they find them in the first place? I can't even recall any mention of a Jheck here in the south, not a single one.'

'There was one,' said Spindle. 'Hired as a scout, I think. Spent all his time in brothels, so he was dismissed. A few years ago now.'

'Balk ran brothels back then?'

This time, Spindle's grunt was almost a laugh. 'Not that one, I don't think. Answer is, I don't know how that contract happened. More to the point, we want to know why it happened. What do the Jheck need with mercenaries?'

'And Rayle had nothing to report?'

'If she did, it was to the captain,' Spindle said, shrugging. 'Obviously, neither Gruff nor Sevitt was satisfied with what she had to say.'

'I wonder,' said Oams, 'if we'd hit Balk with all we had the first time, this might've turned out differently.'

'Holding back is what we do when it's to our advantage.'

Oams scowled. 'Sevitt likes her games. That first clash with Balk's Company all those months ago cost us marines.' *Friends, comrades.*

'Sometimes it's our job to die, Oams,' Spindle said. He began repacking his kit.

'I was scared shitless riding in,' admitted Oams. 'The Fist kept holding me back. I didn't like it, Sergeant.'

'We follow orders,' said Spindle, leaning over the eaves to drop his kit bag to the ground below. He quickly clambered down after it.

Oams followed suit. 'Benger's such an idiot, breathing red dust like that. This forest could be hairy, Sergeant.'

'Aye.'

They set off, out of the farmyard, over the road, and began making their way across Balk's old encampment. Oams fixed his gaze on the hundreds of bodies at the tree-line and he shivered.

'We had Balk's Company in our pocket,' he said as they crossed the vacated, littered pasture. 'Then Gruff just lets them go?'

'It wouldn't have been as easy as you think,' said Spindle. 'Aye, that Wilder attack got stopped, Oams. But even the new squads were spent. Lucky for us the enemy was broken by then. Anyway, we're here to find the answers, so stop trying to second-guess this.'

'What a confused mess,' Oams said, mostly under his breath.

But Spindle clearly heard him. 'Can you tell me why, Oams?'

'No.'

'Neither can I. Something's missing. It may seem over, but it isn't, not by a long shot. We find Balk and his employer, and we ask them a few questions. They answer us and then we leave. That's our mission. The sooner we're back with our people, the happier I'll be.'

'The surviving Wilders won't be happy with Balk,' Oams mused. 'Or the Jheck for that matter, if you're right about them being here, but choosing not to fight.'

'Aye, they won't be happy at all.'

'And if they're still hanging around?'

'I doubt they are.'

'Stillwater would've been better for this.'

'Aye,' Spindle said as he led Oams towards the notch, 'let's have Stillwater do the diplomacy thing. Good idea.'

Oams sighed again. 'For the sneaky part, I meant.' *No, I meant 'not you', Spindle. Balk's mercenaries hate you with a passion. And so we just walk into their camp? Fucking madness.*

But something had relented in Spindle and he let out a ragged sigh. 'She can rest with the others when they get to Culvern, Oams. She's earned it. They've all earned it.' He paused before the notch, eyes on the bloated, rotting bodies to either side.

'Fucking Fourth Company,' said Oams. 'Dead air. Must have been an awful thing to see, all these people suffocating to death. I should have been with you all.'

Spindle grimaced, something in his posture making him suddenly look old. 'Gruff led out three broken squads, Oams. You didn't miss anything good.' He passed a hand over his eyes. 'What was it all for? Why didn't they retreat? Step around us, or just . . . *run away?*'

Oams hesitated, but then he had to ask. 'And you, Sergeant? Are you broken as well?'

'Ah, Oams,' said Spindle, 'I've been broken for years.' He set out, passing between the piled bodies.

Oams watched him for a moment, and then followed. 'Sometimes,' he whispered, 'I *hate* my job.'

'Lord Gower,' said the Jheck who had come out from the forest, 'when War-Bitch came to us and told us you were coming, when she led your clans to our camps, I knew that our world had truly ended. Dead is the past, dead the feuds and the hatred, dead the old ways of our dens and packs. Now here I stand, facing my rival, and to you I offer my throat.'

Gower was silent for a half-dozen breaths, and then he said, 'Lord Casnock of the White Jheck, it is as you say. Dead is the past. To you I offer my throat.' He stepped forward then. The two Jheck lords clasped wrists.

Nilghan muttered something under his breath, then voiced a harsh laugh. 'Now I have seen everything! Bellies to scratch on all sides! Casnock, you crag-goat, who is this southlander at your side?'

Rant brought his hand to his knife yet again, awaiting the White Jheck's burst of anger.

Instead, Casnock offered Nilghan a comical skew-eyed expression and said, 'The rat-tailed marmot speaks. Indeed, wonders never cease. Gower, why have you not killed your brother, who so longs for your title he came to me a year past with offers of secret alliance?'

Gower glanced over at his brother. 'He grovels to everyone, Casnock. Pity is all I can muster when setting eyes upon my brother.'

'The southlander!' Nilghan insisted with a growl.

She spoke, 'I am Lieutenant Ara of Balk's Company. We are encamped half a league away, in the forest, with all of your kind.'

'Allies?' Nilghan demanded.

'Allies,' she agreed. 'More specifically, we are to provide you an escort into the southlands, as you seek a new homeland.'

But Nilghan sneered. 'A mercenary company claims to be able to protect us from the Malazan Empire. Madness. Casnock, you have been deceived. How many gold fleeces did this cost you? These vaga-bonds will abandon you at first sight of a Malazan banner! You and my brother are fools, and so is War-Bitch! We shall have to fight for every step we take. The lifeless bodies of our kin shall strew a trail for a hundred leagues behind us, until none are left!'

'The Malazan Empire,' said Lieutenant Ara, 'honours the legality of contracts. When so informed, their marines permitted us to join the

Jheck. We took no part in the battle at Silver Lake. But if you would run wild through the empire, Jheck, no one can protect you, least of all a company of mercenaries.'

'As War-Bitch advises,' said Casnock, glaring at Nilghan, 'we travel at night, in silence if at all possible. We avoid settlements.'

'And eat what, grass and flowers?'

Rant saw the lord of the White Jheck wince. 'Trade and barter, we hope,' he said after a moment. Then his shoulders fell, and he said, 'And yes, Nilghan, we may well starve.'

'We can discuss details in the camp,' said Ara, clearly uncomfortable with either what had been said, or all the dead bodies surrounding them. 'My company occupies an old logger clearing. Cook-pits have been dug. If you would arrive in time for a modest feast, we'd best get moving.'

'A moment,' said Casnock. 'Who are these Teblor? Do they seek to join us? Those dogs will be trouble.'

Gower spoke. 'They are all with us. The dogs are bound to the one they protect.'

Delas Fana then said, 'We shall camp apart, not far, but not too close, lest there be any misunderstanding. Lord Gower, I assume you and your brother will join your clans?'

'I will,' said Gower. 'But not Nilghan. He is banished from all kin for the duration of one year. For being an ass.'

'And I'll not miss a single moment of your company!' Nilghan snapped, crossing his brawny, hairy arms.

'Better to mangle the marmot's scrawny neck, Gower.'

'He'll serve a purpose in the Teblor camp,' said Gower, shrugging. 'Keeping away other Jheck.'

'By smell alone, I'm sure.'

The lieutenant was the first to pass through the notch and into the forest beyond. Rant and Delas Fana both dismounted to join Pake Gild who still led her horse with an unconscious Valoc on the travois. The horses were not too pleased passing through the notch but settled immediately afterwards.

Rant found himself thinking of the dead caribou he'd seen in the lake, so long ago now. Bloated like these bodies. The Wilders were small people in Rant's eyes, but heat and gases had made them giants. Death was indifferent to size. He saw no wounds on any of the corpses, just swollen blue-tinted faces with burst veins on cheeks and foreheads. The emptiness of their eyes told him stories he didn't want to know, whispering of the world as it was, which was nothing like the world Rant had once known, the one he had believed to be no different from anywhere else.

Silver Lake, the town that had been all he'd known, was now just one more stain of ash on the ground. These bodies ringed it like an offering. If so, which god looked down right now, with pleased, satisfied eyes?

They moved deeper into the forest, passing one abandoned camp after another, skirting heaps of rubbish and discarded weapons. They found the bodies of Wilder elders and the lame, arranged in even rows beside some of these camps. Their throats had been slit and the expressions on their faces seemed peaceful, almost relieved. Burdens, explained Nilghan, to a fleeing people.

After a time, Pake Gild's hand rested on Rant's arm. 'You are descending into shock, Rant. I can see it in your eyes, your face. These horrors are surpassing for us all. Is there no end to it? But I tell you, there is. Somewhere ahead, sometime soon.'

'I will protect everyone,' said Rant, only now realizing how tightly he gripped the handle of his knife. 'All the Jheck. These mercenaries. No more dying. It has to end.'

'I fear you overreach,' said Pake Gild. 'Your father was one for vast, terrible vows. Do not fall into that trap, for as Valoc here might tell you, each and every vow is announced by the click of yet another shackle. Leave your future free of such things, Rant.'

'I see one god before us all,' said Rant, 'and he has my father's face.'

'Karsa is not to blame for this.'

'Isn't he? I am not so sure, Pake Gild. I feel his shadow over all of this. All that he has turned away from now haunts us. My future is not free. We are all on his path.'

She squeezed his arm, then released him.

Rant shook his head. 'I don't know what to do, Pake Gild. I still wish to find my mother, but she will not be among these Jheck, or those mercenaries.'

'No, but the mercenaries may possess information on where the residents of Silver Lake went. We will ask them.'

They continued on, but a strange unease now accompanied Rant. Through the hand that gripped the knife's handle, he felt waves of alarm, radiating up from the blade. There was a wind now, high in the canopy overhead, coming down from the north, the wrong direction for this time of year. On occasion, it curled down through the branches, the air unseasonably cold.

'It feels wrong to be in a forest,' said Rant.

'I feel it too,' said Pake Gild. 'We should not linger here long.'

They came upon the first small camps of Jheck. The White and Black tribes seemed to be all mixed together. Most were sembled, but others remained veered, and Rant's dogs had drawn in close around him. Sculp walked on his left, at times brushing against him. For the first time, Rant saw pups and children. It seemed hunger was already an issue, with thin limbs and bloated bellies.

Both Gower and Casnock slowed up as kin gathered. Questions and answers in the Jheck tongue, growing heated. At a gesture, Lieutenant Ara invited the Teblor to continue onward. A short time later they reached the clearing where the mercenaries had raised their tents.

Rant saw the cook-pits. The huge carcasses skewered over them were horse.

'No, Rant,' said Pake Gild in a low tone, 'we should not stay here for long.'

Delas Fana strode back to them, leaving a bemused Nilghan in her wake. 'I don't like this,' she said. 'Mercenary companies are not to be trusted. Gower and Casnock should be getting their people moving. South, as quickly as possible. Instead, they are besieged, arguing with dozens of Nilghans. And where is this War-Bitch goddess?'

Rant looked around, studying the southlander mercenaries. They all seemed tense and unhappy. They held on to their weapons and remained in whatever armour they owned. There were saddles on the ground but no horses.

Lieutenant Ara approached. 'Rest here. You are safe. We will soon eat.'

'You killed your own horses,' said Delas Fana.

'It was necessary.'

'You need to get everyone moving.'

Ara nodded. 'Hopefully, now that Lord Gower is here, he and Casnock can begin to organize their people.'

'Has their goddess appeared?'

The woman smiled. 'By words alone. It's my thought that she doesn't even exist, to be honest. Rather, Casnock and now Gower will use her to enforce their will.'

Some renewed commotion drew their attention. Jheck warriors appeared from the west side of the camp, and a moment later Rant saw Casnock, and then Gower, and with them were two men. Many weapons were out among the Jheck.

Ara swore under her breath. 'I don't believe this.' She turned, caught another southlander's attention. 'Irik, get Commander Balk here. Quickly!'

Rant remembered those uniforms, although it had been years since he'd last seen them. 'They are Malazan marines,' he said to Pake Gild and Delas Fana.

A groaning sound came from the travois, followed by Valoc's frail voice. 'Don't let them see me.'

Delas Fana moved round to crouch beside Valoc. 'You are safe,' she said. 'I promise you this.'

411

'Marines . . .'

'Only two of them.'

A strangled laugh answered her, and then Valoc said, 'Six, two, as if it makes a difference.'

'The Jheck surround them,' said Delas Fana. 'Valoc, here, let me unbind you.'

'No point, Delas Fana. I cannot run. I don't know why you took me away from my kin. I wanted to die there. Leave me here or take me back. Is it far? Perhaps I can crawl.'

'Enough, Valoc,' Delas Fana said in a hard tone. 'Self-pity ill suits a Teblor warrior.'

'You don't understand, Delas Fana. You can't.'

'Oh, and why is that?'

'Because you are Uryd. You have not lived the life of a Sunyd.' A hand waved, feebly. 'Remove the trap, please. It bites. How it bites!'

Rant turned away. Something about Valoc disturbed him deeply, as if when Rant looked upon him he saw instead a mirror reflection, distorted but still recognizable. His own face, his own body, and the limb that was both there and not there, like the time in the lake or lying in Damisk's boat, trapped between numbness and agony.

The man who must be Commander Balk had arrived and now stood beside Lieutenant Ara, watching as Casnock led the two marines over. Behind them, Gower and Nilghan were arguing in their own language.

'Sergeant Spindle,' said the mercenary commander. 'This is unexpected.'

'Balk,' the marine named Spindle replied with a nod. 'Is this Lord Casnock your employer?'

'He is.'

Nodding again, Spindle turned to the lord of the White Jheck. 'May I ask, Lord Casnock, your need for a mercenary company?'

The lord scowled. 'Why should I answer you? Do you not understand such hirings? Is it not a civilized thing to offer coin for the service of swords? Gold for blood? The borrowed blade?'

'Oh,' said Spindle, 'that part we understand well, and indeed, we will honour it. As I'm sure Commander Balk told you.'

'Then what else is there for you to know?'

'Well,' said Spindle, 'that depends, Lord Casnock. You are already within the borders of the Malazan Empire. Your people – there are thousands here, are there not?'

'All the Jheck who remain alive are here,' said a voice behind the two marines, and Gower stepped into view, trailed by Nilghan. 'White-furred and black, silver and rust.'

'A migration, Lord? Or an invasion?'

Gower grimaced. 'Both, I suspect.'

Spindle faced Casnock again. He glanced at Commander Balk as he said, 'Eleven hundred mercenaries will not make much difference, I'm afraid. The Malazan Empire does not appreciate invasions and will respond in force.'

Balk snorted. 'Oh, you appreciate invasions well enough, Sergeant, when it's you doing the invading.'

'Those days are done,' Spindle calmly replied, eyes narrowing on Casnock. 'You might have fared better by not hiring this company. The lands south might be imperial, but they're sparsely populated. Moving by stealth, you might have penetrated deep into the territory, found some success. But in the end, we'd have to stop you, to protect our citizens. On the day of your last stand, do you really think Commander Balk will fall at your side? Mercenary companies are not about last stands, Lord Casnock.'

Some deep emotion had taken Casnock – he was nothing like Gower in this, Rant could see, who held things hidden behind cool, cunning eyes. But the lord of the White Jheck seemed to be near weeping. Voice trembling, he said, 'The waters rose. We lost our land. There is nowhere else to go.' He waved his hands. 'Look at us! Hairy savages, wild beasts, feared by all. The southlands are civilized. We are your season of the hunt and you will come out by the thousands, wolf-pelts to harvest.' He drew a long, shaky breath, his eyes glistening. 'To pass through is all we can hope for. But to then be hunted day and night, our elders and our children slain when flight is impossible, forever seeking a place empty of your people, how far would we have to travel? How many of us would be left when at last we found a new home? No, we required an escort. Southlanders.'

Spindle turned to Balk. 'Your company chooses this?'

Balk nodded.

'Commander,' said Spindle, 'my apologies. This is slowly becoming clearer. The problem I am seeing is that it was you, Andrison Balk, advising Lord Casnock or his messengers on your old enemy, the Malazan Empire. Nevertheless, this was a worthy contract.'

Balk blinked, and then nodded a second time. 'Thank you, Sergeant. I think.'

'I wish you'd told us.'

'I was ordered not to.' Balk gestured towards Casnock. 'For reasons he has just explained.'

'We meant to pass unseen if possible,' said the Jheck. He sighed heavily, looking utterly defeated. 'No choice. Who in the south would accept us?'

Spindle's gaze was level, steady as he regarded the Jheck lord, as he answered quietly, 'We would.'

The lord frowned. 'You, a simple soldier, you speak for your empire?'

'Aye, I do. More to the point, we will find you a place to live, and we will provide provisions for the journey to that place.'

Bewildered, Casnock glanced at Balk, who shrugged and said, 'I am no friend to the Malazan Empire. Nor would I trust its governors. What Spindle said about my advice was, sadly, accurate.' He hesitated, and then added, 'But these marines, the gods help me, I trust them. I trust this man, too. We sighted their approaching battalions. They could have annihilated us. Instead, they accepted the truth of this contract. They let us go. Despite . . .' he hesitated, '. . . everything.'

Spindle said to Balk, 'Provide their escort, Commander. We will link up with you when we can with resupply. Word will go out that you are sanctioned in your task of protecting these displaced people. The lands of the Malazan Empire are both safe passage and potential home. There will be no season of the hunt. Mind you,' he added, 'don't fuck this up. No raiding.'

'I hear you, Sergeant,' said Balk.

Spindle returned his attention to Casnock. 'Lord? Do you promise to keep your packs under control?'

But Casnock was in no state to reply. Hands to his face, he turned away. Instead, it was Gower who answered the sergeant. 'We do. Who among us would risk the wrath of War-Bitch?'

Spindle nodded. He glanced at his companion. 'I think it's time to leave.'

At a gesture from Gower, the Jheck pulled away from the two marines. Balk then turned to one of his aides. 'Get these two Malazans an escort back to the tree-line. There are still a few Wilders about and they're desperate enough to be dangerous. I don't want this agreement made by the sergeant not to reach his Fist. Our damned lives depend upon it.'

The aide moved off.

Rant thought to speak to these Malazan marines, but suddenly, he was once more the child he had been, bloodied by stones and kneeling in the street. The shadow falling upon him, the lone marine stepping in between Rant and his so-called friends. And then the calloused hand reaching down to help him to his feet. The pangs of excruciating shyness taking all words or thought from the child's mind.

Instead he simply watched, remaining at a distance and unable to draw even a single step closer, as the two marines made their way back to the clearing's edge, and there, three mercenaries arrived to provide their escort.

Beside Rant, Pake Gild said, 'Gower wishes to speak with us, I think. Casnock as well, but he's not yet . . . ready. The fear haunting him must have been a terrible burden.'

'They lost their homeland,' Rant said. 'They had nowhere to go. They are strangers, and so much of the world,' he added, thinking of the Teblor tribes, 'hates strangers.'

'I hope that marine wasn't lying.'

Rant said nothing, his gaze lingering on the place where they had re-entered the forest with their escort.

Lieutenant Ara left Balk's side and approached. 'You are invited to eat, Teblor.'

As they moved to accept Ara's inviting gesture, Rant's hand closed again about the handle of his knife. Thinking of the child he once was, and the uniform he remembered so well.

The worn grip felt like ice in his palm. A faint shudder ran through him, and he frowned.

Bray timed it perfectly. They were halfway back out of the forest, well away from the last of the Jheck camps. The two Malazans were having a low conversation about something, when Bray's mailed fist took the one named Oams in the side of the head, and then, as Spindle turned, his hand already drawing his sword, Bray slammed a punch into his face, shattering the nose and knocking the man unconscious. As he collapsed, Sugal moved up.

'Gag the fuckers, quick. Bind them up, Bray, get all their fucking weapons. Gods below, this is going to be fun.'

'I want this one,' said Bray, kneeling over Oams. 'I'm not into your shit. I'll do him as soon as he's awake. I want him to see me put my knife-point to his forehead, between the eyes, and then I'll start pushing it down.'

'A waste,' muttered Stick, looking jumpy, her eyes bright.

Sugal finished gagging the sergeant. He paused to smile down at that broken, bloody face. 'Oh, this is going to be fun. Stick, there's an old shack just up this side trail, by the wood stacks. Let's drag him there.'

'I can't wait,' whispered Stick, wiping at her lips. 'This is going to be so good.'

'Bray,' said Sugal, 'meet us up there when you're finished.'

'I will.'

Stick laughed. 'Then you can watch how it's supposed to be done. Knife in the brain? Too fucking easy by far.'

Sugal paused. 'You catch any of that between Balk and these bastards? I was too far away.'

Stick kept licking her lips. Sugal wondered if she was hiding something. In answer to his question she shook her head. 'Fucking conversations, all bullshit courtesy. Balk playing the highborn for all it's worth. Noble this and noble that. Don't worry about any of it. I got Balk all wrapped up and not just between my legs. We'll do Ara tonight, when we get back. Then we'll soak the Jheck for all they got. We'll make it perfect.'

They got Spindle's limp form between them and set off up the side trail.

'Fucking couldn't believe it,' said Sugal, already breathing hard. 'Balk just ordering us into the fucking forest. Even after they went and killed our mages. We're not the only ones feeling betrayed, I'm sure of it. We should've killed them all.'

'Those mines,' said Stick.

Sugal snorted. 'Send a hundred ahead in the first wave. The ones so stupid they'll do whatever Balk tells them to do. Walk out there, fools, blow up those mines for us, one boot at a time. Get rid of those mines just like that, then in we go. Even their magic couldn't have saved them – you saw it, Stick, they damn near stumbled out through the gate.'

'Hit them there and then,' said Stick, 'and nobody crosses that field of mines at all.'

'Good point. But we were in the trees by then, remember. I'm saying we could've taken them right in town. Get some still alive and roast them slowly in all the burning shit. Balk's got to go.'

'He will. And I'll make the night last with him, too. Taking away my wine, the fucking shit. Then we strand all those filthy dogs—'

'Wolves.'

'Whatever. Put out the word wherever we pass through. A fortune in wolf-pelts for the taking.'

'Did you see those fleeces? How do they turn them into gold like that?'

'No idea and who cares,' gasped Stick. 'I see the shed.'

Oams felt a fierce pain in his head. He opened his eyes, but they weren't working right. He was being jostled, dragged through underbrush by his boots. Things spun crazily and he could taste vomit in his mouth, which was partly full of sodden wool. He groaned.

The pulling stopped, his heels thumping as they were released. Then a broad, blunt, bearded face was looking down on him, breaths harshly whistling through a crooked nose.

'Awake,' the man said. 'Good. Decided to drag you off the trail, just in case. Now we're good and alone. That knife to Balk's throat, you got to pay for that.'

Oams frowned. What was the man talking about? He tried to speak, realized that he was gagged.

The man tugged the wool cloth away. 'Got something to say? Don't scream. I won't abide screaming.'

'Healer,' Oams requested. 'I think I fell. Did I fall? Did something happen?'

The man slapped him hard. 'Clear your head, fucker. I want you to get what I'm going to do to you.'

Vision slowly steadying, Oams watched as the man drew out a large hunting knife. 'What's that for?'

'Killing,' answered the man.

'Who?'

'You.'

'Oh.' Oams tried to bring up a hand, to hold against the side of his head, where he felt blood leaking down into his ear, but the hand wouldn't move, and now he felt the leather strips binding his wrists together. Then he blinked. And blinked a second time. 'Careless,' he said.

'More like stupid.'

'If you say so.'

The man grinned. 'I do.'

'I don't think you get it,' Oams said, his head pounding.

The man frowned. 'I'm going to kill you now. What's not to get?'

'I think,' Oams said, his words slightly slurring, but his vision suddenly sharp, 'her name is Tangle-Witch.'

'What? Who?'

She filled the whole space behind the man. A wind was thrashing in the trees high above, last autumn's wet leaves spinning into the air as icy gusts reached down to rake the trail. She loomed, not quite solid, but solid enough.

'Behind you,' Oams said.

He watched as the man was suddenly grasped at the wrists and yanked upward, off his feet.

Bones snapped and the man's mouth opened wide in a scream that, curiously, made no sound at all. Then both arms were torn from their sockets at the shoulder, leaving the man to fall.

The timing of that had to be perfect. How did she manage it?

He landed with a wet thump, legs spasmodically kicking Oams in the shins.

The red-haired apparition showed Oams an expression of grief and horror, before returning her attention to the mercenary. He'd been a big man, wide and muscled. Those shoulder muscles now flapped wetly as blood spat out, white tendons dangling like a marionette's strings. She collected up one leg by the ankle, set a wide, bare, taloned foot against the man's crotch.

Pulling his leg off took some time. Flinging it aside, she set to to do it again with the other leg.

Oams was pretty certain the man was dead by then. At least, he hoped so.

Rolling onto one side, he looked around. Wasn't he with someone? There'd been others, he was sure of it. He struggled against his bindings – there were ones around his ankles as well.

'Oh fuck,' he murmured. *Spindle. The other two, they've got Spindle.*

'Sweet lady,' he said, 'cut my bindings, please! I need to get up. I need to get to Spindle—'

Instead, she picked him up as one would a child, pressed him savagely against her chest.

Oams felt more nipples than he expected, one against his undamaged temple, another on his jawline, and yet another down by his neck. He tried to twist free. 'Gods below, just untie me! I'm begging you!'

She sat, partly on the dead mercenary's limbless torso, and began rocking and then crooning.

'Untie me,' Oams whispered.

She hugged him all the tighter.

The shed wasn't much of a shed, more a lean-to intended to cover cut logs as they seasoned. But with the wind working up and all the leaves and twigs whipping down from shredded branches, any shelter would do.

Stick knelt on Spindle's chest, playing with her knives in front of the sergeant's open eyes. 'Yes,' she said in a low murmur, 'you stay awake for me. We're going to take all night, you and me.'

'And me,' Sugal added. 'He ain't all yours, you know.'

'I got his face and neck and chest,' snapped Stick. 'Then his cock and balls.'

'Not leaving me much,' Sugal said.

'Hands, feet, behind the knees, the places that hurt like fuck. Be creative.' She leaned in close to Spindle's face. 'Doing Balk a favour here, you understand. It's not personal.' She snorted a laugh. 'Never is, actually. It's just that I'm an artist, right? I sculpt. With knives. And all the appreciation I'll ever need, why, I'll find it in your eyes.'

'Just get started – what's that—'

Sugal stumbled or something behind Stick, probably tripping on a fallen branch. But Stick didn't care. She heard him grunt and then gasp, and a familiar sound made her stiffen. *That's a knife-blade leaving flesh.*

She whipped around, both knives slashing.

There was a flicker of something the colour of copper, then terrible pain in her wrists. She fell back, staring at the stumps where her hands were supposed to be.

Another flash, right into her face, and suddenly, a void of nothing, into which she sank, screaming all the way.

It was difficult to make out, as blood from his broken nose crusted around his eyes. His head had, at some point – probably when they carried him – hung upside down. But Spindle thought he recognized his saviour.

In the camp they'd just left. A young Teblor warrior. He'd been with two Teblor women, standing well back. Spindle had noticed some kind of yearning in his face, and how the youth's eyes had tracked him and Oams. A few curious moments, but nothing came of it.

Now, after knife-work too fast to even follow, he was kneeling beside Spindle, cutting his bindings. Teblor hounds appeared on all sides, one of them collecting up one of Stick's hands. It began chewing, bones crunching.

The youth then leaned close and said something that left Spindle confused, uncertain how to respond even if he could. Then his hands were at last free and he reached up to pull away the gag.

But the youth had already withdrawn. Gesturing to his dogs, he set off back to the camp without another word.

Spindle slowly sat up. His thoughts were muddy, his headache ferocious. His broken nose throbbed and the swelling was getting worse around his eyes.

Sudden thrashing made him lift his gaze, to find Oams stumbling towards him. One side of the man's head was drenched in blood.

'Sergeant! Fuck, you're alive. Thank – who, ow, Stillwater's here? Fuck, those are the cleanest cuts I've ever seen. Spindle? How did I get here? What happened? Where is she?'

'Sit down,' Spindle said in a dry rasp. 'I need to bind your head. That's a bad one.'

'Who was that I saw – I saw someone, kneeling right over you. Thought, are they kissing? But I mean, Stillwater? Have you lost your wits?'

'No, Oams, but you have. Not Stillwater. That was a Teblor from the camp we just left. The young one, a boy, I think. Hard to tell with them, though.'

'So he killed these two, and then kissed you?'

'No kiss. Just words. I didn't get them. Still don't. But even so, they were the sweetest words I've ever heard.'

Oams pawed at one side of his face. 'Well. Do I fucking have to ask, Spindle?'

'That's more like you, Oams. You do realize that it entertains me to feed you mere scraps of information, right?'

Oams sat on the mulch. 'Bastard,' he muttered, looking down at the blood smeared on his palm.

'Anyway,' Spindle said with a shake of his head. 'He leant down close, as you saw, and all he said to me was: *"For the knife."*'

Oams frowned at the sergeant. 'That . . . makes no sense.'

'How'd you get away, Oams?'

'No idea. Can't remember fuck all. Just came to beside a freshly dismembered body, and something had chewed through my bindings. With a whole lot of spit left behind.' He touched his temple tenderly. 'Was that a punch?'

'It was.' Spindle slowly rose. 'A fist wrapped inside mail. I'll bandage your head, and then we've got to move.'

'We in a hurry?'

'More than we know, Oams.'

'That makes no sense either, Sergeant.' He shook his head, then winced. 'Was this by Balk's order?'

Frowning, Spindle sighed. 'Can't see how that would make any sense, Oams. Though from what the woman said, they were doing it for him.'

'A few more questions for that bastard, then,' said Oams.

'Aye, but later. We need to get back to that barn and our horses and ride to Culvern. I don't like this wind at all.' Spindle slowly climbed to his feet. 'Can you walk, Oams?'

'Maybe.'

'Can you run?'

'Gods below.' Oams clambered upright and stood, weaving slightly. 'I'll try. "For the knife", he said?'

Spindle nodded. '"For the knife."'

Oams looked away. 'Huh.'

'Stay close, Oams. I don't want to lose you.'

His memory wasn't working well. Oams recalled staggering through wind-whipped woods. A few spats of icy rain. Then out into a clearing – Balk's old camp. Then, an unknown amount of time later, they'd saddled their horses and mounted up and were now riding at a canter down Culvern Road.

At some point, Spindle had glanced to the right, and had then twisted in his saddle to look northwest. 'Gods below!'

Oams had stared at his sergeant, trying to recall what they were doing here, wondering if he should ask about what Spindle had just seen. Enemy forces? In this storm? With its growing roar? Or was that—

Finally, he followed Spindle's gaze.

The northwest flatland looked somehow wrong. Terribly wrong. What was he seeing? 'Sergeant?'

'Floodwaters! Follow me!'

The sergeant turned down off the road, shifting their direction towards the southeast. Oams followed, and they pushed their horses into a gallop across a ploughed field.

That heaving, foaming wall of water was coming at an angle – and this was why they'd left the road, were now riding slightly inland. Oams nodded to himself. That made sense. Good thing Spindle was in charge. Oams didn't even know where they were, wasn't quite sure what was happening, or where all that water came from.

'We won't outrun it,' Spindle shouted.

'Won't we? It's still far away, isn't it?' Oams twisted to look behind them. In time to see the flood slam into the farmstead they'd left not too long ago. The barn exploded, shattered planks of wood flying skyward. 'No, it's closer,' he said.

'Fuck!'

Oams nodded. That was the right word for this, wasn't it. The roaring sound got louder.

He knew he was slipping into and out of awareness as they rode on in front of the water. It was like a nightmare he kept falling back into. At one point, he saw that they were managing to maintain the gap between them and that roaring, towering wall. But in the next moment the horses had begun to tire, and in a flash of cold clarity, Oams knew they were done for. No outrunning their fate this time. Even the damned witch who haunted him could do nothing now.

'*Fuck! Hang on, Oams! Just hang on!*'

'What? Why—'

Both horses screamed.

Then the ground was passing beneath them in a blur, and Oams could hear, cutting through the roar, Spindle's harsh voice, unleashing a stream of bitter hate. It shocked Oams, and then he was shocked a second time, when he realized that all that hate coming from Spindle was not directed at anyone but himself. It made no sense.

Then it did, as the horses screamed again, and in a surge, they began running as they'd never run before. They ran faster than seemed possible. They slowly began to pull further away from that raging, tumbling wall of water. Oams held on as best he could.

He knew, if but vaguely, about Spindle's sorcery. How it agitated animals of all sorts. Which was why Spindle never used it, why he hated it, in fact. But it'd never occurred to Oams just what that sorcery did – one could hardly ask a dog, could one? Or a horse, for that matter.

The horses ran until blood replaced the lathered sweat on their sleek hides. They ran until that hide began splitting in widening gashes as the muscles beneath – swollen and engorged – began to erupt, tearing themselves apart. They ran until bones started splintering.

For a time, Oams was certain that those horses ran while dead. He clung on, pain bounding through his skull. How long could this go on? It would end – it had to – and then? Then . . . his mind went away again.

CHAPTER TWENTY-TWO

What gesture will you make, to announce to all the true colour
of your soul? How long will we all wait for you to find your
courage?

On the Bed Where I Die
Jalstin Peff

BLANKET AND FOLIBORE CORNERED CORPORAL SNACK DOWN AT
the latrine. Stillwater was just coming from there, relieved that
no beady eyes were looking up at her from beneath the board she
had been sitting on. What a ridiculous world, when you had to check
before you pissed.

Snack was looking distraught. Stillwater had never been distraught
herself, but she'd seen it in plenty of faces, mostly just moments before
she stuck a knife in them. 'This looks,' she said, coming up to the three
men, 'like bullying. What's the poor corporal done now?'

'We just want answers,' said Folibore.

'Asked a question, that's all,' Blanket added. 'Didn't think it was
going to make him cry.'

Now all three of them were looking distraught.

Sighing, Stillwater regarded them. 'I knew three boys once. They
accidentally burned down a stable. Empty, luckily for them, but there
was still talk of stringing them up, on account of, you know, property damage. Playing with mage-fire or something, or so they admitted
after I volunteered to question them.'

Three shocked expressions looked back at her.

'You took a knife to three little boys?' Folibore asked, face starting
to crumple.

'Didn't have to,' she replied with an eye-roll. 'You're missing the point. So I'll just ask: who did you set on fire, Corporal?'

'Nobody that wasn't threatening to gut me,' Snack replied. 'It was my traps.'

'Wolf-traps,' Blanket elaborated. 'He had dozens of them. You were there, Stillwater. You saw what happened. Those damned things are for wolves and even then, gods below, what a cruel and heartless thing to do. Against people – even Teblor – that's just . . .' His mouth worked a bit longer, but he was clearly at a loss.

'So we wanted to know what he was thinking,' Folibore explained. 'Then he starts crying.'

'I'm not crying, Folibore. I'm *upset*. It's different.'

'Poor Snack,' said Stillwater. 'He's upset. Can't you see that?'

A signal horn from the marine camp behind them announced that it was time to strike the tents. Finally, it seemed, the town of Culvern was ready for them. And not too soon, either, since scouts had sighted a Teblor force on its way.

At Stillwater's effort at commiseration, Snack turned on her. 'It's all your fault, Stillwater!'

'Me? I didn't do nothing, or if I did you're still alive so count yourself lucky because next time I won't be so careless.'

'I've been trying to tell my story for months and months, damn you! But no! You always shut me down. Boring, you kept saying!'

'Oh, that story. Well, aye, it *was* boring.'

'How can you know that if you never heard it?'

She shrugged. 'Because, Snack, *you're* boring.'

'That story, you soulless assassin cow, is *about the traps*!'

'The ones you collect and carry everywhere? Why didn't you say so in the first place? You wouldn't believe all the speculations and weird ideas people come up with about you and your stupid traps. Well, I don't think they're weird, but everyone else does.'

Snack clutched the hair over his ears and pulled until his face flattened out, eyes bulging.

'Besides,' continued Stillwater, 'it's probably *still* boring.' She turned to leave.

'Stand right there, soldier! That's a fucking order!'

She faced him again in surprise. 'You're ordering me to get bored to death? That's just vicious.'

'I was a child,' Snack said. 'Playing in the forest behind the pasture that I wasn't allowed in because of the sheep—'

'That makes sense,' Folibore said to Blanket and they nodded at each other.

'Gods below, Snack,' said Stillwater. 'Sheep? And you just a boy?'

'On account of the lambs, damn you all! That must have been what brought the wolves, right? There I was, playing, and suddenly I was climbing a fucking tree as fast as I could. And they wanted me! They hung around all day and all night even. And I had to – well, I had to, right? But it wasn't much of a tree, not really, and not one branch I could reach would take my weight—'

'And you just a boy?' Stillwater asked, frowning. 'You sure it wasn't a sapling? And if so, it couldn't have been very tall, could it. You said wolves? You sure they weren't foxes?'

'Or puppies,' Blanket suggested.

'Good point,' agreed Folibore. 'Fox puppies and wolf puppies look pretty much the same. I think.'

'I was traumatized! I still have nightmares about it!' Snack pointed at Stillwater. 'And there was talk of Jheck in that army. Wolves! But you – you've never had nightmares, have you? Being so fucking *insane.*'

She crossed her arms and leaned on one leg, hip cocked. 'I'm having one now.'

The horn sounded a second time, and everyone turned to face the camp. 'Now look,' moaned Folibore. 'All the tents are down except those ones, because those ones are ours.'

'Look at Drillbent,' said Stillwater, 'trying to take them all down. He'd get it done a lot faster if he wasn't swearing so much.'

'And actually just doing them one at a time,' Blanket added, 'instead of all at once. There's Anyx Fro. What's she doing?'

'Watching,' answered Stillwater. 'Maybe supervising.'

'No wonder Drillbent's swearing,' said Folibore. 'Anyx Fro's not very good at supervising. Look! She's pointing him to the next tent and the last one's still a mess.'

'Uh oh,' said Blanket. 'He's now armed with a tent pole. This could get ugly, my friends, since Anyx can't run a straight line to save her life, even when it might save her life.'

Stillwater turned to Snack and gave him her biggest smile. 'That was a great story, sir. But don't you think you'd better help your sergeant with those tents?'

'I don't like forests! Because I don't like wolves! I wasn't expecting those damned Teblor to be there!'

'Really?' Folibore asked, eyebrows lifting. 'I mean, they were *everywhere.*'

'I was panicking. All those nightmares, they were getting worse and worse!'

'Now I see,' said Stillwater. 'You've gone and left them all behind, haven't you? Poor Snack, now fated to be a snack – hey, is that why you're named that?' Her shoulders slumped. 'But it seems so . . . obvious, you know? On account of the wolves.'

A horn announced an imminent attack, temporarily breaking up the conversation, as they all turned now to look northward.

'That's the messiest charge I've ever seen,' observed Folibore.

Marines were forming a line with their backs to the town's low wall, and now Drillbent was shrieking and pointing at them.

'We should get going,' said Stillwater. 'I've misplaced my shield and it looks like I'll need it.'

They set out to rejoin their sergeant and Anyx Fro, who was now unpacking her Iron Maw, and since she had spent most of the morning packing it in the first place, Stillwater could guess at the words coming from Fro's mouth which didn't stop moving despite all the ruckus erupting around her.

'No time to get behind the walls,' Snack observed. 'We got us another fight on our hands.'

'That last one wasn't a fight,' replied Blanket. 'These are mounted Teblor and, Icari's fury, are those giant dogs?'

'Could be small horses,' Folibore suggested. 'No, sorry, they're not small horses. They're Teblor war-dogs.'

'Way to go, Corporal,' said Stillwater as they reached the mess that was their camp, 'where are all your traps when we actually need them? Oh, I know. In the forest!'

'One day,' hissed Snack, 'I swear I'll do a First Squad on you, Stillwater.'

'Really, Corporal!' said Folibore, shocked. 'We don't talk about the First Squad, ever!'

Stillwater walked over to Anyx Fro. And sure enough, she was cursing something fierce. 'Give it up,' Stillwater said. 'You'll never have it assembled in time.'

Anyx Fro fell silent. She stared down at the various pieces on the ground at her feet, and then at the huge barrel in her arms. Her bulging cheek shifted and rippled. 'You're right. I'll just have to hold it like this.'

'That'll work,' said Stillwater, nodding. 'Not at all, I mean.'

'Get your damned gear and get in the ranks!' Drillbent bellowed.

'But the tents—'

Despite the haste, there wasn't much jostling. Everyone knew their place. Stillwater was the only marine without a shield, but she wasn't too worried about that. Those poor Teblor would never reach them.

She'd seen it before, though not here on Genabackis, and even with only half a legion of Malazan marines, the wall of sorcery they could deliver was devastating.

But then a note of worry was voiced, possibly by Folibore, who knew all kinds of obscure things, and it ran like wildfire through the ranks.

Teblor are resistant to magic. So are their horses. So are their war-dogs.

Suddenly, Stillwater wished she'd found her shield. Oh, and her short-sword. Sighing, she drew her knives. 'Word of warning,' she called out, 'I might go sneaky.'

'Even though she's not a mage or anything,' Anyx Fro called out immediately after, grunting as she adjusted the huge iron barrel in her arms, 'Stillwater's diving into her warren like a cowardly rat!'

Catcalls sounded on all sides.

Stillwater's mind scrambled for a retort or something, but she never got the chance, for someone close behind her said in a deadpan tone, 'They're not charging.'

Since that was a strange thing to say, Stillwater shifted her attention to the approaching Teblor army, moving in a ragged wall across the flat farmland.

Suddenly, that observation was being shouted up and down the ranks, and the horns that blared then announced a sudden change of plans. Bewildered, Stillwater turned to Anyx Fro. 'What was that signal? We're retreating? We'll get cut to pieces!'

'No we won't,' said Folibore, quickly slinging his shield back over his shoulder. 'That came from a watchtower. Look at the horizon behind them!'

What? Stillwater squinted. The horizon-line had lost its sharp demarcation, vanishing inside a hazy bank of something like smoke or fog. She looked again at the approaching Teblor. No, not charging.

Fleeing.

'That's water!' someone shouted. 'A wall of water!'

Stillwater studied that fast-approaching band of white, brown and grey. 'If that's a wall,' she muttered, 'it's pretty high.'

'Higher than Culvern's fucking walls,' Anyx Fro said, dropping her Iron Maw. 'We're all fucked.'

'Maybe not all of us,' said Folibore, shrugging out of his chain hauberk.

'What do you mean?' Anyx Fro asked.

'The barges on the river,' Folibore replied. 'Town's already mostly evacuated, remember. Battalions came in on them and they can go out on them, too.'

'Riding that *fucking wave?*' Anyx Fro demanded in disbelief. 'Give it up, Folibore – we really are fucked.'

'Got to agree with Anyx on this one,' said Stillwater, sheathing her knives. The foremost Teblor riders were now within two or so thousand paces. She could see that all riders were doubled up, carrying non-combatants. Now she saw war-dogs, many with children clinging to them, skinny arms wrapped about brawny necks.

Some horses were going down. Dogs as well. They'd been running for a long time.

Culvern's massive gates were squealing open. The battalions began breaking into their squads, most of them heading for their piles of gear lined up in rows against Culvern's stone wall. Then captains and sergeants in the front ranks bellowed a change of orders.

'First three ranks, drop all shields and sheathe swords! Advance on the double!'

Benger was tugging at So Bleak's arm even before he managed to drop his kit bag. 'Leave it, soldier! Let's move!' An instant later, So Bleak was running forward alongside Benger. There was no need to ask for an explanation. Those first three ranks, still facing the mass of Teblor while awaiting the command to make their way through the gate, could see all too clearly the tragedy unfolding before them.

Exhaustion was dragging down horses and dogs. Children were tumbling away from animals falling dead from burst hearts. Warriors and their passengers were thrown from stumbling, collapsing horses. The children who could picked themselves up and began running. But many were too injured, lying motionless on the ground to be trampled, or limping as best they could before dust and running forms swallowed them.

So Bleak unclasped his sword belt and flung belt and weapon aside. He could hear a flurry of horn blasts well behind him and knew that those marines who had already entered through the gates were now coming back out. They would form a funnel for the Teblor into the city through the gate, to make their invitation as plain as possible.

Here! Into the city! Behind the walls!

So Bleak could see that wall of water now. He knew that the town's stone walls weren't high enough.

The barges! Enough room for the refugees? Most of them? Half?

Aye, if we marines don't join them.

Suddenly, he was among the Teblor. Chaos, dust, stumbling figures on all sides. A marine was yelling, voice hoarse, *'The gates! Go through the gates!'*

A Teblor warrior was on her knees directly in front of So Bleak. He ran up to the woman. 'Almost there! Come on, get on your feet!' He grasped her by an arm and sought to lift her. 'Gods, help me!'

Then, with her help, he had her upright. The agony he saw in the woman's face made her seem ancient. Her eyes were blank, her lips crusted in black dust and her mouth open as her chest heaved. She kept twisting as So Bleak sought to get her facing the gate – he realized that she was looking for someone, the pain in her face now shifting into anguish.

'We'll get them!' So Bleak yelled at her. 'Just go! We'll get them all!'

Another warrior appeared and took the woman by a wrist. They staggered in the right direction and So Bleak wheeled round.

He saw a child on hands and knees and rushed over. At least this one was small enough to carry. Possibly.

On all sides, more and more marines were running into the mob, disappearing into rolling dust.

The Teblor youth was screaming as Blanket and Snack pulled him out from under a dead horse, with Folibore trying to lift part of the animal's lathered carcass. The rider the youth had shared the saddle with was lying nearby, dead, head at an impossible angle. Stillwater could see that the survivor's right leg was dislocated, the joint pulled from the hip socket and jutting out just below the leather belt. She moved alongside Folibore and threw her strength into his efforts.

A final shriek and the youth was free, being dragged away until his frenzied writhing pulled him loose from the grip of the two marines. Then Blanket shouted something to Snack who fell bodily on top of the Teblor, pinning him while Blanket grasped the dislocated leg and pushed the ball joint back into its socket.

The youth's struggles ceased, head lolling. Snack helped get his limp body across Blanket's shoulders and then the big heavy was staggering back towards the distant gate.

Stillwater grasped Folibore's arm. 'Go with Blanket – no way he'll be able to carry that ox all the way!'

Wiping at his face, Folibore then reached with his other hand and cupped Stillwater's chin, his calloused fingers up along her jawline. He met her eyes. 'It's been a sweet pleasure, Stillwater,' he said. 'Now be sure you use that warren of yours and bail before it's too late.'

Stillwater pulled her face away. 'Fuck you, Folibore. I'll see you on the barges.' She quickly moved away, collecting up Anyx Fro before plunging into the dust cloud. 'We look for the little ones, Anyx, ones we can carry, got it?'

'Throw them into your fucking warren, Still!'

'You've lost your mind. There's nasty shit in that realm! Come on!'

'Better than drowning!'

'Getting torn to pieces by a Hound of Shadow? I don't think so!'

'Stillwater!'

She stopped, looked back at Anyx Fro, and then at Creature's little bullet head thrusting up between the woman's breasts, eyes fixed on her. 'Ah, fuck it.'

There was now so much dust that it was impossible to see where they were. Stillwater was fairly certain she knew the direction of the gate. But she saw children running the wrong way, while others simply stood, dazed, uncomprehending.

'Start collecting them up,' she said. 'Get them to hold hands and stay with me – gods below, how many fucking children are there?' She saw one, a girl about her own height, who was carrying a puppy in her arms. 'You! Over here! Quickly!'

'Stillwater – we're still going the wrong way! We should be dragging them back that way!'

'I know. But we need to collect up more. There – get that grown-up Teblor to help us! You! With the broken arm! Can you understand Nathii? Never mind – over here, with us, damn you – no, I know it's the wrong way. We're collecting children! Come on!'

Benger saw Stillwater. And then Anyx Fro, with a crowd around them both. 'Daint, Paltry Skint, follow me!'

They headed to intercept the two women, who seemed to have rounded up a full dozen Teblor, young, old, even a pregnant woman. Just beyond them, Clay Plate arrived as well, one child small enough to carry in one arm, the other on his opposite hip with her arms wrapped about his neck.

Daint was carrying a Teblor baby, still wrapped in cloth, its tiny hands closed into fists as it wailed. Paltry was with the young girl who'd been with the baby, while Benger was holding a small hand that gripped his with surprising strength, the boy's moccasin-clad feet repeatedly kicking at Benger's heels.

Reaching Stillwater, Benger said, 'You're all going the wrong way, you fools!'

'No we're not,' snapped Stillwater. 'We're collecting more!'

'There's no time—'

'No fucking kidding there's no time, Benger! Can't you hear it?'

He could. That wall of water was closing fast. He stared at Stillwater, and then he swore. 'You must be insane! Emurlahn? *Fucking Emurlahn?*'

'Just take charge afterwards, Benger,' said Stillwater.

'The Hounds—'

'*Leave the fucking Hounds to me,*' she said.

Benger would have said more, until he saw the look in her eyes.

'Everyone! Grasp hands! Hold on tight!' Stillwater reached back and got a handful of Anyx Fro's jerkin. 'Ow!' There was Creature, jaws fastened on her hand. 'Get this little shit off me, Anyx Fro!'

'Give him a treat!'

'I haven't got a treat!'

'Then . . . I don't know!'

Snarling, Stillwater moved in, intending to bite the animal's head off if she could. Creature let go and vanished down Anyx Fro's shirt. Stillwater whirled round. The roar of the approaching water was deafening, the ground trembling underfoot, as if being repeatedly pounded by something. 'Follow me!'

She opened the warren into Emurlahn, plunged in, dragging Anyx Fro – and hopefully everyone else – behind her. Five paces, ten, and then twenty and more.

'All through!' came Benger's shout well behind her.

She slammed shut the portal, let go of Anyx Fro and then stumbled to her knees.

The sudden silence made the eerie gloom of Emurlahn even more oppressive. Stillwater lifted her gaze, vision piercing the reality of this realm, seeing instead the world they'd just left.

Swirling, rushing chaos. She saw bodies tumbling past, whipped so hard they spurted blood. She saw enormous boulders bounding and rolling in the savage current. And that world was darkening with every breath, as the deluge grew. Silts in spinning clouds, remnants of farmhouses and barns, fence posts and twisted wire, branches and uprooted trees.

A hand on her shoulder, gripping hard. Benger's rasping voice in her ear. 'What do you see?'

'Bodies.'

'Marines?'

'Marines, Teblor, dogs, horses, things I can't even identify . . .'

He shook her. 'Snap out of it, Stillwater. Get your eyes back on what's here. You need to choose a path.'

Blinking, she rubbed at her face and then stood. 'Right. You're right.' She looked around and then pointed. 'There, the forest. You need to hide.'

After a quizzical look, Benger went to the others, all huddled in a group: the four Teblor warriors, a woman and three men, all kneeling on the damp ground, chests heaving, heads down as they fought to recover; the pregnant woman who seemed to have lost consciousness, but Clay Plate was next to her; and almost a score of children standing or sitting, dazed and uncomprehending. The only marines were Anyx Fro, Clay Plate, Benger and Daint.

Stillwater watched Benger now addressing them all, his tone low.

She swung round to scan the horizon. The line of forest was vast. One of the ancient ones, she could see, with enormous twisted trees and a denuded, lifeless floor she knew would be damp and fetid. She preferred to stay out of places like that, since they seemed to be crammed with carnivores, some on the ground, others in the trees.

Opposite the forest, the plain they were on stretched out, terminating in a line of undulating, barren hills.

'We're ready,' Benger whispered behind her.

Stillwater turned. 'What have you got back?'

He scowled. 'Fuck all. This may be permanent. And I talked to Clay and Daint and Anyx – we don't think we can get us out of here. It's all down to you. We lose you, Still, and we're finished.'

'Maybe, maybe not,' she replied. 'Nothing here's got your scent, not yet anyway. And when I say "scent" I don't just mean how bad you all smell. I mean the imprint of your soul, your life force, all that shit. That's why—'

A distant howl interrupted her, coming from the direction of the hills. Stillwater sighed. 'That's Pallid, that's the one who's got my scent like an itch in his nose. Or her nose. I never bothered to check. She or he knows I'm here, Benger. That's why you all have to get away from me, get into that forest, just out of sight – no deeper. Stay there and don't none of you make a sound.'

'And then?'

'Then Pallid might just leave, after.'

'After what?'

'We're wasting time we don't have, Benger.'

'Stillwater, you can't fight a Hound of Shadow.'

'We're old friends, me and Pallid,' said Stillwater. 'Been dancing for years.' She shrugged. 'Now it's time to see who takes who home for the royal fuck-over.'

'Still—'

'Get them into the woods, Benger.' She reached up and began untying her scarf. 'Is it possible to assassinate a Hound of Shadow? Probably not. How about just inconvenience one?' She got the scarf free and stuffed it under her belt, and then smiled at Benger. 'Let's find out!'

He was about to add something, but she didn't give him the chance, setting off, straight across the plain. The howl sounded a second time, so deep it reverberated in her chest. Stillwater nodded, adjusted her course slightly to head straight for it. 'Poor Pallid,' she whispered. But her mouth was dry. Better, she decided, than full of water. That had looked like a whole damned ocean coming down on them. Where'd all the water come from?

'What a crazy day,' she said aloud as she continued on.

At thirty or so paces she glanced back. The refugees were almost at the tree-line. A moment later the first of them vanished among the black boles.

Stillwater fixed her attention back on the way ahead. Was that something on that hill's slope? Coming fast, now down to the base and momentarily out of sight. She continued jogging, drawing out her knives.

'Caribou and giant rats, birds in the sky, all that thunder a few nights ago. What the fuck were we thinking? Oh, I know. Nothing! That's what. Barbarians invading from the north! Well, no kidding. Gods, we were about to hammer them with magic. Not that it would've worked, if what Folibore said was true. Toblakai shrugged that shit off. So it would've got real messy, back to throwing cheap cussers and hoping for the best.

'Instead, well, only one thing to do. Change the orders. Stay decent, that's all, just stay decent.'

For all she knew, those four marines behind her were the only ones left. Everyone else was already dead. 'Poor everyone else.'

And there was Pallid, coming straight for her. Teblor war-dogs were pretty big. So was Pallid, only Pallid was heavier, wider. 'Oh. No, got that wrong. Pallid's bigger than any Teblor war-dog. Must be a perspective thing. And, um, faster, too.'

The distant dot wasn't a dot any longer. Pallid was coming at full charge.

Stillwater began to sprint. She held up both knives. 'Look at these!' she yelled. 'I'm going to stick them in your eyes!' She kept waving them as she ran.

The enormous beast surged towards her, lips stretched back, all its teeth bared. Its eyes blazed like fist-sized coals. It was lowering its head to a level that matched her eyes. It was intending, she realized, to bite her head off.

'Come on, then!' she shrieked, still gauging its speed. And gods below, it was *fast*.

Stillwater sheathed her knives, making sure both blades locked in their scabbards. She had an instant to raise her hands and then Pallid was upon her like a runaway carriage. 'With teeth!'

She dived down at the last moment, down into the tangle of its forelimbs. Her hands shot out as jaws snapped shut directly above her, her left one finding only air. Then her right hand closed about a foreleg, just above the paw. Not entirely closed, of course, since her hand wasn't big enough for that. But she held on long enough—

— to drag that fucking Hound back into the world she'd just left.

'Gods below,' hissed Benger. He was lying in deep shadows at the forest's edge, along with Anyx Fro, Daint and Clay Plate.

Anyx Fro seemed to choke on something. 'Did she just . . .'

'Oh fuck,' groaned Clay Plate.

Then Daint said, 'Hey, I didn't know she was a mage.'

'Says the man with a brick for a brain,' snapped Anyx Fro. 'How do you think we got here in the first place, Daint?'

Somewhat peevishly, Daint replied, 'If I knew where we were, why, I'd have an answer to that, wouldn't I? Was it you, Clay Plate? I thought it was you. I mean, my warren's Serc, after all, so I don't think it was me. Was it me?'

Benger rubbed his face. 'That's it, then. Fucking Stillwater. Brilliant, aye, but still . . .'

They fell silent then, eyes on an empty plain.

Detonations! Icy cold! Piercing agony in both ears – she released her hold and clawed at her ears as she was rushed through freezing, black, gravel-filled water under vast pressure, spinning and tumbling over a bottom that was no longer a ploughed field. Instead, it seemed to be a bed of boulders. She struck one after another, screaming her pain in a thrash of bubbles and nothing else.

She caught a glimpse of something that might be Pallid, borne away into the gloom.

A rock smacked into her forehead, almost stunning her.

Stillwater opened her warren again before another one knocked her senseless, and spilled out, rolling across hard, dry ground. Coughing, choking, so cold she could barely feel her limbs.

Good thing, too, she decided as she caught a glimpse of the ravaging those limbs had taken. When she stopped rolling, she was lying on her stomach, a good position to stay in as she spat more water out from her lungs, and then added a bit of vomit to finish things off.

The ground trembled.

Fuck! Stillwater clambered upright, wavered as her balance was all off, and then carefully steadied herself.

Pallid was about two hundred paces away – downstream in the other world – slowly gathering itself on shaky legs. She saw it lift its head and the two red eyes found her.

Stillwater staggered towards the Hound. 'That's right! Let's do it again, you fat pig!' She was pretty sure she'd shouted that challenge, but deathly silence filled her head. Her ears, she realized, were broken somewhere inside.

No matter. She only hoped Pallid could hear, especially what she next shouted as she ran, wobbling, towards the beast. 'Again and again! A thousand times! In and out! In and out! It'll be such fun!'

To her astonishment, Pallid backed away from her.

'Get back here!' Stillwater screamed.

Pallid backed still further, and then the Hound of Shadow wheeled round and ran.

'Come back, you fucker! Oh, gods, the pain in my head! I'm broken! Injured! I'm dying!' She stumbled on a tuft of something, fell to the ground, arms still reaching for the now distant Hound. 'Come back!' she moaned.

A shadow fell over her and she blinked, lifting her head to look up.

Anyx Fro almost died. Laughing, a huge lump of rustleaf slid down and blocked everything in her throat. As she was thrashing about, Creature's head popped up to see what was going on, and then vanished again. Clay Plate needed to pull her up into an embrace from behind, rhythmically squeezing her chest – Creature along with it – while Benger jammed his finger into her mouth, trying to dig out the plug.

By the time the two succeeded in dislodging the wad of slimy brown goo, Anyx Fro had passed out. Clay Plate knelt beside her. 'She'll live,' he pronounced. Then he peered down between her breasts.

'Really, Clay?' Benger asked.

'That fucking weasel is still alive, dammit.'

'Oh, right. Sorry.'

In the meantime, Daint had been staring out onto the plain. 'Where'd she go?' he asked.

Benger turned. 'What? You mean—'

'I mean,' Daint said in a growl that bespoke fraying patience, 'where'd she go? She took the Hound with her, and then they both came back, and then the Hound ran off, and then she fell over and now she's gone again.'

He was right. Benger rose and stepped out for a better look. No Hound, no Stillwater.

'Shit,' Clay Plate muttered. 'Did she bail on us? I can't believe – she bailed on us!'

'That makes no sense,' Benger objected. 'She wouldn't go back into that flood on purpose. Maybe it was another Hound and we missed it.'

'I didn't miss nothing,' said Daint. 'I was watching the whole time. She sat up, seemed to be waving her hands in the air, and then just disappeared.'

'That's us done for,' croaked Anyx Fro, who'd regained her senses and was lying on her back on the ground behind them.

Sighing, Benger returned to the gloomy shadows. 'Let's get back to the others. Tell them Stillwater got rid of the Hound. That one, anyway.'

'Don't add that bit about "that one anyway", Benger,' advised Anyx Fro, slowly sitting up. She reached for her pouch of rustleaf and began stuffing her mouth again. 'Those kids are scared enough by your face, why add to the horror?'

The voice spoke in her head. *'Nice tattoo.'*

Blinking, Stillwater sat up and looked around. Some kind of shadow had enveloped her, and she wasn't where she'd been a moment ago. Now she was on a hilltop that was surrounded by a low stone wall mostly covered in lichen and moss. A single stone column rose from the centre, so weathered it looked more like a denuded tree trunk. Standing before it and facing her was a pretty good-looking man wearing light leather armour, deer-hide leggings, well-worn boots, a plain knife at one hip and a coiled length of rope at the other. He was smiling and his black hair was long and insultingly clean.

Still soaking wet, Stillwater had begun shivering. 'Can you hear me? I can't.'

'No need to shout, Lady Therose Deshar.'

She got shakily to her feet and brushed feebly at her leggings. 'Lady? What the fuck do you mean by that and how do you know that name? I left that name behind. And look at you! Who do you think you are? Cotillion? Nice try, but I've seen the statues. You're not half bad but he's way better looking.'

'The title is yours to inherit, Lady Deshar, should you elect to return to your family estate and resume the life you left behind. A place as well on the Untan Council of Magistrates—'

'I gave up advocacy and the law,' she replied. 'Too cut-throat for my tastes. Am I dreaming? Did I pass out? Or am I actually dead and if I am, doesn't that Hound *ever* give up the chase? I'm dead already! Leave me alone! Wait! Are you Iskar Jarak? You can't be, I've seen his statues too. He was way better looking as well, unless you went and shaved off your beard, which – and I'm trying to be helpful here – was a mistake.'

The man slowly cocked his head. *'Is this an act?'*

'Is what an act? What am I doing here? I got people to save. Is this Emurlahn? It looks like Emurlahn.'

'Emurlahn. A curious identification. I daresay you've inadvertently picked it up from a barrow you should never have broken into, or has that not even occurred to you? Naming this warren in the language of the Tiste Edur.'

Stillwater shrugged. 'Meanas, Emurlahn, whatever. Are you some vagabond or something? Some pathetic wanderer like Edgewalker, only not as rotten?'

'Wanderer? That suffices. My curiosity, while far from satisfied, now yields to exasperation. You wish to return to your companions? Interlopers all? Very well. I will distract the Hounds from you, for a while. A few days, perhaps?'

'If that's long enough to get us away from the fucking ocean that just landed on us, then good, that's perfect. Go and distract the Hounds.'

He raised his hands, and then hesitated. *'By the way, Pallid now admires you, Stillwater, and by the tattoo around your throat, you have leave to visit Emurlahn. Within limits, that is, which do not include looting the realm's ancient barrows.'*

'Wouldn't even think of it,' she replied, eyes wide.

He studied her for a moment longer.

She maintained her wide-eyed innocence, unblinking.

He gestured and vanished.

No, she must have, because now she was back where she'd started, on that infernal plain. Still shivering, still bruised, still dizzy, still deaf. She lifted her head and said, 'Thanks a whole lot for almost nothing, Cotillion.'

She faced the forest, saw no one. 'Typical. "Oh, poor Stillwater's dead! Let's get out of here."' She set off to find their trail.

In the ancient circle known as Silcha's Last Vow, the god Cotillion stood alone for a time, contemplating the strange conversation just past.

Shadows coalesced beside him into something akin to a cloaked, hooded figure, leaning on a cane. 'You believe her?' it asked Cotillion in a whispery voice.

He grunted. 'What's not to believe?'

Rasping laughter answered him. 'Indeed, as you tracked her all these years, witness to all that she has done, all that she has survived. What's not to believe? Why, I think the answer might be: *all of it.*'

Cotillion shrugged. 'That's the thing with mortals,' he said. 'Some are simply born with . . . something.'

'Do you always pay so much attention to all who tattoo themselves in your name?'

'No. But she reminded me of someone, long ago.'

'That's . . . unnerving, Cotillion.'

'Sorry?'

'Just so,' the god Shadowthrone snapped in irritation. He began to dissolve and moments later was gone.

Cotillion remained for a little while longer. Eventually he shook his head. 'On second thought,' he said to no one, 'nothing like her at all.'

Daint had a nose for things, so when he announced that they were being followed, Benger called everyone to a halt and then had them gather round. 'We got some knives among us,' he said, 'but nothing else.' He squinted at the Teblor warriors. 'Any of you up for a fight if it comes to that?'

The woman and the three men were silent. After a moment the pregnant woman, standing off to one side, spoke. 'We do not understand you.'

Benger frowned. 'What?'

'We came to slay you all. Though I knew I would not be fighting, all my kin would. We are Rathyd, unconquered and avowed enemies of the southlanders who enslaved the Sunyd and destroyed them. I expected to walk over your broken bodies at the end of this day.' She shook her head, now regarding all four marines. 'Then we saw the water and all thoughts of war vanished. Not enough horses, not enough time, and then you were among us. Saving us. We do not understand you.'

'That wall of water,' said Anyx Fro, 'doesn't give a shit who's in front of it. As senseless as a mountain falling on our heads.'

A male warrior spoke rapidly to the pregnant woman in their own tongue. She replied and then said to the marines, 'You could have run. Kadarast saw others, soldiers like you, guiding the Rathyd into the town. Those soldiers could not have survived. Nor was the town's wall high enough. What was the point of it all?'

Benger shrugged. 'We had barges. There was a chance. Not much of one, but we had to try.'

'And not save yourselves? This makes no sense.'

'No,' Benger admitted, 'I suppose not.'

'If your soldiers had gone through the gate and closed it behind them, perhaps they would have had time to get to these barges of yours.'

Benger glanced at his fellow marines. They all looked as uncomfortable as he felt. Then Clay Plate cleared his throat and said, 'You stopped being the enemy. We saw that.'

'If not enemies, then what?'

'Refugees,' said Anyx Fro. 'I mean, no wonder you all invaded. Your homeland is under water, gone for ever. What choice did you have?' She chewed for a bit and then sent out a brown stream. 'Like I said. Refugees. What kind of person turns a back on that? Not us.'

The woman blinked. She turned and addressed the other Rathyd, her words drawing in a few of the older youths. When at last she was done, the four warriors began their own discussion that quickly grew heated.

'What now?' Benger asked the pregnant woman. 'We haven't got time for this, and besides, Stillwater warned us to stay quiet. This forest ain't as empty as it looks.'

'Stillwater? The woman who attacked Demon-hound? Who gave her life for us?'

'We don't know she's dead,' said Anyx Fro. 'In fact, I doubt she is. There's nobody more slippery than Stillwater. In fact,' she added, 'here she is now, the miserable cow. Now we know who was following us.'

Benger turned to track Anyx Fro's – and now Creature's – gaze and sure enough there was Stillwater, striding unevenly out from the trees. 'I see you all jabbering!' she shouted. 'Didn't I tell you to be quiet? There's monsters in here! Clay Plate! I'm deaf! My ears exploded! I'm dying! Worse, I walk like Anyx Fro! Heal me!'

Clay Plate walked over and placed a hand across Stillwater's mouth, mercifully shutting her up. The eyes above the hand widened and then narrowed. Clay Plate shook his head and put two fingers to his lips. Stillwater nodded.

'She's right,' the healer said after a moment's concentration, 'they really did explode. This is going to take some work. To be honest, we need Benger's High Denul.'

'Well,' snapped Benger, 'Benger ain't got it right now. So do what you can. Get rid of the pain at least. Burst ears hurt, a lot. Had my right one do that once, when I was too close to a cusser – that's why she's looking so agitated. Can't concentrate and can't walk straight.'

'That I can do,' said Clay Plate.

'If it's concentration you're hoping for,' remarked Anyx Fro, 'even High Denul won't work. This is Stillwater, remember?'

The Teblor warrior named Kadarast spoke to the pregnant woman. She slowly nodded, her eyes wide, and then turned to the marines. 'It is decided,' she said. 'These warriors of the Rathyd wish to be marines.'

'I'm sorry, but what?' Benger asked.

'You have humbled them. You have humbled us. We are unfamiliar with such feelings. The Rathyd are sworn to defend their kin, and all Teblor children no matter what tribe they belong to, because it is the way. But you soldiers, you *marines*, you choose to defend even those not of your tribe, or even your people. We are inspired to answer in kind. In your eyes we ceased to be the enemy. In our eyes now, and for ever more, you cease to be ours.'

'This is getting complicated,' said Anyx Fro to the pregnant woman. 'How about we pick it up later, once we're out of this mess. Besides, a few days and nights in our grunting, farting company – I'm looking at you, Daint – and you're bound to come to your senses.'

'It's not hurting but I still can't hear me!' Stillwater screamed.

Benger dragged Clay Plate away and took his place facing Stillwater. He began hand-signalling in the Marine's Cant.

'I'm screaming?' she shouted. 'Really? Okay, how about I whisper like this? No, I *am* whispering. Quieter? You sure? Like this? Okay, fine. Here's what we do now, folks – you all listening? One, get out of this forest, back the way we came. Two, do it fast and hope nothing's caught our scent. Three, we've got two days free of any Hounds, so we need to make use of them by double-timing south and yes, I know which way south is. Five, I can – what? I missed "four"? So what, I'll get back to it. Five, I can peek every now and then, so I'll know when we're past the floodwaters. As soon as we are, we go through. Now, back to four. Four, the Hounds aren't the only horrible monsters here, so we may still run out of luck. That's why everybody keeps it down, understood?'

'Ask her how she made the deal with the Hounds,' Anyx Fro said to Benger.

His hands danced about.

Stillwater scowled. 'How was I supposed to know all Pallid wanted was a bath?'

CHAPTER TWENTY-THREE

It is a necessary conceit to believe things cannot change beyond all recognition. To greet the day to come as if it was but a shadow cast forward by the day just done, is how we fashion the links of the chain that we call our lives.

But it is in the moment when the world shows a new face, when the chain twists, buckles and binds, when rain turns into fire, water into stone, land into sea, that we must acknowledge a most unpleasant truth.

Continuity is an illusion. Unseen forces work to their own ends. On this day, then, I was one among many, witnessing my nation torn asunder by a clash of worlds. Neighbours took on the guise of demons. Husbands into tyrants, children into mute victims from whom all hope was stripped away, wives and mothers who stood like islands in a sea of storms, the waves rising ever higher.

What changed was no natural calamity, although those were soon to come. The death in question, precipitating the end to all reason, was an event barely noticed.

A nation depends upon its beliefs, the foundation stones of myths into which all manner of faith is instilled. The cynic is the myth-slayer, relentless in all discourse to disaffect the veracity of honest things. This one lives solely in the present, the disbeliever in the future, the denier of the past. Dead are the destroying eyes, empty the embittered words, relentless the fist in the faces of all who suffer.

The cynic is tormentor and tormented both. Amidst the heaped bodies you will find no sign announcing them, nothing to tell you that the first world destroyed was within each of them. All that followed was a continuity of loss and despair leading to the bitter desire to cast outward the foul seeds born within.

Alas, the changed world they wrought did not spare a single one.

Prelude to The Uprising,
A History of Collapse
Syrin ben Illant

FOLIBORE HELD UP A HAND, BEGAN TAPPING FINGERS. 'SPINDLE, Oams, Benger, Daint, Anyx Fro and . . .' He grunted, frowning. Then his frown cleared, and he held up his other hand. 'Stillwater. Did I miss anyone?'

Blanket considered, slowly scratching at his mud-flecked beard.

Corporal Snack muttered a curse and then said, 'Stop fucking around, you two. We know who we lost and yes, Folibore, you can count to at least fifteen. Playing at being idiots has turned into a habit with you heavies, and it makes me want to drive an axe through your skull. So leave it and let us grieve, will you?'

Folibore sighed, shrugged at Blanket, who sighed and shrugged back.

The barge they were on was half-filled. It had been the last one being loaded before time ran out and it had to be cut free. Even then, as the flood smashed into and then over Culvern's walls, knocking down building after building, the sudden swell that lifted them out of the river had sent a dozen or more Teblor and marines over the side, none of whom were seen again.

'Leave them be,' said Sergeant Drillbent, his eyes on the swirling, refuse-cluttered currents. 'All we know is we saw none of them on the barges or going over any either. Spindle and Oams, well, they didn't stand a chance and let's hope it was quick. The others?' He jutted his chin towards the waters and said nothing more.

The sky overhead was grey and low. Rain periodically pelted them, occasionally tasting of salt. As for the flood itself, it was saltwater without any doubt, and viciously cold.

They'd lost sight of the other barges sometime in the night just past and were now alone, slightly fewer than five hundred bedraggled Teblor and marines, with a ratio of about four Teblor to one marine. The two battalions had been hit hard. Half the XIVth Legion was effectively no longer a coherent fighting force. No armour, no supplies, and not a single short-sword to be found.

The flood continued on, southward, swallowing everything in sight, but the current was palpably slowing. Drillbent straightened and made his way past sitting or lying figures, gripping the handrail as he worked his way towards the stern. There was no high deck on these barges, and the single tiller required two people on it at all times to slow the craft's spin, though that had eased up as well since they were taking on water through seams in the hull. Accordingly, at the moment, the stern was now forward, not aft.

Gulls wheeled over them, riding confused winds. Occasionally, a flock would descend to fight over the bloated carcass of a dead animal or person, their cries too much like laughter for Drillbent's liking.

He reached the deck near the tiller where Captain Gruff and Sergeant Shrake sat with Captain Hayfire from the 3rd Company, who'd lost all of her sergeants and most of her squads. Her weathered face was a lined map of dismay and she hadn't spoken in a while.

Everyone was cold, their clothes wet. Gruff was still wearing his otataral-treated hauberk, now blotchy and salt-crusted.

'Captain,' said Drillbent as he arrived. 'I ran through the list again and nobody saw any of them anywhere near the barges.'

'A grim day indeed,' Gruff said with a sigh. 'Even Hayfire's sweet reunion with Rayle could do little to enliven spirits, although more so for us than them, alas.' He paused, and then said, 'Grief surrounds us in countless, unidentifiable shapes floating aimlessly by. Worse, our failure shouts its scorn in every drowned Teblor drifting past. Not enough time, not enough barges, our salvation proving deadly in the one that overturned, and here, barely half filled – I will never scrub from my eyes the sight of the crush on the landing as the water engulfed them all. All those faces, all the hands reaching for us. I fear, my friends, I am broken, truly broken.'

No one spoke for a time. The barge shuddered briefly as its hull scraped along something, possibly a roof from a farmhouse or a barn. Then the current pulled it past and it seemed the barge settled a hand's width lower in the water as it floated free.

Hayfire surprised them all by speaking. 'So start putting yourself back together, Gruff. Fuck the lament. We did what we could. Aye, it mostly went wrong, but it could have been worse. Without the town to break that front wave, not one barge would have survived. We just ran out of time and that's not our fault.'

'We should've sniffed it out,' said Sergeant Shrake. She'd lost her helmet and her hair was unbound, lifting in the gusts of wind. She looked ten years older than she had two days ago. 'All those tribes moving down like that. There was a reason for it, and nobody asked what it might be.'

'Asking might not have given us an answer,' said Drillbent. 'The only way would have been an expedition into the north, and that would have had to carve a path through thousands of Wilders just to get to where that answer might be found. We knew they were coming. We didn't know why.'

'This was written of,' announced Gruff.

'Sir?' Drillbent asked. 'What do you mean?'

'The end of the Imass Pogrom against the Jaghut, Sergeant. The end of that war, and with it, the relinquishing of Omtose Phellack and all the walls of ice and fields of lifeless snow that held at bay the T'lan Imass from the last Jaghut strongholds. It was conjectured that the great thaw might have consequences.'

Drillbent grunted. 'You mean some hoary scholar with cobwebs in her hair muttered something about a melt in some obscure treatise? Well, damn me, why didn't anyone pay attention to that warning?'

'Many reasons,' Gruff answered, apparently too tired or too distraught to catch Drillbent's acidic sarcasm. 'Scholars never speak loudly, not on paper and not in person. And even if one did, those in power are disinclined to pay heed. They have more immediate concerns, my dear, than some hypothetical blathering from a scholar. On a grander scale,' he continued, 'imperial education squints at all the wrong things.'

It turned out that Paltry Skint was sitting nearby, and at Gruff's last statement she lifted her head and said, 'Now that's an interesting thing to say, Captain. Care to explain?'

'In common language, Paltry, or in the language of the heavy?'

Paltry Skint's brows lifted. 'Why, sir, if you dare give the heavy a try, then you dare also my opinion on how well you did. Are you certain?'

Gruff's smile was weary, but appreciative nonetheless. 'Dearest Paltry, have you ever known me not to rise to the occasion? Harken then, as I elevate this discourse beyond all reason. Heavy the cant, see this flower bloom!'

Paltry Skint snorted. 'Sweet the scent? Or something to dread? Go.'

Drillbent groaned and turned to lean on the rail, eyes fixing on the south horizon. Muddy water and nothing but. Behind him, Gruff had begun, but Drillbent was only half listening.

'. . . the proclivity towards overspecialization ever narrows the focus of the mind, darling, and with each narrowing increment the interconnected relationships among all forms of knowledge and learning cease to obtain, indeed, cease to matter. A career devoted to a single cog loses sight of the machinery, forgets the purpose of the mill, grows deaf to the water in the vast wheel, and thinks nothing of the grain's birth in the bread devoured. How fare I thus far?'

'You leave me breathless, sir,' Paltry Skint replied. 'But without intimate knowledge of the cog, the machinery may not work, the mill wheel not spin, the energy of the water churns past, lost to all purposes but its own.'

'I dare not deny your point, sweetness, yet to voice it in objection to mine seems strangely amiss.'

'Aye, I suppose it is, sir. A proper education, after all, must perforce embrace both extremes.'

'And all that lies in between. I daresay—'

'I see something,' Drillbent cut in, straightening and holding a hand up to shade his eyes. 'Land? Hills?'

The others were quickly at the rail.

'Well spotted, Sergeant,' said Gruff. 'Those are indeed the Blued Spine Hills. And do I not see . . . why, yes, barges drawn up. Landfall, my friends, is now imminent.'

Drillbent knew that Gruff had the sharpest eyes in the company, so he did not doubt his captain for a moment. 'We're riding damned low, sir. I hope we make it.'

'Should we run aground, they will see our plight, I'm sure,' said Gruff. 'The hillsides are crawling, the ridge itself lined with refugees. Runners will have been sent south to Blued, hopefully by warren. More immediately, I see slight hints of smoke. Fires have been lit. Perhaps we'll not all die of exposure after all.'

Drillbent pushed off from the rail. 'I'll spread the word, sir, lest everyone on board decides to rush here to see.'

'Sound thinking, Sergeant. And at a propitious moment we'll have to swing the barge around and seek to steer our way to the softest landing possible.'

Not too far from this group of marines, Hestalan of the Rathyd lay on the deck with her face hidden in the crook of her arm and her eyes full of tears. She was among the very few Rathyd on this barge who understood Nathii, and indeed Malazan. Her village had held a refugee from the south, a Malazan deserter, who'd lived out his years among the Rathyd, initially barely tolerated but eventually wholly welcomed. The man had died of a fever two years past, the village mourning his passing as if he had been one of their own. Hestalan remembered him well, as he had spent almost ten years in her own household.

These marines were strange. How many fists to the face could they take, only to rise one more time? As if to defy the will of the world was all that they lived for. And there they were, the officers and the sergeants, beating themselves over having failed to save more Teblor.

Little was said of their own grief, their lost comrades. Names offered in a list and nothing more. And just like that, that harrowing subject was done with, dispensed. No, what clawed at their souls were all the Rathyd they'd not saved from the flood, the same Rathyd they would have killed without compunction in battle.

Just before dawn, Bagidde, who had been holding her from behind to share body heat, had begun whispering in her ear, making the observation that the enemy were so few on this barge, it would be easy to simply throw them all over the side, easy, he repeated, to kill them all, for were they not the enemy?

Hestalan had asked him to roll over, so that she could embrace him from behind as he had done to her, sharing heat. She was a moment or two before moving into position, and in the mutual repositioning he hadn't noticed the cord in her right hand, nor her drawing it around his neck. After that, it was simple and quickly done, killing her old friend where he lay.

Before light arrived, Hestalan lifted and dragged Bagidde's body to the rail, leaned it over, and then flipped it into the water.

A voice from the darkness behind her murmured something, a few Malazan words of commiseration that her friend had not survived. She had grunted her thanks and then returned to her place on the deck.

This was the thing about saving people. Some could not shift their thinking in the face of a world overturned, enemy to saviour, foe to friend, and thought still in the old ways where violence was close at hand, along with the lust for killing. Hestalan understood it but did not share it. That overturned world had shown her a god's hidden face, hidden because she had been blind to it all her life. Well, blind no longer.

I will die for these marines. I will kill for them, too. Bagidde could not understand, could not make the heart's journey. And I knew he never would, that he'd be sowing dissension without surcease. I knew, yes, what needed doing.

The marines had failed to save all the Rathyd. To have expected to do so was madness, but such glorious, stunning madness that she wept, and was still weeping, her own face hidden, cheek against the damp deck.

Kin and stranger alike no doubt imagined her grieving for Bagidde's sudden, inexplicable death, and so they left her alone for now. Soon, however, she knew a marine would come by, kneel down, and offer her a drink from a waterskin – precious and dwindling as that water might be – and then leave, after a brief settling of one hand on her shoulder, or back, that touch of commiseration.

She knew it was coming. She knew what it meant. It meant *everything*.

*   *   *

446

Oams said nothing because there was nothing to say. His head still ached and occasionally he still lost his sense of things, falling into confusion. They sat on a bank above the water on what used to be a hill. Behind them the land climbed still higher. Far to the west were streaks of white smoke above the ridge line, telling him that others had made it.

Vague visions haunted Oams. That wild ride that seemed to be endless. A waking nightmare, broken up again and again by empty blankness. When his mind returned, he and Spindle were now on their feet, less than a thousand paces from this hillside. The carcasses of the horses, he supposed, were somewhere on the plain behind them. He didn't turn to look.

Now, with the clouds finally parting overhead and a small measure of warmth seeping down upon them, Oams sat a few paces away from his sergeant. As the man wept for the horses. And wept. And wept.

What could Oams say? Nothing.

In a while, in however long it took, Spindle would fall silent. He'd wipe the mess from his face and then stand. Oams would join him, still saying nothing, and they'd set out westward. To find their friends.

Was there any point in thanking dead things? Oams didn't know, but it wouldn't stop him, not for a moment. He would whisper his thanks whenever the moment felt right. He had a lifetime to do it, a lifetime of remembering. In the realm of dead things, if such a thing existed, two beasts might lift heads at his words of gratitude, up from the sweet grasses, lift them high, and bathe in the bright light and soothing warmth of his prayers.

He hoped it was like that, anyway. It'd be a shame if it wasn't.

* * *

There had been no shelter at first, but then the new shoreline grew cluttered with driftwood. Branches and entire trees lying in thick mud, remnants of farm buildings and the like. So Bleak had joined a team of marines from the other battalion in collecting this material. Instead of tents, then, they built wooden huts. The first problem was the lack of tools. All of their kits had been lost. Some creative magic took the place of those tools for the first day and a half, before the company's old train appeared from the south road, bringing news of a relief force on the way from Blued, along with the wagon loaded with the company's heavier engineering tools.

The huts were elaborated on, sometimes rebuilt from scratch. They became houses. The encampment, while ordered in a military grid, soon began to look like a town. Three teams of marines had merged to raise up a proper barracks and longhall, anticipating food and drink on the way. So Bleak found himself, with a few others, pushing chinking between the logs of each house; canvas munition sacks were filled with mud and brought up to where they worked. Luckily, it was summer, and exposure wasn't as big a risk as it might have been, but the new icy sea had dropped temperatures considerably, especially at night. That, and the lack of bedding, had meant that each shelter required a fire-pit and proper ventilation.

The chinking dried quickly in the sun that finally reappeared overhead, the last of the clouds burning away. So Bleak now found himself working alongside Storp, the old tavern-keeper from Silver Lake. Neither seemed inclined to talk much, and So Bleak was content with that.

He knew what the survivors from his company were probably saying. The curse of So Bleak lived on. Wherever he went, disaster and death followed, thinning the ranks around him. He knew the look he'd see in their eyes. Better to stay away, and maybe, as soon as possible, put in for a transfer.

They moved on to the next house, this one slightly larger as it now housed a family of Rathyd. The Teblor were huge, towering over all the marines. Two youths were sitting outside the entrance, on a discarded core-rotted log. It was hard to see them as children, since both were taller than So Bleak. Hunger and shock made them listless, watching dully as Storp dragged close another sack, then opened the burlap mouth in time for So Bleak to reach in for two handfuls of the cold, wet clay.

'You not ask for help,' said one of the youths, a girl with blonde hair and glints of silver in her blue eyes. Her brother looked at her without comprehension.

It was a moment before So Bleak realized that she'd spoken heavily accented Nathii. 'Ah,' he replied, 'we're used to working together. We're always building, everywhere we go. Forts, trenches, masonry, carpentry . . .' He stopped, seeing that she'd understood only a few of those words. He shrugged. 'Leave it to us, we're fine.'

Beside him, Storp said, 'You're not fine at all, soldier.'

Startled, So Bleak frowned. 'Well, as best as can be, I guess.'

'Not even that,' the grizzled veteran muttered. 'You're the one called So Bleak, right? Bouncing through legions like Oponn's own coin. Did you lose your whole squad again?'

Wincing, So Bleak turned his attention to slapping clay into the joins between logs. 'A couple.'

'Clay Plate and Daint.'

'You already know, then, so why twist the knife?'

'Is that what this is? So, I'm just wondering.'

Annoyed, So Bleak turned to face the old man. 'What?'

'Well, who made you Hood reborn? That's all.'

'I wish I knew,' answered So Bleak.

Storp scowled up at him. 'Arrogant punk. *I* ain't calling you Hood reborn, soldier. *You* are. All convinced the whole fucking world coming down is somehow all down to you. It ain't.'

'You haven't been through so many squads—'

'Now you're pissing not knowing which way the wind's blowing, soldier. I was part of the Bridgeburners. An auxiliary, aye, but I knew them. I knew their faces. Their names. And I'd have died with them in the tunnels of Pale, if I hadn't been attached to garrison duty in Mott. So what did that make me? Hood's spunky spawn?' He shook his head and spat. 'No, it didn't. All it meant – all it *ever* meant – was that I was lucky. And, it turns out, so are you. So, is luck something you steal from others? Oponn alone knows. You, being just one more witless mortal, you take what you're given and that's that.'

So Bleak looked down at his mud-encrusted hands. 'Apologies, Storp. I guess you see it that way and I'm happy for you. No, truly. It's my squad-mates—'

'Aye, the ones asking after you? The ones who hunted me down and told me to keep an eye on you? Those ones?'

So Bleak stared at the man.

'You think they'd wax you at every turn if they didn't give a shit? Or thought you actually cursed or something? You ain't cursed. They checked, I'm sure. Marines know it's a nasty world that's one long list of random shit happening randomly, and being shit, it stinks.' He straightened and wiped at his brow, glancing up the sloped street. 'Now regulars, they're different. Superstitious as fuck, those ones. But mostly you don't got to deal with them any more. Exceptin' right now.'

So Bleak turned to follow Storp's gaze. The three soldiers pulling a roughly made – but actually wheeled – cart towards them he thought he knew, though it took a moment to identify them. *Damn, these ones.* He brushed dried mud from his hands and spoke. 'No, I still don't owe you all a drink.'

The youngest of the three sisters gave a lopsided shrug. 'That was my sisters being shits, Marine. When we had the leisure to be shits, that is.'

The cart was loaded with more sacks of clay. The oldest of the sisters, who So Bleak recalled was named Flown, said, 'We know enough to stay on the outside when you marines are building stuff. Ignorant regulars like us know we'd just get in your way and slow you down.'

Her sisters began unloading the sacks.

'But slinging mud,' Flown continued, 'why, that's one thing we're good at, right? Good to see you, Storp. Glad you made it.'

'Thanks, Flown. But be warned. This is no time for Lope to go all sniffy again. Same for you, Amiss. Not here, not with this marine.'

Flown sighed. 'Didn't need to tell us that, Storp. In fact, we're here to make amends.'

Storp grunted.

Lope laughed. 'I know, we're all awkward here, right? It's because we're not used to feeling ashamed, that's all. We're even less used to apologizing.'

'Forget it,' said So Bleak. 'No harm was done. Thanks for the clay.'

'Well,' said the second sister, Amiss, 'jamming clay between logs isn't hard. We can see how it's done. Your sergeant's looking for you, So Bleak. She's over by the longhall. Try the equipment shack behind the log-pile.'

When So Bleak hesitated, Storp said, 'Go on, I'm going to enjoy watching these three regulars working for a change. This way, I can keep reminding them of the last tab which they left unpaid.'

'All right.' So Bleak eyed the sisters, and then Storp, and lastly the two Teblor children, who had been watching if not understanding much. 'I guess I'll go, then.'

He headed off.

The work-crew at the longhall was mostly along the front wall, which was nearing completion. So Bleak moved past them, around the skeletal framework of the side, and then crossed to the back of the log-pile. He saw the shed, but its flimsy driftwood-planked door was closed.

So Bleak looked around, saw no one. Well, she was probably busy, dragging the squad off somewhere to strip bark or collect shavings for kindling.

The shed door opened. 'Get the fuck in here, soldier.'

So Bleak went over. 'Must be a bit crowded in—'

She grabbed him by the collar and pulled him into the gloom. Slammed the door shut. 'Get out of those clothes quick. I've waited long enough.' All at once, her hands were all over him, her lips pressing hard against his.

We're both going to regret this. But it's today and we're still alive. Can a marine expect anything more than that?

Then the last of their clothes had been stripped away and it was past stopping, especially when Shrake pushed between his lips a mouthful of clean but salty hair.

* * *

It was important to keep things secret, no time to be careless, so Stillwater led her group into a strange, slow dance between saggy wooden houses only she could see. Behind her, Clay Plate was asking, cautiously, whether she'd taken another blow to the head, or was her balance getting bad again, or maybe Anyx Fro's inability to walk straight was actually some kind of infection and now she'd caught it, and, oh, might be worth checking that weasel bite, too, since didn't weasels zigzag when running? So Stillwater was wondering, and looking, to see if she could pluck them all back into the real world in such a way that Clay Plate would materialize over a latrine trench.

No such luck. They were in the wrong place for that, since she seemed to have taken them to the centre of this makeshift town. Oddly enough, this presented her with the perfect place to fashion the shift.

More marines had survived than she'd expected. Better still, they'd been busy and so no one in her group would have to sleep any more without shelter, in the cold, surrounded by monsters, weasels and Daint's snoring. It felt good knowing that everyone left was just getting on with things. The world was all about getting fists to the face, after all. How was this any different?

She found a place that seemed quiet enough and halted everyone behind her. She paused and looked back at them. Amazing they'd all survived. No Hounds, and even the monsters that looked in on them weren't especially hungry. She knew they were seeing nothing but Emurlahn's bleak, blasted landscape: the dun hills, the plains, distant stands of strange-looking trees. She knew as well that they were exhausted – no one had slept well. Worst of all, Anyx Fro was getting low on her supply of rustleaf, and when she had to do without, bad things happened, usually to other people.

Stillwater sighed. Benger was staring at her with a demented look on his wide, ugly face. Clay Plate was carrying a Teblor child, since there were more children than adults in this crowd and every Teblor adult had a smaller version in their arms. One girl still carried a puppy. Even Anyx Fro had a child by the hand, a toddler who'd taken to stuffing grass into her mouth to have the same cheek-bulge as Anyx Fro. Daint, near the back, had decided to sit down for some unknown reason.

'What do you see, Stillwater?' Benger asked.

'Ghosts,' she replied.

'Oh great,' snapped Anyx Fro, 'now you've walked us all into the realm of Death.'

'Not that kind of ghosts,' Stillwater replied. 'They're alive, just looking ghostly from this side.'

'Marines?' Benger asked.

She nodded. 'Aye. So I'm going to open the way back and we can just walk through the same way we came in here. So link up, everybody. And you, Benger, grab hold of me, just make sure that the bit of me you grab hold of won't force me to stick a knife in your eye.'

'I wouldn't.'

'You wouldn't?'

'Well, I won't. I promise. I mean, you're adorable and all that, but in a deadly, terrifying way.'

She frowned at him for a moment, wondering what all that meant. Then, with a shrug, she swung round. 'Now, follow me,' she said, fashioning a portal with two faint gestures from her hands. Warm, salty air blew in across her face. Smelled good, except for a slight undercurrent of something unpleasant.

She strode forward, out onto a grassy expanse atop a hill. A pile of freshly trimmed logs was stacked to her right, a heap of brush pushed up against it. Opposite was a shack, from which strange sounds emerged.

Daint was suddenly at her side, then past, walking up to the shed. He opened the door, peered in for a moment, and then leaned back and closed it behind him.

'Well?' Stillwater demanded.

He shrugged and then said, 'We're home, and all is well.'

Heavies were a confusing lot, weren't they? She didn't get them at all. 'Let's head back round to the front street, or track, or whatever you want to call it. I saw some of our squad-mates down near the shoreline.'

'You did?' Anyx Fro demanded. 'And you didn't say anything?'

'Yes, and why, yes. Come on.'

Once more, she led the way.

Some commotion across the way made Folibore look up. He had been thinking about . . . wait, what had he been thinking about? He scratched his beard, eyes narrowing as he saw a Teblor woman scream and run into a milling crowd, and suddenly she was backing out from that same crowd, only this time she held a child tight in her arms and her screams turned into wailing that was being picked up by other Teblor. The wailing, he realized, was supposed to be a happy sound.

At his side, Blanket grunted. 'Is that Stillwater I see? And Benger. Anyx and Daint.'

Both heavies rose to their feet. 'I'll get the sergeant and the corporal,' said Blanket. Before leaving, he punched Folibore on the arm. 'Squad's back.'

Folibore nodded. 'Squad's back,' he answered, although Blanket had already left.

Stillwater marched up. 'Thought you were dead,' she said.

Smiling, Folibore said, 'You never fail to brighten my day, Stillwater.'

She scowled. 'What now?'

'Now nothing,' he replied, stepping forward and wrapping her in a bear hug.

She squirmed a moment in his grip, then relented.

'Gods,' he murmured, 'what's that smell?'

'How should I know? Wet dog?'

It was near dusk when Captain Gruff led Drillbent and Shrake along the shoreline to the moored barge where Fist Sevitt had made her headquarters. They climbed the ramp to the deck to find the woman alone and leaning on the stern rail.

Drillbent had of course seen the Fist before, but only at a distance. She had once been a marine. He knew that much. Probably a heavy, since she looked beefy enough to shield-knock just about anybody to the ground, then finish the whole thing off with a heel to the head.

When she turned, Drillbent was surprised to see that her face was covered in freckles. At a distance, he'd thought her Kanese, but no, she was Falari. Did it make any difference? Well, no. But yes, too. Most people didn't think of Kanese as holding much of a place in the Malazan military. They were mostly artists, after all. And philosophers and scholars and whatnot. That had tainted Drillbent's view of the Legion's Fist, when it probably shouldn't have.

Instead, she was Falari, and if any people at all had carved out a big place in the history of the Malazan military, it was the Falari. *Stormy, Gesler, Iyerback, Callis Vantage, the list goes on and on.*

Her expression was grave as she studied the three of them.

'Fist?' Gruff asked in concern. 'Is all well?'

'Of course not, Captain,' Sevitt replied. 'But I am pleased to hear that some of your lost comrades have been found. I was always worried that I'd sent you and your three squads into something they'd never come back from.'

'All manageable, ma'am,' said Gruff. 'We'll soon have to send scouts to determine the fate of Balk's Company. Our Nerruse mages tell us that the greatest force of the inundation was west of here. Also, the forest likely slowed the rush of water. I suspect we've not seen the last of that company.'

She nodded. 'West of here, yes.' She paused, and then slowly straightened, before meeting Gruff's eyes. Her tone shifted into the formal. 'I am afraid that I must inform you of the loss of the two battalions stationed at Ninsano Moat. It seems the flood there was far more violent than what we faced.'

'No survivors, ma'am?'

'None that we know of, no. It seems that the casualties also include two entire armies consisting of northern tribals and Teblor. These Rathyd here in our midst may well be the last of their kind.'

Shrake plucked at Drillbent's arm and he shot her a glance. She nodded eastward. 'Two figures,' she said quietly, 'on foot.'

He squinted in that direction. It was too dark to make out any details.

'I know,' said Sevitt in a harsh tone, 'grief is the marine's mistress. I get it. What I also get,' she added, turning back to gaze out over the new sea, 'is what will come of it.'

Gruff asked, 'Sergeants, just what has so captured your – ah, dear me.' He turned back to Sevitt. 'Fist, I am pleased to report no losses among my three squads.'

She glanced over a shoulder, eyes narrowing, and then nodded. 'Very good, Captain. One last thing, please convey my order to begin preparations for our immediate departure. And that includes all the refugees.'

'Immediate, ma'am?'

'Yes. We should be on the south road to Blued by midday if possible, with the refugees at the forefront, as far away from this shoreline as possible.'

Drillbent frowned, wondering what he had missed. Glancing at his captain, he saw how pale the man had suddenly become.

'Understood, ma'am.'

'Dismissed.'

Gruff gestured Drillbent and Shrake towards the ramp. They reached the shoreline and approached the two figures walking slowly their way.

'How fares Benger?' Gruff asked quietly. 'His powers have returned yet?'

'Getting there, he says,' Shrake answered. 'For now, there's only Clay Plate. Of course, among the other squads—'

'Only if absolutely necessary,' Gruff said. 'Oams is one of ours, after all. But dearest of the gods, he looks a mess.'

Spindle, Drillbent observed silently, didn't look much better.

'We may need wagons for them on the march tomorrow,' said Shrake.

Their captain snorted. 'Darling, you know damned well that neither will hitch a ride. No, we marched out together and we'll march back the same way. Until your knee acts up, of course, but that's to be expected.'

Shrake grimaced at Drillbent, but then shrugged. 'Always making a point, sir?'

He nodded, his eyes glistening. 'The only one we ever make.'

CHAPTER TWENTY-FOUR

Ask not the hero about heroism
Forgive the unwillingness
To lock gazes while you search
For what cannot be explained

Seen by one or none the underside
Leaking veins and the litany of lesions
All the errors that cannot be taken back
Missed opportunities and all that was witnessed

Here are the bloody roots in nightmare tangle
In the reaching hands that were missed
Consider this a torment unseen
All that was and wasn't done gathered up

This past is not past and a world of clutter
Makes a maze behind those eyes
You cannot go there, where thoughts devour
Their own tails inside out round and round

What a thing to admire, this roiling confusion
The disbelief in shying eyes, faint suspicion
Across this chasm no bridge is possible
Ask not and leave the hero to spare you

In unguarded moment a fleeting glance,
Flitting search for who are you and what do you want?
It is this grinding return
To the impossible solitude – this *impossible* solitude

Wishing this dubious fame on no one
Lives saved, lives lost, the equation
Means less than nothing, is not even reached
And then is now, is always, is right and is wrong, *always*

Burning with shame, shuddering guilt
Ask not a thing of the hero who will tell you
It was not enough, is never enough
And will never be enough

Ask Not
Gaereslan

'*L*ET US TAKE A JOURNEY.'
The voice was barely a whisper in Rant's mind. He had thought that an iron blade was a prison of silence for the soul trapped within it. She had told him as much, he recalled. But now, in his head, she spoke.

'*Let us take a journey, son of Karsa Orlong. There is little of the God with the Broken Face who now infuses you that can be said to be gifts. Your strength is your own, and so too your doubts. Yet your soul now floats free of most mortal constraints, freeing us both in ways unimagined. Will you travel with me?*'

They were encamped on high ground, leagues south of the flooded forest. The Jheck were starving. The company of mercenaries had sent out parties to distant settlements, loaded down with Jheck gold. Delas Fana had wondered if any of those troops would ever return. There had been talk of killing the Teblor horses and Pake Gild was urging them to leave soon, before in the madness of hunger the Jheck rose up against them.

As far as Rant understood, the nearest cities were to the west, but many leagues distant. There had been a moment of evident consternation shortly after the two Malazan marines had departed. Commander Balk had sent squads into the forest in pursuit. Rant had slipped past one such squad on his return to the Jheck camp.

He'd yet to speak of that day. Something made him reticent. He had killed two of Balk's mercenaries, after all, and perhaps that was it. He felt bad about that, but then, he did not think he trusted Balk, either. The two men and one woman who guided the marines back into the forest had intended to kill them. Was this by Balk's command? What was the meaning, then, of the squads he'd sent after them? The whole incident confused Rant.

He'd seen little of Gower and Nilghan since everyone's panicked withdrawal from the flooding forest. The rising waters had been swift, but not so much that they could not outrun the advance. It was Delas Fana's opinion that the forest itself did much to slow it down. She was fearful of what had happened in the west.

They would depart soon, then, riding west along the spine of the hills. It was possible that they would be riding into a war. Rant felt sad when he thought of saying goodbye to his two oldest friends, but he could see that they were busy now, too busy for him, and that made sense. The plight of their people would be their only concern. Gower had even relented with regard to his brother, dismissing his banishment.

Rant was sitting alone at the moment, a short distance from the small camp Pake Gild had made for the three of them along with the ex-slave Sunyd, Valoc, keeping their horses close by. His back was to a boulder perched on the edge of a hill, facing north. The flood had not reached this part of the plain, but he could just make out the glitter of waves in the distance. All the land, including the plain, said Delas Fana, was higher here than it was in the west.

The sun was edging towards the horizon and the day's warmth lingered. Rant closed his eyes, and said, 'Yes. I will travel with you.'

Abruptly he was lifted skyward, but only in his mind, as he looked down for a brief instant and saw his own body seated there, back to the boulder, motionless, looking like a corpse. *Am I dead?*

'*No. You will return unharmed. Your body below is a small receptacle, Rant, limiting how much of your soul can fit within it. Further, it is bound by laws restricting your senses. Such laws are necessary, for when within your body, you must concern yourself with its safety, its survival. These are not the soul's laws, however. All of this, Rant, is true for all mortals.*'

They were still rising, the landscape below dwindling, spreading ever wider. Rant felt a thrill of exhilaration. *We are flying. This is what it feels like to fly. I remember your wings, Three. You have known this all your life, long ago.*

'*And so the world is unveiled,*' she replied. '*A change of perspective, and with it, a new understanding. In this place, Rant, time can be unravelled. We can choose what we see.*'

He wasn't sure what she meant by that. And then, as their climb slowed, they began winging into the northwest.

'*Back, then,*' she whispered. '*To see what there is to see. You may wonder why this is necessary. Be patient. When the reason is revealed, you will know it.*'

He could see a vast sweep of water below. In the forest, they had brushed against the mere edges of the catastrophe, but now, here, all was revealed. The land was gone. Silver Lake, the high ridges of folded bedrock rising from its north shore, had completely disappeared. The peaks of the mountains to the northwest were now islands, and water still foamed in wild currents around them. The new sea stretched into the west as far as he could see.

'This is as it is now, Rant.'

It was . . . terrible.

'Omtose Phellack is relinquished. The ancient magic crumbles. Let us see now what has just passed.'

The world below seemed to dissolve into a grey tumult. It took a long moment before Rant understood what he was seeing. The flood in reverse. They now winged northward, and Rant stared down, witnessing the horrifying inundation below, as it crawled back, folded into what had been gushing torrents in mountain passes.

'Can you see, to the northeast, Rant, that white line? This is the wall of ice that had been holding back the northern sea. But look to your left, northwest, where that wall fills the high passes of the mountains. This was where the heart of Omtose Phellack was, locked into caverns in the mountains themselves, in places surrounded by the broken bones of T'lan Imass, by the scattered remnants of Forkrul Assail. By the woven madness of Icarium's magic.'

The words and strange names meant nothing to Rant, but he had no interest in interrupting her description. They were nearing such a blocked pass, where the sheer wall of ice slowly reassembled itself.

'It broke here first,' said Three. 'A single, narrow chute for an entire sea to flow through. You saw the result of that. How the breaking here eased the pressure on the wall of ice to the northeast. See, too, how the waters backed northward, to gnaw at the wall from both sides, and how the ice began its slow crumble ever eastward, releasing yet more waters into the south.'

Suddenly they were reversing their route, moving faster than ever before.

'But now, Rant, let us look more closely at the flat tundra directly north of the great inland forest where you found temporary refuge. Where the floodwaters rushed down to that tree-line . . . here, north and east of the town where you were born . . .'

They were descending now, more details appearing of the tundra, its broad sinkholes, its eskers and low mounds, and there, standing upon one rise, a lone figure, long silver hair flowing in a raging wind, her arms outstretched.

'War-Bitch, child of the Wolves of Winter, the last of the ancient Beast Gods of the Holds. The flood that came to your forest, Rant, should have arrived with much greater force, much greater speed. And in that high wave, sweeping through, gathering up trees and branches and all else, you would not have survived. Not one of you.

'Your Jheck companions wonder where War-Bitch has gone. Look on, then, son of Karsa Orlong. Even I don't understand this, because she has not the strength to do what she did. I don't understand at all. Look on, Rant Bloodcurse, and witness.'

And so he did. As this lone woman, so beautiful, so strong and wild, drew all the power she possessed, to hold back an entire sea. And then, as she began to fail, she struggled to slow its mad, rushing flow, even as the hill she stood upon became an island, and the waters rose around her, seeking to crush her, sweep away her broken body.

Still she battled on against the world.

Saving us. Saving us all.

Once more, time began working backwards, to the moment before that towering onrush reached War-Bitch and swept past to either side.

'Here, then, this moment. Something impossible happens. Will you, perhaps, see what I cannot?'

He found himself hovering just above a hollow whirlpool that led down to War-Bitch and the small span of hilltop upon which she stood.

'Is this not inevitable? Look on. I do not understand. Now, must we not see her die?'

Later, Rant did not think Three expected what was coming. He did not think she could have imagined the storm that erupted from his soul, how it tore out all of the anger that had once been within him, and then within the Malazan knife. The anger of a childhood in torment, when the child itself knows and understands *none of it*. The reasons for the hatred, the spite, the cruel words, the swirling unseen sea of blind malice in which he drowned daily, nightly, every living moment.

There were so many things that could be done with that anger. It could become violent. It could be passed onward to the next victim. It could be turned inward, devouring the soul. It could rage for an entire lifetime, simmering beneath a placid surface, at risk of erupting at any moment.

Its power was raw and vicious, blinding and maddening.

Rant took it all into an embrace. He would do with it none of the easy things one could do. He was not the child he had once been, and never would be again.

The anger then expanded, reaching for countless other sources, other places, all the wounded souls of children made to suffer. He drew from the Teblor tribes, with all their savage and savagely harsh laws, that took children into their own embrace, but one of blood and hate. Laws of rape, laws of raids and murder, laws of the seeds of blood-oil.

He took, also, the suffering that lived without anger, when anger itself was beyond a child's reach – too many years ahead before it could find its expression – in terrible, wounded and wounding ways. The planted seeds, in the moments before heat and urgency burst them open.

Rant gathered it up, folding everything into his embrace. Then he released it. Making his own sea, his own vortex of raging currents, enough to reach down, enough to break time itself.

As she failed. As she died.

But he would have none of that.

*   *   *

War-Bitch felt herself faltering. In these last moments, defiant against the impossible, she was drawing upon the last vestiges of worship, from Gower, from Casnock, from the few hundred Jheck who still believed in her. But they were not enough. Without the gift of belief from all of the Jheck, there was simply not enough power available to her. Too few the currents between them, too thin these linking threads of worship, love and service.

Most of the new gods did not understand this. They did not understand the necessity of service, there in the hands – or paws – of the god. They did not understand the notion of *giving back*. But then, god or mortal, few did.

To be believed in is an obligation. Only by heeding that obligation are you made worthy of that belief.

Had she done enough? *No.* The torrent towered above her, a mass of white water and enormous, tumbling sections of ice, and then roared over and around her. It crushed everything in its path, devoured without pause the stunted line of trees that marked the northernmost reaches of the great forest. Swept onward, southward, uprooting the entire forest, tree by tree, carrying thick, churning walls of deadly detritus.

She had failed.

Slowly, her arms began sinking down, the hollow whirlpool narrowing around her.

Well, at least I got a good fuck in, before—

Sudden warmth, sweeping in like an embrace from behind. She felt herself lifted from her feet, thick, muscled arms holding her tight.

A face pressed against her left cheek and the thick hair on that side. A voice whispered in her ear.

'There will be no dying here.'

Her answering laugh was harsh. 'Stranger, my thanks, but far, far too late—'

'*I am going to give you something—*'

'Too late! It has swept past! Even now all my children are dying—'

'*We will turn it back,*' the voice said.

Everything about that voice defied reason. It was too calm, too sure of itself. But more than that. Something else about it sounded all wrong. She struggled to understand, even as she felt the strength of those arms, the heat of his breath against her cheek.

'*I have with me something. It comes from all of us who never understood, who still don't, and maybe never will. What else could be expected? We weren't ready for any of it.*

'*The twisting faces of the grown-ups. Strangers, or fathers, or mothers, the hands yanking on our arms, striking our faces. All the things they said that hurt us, broke us down inside. All the wars against what we were inside, what we were born with. All the stones thrown, all the kicks and all the fists – do you see?*'

She could hear the pain in his voice, but it wasn't simply his own pain. Had he gathered an entire world's worth? Was such a thing even possible?

'*Not knowing; it sinks into the ground, and the bedrock. Not knowing paints the walls of the small rooms, the loft and its too-small bed. Not knowing makes the light coming in through the window dull and cold, because it's not there for you at all.*'

That pain had narrowed down, and it hurt her chest to hear it.

'*So here, for you, is this anger. I've gathered it all up. It's yours.*'

'I am not your god,' she said.

'*I don't care.*'

'You can't just—'

What filled her being then was as vast as it was devastating. It swept away her objections. Visions rushed into her, a multitude of fragmented scenes, all from a child's point of view. She beheld the uncomprehending eyes of children as violence flared around them. And, rising from her own soul, she saw those same eyes, there in every creature slain, by human or beast of the wild – it mattered not which did the killing, because either way, in the end, the innocent did nothing but die. And so it followed, that to *survive* was to kill one's own innocence.

The innocent, she repeated to herself, *do nothing but die.*

She now understood the thing about the voice speaking to her, the thing that had so confused her. These arms wrapped about her deceived. This height and this strength fed the illusion yet more, leaving her floundering.

The voice, she realized, was that of a child.

As the power poured out from him into her, and from her outwards, the world began to change. She watched, almost beyond comprehension, as time reversed around them. Back, and back yet further, until once more she faced a wall of water.

But this time, as it surged towards her, she took this child's belief – and so swiftly did it flow that she had no chance to glean its details – and lifted it into a wall. Before her eyes, it was the clearest ice, blazing, as if devouring all the light the sun had to offer. So pure, it blinded her.

The torrent of the onrushing sea struck it, and almost instantly, its wild fury abated, as if drained of all power. The new icy wall almost immediately began to crumble, fissures forming, water pouring through, but with little of the energy it had once possessed.

She watched in what seemed a place outside of time, even as she witnessed the now ebbing progression of the flood, slowly surging its way into the forest. Her island remained immune to all of it. She realized, eventually, that she was between breaths. Trapped there.

'Can I die now?' she asked.

The child said, 'No. I won't let you. I'm tired of letting people die.'

'People?'

'Or gods.'

'You can't stop them all, child. And oh, I would name you, but I dare not invoke the blood you share. What do I know of your father's aspect, after all?'

'More than I know of it,' he said, somewhat forlornly. 'But one day, I will find out.'

'And then?'

He sighed. 'I don't know.'

'These children you've taken from, they don't worship me.'

'What I took was what they left behind. Leave behind, even now. When you are in that moment, I think, that moment of not knowing, of not understanding, all you can do is . . . is put it down. Leave it lying there. And you walk away.'

She shook her head. 'You didn't leave it, child. You know that, don't you?' She paused, and then gasped. 'Ah, I'm sorry. I didn't understand. I am wrong. You *do* leave it behind, don't you?'

He nodded, his beardless skin soft against her cheek. 'That's why I gathered it all up. All that not knowing. Because it has another name.'

'Innocence,' she whispered. *The one thing we all leave behind, alas. The one thing we all walk away from, sooner or later. Oh yes, you can look back and call it ignorance instead. But you do that because you've forgotten what you lost.*

'Leaving it behind is hard,' said the son of Karsa Orlong. 'No, not hard. It makes you mad. Angry, I mean. Only you don't know it.'

She understood. 'You don't connect that anger with the act of leaving your innocence behind,' she said, and then added, 'Few of us ever do.'

Her raised hands began settling. Time flowed forward once more. The flood was now back into the forest behind her, but more akin to a river overflowing its banks in a spring thaw. This would be survivable. They'd be able to outrun this. And she was alive, when she knew she wasn't supposed to be. New possibilities opened to her then, as bright and pure and clear as the ice he had given to her.

Slowly, his arms eased their embrace. She wanted to step free, to turn around and look into his eyes, but his hands now settled on her shoulders, effortlessly holding her in place. 'I shouldn't be here,' he said.

Then he was gone.

War-Bitch looked around. The waters surrounding her wanted to sweep in, drown this remnant isle.

'Guess I'd better leave,' she said under her breath, pleased indeed that such breaths proceeded normally. In, out, in, out.

New possibilities. It turned out that Gower had given her one, although she'd cast it away not too long ago. Pointless, irrelevant, at least back then. But now . . . *Well then, let me take some of that purity with me, the bright gift we all know but so often forget. And so, to be a mother again.*

And this time, with my brood of godlings, it will be different.

She lifted her head. 'Thank you, Rant Bloodcurse.'

'Unexpected,' was all Three said, before relinquishing him. Rant opened his eyes, and it seemed that barely a moment had passed since she'd taken him out of this body. His limbs remained supple, the boulder at his back not yet biting.

Hearing someone approach, Rant climbed to his feet and stepped around the boulder.

He saw Gower and Nilghan, both drawing up short as he appeared in front of them.

'He has a way about him,' Nilghan muttered. 'Quiet as a hare underfoot, a fawn in the grasses.'

'I am pleased to see you both,' said Rant. 'We are leaving here tomorrow.'

Nodding, Gower said, 'And timely indeed that you get away as soon as you can. I'd even suggest leaving tonight, in night's deepest well of darkness.'

'This is why,' said Nilghan, 'we are here, pup.'

'To say our goodbyes,' Gower explained.

Rant glanced away, uncomfortable. 'I don't like goodbyes.'

'Some are better than others,' said Nilghan. 'When I left the great den of the southlanders, my back was straight, and my head was held high. I was the Jheck, after all, who had survived living in the midst of the enemy and their awful crowded streets and silly laws. I defied their corrupting ways—'

Gower snorted. 'Mostly.'

Nilghan glared at his brother, and then grunted a laugh. 'Mostly, then.' He faced Rant once more. 'War-Bitch flung a mountain on you, pup. All those expectations. Telling us it was you who would save us. That was unfair and it's good she's gone, assuming she ever existed anywhere but in my brother's empty head.

'But we are done with all of that now,' he continued. 'And if we must break into our packs and take our chances on the Rhivi Plains, why, some of us will survive. I am sure of it.'

Gower cut in before Nilghan could resume. 'That marine who said the empire would help is probably dead, drowned. Or stranded somewhere on the roof of a barn. Balk has little faith and as we can see, we are on our own.'

'We survived only to die more slowly,' said Nilghan, showing his teeth in a defiant grin. 'But don't worry about me and this fat lord at my side, Rant. We shall make it even if none of our kin do.'

'You are not helping this moment, brother,' said Gower, moving over to the boulder to lean against it, his arms crossing. 'I believe War-Bitch has died. I believe this flood was slowed by her hands. I saw strange things in my dreams, at least until last night, when all was silent, all was dark. She is gone, and of her faith in you, Rant, well, you may not see it as I do – my brother doesn't, it's obvious – but had we not journeyed with you, we might all be dead now. So in my mind, you did save us.'

'She lives,' Rant said to Gower.

His smile was faint. 'For you, friend, I shall hold out hope for a few more days, then. Besides, faith is often answered with silence and what are we to make of that?'

Rant frowned. 'I do not like the thought of leaving you,' he said. 'But Pake Gild says the horses are at risk, even with the Teblor hounds guarding them. We too are without food, and the dogs continue to leave us to hunt on the shore.'

'As some of our packs have sought to do,' said Gower, nodding. 'But there are hardly any carcasses coming out from the flooded forest. It is strange.'

'Not so strange,' said Nilghan. He was staring northward. 'The water is too still. No currents, no tides. The dead forest animals remain in the forest, tangled in branches. This is my thought and it is a sound one.'

'Probably,' Gower agreed. He pushed himself off from the boulder and approached Rant. 'Let us then clasp forearms, Rant Bloodcurse, in the manner of the southlanders. It is a good gesture, I think. Ride quickly west. It's said there is a road cutting through the hills. Find it and travel south and you will come to a city—'

'A great den,' said Nilghan, 'called Owndos. Beware the women who demand money after playing with your penis. They understand nothing of privilege.'

Rant and Gower clasped wrists for a brief moment. Then Gower released his hold and stepped back. He turned away with a hand to his face and began walking to the Jheck camp. Rant stared after him, wondering at how brief their goodbye had been. Then it occurred to him that Gower had just been getting the moment over with, because of his worries about his kin.

Nilghan grinned at Rant. 'My brother is foolish in many things, but in this he is wise. Let us be done with this quickly, pup. I will say only this. That last was the final time I call you pup, for you are one no longer. I forgive you for punching me in the face, too, making you the only one I have ever forgiven for such a thing. This day, I say goodbye to Rant Bloodcurse.' He dipped his shaggy head and then turned and walked after his brother.

After a few paces, however, he swung round and said, 'His wives are jealous that you have stolen his heart. Oh, not as another bitch would, but they have never known their husband to have any friends. Until you, that is.' Then he waved and continued on.

Now three of his friends had left him. His first three. This, then, must be what life would be like. Distractions would take them away one by one. Their interest would be temporary, quickly wearing thin. He'd seen the same among the children in Silver Lake, how so many of them grew apart from one another, how each went off to make their own life.

And was he not doing the same? Were they not about to leave? There was Pake Gild now, a woman nestled between his hearts. There was his half-sister, Delas Fana. He wondered how frail that binding might be, especially since she had seemed so distant of late. He thought she might be worried, but she'd not confided in him. And why would she? Although in terms of actual age they were very close, he saw her as a grown woman. She had been to many places and seen unimaginable things.

It made sense that she'd see him as little more than a near-child, unwise in all the ways that mattered. Compared to her, he hadn't done much, after all.

Three friends found, three friends gone.

He wiped at his eyes, then let one hand settle on the pommel of his knife. *And you? Will I one day lose you, too?*

And in his head, her voice replied, 'Never.'

Balk sat on the cot, his face buried in his hands. He'd said nothing, nor even moved, in some time. Tired of waiting for a response, Ara left, returning a short time later with a folding stool. She sat opposite him, waited for a few more breaths, and then said, 'You did all you could, Andrison. We don't know what happened in that forest. How could the three bodies we found not be a good outcome? The marines survived.'

His hands fell away and he lifted his gaze. 'Thinking I'd sent three assassins as their escort.'

'And what if you did?' she retorted.

His eyes widened.

Ara glanced away, swearing under her breath. 'Fucking men,' she muttered. Then she leaned forward and met his eyes. 'Sergeant Spindle made his promise to Lord Casnock. To the Jheck. Not to you, Andrison.'

'You actually think they escaped the flood?'

'A three-legged dog could have escaped that flood. We could hear it coming long before we even saw it. Besides, I doubt they came all the way to us without having horses stashed nearby. So yes, I think they survived.'

'And all that Delas Fana told us? The invasion? The war to the west?' One of his hands made a cutting gesture. 'Spindle probably rode into a nightmare. The Malazans will have other things on their minds, don't you think?'

'That's possible,' she conceded.

'Not just possible, but likely.' Abruptly, Balk rose. He paced a few times, only to return to the cot, where he sat, forearms on his thighs as he stared at the dusty floor. 'It's probably a good thing my company is being dismantled, one troop at a time. The only thing that stings, Ara, is something that shouldn't. I mean, I know better, passing over raw gold – that's not even mine to give – in the idiotic hope that I have at least *one* loyal follower in my company.'

'One wouldn't have been enough,' Ara commented. 'The others would just cut the fool down.'

'I know that!' he snapped.

'But there was nothing else you could do, barring us both leading three or four of the least treacherous of them, with you watching my back and me watching yours, and if we did that, well, not one of your mercenaries would be here when we got back.'

'Instead, I made them rich and sent them off with a fucking hand-shake.'

'Yes, that's how it seems to have turned out,' Ara admitted.

'What if we marched straight to Owndos?' Balk asked, slowly straightening.

'With thousands of shapeshifting savages in tow? Well, if word from Spindle somehow got down there . . . but even then, the local governor might decide he never saw the orders, and with no marines garrisoned there, well, he'd close those gates to us for sure. Until the Jheck rioted, and then there'd be slaughter, and whatever agreement we had with the Malazan military won't be worth a thing.'

He slumped back down. 'Sometimes I hate your relentless logic, Ara.'

'You ready to listen, then?'

'To what?'

'My advice.'

He studied her for a long moment, and then said, 'Go on.'

'Disband the company. Pay them up, enough to make them happy, and send them off. *They* can go to Owndos, or Blued, or even into the south.'

'I won't abandon the Jheck. They hired us to protect them, to escort them!'

'The Jheck are about to veer, Balk, all of them. Then disperse in packs, each one starving and desperate. They will head off and slaughter until they're in turn slaughtered. Without food, there is no fulfilling this contract. How can you not see that?'

'Oh, I see it all right, Ara. But I mean to hold on, until the last possible moment. So, no more talk of disbanding, please.'

'And foraging parties, loaded down with Jheck gold?'

'No more of those, either.'

'And when the Jheck confederacy dissolves in chaos and carnage?'

His eyes widened on her. 'You think they'll feed on *us?*'

She shrugged. 'If I was a starving wolf, I'd not hesitate. Would you?' She sighed. 'And this is why your troops are getting so damned nervous. It's why bands of them are offering you a final salute and walking off.'

'We hold on,' Balk said.

'Fine.' Ara stood, collected up the folding stool. 'I'm off to do a head-count.'

'Just to cheer you up,' he mumbled, gaze on the floor again.

She thought to reply to that, decided not to, and quietly left.

*

467

Dawn was just arriving when Rant mounted, collected up the lone rein, and looked to Pake and Delas Fana. It was chilly, cold air coming down from the north, but the sky overhead was free of clouds and so the day would be warm, perhaps even hot. His gaze then shifted to Valoc, lying on the travois behind Pake's horse. His eyes were open, but he hadn't spoken in days, and he was wan and gaunt. Rant looked away.

It had been an uneasy night. Packs of veered Jheck howled in the darkness, off hunting for whatever could be found. Sleep came reluctantly to Rant, but he could not track down the source of his restlessness. Much later in the night, Pake Gild came to him, asking to be held. He did so, and eventually fell into slumber with her in his arms.

Then they were awoken before the eastern sky had even begun to pale. Something had happened. There had been a commotion of some sort, something that set all the Jheck into a frenzy of activity, until howls reverberated in a savage roar.

Delas Fana told Rant to stand guard with her while Pake Gild quickly saddled the horses. Sculp and the other dogs stood with heads lifted, noses testing the cool breeze coming down from the north.

'They've all veered,' Delas Fana said quietly. 'We knew it was coming.'

'But the howling is moving away from us,' Rant observed.

'You're right. It is. Odd. They're all going north.'

Pake Gild came over. 'I think we're safe for now,' she said. 'But since we're up and saddled, let us eat whatever we have left and then be off. We will stay on the ridge and then, if we're able, make our way down to flatter land. Once there, we should get plenty of distance covered. The following day for Owndos, Delas Fana?'

She nodded. 'I think so. To whatever welcome may come when we get there.'

Suddenly, all the hounds were on the move, running north.

'That's not good,' muttered Delas Fana.

Pake Gild shrugged and then set to making a small fire.

Now they were ready to depart and still the Teblor hounds had not returned. Their inexplicable absence stung Rant's hearts. He had grown used to their presence, to the protective circle they would make around the three Teblor and their horses.

'We've waited long enough,' Pake Gild announced. 'They can find us again, if they're of a mind to. Delas Fana, will you lead us?'

Nodding, Delas Fana nudged her mount's flanks and set off. Rant fell in behind her, with Pake Gild behind him.

He took a moment to glance back at the now empty Jheck camp. It looked like a battlefield without the bodies, with all the gear abandoned and scattered everywhere. He saw a small gathering of mercenaries, Balk and Ara among them. They seemed to be about to depart.

'Have faith in Gower and Nilghan,' said Pake Gild, with a slight smile. 'They are survivors.'

'I know,' said Rant. 'But I grieve for all that they have lost.'

'And are perhaps losing even now,' she added.

He turned and set his gaze on the hills ahead, a deep, aching heaviness settling in his chest. It was hard, he decided, losing friends. Damisk had been his first, the first friend he'd ever had, and the first one lost. That friendship had been born with a hand reaching up, out of icy water. That seemed a long time ago. Without the hand that met his in that last, desperate moment, he would never have met Gower, or Nilghan. He would not now be riding with these Teblor women. His life had begun a second time that day.

Some fathers, he realized, were not of the blood.

Balk led the way as they tracked the mass exodus of Jheck. The night just past had been terrifying. Many of the mercenaries, awakened to the wild howling, had simply fled the camp. Four had attempted to loot the gold supply, only to panic when finding themselves in the midst of wolves snapping and growling on all sides.

By dawn, Ara was standing beside Balk, surveying the remnants of the camp. Glancing to the west, she saw the four Teblor making a quick exit, and silently wished them luck.

'Let's find out where they all went,' said Balk.

Now they walked the dusty plain in a small group, retracing their flight from the flooded forest.

By mid-morning they caught sight of something directly ahead, close to the shoreline. Wolves in their thousands, the sky above crowded with ravens and, surprisingly, gulls.

'They are feeding,' said Ara.

Balk glanced back at her, his face flushed. 'On carcasses. Can you see it, Ara? Carcasses heaped along the shore – I'd thought them dunes at first, which made no sense.'

'They're feeding on drowned animals?'

He grinned. 'Ara, right now, they're *wolves*. So, why not?'

A mercenary behind Ara spat a curse and then, in a low tone, said, 'Easy enough for them, I suppose. Bloated, rotting carcasses . . . the gods spare me.'

Another answered, 'Bloated or not, I'm of a mind to do the same fucking thing.'

They drew ever nearer, and Ara could now see that some of the Jheck had sembled, bellies swollen, gaits wide, and were all making their way towards a modest hill, where stood a tall woman with silver-white hair.

'Don't think I saw that one in the camp,' the first soldier said. 'I would've noticed with a body like that!'

Balk elected to lead them towards the same mound, where a gathering of well-fed Jheck was assembling. Gower was among them. Casnock as well. Balk pointed westward and Ara looked there to see the Teblor dogs around the carcass of a bhederin, ignoring and being ignored by the wolves working on carcasses of their own.

They drew up closer. Casnock took note of them and with a wave gestured them through the press of satiated Jheck.

'War-Bitch,' he said, his face splashed in blood, his beard flecked with bits of meat. Flies buzzed everywhere. 'Do you see our beloved goddess? She gathered us a feast!'

'How spoiled was the meat?' Balk immediately asked.

'Some not spoiled at all – we avoided those for the most part, Commander, with you in mind. Soon, we will butcher them for you. We will make fires. We will smoke the meat. This has won us many days, has it not?'

Balk slowly nodded, and then he said, 'I am sorry, Lord Casnock. I've lost half my company.'

'No matter. More pay for the rest of you, then.'

'You still wish our escort?'

'We do, Commander. You did not abandon us, and that we will not forget. Now, join us here, so that we may hear our goddess speak.'

Gower looked on her with more love in his heart than was probably healthy. He'd caught her gaze more than once, however, lingering on him. Or perhaps that was only his imagination. A sour comment from his oldest wife suggested otherwise.

He now stood facing the goddess, his belly aching and heavy. The stench of rotting meat was sweet in the air.

War-Bitch seemed to be displaying some confusion, casting her gaze about. Finally, frowning, she met Gower's eyes. 'Where are they, then?'

'Who, Goddess?'

'The Teblor! Where is Rant Bloodcurse?'

Nilghan spoke up. 'Gone, War-Bitch, into the west. We said our fare-wells yesterday. You said he would save us, but it was you after all, Goddess. We were fools to doubt! I was a fool!'

'I can die now,' Gower said under his breath.

'You are still a fool, Nilghan,' said War-Bitch. 'I told the chosen among you that Rant Bloodcurse, this bastard child of the God with the Shattered Face, would be our salvation. I knew not how, but I knew it nonetheless.' She paused, scanning faces. 'You think he did little for you? You think he did nothing? Gather closer, children, hear my words. Pass my words to those behind you, and let this tale be told!' She met Gower's eyes and smiled, and there was something in that smile that bespoke the wisdom of century upon century. At the same time, Gower saw something reborn, something he could not quite identify. The smile took away his breath.

'Let me tell you a tale,' she began, 'one to bring hope to the future. It begins as it ends. With a child . . .'

EPILOGUE

To be believed in is an obligation. Only by heeding that
obligation are you made worthy of that belief.

War-Bitch, Goddess of the Jheck

NINETEEN UNHAPPY HORSES CARRIED THEIR RIDERS DOWN TO
the shoreline of the new sea. For once, however, Spindle knew
that he was not the cause of their unhappiness. The sorcery
within him was particularly subdued this day, still half-buried in the
ashes of his grief over what he had done to their mounts during their
flight from the flood.

The raucous roar of gulls and ravens reached them long before they
came within sight of the shore. Fist Sevitt had known this was coming.
The orders to quit the camp they had been making for the surviving
marines and the refugees had come in time. The dismantling had gone
quickly, efficiently, and even now a new town was emerging on a pair
of flat-topped hills about a league to the south. A battalion of Malazan
heavy engineers had arrived from Blued to begin road construction.
Until that was done, however, the relief trains would continue to be
slow in arriving, traversing what amounted to a goat-track wending up
into the hills.

This work was tiring, but it was clean and honest. The building up of
civilization seemed worthy, as far as Spindle was concerned. Proof that
humanity could rise yet again after having been driven to its knees, a
not uncommon occurrence. *Aye, we're a stubborn lot.*

He thought back to his farewell with Bliss Rolly the previous morning.
She and her regulars were part of the escort accompanying the supply
wagons setting out eastward, to link up with Balk's Company and the
refugee Jheck. There was something solid about Bliss Rolly, something

implacable and indefatigable. Spindle was surprised at how deep his feelings for her went, and indeed, he was somewhat frightened by that depth, and what it might mean.

Seeing him approaching where she stood close to the lead wagon, she had smiled, tanned skin crinkling around her eyes. 'I was hoping you'd come,' she said.

'I'm sorry I've only managed it now, when you're about to leave.'

'Just as well,' she said, glancing away.

Spindle thought about that, and then he nodded. 'It was just the one night, right? Meant nothing. Don't worry, I get it.'

She quickly looked back at him, eyes flashing. 'Don't be an idiot, Spindle. I'd spent a day and a night and half the next day thinking you were dead. I don't think I have *ever* cried more tears or laid down more curses at *anything* than I did at that damned sea. Then it was another day and a half to fucking recover, so I'm glad you didn't see me in that state.'

Oh.

Spindle managed to clear his throat, hoping she saw no sign of how hard his heart was beating. 'Will you be staying with the Jheck migration, then?'

She nodded. 'For a while, just to make certain Balk's got nothing nasty planned.' Her head cocked slightly. 'Did I hear something about an attempt to kill you and Oams?'

Spindle shrugged. 'We made it out.'

'What was Balk thinking?'

'I'm beginning to suspect it was a few rogue mercenaries, taking things into their own hands. Either way, the empire doesn't give a shit about Balk and his company.'

Bliss ran both hands through her hair. She'd cut it back some time ago but now it was growing long again. 'Different story for the Jheck.'

'Aye, it is. What worth an empire that turns its back on helpless people, its own citizens or otherwise? I wouldn't wear this uniform if it was any other way.'

She grinned. 'I prefer you wearing nothing.' The grin then faded. 'We'll see each other again, Spin?'

'I hope so,' he replied. 'In fact,' he added, 'I might be getting a bit old for this marine stuff. Was thinking of surrendering my commission.'

Her brows lifted. 'Really?'

His old paranoia resurrected itself, making his reply vague. 'There're ... rumours, Bliss, that maybe a few Bridgeburners are still breathing, down in Darujhistan.'

Her gaze narrowed. 'Deserters?'

'That's a charge I won't abide,' Spindle said. 'Dujek Onearm officially disbanded us at Black Coral.'

'I believe you,' Bliss said. 'But Dujek's decision wasn't sanctioned back then, and still hasn't been as far as I know. Be careful, Spin. Find a defendable house, preferably with multiple exits, and to begin with, stay close to your friends.'

'To begin with?'

'Aye, to begin with.'

He searched her eyes, and then asked, 'You mean, until you get there?'

'I'll make a quick wit of you yet,' she said. And then she stepped close, cupped the back of his head, and drew him in for a long kiss.

Catcalls erupted from the nearby regulars.

But Spindle didn't care, and, quick wit that he was, he knew she didn't either.

The gulls and ravens were deafening as the three squads rode within sight of the shoreline. Captain Gruff, in the lead, reined in at the ridge just before the hill began its slope down to the water.

Oams watched Spindle draw up beside the captain, and then each rider in turn did the same, forming a line facing the new sea and its final bitter gift. Horses tossed their heads and shifted about for a time until finally settling. The stench was overpowering.

It was well, Oams decided, that Fist Sevitt had made certain the refugees were at the front of the withdrawal to the new camp site well inland. They'd not seen this, and he hoped they never would.

There were remnants of uniforms among the thousands of corpses that now marked the division between land and sea, but for the most part, the dead weren't soldiers. They were Teblor. They were Ganrel. They were Wilders and Saemdhi, Bright Knot and Jhinan, Fildasz and Brethen, and countless other peoples beyond identification.

Looking to the left, Oams could see that grisly wrack continuing on for as far as his eyes could discern. To the right, the sea's shoreline curled northward, and there the bodies were mixed among uprooted trees, branches and massive mats and mounds of leaves.

No one spoke. They weren't here to speak.

But Oams felt the failure like a stone in his chest. Still, he would not look away. Like the others, he studied the scene below, detail after detail, searing it onto his soul. There were reasons for doing this. No doubt they would make no sense to most people. At times, they made no sense to Oams, either. None of those reasons were easy to put into words.

To bear witness, perhaps. Because to do otherwise would not only be the act of a coward, it would also be an act of disrespect. And it was not just the bodies of Malazan marines below – the bodies of friends and comrades lost – but all the others as well. Especially the children, and there were so many children.

What sort of person could turn away from such a scene? Shutting off all feeling, all humanity?

It was a ritual, he eventually decided, but a ritual in the proper sense of the term. Not quite a rite of passage – that would be too ghastly a price from any one place to the next – but something that simply needed to be done.

You do not turn away.

You do not rush back to your own life, your own world, and tell yourself that your family, your loved ones, are all that matters. Were they indeed all that mattered, then in your world not one person who's not you or your family would give a flying fuck about you, or them. And in a world like that, why, it might well be better to be dead than alive.

Or it was something else. He might be way off in his thinking and there was reason to suspect that he was. After all, those very thoughts left him seething with rage. And fear – fear that such a world was possible, that such a world could in fact exist. Fear, yes, that such a world could be found even here in his own world, in a land and among people not too far away.

Cowardice had a hundred thousand faces, after all. In most of them, the eyes were squeezed shut.

No matter. None of that belonged to a marine of the Malazan Empire. And this was why they were here, beneath a hot sun and wheeling birds, sitting in saddles on almost motionless horses, saying nothing and not one of them turning away, not for a moment.

Reminders, Oams decided, were important. They'd done what they could. It wasn't enough. They'd made mistakes. Far too many mistakes. Some of those bodies down there had died to Malazan munitions and Malazan sorcery, after all. And this was another lesson. Mistakes cost lives. Any commander waving a hand at that earned a knife in the back.

The same, as far as Oams was concerned, for any ruler.

So far, Emperor Mallick had played it straight. It may not have started well, but the messes were cleaned up, eventually, and peace had come to the empire. But that was no reason to be complacent. Power always corrupted, after all, and that might one day come to an emperor; even one who was a Jhistal priest. And if that day came, well, not even an emperor was safe from a knife in the back.

Aye, good old Oams. Got the Claw written all over him, right?

Well, no. The Claw don't deal with internal matters. Not at that level, anyway.

Good old Oams. Mallick's gone bad. What're you going to do about it?

Oams reached up a hand to brush at the space just below his throat, feeling his hard sternum beneath the thin cotton shirt he now wore. There was nothing there, of course. Nothing hanging from a leather string, or silver chain. Those days were long gone.

Well, boys and girls? I'll go and do what needs doing.

We always have, and we always will.

Poor everyone, Stillwater thought, after having given up counting marine uniforms down below, which was after she'd given up trying to count dead Wilders and Teblor, which was after she'd given up trying to count dead children.

Nature was mean, she decided. It just didn't give a fuck. But people had Nature in each of them, too, and if it was in charge, why, they had the same not-giving-a-fuck attitude. Given the choice, she'd kill all of those ones. Quickly and efficiently, since there'd be so many of them.

She was back in her *very first* uniform and that made her feel complete again. A real miracle, the way Blowlant had somehow found it in that giant sea out there, then dried it out, repaired it, got Varbo to oil it up good, and offer it to Sarlis to present it to her with all their compliments.

It was good to have people like that looking out for you. The kind who went through life quietly, sincerely and consistently. *People*, she realized with a start, *just like me*.

When Captain Gruff at last gathered up his reins and wheeled his mount, setting out for the return journey, Spindle waved the others on. They didn't hesitate and a short time later, Spindle was alone.

The dead didn't need to accuse, but they did it anyway. They did it in their own way. No words, obviously, and no gestures, either. They did it by not moving, by the lifeless faces and the empty eyes, the pale flesh – all the signs of their souls' absence.

It would take a very special fool to look upon two bodies, one living and one dead, and think the only difference between them was that one breathed and moved and the other did not.

This was a sea of souls, now. Although he'd heard the cartographers in the engineer battalion already giving it a name, he didn't think theirs would stick. Because those engineers had not come out here to see for themselves as the marines had done. No, it would acquire a different name, a proper one. Officials might fight it, but probably not for very long. It would come when the surveyors finally arrived to measure and map the shoreline.

By then, it'd be a sea of bones.

That, he decided, would be a fitting name. Better than his own 'sea of souls', because by then, those souls would be long gone.

He lifted his gaze, out onto the glittering, wavy surface. He tried to imagine spears of sunlight filtering down through the icy waters, and down, faintly illuminating the old Malazan roads, the abandoned forts and the barrows. The legacy of short-lived conquest. In a way, as foolish as anything a mortal could do, to think of ownership of what could not be owned, and to fight one another for the right of it.

The more powerful forces simply bided their time. They were, after all, the true masters of conquest.

He remained for a while longer, content in being alone, so that no others could see his tears. Eventually, his weeping ended, and the onshore breeze dried his cheeks and beard. He collected up his reins and swung his horse around.

Time to return to his marines.

This ends the First Tale of Witness

ABOUT THE AUTHOR

STEVEN ERIKSON is an archaeologist and anthropologist and a graduate of the Iowa Writers' Workshop. His *New York Times* bestselling Malazan Book of the Fallen has met with widespread acclaim and established him as a major voice in fantasy fiction. He lives in Canada.